A TREASURY OF CLASSIC MYSTERY STORIES

A TREASURY OF CLASSIC MYSTERY STORIES

FALL RIVER PRESS

New York

FALL RIVER PRESS

New York

An Imprint of Sterling Publishing Co., Inc.
1166 Avenue of the Americas
New York, NY 10036

ISBN 978-1-4351-6285-3

Manufactured in the United States of America

6 8 10 9 7 5

sterlingpublishing.com

CONTENTS

Introduction   vii

Missing!—Émile Gaboriau   1

The Traveller's Story of a Terribly Strange Bed—Wilkie Collins   16

The Murders in the Rue Morgue—Edgar Allan Poe   29

The Ten-Thirty Folkestone Express—Sax Rohmer   56

The Fenchurch Street Mystery—Baroness Orczy   76

The Invisible Man—G. K. Chesterton   90

The Murder of Bennett Sandman—Edgar Wallace   104

The S. S.—M. P. Shiel   115

The Mysterious Card—Cleveland Moffett   140

The Hound of the Baskervilles—Arthur Conan Doyle   161

The Ivy Cottage Mystery—Arthur Morrison   285

The Tragedy at Brookbend Cottage—Ernest Bramah   304

A Case of Premeditation—R. Austin Freeman   322

The Scarlet Thread—Jacques Futrelle   345

The Red Silk Scarf—Maurice Leblanc   371

The Business Minister—H. C. Bailey   390

The Big Bow Mystery—Israel Zangwill   427

Room Number 3—Anna Katharine Green   516

The Doomdorf Mystery—Melville Davisson Post   557

The Poisoned Pen—Arthur B. Reeve   568

Justice Ends at Home—Rex Stout   584

The Rope of Fear—Mary E. Hanshew and Thomas W. Hanshew   633

The Mysterious Affair at Styles—Agatha Christie   648

Original Sources   791

INTRODUCTION

BLAME IT ALL ON EDGAR ALLAN POE. IN 1841, POE PLACED HIS STORY "THE Murders in the Rue Morgue" in the April issue of *Graham's Magazine*. Regarded as the first modern tale of detection the story introduced C. Auguste Dupin, a dilettante detective, and it featured all of the elements that we associate with the classic mystery story: the discovery of a puzzling crime, the parsing of legitimate clues from a welter of red herrings and misinformation, the application of rigorous logic to interpret those clues and reconstruct the events of the crime, and the apprehension of the criminal (who is often someone entirely above suspicion). "The Murders in the Rue Morgue" was the first of three stories to feature Dupin—the others were The Mystery of Marie Rogêt" and "The Purloined Letter," both classics in their own right—and its importance to the mystery canon cannot be overestimated. Years later, in his first tale of Sherlock Holmes, Arthur Conan Doyle—who praised Poe's three tales of detection as "a model for all time"—would have his soon-to-be legendary detective egotistically distinguish himself from Poe's by commenting, "Dupin was a very inferior fellow. . . . He had some analytical genius, no doubt; but he was by no means such a phenomenon as Poe appeared to imagine."

Certainly, writers wrote mysteries before Poe did—the gothic novels published at the turn of the nineteenth century abounded with mysteries and subterfuges, usually revealed to be the handiwork of their villains—but Poe provided his mysteries with a structure and their solutions with a rationale that became the framework for classic mystery fiction. *A Treasury of Classic Mystery Stories* celebrates Poe and his achievement through his own classic tale and the stories of twenty-two other authors who wrote mystery fiction in his wake. The authors represented in this anthology are among the most talented and best-known writers to turn their hands to the mystery tale.

Like Poe's story many of the selections included here are tales of detection whose crime solvers have their own unique personalities. Father Brown in G. K. Chesterton's "The Invisible Man" is a Catholic priest who often appreciates the spiritual side of crimes. Max Carrados in Ernest Bramah's "The Tragedy at Brookbend Cottage" is a blind man who has trained his other senses to help him perceive clues that others miss. The nameless man in the corner in Baroness Orczy's "The Fenchurch Street Mystery" is an amateur sleuth who processes clues related to him second-hand and solves crimes without leaving his seat. The crime of murder dominates these stories, as well it might, murder being the most unthinkable, and thus frequently the most puzzling of all crimes to solve—especially if the murderer is skilled at covering his tracks and deflecting attention from himself. But it's often the circumstances of the murder that make the story compelling. Israel Zangwill's "The Big-Bow Mystery" virtually inaugurated the subgenre of the locked-room mystery, a story type that presents the reader with a crime committed in a room that it appears no one could have entered or left, and that taxes the intelligence of those at the scene to determine which details are clues that point to a solution. In several of these stories, the crimes committed are fraught with elements of the supernatural that sometimes are or aren't rationalized away. Arthur Conan Doyle's classic Sherlock Holmes adventure "The Hound of the Baskervilles" and Cleveland Moffett's "The Mysterious Card" represent the opposite extremes of this story type.

The authors in this anthology all hail from America, England, and the European continent. Especially notable is British writer Agatha Christie, whose novel *The Mysterious Affair at Styles* introduced detective Hercule Poirot to the world. Poirot would feature in thirty-three of her mystery novels and he became so well-known to readers that, when Christie killed him off in *Curtain* (1975), he merited a front-page obituary in the *New York Times*. Rex Stout's "Justice Ends at Home" introduces attorney Simon Leg and his assistant Dan Culp, forerunners of Stout's detective Nero Wolfe and his assistant Archie Goodwin. Stout's story was published in the general fiction pulp magazine *All-Story Weekly*, but this tale of detection can be read as an anticipation of the mystery tale as it would flourish in the crime and mystery pulps, notably *Black Mask* and other magazines where the hardboiled detective story came into vogue. The variety and diversity of all the stories in this volume are a testament to imaginative possibilities for the mystery tale, and to the many ways in which it has, for nearly two centuries, entertained readers and invited them to match their wits with expert crime solvers to unravel the world's most challenging mysteries.

MISSING!

Émile Gaboriau

ONE SUNDAY AFTERNOON, NOT LONG AGO, THE WHOLE DISTRICT OF the Marais—that busy quarter of Paris which now-a-days is but one vast workshop from the Temple to the Rue Saint Antoine, from the Bastille to the Rue Turbigo—was in a state of most unwonted excitement. Bustling as it may be on week-days, when all the bronze factories re-echo to the sound of toil, when the heavy vans roll over the pavement from druggist's to toy-dealer's, taking at each halt some fresh consignment for despatch by rail, when work-people and customers crowd the thousand and one establishments where every description of *"article de Paris"* is produced for a value of many millions of francs per annum—on Sundays, at least, the Marais usually relapses into silence. Were it not for the multitudinous inscriptions which cover all the houses from garret to basement chronicling the names of manufacturers, dealers and commission agents, one might fancy oneself in the old times, when the Marais was inhabited solely by the *rentier* class, by worthy old couples retired from business on fairly decent incomes, or by relics of the ancient nobility, scarcely wealthy enough to reside in the Faubourg St. Germain. Such, indeed, was the Marais fifty years ago—a quiet and secluded district—and thus have Honoré de Balzac and Paul de Kock described it in their novels. But, now-a-days, it is a vast hive of industry, whence peace and quiet are utterly banished during the six days set apart for toil. It is only on the Sabbath, when workshops and store-rooms are closed, when the week-day toilers are making merry in their native Belleville, or chinking glasses in the *bosquets* of Montreuil, that it regains a semblance of its old tranquillity.

And yet, on the particular Sunday we have mentioned, the usual "Sabbath-hush" was wanting. True enough, no heavily laden vans were rolling through the narrow streets; no din of hammers and anvils came from the closed *ateliers*. The foot-ways were not bestrewn with packing cases, and no crowd of commissionnaires and receivers, clerks and commercial travellers, hurried hither and thither peripatetically proving the truth of the axiom that "Time is money." But then, there were unusually animated groups of customers in all the wine shops, unwonted knots of people at the street corners, gatherings of housewives in front of the fruiterers' stores, and conclaves of door-keepers and kindred scandal-mongers in every convenient alley.

Something very extraordinary must have happened, as passers-by correctly opined. The fact is, that one of the most honourable manufacturers the Rue du Roi de Sicile had disappeared, and all efforts to find him had so far proved unsuccessful. The grocer at the corner of the Rue St. Louis possessed full information on the subject— information obtained first hand from the cook of the missing gentleman—and his shop was most extensively patronised that afternoon, even by people who pretended that he mixed dust with his pepper, and sweetened his jam with glucose. For once in a way, they put up with his adulterations to enjoy the benefit of his conversation. "It was yesterday evening," repeated the worthy grocer over and over again, as he assisted in weighing pounds of sugar and penn'orths of salt, "yesterday evening just after dinner, our neighbour M. Jandidier went down to his cellar to get up a bottle of old wine, and since then no one has seen him. The cellar door was found wide open, but M. Jandidier had disappeared, vanished, evaporated!"

From time to time it happens that mysterious disappearances are spoken of. Alarm is spread in various directions, and prudent people invest money in sword sticks and revolvers. But as a rule the police shrug their shoulders when these occurrences are mentioned. They are acquainted with the "seamy side" of the cunningly embroidered canvas. They start an investigation and discover the truth, so different to popular exaggeration: in lieu of a romance, they come upon some sad story.

However, to a certain extent the grocer of the Rue Saint Louis spoke the truth. It was a fact that M. Jandidier, who did a most extensive business as a manufacturer of imitation jewellery, had altogether disappeared since the previous night.

M. Théodore Jandidier was some fifty-eight years old. He was very tall and very bald, gifted with fairly good manners and deportment, and according to popular report, possessed of a very considerable fortune. This was not to be wondered at, for in Paris the trade in imitation jewellery is simply enormous, and some manufacturers like the Bourguignons and others, whose creations are exported all over the world, are simply millionaires. One could not say as much concerning M. Jandidier, but he was, nevertheless, a man of means. A pretty little collection of scrip and bonds were said to yield him an income of twenty thousand francs a year, and his business brought him an average annual profit of another fifty thousand. He was esteemed and liked in the neighbourhood, for his probity was above all question, and his morals perfectly exemplary. When five-and-thirty, he had married a portionless cousin, who had proved a happy and faithful wife.

This worthy couple possessed an only daughter named Thérèse, who was literally idolised by her father. At one time it had been said that she was to marry M. Gustave Schmidt, the eldest son of the senior partner in the great banking house of Schmidt,

Gubenheim, and Worb, but somehow or other—no one knew why—the marriage had been broken off; and this had caused all the more surprise, as the young folks were apparently very much in love with each other.

Some friends of the Jandidier family pretended that old Schmidt, the father, the most avaricious of all our Parisian financiers, and an inveterate "fleecer," had required that Mademoiselle Thérèse should bring her husband a preposterously large dowry, such as her father could not possibly furnish despite his comparative wealth. However, this was only a rumour which nothing had so far authenticated.

On this Sunday afternoon, when the news of M. Jandidier's disappearance spread through the Marais, all the incidents of his past life which the gossips were acquainted with, were duly recorded and submitted to public appreciation. A hundred stories of his honesty and good nature were told. He had been an honour to the district, an excellent worthy man in every respect. Given his rigid morals, it was altogether impossible to imagine that he had "gone off on the loose." His family ties were too strong for him to have abandoned his wife and daughter. No, he must have fallen a victim to some base scoundrel—he must have received a foul blow; and the honour of the Marais required that his remains should be recovered and fittingly interred, and that his murderer should be brought to justice.

So thus, during that Sunday afternoon, the rumours flew through the district, spreading in every ear and growing on every tongue, till, at last, having learned the reports from his agents, the district commissary of police considered it his duty to repair to the missing gentleman's residence with the view of obtaining precise information.

He was ushered into the grand drawing-room which was in a state of semi-obscurity, the shutters being half closed and the curtains drawn. Both Madame Jandidier and her daughter were distracted with grief, and he had considerable difficulty in calming them and inducing them to answer his questions. However, he was at length placed in possession of these particulars.

On the previous evening (Saturday) M. Jandidier had dined as usual with his family. He had made, however, but a poor meal, for he was troubled with a bad headache. After dinner he had gone down stairs—not to the wine cellar as the grocer of the Rue Saint Louis pretended—but to his warehouse, where a couple of *employés* were still at work. Having given them some orders, he retired for a short time into his private-room, occupied himself, no doubt, with various business matters, and then came up stairs again and told his wife that he was going out for a stroll. From that stroll he had never returned.

The commissary of police carefully noted down these particulars, and then asked Madame Jandidier if he could not speak with her alone for a few minutes. She looked at him with some surprise but finally signified her assent, and Mademoiselle Thérèse discreetly left the room.

"You must excuse the question I am about to ask you, madame," exclaimed the commissary, as the young lady closed the door behind her. "But this is a serious affair, and if we, the officials of justice, are to clear up the mystery, we must know the whole truth. Excuse my indiscretion, I beg you, but can you tell me whether M. Jandidier, your husband, ever had—to your knowledge—what shall I say? Well, any passing fancy, any feminine acquaintance away from home?"

Madame Jandidier sprang to her feet as if impelled by a spring. Anger had dried her tears, and it was in a snappish voice that she answered, "I have been married three-and-twenty years, monsieur. Never on any one occasion has my husband given cause for such a supposition. If I was not with him of an evening, he never returned home later than ten o'clock."

"Well, madame, was your husband in the habit of frequenting any club?" asked the commissary. "Had he any special café where he met his friends?"

"I should not have allowed such habits," curtly replied the lady.

"Do you know if he was accustomed to carry large sums about his person, madame?"

"On that point I can give you no information. I have always attended to my household, and not to my husband's business affairs."

The commissary found it impossible to obtain any further information, for the worthy dame's grief was now blended with a strong admixture of anger and resentment. The supposition that her husband might have a mistress revolted her feelings as a wife, and the barely veiled insinuation that he might frequent a club, and no doubt gamble there, incensed her as an attack on his recognised probity and integrity. However, despite Madame Jandidier's stiff air, the commissary thought it only right to try and assuage her affliction by repeating a few hackneyed "compliments of condolence," and then, with a profound bow, he retired.

Before leaving the house, however, he considered it his duty to question the servants, and their statements which generally corroborated Madame Jandidier's, made him feel somewhat anxious. He began to think that a crime had really been committed.

A few hours later he sent his report to the Prefecture of Police, and the same evening the case was submitted to the consideration of the Public Prosecutor. The latter, in his turn, delegated an investigating magistrate to examine the affair, and on the Monday morning the famous detective Retiveau, better known in the Rue de Jérusalem by his nickname of "Maître Magloire," received orders to scour Paris, and if needs be, the provinces, in search of M. Jandidier—or his corpse. A capital photograph of the manufacturer, taken only a short time previously, was handed to the detective, who at once commenced his difficult task,

II

Maître Magloire was a man of no little energy, and a fervent believer in the value of time. His alacrity was proverbial, so that the investigating magistrate, intrusted with the Jandidier affair, was by no means surprised when, on the Monday afternoon, his usher announced that the detective wished to speak with him, having already obtained some important information.

The magistrate at once gave orders for the police agent to be admitted. "Here already, M. Magloire," said he. "So you have fresh news, eh?"

"I am on the scent, monsieur."

"Well, tell me what you have ascertained."

"To begin, monsieur, I have learned that M. Jandidier did not leave home at half-past six on Saturday evening, but at seven o'clock precisely."

"Precisely?"

"Well, yes. My information comes from a clock-maker, in the immediate neighbourhood of M. Jandidier's house. This clock-maker knew him well, and noticed that he paused in front of his shop. In fact, M. Jandidier pulled out his watch and compared time with the clock above the door. The circumstance induced the clock-maker to look at the time himself, and he recollects perfectly well that it was then exactly two minutes past seven. Those two minutes would have amply sufficed for M. Jandidier to walk from his house as far as this shop. It is fortunate that he should have paused to compare time, for this apparently trivial circumstance has guided me to all my subsequent discoveries. For instance, the clock-maker noticed that M. Jandidier was munching an unlighted cigar. It occured to me that he must ultimately have lighted it, and I asked myself where and how? Had he a box of lucifers in his pocket? No; for I learned at his house that a little silver-plated box he usually carried about with him, had been found on the mantel-shelf in his room since his disappearance. In this case, I reasoned, he must probably have gone into some tobacconist's shop to get a light."

"Yes, no doubt," opined the magistrate.

"I had considerable difficulty in finding the shop in question," resumed the detective; "but as the course taken by M. Jandidier from his residence to the clock-maker's shop seemed to indicate that he was going towards the boulevards, I went in that direction. To my delight, just as I reached the Boulevard du Temple, sure enough I came upon a tobacconist's shop. I went in and made inquiries. The woman behind the counter was well acquainted with M. Jandidier, and she recollected perfectly that he came in on Saturday evening to get a light. She was all the more certain on the point for, at the same time, he purchased a packet of *londrès extra*, which greatly surprised her, as he usually smoked very cheap cigars."

"How did he seem?"

"The woman told me that he looked pre-occupied. I obtained from her an important piece of information, which shows that Madame Jandidier was altogether wrong when she told the commissary of police that her husband did not go to any particular café. However, husbands don't always tell everything to their wives; and according to the tobacconist, M. Jandidier frequently went to the Café Turc, which is hard-by. I went there and questioned the waiters. Two of them remembered having seen him on Saturday evening. He drank two small glasses of brandy neat, and talked with some friends who were there. He seemed sad. The waiter who served at his table told me that he and his friends talked all the while about life insurances. It was half-past eight when he went away, accompanied by one of his friends, M. Blandureau, a merchant of the neighbourhood. I immediately went to M. Blandureau's ware-house and questioned him. He told me that on Saturday evening he walked down the boulevards with M. Jandidier, as far as the corner of the Rue de Richelieu, where M. Jandidier left him, saying that he had business to attend to. He was not at all in his usual frame of mind, M. Blandureau tells me; he seemed out of sorts and worried with melancholy presentiments."

"Very good, so far," muttered the magistrate.

"On leaving M. Blandureau," continued Maître Magloire, "I returned to the Rue du Roi de Sicile to inquire of the people of the house if M. Jandidier had, to their knowledge, any customers or friends, might be even a mistress, in the Rue de Richelieu. I more particularly questioned the man-servant who generally did his master's errands, but all he could tell me was that M. Jandidier's tailor lived in that street. I thought it, after all, advisable to go and see this tailor. 'Yes,' said he, 'M. Jandidier came to see me on Saturday. He came to order a pair of trousers. It was past nine o'clock.' It seems that whilst he was being measured a button fell from his waistcoat, and he asked the tailor to sew it on again. For this to be done, he took off his coat, and at the same time removed a packet of papers and a note-book from the breast-pocket. Holding these papers in his hand he half sorted them, and the tailor noticed that they comprised several bank notes."

"Ah! That's a clue. So he had a large sum on his person?"

"Large? Well not so, perhaps, for a man of his position; but still a fair amount. The tailor thinks there must have been twelve or fourteen hundred francs in notes."

"Continue," said the investigating magistrate.

"While the button of his waistcoat was being sewn on again, M. Jandidier suddenly left off sorting his papers and complained of indisposition. The tailor had already noticed that he looked far from well; and at his customer's request he dispatched an apprentice to fetch a cab. M. Jandidier said that he had to go as far as the Halle aux Vins to see one of his work people who lived hard-by. Unfortunately the apprentice could not tell me the number of the cab he fetched, but on the other hand he recollected that it had yellow wheels, and was drawn by a big black horse. The yellow wheels proved that the vehicle did not come from the stables of the Cab Company, but that it belonged to some petty job-master. I sent a circular note to all the authorised cabkeepers, and a few hours ago I had the satisfaction of learning that the vehicle in question was No. 6,007. The driver remembered that on Saturday evening he was hailed by a lad in the Rue de Richelieu, and that for ten minutes or so he waited outside the shop of a tailor named Gouin. I asked him if he would be able to recognise the gentleman he drove to the Halle aux Vins, and he told me that he thought he would. Thereupon, I showed him five photographs, and he at once picked out M. Jandidier's portrait. There was a bright moonlight on Saturday evening, he said, and whilst the gentleman was counting out the money to pay his fare he had a good look at him."

Maître Magloire paused and noted with satisfaction the approbative expression on the magistrate's face.

"Well," said he, "this cabby drove M. Jandidier to the immediate vicinity of the Halle aux Vins, to No. 48, in the Rue d'Arras-Saint Victor; and in this house there lives a workman, whom M. Jandidier employed, a workman of the name of Jules Tarot."

The significant manner in which Maître Magloire articulated these words "Jules Tarot" was well calculated to impress the investigating magistrate.

"Have you any suspicions?" asked the latter, giving the detective a keen look.

"Not precisely; but still here are the facts. On reaching the Rue d'Arras, M. Jandidier discharged his cab. He asked the doorkeeper if Tarot was at home, and on receiving an affirmative reply he went upstairs. It was then about ten o'clock. Half an hour afterwards the doorkeeper went to bed, and he was just falling asleep when he heard Tarot come down stairs. Tarot called to him to pull the rope which opens the door, and, thanks to the night light, the doorkeeper perceived that the workman was accompanied by the gentleman who had called. They went out together; and shortly after midnight Tarot returned home alone."

"And M. Jandidier?" asked the magistrate.

"Ah! I have been unable to trace him any further," replied Maître Magloire.

"That seems significant; suspicious even."

"Yes, monsieur. I fancy it's a bad job. Of course I could not question Tarot; it would have put him on his guard."

"Have you found out what kind of man this fellow Tarot is?"

"Oh! On that point I questioned the doorkeeper. Tarot, he told me, is a mother-of-pearl worker. He polishes the shells, and is most skilful in imparting the proper macreous iridescence. Altogether, he seems to be a clever fellow, and he and his wife together—for he has taught her the work—earn at times as much as a hundred francs a week."

"So they are well off, for people of their class."

"Well, no, monsieur. They are both of them young, both of them Parisians born and bred, they have no children, and so they amuse themselves. Not content with Sunday relaxation and pleasure, they habitually make Monday a fête day, after the fashion of so many workpeople, and the result is, that long before pay day arrives they are desperately hard up."

"H'm," said the magistrate, stroking his chin with a pensive air. "All this seems very suspicious—very suspicious indeed. So the Tarots lead rather a loose life? Their purse is often empty; and very likely they are in debt. Those twelve hundred francs that M. Jandidier had about him, no doubt, excited their covetousness. He probably called on Tarot to intrust him with some work, and no doubt pulled out his pocket-book to make a memorandum. Tarot must have seen the bank notes. And no trace, you say, can be found of M. Jandidier after he left the house with his workman at eleven o'clock at night?"

"No, monsieur, no trace at all," answered the detective. "I have made diligent inquiries in all directions but without result."

"Very strange, very suspicious," muttered the magistrate; and then in a louder key he added: "I must say, M. Magloire, that you have conducted this inquiry admirably. Guided by M. Jandidier's unlighted cigar, you have traced him to—well, to the man who is probably his murderer. Yes, his murderer, I have very strong suspicions on the point."

A brief pause ensued, and then the magistrate asked: "Was Tarot at home when you made these inquiries this afternoon?"

"Oh, no, monsieur. He and his wife had gone off. It's Monday, remember."

"Are you certain that they had merely gone off holiday-making?"

"Why, yes, monsieur; the doorkeeper said they had left early in the morning with a couple of friends, two of Tarot's comrades, I believe. They were going to picnic near Chaville."

"Ah! That was a splendid opportunity to make a perquisition in their absence, Maître Magloire."

"Certainly, monsieur, but I had no search warrant, and besides, it was only an hour or so ago that I went to the Rue d'Arras."

"I suppose that doorkeeper is to be depended upon?"

"Oh, yes, monsieur. He's affiliated at the Prefecture, No. 920."*

"Then he's safe. Did you leave him any instructions as to what he ought to do, if the Tarots returned home before you saw him again?"

"I did better than that, monsieur, I left a comrade at the house to wait and watch."

"Very good. Well, M. Magloire, we must have a perquisition; and here are a couple of warrants which you can use if occasion requires. Be here at eight o'clock to-morrow morning."

So saying, the magistrate returned to some documents he had been perusing when the detective arrived. The latter pocketed the warrants, made a deep bow, and hastened out of the room.

III

It was already six o'clock, and before repairing to the Rue d'Arras-Saint-Victor it was necessary that Maître Magloire should call at the office of the district commissary of police, show him his instructions, and request him to preside at the perquisition. As the commissary was away at his dinner, some little time was lost. "We must have a locksmith," the detective reflected, "for the Tarots will hardly have returned, and it will be necessary to force open the door." A locksmith was accordingly procured, a couple of *gardiens de la Paix* were summoned to serve as an escort, and on the commissary's return the party set off.

At the corner of the street the detective asked his companions to wait a moment, and then went ahead. It was necessary that he should reconnoitre the ground, and ascertain from the comrade whom he had left with the doorkeeper if anything noteworthy had occurred during his absence.

As he entered the house he heard heavy steps climbing the stairs, and a man and a woman singing a gay refrain. "Have they returned?" thought Maître Magloire, and he hurried into the doorkeeper's room.

His comrade was there, and on perceiving him raised his fore-finger to his lips: "Hush, they've just come home. They are only halfway up stairs."

"They are singing loud enough," rejoined Maître Magloire in an undertone. "I must say that they are unusually gay for—for murderers."

---

*It should be remembered that a very large number of Parisian doorkeepers or concierges are secret agents of the Prefecture de Police.—[Trans.]

"Oh!" replied his comrade. "The wine has got into their heads. As for their gaiety we'll see about that by-and-bye."

Despite this rejoinder Magloire remained for a moment pensive. "Am I mistaken?" he asked himself. "But, then——" However, his hesitation was of short duration. "At all events we must clear up the mystery," he added, and leaving the house he went in search of the commissary.

Joyful the Tarots had certainly seemed as they climbed the stairs, singing a popular ditty. They were laden with field flowers, which the wife tastefully arranged in two large blue vases as soon as they had entered their lodging.

"Now, Clementina," called the husband, "you must make haste with the supper, or else the concert will be over by the time we get there."

Both Tarot and his wife were very partial to the entertainments given at a little café concert in the neighbourhood, and it was with the view of going there that evening, that they had returned so early from their excursion.

"Oh! I've only the stew to warm," answered the wife; "but, Eugène, while I light the fire would you mind running down to fetch a quart of wine?"

The husband took an empty bottle from a corner in the kitchen and went toward the outer door of the apartment, but when only halfway he paused with surprise.

Rat-tat-tat, rat-tat-tat. Some very noisy visitor indeed demanded admittance.

"Who's there?" cried Tarot.

"Open, in the name of the law," answered a stern voice.

Husband and wife turned pale with terror.

"Open, in the name of the law," repeated the same voice.

Still Tarot did not budge. Fear seemed to root him to the spot.

There was no further parleying, for at that moment Maître Magloire perceived that the key had been left in the door outside. So he just turned it and walked in, followed by his comrade and the commissary of police.

On perceiving the latter functionary, whose stomach was spanned with his broad tricolour sash of office, Tarot and his wife were seized with a nervous trembling, of which Maître Magloire took careful note.

"Why did'nt you open the door?" sternly asked the commissary of police.

"I was so surprised—monsieur—I didn't know—I—" stammered Tarot.

"Ah, you look as if you had something on your conscience," retorted the functionary, "I suppose you know what has brought us here?"

Tarot gave the commissary an anxious look, and stammered an incomprehensible answer.

"We have come to make a perquisition," said Maître Magloire. "Do you know that your employer, M. Jandidier of the Rue du Roi de Sicile, has disappeared? He was last seen in your company late on Saturday night."

Both Tarot and his wife were too overwhelmed to speak.

"Come give us the keys of all your drawers and cupboards," said the commissary; and as the wife timidly drew them from her pocket he added, turning to the detective: "There you are, Maître Magloire, you may set about your task."

The search was a protracted and a difficult one, for dusk had now set in, and a careful scrutiny could scarcely be made by lamp light. However, all the drawers were turned out, and all the cupboards carefully explored. Magloire ferreted in every nook and corner, ripped up the mattresses and pillows on the bed, tried the stuffing of the chairs, but all to no avail. Nothing suspicious could be found.

"It's singular," muttered the detective; and he once more asked himself, "Have I been mistaken after all?"

At this moment it occurred to him to look at the Tarots who stood by, watching the proceedings in silence. Perhaps their demeanour might give him a clue; otherwise he and his companions would have no other resource but to apologise and withdraw. At first he observed nothing particular, save an expression of affright in their looks, but as he carefully followed the direction of the wife's glance, he noticed that it was fixed on a birdcage hanging near the window. "Eureka!" he cried, "I have it!"

Springing towards the cage he unhooked it, and careless of the canary roosting on the perch, he examined it in every sense. As in most cages there was a movable floor which drew out to admit of proper cleansing, and sure enough, between the thin boards, Maître Magloire found a sum of twelve hundred francs in bank notes.

The Tarots exchanged looks of terror. The husband seemed overwhelmed, but the wife broke out into piteous lamentations, repeating again and again that she and her husband were innocent.

However, the commissary and Magloire paid little or no attention to her wailings. "You had much better make a clean breast of it," exclaimed the detective, "instead of kicking up that row." Whereupon both husband and wife answered in piteous tones: "Oh! we are innocent, sir, we are innocent!"

This time the detective shrugged his shoulders. "In the name of the law, I arrest you," said he. "I charge you with the murder of M. Jandidier." And he called to the two *gardiens de la Paix*, waiting below, to come upstairs.

The Tarots showed no signs of resistance, but as they were charged with a capital offence, the commissary thought it prudent to have them hand-cuffed. They passively allowed themselves to be removed to a cab which was sent for, and half an hour later they crossed the threshold of the Dépôt, and were duly locked into separate cells.

Magloire was fairly elated, and, forgetful of discipline, hurried off to the private residence of the investigating magistrate, to acquaint him with the capture and the recovery of M. Jandidier's money. The magistrate was pleased to express his approval, and renewed the appointment for the following morning at his office at the Palais de Justice.

The Tarots were interrogated separately. They both looked pale and careworn when they entered the magistrate's office, but, after passing the night under lock and key in a prison cell, this was only natural. However, they had both found their tongues again, and apparently they had preconcerted a system of defence, for their answers were identical.

They admitted that M. Jandidier had called on them on the Saturday evening. He seemed very poorly, and they asked him if he would not like to take a drop of something, but he refused the offer.

"What was the object of his visit?" asked the magistrate.

"He wished us to execute an important order, and proposed that we should take workpeople on our own account."

"That's singular. Had he not numerous workmen of his own?"

"Yes, but he said that his health was failing him, that he could no longer give his usual attention to business, and should prefer to transfer the order to us."

"And what was your answer?"

"We told him that we lacked the capital to execute it."

"Ah!—ah! And what then?"

"Why, he replied, 'Oh, that's of no consequence. I'll advance you enough money'; and he pulled out his pocket-book, and laid twelve hundred francs in bank notes on the table."

"Had he so much confidence as that in you?"

"Well, he knew we worked fairly well."

"Yes, but you have dissipated habits. You spend your money faster than you earn it. Your story is altogether improbable. M. Jandidier must have known how prodigal you both were. Well, did you at least give him a receipt?"

"Yes, monsieur."

"Who signed it?"

"We both did."

"H'm, and what then?"

"After that," answered Tarot, "M. Jandidier asked me to see him further on. He said he was going in the direction of the Faubourg St. Antoine."

"And where did you leave him?"

"At the Place de la Bastille. We crossed the Constantine foot bridge and followed the canal."

"Ah! you followed the canal?" exclaimed the magistrate, eyeing Tarot attentively. "And you reached the Place de la Bastille safely?"

"Certainly we did, monsieur," answered the workman, with a flushed face.

Naturally enough, the magistrate asked both the husband and the wife to explain why they had hidden the money in the birdcage, and they each gave the same answer. On the Sunday night, as they were going home, Tarot met a comrade who, while he was playing cards in a wine-shop in the Marais during the afternoon, had heard of M. Jandidier's disappearance. The news greatly frightened them, and Tarot said to his wife, "If it were known that he came here on Saturday night, it would be a bad job for us. Didn't we cross the bridge together, and walk along the banks of the canal? The police would certainly suspect me, and if those twelve hundred francs were found in our possession, we should be altogether lost."

"We didn't sleep all Sunday night," said Tarot's wife; "we lay awake thinking about M. Jandidier. And we certainly shouldn't have gone out on the Monday, if one of my husband's cousins hadn't come to fetch us according to arrangement. However, in the country we almost forgot about the matter, and as the detective says, we were no doubt gay when we came home. Before going out, I wanted to burn the ban notes, but Tarot wouldn't let me. He meant to refund the money to M. Jandidier's family, he said; and besides, as he explained, we might have put ourselves in a bad position by destroying the notes, for, even if M. Jandidier were dead, his body might be found with our receipt in his pocket, and then we should have to refund the money; and how could we do so if the notes were destroyed?"

The magistrate listened attentively to this explanation, which was plausible if not probable, and the prisoners' line of defence struck him as a very artful one. "How did you know," he asked at length, "how did you know that M. Jandidier's body had not been found when the police searched your place? It might have been recovered, and the detectives might have had your receipt with them. It was your duty to produce that money at once. Why didn't you do so?"

"We didn't know what to do or what to think, monsieur; we were too frightened."

"Innocent persons have no reason to feel frightened," sententiously retorted the magistrate. "Justice knows how to distinguish between the innocent and the guilty."

He said this, and yet, at that very moment, he was asking himself in sore perplexity, "Are these people culpable or not?" After all, there was nothing to corroborate the explanation of the Tarots, and it was utterly impossible for him to content himself with their mere word. A further search must be made for M. Jandidier. Perhaps his body might be found, and then it would be possible to form a positive opinion. In the meanwhile, the workman and his wife must be retained in custody.

IV

A week elapsed, and the magistrate was still in the same perplexity. The Tarots had each been re-examined three times, but nothing fresh had been elicited from them, and their later statements failed to contradict their earlier version. Were they innocent, then? Or had they merely cleverly preconcerted a plausible system of defence?

M. Jandidier's remains had been searched for far and wide. The Seine and the canal had been dragged. The missing manufacturer's photograph had been sent all over France, but utterly without result. In this situation, the magistrate asked himself what course he ought to pursue. If he sent the prisoners to the assizes they would very likely be acquitted for want of sufficient proofs, especially if they were defended by a skilful advocate. No doubt there was the circumstance of those twelve hundred francs found in their possession; but would that suffice to ensure a conviction? The prisoners explained their possession of this money in a most artful fashion, and, besides, the true *corpus délicti* was wanting. What should the magistrate do then?

He was asking himself this question for the hundredth time, when a strange, almost incredible report reached his ears. The well known firm of Jandidier *ainé* had suspended payment, and was going into bankruptcy! "Who would have expected that!" grumbled the magistrate. "Well, perhaps, we are coming to the truth."

On the morrow a detective who had been duly instructed, brought him a full report of circumstances which none of M. Jandidier's family had ever dreamed of. The revelation was an astounding one, and had caused immense surprise throughout the district of the Marais where M. Jandidier had been so respected and esteemed. In fact, the man whom the denizens of the Rue du Roi de Sicile so delighted to honour, the idol of the trade in imitation jewellery, had fallen from his pedestal with a crash. People had imagined he was wealthy, and yet in reality he was ruined—utterly ruined: and during the last three years he had only kept up his credit by means of expedients. Less than a thousand francs had been found in his safe, and on the Saturday after his disappearance, bills for sixty-seven thousand five hundred francs were presented for payment by the Bank of France. Yes, Jandidier, the man of severe morality, gambled at the Bourse; the virtuous husband kept a mistress!

The magistrate could scarcely believe his ears, and was giving vent to his astonishment when Maître Magloire appeared, quite out of breath.

"You know the news, monsieur?" asked the detective as he crossed the threshold.

"Yes, I have just been told everything."

"The Tarots are innocent!"

"I think so—and yet that visit Jandidier paid them—how do you explain that visit?"

The detective sighed. "Ah, monsieur," said he, "I was a fool, as my colleague, Monsieur Lecoq, has just shown me. You will recollect that at the Café Turc, Jandidier and his friends talked all the time about life assurances?"

"Yes, I remember; but what connection—"

"Ah! monsieur, that was the point I ought to have kept in mind! Jandidier's life was assured for 200,000 francs."

"Indeed!"

"Yes, and as you are aware, monsieur, in France assurance companies don't pay when the holder of a policy commits suicide. Now, Jandidier was no doubt anxious to provide for his family; and so he made it appear as if he had been murdered, in hopes that the companies would pay his wife."

"Do you think he has destroyed himself?"

"I cannot say, monsieur. At all events we cannot find his remains. May be he has simply taken himself off. And yet I don't know; he can only have had very little money with him, and at his age a man scarcely has the courage to begin life over again. At all events, he certainly laid a trap for poor Tarot, and would have sent him to the guillotine for the sake of his policies being paid."

"What a scamp!" growled the magistrate; and he took up his pen to sign an order for the release of the workman and his wife.

Thanks to M. Gustave Schmidt—of the great house of Schmidt, Gubenheim, and Worb—the firm of Jandidier did not go into bankruptcy. Old Schmidt had just died, most opportunely, and M. Gustave was able to dispose of the paternal inheritance as he pleased, and more than that, he means to dispose of himself as well, for the papers announced that he and Mademoiselle Thérèse Jandidier are to be married next month.

Tarot and his wife have set up in business, thanks to the twelve hundred francs returned to them at M. Gustave's request; and, mindful of the investigating magistrate's reproaches anent their "prodigality," and "dissipated habits," they have quite given up "merry-making" Mondays.

But what has become of M. Jandidier? Is he dead, or has he gone to America? If any of our readers are acquainted with his whereabouts they may communicate with the authorities, who offer a thousand franc reward!

THE TRAVELLER'S STORY OF A TERRIBLY STRANGE BED

Wilkie Collins

SHORTLY AFTER MY EDUCATION AT COLLEGE WAS FINISHED, I HAPPENED TO BE staying at Paris with an English friend. We were both young men then, and lived, I am afraid, rather a wild life, in the delightful city of our sojourn. One night we were idling about the neighbourhood of the Palais Royal, doubtful to what amusement we should next be-take ourselves. My friend proposed a visit to Frascati's; but his suggestion was not to my taste. I knew Frascati's, as the French saying is, by heart; had lost and won plenty of five-franc pieces there, merely for amusement's sake, until it was amusement no longer, and was thoroughly tired, in fact, of all the ghastly respectabilities of such a social anomaly as a respectable gambling-house. "For Heaven's sake," said I to my friend, "let us go somewhere where we can see a little genuine, blackguard, poverty-stricken gaming, with no false gingerbread glitter thrown over it at all. Let us get away from fashionable Frascati's, to a house where they don't mind letting in a man with a ragged coat, or a man with no coat, ragged or otherwise."—"Very well," said my friend, "we needn't go out of the Palais Royal to find the sort of company you want. Here's the place just before us; as blackguard a place, by all report, as you could possibly wish to see." In another minute we arrived at the door, and entered the house, the back of which you have drawn in your sketch.

When we got up stairs, and had left our hats and sticks with the doorkeeper, we were admitted into the chief gambling-room. We did not find many people assembled there. But, few as the men were who looked up at us on our entrance, they were all types—lamentably true types—of their respective classes.

We had come to see blackguards; but these men were something worse. There is a comic side, more or less appreciable, in all blackguardism—here there was nothing but tragedy—mute, weird tragedy. The quiet in the room was horrible. The thin, haggard, long-haired young man, whose sunken eyes fiercely watched the turning up of the cards, never spoke; the flabby, fat-faced, pimply player, who pricked his piece of pasteboard perseveringly, to register how often black won, and how often red—never spoke; the dirty, wrinkled old man, with the vulture eyes and the darned greatcoat, who had lost his last *sou*, and still looked on desperately, after he could play no longer—never spoke. Even the voice of the croupier sounded as if it were strangely dulled and thickened in the atmosphere of the room. I had entered the place to laugh; but the spectacle before me was something to weep over. I soon found it necessary to take refuge in excitement from the depression of spirits which was fast stealing on me. Unfortunately I sought the nearest excitement, by going to the table, and beginning to play. Still more unfortunately, as the event will show, I won—won prodigiously; won incredibly; won at such a rate, that the regular players at the table crowded round me; and staring at my stakes with hungry, superstitious eyes, whispered to one another, that the English stranger was going to break the bank.

The game was *Rouge et Noir*. I had played at it in every city in Europe, without, however, the care or the wish to study the Theory of Chances—that philosopher's stone of all gamblers! And a gambler, in the strict sense of the word, I had never been. I was heart-whole from the corroding passion for play. My gaming was a mere idle amusement. I never resorted to it by necessity, because I never knew what it was to want money. I never practised it so incessantly as to lose more than I could afford, or to gain more than I could coolly pocket without being thrown off my balance by my good luck. In short, I had hitherto frequented gambling-tables—just as I frequented ball-rooms and opera-houses—because they amused me, and because I had nothing better to do with my leisure hours.

But on this occasion it was very different—now, for the first time in my life, I felt what the passion for play really was. My success first bewildered, and then, in the most literal meaning of the word, intoxicated me. Incredible as it may appear, it is nevertheless true, that I only lost when I attempted to estimate chances, and played according to previous calculation. If I left everything to luck, and staked without any care or consideration, I was sure to win—to win in the face of every recognised probability in favour of the bank. At first, some of the men present ventured their money safely enough on my colour; but I speedily increased my stakes to sums which they dared not risk. One after another they left off playing, and breathlessly looked on at my game.

Still, time after time, I staked higher and higher, and still won. The excitement in the room rose to fever pitch. The silence was interrupted by a deep, muttered chorus of oaths and exclamations in different languages, every time the gold was shovelled across to my side of the table—even the imperturbable croupier dashed his rake on the floor in a (French) fury of astonishment at my success. But one man present preserved his self-possession; and that man was my friend. He came to my side, and whispering in English, begged me to leave the place satisfied with what I had already gained. I must do him the justice to say, that he repeated his warnings and entreaties several times; and only left me and went away, after I had rejected his advice (I was to all intents and purposes gambling-drunk) in terms which rendered it impossible for him to address me again that night.

Shortly after he had gone, a hoarse voice behind me cried:—"Permit me, my dear sir!—permit me to restore to their proper place two Napoleons which you have dropped. Wonderful luck, sir! I pledge you my word of honour as an old soldier, in the course of my long experience in this sort of thing, I never saw such luck as yours!—never! Go on, sir—*Sacré mille bombes*! Go on boldly, and break the bank!"

I turned round and saw, nodding and smiling at me with inveterate civility, a tall man, dressed in a frogged and braided surtout.

If I had been in my senses, I should have considered him, personally, as being rather a suspicious specimen of an old soldier. He had goggling blood-shot eyes, mangy mustachios, and a broken nose. His voice betrayed a barrack-room intonation of the worst order, and he had the dirtiest pair of hands I ever saw—even in France. These little personal peculiarities exercised, however, no repelling influence on me. In the mad excitement, the reckless triumph of that moment, I was ready to "fraternize" with anybody who encouraged me in my game. I accepted the old soldier's offered pinch of snuff; clapped him on the back, and swore he was the honestest fellow in the world—the most glorious relic of the Grand Army that I had ever met with. "Go on!" cried my military friend, snapping his fingers in ecstasy,—"Go on, and win! Break the bank—*Mille tonnerres*! my gallant English comrade, break the bank!"

And I *did* go on—went on at such a rate, that in another quarter of an hour the croupier called out: "Gentlemen! the bank has discontinued for to-night," All the notes, and all the gold in that "bank," now lay in a heap under my hands; the whole floating capital of the gambling-house was waiting to pour into my pockets!

"Tie up the money in your pocket-handkerchief, my worthy sir," said the old soldier, as I wildly plunged my hands into my heap of gold. "Tie it up, as we used to tie up a bit of dinner in the Grand Army; your winnings are too heavy for any breeches pockets that ever were sewed. There! that's it!—shovel them in, notes and all! *Credié*! what luck!—Stop! another Napoleon on the floor! *Ah! sacré petit polisson de Napoleon*! have I found thee at last? Now then, sir—two tight double knots each way with your honourable permission, and the money's safe. Feel it! feel it, fortunate sir! hard and round as a cannon ball—*Ah, bah*! if they had only fired such cannon balls at us at Austerlitz—*nom d'une pipe*! if they only had! And now, as an ancient grenadier, as an ex-brave of the French army, what remains for me to do? I ask what? Simply this: to entreat my valued English friend to drink a bottle of champagne with me, and toast the goddess Fortune in foaming goblets before we part!"

Excellent ex-brave! Convivial ancient grenadier! Champagne by all means! An English cheer for an old soldier! Hurrah! hurrah! Another English cheer for the goddess Fortune! Hurrah! hurrah! hurrah!

"Bravo! the Englishman; the amiable, gracious Englishman, in whose veins circulates the vivacious blood of France! Another glass? *Ah, bah!*—the bottle is empty! Never mind! *Vive le vin*! I, the old soldier, order another bottle, and half-a-pound of *bon-bons* with it!"

"No, no, ex-brave; never—ancient grenadier! *Your* bottle last time; *my* bottle this. Behold it! Toast away! The French Army!—the great Napoleon!—the present company! the croupier! the honest croupier's wife and daughters—if he has any! the Ladies generally! Everybody in the world!"

By the time the second bottle of champagne was emptied, I felt as if I had been drinking liquid fire—my brain seemed all a-flame. No excess in wine had ever had this effect on me before in my life. Was it the result of a stimulant acting upon my system when I was in a highly excited state? Was my stomach in a particularly disordered condition? Or was the champagne amazingly strong?

"Ex-brave of the French Army!" cried I, in a mad state of exhilaration, "*I* am on fire! how are *you*? You have set me on fire! Do you hear; my hero of Austerlitz? Let us have a third bottle of champagne to put the flame out!"

The old soldier wagged his head, rolled his goggle eyes, until I expected to see them slip out of their sockets; placed his dirty forefinger by the side of his broken nose; solemnly ejaculated "Coffee!" and immediately ran off into an inner room.

The word pronounced by the eccentric veteran seemed to have a magical effect on the rest of the company present. With one accord they all rose to depart. Probably they had expected to profit by my intoxication; but finding that my new friend was benevolently bent on preventing me from getting dead drunk, had now abandoned all hope of thriving pleasantly on my winnings. Whatever their motive might be, at any rate they went away in a body.

When the old soldier returned, and sat down again opposite to me at the table, we had the room to ourselves. I could see the croupier, in a sort of vestibule which opened out of it, eating his supper in solitude. The silence was now deeper than ever.

A sudden change, too, had come over the "ex-brave." He assumed a portentously solemn look; and when he spoke to me again, his speech was ornamented by no oaths, enforced by no finger-snapping, enlivened by no apostrophes or exclamations.

"Listen, my dear sir," said he, in mysteriously confidential tones—"listen to an old soldier's advice. I have been to the mistress of the house (a very charming woman, with a genius for cookery!) to impress on her the necessity of making us some particularly strong and good coffee. You must drink this coffee in order to get rid of your little amiable exaltation of spirits before you think of going home—you *must*, my good and gracious friend! With all that money to take home to-night, it is a sacred duty to yourself to have your wits about you. You are known to be a winner to an enormous extent by several gentlemen present to-night, who, in a certain point of view, are very worthy and excellent fellows; but they are mortal men, my dear sir, and they have their amiable weaknesses! Need I say more? Ah, no, no! you understand me! Now, this is what you must do—send for a cabriolet when you feel quite well again—draw up all the windows when you get into it—and tell the driver to take you home only through the large and well-lighted thoroughfares. Do this; and you and your money will be safe. Do this; and to-morrow you will thank an old soldier for giving you a word of honest advice."

Just as the ex-brave ended his oration in very lachrymose tones, the coffee came in, ready poured out in two cups. My attentive friend handed me one of the cups with a bow. I was parched with thirst, and drank it off at a draught. Almost instantly afterwards, I was seized with a fit of giddiness, and felt more completely intoxicated than ever. The room whirled round and round furiously; the old soldier seemed to be regularly bobbing up and down before me like the piston of a steam-engine. I was half deafened by a violent singing in my ears; a feeling of utter bewilderment, helplessness, idiocy, overcame me. I rose from my chair, holding on by the table to keep my balance; and stammered out, that I felt dreadfully unwell—so unwell that I did not know how I was to get home.

"My dear friend," answered the old soldier, and even his voice seemed to be bobbing up and down as he spoke—"my dear friend, it would be madness to go home in *your* state; you would be sure to lose your money; you might be robbed and murdered with the greatest ease. *I* am going to sleep here: do *you* sleep here, too—they make up capital beds in this house—take one; sleep off the effects of the wine, and go home safely with your winnings to-morrow—to-morrow, in broad daylight."

I had but two ideas left:—one, that I must never let go hold of my handkerchief full of money; the other, that I must lie down somewhere immediately, and fall off into a comfortable sleep. So I agreed to the proposal about the bed, and took the offered arm of the old soldier, carrying my money with my disengaged hand. Preceded by the croupier, we passed along some passages and up a flight of stairs into the bed-room which I was to occupy. The ex-brave shook me warmly by the hand; proposed that we should breakfast together, and then, followed by the croupier, left me for the night.

I ran to the wash-hand stand; drank some of the water in my jug; poured the rest out, and plunged my face into it—then sat down in a chair and tried to compose myself. I soon felt better. The change for my lungs, from the fetid atmosphere of the gambling-room to the cool air of the apartment I now occupied; the almost equally refreshing change for my eyes, from the glaring gas-lights of the "Salon" to the dim, quiet flicker of one bedroom candle; aided wonderfully the restorative effects of cold water. The giddiness left me, and I began to feel a little like a reasonable being again. My first thought was of the risk of sleeping all night in a gambling-house; my second, of the still greater risk of trying to get out after the house was closed, and of going home alone at night, through the streets of Paris with a large sum of money about me. I had slept in worse places than this on my travels, so I determined to lock, bolt, and barricade my door, and take my chance till the next morning.

Accordingly, I secured myself against all intrusion; looked under the bed, and into the cupboard; tried the fastening of the window; and then, satisfied that I had taken every proper precaution, pulled off my upper clothing, put my light, which was a dim one, on the hearth among a feathery litter of wood ashes, and got into bed, with the handkerchief full of money under my pillow.

I soon felt not only that I could not go to sleep, but that I could not even close my eyes. I was wide awake, and in a high fever. Every nerve in my body trembled—every one of my senses seemed to be preternaturally sharpened. I tossed and rolled, and tried every kind of position, and perseveringly sought out the cold corners of the bed, and all to no purpose. Now, I thrust my arms over the clothes; now, I poked them under the clothes; now, I violently shot my legs straight out down to the bottom of the bed; now, I convulsively coiled them up as near my chin as they would go; now, I shook out my crumpled pillow, changed it to the cool side, patted it flat, and lay down quietly on my back; now, I fiercely doubled it in two, set it up on end, thrust it against the board of the bed, and tried a sitting-posture. Every effort was in vain; I groaned with vexation, as I felt that I was in for a sleepless night.

What could I do? I had no book to read. And yet, unless I found out some method of diverting my mind, I felt certain that I was in the condition to imagine all sorts of horrors; to rack my brain with forebodings of every possible and impossible danger; in short, to pass the night in suffering all conceivable varieties of nervous terror.

I raised myself on my elbow, and looked about the room—which was brightened by a lovely moonlight pouring straight through the window—to see if it contained any pictures or ornaments that I could at all clearly distinguish. While my eyes wandered from wall to wall, a remembrance of Le Maistre's delightful little book, "Voyage autour de ma Chambre," occurred to me. I resolved to imitate the French author, and find occupation and amusement enough to relieve the tedium of my wakefulness, by making a mental inventory of every article of furniture I could see, and by following up to their sources the multitude of associations which even a chair, a table, or a wash-hand stand may be made to call forth.

In the nervous unsettled state of my mind at that moment, I found it much easier to make my inventory than to make my reflections, and thereupon soon gave up all hope of thinking in Le Maistre's fanciful track—or, indeed, of thinking at all. I looked about the room at the different articles of furniture, and did nothing more.

There was, first, the bed I was lying in; a four-post bed, of all things in the world to meet with in Paris!—yes, a thorough clumsy British four-poster, with the regular top lined with chintz—the regular fringed valance all round—the regular stifling unwholesome curtains, which I remembered having mechanically drawn back against the posts without particularly noticing the bed when I first got into the room. Then there was the marble-topped wash-hand stand, from which the water I had spilt, in my hurry to pour it out, was still dripping, slowly and more slowly, on to the brick-floor. Then two small chairs, with my coat, waistcoat, and trousers flung on them. Then a large elbow-chair covered with dirty-white dimity, with my cravat and shirt-collar thrown over the back. Then a chest of drawers with two of the brass handles off, and a tawdry, broken china inkstand placed on it by way of ornament for the top. Then the dressing-table, adorned by a very small looking-glass, and a very large pin-cushion. Then the window—an unusually large window. Then a dark old picture, which the feeble candle dimly showed me. It was the picture of a fellow in a high Spanish hat, crowned with a plume of towering feathers. A swarthy sinister ruffian, looking upward, shading his eyes with his hand, and looking intently upward—it might be at some tall gallows at which he was going to be hanged. At any rate, he had the appearance of thoroughly deserving it.

This picture put a kind of constraint upon me to look upward too—at the top of the bed. It was a gloomy and not an interesting object, and I looked back at the picture. I counted the feathers in the man's hat—they stood out in relief—three white, two green. I observed the crown of his hat, which was of a conical shape, according to the fashion supposed to have been favoured by Guido Fawkes. I wondered what he was looking up at. It couldn't be at the stars; such a desperado was neither astrologer nor astronomer. It must be at the high gallows, and he was going to be hanged presently. Would the executioner come into possession of his conical crowned hat and plume of feathers? I counted the feathers again—three white, two green.

While I still lingered over this very improving and intellectual employment, my thoughts insensibly began to wander. The moonlight shining into the room reminded me of a certain moonlight night in England—the night after a picnic party in a Welsh valley. Every incident of the drive homeward, through lovely scenery, which the moonlight made lovelier than ever, came back to my remembrance, though I had never given the picnic a thought for years; though, if I had *tried* to recollect it, I could certainly have recalled little or nothing of that scene long past. Of all the wonderful faculties that help to tell us we are immortal, which speaks the sublime truth more eloquently than memory? Here was I, in a strange house of the most suspicious character, in a situation of uncertainty, and even of peril, which might seem to make the cool exercise of my recollection almost out of the question; nevertheless, remembering, quite involuntarily, places, people, conversations, minute circumstances of every kind, which I had thought forgotten for ever, which I could not possibly have recalled at will even under the most favourable auspices. And what cause had produced in a moment the whole of this strange, complicated, mysterious effect? Nothing but some rays of moonlight shining in at my bedroom window.

I was still thinking of the picnic—of our merriment on the drive home—of the sentimental young lady who *would* quote Childe Harold because it was moonlight. I was absorbed by these past scenes and past amusements, when, in an instant, the thread on which my memories hung snapped asunder: my attention immediately came back to present things more vividly than ever, and I found myself, I neither knew why nor wherefore, looking hard at the picture again.

Looking for what?

Good God, the man had pulled his hat down on his brows!—No! the hat itself was gone! Where was the conical crown? Where the feathers—three white, two green? Not there! In place of the hat and feathers, what dusky object was it that now hid his forehead, his eyes, his shading hand?

Was the bed moving?

I turned on my back and looked up. Was I mad? drunk? dreaming? giddy again? or was the top of the bed really moving down—sinking slowly, regularly, silently, horribly, right down throughout the whole of its length and breadth—right down upon Me, as I lay underneath?

My blood seemed to stand still. A deadly paralyzing coldness stole all over me, as I turned my head round on the pillow, and determined to test whether the bed-top was really moving or not, by keeping my eye on the man in the picture.

The next look in that direction was enough. The dull, black, frowsy outline of the valance above me was within an inch of being parallel with his waist. I still looked breathlessly. And steadily, and slowly—very slowly—I saw the figure, and the line of frame below the figure, vanish, as the valance moved down before it.

I am, constitutionally, anything but timid. I have been on more than one occasion in peril of my life, and have not lost my self-possession for an instant; but when the conviction first settled on my mind that the bed-top was really moving, was steadily and continuously sinking down upon me, I looked up shuddering, helpless, panic-stricken, beneath the hideous machinery for murder, which was advancing closer and closer to suffocate me where I lay.

I looked up, motionless, speechless, breathless. The candle, fully spent, went out; but the moonlight still brightened the room. Down and down, without pausing and without sounding, came the bed-top, and still my panic-terror seemed to bind me faster and faster to the mattress on which I lay—down and down it sank, till the dusty odour from the lining of the canopy came stealing into my nostrils.

At that final moment the instinct of self-preservation startled me out of my trance, and I moved at last. There was just room for me to roll myself sideways off the bed. As I dropped noiselessly to the floor, the edge of the murderous canopy touched me on the shoulder.

Without stopping to draw my breath, without wiping the cold sweat from my face, I rose instantly on my knees to watch the bed-top. I was literally spell-bound by it. If I had heard footsteps behind me, I could not have turned round; if a means of escape had been miraculously provided for me, I could not have moved to take advantage of it. The whole life in me was, at that moment, concentrated in my eyes.

It descended—the whole canopy, with the fringe round it, came down—down—close down; so close that there was not room now to squeeze my finger between the bed-top and the bed. I felt at the sides, and discovered that what had appeared to me from beneath to be the ordinary light canopy of a four-post bed, was in reality a thick, broad mattress, the substance of which was concealed by the valance and its fringe. I looked up and saw the four posts rising hideously bare. In the middle of the bed-top was a huge wooden screw that had evidently worked it down through a hole in the ceiling, just as ordinary presses are worked down on the substance selected for compression. The frightful apparatus moved without making the faintest noise. There had been no creaking as it came down; there was now not the faintest sound from the room above. Amid a dead and awful silence I beheld before me—in the nineteenth century, and in the civilized capital of France—such a machine for secret murder by suffocation as might have existed in the worst days of the Inquisition, in the lonely inns among the Hartz Mountains, in the mysterious tribunals of Westphalia! Still, as I looked on it, I could not move, I could hardly breathe, but I began to recover the power of thinking, and in a moment I discovered the murderous conspiracy framed against me in all its horror.

My cup of coffee had been drugged, and drugged too strongly. I had been saved from being smothered by having taken an overdose of some narcotic. How I had chafed and fretted at the fever-fit which had preserved my life by keeping me awake! How recklessly I had confided myself to the two wretches who had led me into this room, determined, for the sake of my winnings, to kill me in my sleep by the surest and most horrible contrivance for secretly accomplishing my destruction! How many men, winners like me, had slept, as I had proposed to sleep, in that bed, and had never been seen or heard of more! I shuddered at the bare idea of it.

But, erelong, all thought was again suspended by the sight of the murderous canopy moving once more. After it had remained on the bed—as nearly as I could guess—about ten minutes, it began to move up again. The villains who worked it from above evidently believed that their purpose was now accomplished. Slowly and silently, as it had descended, that horrible bed-top rose towards its former place. When it reached the upper extremities of the four posts, it reached the ceiling too. Neither hole nor screw could be seen; the bed became in appearance an ordinary bed again—the canopy an ordinary canopy, even to the most suspicious eyes.

Now, for the first time, I was able to move—to rise from my knees—to dress myself in my upper clothing—and to consider of how I should escape. If I betrayed, by the smallest noise, that the attempt to suffocate me had failed, I was certain to be murdered. Had I made any noise already? I listened intently, looking towards the door.

No! no footsteps in the passage outside—no sound of a tread, light or heavy, in the room above—absolute silence everywhere. Besides locking and bolting my door, I had moved an old wooden chest against it, which I had found under the bed. To remove this chest (my blood ran cold as I thought what its contents *might* be!) without making some disturbance was impossible; and, moreover, to think of escaping through the house, now barred up for the night, was sheer insanity. Only one chance was left me—the window. I stole to it on tiptoe.

My bedroom was on the first floor, above an *entresol*, and looked into the back street, which you have sketched in your view. I raised my hand to open the window, knowing that on that action hung, by the merest hair's-breadth, my chance of safety. They keep vigilant watch in a House of Murder. If any part of the frame cracked, if the hinge creaked, I was a lost man! It must have occupied me at least five minutes, reckoning by time—five *hours*, reckoning by suspense—to open that window. I succeeded in doing it silently—in doing it with all the dexterity of a housebreaker—and then looked down into the street. To leap the distance beneath me would be almost certain destruction! Next, I looked round at the sides of the house. Down the left side ran the thick water-pipe which you have drawn—it passed close by the outer edge of the window. The moment I saw the pipe, I knew I was saved. My breath came and went freely for the first time since I had seen the canopy of the bed moving down upon me!

To some men the means of escape which I had discovered might have seemed difficult and dangerous enough——to *me* the prospect of slipping down the pipe into the street did not suggest even a thought of peril. I had always been accustomed, by the practice of gymnastics, to keep up my schoolboy powers as a daring and expert climber; and knew that my head, hands, and feet would serve me faithfully in any hazards of ascent or descent. I had already got one leg over the window-sill, when I remembered the handkerchief filled with money under my pillow. I could well have afforded to leave it behind me, but I was revengefully determined that the miscreants of the gambling-house should miss their plunder as well as their victim. So I went back to the bed and tied the heavy handkerchief at my back by my cravat.

Just as I had made it tight and fixed it in a comfortable place, I thought I heard a sound of breathing outside the door. The chill feeling of horror ran through me again as I listened. No! dead silence still in the passage——I had only heard the night-air blowing softly into the room. The next moment I was on the window-sill——and the next I had a firm grip on the water-pipe with my hands and knees.

I slid down into the street easily and quietly, as I thought I should, and immediately set off at the top of my speed to a branch "Prefecture" of Police, which I knew was situated in the immediate neighbourhood. A "Sub-prefect," and several picked men among his subordinates, happened to be up, maturing, I believe, some scheme for discovering the perpetrator of a mysterious murder which all Paris was talking of just then. When I began my story, in a breathless hurry and in very bad French, I could see that the Sub-prefect suspected me of being a drunken Englishman who had robbed somebody; but he soon altered his opinion as I went on, and before I had anything like concluded, he shoved all the papers before him into a drawer, put on his hat, supplied me with another (for I was bare-headed), ordered a file of soldiers, desired his expert followers to get ready all sorts of tools for breaking open doors and ripping up brick-flooring, and took my arm, in the most friendly and familiar manner possible, to lead me with him out of the house. I will venture to say, that when the Sub-prefect was a little boy, and was taken for the first time to the Play, he was not half as much pleased as he was now at the job in prospect for him at the gambling-house!

Away we went through the streets, the Sub-prefect cross-examining and congratulating me in the same breath as we marched at the head of our formidable *posse comitatus*. Sentinels were placed at the back and front of the house the moment we got to it; a tremendous battery of knocks was directed against the door; a light appeared at a window; I was told to conceal myself behind the police——then came more knocks, and a cry of "Open in the name of the law!" At that terrible summons bolts and locks gave way before an invisible hand, and the moment after the Sub-prefect was in the passage, confronting a waiter half-dressed and ghastly pale. This was the short dialogue which immediately took place:—

"We want to see the Englishman who is sleeping in this house?"

"He went away hours ago."

"He did no such thing. His friend went away; *he* remained. Show us to his bedroom!"

"I swear to you, Monsieur le Sous-prefet, he is not here! he—"

"I swear to you, Monsieur le Garçon, he is. He slept here—he didn't find your bed comfortable—he came to us to complain of it—here he is among my men—and here am I ready to look for a flea or two in his bedstead. Renaudin! (calling to one of the subordinates, and pointing to the waiter) collar that man, and tie his hands behind him. Now, then, gentlemen, let us walk up stairs!"

Every man and woman in the house was secured—the "Old Soldier" the first. Then I identified the bed in which I had slept, and then we went into the room above. No object that was at all extraordinary appeared in any part of it. The Sub-prefect looked round the place, commanded everybody to be silent, stamped twice on the floor, called for a candle, looked attentively at the spot he had stamped on, and ordered the flooring there to be carefully taken up. This was done in no time. Lights were produced, and we saw a deep raftered cavity between the floor of this room and the ceiling of the room beneath. Through this cavity there ran perpendicularly a sort of case of iron thickly greased; and inside the case appeared the screw, which communicated with the bed-top below. Extra lengths of screw, freshly oiled; levers covered with felt; all the complete upper works of a heavy press—constructed with infernal ingenuity so as to join the fixtures below, and when taken to pieces again to go into the smallest possible compass—were next discovered and pulled out on the floor. After some little difficulty the Sub-prefect succeeded in putting the machinery together, and, leaving his men to work it, descended with me to the bedroom. The smothering canopy was then lowered, but not so noiselessly as I had seen it lowered. When I mentioned this to the Sub-prefect, his answer, simple as it was, had a terrible significance. "My men," said he, "are working down the bed-top for the first time—the men whose money you won were in better practice."

We left the house in the sole possession of two police agents—every one of the inmates being removed to prison on the spot. The Sub-prefect, after taking down my "*procès-verbal*" in his office, returned with me to my hotel to get my passport. "Do you think," I asked, as I gave it to him, "that any men have really been smothered in that bed, as they tried to smother me?"

"I have seen dozens of drowned men laid out at the Morgue," answered the Sub-prefect, "in whose pocket-books were found letters, stating that they had committed suicide in the Seine, because they had lost everything at the gaming-table. Do I know how many of those men entered the same gambling-house that *you* entered? won as *you* won? took that bed as *you* took it? slept in it? were smothered in it? and were privately thrown into the river, with a letter of explanation written by the murderers and placed in their pocket-books? No man can say how many or how few have suffered the fate from which you have escaped. The people of the gambling-house kept their bedstead machinery a secret from *us*—even from the police! The dead kept the rest of the secret for them. Good night, or rather good morning, Monsieur Faulkner! Be at my office again at nine o'clock—in the meantime, *au revoir*!"

The rest of my story is soon told. I was examined and re-examined; the gambling-house was strictly searched all through from top to bottom; the prisoners were separately interrogated; and two of the less guilty among them made a confession. *I* discovered that the Old Soldier was the master of the gambling-house—*justice* discovered that he had been drummed out of the army as a vagabond years ago; that he had been guilty of all sorts of villanies since; that he was in possession of stolen property, which the owners identified; and that he, the croupier, another accomplice, and the woman who had made my cup of coffee, were all in the secret of the bedstead. There appeared some reason to doubt whether the inferior persons attached to the house knew anything of the suffocating machinery; and they received the benefit of that doubt, by being treated simply as thieves and vagabonds. As for the Old Soldier and his two head-myrmidons, they went to the galleys; the woman who had drugged my coffee was imprisoned for I forget how many years; the regular attendants at the gambling-house were considered "suspicious," and placed under "surveillance"; and I became, for one whole week (which is a long time), the head "lion" in Parisian society. My adventure was dramatised by three illustrious playmakers, but never saw theatrical daylight; for the censorship forbade the introduction on the stage of a correct copy of the gambling-house bedstead.

One good result was produced by my adventure which any censorship must have approved:—it cured me of ever again trying *Rouge et Noir* as an amusement. The sight of a green cloth, with packs of cards and heaps of money on it, will henceforth be for ever associated in my mind with the sight of a bed-canopy descending to suffocate me in the silence and darkness of the night.

THE MURDERS IN THE RUE MORGUE

Edgar Allan Poe

What song the Syrens sang, or what name Achilles assumed when he hid himself among women, although puzzling questions, are not beyond *all conjecture*.

Sir Thomas Browne

THE MENTAL FEATURES DISCOURSED OF AS THE ANALYTICAL, ARE, IN themselves, but little susceptible of analysis. We appreciate them only in their effects. We know of them, among other things, that they are always to their possessor, when inordinately possessed, a source of the liveliest enjoyment. As the strong man exults in his physical ability, delighting in such exercises as call his muscles into action, so glories the analyst in that moral activity which *disentangles*. He derives pleasure from even the most trivial occupations bringing his talent into play. He is fond of enigmas, of conundrums, of hieroglyphics; exhibiting in his solutions of each a degree of acumen which appears to the ordinary apprehension præternatural. His results, brought about by the very soul and essence of method, have, in truth, the whole air of intuition.

The faculty of re-solution is possibly much invigorated by mathematical study, and especially by that highest branch of it which, unjustly, and merely on account of its retrograde operations, has been called, as if *par excellence*, analysis. Yet to calculate is not in itself to analyse. A chess-player, for example, does the one without effort at the other. It follows that the game of chess, in its effects upon mental character, is greatly misunderstood. I am not now writing a treatise, but simply prefacing a some-what peculiar narrative by observations very much at random; I will, therefore, take occasion to assert that the higher powers of the reflective intellect are more decid-edly and more usefully tasked by the unostentatious game of draughts than by all the elaborate frivolity of chess. In this latter, where the pieces have different and *bizarre* motions, with various and variable values, what is only complex is mistaken (a not unusual error) for what is profound. The *attention* is here called powerfully into play. If it flag for an instant, an oversight is committed, resulting in injury or defeat. The possible moves being not only manifold but involute, the chances of such oversights are multiplied; and in nine cases out of ten it is the more concentrative rather than the more acute player who conquers. In draughts, on the contrary, where the moves are *unique* and have but little variation, the probabilities of inadvertence are diminished, and the mere attention being left comparatively unemployed, what advantages are obtained by either party are obtained by superior *acumen*. To be less abstract—Let us suppose a game of draughts where the pieces are reduced to four kings, and where, of course, no oversight is to be expected. It is obvious that here the victory can be decided (the players being at all equal) only by some *recherché* movement, the result of some strong exertion of the intellect. Deprived of ordinary resources, the analyst throws himself into the spirit of his opponent, identifies himself therewith, and not unfrequently sees thus, at a glance, the sole methods (sometimes indeed absurdly simple ones) by which he may seduce into error or hurry into miscalculation.

Whist has long been noted for its influence upon what is termed the calculating power; and men of the highest order of intellect have been known to take an apparently unaccountable delight in it, while eschewing chess as frivolous. Beyond doubt there is nothing of a similar nature so greatly tasking the faculty of analysis. The best chess-player in Christendom *may* be little more than the best player of chess; but proficiency in whist implies capacity for success in all those more important undertakings where mind struggles with mind. When I say proficiency, I mean that perfection in the game which includes a comprehension of *all* the sources whence legitimate advantage may be derived. These are not only manifold but multiform, and lie frequently among recesses of thought altogether inaccessible to the ordinary understanding. To observe attentively is to remember distinctly; and, so far, the concentrative chess-player will do very well at whist; while the rules of Hoyle (themselves based upon the mere mechanism of the game) are sufficiently and generally comprehensible. Thus to have a retentive memory, and to proceed by "the book," are points commonly regarded as the sum total of good playing. But it is in matters beyond the limits of mere rule that the skill of the analyst is evinced. He makes, in silence, a host of observations and inferences. So, perhaps, do his companions; and the difference in the extent of the information obtained, lies not so much in the validity of the inference as in the quality of the observation. The necessary knowledge is that of *what* to observe. Our player confines himself not at all; nor, because the game is the object, does he reject deductions from things external to the game. He examines the countenance of his partner, comparing it carefully with that of each of his opponents. He considers the mode of assorting the cards in each hand; often counting trump by trump, and honor by honor, through the glances bestowed by their holders upon each. He notes every variation of face as the play progresses, gathering a fund of thought from the differences in the expression of certainty, of surprise, of triumph, or of chagrin. From the manner of gathering up a trick he judges whether the person taking it can make another in the suit. He recognises what is played through feint, by the air with which it is thrown upon the table. A casual or inadvertent word; the accidental dropping or turning of a card, with the accompanying anxiety or carelessness in regard to its concealment; the counting of the tricks, with the order of their arrangement; embarrassment, hesitation, eagerness or trepidation—all afford, to his apparently intuitive perception, indications of the true state of affairs. The first two or three rounds having been played, he is in full possession of the contents of each hand, and thenceforward puts down his cards with as absolute a precision of purpose as if the rest of the party had turned outward the faces of their own.

The analytical power should not be confounded with simple ingenuity; for while the analyst is necessarily ingenious, the ingenious man is often remarkably incapable of analysis. The constructive or combining power, by which ingenuity is usually manifested, and to which the phrenologists (I believe erroneously) have assigned a separate organ, supposing it a primitive faculty, has been so frequently seen in those whose intellect bordered otherwise upon idiocy, as to have attracted general observation among writers on morals. Between ingenuity and the analytic ability there exists a difference far greater, indeed, than that between the fancy and the imagination, but of a character very strictly analogous. It will be found, in fact, that the ingenious are always fanciful, and the *truly* imaginative never otherwise than analytic.

The narrative which follows will appear to the reader somewhat in the light of a commentary upon the propositions just advanced.

Residing in Paris during the spring and part of the summer of 18—, I there became acquainted with a Monsieur C. Auguste Dupin. This young gentleman was of an excellent—indeed of an illustrious family, but, by a variety of untoward events, had been reduced to such poverty that the energy of his character succumbed beneath it, and he ceased to bestir himself in the world, or to care for the retrieval of his fortunes. By courtesy of his creditors, there still remained in his possession a small remnant of his patrimony; and, upon the income arising from this, he managed, by means of a rigorous economy, to procure the necessaries of life, without troubling himself about its superfluities. Books, indeed, were his sole luxuries, and in Paris these are easily obtained.

Our first meeting was at an obscure library in the Rue Montmartre, where the accident of our both being in search of the same very rare and very remarkable volume, brought us into closer communion. We saw each other again and again. I was deeply interested in the little family history which he detailed to me with all that candor which a Frenchman indulges whenever mere self is his theme. I was astonished, too, at the vast extent of his reading; and, above all, I felt my soul enkindled within me by the wild fervor, and the vivid freshness of his imagination. Seeking in Paris the objects I then sought, I felt that the society of such a man would be to me a treasure beyond price; and this feeling I frankly confided to him. It was at length arranged that we should live together during my stay in the city; and as my worldly circumstances were somewhat less embarrassed than his own, I was permitted to be at the expense of renting, and furnishing in a style which suited the rather fantastic gloom of our common temper, a time-eaten and grotesque mansion, long deserted through superstitions into which we did not inquire, and tottering to its fall in a retired and desolate portion of the Faubourg St. Germain.

Had the routine of our life at this place been known to the world, we should have been regarded as madmen—although, perhaps, as madmen of a harmless nature. Our seclusion was perfect. We admitted no visitors. Indeed the locality of our retirement had been carefully kept a secret from my own former associates; and it had been many years since Dupin had ceased to know or be known in Paris. We existed within ourselves alone.

It was a freak of fancy in my friend (for what else shall I call it?) to be enamored of the Night for her own sake; and into this *bizarrerie*, as into all his others, I quietly fell; giving myself up to his wild whims with a perfect *abandon*. The sable divinity would not herself dwell with us always; but we could counterfeit her presence. At the first dawn of the morning we closed all the massy shutters of our old building; lighting a couple of tapers which, strongly perfumed, threw out only the ghastliest and feeblest of rays. By the aid of these we then busied our souls in dreams—reading, writing, or conversing, until warned by the clock of the advent of the true Darkness. Then we sallied forth into the streets, arm in arm, continuing the topics of the day, or roaming far and wide until a late hour, seeking, amid the wild lights and shadows of the populous city, that infinity of mental excitement which quiet observation can afford.

At such times I could not help remarking and admiring (although from his rich ideality I had been prepared to expect it) a peculiar analytic ability in Dupin. He seemed, too, to take an eager delight in its exercise—if not exactly in its display—and did not hesitate to confess the pleasure thus derived. He boasted to me, with a low chuckling laugh, that most men, in respect to himself, wore windows in their bosoms, and was wont to follow up such assertions by direct and very startling proofs of his intimate knowledge of my own. His manner at these moments was frigid and abstract; his eyes were vacant in expression; while his voice, usually a rich tenor, rose into a treble which would have sounded petulantly but for the deliberateness and entire distinctness of the enunciation. Observing him in these moods, I often dwelt meditatively upon the old philosophy of the Bi-Part Soul, and amused myself with the fancy of a double Dupin—the creative and the resolvent.

Let it not be supposed, from what I have just said, that I am detailing any mystery, or penning any romance. What I have described in the Frenchman, was merely the result of an excited, or perhaps of a diseased intelligence. But of the character of his remarks at the periods in question an example will best convey the idea.

We were strolling one night down a long dirty street, in the vicinity of the Palais Royal. Being both, apparently, occupied with thought, neither of us had spoken a syllable for fifteen minutes at least. All at once Dupin broke forth with these words:

"He is a very little fellow, that's true, and would do better for the *Théâtre des Variétés*."

"There can be no doubt of that," I replied unwittingly, and not at first observing (so much had I been absorbed in reflection) the extraordinary manner in which the speaker had chimed in with my meditations. In an instant afterward I recollected myself, and my astonishment was profound.

"Dupin," said I, gravely, "this is beyond my comprehension. I do not hesitate to say that I am amazed, and can scarcely credit my senses. How was it possible you should know I was thinking of ——?" Here I paused, to ascertain beyond a doubt whether he really knew of whom I thought.

"—— of Chantilly," said he, "why do you pause? You were remarking to yourself that his diminutive figure unfitted him for tragedy."

This was precisely what had formed the subject of my reflections. Chantilly was a *quondam* cobbler of the Rue St. Denis, who, becoming stage-mad, had attempted the *rôle* of Xerxes, in Crébillon's tragedy so called, and been notoriously Pasquinaded for his pains.

"Tell me, for Heaven's sake," I exclaimed, "the method—if method there is—by which you have been enabled to fathom my soul in this matter." In fact I was even more startled than I would have been willing to express.

"It was the fruiterer," replied my friend, "who brought you to the conclusion that the mender of soles was not of sufficient height for Xerxes *et id genus omne*."

"The fruiterer!—you astonish me—I know no fruiterer whomsoever."

"The man who ran up against you as we entered the street—it may have been fifteen minutes ago."

I now remembered that, in fact, a fruiterer, carrying upon his head a large basket of apples, had nearly thrown me down, by accident, as we passed from the Rue C——

into the thoroughfare where we stood; but what this had to do with Chantilly I could not possibly understand.

There was not a particle of *charlâtanerie* about Dupin. "I will explain," he said, "and that you may comprehend all clearly, we will first retrace the course of your meditations, from the moment in which I spoke to you until that of the *rencontre* with the fruiterer in question. The larger links of the chain run thus—Chantilly, Orion, Dr. Nichols, Epicurus, Stereotomy, the street stones, the fruiterer."

There are few persons who have not, at some period of their lives, amused themselves in retracing the steps by which particular conclusions of their own minds have been attained. The occupation is often full of interest; and he who attempts it for the first time is astonished by the apparently illimitable distance and incoherence between the starting-point and the goal. What, then, must have been my amazement when I heard the Frenchman speak what he had just spoken, and when I could not help acknowledging that he had spoken the truth. He continued:

"We had been talking of horses, if I remember aright, just before leaving the Rue C——. This was the last subject we discussed. As we crossed into this street, a fruiterer, with a large basket upon his head, brushing quickly past us, thrust you upon a pile of paving-stones collected at a spot where the causeway is undergoing repair. You stepped upon one of the loose fragments, slipped, slightly strained your ankle, appeared vexed or sulky, muttered a few words, turned to look at the pile, and then proceeded in silence. I was not particularly attentive to what you did; but observation has become with me, of late, a species of necessity.

"You kept your eyes upon the ground—glancing, with a petulant expression, at the holes and ruts in the pavement, (so that I saw you were still thinking of the stones,) until we reached the little alley called Lamartine, which has been paved, by way of experiment, with the overlapping and riveted blocks. Here your countenance brightened up, and, perceiving your lips move, I could not doubt that you murmured the word 'stereotomy,' a term very affectedly applied to this species of pavement. I knew that you could not say to yourself 'stereotomy' without being brought to think of atomies, and thus of the theories of Epicurus; and since, when we discussed this subject not very long ago, I mentioned to you how singularly, yet with how little notice, the vague guesses of that noble Greek had met with confirmation in the late nebular cosmogony, I felt that you could not avoid casting your eyes upward to the great *nebula* in Orion, and I certainly expected that you would do so. You did look up; and I was now assured that I had correctly followed your steps. But in that bitter *tirade* upon Chantilly, which appeared in yesterday's '*Musée*,' the satirist, making some disgraceful allusions to the cobbler's change of name upon assuming the buskin, quoted a Latin line about which we have often conversed. I mean the line

Perdidit antiquum litera prima sonum

I had told you that this was in reference to Orion, formerly written Urion; and, from certain pungencies connected with this explanation, I was aware that you could not have forgotten it. It was clear, therefore, that you would not fail to combine the two ideas of Orion and Chantilly. That you did combine them I saw by the character of the smile which passed over your lips. You thought of the poor cobbler's immolation. So far, you had been stooping in your gait; but now I saw you draw yourself up to your full height. I was then sure that you reflected upon the diminutive figure of Chantilly. At this point I interrupted your meditations to remark that as, in fact, he *was* a very little fellow—that Chantilly—he would do better at the *Théâtre des Variétés*."

Not long after this, we were looking over an evening edition of the "Gazette des Tribunaux," when the following paragraphs arrested our attention.

"EXTRAORDINARY MURDERS.—This morning, about three o'clock, the inhabitants of the Quartier St. Roch were aroused from sleep by a succession of terrific shrieks, issuing, apparently, from the fourth story of a house in the Rue Morgue, known to be in the sole occupancy of one Madame L'Espanaye, and her daughter, Mademoiselle Camille L'Espanaye. After some delay, occasioned by a fruitless attempt to procure admission in the usual manner, the gateway was broken in with a crowbar, and eight or ten of the neighbors entered, accompanied by two *gendarmes*. By this time the cries had ceased; but, as the party rushed up the first flight of stairs, two or more rough voices, in angry contention, were distinguished, and seemed to proceed from the upper part of the house. As the second landing was reached, these sounds, also, had ceased, and everything remained perfectly quiet. The party spread themselves, and hurried from room to room. Upon arriving at a large back chamber in the fourth story, (the door of which, being found locked, with the key inside, was forced open,) a spectacle presented itself which struck every one present not less with horror than with astonishment.

"The apartment was in the wildest disorder—the furniture broken and thrown about in all directions. There was only one bedstead; and from this the bed had been removed, and thrown into the middle of the floor. On a chair lay a razor, besmeared with blood. On the hearth were two or three long and thick tresses of grey human hair, also dabbled in blood, and seeming to have been pulled out by the roots. Upon the floor were found four Napoleons, an ear-ring of topaz, three large silver spoons, three smaller of *métal d'Alger*, and two bags, containing nearly four thousand francs in gold. The drawers of a *bureau*, which stood in one corner, were open, and had been, apparently, rifled, although many articles still remained in them. A small iron safe was discovered under the *bed* (not under the bedstead). It was open, with the key still in the door. It had no contents beyond a few old letters, and other papers of little consequence.

"Of Madame L'Espanaye no traces were here seen; but an unusual quantity of soot being observed in the fire-place, a search was made in the chimney, and (horrible to relate!) the corpse of the daughter, head downward, was dragged therefrom; it having been thus forced up the narrow aperture for a considerable distance. The body was quite warm. Upon examining it, many excoriations were perceived, no doubt occasioned by the violence with which it had been thrust up and disengaged. Upon the face were many severe scratches, and, upon the throat, dark bruises, and deep indentations of finger nails, as if the deceased had been throttled to death.

"After a thorough investigation of every portion of the house, without farther discovery, the party made its way into a small paved yard in the rear of the building, where lay the corpse of the old lady, with her throat so entirely cut that, upon an attempt to raise her, the head fell off. The body, as well as the head, was fearfully mutilated—the former so much so as scarcely to retain any semblance of humanity.

"To this horrible mystery there is not as yet, we believe, the slightest clew."

The next day's paper had these additional particulars.

"*The Tragedy in the Rue Morgue*. Many individuals have been examined in relation to this most extraordinary and frightful affair." [The word '*affaire*' has not yet, in France, that levity of import which it conveys with us,] "but nothing whatever has transpired to throw light upon it. We give below all the material testimony elicited.

"*Pauline Dubourg*, laundress, deposes that she has known both the deceased for three years, having washed for them during that period. The old lady and her daughter seemed on good terms—very affectionate towards each other. They were excellent pay. Could not speak in regard to their mode or means of living. Believed that Madame L. told fortunes for a living. Was reputed to have money put by. Never met any persons in the house when she called for the clothes or took them home. Was sure that they had no servant in employ. There appeared to be no furniture in any part of the building except in the fourth story.

"*Pierre Moreau*, tobacconist, deposes that he has been in the habit of selling small quantities of tobacco and snuff to Madame L'Espanaye for nearly four years. Was born in the neighborhood, and has always resided there. The deceased and her daughter had occupied the house in which the corpses were found, for more than six years. It was formerly occupied by a jeweller, who under-let the upper rooms to various persons. The house was the property of Madame L. She became dissatisfied with the abuse of the premises by her tenant, and moved into them herself, refusing to let any portion. The old lady was childish. Witness had seen the daughter some five or six times during the six years. The two lived an exceedingly retired life—were reputed to have money. Had heard it said among the neighbors that Madame L. told fortunes—did not believe it. Had never seen any person enter the door except the old lady and her daughter, a porter once or twice, and a physician some eight or ten times.

"Many other persons, neighbors, gave evidence to the same effect. No one was spoken of as frequenting the house. It was not known whether there were any living connexions of Madame L. and her daughter. The shutters of the front windows were seldom opened. Those in the rear were always closed, with the exception of the large back room, fourth story. The house was a good house—not very old.

"*Isidore Musèt, gendarme*, deposes that he was called to the house about three o'clock in the morning, and found some twenty or thirty persons at the gateway, endeavoring to gain admittance. Forced it open, at length, with a bayonet—not with a crowbar. Had but little difficulty in getting it open, on account of its being a double or folding gate, and bolted neither at bottom nor top. The shrieks were continued until the gate was forced—and then suddenly ceased. They seemed to be screams of some person (or persons) in great agony—were loud and drawn out, not short and quick. Witness led the way up stairs. Upon reaching the first landing, heard two voices in loud and angry contention—the one a gruff voice, the other much shriller—a very strange voice. Could distinguish some words of the former, which was that of a Frenchman. Was positive that it was not a woman's voice. Could distinguish the words '*sacré*' and '*diable*.' The shrill voice was that of a foreigner. Could not be sure whether it was the voice of a man or of a woman. Could not make out what was said, but believed the language to be Spanish. The state of the room and of the bodies was described by this witness as we described them yesterday.

"*Henri Duval*, a neighbor, and by trade a silver-smith, deposes that he was one of the party who first entered the house. Corroborates the testimony of Musèt in general. As soon as they forced an entrance, they reclosed the door, to keep out the crowd, which collected very fast, notwithstanding the lateness of the hour. The shrill voice, this witness thinks, was that of an Italian. Was certain it was not French. Could not be sure that it was a man's voice. It might have been a woman's. Was not acquainted with the Italian language. Could not distinguish the words, but was convinced by the intonation that the speaker was an Italian. Knew Madame L. and her daughter. Had conversed with both frequently. Was sure that the shrill voice was not that of either of the deceased.

"—— *Odenheimer, restaurateur*. This witness volunteered his testimony. Not speaking French, was examined through an interpreter. Is a native of Amsterdam. Was passing the house at the time of the shrieks. They lasted for several minutes— probably ten. They were long and loud—very awful and distressing. Was one of those who entered the building. Corroborated the previous evidence in every respect but one. Was sure that the shrill voice was that of a man—of a Frenchman. Could not distinguish the words uttered. They were loud and quick—unequal—spoken apparently in fear as well as in anger. The voice was harsh—not so much shrill as harsh. Could not call it a shrill voice. The gruff voice said repeatedly '*sacré*,' '*diable*,' and once '*mon Dieu*.'

"*Jules Mignaud*, banker, of the firm of Mignaud et Fils, Rue Deloraine. Is the elder Mignaud. Madame L'Espanaye had some property. Had opened an account with his banking house in the spring of the year —— (eight years previously). Made frequent deposits in small sums. Had checked for nothing until the third day before her death, when she took out in person the sum of 4000 francs. This sum was paid in gold, and a clerk sent home with the money.

"*Adolphe Le Bon*, clerk to Mignaud et Fils, deposes that on the day in question, about noon, he accompanied Madame L'Espanaye to her residence with the 4000 francs, put up in two bags. Upon the door being opened, Mademoiselle L. appeared and took from his hands one of the bags, while the old lady relieved him of the other. He then bowed and departed. Did not see any person in the street at the time. It is a bye-street—very lonely.

"*William Bird*, tailor deposes that he was one of the party who entered the house. Is an Englishman. Has lived in Paris two years. Was one of the first to ascend the stairs. Heard the voices in contention. The gruff voice was that of a Frenchman. Could make out several words, but cannot now remember all. Heard distinctly '*sacré*' and '*mon Dieu*.' There was a sound at the moment as if of several persons struggling—a scraping and scuffling sound. The shrill voice was very loud—louder than the gruff one. Is sure that it was not the voice of an Englishman. Appeared to be that of a German. Might have been a woman's voice. Does not understand German.

"Four of the above-named witnesses, being recalled, deposed that the door of the chamber in which was found the body of Mademoiselle L. was locked on the inside when the party reached it. Every thing was perfectly silent—no groans or noises of any kind. Upon forcing the door no person was seen. The windows, both of the back and front room, were down and firmly fastened from within. A door between the two rooms was closed, but not locked. The door leading from the front room into the passage was locked, with the key on the inside. A small room in the front of the house, on the fourth story, at the head of the passage, was open, the door being ajar. This room was crowded with old beds, boxes, and so forth. These were carefully removed and searched. There was not an inch of any portion of the house which was not carefully searched. Sweeps were sent up and down the chimneys. The house was a four story one, with garrets (*mansards*). A trap-door on the roof was nailed down very securely—did not appear to have been opened for years. The time elapsing between the hearing of the voices in contention and the breaking open of the room door, was variously stated by the witnesses. Some made it as short as three minutes—some as long as five. The door was opened with difficulty.

"*Alfonzo Garcio*, undertaker, deposes that he resides in the Rue Morgue. Is a native of Spain. Was one of the party who entered the house. Did not proceed up stairs. Is nervous, and was apprehensive of the consequences of agitation. Heard the voices in contention. The gruff voice was that of a Frenchman. Could not distinguish what was said. The shrill voice was that of an Englishman—is sure of this. Does not understand the English language, but judges by the intonation.

"*Alberto Montani*, confectioner, deposes that he was among the first to ascend the stairs. Heard the voices in question. The gruff voice was that of a Frenchman. Distinguished several words. The speaker appeared to be expostulating. Could not make out the words of the shrill voice. Spoke quick and unevenly. Thinks it the voice of a Russian. Corroborates the general testimony. Is an Italian. Never conversed with a native of Russia.

"Several witnesses, recalled, here testified that the chimneys of all the rooms on the fourth story were too narrow to admit the passage of a human being. By 'sweeps' were meant cylindrical sweeping-brushes, such as are employed by those who clean chimneys. These brushes were passed up and down every flue in the house. There is no back passage by which any one could have descended while the party proceeded up stairs. The body of Mademoiselle L'Espanaye was so firmly wedged in the chimney that it could not be got down until four or five of the party united their strength.

"*Paul Dumas*, physician, deposes that he was called to view the bodies about day-break. They were both then lying on the sacking of the bedstead in the chamber where Mademoiselle L. was found. The corpse of the young lady was much bruised and excoriated. The fact that it had been thrust up the chimney would sufficiently account for these appearances. The throat was greatly chafed. There were several deep scratches just below the chin, together with a series of livid spots which were evidently the impression of fingers. The face was fearfully discolored, and the eye-balls protruded. The tongue had been partially bitten through. A large bruise was discovered upon the pit of the stomach, produced, apparently, by the pressure of a knee. In the opinion of M. Dumas, Mademoiselle L'Espanaye had been throttled to death by some person or persons unknown. The corpse of the mother was horribly mutilated. All the bones of the right leg and arm were more or less shattered. The left *tibia* much splintered, as well as all the ribs of the left side. Whole body dreadfully bruised and discolored. It was not possible to say how the injuries had been inflicted. A heavy club of wood, or a broad bar of iron—a chair—any large, heavy, and obtuse weapon would have produced such results, if wielded by the hands of a very powerful man. No woman could have inflicted the blows with any weapon. The head of the deceased, when seen by witness, was entirely separated from the body, and was also greatly shattered. The throat had evidently been cut with some very sharp instrument—probably with a razor.

"*Alexandre Etienne*, surgeon, was called with M. Dumas to view the bodies. Corroborated the testimony, and the opinions of M. Dumas.

"Nothing farther of importance was elicited, although several other persons were examined. A murder so mysterious, and so perplexing in all its particulars, was never before committed in Paris—if indeed a murder has been committed at all. The police are entirely at fault—an unusual occurrence in affairs of this nature. There is not, however, the shadow of a clew apparent."

The evening edition of the paper stated that the greatest excitement still continued in the Quartier St. Roch—that the premises in question had been carefully re-searched, and fresh examinations of witnesses instituted, but all to no purpose. A postscript, however, mentioned that Adolphe Le Bon had been arrested and imprisoned—although nothing appeared to criminate him, beyond the facts already detailed.

Dupin seemed singularly interested in the progress of this affair—at least so I judged from his manner, for he made no comments. It was only after the announcement that Le Bon had been imprisoned, that he asked me my opinion respecting the murders.

I could merely agree with all Paris in considering them an insoluble mystery. I saw no means by which it would be possible to trace the murderer.

"We must not judge of the means," said Dupin, "by this shell of an examination. The Parisian police, so much extolled for *acumen*, are cunning, but no more. There is no method in their proceedings, beyond the method of the moment. They make a vast parade of measures; but, not unfrequently, these are so ill adapted to the objects proposed, as to put us in mind of Monsieur Jourdain's calling for his *robe-de-chambre—pour mieux entendre la musique*. The results attained by them are not unfrequently surprising, but, for the most part, are brought about by simple diligence and activity. When these qualities are unavailing, their schemes fail. Vidocq, for example, was a good guesser, and a persevering man. But, without educated thought, he erred continually by the very intensity of his investigations. He impaired his vision by holding the object too close. He might see, perhaps, one or two points with unusual clearness, but in so doing he, necessarily, lost sight of the matter as a whole. Thus there is such a thing as being too profound. Truth is not always in a well. In fact, as regards the more important knowledge, I do believe that she is invariably superficial. The depth lies in the valleys where we seek her, and not upon the mountain-tops where she is found. The modes and sources of this kind of error are well typified in the contemplation of the heavenly bodies. To look at a star by glances—to view it in a side-long way, by turning toward it the exterior portions of the *retina* (more susceptible of feeble impressions of light than the interior), is to behold the star distinctly—is to have the best appreciation of its lustre—a lustre which grows dim just in proportion as we turn our vision *fully* upon it. A greater number of rays actually fall upon the eye in the latter case, but, in the former, there is the more refined capacity for comprehension. By undue profundity we perplex and enfeeble thought; and it is possible to make even Venus herself vanish from the firmanent by a scrutiny too sustained, too concentrated, or too direct.

"As for these murders, let us enter into some examinations for ourselves, before we make up an opinion respecting them. An inquiry will afford us amusement," [I thought this an odd term, so applied, but said nothing] "and, besides, Le Bon once rendered me a service for which I am not ungrateful. We will go and see the premises with our own eyes. I know G——, the Prefect of Police, and shall have no difficulty in obtaining the necessary permission."

The permission was obtained, and we proceeded at once to the Rue Morgue. This is one of those miserable thoroughfares which intervene between the Rue Richelieu and the Rue St. Roch. It was late in the afternoon when we reached it; as this quarter is at a great distance from that in which we resided. The house was readily found; for there were still many persons gazing up at the closed shutters, with an objectless curiosity, from the opposite side of the way. It was an ordinary Parisian house, with a gateway, on one side of which was a glazed watch-box, with a sliding panel in the window, indicating a *loge de concierge*. Before going in we walked up the street, turned down an alley, and then, again turning, passed in the rear of the building—Dupin, meanwhile, examining the whole neighborhood, as well as the house, with a minuteness of attention for which I could see no possible object.

Retracing our steps, we came again to the front of the dwelling, rang, and, having shown our credentials, were admitted by the agents in charge. We went up stairs—into the chamber where the body of Mademoiselle L'Espanaye had been found, and where both the deceased still lay. The disorders of the room had, as usual, been suffered to exist. I saw nothing beyond what had been stated in the "Gazette des Tribunaux." Dupin scrutinized every thing—not excepting the bodies of the victims. We then went into the other rooms, and into the yard; a *gendarme* accompanying us throughout. The examination occupied us until dark, when we took our departure. On our way home my companion stepped in for a moment at the office of one of the daily papers.

I have said that the whims of my friend were manifold, and that *Je les ménagais:*— for this phrase there is no English equivalent. It was his humor, now, to decline all conversation on the subject of the murder, until about noon the next day. He then asked me, suddenly, if I had observed any thing *peculiar* at the scene of the atrocity.

There was something in his manner of emphasizing the word "peculiar," which caused me to shudder, without knowing why.

"No, nothing *peculiar*," I said; "nothing more, at least, than we both saw stated in the paper."

"The 'Gazette,'" he replied, "has not entered, I fear, into the unusual horror of the thing. But dismiss the idle opinions of this print. It appears to me that this mystery is considered insoluble, for the very reason which should cause it to be regarded as easy of solution—I mean for the *outré* character of its features. The police are confounded by the seeming absence of motive—not for the murder itself—but for the atrocity of the murder. They are puzzled, too, by the seeming impossibility of reconciling the voices heard in contention, with the facts that no one was discovered up stairs but the assassinated Mademoiselle L'Espanaye, and that there were no means of egress without the notice of the party ascending. The wild disorder of the room; the corpse thrust, with the head downward, up the chimney; the frightful mutilation of the body of the old lady; these considerations, with those just mentioned, and others which I need not mention, have sufficed to paralyze the powers, by putting completely at fault the boasted *acumen*, of the government agents. They have fallen into the gross but common error of confounding the unusual with the abstruse. But it is by these devia- tions from the plane of the ordinary, that reason feels its way, if at all, in its search for the true. In investigations such as we are now pursuing, it should not be so much asked 'what has occurred,' as 'what has occurred that has never occurred before.' In fact, the facility with which I shall arrive, or have arrived, at the solution of this mystery, is in the direct ratio of its apparent insolubility in the eyes of the police."

I stared at the speaker in mute astonishment.

"I am now awaiting," continued he, looking toward the door of our apartment— "I am now awaiting a person who, although perhaps not the perpetrator of these butcheries, must have been in some measure implicated in their perpetration. Of the worst portion of the crimes committed, it is probable that he is innocent. I hope that

I am right in this supposition; for upon it I build my expectation of reading the entire riddle. I look for the man here—in this room—every moment. It is true that he may not arrive; but the probability is that he will. Should he come, it will be necessary to detain him. Here are pistols; and we both know how to use them when occasion demands their use."

I took the pistols, scarcely knowing what I did, or believing what I heard, while Dupin went on, very much as if in a soliloquy. I have already spoken of his abstract manner at such times. His discourse was addressed to myself; but his voice, although by no means loud, had that intonation which is commonly employed in speaking to some one at a great distance. His eyes, vacant in expression, regarded only the wall.

"That the voices heard in contention," he said, "by the party upon the stairs, were not the voices of the women themselves, was fully proved by the evidence. This relieves us of all doubt upon the question whether the old lady could have first destroyed the daughter, and afterward have committed suicide. I speak of this point chiefly for the sake of method; for the strength of Madame L'Espanaye would have been utterly unequal to the task of thrusting her daughter's corpse up the chimney as it was found; and the nature of the wounds upon her own person entirely preclude the idea of self-destruction. Murder, then, has been committed by some third party; and the voices of this third party were those heard in contention. Let me now advert—not to the whole testimony respecting these voices—but to what was *peculiar* in that testimony. Did you observe any thing peculiar about it?"

I remarked that, while all the witnesses agreed in supposing the gruff voice to be that of a Frenchman, there was much disagreement in regard to the shrill, or, as one individual termed it, the harsh voice.

"That was the evidence itself," said Dupin, "but it was not the peculiarity of the evidence. You have observed nothing distinctive. Yet there *was* something to be observed. The witnesses, as you remark, agreed about the gruff voice; they were here unanimous. But in regard to the shrill voice, the peculiarity is—not that they disagreed—but that, while an Italian, an Englishman, a Spaniard, a Hollander, and a Frenchman attempted to describe it, each one spoke of it as that *of a foreigner*. Each is sure that it was not the voice of one of his own countrymen. Each likens it—not to the voice of an individual of any nation with whose language he is conversant—but the converse. The Frenchman supposes it the voice of a Spaniard, and 'might have distinguished some words *had he been acquainted with the Spanish*.' The Dutchman maintains it to have been that of a Frenchman; but we find it stated that '*not understanding French this witness was examined through an interpreter*.' The Englishman thinks it the voice of a German, and '*does not understand German*.' The Spaniard 'is sure' that it was that of an Englishman, but 'judges by the intonation' altogether, '*as he has no knowledge of the English.*' The Italian believes it the voice of a Russian, but '*has never conversed with a native of Russia.*' A second Frenchman differs, moreover, with the first, and is positive that the voice was that of an Italian; but, *not being cognizant of that tongue*, is, like the Spaniard, 'convinced by the intonation.' Now, how strangely unusual must that voice have really been, about which such testimony as this *could* have been elicited!—in whose *tones*, even, denizens of the five great divisions of Europe could recognise nothing familiar! You will say that it might have been the voice of an Asiatic—of an African. Neither Asiatics nor Africans abound in Paris; but, without denying the inference, I will now merely call your attention to three points. The voice is termed by one witness 'harsh rather than shrill.' It is represented by two others to have been 'quick and *unequal.*' No words—no sounds resembling words—were by any witness mentioned as distinguishable.

"I know not," continued Dupin, "what impression I may have made, so far, upon your own understanding; but I do not hesitate to say that legitimate deductions even from this portion of the testimony—the portion respecting the gruff and shrill voices—are in themselves sufficient to engender a suspicion which should give direction to all farther progress in the investigation of the mystery. I said 'legitimate deductions'; but my meaning is not thus fully expressed. I designed to imply that the deductions are the *sole* proper ones, and that the suspicion arises *inevitably* from them as the single result. What the suspicion is, however, I will not say just yet. I merely wish you to bear in mind that, with myself, it was sufficiently forcible to give a definite form—a certain tendency—to my inquiries in the chamber.

"Let us now transport ourselves, in fancy, to this chamber. What shall we first seek here? The means of egress employed by the murderers. It is not too much to say that neither of us believe in præternatural events. Madame and Mademoiselle L'Espanaye were not destroyed by spirits. The doers of the deed were material, and escaped materially. Then how? Fortunately, there is but one mode of reasoning upon the point, and that mode *must* lead us to a definite decision.—Let us examine, each by each, the possible means of egress. It is clear that the assassins were in the room where Mademoiselle L'Espanaye was found, or at least in the room adjoining, when the party ascended the stairs. It is then only from these two apartments that we have to seek issues. The police have laid bare the floors, the ceilings, and the masonry of the walls, in every direction. No *secret* issues could have escaped their vigilance. But, not trusting to *their* eyes, I examined with my own. There were, then, *no* secret issues. Both doors leading from the rooms into the passage were securely locked, with the keys inside. Let us turn to the chimneys. These, although of ordinary width for some eight or ten feet above the hearths, will not admit, throughout their extent, the body of a large cat. The impossibility of egress, by means already stated, being thus absolute, we are reduced to the windows. Through those of the front room no one could have escaped without notice from the crowd in the street. The murderers *must* have passed, then, through those of the back room. Now, brought to this conclusion in so unequivocal a manner as we are, it is not our part, as reasoners, to reject it on account of apparent impossibilities. It is only left for us to prove that these apparent 'impossibilities' are, in reality, not such.

"There are two windows in the chamber. One of them is unobstructed by furniture, and is wholly visible. The lower portion of the other is hidden from view by the head of the unwieldy bedstead which is thrust close up against it. The former was found securely fastened from within. It resisted the utmost force of those who endeavored to raise it. A large gimlet-hole had been pierced in its frame to the left, and a very stout nail was found fitted therein, nearly to the head. Upon examining the other window, a similar nail was seen similarly fitted in it; and a vigorous attempt to raise this sash, failed also. The police were now entirely satisfied that egress had not been in these directions. And, *therefore*, it was thought a matter of supererogation to withdraw the nails and open the windows.

"My own examination was somewhat more particular, and was so for the reason I have just given—because here it was, I knew, that all apparent impossibilities *must* be proved to be not such in reality.

"I proceeded to think thus—*à posteriori*. The murderers did escape from one of these windows. This being so, they could not have re-fastened the sashes from the inside, as they were found fastened;—the consideration which put a stop, through its obviousness, to the scrutiny of the police in this quarter. Yet the sashes *were* fastened. They *must*, then, have the power of fastening themselves. There was no escape from this conclusion. I stepped to the unobstructed casement, withdrew the nail with some difficulty, and attempted to raise the sash. It resisted all my efforts, as I had anticipated. A concealed spring must, I now knew, exist; and this corroboration of my idea convinced me that my premises, at least, were correct, however mysterious still appeared the circumstances attending the nails. A careful search soon brought to light the hidden spring. I pressed it, and, satisfied with the discovery, forbore to upraise the sash.

"I now replaced the nail and regarded it attentively. A person passing out through this window might have reclosed it, and the spring would have caught—but the nail could not have been replaced. The conclusion was plain, and again narrowed in the field of my investigations. The assassins *must* have escaped through the other window. Supposing, then, the springs upon each sash to be the same, as was probable, there *must* be found a difference between the nails, or at least between the modes of their fixture. Getting upon the sacking of the bedstead, I looked over the head-board minutely at the second casement. Passing my hand down behind the board, I readily discovered and pressed the spring, which was, as I had supposed, identical in character with its neighbor. I now looked at the nail. It was as stout as the other, and apparently fitted in the same manner—driven in nearly up to the head.

"You will say that I was puzzled; but, if you think so, you must have misunderstood the nature of the inductions. To use a sporting phrase, I had not been once 'at fault.' The scent had never for an instant been lost. There was no flaw in any link of the chain. I had traced the secret to its ultimate result,—and that result was *the nail*. It had, I say, in every respect, the appearance of its fellow in the other window; but this fact was an absolute nullity (conclusive as it might seem to be) when compared with the consideration that here, at this point, terminated the clew. 'There *must* be something wrong,' I said, 'about the nail.' I touched it; and the head, with about a quarter of an inch of the shank, came off in my fingers. The rest of the shank was in the gimlet-hole, where it had been broken off. The fracture was an old one (for its edges were incrusted with rust), and had apparently been accomplished by the blow of a hammer, which had partially imbedded, in the top of the bottom sash, the head portion of the nail. I now carefully replaced this head portion in the indentation whence I had taken it, and the resemblance to a perfect nail was complete—the fissure was invisible. Pressing the spring, I gently raised the sash for a few inches; the head went up with it, remaining firm in its bed. I closed the window, and the semblance of the whole nail was again perfect.

"The riddle, so far, was now unriddled. The assassin had escaped through the window which looked upon the bed. Dropping of its own accord upon his exit (or perhaps purposely closed), it had become fastened by the spring; and it was the retention of this spring which had been mistaken by the police for that of the nail,—farther inquiry being thus considered unnecessary.

"The next question is that of the mode of descent. Upon this point I had been satisfied in my walk with you around the building. About five feet and a half from the casement in question there runs a lightning-rod. From this rod it would have been impossible for any one to reach the window itself, to say nothing of entering it. I observed, however, that the shutters of the fourth story were of the peculiar kind called by Parisian carpenters *ferrades*—a kind rarely employed at the present day, but frequently seen upon very old mansions at Lyons and Bourdeaux. They are in the form of an ordinary door, (a single, not a folding door) except that the upper half is latticed or worked in open trellis—thus affording an excellent hold for the hands. In the present instance these shutters are fully three feet and a half broad. When we saw them from the rear of the house, they were both about half open—that is to say, they stood off at right angles from the wall. It is probable that the police, as well as myself, examined the back of the tenement; but, if so, in looking at these *ferrades* in the line of their breadth (as they must have done), they did not perceive this great breadth itself, or, at all events, failed to take it into due consideration. In fact, having once satisfied themselves that no egress could have been made in this quarter, they would naturally bestow here a very cursory examination. It was clear to me, however, that the shutter belonging to the window at the head of the bed, would, if swung fully back to the wall, reach to within two feet of the lightning-rod. It was also evident that, by exertion of a very unusual degree of activity and courage, an entrance into the window, from the rod, might have been thus effected.—By reaching to the distance of two feet and a half (we now suppose the shutter open to its whole extent) a robber might have taken a firm grasp upon the trellis-work. Letting go, then, his hold upon the rod, placing his feet securely against the wall, and springing boldly from it, he might have swung the shutter so as to close it, and, if we imagine the window open at the time, might even have swung himself into the room.

"I wish you to bear especially in mind that I have spoken of a *very* unusual degree of activity as requisite to success in so hazardous and so difficult a feat. It is my design to show you, first, that the thing might possibly have been accomplished:—but, secondly and *chiefly*, I wish to impress upon your understanding the *very extraordinary*—the almost præternatural character of that agility which could have accomplished it.

"You will say, no doubt, using the language of the law, that 'to make out my case,' I should rather undervalue, than insist upon a full estimation of the activity required in this matter. This may be the practice in law, but it is not the usage of reason. My ultimate object is only the truth. My immediate purpose is to lead you to place in juxta-position, that *very unusual* activity of which I have just spoken, with that *very peculiar* shrill (or harsh) and *unequal* voice, about whose nationality no two persons could be found to agree, and in whose utterance no syllabification could be detected."

At these words a vague and half-formed conception of the meaning of Dupin flit-ted over my mind. I seemed to be upon the verge of comprehension, without power to comprehend—as men, at times, find themselves upon the brink of remembrance, without being able, in the end, to remember. My friend went on with his discourse.

"You will see," he said, "that I have shifted the question from the mode of egress to that of ingress. It was my design to convey the idea that both were effected in the same manner, at the same point. Let us now revert to the interior of the room. Let us survey the appearances here. The drawers of the bureau, it is said, had been rifled, although many articles of apparel still remained within them. The conclusion here is absurd. It is a mere guess—a very silly one—and no more. How are we to know that the articles found in the drawers were not all these drawers had originally contained? Madame L'Espanaye and her daughter lived an exceedingly retired life—saw no company—seldom went out—had little use for numerous changes of habiliment. Those found were at least of as good quality as any likely to be possessed by these ladies. If a thief had taken any, why did he not take the best—why did he not take all? In a word, why did he abandon four thousand francs in gold to encumber himself with a bundle of linen? The gold *was* abandoned. Nearly the whole sum mentioned by Monsieur Mignaud, the banker, was discovered, in bags, upon the floor. I wish you, therefore, to discard from your thoughts the blundering idea of *motive*, engendered in the brains of the police by that portion of the evidence which speaks of money delivered at the door of the house. Coincidences ten times as remarkable as this (the delivery of the money, and murder committed within three days upon the party receiving it), happen to all of us every hour of our lives, without attracting even momentary notice. Coincidences, in general, are great stumbling-blocks in the way of that class of thinkers who have been educated to know nothing of the theory of probabilities—that theory to which the most glorious objects of human research are indebted for the most glorious of illustration. In the present instance, had the gold been gone, the fact of its delivery three days before would have formed something more than a coincidence. It would have been corroborative of this idea of motive. But, under the real circumstances of the case, if we are to suppose gold the motive of this outrage, we must also imagine the perpetrator so vacillating an idiot as to have abandoned his gold and his motive together.

"Keeping now steadily in mind the points to which I have drawn your attention—that peculiar voice, that unusual agility, and that startling absence of motive in a murder so singularly atrocious as this—let us glance at the butchery itself. Here is a woman strangled to death by manual strength, and thrust up a chimney, head downward. Ordinary assassins employ no such modes of murder as this. Least of all, do they thus dispose of the murdered. In the manner of thrusting the corpse up the chimney, you will admit that there was something *excessively outré*—something altogether irreconcilable with our common notions of human action, even when we suppose the actors the most depraved of men. Think, too, how great must have been that strength which could have thrust the body *up* such an aperture so forcibly that the united vigor of several persons was found barely sufficient to drag it *down*!

"Turn, now, to other indications of the employment of a vigor most marvellous. On the hearth were thick tresses—very thick tresses—of grey human hair. These had been torn out by the roots. You are aware of the great force necessary in tearing thus from the head even twenty or thirty hairs together. You saw the locks in question as well as myself. Their roots (a hideous sight!) were clotted with fragments of the flesh of the scalp—sure token of the prodigious power which had been exerted in uproot-ing perhaps half a million of hairs at a time. The throat of the old lady was not merely cut, but the head absolutely severed from the body: the instrument was a mere razor. I wish you also to look at the *brutal* ferocity of these deeds. Of the bruises upon the body of Madame L'Espanaye I do not speak. Monsieur Dumas, and his worthy coadjutor Monsieur Etienne, have pronounced that they were inflicted by some obtuse instru-ment; and so far these gentlemen are very correct. The obtuse instrument was clearly the stone pavement in the yard, upon which the victim had fallen from the window which looked in upon the bed. This idea, however simple it may now seem, escaped the police for the same reason that the breadth of the shutters escaped them—because, by the affair of the nails, their perceptions had been hermetically sealed against the possibility of the windows having ever been opened at all.

"If now, in addition to all these things, you have properly reflected upon the odd disorder of the chamber, we have gone so far as to combine the ideas of an agility astounding, a strength superhuman, a ferocity brutal, a butchery without motive, a *grotesquerie* in horror absolutely alien from humanity, and a voice foreign in tone to the ears of men of many nations, and devoid of all distinct or intelligible syllabifica-tion. What result, then, has ensued? What impression have I made upon your fancy?"

I felt a creeping of the flesh as Dupin asked me the question. "A madman," I said, "has done this deed—some raving maniac, escaped from a neighboring *Maison de Santé.*"

"In some respects," he replied, "your idea is not irrelevant. But the voices of mad-men, even in their wildest paroxysms, are never found to tally with that peculiar voice heard upon the stairs. Madmen are of some nation, and their language, however inco-herent in its words, has always the coherence of syllabification. Besides, the hair of a madman is not such as I now hold in my hand. I disentangled this little tuft from the rigidly clutched fingers of Madame L'Espanaye. Tell me what you can make of it."

"Dupin!" I said, completely unnerved; "this hair is most unusual—this is no *human* hair."

"I have not asserted that it is," said he; "but, before we decide this point, I wish you to glance at the little sketch I have here traced upon this paper. It is a *fac-simile* drawing of what has been described in one portion of the testimony as 'dark bruises, and deep indentations of finger nails,' upon the throat of Mademoiselle L'Espanaye, and in another, (by Messrs. Dumas and Etienne,) as a 'series of livid spots, evidently the impression of fingers.'

"You will perceive," continued my friend, spreading out the paper upon the table before us, "that this drawing gives the idea of a firm and fixed hold. There is no *slipping* apparent. Each finger has retained—possibly until the death of the victim—the fearful grasp by which it originally imbedded itself. Attempt, now, to place all your fingers, at the same time, in the respective impressions as you see them."

I made the attempt in vain.

"We are possibly not giving this matter a fair trial," he said. "The paper is spread out upon a plane surface; but the human throat is cylindrical. Here is a billet of wood, the circumference of which is about that of the throat. Wrap the drawing around it, and try the experiment again."

I did so; but the difficulty was even more obvious than before. "This," I said, "is the mark of no human hand."

"Read now," replied Dupin, "this passage from Cuvier."

It was a minute anatomical and generally descriptive account of the large fulvous Ourang-Outang of the East Indian Islands. The gigantic stature, the prodigious strength and activity, the wild ferocity, and the imitative propensities of these mammalia are sufficiently well known to all. I understood the full horrors of the murder at once.

"The description of the digits," said I, as I made an end of reading, "is in exact accordance with this drawing. I see that no animal but an Ourang-Outang, of the species here mentioned, could have impressed the indentations as you have traced them. This tuft of tawny hair, too, is identical in character with that of the beast of Cuvier. But I cannot possibly comprehend the particulars of this frightful mystery. Besides, there were *two* voices heard in contention, and one of them was unquestionably the voice of a Frenchman."

"True; and you will remember an expression attributed almost unanimously, by the evidence, to this voice,—the expression, '*mon Dieu!*' This, under the circumstances, has been justly characterized by one of the witnesses (Montani, the confectioner,) as an expression of remonstrance or expostulation. Upon these two words, therefore, I have mainly built my hopes of a full solution of the riddle. A Frenchman was cognizant of the murder. It is possible—indeed it is far more than probable—that he was innocent of all participation in the bloody transactions which took place. The Ourang-Outang may have escaped from him. He may have traced it to the chamber; but, under the agitating circumstances which ensued, he could never have re-captured it. It is still at large. I will not pursue these guesses—for I have no right to call them more—since the shades of reflection upon which they are based are scarcely of sufficient depth to be appreciable by my own intellect, and since I could not pretend to make them intelligible to the understanding of another. We will call them guesses then, and speak of them as such. If the Frenchman in question is indeed, as I suppose, innocent of this atrocity, this advertisement, which I left last night, upon our return home, at the office of 'Le Monde,' (a paper devoted to the shipping interest, and much sought by sailors,) will bring him to our residence."

He handed me a paper, and I read thus:

CAUGHT—*In the Bois de Boulogne, early in the morning of the* —— *inst.,* (the morning of the murder,) *a very large, tawny Ourang-Outang of the Bornese species. The owner, (who is ascertained to be a sailor, belonging to a Maltese vessel,) may have the animal again, upon identifying it satisfactorily, and paying a few charges arising from its capture and keeping. Call at No.* ——, *Rue* ——, *Faubourg St. Germain—au troisiême.*

"How was it possible," I asked, "that you should know the man to be a sailor, and belonging to a Maltese vessel?"

"I do *not* know it," said Dupin. "I am not sure of it. Here, however, is a small piece of ribbon, which from its form, and from its greasy appearance, has evidently been used in tying the hair in one of those long *queues* of which sailors are so fond. Moreover, this knot is one which few besides sailors can tie, and is peculiar to the Maltese. I picked the ribbon up at the foot of the lightning-rod. It could not have belonged to either of the deceased. Now if, after all, I am wrong in my induction from this ribbon, that the Frenchman was a sailor belonging to a Maltese vessel, still I can have done no harm in saying what I did in the advertisement. If I am in error, he will merely suppose that I have been misled by some circumstance into which he will not take the trouble to inquire. But if I am right, a great point is gained. Cognizant although innocent of the murder, the Frenchman will naturally hesitate about replying to the advertisement— about demanding the Ourang-Outang. He will reason thus:—'I am innocent; I am poor; my Ourang-Outang is of great value—to one in my circumstances a fortune of itself—why should I lose it through idle apprehensions of danger? Here it is, within my grasp. It was found in the Bois de Boulogne—at a vast distance from the scene of that butchery. How can it ever be suspected that a brute beast should have done the deed? The police are at fault—they have failed to procure the slightest clew. Should they even trace the animal, it would be impossible to prove me cognizant of the murder, or to implicate me in guilt on account of that cognizance. Above all, *I am known*. The advertiser designates me as the possessor of the beast. I am not sure to what limit his knowledge may extend. Should I avoid claiming a property of so great value, which it is known that I possess, I will render the animal at least, liable to suspicion. It is not my policy to attract attention either to myself or to the beast. I will answer the advertisement, get the Ourang-Outang, and keep it close until this matter has blown over.'"

At this moment we heard a step upon the stairs.

"Be ready," said Dupin, "with your pistols, but neither use them nor show them until at a signal from myself."

The front door of the house had been left open, and the visiter had entered, without ringing, and advanced several steps upon the staircase. Now, however, he seemed to hesitate. Presently we heard him descending. Dupin was moving quickly to the door, when we again heard him coming up. He did not turn back a second time, but stepped up with decision, and rapped at the door of our chamber.

"Come in," said Dupin, in a cheerful and hearty tone.

A man entered. He was a sailor, evidently,—a tall, stout, and muscular-looking person, with a certain dare-devil expression of countenance, not altogether unprepossessing. His face, greatly sunburnt, was more than half hidden by whisker and *mustachio*. He had with him a huge oaken cudgel, but appeared to be otherwise unarmed. He bowed awkwardly, and bade us "good evening," in French accents, which, although somewhat Neufchatelish, were still sufficiently indicative of a Parisian origin.

"Sit down, my friend," said Dupin. "I suppose you have called about the Ourang-Outang. Upon my word, I almost envy you the possession of him; a remarkably fine, and no doubt a very valuable animal. How old do you suppose him to be?"

The sailor drew a long breath, with the air of a man relieved of some intolerable burden, and then replied, in an assured tone:

"I have no way of telling—but he can't be more than four or five years old. Have you got him here?"

"Oh no; we had no conveniences for keeping him here. He is at a livery stable in the Rue Dubourg, just by. You can get him in the morning. Of course you are prepared to identify the property?"

"To be sure I am, sir."

"I shall be sorry to part with him," said Dupin.

"I don't mean that you should be at all this trouble for nothing, sir," said the man. "Couldn't expect it. Am very willing to pay a reward for the finding of the animal— that is to say, any thing in reason."

"Well," replied my friend, "that is all very fair, to be sure. Let me think!—what should I have? Oh! I will tell you. My reward shall be this. You shall give me all the information in your power about these murders in the Rue Morgue."

Dupin said the last words in a very low tone, and very quietly. Just as quietly, too, he walked toward the door, locked it, and put the key in his pocket. He then drew a pistol from his bosom and placed it, without the least flurry, upon the table.

The sailor's face flushed up as if he were struggling with suffocation. He started to his feet and grasped his cudgel; but the next moment he fell back into his seat, trembling violently, and with the countenance of death itself. He spoke not a word. I pitied him from the bottom of my heart.

"My friend," said Dupin, in a kind tone, "you are alarming yourself unnecessarily—you are indeed. We mean you no harm whatever. I pledge you the honor of a gentleman, and of a Frenchman, that we intend you no injury. I perfectly well know that you are innocent of the atrocities in the Rue Morgue. It will not do, however, to deny that you are in some measure implicated in them. From what I have already said, you must know that I have had means of information about this matter—means of which you could never have dreamed. Now the thing stands thus. You have done nothing which you could have avoided—nothing, certainly, which renders you culpable. You were not even guilty of robbery, when you might have robbed with impunity. You have nothing to conceal. You have no reason for concealment. On the other hand, you are bound by every principle of honor to confess all you know. An innocent man is now imprisoned, charged with that crime of which you can point out the perpetrator."

The sailor had recovered his presence of mind, in a great measure, while Dupin uttered these words; but his original boldness of bearing was all gone.

"So help me God," said he, after a brief pause, "I *will* tell you all I know about this affair;—but I do not expect you to believe one half I say—I would be a fool indeed if I did. Still, I *am* innocent, and I will make a clean breast if I die for it."

What he stated was, in substance, this. He had lately made a voyage to the Indian Archipelago. A party, of which he formed one, landed at Borneo, and passed into the interior on an excursion of pleasure. Himself and a companion had captured the Ourang-Outang. This companion dying, the animal fell into his own exclusive possession. After great trouble, occasioned by the intractable ferocity of his captive during the home voyage, he at length succeeded in lodging it safely at his own residence in Paris, where, not to attract toward himself the unpleasant curiosity of his neighbors, he kept it carefully secluded, until such time as it should recover from a wound in the foot, received from a splinter on board ship. His ultimate design was to sell it.

Returning home from some sailors' frolic on the night, or rather in the morning of the murder, he found the beast occupying his own bed-room, into which it had broken from a closet adjoining, where it had been, as was thought, securely confined. Razor in hand, and fully lathered, it was sitting before a looking-glass, attempting the operation of shaving, in which it had no doubt previously watched its master through the key-hole of the closet. Terrified at the sight of so dangerous a weapon in the possession of an animal so ferocious, and so well able to use it, the man, for some moments, was at a loss what to do. He had been accustomed, however, to quiet the creature, even in its fiercest moods, by the use of a whip, and to this he now resorted. Upon sight of it, the Ourang-Outang sprang at once through the door of the chamber, down the stairs, and thence, through a window, unfortunately open, into the street.

The Frenchman followed in despair; the ape, razor still in hand, occasionally stopping to look back and gesticulate at its pursuer, until the latter had nearly come up with it. It then again made off. In this manner the chase continued for a long time. The streets were profoundly quiet, as it was nearly three o'clock in the morning. In passing down an alley in the rear of the Rue Morgue, the fugitive's attention was arrested by a light gleaming from the open window of Madame L'Espanaye's chamber, in the fourth story of her house. Rushing to the building, it perceived the lightning-rod, clambered up with inconceivable agility, grasped the shutter, which was thrown fully back against the wall, and, by its means, swung itself directly upon the headboard of the bed. The whole feat did not occupy a minute. The shutter was kicked open again by the Ourang-Outang as it entered the room.

The sailor, in the meantime, was both rejoiced and perplexed. He had strong hopes of now recapturing the brute, as it could scarcely escape from the trap into which it had ventured, except by the rod, where it might be intercepted as it came down. On the other hand, there was much cause for anxiety as to what it might do in the house. This latter reflection urged the man still to follow the fugitive. A lightning-rod is ascended without difficulty, especially by a sailor; but, when he had arrived as high as the window, which lay far to his left, his career was stopped; the most that he could accomplish was to reach over so as to obtain a glimpse of the interior of the room. At this glimpse he nearly fell from his hold through excess of horror. Now it was that those hideous shrieks arose upon the night, which had startled from slumber the inmates of the Rue Morgue. Madame L'Espanaye and her daughter, habited in their night clothes, had apparently been occupied in arranging some papers in the iron chest already mentioned, which had been wheeled into the middle of the room. It was open, and its contents lay beside it on the floor. The victims must have been sitting with their backs toward the window; and, from the time elapsing between the ingress of the beast and the screams, it seems probable that it was not immediately perceived. The flapping-to of the shutter would naturally have been attributed to the wind.

As the sailor looked in, the gigantic animal had seized Madame L'Espanaye by the hair, (which was loose, as she had been combing it,) and was flourishing the razor about her face, in imitation of the motions of a barber. The daughter lay prostrate and motionless; she had swooned. The screams and struggles of the old lady (during which the hair was torn from her head) had the effect of changing the probably pacific purposes of the Ourang-Outang into those of wrath. With one determined sweep of its muscular arm it nearly severed her head from her body. The sight of blood inflamed its anger into phrenzy. Gnashing its teeth, and flashing fire from its eyes, it flew upon the body of the girl, and imbedded its fearful talons in her throat, retaining its grasp until she expired. Its wandering and wild glances fell at this moment upon the head of the bed, over which the face of its master, rigid with horror, was just discernible. The fury of the beast, who no doubt bore still in mind the dreaded whip, was instantly converted into fear. Conscious of having deserved punishment, it seemed desirous of concealing its bloody deeds, and skipped about the chamber in an agony of nervous agitation; throwing down and breaking the furniture as it moved, and dragging the bed from the bedstead. In conclusion, it seized first the corpse of the daughter, and thrust it up the chimney, as it was found; then that of the old lady, which it immediately hurled through the window headlong.

As the ape approached the casement with its mutilated burden, the sailor shrank aghast to the rod, and, rather gliding than clambering down it, hurried at once home— dreading the consequences of the butchery, and gladly abandoning, in his terror, all solicitude about the fate of the Ourang-Outang. The words heard by the party upon the staircase were the Frenchman's exclamations of horror and affright, commingled with the fiendish jabberings of the brute.

I have scarcely anything to add. The Ourang-Outang must have escaped from the chamber, by the rod, just before the breaking of the door. It must have closed the window as it passed through it. It was subsequently caught by the owner himself, who obtained for it a very large sum at the *Jardin des Plantes*. Le Bon was instantly released, upon our narration of the circumstances (with some comments from Dupin) at the *bureau* of the Prefect of Police. This functionary, however well disposed to my friend, could not altogether conceal his chagrin at the turn which affairs had taken, and was fain to indulge in a sarcasm or two, about the propriety of every person minding his own business.

"Let him talk," said Dupin, who had not thought it necessary to reply. "Let him discourse; it will ease his conscience. I am satisfied with having defeated him in his own castle. Nevertheless, that he failed in the solution of this mystery, is by no means that matter for wonder which he supposes it; for, in truth, our friend the Prefect is somewhat too cunning to be profound. In his wisdom is no *stamen*. It is all head and no body, like the pictures of the Goddess Laverna,—or, at best, all head and shoulders, like a codfish. But he is a good creature after all. I like him especially for one master stroke of cant, by which he has attained his reputation for ingenuity. I mean the way he has '*de nier ce qui est, et d'expliquer ce qui n'est pas.*'"*

---

*Rousseau—Nouvelle Heloise.

THE TEN-THIRTY
FOLKESTONE EXPRESS

Sax Rohmer

I

I glanced at the clock on the mantelpiece and noted that one A.M. was already past. My work began to worry me, my brain was growing dull, and I decided that the article upon which I was engaged could not be finished that night as I had hoped.

My hand was actually upon the switch of the table-lamp, when a familiar whistle reached me from the roadway—two bars of an Oriental strain which bore my memory back to Cairo. That summons, so wholly unexpected, brought me to my feet in a trice; and, the household having long since retired, I ran to the door and opened it—to admit a ruddy-faced, clean-shaven man, whose well-cut tweed suit served to show off his spare but athletic figure, and whose blue eyes shone the more brightly from contrast with the sunburnt skin.

"Rider!" I cried—and gripped his extended hand.

"Rider, it is!" he said, with the odd, one-sided smile which I knew.

I drew him back to the study, seated him in the armchair, and brought out whisky, siphon, and cigars, with a celerity which only reflected the delight occasioned by his arrival.

Rider helped himself liberally, without apology, his unhandsome countenance revealing keen appreciation of my hospitality.

"My dear man!" I cried, "it is sheer luck that you did not find me in bed and asleep!"

"We are brother owls," he replied, the blue eyes twinkling. "I gambled on finding you up, and my plunge was justified."

How good it was to hear his drawling voice again. Ours was a true, if peculiar friendship. To the confusion of those who claim that our secret service is conducted by glorified constables, I advance the instance of my friend, Rider. "Rider Pasha" they called him in Egypt, and, although he was a popular member of both the Cairo clubs, I could swear that not another member knew the exact nature of his duties, his official position, or true sphere of activity. Furthermore, I am ignorant of these matters to this day. Yet I knew and have evidence to prove, that Rider Pasha is a secret service agent—a higher detective. As one of his most intimate friends, I can add that I have not the remotest idea to which Government department he is really attached.

"I didn't know you had left Cairo," I said, watching him as he smoked and drank with that appearance of satisfaction peculiarly Rider's own.

"My good chap," he replied, "I have been in Cape Town, in Rangoon, in Hong-Kong, in St. Petersburg, and in Paris, since you last saw me at the Turf Club in Cairo!"

"And now?"

"Now, as you see, I am in London."

"And the business?"

"The business, my boy, at the moment, is murder."

"*Murder!*"

"You have based some ripping yarns upon former inquiries of mine, and, incidentally, have brought your powerful, if undisciplined imagination, usefully to bear upon the business side of certain cases; I invite your co-operation once more; because—A—" (He ticked off the point on his finger) "the present case is one wherein I rank your views above those of a constable; and—B—" (He raised a second finger) "it is a mystery which I feel sure, suitably disguised, will make excellent copy."

"You spoke of murder—"

"Murders, you were about to say, are outside my province?"

"This particular one—"

"I have a cab at the corner, and I am about to ask you to come and see the body!"

"The body! What! now?"

"At this very moment! Are you coming?"

Undoubtedly I was going; for a case in which Rider was concerned must necessarily be of exceptional interest. Ignorant as I was of his real official position, I knew, or had divined, that he was no ordinary detective. This murder of which he spoke must therefore possess a political interest.

Three minutes later we were in the cab, which waited at the corner, and were speeding I knew not where, for Rider had merely given the direction: "Back again."

Our course, then, lay southward, in a line, roughly, following the railroad. It took us through the more desirable suburbs into a network of slummy streets. At the end of one of these, occupied by a long block of dwellings bearing the title "Morley's Buildings," we stopped.

"It is the third house," said Rider, taking my arm and pointing. "You see the light shining from the window there?"

I glanced up at the window indicated—it was otherwise no different from those adjoining it—and noted that a light showed through the dingy blind.

"We do not enter the house," continued my companion, "but we proceed to the corner."

This we did; and the block proved to terminate upon a stretch of waste land. That is to say, there was a gap, with some kind of factory rising dimly beyond, and on the right through the gap a dismal patch, a hundred yards or more in extent, with the telegraph poles and network of wires bounding it which showed that a railway embankment ran parallel with Morley's Buildings.

Rounding the angle of the end house, Rider and I stumbled through the rank weeds for some fifty or sixty yards. A light flashed suddenly in my face; a constable was directing his lantern upon me.

"All right, officer!" said Rider.

The constable raised his hand in salute.

"Nothing suspicious?"

"Nothing sir."

"Look!" said Rider. Then:—"Shine your lantern on him, constable."

As Rider pulled my arm I looked down into the tangled mass of weeds and grasses.

A man was there, almost at my feet—a man who wore rough and ragged clothes and who lay, or rather half knelt, with his elbows dug into the soil and his head lowered grotesquely so that his face was hidden. He seemed to be crouching, as if for a catlike spring. But the back of his skull showed, in the light of the bull's-eye, as one ghastly wound—a blurr of blood-matted hair and shattered bone, difficult adequately to describe, frightful to remember, impossible to forget.

"Dead!"

"Over an hour, sir."

It was the constable who had answered me.

"About twelve o'clock, then?"

"According to the doctor," said Rider, grimly, "yes. His wife found him."

Momentarily I was too horrified to speak. Then:—

"Who is he?" I asked huskily.

"He is, or was," answered Rider, "one Dan Wiley; something of an undesirable, but none the less, poor devil!—"

"And he lived?"

"At number 3, where you saw the light in the window. His wife is up there. I pity her."

"He was drunk, sir—" began the constable—

"Yes," interrupted Rider; "he reeks of drink now, but—" he pointed significantly—"it was not drink that killed him."

Another silence; then:——

"What are the particulars?" I asked, and began to move away.

"Don't go yet!" snapped Rider, taking my arm. "I want to ask you if you notice anything peculiar——"

"In what way?"

"Just study the scene; I won't prejudice your views; but just take in all the details whilst I tell you what I know."

A sense of nausea was assailing me; but I repelled it and sought to do as Rider directed. Meanwhile he continued:——

"Dan Wiley was a ne'er-do-well, and one of the most dissolute characters of a dissolute neighborhood. He had no regular work, and was rarely sober. He lived with his wife at number 3 Morley's Buildings. I fancy that the poor woman contributed more largely to the upkeep of the establishment than did the departed. It was his almost nightly custom to get obstreperously drunk at the King's Head in Grenville Street, some little distance off on the other side of the line. On leaving, or being ejected, he would take a short cut home by scrambling over the fence, crossing the railway line, and thence going through this waste patch upon which he was found to-night.

"Sometimes he would fall asleep on the way, but never—so strangely does Providence protect the drunkard—upon the line! On several occasions, however, he has been found asleep on the intervening stretch of waste ground upon which to-night—it was no unusual adventure, poor creature—Mrs. Wiley came out about twelve o'clock to search for her husband. She found him as you see."

"Had there been any quarrel at the public house?"

"None at all. He was only moderately drunk when he left the bar for home, and nothing of an unusual nature had occurred, although he was naturally a quarrelsome man."

"But he is not facing towards——"

"Towards home?" snapped Rider, tensely. "Right! I am glad you noted it. It was the first thing that struck my attention."

"Someone attacked him from behind."

"Someone who came, not from the railway line, but from the direction of Morley's Buildings? Exactly!"

"You have inquired?"——

"I have made such inquiries as were possible without exciting undue suspicion. Do you note anything else of a peculiar nature?"

I shook my head. The brutal and revolting crime sickened me; and I was incapable of considering coolly the circumstances attendant upon it.

"Then we will just have a look around number 3," said Rider, "and afterward, if nothing strikes you, you have my leave to return home."

"Thanks!" I said, ironically. "This is scarcely the sort of case, Rider—"

"Don't be too sure," he interrupted. "It looks a brutally unimaginative affair, I grant you; sordid it is, I admit. But although—and frankly I am disappointed—you have overlooked them, there are points about it which place the crime in a class quite by itself."

I said no more, until, in answer to my friend's knock, a rather slatternly woman, whose plain face was rendered yet less attractive by eyes red with weeping, opened the door. She offered us no greeting, but turned, in a pathetically aloof manner, and walked up the uncarpeted stairs ahead of us.

Rider took my arm again.

"You note the door upon the right?" he whispered. "It communicates with a sort of ground-floor—actually the basement. There are three steps down, and two rooms below. The front one is only a foot or so below the level of the street, the back one is virtually a cellar. One window, high in the wall, looks out upon the waste ground and the railway. The Wileys leased the house, but they only occupied the top floor. The middle floor is vacant and the ground floor, to which I have referred, is rented by one Zahdoff, a cabinet-maker. I have seen Zahdoff; he had merely a nodding acquaintance with his landlord—Dan Wiley; and his limited English vocabulary does not admit of a protracted conversation."

"He is a foreigner?"

"A Polish-Jew, according to his own account."

We mounted the stairs to the top floor; a miserable abode it was.

"You see," said Rider, quietly, "it is typical enough of its kind. The poor woman does charing, and her husband used to drink the proceeds. There is nothing much to learn here. Do you think so?"

I shook my head; and Rider, with a few kindly words to the unhappy woman, who sat in the one practicable chair, staring before her with unseeing eyes, descended the stairs with me.

"The neighborhood knows nothing of the matter as yet," he told me. "We have succeeded in keeping it quiet. But I must make arrangements for the removal of the body to the mortuary."

In the street he stood facing me for a moment.

"I won't ask you to worry about it, to-night," he said: "but in the morning, get all the facts in line, and jot down your impressions. Oh! I am not joking; you have the type of mind which, not being confined in certain grooves, such as mine is, can frequently cast light into dark places. Jot down your impressions; I am most anxious to have them. The cab is waiting at the corner, and is at your service." . . . .

II

I cannot say that I slept well, on my return; for the vision of that splintered skull persistently haunted me. Yet no occasion arose to jot down impressions as Rider had requested, for saving that blood mist of sordid brutality which hung over the affair, there was nothing, so far as I could perceive, in the nature of a clue; there was nothing showing this ghastly crime to be a link in a chain, to be a move in some wider campaign such as would call for the services of Rider Pasha.

Towards dawn, sleep still defying me, I had an idea to which my mind obstinately clung; in short, it occurred to me that Rider, or those who instructed him, must know something of the antecedents of the man Wiley which gave him a certain importance not perceptible to me.

Before I had finished breakfast, Rider appeared carrying a tremendous bundle of newspapers. He waved to me in his airy fashion to continue my meal, and throwing himself into an armchair, began rapidly to scan the columns of the journals.

He quite ignored my remarks until this task was accomplished; then, dropping down the final sheet upon the mound already littered at his feet, he turned to me.

"There was barely time," he said, "to arrange for the suppression of the news, and I feared that it might have found its way into print despite my activities. It has not, however."

"You attach a singular importance to the murder of the man Wiley?"

"Then you are still in the dark?"

"To me it has the appearance of a typical slum crime."

"And you may be right. But yet—there are points . . ."

"I have quite failed to detect them."

"Consider the circumstances: What could be the object of such a crime? Who could profit by it?"

"It is mysterious, certainly."

Rider leant against the mantelpiece, both hands deep in his pockets, and his jaw thrust forward truculently.

"It is!" he snapped.

He stared at me vaguely for some time in silence; then:—

"I want you to come along tonight," he said, "and go over the ground once again with me."

"Why at night?"

"Because, assuming the murderer to reside in the locality—and one may fairly assume so much—I do not wish him to observe us."

A while longer Rider remained, talking of matters purely personal; then, arranging to meet me at a point near to Morley's Buildings, at ten o'clock that night, he left me to my work—which progressed none the more favorably by reason of his visit and the disturbing ideas which it had engendered.

The place which Rider had selected for the rendezvous was a certain tavern, bearing the sign of the Two Feathers. I must explain that I was no stranger to this type of nocturnal adventure; and my costume, when, a few minutes before the appointed hour, I entered the private bar of this establishment, was not of a fashion which I should have chosen for a business visit to Fleet Street.

Rider—an expert—has assured me that I make an excellent loafer; and when on the stroke of the hour my companion joined me in the bar, I was forced to concede that a more undesirable looking ruffian I had never encountered.

Picture us, then, as, typical of Morley's Buildings, we slouched across the open ground behind those unsavory tenements in the direction of the railway line.

A certain sordid activity was noticeable in the street at this comparatively early hour. Many dirty children still continued their play in the gutters beneath a fire of shrewish screams from bedraggled mothers. Lights showed in many of the windows, and practically all the front doors were open.

We were already upon our way to the scene of the crime, when Rider, suddenly tackling me in Rugby fashion, threw me heavily to the ground, and, prostrate upon my body, held me there!

"Not a word!" he hissed in my ear. He loses his drawling speech in moments of action. "I don't think she has seen us!"

I succeeded in raising my head. A vague and shapeless, muffled figure was approaching from the railroad, and must pass close to the spot where we lay amid the tangled vegetation.

Rider's nervous excitement communicating itself to me, I crouched, scarcely breathing, whilst the figure came nearer and nearer, drew level with our hiding-place, and passed on.

It was that of a woman, poorly dressed, and having a furtiveness of manner very singular and noticeable. A vague light had shone upon her face as she passed me; and since this was a strangely dark night, I craned my neck to ascertain from whence the light had come. Instantly I perceived that we lay just without the radius of this faint illumination—which proceeded from a little window partially masked with tangled weeds in one of the houses of Morley's Buildings.

"The basement window of number 3!" whispered Rider—"watch!"

Indeed I was watching to the best of my ability; for vague as the light had been which had illuminated the face of the furtive woman, nevertheless it had served to show me that her clothes were as false a clue to real identity as were our own.

She was very dark and had a pale and distinguished beauty, with large flashing eyes, and a type of clear-cut features which for some reason set me thinking of Vienna. And my imagination was still straying through the brilliantly lighted streets of the Austrian capital, when the mysterious woman gained the window, stooped, and evidently entered into conversation with one who stood in the room within.

"Zahdoff!" whispered Rider in my ear. "Did you see her face?"

"I did," I replied. "She has beauty, of a dark sort—"

"White complexion, with strangely black eyes?"

"Yes."

"From where I lay, I could not see her, unfortunately." His voice spoke of excitement restrained with difficulty. "But, by God! I believe I'm right!" he added, strangely.

"What do you suspect?"

"Impossible to go into that now. Surely even you will admit that this incident lifts the case above the sordid level to which you had assigned it?"

"It is very mysterious—certainly."

"Quiet!" whispered Rider. "See! she is going!"

Indeed, as he spoke, a figure in black silhouette moved across the window and was lost in the shadows of the buildings. Then for a moment it reappeared at the corner—and was lost again.

"Is *he* looking from the window, now?" hissed Rider.

"No," I reported.

"Then come on!"

My companion leapt to his feet, and stood, clutching my arm.

Faintly, in the distance, I heard the drone of a starting motor engine.

"Too late!" he muttered. "Let's see what we can find here," and went on some dozen paces to the spot where Dan Wiley had been found.

"Stand between me and the buildings," he directed.

I did as he desired, and he, kneeling amid the tangled growths, directed the ray of a pocket-lamp upon the ground all about.

"Keep your eye on the window!"

I was watching the window intently, and, even as he spoke, a shaggy head appeared thereat, sharply outlined by the light in the room behind it.

"*Ss!*"

Rider extinguished the lamp as I dropped on my knees beside him. We both turned and looked back at Morley's Buildings.

A man in the basement of number 3 was staring out intently across the patch of waste ground.

"Do you think he saw the light?" whispered Rider.

"Impossible to say, but I think not."

"I hope not," snapped my friend, "for if he did—"

"Well?"

"I am gradually collecting the threads, I think; and unless I am greatly mistaken, we have to deal with one of the cleverest rogues in Europe!"

"But surely you know—"

"I have never set eyes upon his face; his real face, I mean. Few have. He has a reputation—! If I can round him up, it may mean the difference between—"

He paused.

"Between?"

"I must not say too much," added Rider, "more especially as I may be wrong; but—"

The figure vanished from the window, and—

"Come on!" snapped my friend, seizing my arm.

We hastened across to the corner of the buildings and again adopting the slouching gait fashionable in that vicinity, passed along by the houses. The door of number 3 was closed, but from the grated window at our feet, a faint light shone up.

"The worthy cabinet-maker," said Rider, "works late."

Half an hour afterwards we were both seated in my study, and Rider was addressing himself to the whisky and soda with that air of joyous satisfaction peculiarly his own. For my part, although, now, I divined that the murder of Dan Wiley was no common crime, I was completely mystified at all points. The cabinet-making of Zahdoff clearly was but a mask to other more deadly operations. But who *was* Zahdoff? If Rider knew that the man had a criminal history, why was Zahdoff not arrested? Who was the woman with the remarkable eyes? What part did she play in the drama? I scarcely knew where to begin my inquiries; but—

"What do you know of the man called Zahdoff?" I asked abruptly, pushing a box of cigarettes towards Rider.

He glanced up with his odd smile.

"Unfortunately," he replied, "I know nothing; I merely suspect. There is a certain individual of international notoriety who might—it is conceivable—be hidden beneath the bearded Zahdoff. In certain quarters it has been suspected for some time that this individual, whom we will dignify by the title of Colonel X, was concealed in

London. I may even go so far as to state that I came to London expressly to look for him! The death of Dan Wiley presented certain curious features which induced me to glance in that direction. In this way I made the acquaintance of Zahdoff, Polish-Jew and cabinet-maker. He interested me, although I flatter myself that I did not display this interest; but there was not the slightest ground of suspicion; I hadn't a scrap of evidence to connect Zahdoff with the murder, and I hadn't a scrap of evidence to connect Zahdoff with Colonel X. But I have certain instincts or intuitions. Pursuing these random ideas, I blundered upon my first real clue—not necessarily to the murderer of Wiley, but to the identity of Zahdoff with Colonel X!"

"Who is Colonel X?"

"Let us say for the moment that he is head of a gang of international criminals. Although, as I have already mentioned, the appearance of the real Colonel is quite unknown to the secret service men throughout Europe—a tribute to his protean genius—he has been traced on more than one occasion and identified, by reason of his association with a certain woman . . . ."

"Madame X?"

Rider shrugged his shoulders and lighted a cigarette.

"Suppose we give her the benefit of the doubt?" he said, smiling. "At any rate she has been less successful in disguising herself than has the Colonel. She is a woman of considerable beauty, though of a distinctly vampirish sort; a dull white complexion with very dark eyes and very red lips—you know the type?"

"It was she!" I cried, excitedly.

"I am disposed to agree with you."

"Then Zahdoff—"

"Is Colonel X? Again, I think so."

"And Wiley?"

"Wiley is a stumbling block; I cannot disguise that fact. As I have told you, I blundered upon this den of the cabinet-maker—sheerly blundered upon it. I do not claim that in the murder of Dan Wiley I perceived a clue to the whereabouts of the man for whom I was searching; I looked into the case merely because I was on the spot at the time, and because it presented unusual features. If I have found my man, it is more by good luck than by good management."

I crossed the room to where the siphon stood upon the side-table, and, squirting soda into my tumbler, threw to Rider the query:—

"You have spoken several times of these unusual features. What are they?"

"Since your imagination would appear to have lost something of its fertility, they are these:—The entire absence of any motive, and the position of the victim's body."

"He was practically kneeling."

"I am convinced that he was *actually* kneeling at the time that his assailant came upon him from behind. He was kneeling with his head lowered to the ground."

"Well?"

Again Rider shrugged his shoulders.

"I do not know *why* he was in that attitude," he confessed, "but I am determined to find out. Since the *motive* is at present lacking in the scheme, I take it that he was murdered *because* he was kneeling in that way!"

"What?"

"It seems absurd, I know; but I feel that the clue to the labyrinth is dangling before our eyes."

There was a silence of some minutes.

"What steps are you taking?"

"I am arranging to watch Zahdoff."

"Why did you not follow the woman to-night?"

"Because I had not provided against the possibility of having to do so."

"What do you mean?"

"She had a cab or a car waiting in the locality. I heard it drive off. How could I hope to follow?"

"True," I said. "What is the nature of the arrangements you have made?"

"I have leased the vacant floor of number 3," replied Rider; "and some time to-morrow, whilst Zahdoff is absent, for he goes out to purchase certain necessary provisions daily, I shall cut an opening in the boards at a point immediately above the tall cupboard which I noticed in his room, and make a spy-hole in the very dilapidated plaster of his ceiling. It is even possible that some of the existing holes will serve my purpose."

"Can I assist you in any way?" I asked eagerly.

"I am relying upon you," replied Rider. "For my own part I might be called away at any time; I should then look to you to keep watch on our friend until my return. In order to provide against that emergency, I have given out that I have leased the room for myself and my brother and that we are both very irregular characters! A few necessary items of furniture are being installed, and here are your keys!"

Gravely he handed me two door keys, then, screwing his face into that odd smile of his, lighted a second cigarette.

He left at eleven o'clock to return to his temporary chambers, and to resume more decent raiment. About midday, on the morrow it was that I next heard from him. He rang me up.

"My precautions were taken only just in time," he said, "I have my orders for Budapest, and am now off to catch the train! I look to you, brother owl, to devote several evenings during the coming week to the spy-hole at number 3 Morley's Buildings. Oh! I've made it—yes! It has just occurred to me that the real activities of Zahdoff probably do not commence until the neighborhood is sleeping. You understand what I mean?"

"Quite well," I replied, grimly. "I must sleep during the day if I am to remain up half the night!"

"I will communicate with you at the earliest possible moment. Make notes of anything which you may observe; and don't forget to lock the room door when you leave. To spur you to enthusiasm, I may add that *if* Zahdoff is actually identical with Colonel X, his activities are inimical, not merely to individuals, but to the future of the British Empire!"

III

That night I took possession of my apartments in Morley's Buildings. At an hour when the dirty children and their bedraggled watchers had already departed from the gutter-way, I inserted the key in the lock and stepped into the stuffy little passage with its mingled odor of fried bacon and lamp oil. It was perfectly dark as I entered, but at the sound of my footsteps the depressed door on the right opened, and the figure of Zahdoff, the cabinet-maker, was blackly indicated against the light from the room behind him.

Of his height I was unable to judge, since he stood considerably below me, but he possessed a great breadth of shoulder, and with his shaggy hair and bushy whiskers, presented a striking silhouette, markedly leonine in character.

He muttered something which may have been a greeting, to which I responded with a gruff "good-night"—and passed up the stairs.

As I mounted, Zahdoff reclosed his door, and in utter darkness I had to grope my way to the upper apartments. The door communicating with the front room was locked, in which I recognized a precaution of Rider's, since one had to pass through this front room in order to reach that at the back, the real scene of operations.

I lighted a match and surveyed my demesne. The "furniture" to which Rider had referred, consisted of a deal table and two chairs! Entering the second room, I observed a carpet upon the floor, and a pallet bed over by the window. A small rickety table, bearing a common brass lamp, completed the "appointments" of my chambers. I was unaware of Mrs. Wiley's position in the matter; I did not know whether she was our accomplice, or whether she believed me to be a bona fide lodger. Rider had neglected to advise me on this point, and I determined to take no undue risks in regard to my landlady.

Having lowered the dirty linen blind, I rolled up a corner of the carpet and began to search for the spyhole. Since I had never been in Zahdoff's apartments, I did not know upon which side of the room, beneath, the cupboard referred to by Rider was situated; therefore I searched two sides of my floor in vain, but finally I found a section of boarding neatly cut out and readily detachable by means of a little brass screw which had been placed in it for the purpose. I was diplomatic enough to know that to commence operations immediately would be unwise, and I did not even remove the board; in fact I replaced the carpet over it—just as a loud rap sounded at my door!

Lamp in hand, I crossed the front room and threw open the door.

The light shone upon the pale, bearded face of Zahdoff; and a singular face it was—large featured and lined with innumerable furrows. Pale blue eyes he had, seeming abnormally large behind the pebbles of his spectacles, and a high, broad brow; this sufficiently singular countenance was crowned, surrounded, and, as regards the mouth and jaw, masked, by such a riot of reddish-brown hair as I had rarely seen upon any human being.

A moment he confronted me so; then:—

"It is Mr. Grimes?" he said, speaking thickly and with a strong accent—"that gomes to live here?"

"That's me!" I replied in my broadest Cockney.

"I am glad to know my neighbors," continued Zahdoff, and held out an angular and sinewy hand.

I grasped it with my own, which was artificially dirtied, and wondered what this visit might portend. In the next instant its object stood revealed. From a capacious pocket Zahdoff took out a blind-roller.

"You will find that your blind," he explained, thickly, "it is broken—no good. I gome to fix you a new one."

Not an instant did I hesitate. "Right oh! my old buck!" I cried, slapping him boisterously on the shoulder—"get on with it!"

I stood aside for him to enter, and this he did with alacrity. But little more he had to say for himself, whilst, with deft fingers, he took down the old roller (which appeared to me to be in perfect working order) and substituted the new one. I busied myself in the outer room, giving Zahdoff every opportunity to inspect the inner one—for which purpose, I doubted not, he was come. I had taken the precaution, however, of placing the ricketty table directly over the spy-hole, with the lamp upon it!

His act of disinterested kindness performed, Zahdoff retired, casting a final keen glance about ere he did so. I had sufficient confidence in my make-up and acting to believe that he had accomplished nothing by his visit. Shortly afterwards, a great noise of carpentry arose from below, and this continued until long after midnight—when it ceased abruptly. I had locked my outer door and extinguished the lamp. Now I began, cautiously, to raise the blind of the back window; and, as I did so, the roller supplied by Zahdoff emitted a formidable squeak.

With my hand upon the cord, I stopped. Was this squeaking roller installed with design? I had raised the blind no more than three or four inches, and I determined that my best course would be to raise it fully, let it squeak as loudly as it might; for if I desisted on the first squeak, it would show that I had hoped to act secretly; and it might be that this was the purpose of the contrivance.

Amid a perfect wailing, I fully raised the blind. Peering down upon the waste ground, I was in time to see a muffled figure gliding into the shadows of the building.

That my first vigil was rewarded, I ascribed, at the time, to the success of my maneuvres; I am disposed to believe now that Zahdoff's activity was dictated by an imperious need for haste. Lying prone upon the floor, then, with my head thrust tortoise-wise through the opening and my eye but a few inches removed from a rent in the plaster below, I viewed the workshop of Zahdoff that night, and I saw strange things.

As was to be expected, a quantity of timber lay about upon the floor or was piled against the wall. The cupboard, over the top of which I looked, was open; and when first I began my spying, the room below was empty—silent.

Then, *out from the cupboard*, came Zahdoff bearing a basket, evidently heavy. Its contents I was unable to perceive. But if his appearance from the cupboard had surprised me, his next movement was even more mysterious. He lifted the basket on to the ledge of the window, and someone—someone who must have stood outside on the waste ground—received it from him. It vanished . . . and Zahdoff, shouldering a heavy piece of timber, re-entered the cupboard. Silence followed.

Where was he?

Cautiously I stood upright. Zahdoff's cupboard was set in that side of the building backing upon the waste patch; the window also was on this side—as has already been noted—and to the left of the cupboard. I crept to the window and looked out.

This was a moonless night, during the brief heat-wave which visited us in the memorable summer of 1914; but under the blaze of the stars, I saw a vaguely outlined figure returning from the direction of the railway embankment with the basket—now evidently empty! I watched until the bearer of the basket passed in below my window.

It was a woman.

When I returned to the spy-hole—Zahdoff reappeared, dragging a second basket. Tantalizingly enough, although I could see Zahdoff and at times see the basket, I could not, strain as I might, obtain a view of its contents. These mysterious operations, then, I watched far into the night. My weariness, and a certain quality in the atmosphere, warned me that dawn was nigh, when the baskets made their final journey, the woman disappeared, and Zahdoff extinguished the light in his work-shop.

I left the house about five o'clock, locking my door behind me.

On returning home, I slept until late in the morning. A telegraphic message was delivered at midday. It had been tendered in Paris, and read as follows:—

Dan W. may have been listening. Listening." (The word was repeated.) "Wish had perceived this sooner. Search for earth newly turned upon waste ground and embankment. Observe greatest caution. Importance of W.'s case increasing hourly. Expect return any moment.

RIDER

IV

Ensued those dreadful days of suspense—of waiting from hour to hour, almost from minute to minute, for the words of the War Minister which should penetrate to every corner of the civilized world; which should advise the Powers, some to their consternation, others to their gladness, that the sword of Great Britain was unsheathed.

So wholly had I succumbed to the oppression of those anxious hours that the mission entrusted to me by Rider was, I regret to say, temporarily neglected. Three times, now, I had sought my apartments in Morley's Buildings; on each occasion Zahdoff had greeted my entry in truly neighborly fashion; and upon three nights I had watched the pseudo cabinet-maker bearing timber into his cupboard and bearing laden baskets out. I had gone so far, whilst the detective zeal was upon me, as to search the waste ground between the houses and the railroad one morning whilst the occupant of the ground floor was absent. To my notes, bearing upon the murder mystery, I had added, as result, this item:—

"Great quantities of stone, clay, and newly turned soil, have been recently deposited upon the railway embankment behind Morley's Buildings."

Obtuse I must have been at this time; for I frankly confess that up to the moment of the declaration of war I had failed to associate my new discovery with the baskets which nightly came forth from Zahdoff's cupboard, and which were passed through his window to be received by the woman who waited!

Incredible it may appear, but that I may eat of the bread of humility, I confess it.

Swayed by the common excitement which had all England in its grip, I had relegated my amateur detective exploits to the limbo of things forgotten; when one evening some time after Britain's position in the Great Struggle had clearly been defined, I found myself a unit of the crowd thronging Downing Street . . . and I found myself face to face with the woman of Morley's Buildings—the woman whom Rider had suspected of being Madame X!

She was in a nervous hurry, and was very elegantly dressed, so that her really remarkable beauty excited comment on all sides. But she thrust her way resolutely through the crowd and seemed bent upon gaining the end of the street.

Some momentous idea struggled for admission to my brain; and, whilst yet unable to embrace it, I, in turn, forced my way through the throng and followed that conspicuous figure.

I was only in time to see her being driven off in a large and opulently appointed car.

A new turn had been given to my ideas and an hour later I was seated at my study table with my notes opened before me. The nebulous was becoming substantial. If I had been excited before, I was trebly excited now.

Where was Rider? If these new ideas were well-founded, why was he not in London?

Suddenly it came home to me like a thunder-clap, that mighty issues were concerned. It appeared, nightmare fashion, that the structure of the British Empire rested upon my shoulders; so that, mentally and physically, I tottered and grew sick with dread.

My notes before me, I sat, longing ardently for my 'phone bell to ring, or for that familiar whistle to sound from the street.

But the bell did not ring, nor did I hear the whistle.

Ten minutes earlier, a company of Territorials had tramped past, visualizing England's readiness. Full well I knew that Civilization's self tottered upon the brink of an abyss. Already the news had leaked out that a British Expeditionary Force, for the first time since the dread shadow of Napoleon lay across Europe, had landed on the Continent. As a press-man, I knew more of the fact than could be available to the general public; and I knew that the peace of Europe veritably might depend upon the action, not of a field army or an army corps, not of a regiment or a garrison, but upon the action of a single man.

Now I perceived, and perceived with horror, by this process of elimination, that that man might well be—*myself*!

The 'phone bell rang.

With a hand not too steady, I snatched up the receiver—I heard Rider's voice.

"Quick!" he snapped, "I am at Charing Cross. You have been watching Zahdoff?"

"I have!" I cried.

"Particulars! Omit nothing. But be brief."

I spread my notes under my hand and commenced to read through them from the time that I had first entered upon my campaign of espionage. My very soul shuddered when I contemplated what my recent neglect might mean!

Rider never once interrupted me, save by—"yes, go on!" I had almost reached the end of my notes, and I was just explaining how I had found the clay and newly turned earth on the railway embankment, when, upon the drawn casement curtain before me, I perceived a shadow!

My windows were fully opened, and by the light of the street lamp at the end of the front lawn, this shadow was clearly perceptible—for a moment only, but long enough to show me that the shadow was that of a woman—who had fled.

How long had she been crouching outside my open window? Who was she? I could not doubt!

"Go on, go on!" cried Rider—"why do you stop?"

In a great gush of words, I told him. Then:—

"Join me at H Station!" he directed tersely. "I shall be waiting with a car . . ."

It was in a frame of mind unreal, dreamlike, that I performed the journey to meet Rider. The streets through which I passed were dream-streets; the lights, the groups about the paper-shops, the unusual number of khaki coats amid the throng— all were phantoms. I seemed not to belong to this world about me. I was aloof from it, detached; a creature apart, marked out from my fellow men by a mighty responsibility which Fate had cast upon me.

At the station Rider waited, standing beside a powerful touring-car. A Territorial was on guard at the foot of the stairs, a curious group surveying him wonderingly.

"In!" snapped Rider—tossed half a crown to the man who had driven me, and literally dragged me into the car.

The chauffeur started so suddenly as to jerk me back upon the seat. Clearly, he had his orders; and a glance at Rider's face confirmed, if confirmation were necessary, the awful seriousness of our mission that night.

A sort of dusky pallor showed itself through the tan of his skin and his eyes were more nearly gray than blue, widely opened, set, and alight with an expression which I can only describe as one of deliberate ferocity. His fingers as he gripped my arm closed upon it like a steel vise.

"I was detained," he began, rapidly. "These last two weeks have been hell for me! . . . Then, suddenly, with a thousand difficulties to overcome before I could return, I saw that my post was here, in London. God! what I have done to get back! Some day I will tell you . . . . On the way I have pictured everything that you told me just now. I saw what a fool I had been, I saw what it all meant; everything—everything—down to the tiniest item, fitted into the fiendish scheme!" . . . .

"Wiley—"

"He fell asleep there—on the waste ground. He was awakened by the sounds beneath him—"

"*Beneath* him!"

"Damn it, man, damn it! You surely understand? He heard them cutting the *tunnel* below! In his semi-drunken state, some cry escaped him. Then *they* heard *him!* . . . . Whilst he still lay, listening for further sounds, Zahdoff returned to his cellar, selected a heavy piece of timber, and crept around behind Wiley. There was no time for half measures. He knew, to within a day or two, at any rate, when he had to be ready; he dashed Wiley's brains out—"

"Then Zahdoff—"

"Is Dr. von Kotter, the cleverest and most unscrupulous spy in Europe! German War Office . . . ."

Rider spoke the words disconnectedly, all the time gripping my arm with those steely fingers.

"Why, in heaven's name, was I so blind?" he cried. "A search of von Kotter's room would have revealed the whole accursed plot! Now!—"

He pulled out his watch.

"Merciful God!"—the words were barely audible—"only ten minutes!"

The car pulled up with a jerk. Rider threw himself out, dragging me after him. I found myself at the corner of a mean street which I remembered to have passed before in my journeys to Morley's Buildings. Similarly to the latter, it lay parallel with the railway line, but at a rather more northerly point. Rider went racing along it madly, and I followed him. Those grouped about the open doors of the houses stared at us in stupid wonderment; but straight on went my companion, turned to the right, down a narrow courtway, and was out upon a continuation of that belt of waste land which, five hundred yards lower down the line, I knew so well.

A signal-box loomed directly above us. In the light from its windows, Rider consulted his watch.

"Ten-forty-four!" he hissed, breathlessly. "Five minutes!"

Then with a bound he was up on the embankment and scrambling for the ladder of the box!

"*Halt!*"

There was a sentry on duty by the signal-box; Rider had been almost beside him ere he was perceived! Now the man stood with his bayonet but a few inches removed from Rider's chest!

I have never seen such an expression as that which crossed my friend's face: anger and horror mingled in it strangely.

"It is life or death!" he almost screamed at the man. "I am on secret service business here! You understand?" He thrust out a card.

"Halt! you cannot pass!"

"God in heaven! this is awful—I shall go mad! I tell you I *must* enter that box . . . ."

There sounded the distant clang of metal. A groan burst from Rider's lips.

"The signalman has cleared the line!" I heard.

But the bayonet never moved. The man was a private in a London Territorial regiment, and clearly he was doubtful respecting his duty in such a situation. I think he perceived that Rider was in deadly earnest; yet I could not reproach him. He had his orders, and, up to a point, he adhered to them.

"Come on!" shouted Rider—"there is one other chance!"

"Halt!" The sentry stepped in front of my wild-eyed friend. "You cannot move. I must arrest you both and hand you over to the guard!"

Then, in that unlikely spot, a blow was struck and a martyr made for England.

Rider, with a serpentine movement, twisted under the threatening bayonet and delivered the sentry a left-handed blow placed with deadly accuracy upon the jaw! The man pitched forward like a pole-axed bullock and without a cry rolled heavily down the embankment and lay at my feet.

Like a deer, Rider made off, and, with my heart thumping fiercely, I followed. We covered the five hundred yards to Morley's Buildings as one traverses the ground of dreamland. There was no light in Zahdoff's window. Around an angle of the building raced Rider, and into the street. At the door of number 3:

"The key!" he panted.

I thrust the key into his hand, and in a moment he had the door open. Zahdoff's door was closed. Rider threw himself upon it. It was locked!

"Stand back!" he rasped, huskily.

I stood back against the wall, as, pulling a Browning pistol from his hip pocket, he blew out the lock! There was a crash as he kicked the door open. Then we were blundering down the steps and into the darkened, cellar-like room. A beam of light shone out from Rider's pocket-lamp; it shone upon the open door of the mysterious cupboard.

Then I saw that this cupboard was different from other cupboards in that, where the back should have been there showed only a gaping cavity! Rider glanced all about the room and all about the cupboard. Then, for the last time, pulled out his watch.

"Ten-forty-eight! *We have one minute!*"

He leapt into the cavity and went blundering forward. I followed and found my feet upon clay soil. Dimly, in the reflected light of Rider's lamp, I saw that this was a crude passage cut through the damp earth and upheld at intervals by roughly placed timbers. Bent almost double, for the roof was low, Rider pressed on. A dull and distant rumbling came to my ears, and the place seemed to shake.

We were come to the end of the tunnel.

On a wooden ledge, placed across from side to side, stood a square iron box about a foot in diameter, and attached to it was a contrivance which reminded me of a taximeter. Above the ever increasing roar, which, now, I recognized, I could hear the *tick-tick-tick* of the clock-like thing.

"Hold the lamp!"

Rider's voice now was icily cool. He thrust the lamp into my hands, and as I directed the ray upon the machine on the plank, he set to work with deft fingers.

Tick-tick-tick-tick!

What he did, I do not know to this day; I only know that it was well done, that it was executed as though Rider were regulating a watch. My eyes, whilst they perceived the fingers rapidly at work with the mechanism of the machine, yet were fixed upon the clock face set in it . . . . and this registered:—

10:49.

Tick-tick-tick-tick!

I knew that 10:49 must be, almost to a second, the exact time!

Tick-tick!—and the ticking ceased.

It was done!

Rider pulled out from a crevice in the contrivance the ends of two pieces of flex, which descended from the roof . . . and collapsed at my feet.

"Gun-cotton!" he muttered. "Those wires connect to the electric main!"

The muffled roar became deafening. The place about me quivered and rocked. My ears seemed to ache with the sound. Then it grew fainter—more faint—and died away.

I glanced down at Rider. Pallid, his face showed in the lamplight.

"The ten-thirty Folkestone Express!" he whispered hoarsely.

I clutched at the wall to steady myself.

"But—"

"Bearing the Field Marshal commanding the British Expeditionary Force."

Rider Pasha swooned.

THE FENCHURCH STREET MYSTERY

Baroness Orczy

I

The man in the corner pushed aside his glass, and leant across the table.

"Mysteries!" he commented. "There is no such thing as a mystery in connection with any crime, provided intelligence is brought to bear upon its investigation."

Very much astonished Polly Burton looked over the top of her newspaper, and fixed a pair of very severe, coldly inquiring brown eyes upon him.

She had disapproved of the man from the instant when he shuffled across the shop and sat down opposite to her, at the same marble-topped table which already held her large coffee (3d.), her roll and butter (2d.), and plate of tongue (6d.).

Now this particular corner, this very same table, that special view of the magnificent marble hall—known as the Norfolk Street branch of the Aërated Bread Company's depôts—were Polly's own corner, table, and view. Here she had partaken of eleven pennyworth of luncheon and one pennyworth of daily information ever since that glorious never-to-be-forgotten day when she was enrolled on the staff of the *Evening Observer* (we'll call it that, if you please), and became a member of that illustrious and world-famed organisation known as the British Press.

She was a personality, was Miss Burton of the *Evening Observer*. Her cards were printed thus:

> **MISS MARY J. BURTON**
> Evening Observer

She had interviewed Miss Ellen Terry and the Bishop of Madagascar, Mr. Seymour Hicks and the Chief Commissioner of Police. She had been present at the last Marlborough House garden party—in the cloak-room, that is to say, where she caught sight of Lady Thingummy's hat, Miss What-you-may-call's sunshade, and of various other things modistical or fashionable, all of which were duly described under the heading "Royalty and Dress" in the early afternoon edition of the *Evening Observer*.

(The article itself is signed M. J. B., and is to be found in the files of that leading halfpennyworth.)

For these reasons—and for various others, too—Polly felt irate with the man in the corner, and told him so with her eyes, as plainly as any pair of brown eyes]can speak.

She had been reading an article in the *Daily Telegraph*. The article was palpitatingly interesting. Had Polly been commenting audibly upon it? Certain it is that the man over there had spoken in direct answer to her thoughts.

She looked at him and frowned; the next moment she smiled. Miss Burton (of the *Evening Observer*) had a keen sense of humour, which two years' association with the British Press had not succeeded in destroying, and the appearance of the man was sufficient to tickle the most ultramorose fancy. Polly thought to herself that she had never seen anyone so pale, so thin, with such funny light-coloured hair, brushed very smoothly across the top of a very obviously bald crown. He looked so timid and nervous as he fidgeted incessantly with a piece of string; his long, lean, and trembling fingers tying and untying it into knots of wonderful and complicated proportions.

Having carefully studied every detail of the quaint personality Polly felt more amiable.

"And yet," she remarked kindly but authoritatively, "this article, in an otherwise well-informed journal, will tell you that, even within the last year, no fewer than six crimes have completely baffled the police, and the perpetrators of them are still at large."

"Pardon me," he said gently, "I never for a moment ventured to suggest that there were no mysteries to the police; I merely remarked that there were none where intelligence was brought to bear upon the investigation of crime."

"Not even in the Fenchurch Street *mystery*, I suppose," she asked sarcastically.

"Least of all in the so-called Fenchurch Street *mystery*," he replied quietly.

Now the Fenchurch Street mystery, as that extraordinary crime had popularly been called, had puzzled—as Polly well knew—the brains of every thinking man and woman for the last twelve months. It had puzzled her not inconsiderably; she had been interested, fascinated; she had studied the case, formed her own theories, thought about it all often and often, had even written one or two letters to the Press on the subject—suggesting, arguing, hinting at possibilities and probabilities, adducing proofs which other amateur detectives were equally ready to refute. The attitude of that timid man in the corner, therefore, was peculiarly exasperating, and she retorted with sarcasm destined to completely annihilate her self-complacent interlocutor.

"What a pity it is, in that case, that you do not offer your priceless services to our misguided though well-meaning police."

"Isn't it?" he replied with perfect good-humour. "Well, you know, for one thing I doubt if they would accept them; and in the second place my inclinations and my duty would—were I to become an active member of the detective force—nearly always be in direct conflict. As often as not my sympathies go to the criminal who is clever and astute enough to lead our entire police force by the nose.

"I don't know how much of the case you remember," he went on quietly. "It certainly, at first, began even to puzzle me. On the 12th of last December a woman, poorly dressed, but with an unmistakable air of having seen better days, gave information at Scotland Yard of the disappearance of her husband, William Kershaw, of no occupation, and apparently of no fixed abode. She was accompanied by a friend—a fat, oily-looking German—and between them they told a tale which set the police immediately on the move.

"It appears that on the 10th of December, at about three o'clock in the afternoon, Karl Müller, the German, called on his friend, William Kershaw, for the purpose of collecting a small debt—some ten pounds or so—which the latter owed him. On arriving at the squalid lodging in Charlotte Street, Fitzroy Square, he found William Kershaw in a wild state of excitement, and his wife in tears. Müller attempted to state the object of his visit, but Kershaw, with wild gestures, waved him aside, and—in his own words—flabbergasted him by asking him point-blank for another loan of two pounds, which sum, he declared, would be the means of a speedy fortune for himself and the friend who would help him in his need.

"After a quarter of an hour spent in obscure hints, Kershaw, finding the cautious German obdurate, decided to let him into the secret plan, which, he averred, would place thousands into their hands."

Instinctively Polly had put down her paper; the mild stranger, with his nervous air and timid, watery eyes, had a peculiar way of telling his tale, which somehow fascinated her.

"I don't know," he resumed, "if you remember the story which the German told to the police, and which was corroborated in every detail by the wife or widow. Briefly it was this: Some thirty years previously, Kershaw, then twenty years of age, and a medical student at one of the London hospitals, had a chum named Barker, with whom he roomed, together with another.

"The latter, so it appears, brought home one evening a very considerable sum of money, which he had won on the turf, and the following morning he was found murdered in his bed. Kershaw, fortunately for himself, was able to prove a conclusive alibi; he had spent the night on duty at the hospital; as for Barker, he had disappeared, that is to say, as far as the police were concerned, but not as far as the watchful eyes of his friend Kershaw were able to spy—at least, so the latter said. Barker very cleverly contrived to get away out of the country, and, after sundry vicissitudes, finally settled down at Vladivostok, in Eastern Siberia, where, under the assumed name of Smethurst, he built up an enormous fortune by trading in furs.

"Now, mind you, every one knows Smethurst, the Siberian millionaire. Kershaw's story that he had once been called Barker, and had committed a murder thirty years ago was never proved, was it? I am merely telling you what Kershaw said to his friend the German and to his wife on that memorable afternoon of December the 10th.

"According to him Smethurst had made one gigantic mistake in his clever career— he had on four occasions written to his late friend, William Kershaw. Two of these letters had no bearing on the case, since they were written more than twenty-five years ago, and Kershaw, moreover, had lost them—so he said—long ago. According to him, however, the first of these letters was written when Smethurst, alias Barker, had spent all the money he had obtained from the crime, and found himself destitute in New York.

"Kershaw, then in fairly prosperous circumstances, sent him a £10 note for the sake of old times. The second, when the tables had turned, and Kershaw had begun to go downhill, Smethurst, as he then already called himself, sent his whilom friend £50. After that, as Müller gathered, Kershaw had made sundry demands on Smethurst's ever-increasing purse, and had accompanied these demands by various threats, which, considering the distant country in which the millionaire lived, were worse than futile.

"But now the climax had come, and Kershaw, after a final moment of hesitation, handed over to his German friend the two last letters purporting to have been written by Smethurst, and which, if you remember, played such an important part in the mysterious story of this extraordinary crime. I have a copy of both these letters here," added the man in the corner, as he took out a piece of paper from a very worn-out pocket-book, and, unfolding it very deliberately, he began to read:—

Sir,—Your preposterous demands for money are wholly unwarrantable. I have already helped you quite as much as you deserve. However, for the sake of old times, and because you once helped me when I was in a terrible difficulty, I am willing to once more let you impose upon my good nature. A friend of mine here, a Russian merchant, to whom I have sold my business, starts in a few days for an extended tour to many European and Asiatic ports in his yacht, and has invited me to accompany him as far as England. Being tired of foreign parts, and desirous of seeing the old country once again after thirty years' absence, I have decided to accept his invitation. I don't know when we may actually be in Europe, but I promise you that as soon as we touch a suitable port I will write to you again, making an appointment for you to see me in London. But remember that if your demands are too preposterous I will not for a moment listen to them, and that I am the last man in the world to submit to persistent and unwarrantable blackmail.

> I am, sir,
> Yours truly,
> FRANCIS SMETHURST

"The second letter was dated from Southampton," continued the man in the corner calmly, "and, curiously enough, was the only letter which Kershaw professed to have received from Smethurst of which he had kept the envelope, and which was dated. It was quite brief," he added, referring once more to his piece of paper.

Dear Sir,—Referring to my letter of a few weeks ago, I wish to inform you that the *Tsarskoe Selo* will touch at Tilbury on Tuesday next, the 10th. I shall land there, and immediately go up to London by the first train I can get. If you like, you may meet me at Fenchurch Street Station, in the first-class waiting-room, in the late afternoon. Since I surmise that after thirty years' absence my face may not be familiar to you, I may as well tell you that you will recognize me by a heavy Astrakhan fur coat, which I shall wear, together with a cap of the same. You may then introduce yourself to me, and I will personally listen to what you may have to say.

> Yours faithfully,
> FRANCIS SMETHURST

"It was this last letter which had caused William Kershaw's excitement and his wife's tears. In the German's own words, he was walking up and down the room like a wild beast, gesticulating wildly, and muttering sundry exclamations. Mrs. Kershaw, however, was full of apprehension. She mistrusted the man from foreign parts—who, according to her husband's story, had already one crime upon his conscience—who might, she feared, risk another, in order to be rid of a dangerous enemy. Woman-like, she thought the scheme a dishonourable one, for the law, she knew, is severe on the blackmailer.

"The assignation might be a cunning trap, in any case it was a curious one; why, she argued, did not Smethurst elect to see Kershaw at his hotel the following day?

A thousand whys and wherefores made her anxious, but the fat German had been won over by Kershaw's visions of untold gold, held tantalisingly before his eyes. He had lent the necessary £2, with which his friend intended to tidy himself up a bit before he went to meet his friend the millionaire. Half an hour afterwards Kershaw had left his lodgings, and that was the last the unfortunate woman saw of her husband, or Müller, the German, of his friend.

"Anxiously his wife waited that night, but he did not return; the next day she seems to have spent in making purposeless and futile inquiries about the neighbourhood of Fenchurch Street; and on the 12th she went to Scotland Yard, gave what particulars she knew, and placed in the hands of the police the two letters written by Smethurst."

II

The man in the corner had finished his glass of milk. His watery blue eyes looked across at Miss Polly Burton's eager little face, from which all traces of severity had now been chased away by an obvious and intense excitement.

"It was only on the 31st," he resumed after a while, "that a body, decomposed past all recognition, was found by two lightermen in the bottom of a disused barge. She had been moored at one time at the foot of one of those dark flights of steps which lead down between tall warehouses to the river in the East End of London. I have a photograph of the place here," he added, selecting one out of his pocket, and placing it before Polly.

"The actual barge, you see, had already been removed when I took this snapshot, but you will realise what a perfect place this alley is for the purpose of one man cutting another's throat in comfort, and without fear of detection. The body, as I said, was decomposed beyond all recognition; it had probably been there eleven days, but sundry articles, such as a silver ring and a tie pin, were recognisable, and were identified by Mrs. Kershaw as belonging to her husband.

"She, of course, was loud in denouncing Smethurst, and the police had no doubt a very strong case against him, for two days after the discovery of the body in the barge, the Siberian millionaire, as he was already popularly called by enterprising interviewers, was arrested in his luxurious suite of rooms at the Hotel Cecil.

"'To confess the truth, at this point I was not a little puzzled. Mrs. Kershaw's story and Smethurst's letters had both found their way into the papers, and following my usual method—mind you, I am only an amateur, I try to reason out a case for the love of the thing—I sought about for a motive for the crime, which the police declared Smethurst had committed. To effectually get rid of a dangerous blackmailer was the generally accepted theory. Well! did it ever strike you how paltry that motive really was?"

Miss Polly had to confess, however, that it had never struck her in that light.

"Surely a man who had succeeded in building up an immense fortune by his own individual efforts, was not the sort of fool to believe that he had anything to fear from a man like Kershaw. He must have *known* that Kershaw held no damning proofs against him—not enough to hang him, anyway. Have you ever seen Smethurst?" he added, as he once more fumbled in his pocket-book.

Polly replied that she had seen Smethurst's picture in the illustrated papers at the time. Then he added, placing a small photograph before her:

"What strikes you most about the face?"

"Well, I think its strange, astonished expression, due to the total absence of eyebrows, and the funny foreign cut of the hair."

"So close that it almost looks as if it had been shaved. Exactly. That is what struck me most when I elbowed my way into the court that morning and first caught sight of the millionaire in the dock. He was a tall, soldierly-looking man, upright in stature, his face very bronzed and tanned. He wore neither moustache nor beard, his hair was cropped quite close to his head, like a Frenchman's; but, of course, what was so very remarkable about him was that total absence of eyebrows and even eyelashes, which gave the face such a peculiar appearance—as you say, a perpetually astonished look.

"He seemed, however, wonderfully calm; he had been accommodated with a chair in the dock—being a millionaire—and chatted pleasantly with his lawyer, Sir Arthur Inglewood, in the intervals between the calling of the several witnesses for the prosecution; whilst during the examination of these witnesses he sat quite placidly, with his head shaded by his hand.

"Müller and Mrs. Kershaw repeated the story which they had already told to the police. I think you said that you were not able, owing to pressure of work, to go to the court that day, and hear the case, so perhaps you have no recollection of Mrs. Kershaw. No? Ah, well! Here is a snapshot I managed to get of her once. That is her. Exactly as she stood in the box—overdressed—in elaborate crape, with a bonnet which once had contained pink roses, and to which a remnant of pink petals still clung obtrusively amidst the deep black.

"She would not look at the prisoner, and turned her head resolutely towards the magistrate. I fancy she had been fond of that vagabond husband of hers: an enormous wedding-ring encircled her finger, and that, too, was swathed in black. She firmly believed that Kershaw's murderer sat there in the dock, and she literally flaunted her grief before him.

"I was indescribably sorry for her. As for Müller, he was just fat, oily, pompous, conscious of his own importance as a witness; his fat fingers, covered with brass rings, gripped the two incriminating letters, which he had identified. They were his passports, as it were, to a delightful land of importance and notoriety. Sir Arthur Inglewood, I think, disappointed him by stating that he had no questions to ask of him. Müller had been brimful of answers, ready with the most perfect indictment, the most elaborate accusations against the bloated millionaire who had destroyed his dear friend Kershaw, and murdered him in Heaven knows what an out-of-the-way corner of the East End.

"After this, however, the excitement grew apace. Müller had been dismissed, and had retired from the court altogether, leading away Mrs. Kershaw, who had completely broken down.

"Constable D 21 was giving evidence as to the arrest in the meanwhile. The prisoner, he said, had seemed completely taken by surprise, not understanding the cause or history of the accusation against him; however, when put in full possession of the facts, and realising, no doubt, the absolute futility of any resistance, he had quietly enough followed the constable into the cab. No one at the fashionable and crowded Hotel Cecil had even suspected that anything unusual had occurred.

"Then a gigantic sigh of expectancy came from every one of the spectators. The 'fun' was about to begin. James Buckland, a porter at Fenchurch Street railway station, had just sworn to tell all the truth, etc. After all, it did not amount to much. He said that at six o'clock in the afternoon of December the 10th, in the midst of one of the densest fogs he ever remembers, the 5.5 from Tilbury steamed into the station, being just about an hour late. He was on the arrival platform, and was hailed by a passenger in a first-class carriage. He could see very little of him beyond an enormous black fur coat and a travelling cap of fur also.

"The passenger had a quantity of luggage, all marked F. S., and he directed James Buckland to place it all upon a four-wheeled cab, with the exception of a small hand-bag, which he carried himself. Having seen that all his luggage was safely bestowed, the stranger in the fur coat paid the porter, and, telling the cabman to wait until he returned, he walked away in the direction of the waiting-rooms, still carrying his small hand-bag.

" 'I stayed for a bit,' added James Buckland, 'talking to the driver about the fog and that; then I went about my business, seein' that the local from Southend 'ad been signalled.'

"The prosecution insisted most strongly upon the hour when the stranger in the fur coat, having seen to his luggage, walked away towards the waiting-rooms. The porter was emphatic. 'It was not a minute later than 6:15,' he averred.

"Sir Arthur Inglewood still had no questions to ask, and the driver of the cab was called.

"He corroborated the evidence of James Buckland as to the hour when the gentleman in the fur coat had engaged him, and having filled his cab in and out with luggage, had told him to wait. And cabby did wait. He waited in the dense fog—until he was tired, until he seriously thought of depositing all the luggage in the lost property office, and of looking out for another fare—waited until at last, at a quarter before nine, whom should he see walking hurriedly towards his cab but the gentleman in the fur coat and cap, who got in quickly and told the driver to take him at once to the Hotel Cecil. This, cabby declared, had occurred at a quarter before nine. Still Sir Arthur Inglewood made no comment, and Mr. Francis Smethurst, in the crowded, stuffy court, had calmly dropped to sleep.

"The next witness, Constable Thomas Taylor, had noticed a shabbily-dressed individual, with shaggy hair and beard, loafing about the station and waiting-rooms in the afternoon of December the 10th. He seemed to be watching the arrival platform of the Tilbury and Southend trains.

"Two separate and independent witnesses, cleverly unearthed by the police, had seen this same shabbily-dressed individual stroll into the first-class waiting-room at about 6:15 on Tuesday, December the 10th, and go straight up to a gentleman in a heavy fur coat and cap, who had also just come into the room. The two talked together for a while; no one heard what they said, but presently they walked off together. No one seemed to know in which direction.

"Francis Smethurst was rousing himself from his apathy; he whispered to his lawyer, who nodded with a bland smile of encouragement. The employés of the Hotel Cecil gave evidence as to the arrival of Mr. Smethurst at about 9:30 P.M. on Tuesday, December the 10th, in a cab, with a quantity of luggage; and this closed the case for the prosecution.

"Everybody in that court already saw Smethurst mounting the gallows. It was uninterested curiosity which caused the elegant audience to wait and hear what Sir Arthur Inglewood had to say. He, of course, is the most fashionable man in the law at the present moment. His lolling attitudes, his drawling speech, are quite the rage, and imitated by the gilded youth of society.

"Even at this moment, when the Siberian millionaire's neck literally and metaphorically hung in the balance, an expectant titter went round the fair spectators as Sir Arthur stretched out his long loose limbs and lounged across the table. He waited to make his effect—Sir Arthur is a born actor—and there is no doubt that he made it, when in his slowest, most drawly tones he said quietly:

"'With regard to this alleged murder of one William Kershaw, on Wednesday, December the 10th, between 6:15 and 8:45 p.m., your Honour, I now propose to call two witnesses, who saw this same William Kershaw alive on Tuesday afternoon, December the 16th, that is to say, six days after the supposed murder.'

"It was as if a bombshell had exploded in the court. Even his Honour was aghast, and I am sure the lady next to me only recovered from the shock of surprise in order to wonder whether she need put off her dinner party after all.

"As for me," added the man in the corner, with that strange mixture of nervousness and self-complacency which had set Miss Polly Burton wondering, "well, you see, *I* had made up my mind long ago where the hitch lay in this particular case, and I was not so surprised as some of the others.

"Perhaps you remember the wonderful development of the case, which so completely mystified the police—and in fact everybody except myself. Torriani and a waiter at his hotel in the Commercial Road both deposed that at about 3:30 P.M. on December the 10th a shabbily-dressed individual lolled into the coffee-room and ordered some tea. He was pleasant enough and talkative, told the waiter that his name was William Kershaw, that very soon all London would be talking about him, as he was about, through an unexpected stroke of good fortune, to become a very rich man, and so on, and so on, nonsense without end.

"When he had finished his tea he lolled out again, but no sooner had he disappeared down a turning of the road than the waiter discovered an old umbrella, left behind accidentally by the shabby, talkative individual. As is the custom in his highly respectable restaurant, Signor Torriani put the umbrella carefully away in his office, on the chance of his customer calling to claim it when he discovered his loss. And sure enough nearly a week later, on Tuesday, the 16th, at about 1 P.M., the same shabbily-dressed individual called and asked for his umbrella. He had some lunch, and chatted once again to the waiter. Signor Torriani and the waiter gave a description of William Kershaw, which coincided exactly with that given by Mrs. Kershaw of her husband.

"Oddly enough he seemed to be a very absent-minded sort of person, for on this second occasion, no sooner had he left than the waiter found a pocket-book in the coffee-room, underneath the table. It contained sundry letters and bills, all addressed to William Kershaw. This pocket-book was produced, and Karl Müller, who had returned to the court, easily identified it as having belonged to his dear and lamented friend 'Villiam.'

"This was the first blow to the case against the accused. It was a pretty stiff one, you will admit. Already it had begun to collapse like a house of cards. Still, there was the assignation, and the undisputed meeting between Smethurst and Kershaw, and those two and a half hours of a foggy evening to satisfactorily account for."

The man in the corner made a long pause, keeping the girl on tenterhooks. He had fidgeted with his bit of string till there was not an inch of it free from the most complicated and elaborate knots.

"I assure you," he resumed at last, "that at that very moment the whole mystery was, to me, as clear as daylight. I only marvelled how his Honour could waste his time and mine by putting what he thought were searching questions to the accused relating to his past. Francis Smethurst, who had quite shaken off his somnolence, spoke with a curious nasal twang, and with an almost imperceptible soupçon of foreign accent. He calmly denied Kershaw's version of his past; declared that he had never been called Barker, and had certainly never been mixed up in any murder case thirty years ago.

" 'But you knew this man Kershaw,' persisted his Honour, 'since you wrote to him?'

" 'Pardon me, your Honour,' said the accused quietly, 'I have never, to my knowledge, seen this man Kershaw, and I can swear that I never wrote to him.'

" 'Never wrote to him?' retorted his Honour warningly. 'That is a strange assertion to make when I have two of your letters to him in my hands at the present moment.'

" 'I never wrote those letters, your Honour,' persisted the accused quietly, 'they are not in my handwriting.'

" 'Which we can easily prove,' came in Sir Arthur Inglewood's drawly tones, as he handed up a packet to his Honour, 'here are a number of letters written by my client since he has landed in this country, and some of which were written under my very eyes.'

"As Sir Arthur Inglewood had said, this could be easily proved, and the prisoner, at his Honour's request, scribbled a few lines, together with his signature, several times upon a sheet of note-paper. It was easy to read upon the magistrate's astounded countenance, that there was not the slightest similarity in the two handwritings.

"A fresh mystery had cropped up. Who, then, had made the assignation with William Kershaw at Fenchurch Street railway station? The prisoner gave a fairly satisfactory account of the employment of his time since his landing in England.

" 'I came over on the *Tsarkoe Selo*,' he said, 'a yacht belonging to a friend of mine. When we arrived at the mouth of the Thames there was such a dense fog that it was twenty-four hours before it was thought safe for me to land. My friend, who is a Russian, would not land at all; he was regularly frightened at this land of fogs. He was going on to Madeira immediately.

" 'I actually landed on Tuesday, the 10th, and took a train at once for town. I did see to my luggage and a cab, as the porter and driver told your Honour; then I tried to find my way to a refreshment-room, where I could get a glass of wine. I drifted into the waiting-room, and there I was accosted by a shabbily-dressed individual, who began telling me a piteous tale. Who he was I do not know. He *said* he was an old soldier who had served his country faithfully, and then been left to starve. He begged of me to accompany him to his lodgings, where I could see his wife and starving children, and verify the truth and piteousness of his tale.

"'Well, your Honour,' added the prisoner with noble frankness, 'it was my first day in the old country. I had come back after thirty years with my pockets full of gold, and this was the first sad tale I had heard; but I am a business man, and did not want to be exactly "done" in the eye. I followed my man through the fog, out into the streets. He walked silently by my side for a time. I had not a notion where I was.

"'Suddenly I turned to him with some question, and realised in a moment that my gentleman had given me the slip. Finding, probably, that I would not part with my money till I *had* seen the starving wife and children, he left me to my fate, and went in search of more willing bait.

"'The place where I found myself was dismal and deserted. I could see no trace of cab or omnibus. I retraced my steps and tried to find my way back to the station, only to find myself in worse and more deserted neighbourhoods. I became hopelessly lost and fogged. I don't wonder that two and a half hours elapsed while I thus wandered on in the dark and deserted streets; my sole astonishment is that I ever found the station at all that night, or rather close to it a policeman, who showed me the way.'

"'But how do you account for Kershaw knowing all your movements?' still persisted his Honour, 'and his knowing the exact date of your arrival in England? How do you account for these two letters, in fact?'

"'I cannot account for it or them, your Honour,' replied the prisoner quietly. 'I have proved to you, have I not, that I never wrote those letters, and that the man—er—Kershaw is his name?—was not murdered by me?'

"'Can you tell me of anyone here or abroad who might have heard of your movements, and of the date of your arrival?'

"'My late employés at Vladivostock, of course, knew of my departure, but none of them could have written these letters, since none of them know a word of English.'

"'Then you can throw no light upon these mysterious letters? You cannot help the police in any way towards the clearing up of this strange affair?'

"'The affair is as mysterious to me as to your Honour, and to the police of this country.'

"Francis Smethurst was discharged, of course; there was no semblance of evidence against him sufficient to commit him for trial. The two overwhelming points of his defence which had completely routed the prosecution were, firstly, the proof that he had never written the letters making the assignation, and secondly, the fact that the man supposed to have been murdered on the 10th was seen to be alive and well on the 16th. But then, who in the world was the mysterious individual who had apprised Kershaw of the movements of Smethurst, the millionaire?"

III

The man in the corner cocked his funny thin head on one side and looked at Polly; then he took up his beloved bit of string and deliberately united every knot he had made in it. When it was quite smooth he laid it out upon the table.

"I will take you, if you like, point by point along the line of reasoning which I followed myself, and which will inevitably lead you, as it led me, to the only possible solution of the mystery.

"First take this point," he said with nervous restlessness, once more taking up his bit of string, and forming with each point raised a series of knots which would have shamed a navigating instructor, "obviously it was *impossible* for Kershaw not to have been acquainted with Smethurst, since he was fully apprised of the latter's arrival in England by two letters. Now it was clear to me from the first that *no one* could have written those two letters except Smethurst. You will argue that those letters were proved not to have been written by the man in the dock. Exactly. Remember, Kershaw was a careless man—he had lost both envelopes. To him they were insignificant. Now it was never *disproved* that those letters were written by Smethurst."

"But—" suggested Polly.

"Wait a minute," he interrupted, while knot number two appeared upon the scene; "it was proved that six days after the murder William Kershaw was alive, and visited the Torriani Hotel, where already he was known, and where he conveniently left a pocket-book behind, so that there should be no mistake as to his identity; but it was never questioned where Mr. Francis Smethurst, the millionaire, happened to spend that very same afternoon."

"Surely, you don't mean—?" gasped the girl.

"One moment, please," he added triumphantly. "How did it come about that the landlord of the Torriani Hotel was brought into court at all? How did Sir Arthur Inglewood, or rather his client, know that William Kershaw had on those two memorable occasions visited the hotel, and that its landlord could bring such convincing evidence forward that would for ever exonerate the millionaire from the imputation of murder?"

"Surely," she argued, "the usual means, the police—"

"The police had kept the whole affair very dark until the arrest at the Hotel Cecil. They did not put into the papers the usual: 'If anyone happens to know of the whereabouts, etc., etc.' Had the landlord of that hotel heard of the disappearance of Kershaw through the usual channels, he would have put himself in communication with the police. Sir Arthur Inglewood produced him. How did Sir Arthur Inglewood come on his track?"

"Surely, you don't mean——?"

"Point number four," he resumed imperturbably, "Mrs. Kershaw was never requested to produce a specimen of her husband's handwriting. Why? Because the police, clever as you say they are, never started on the right tack. They believed William Kershaw to have been murdered; they looked for William Kershaw."

"On December the 31st, what was presumed to be the body of William Kershaw was found by two lightermen: I have shown you a photograph of the place where it was found. Dark and deserted it is in all conscience, is it not? Just the place where a bully and a coward would decoy an unsuspecting stranger, murder him first, then rob him of his valuables, his papers, his very identity, and leave him there to rot. The body was found in a disused barge which had been moored some time against the wall, at the foot of these steps. It was in the last stages of decomposition, and, of course, could not be identified; but the police would have it that it was the body of William Kershaw.

"It never entered their heads that it was the body of *Francis Smethurst, and that William Kershaw was his murderer.*

"Ah! it was cleverly, artistically conceived! Kershaw is a genius. Think of it all! His disguise! Kershaw had a shaggy beard, hair, and moustache. He shaved up to his very eyebrows! No wonder that even his wife did not recognise him across the court; and remember she never saw much of his face while he stood in the dock. Kershaw was shabby, slouchy, he stooped. Smethurst, the millionaire, might have served in the Prussian Army.

"Then that lovely trait about going to revisit the Torriani Hotel. Just a few days' grace, in order to purchase moustache and beard and wig, exactly similar to what he had himself shaved off. Making up to look like himself! Splendid! Then leaving the pocket-book behind! He! he! he! Kershaw was not murdered! Of course not. He called at the Torriani Hotel six days after the murder, whilst Mr. Smethurst, the millionaire, hobnobbed in the park with duchesses! Hang such a man! Fie!"

He fumbled for his hat. With nervous, trembling fingers he held it deferentially in his hand whilst he rose from the table. Polly watched him as he strode up to the desk, and paid twopence for his glass of milk and his bun. Soon he disappeared through the shop, whilst she still found herself hopelessly bewildered, with a number of snap-shot photographs before her, still staring at a long piece of string, smothered from end to end in a series of knots, as bewildering, as irritating, as puzzling as the man who had lately sat in the corner.

THE INVISIBLE MAN

G. K. Chesterton

IN THE COOL BLUE TWILIGHT OF TWO STEEP STREETS IN CAMDEN TOWN, THE shop at the corner, a confectioner's, glowed like the butt of a cigar. One should rather say, perhaps, like the butt of a firework, for the light was of many colours and some complexity, broken up by many mirrors and dancing on many gilt and gaily-coloured cakes and sweetmeats. Against this one fiery glass were glued the noses of many gutter-snipes, for the chocolates were all wrapped in those red and gold and green metallic colours which are almost better than chocolate itself; and the huge white wedding-cake in the window was somehow at once remote and satisfying, just as if the whole North Pole were good to eat. Such rainbow provocations could naturally collect the youth of the neighbourhood up to the ages of ten or twelve. But this corner was also attractive to youth at a later stage; and a young man, not less than twenty-four, was staring into the same shop window. To him, also, the shop was of fiery charm, but this attraction was not wholly to be explained by chocolates; which, however, he was far from despising.

He was a tall, burly, red-haired young man, with a resolute face but a listless manner. He carried under his arm a flat, grey portfolio of black-and-white sketches, which he had sold with more or less success to publishers ever since his uncle (who was an admiral) had disinherited him for Socialism, because of a lecture which he had delivered against that economic theory. His name was John Turnbull Angus.

Entering at last, he walked through the confectioner's shop to the back room, which was a sort of pastry-cook restaurant, merely raising his hat to the young lady who was serving there. She was a dark, elegant, alert girl in black, with a high colour and very quick, dark eyes; and after the ordinary interval she followed him into the inner room to take his order.

His order was evidently a usual one. "I want, please," he said with precision, "one halfpenny bun and a small cup of black coffee." An instant before the girl could turn away he added, "Also, I want you to marry me."

The young lady of the shop stiffened suddenly and said, "Those are jokes I don't allow."

The red-haired young man lifted grey eyes of an unexpected gravity.

"Really and truly," he said, "it's as serious—as serious as the halfpenny bun. It is expensive, like the bun; one pays for it. It is indigestible, like the bun. It hurts."

The dark young lady had never taken her dark eyes off him, but seemed to be studying him with almost tragic exactitude. At the end of her scrutiny she had something like the shadow of a smile, and she sat down in a chair.

"Don't you think," observed Angus, absently, "that it's rather cruel to eat these halfpenny buns? They might grow up into penny buns. I shall give up these brutal sports when we are married."

The dark young lady rose from her chair and walked to the window, evidently in a state of strong but not unsympathetic cogitation. When at last she swung round again with an air of resolution she was bewildered to observe that the young man was carefully laying out on the table various objects from the shop-window. They included a pyramid of highly coloured sweets, several plates of sandwiches, and the two decanters containing that mysterious port and sherry which are peculiar to pastry-cooks. In the middle of this neat arrangement he had carefully let down the enormous load of white sugared cake which had been the huge ornament of the window.

"What on earth are you doing?" she asked.

"Duty, my dear Laura," he began.

"Oh, for the Lord's sake, stop a minute," she cried, "and don't talk to me in that way. I mean, what is all that?"

"A ceremonial meal, Miss Hope."

"And what is *that*?" she asked impatiently, pointing to the mountain of sugar.

"The wedding-cake, Mrs. Angus," he said.

The girl marched to that article, removed it with some clatter, and put it back in the shop window; she then returned, and, putting her elegant elbows on the table, regarded the young man not unfavourably but with considerable exasperation.

"You don't give me any time to think," she said.

"I'm not such a fool," he answered; "that's my Christian humility."

She was still looking at him; but she had grown considerably graver behind the smile.

"Mr. Angus," she said steadily, "before there is a minute more of this nonsense I must tell you something about myself as shortly as I can."

"Delighted," replied Angus gravely. "You might tell me something about myself, too, while you are about it."

"Oh, do hold your tongue and listen," she said. "It's nothing that I'm ashamed of, and it isn't even anything that I'm specially sorry about. But what would you say if there were something that is no business of mine and yet is my nightmare?"

"In that case," said the man seriously, "I should suggest that you bring back the cake."

"Well, you must listen to the story first," said Laura, persistently. "To begin with, I must tell you that my father owned the inn called the 'Red Fish' at Ludbury, and I used to serve people in the bar."

"I have often wondered," he said, "why there was a kind of a Christian air about this one confectioner's shop."

"Ludbury is a sleepy, grassy little hole in the Eastern Counties, and the only kind of people who ever came to the 'Red Fish' were occasional commercial travellers, and for the rest, the most awful people you can see, only you've never seen them. I mean little, loungy men, who had just enough to live on and had nothing to do but lean about in bar-rooms and bet on horses, in bad clothes that were just too good for them. Even these wretched young rotters were not very common at our house; but there were two of them that were a lot too common—common in every sort of way. They both lived on money of their own, and were wearisomely idle and over-dressed. But yet I was a bit sorry for them, because I half believe they slunk into our little empty bar because each of them had a slight deformity; the sort of thing that some yokels laugh at. It wasn't exactly a deformity either; it was more an oddity. One of them was a surprisingly small man, something like a dwarf, or at least like a jockey. He was not at all jockeyish to look at, though; he had a round black head and a well-trimmed black beard, bright eyes like a bird's; he jingled money in his pockets; he jangled a great gold watch chain; and he never turned up except dressed just too much like a gentleman to be one. He was no fool though, though a futile idler; he was curiously clever at all kinds of things that couldn't be the slightest use; a sort of impromptu conjuring; making fifteen matches set fire to each other like a regular firework; or cutting a banana or some such thing into a dancing doll. His name was Isidore Smythe; and I can see him still, with his little dark face, just coming up to the counter, making a jumping kangaroo out of five cigars.

"The other fellow was more silent and more ordinary; but somehow he alarmed me much more than poor little Smythe. He was very tall and slight, and light-haired; his nose had a high bridge, and he might almost have been handsome in a spectral sort of way; but he had one of the most appalling squints I have ever seen or heard of. When he looked straight at you, you didn't know where you were yourself, let alone what he was looking at. I fancy this sort of disfigurement embittered the poor chap a little; for while Smythe was ready to show off his monkey tricks anywhere, James Welkin (that was the squinting man's name) never did anything except soak in our bar parlour, and go for great walks by himself in the flat, grey country all round. All the same, I think Smythe, too, was a little sensitive about being so small, though he carried it off more smartly. And so it was that I was really puzzled, as well as startled, and very sorry, when they both offered to marry me in the same week.

"Well, I did what I've since thought was perhaps a silly thing. But, after all, these freaks were my friends in a way; and I had a horror of their thinking I refused them for the real reason, which was that they were so impossibly ugly. So I made up some gas of another sort, about never meaning to marry anyone who hadn't carved his way in the world. I said it was a point of principle with me not to live on money that was just inherited like theirs. Two days after I had talked in this well-meaning sort of way, the whole trouble began. The first thing I heard was that both of them had gone off to seek their fortunes, as if they were in some silly fairy tale.

"Well, I've never seen either of them from that day to this. But I've had two letters from the little man called Smythe, and really they were rather exciting."

"Ever heard of the other man?" asked Angus.

"No, he never wrote," said the girl, after an instant's hesitation. "Smythe's first letter was simply to say that he had started out walking with Welkin to London; but Welkin was such a good walker that the little man dropped out of it, and took a rest by the roadside. He happened to be picked up by some travelling show, and, partly because he was nearly a dwarf, and partly because he was really a clever little wretch, he got on quite well in the show business, and was soon sent up to the Aquarium, to do some tricks that I forget. That was his first letter. His second was much more of a startler, and I only got it last week."

The man called Angus emptied his coffee-cup and regarded her with mild and patient eyes. Her own mouth took a slight twist of laughter as she resumed, "I suppose you've seen on the hoardings all about this 'Smythe's Silent Service'? Or you must be the only person that hasn't. Oh, I don't know much about it, it's some clockwork invention for doing all the housework by machinery. You know the sort of thing: 'Press a Button—A Butler who Never Drinks.' 'Turn a Handle—Ten Housemaids who Never Flirt.' You must have seen the advertisements. Well, whatever these machines are, they are making pots of money; and they are making it all for that little imp whom I knew down in Ludbury. I can't help feeling pleased the poor little chap has fallen on his feet; but the plain fact is, I'm in terror of his turning up any minute and telling me he's carved his way in the world—as he certainly has."

"And the other man?" repeated Angus with a sort of obstinate quietude.

Laura Hope got to her feet suddenly. "My friend," she said, "I think you are a witch. Yes, you are quite right. I have not seen a line of the other man's writing; and I have no more notion than the dead of what or where he is. But it is of him that I am frightened. It is he who is all about my path. It is he who has half driven me mad. Indeed, I think he has driven me mad; for I have felt him where he could not have been, and I have heard his voice when he could not have spoken."

"Well, my dear," said the young man, cheerfully, "if he were Satan himself, he is done for now you have told somebody. One goes mad all alone, old girl. But when was it you fancied you felt and heard our squinting friend?"

"I heard James Welkin laugh as plainly as I hear you speak," said the girl, steadily. "There was nobody there, for I stood just outside the shop at the corner, and could see down both streets at once. I had forgotten how he laughed, though his laugh was as odd as his squint. I had not thought of him for nearly a year. But it's a solemn truth that a few seconds later the first letter came from his rival."

"Did you ever make the spectre speak or squeak, or anything?" asked Angus, with some interest.

Laura suddenly shuddered, and then said, with an unshaken voice, "Yes. Just when I had finished reading the second letter from Isidore Smythe announcing his success, just then, I heard Welkin say, 'He shan't have you, though.' It was quite plain, as if he were in the room. It is awful; I think I must be mad."

"If you really were mad," said the young man, "you would think you must be sane. But certainly there seems to me to be something a little rum about this unseen gentleman. Two heads are better than one—I spare you allusions to any other organs—and really, if you would allow me, as a sturdy, practical man, to bring back the wedding-cake out of the window—"

Even as he spoke, there was a sort of steely shriek in the street outside, and a small motor, driven at devilish speed, shot up to the door of the shop and stuck there. In the same flash of time a small man in a shiny top hat stood stamping in the outer room.

Angus, who had hitherto maintained hilarious ease from motives of mental hygiene, revealed the strain of his soul by striding abruptly out of the inner room and confronting the new-comer. A glance at him was quite sufficient to confirm the savage guesswork of a man in love. This very dapper but dwarfish figure, with the spike of black beard carried insolently forward, the clever unrestful eyes, the neat but very nervous fingers, could be none other than the man just described to him: Isidore Smythe, who made dolls out of banana skins and match-boxes; Isidore Smythe, who made millions out of undrinking butlers and unflirting housemaids of metal. For a moment the two men, instinctively understanding each other's air of possession, looked at each other with that curious cold generosity which is the soul of rivalry.

Mr. Smythe, however, made no allusion to the ultimate ground of their antagonism, but said simply and explosively. "Has Miss Hope seen that thing on the window?"

"On the window?" repeated the staring Angus.

"There's no time to explain other things," said the small millionaire shortly. "There's some tomfoolery going on here that has to be investigated."

He pointed his polished walking-stick at the window, recently depleted by the bridal preparations of Mr. Angus; and that gentleman was astonished to see along the front of the glass a long strip of paper pasted, which had certainly not been on the window when he had looked through it some time before. Following the energetic Smythe outside into the street, he found that some yard and a half of stamp paper had been carefully gummed along the glass outside, and on this was written in straggly characters, "If you marry Smythe, he will die."

"Laura," said Angus, putting his big red head into the shop, "you're not mad."

"It's the writing of that fellow Welkin," said Smythe gruffly. "I haven't seen him for years, but he's always bothering me. Five times in the last fortnight he's had threatening letters left at my flat, and I can't even find out who leaves them, let alone if it is Welkin himself. The porter of the flats swears that no suspicious characters have been seen, and here he has pasted up a sort of dado on a public shop window, while the people in the shop—"

"Quite so," said Angus modestly, "while the people in the shop were having tea. Well, sir, I can assure you I appreciate your common sense in dealing so directly with the matter. We can talk about other things afterwards. The fellow cannot be very far off yet, for I swear there was no paper there when I went last to the window, ten or fifteen minutes ago. On the other hand, he's too far off to be chased, as we don't even know the direction. If you'll take my advice, Mr. Smythe, you'll put this at once in the hands of some energetic inquiry man, private rather than public. I know an extremely clever fellow, who has set up in business five minutes from here in your car. His name's Flambeau, and though his youth was a bit stormy, he's a strictly honest man now, and his brains are worth money. He lives in Lucknow Mansions, Hampstead."

"That is odd," said the little man, arching his black eyebrows. "I live, myself, in Himylaya Mansions, round the corner. Perhaps you might care to come with me; I can go to my rooms and sort out these queer Welkin documents, while you run round and get your friend the detective."

"You are very good," said Angus politely. "Well, the sooner we act the better."

Both men, with a queer kind of impromptu fairness, took the same sort of formal farewell of the lady, and both jumped into the brisk little car. As Smythe took the handles and they turned the great corner of the street, Angus was amused to see a gigantesque poster of "Smythe's Silent Service," with a picture of a huge headless iron doll, carrying a saucepan with the legend, "A Cook Who is Never Cross."

"I use them in my own flat," said the little black-bearded man, laughing, "partly for advertisements, and partly for real convenience. Honestly, and all above board, those big clockwork dolls of mine do bring you coals or claret or a timetable quicker than any live servants I've ever known, if you know which knob to press. But I'll never deny, between ourselves, that such servants have their disadvantages, too."

"Indeed?" said Angus; "is there something they can't do?"

"Yes," replied Smythe coolly; "they can't tell me who left those threatening letters at my flat."

The man's motor was small and swift like himself; in fact, like his domestic service, it was of his own invention. If he was an advertising quack, he was one who believed in his own wares. The sense of something tiny and flying was accentuated as they swept up long white curves of road in the dead but open daylight of evening. Soon the white curves came sharper and dizzier; they were upon ascending spirals, as they say in the modern religions. For, indeed, they were cresting a corner of London which is almost as precipitous as Edinburgh, if not quite so picturesque. Terrace rose above terrace, and the special tower of flats they sought, rose above them all to almost Egyptian height, gilt by the level sunset. The change, as they turned the corner and entered the crescent known as Himylaya Mansions, was as abrupt as the opening of a window; for they found that pile of flats sitting above London as above a green sea of slate. Opposite to the mansions, on the other side of the gravel crescent, was a bushy enclosure more like a steep hedge or dyke than a garden, and some way below that ran a strip of artificial water, a sort of canal, like the moat of that embowered fortress. As the car swept round the crescent it passed, at one corner, the stray stall of a man selling chestnuts; and right away at the other end of the curve, Angus could see a dim blue policeman walking slowly. These were the only human shapes in that high suburban solitude; but he had an irrational sense that they expressed the speechless poetry of London. He felt as if they were figures in a story.

The little car shot up to the right house like a bullet, and shot out its owner like a bomb shell. He was immediately inquiring of a tall commissionaire in shining braid, and a short porter in shirt sleeves, whether anybody or anything had been seeking his apartments. He was assured that nobody and nothing had passed these officials since his last inquiries; whereupon he and the slightly bewildered Angus were shot up in the lift like a rocket, till they reached the top floor.

"Just come in for a minute," said the breathless Smythe. "I want to show you those Welkin letters. Then you might run round the corner and fetch your friend." He pressed a button concealed in the wall, and the door opened of itself.

It opened on a long, commodious ante-room, of which the only arresting features, ordinarily speaking, were the rows of tall half-human mechanical figures that stood up on both sides like tailors' dummies. Like tailors' dummies they were headless; and like tailors' dummies they had a handsome unnecessary humpiness in the shoulders, and a pigeon-breasted protuberance of chest; but barring this, they were not much more like a human figure than any automatic machine at a station that is about the human height. They had two great hooks like arms, for carrying trays; and they were painted pea-green, or vermillion, or black for convenience of distinction; in every other way they were only automatic machines and nobody would have looked twice at them. On this occasion, at least, nobody did. For between the two rows of these domestic dummies lay something more interesting than most of the mechanics of the world. It was a white, tattered scrap of paper scrawled with red ink; and the agile inventor had snatched it up almost as soon as the door flew open. He handed it to Angus without a word. The red ink on it actually was not dry, and the message ran, "If you have been to see her to-day, I shall kill you."

There was a short silence, and then Isidore Smythe said quietly, "Would you like a little whisky? I rather feel as if I should."

"Thank you; I should like a little Flambeau," said Angus, gloomily. "This business seems to me to be getting rather grave. I'm going round at once to fetch him."

"Right you are," said the other, with admirable cheerfulness. "Bring him round here as quick as you can."

But as Angus closed the front door behind him he saw Smythe push back a button, and one of the clockwork images glided from its place and slid along a groove in the floor carrying a tray with syphon and decanter. There did seem something a trifle weird about leaving the little man alone among those dead servants, who were coming to life as the door closed.

Six steps down from Smythe's landing the man in shirt sleeves was doing something with a pail. Angus stopped to extract a promise, fortified with a prospective bribe, that he would remain in that place until the return with the detective, and would keep count of any kind of stranger coming up those stairs. Dashing down to the front hall he then laid similar charges of vigilance on the commissionaire at the front door, from whom he learned the simplifying circumstances that there was no back door. Not content with this, he captured the floating policeman and induced him to stand opposite the entrance and watch it; and finally paused an instant for a pennyworth of chestnuts, and an inquiry as to the probable length of the merchant's stay in the neighbourhood.

The chestnut seller, turning up the collar of his coat, told him he should probably be moving shortly, as he thought it was going to snow. Indeed, the evening was growing grey and bitter, but Angus, with all his eloquence, proceeded to nail the chestnut man to his post.

"Keep yourself warm on your own chestnuts," he said earnestly. "Eat up your whole stock; I'll make it worth your while. I'll give you a sovereign if you'll wait here till I come back, and then tell me whether any man, woman, or child has gone into that house where the commissionaire is standing."

He then walked away smartly, with a last look at the besieged tower.

"I've made a ring round that room, anyhow," he said. "They can't all four of them be Mr. Welkin's accomplices."

Lucknow Mansions were, so to speak, on a lower platform of that hill of houses, of which Himylaya Mansions might be called the peak. Mr. Flambeau's semi-official flat was on the ground floor, and presented in every way a marked contrast to the American machinery and cold hotel-like luxury of the flat of the Silent Service. Flambeau, who was a friend of Angus, received him in a rococo artistic den behind his office, of which the ornaments were sabres, harquebuses, Eastern curiosities, flasks of Italian wine, savage cooking-pots, a plumy Persian cat, and a small dusty-looking Roman Catholic priest, who looked particularly out of place.

"This is my friend Father Brown," said Flambeau. "I've often wanted you to meet him. Splendid weather, this; a little cold for Southerners like me."

"Yes, I think it will keep clear," said Angus, sitting down on a violet-striped Eastern ottoman.

"No," said the priest quietly, "it has begun to snow."

And, indeed, as he spoke, the first few flakes, foreseen by the man of chestnuts, began to drift across the darkening window-pane.

"Well," said Angus heavily. "I'm afraid I've come on business, and rather jumpy business at that. The fact is, Flambeau, within a stone's throw of your house is a fellow who badly wants your help; he's perpetually being haunted and threatened by an invisible enemy—a scoundrel whom nobody has even seen." As Angus proceeded to tell the whole tale of Smythe and Welkin, beginning with Laura's story, and going on with his own, the supernatural laugh at the corner of two empty streets, the strange distinct words spoken in an empty room, Flambeau grew more and more vividly concerned, and the little priest seemed to be left out of it, like a piece of furniture. When it came to the scribbled stamp-paper pasted on the window, Flambeau rose, seeming to fill the room with his huge shoulders.

"If you don't mind," he said, "I think you had better tell me the rest on the nearest road to this man's house. It strikes me, somehow, that there is no time to be lost."

"Delighted," said Angus, rising also, "though he's safe enough for the present, for I've set four men to watch the only hole to his burrow."

They turned out into the street, the small priest trundling after them with the docility of a small dog. He merely said, in a cheerful way, like one making conversation, "How quick the snow gets thick on the ground."

As they threaded the steep side streets already powdered with silver, Angus finished his story; and by the time they reached the crescent with the towering flats, he had leisure to turn his attention to the four sentinels. The chestnut seller, both before and after receiving a sovereign, swore stubbornly that he had watched the door and seen no visitor enter. The policeman was even more emphatic. He said he had had experience of crooks of all kinds, in top hats and in rags; he wasn't so green as to expect suspicious characters to look suspicious; he looked out for anybody, and, so help him, there had been nobody. And when all three men gathered round the gilded commissionaire, who still stood smiling astride of the porch, the verdict was more final still.

"I've got a right to ask any man, duke or dustman, what he wants in these flats," said the genial and gold-laced giant, "and I'll swear there's been nobody to ask since this gentleman went away."

The unimportant Father Brown, who stood back, looking modestly at the pavement, here ventured to say meekly, "Has nobody been up and down stairs, then, since the snow began to fall? It began while we were all round at Flambeau's."

"Nobody's been in here, sir, you can take it from me," said the official, with beaming authority.

"Then I wonder what that is?" said the priest, and stared at the ground blankly like a fish.

The others all looked down also; and Flambeau used a fierce exclamation and a French gesture. For it was unquestionably true that down the middle of the entrance guarded by the man in gold lace, actually between the arrogant, stretched legs of that colossus, ran a stringy pattern of grey footprints stamped upon the white snow.

"God!" cried Angus involuntarily, "the Invisible Man!"

Without another word he turned and dashed up the stairs, with Flambeau following; but Father Brown still stood looking about him in the snow-clad street as if he had lost interest in his query.

Flambeau was plainly in a mood to break down the door with his big shoulders; but the Scotchman, with more reason, if less intuition, fumbled about on the frame of the door till he found the invisible button; and the door swung slowly open.

It showed substantially the same serried interior; the hall had grown darker, though it was still struck here and there with the last crimson shafts of sunset, and one or two of the headless machines had been moved from their places for this or that purpose, and stood here and there about the twilit place. The green and red of their coats were all darkened in the dusk; and their likeness to human shapes slightly increased by their very shapelessness. But in the middle of them all, exactly where the paper with the red ink had lain, there lay something that looked like red ink spilt out of its bottle. But it was not red ink.

With a French combination of reason and violence Flambeau simply said "Murder!" and, plunging into the flat, had explored every corner and cupboard of it in five minutes. But if he expected to find a corpse he found none. Isidore Smythe was not in the place, either dead or alive. After the most tearing search the two men met each other in the outer hall, with streaming faces and staring eyes. "My friend," said Flambeau, talking French in his excitement, "not only is your murderer invisible, but he makes invisible also the murdered man."

Angus looked round at the dim room full of dummies, and in some Celtic corner of his Scotch soul a shudder started. One of the life-size dolls stood immediately overshadowing the blood stain, summoned, perhaps, by the slain man an instant before he fell. One of the high-shouldered hooks that served the thing for arms, was a little lifted, and Angus had suddenly the horrid fancy that poor Smythe's own iron child had struck him down. Matter had rebelled, and these machines had killed their master. But even so, what had they done with him?

"Eaten him?" said the nightmare at his ear; and he sickened for an instant at the idea of rent, human remains absorbed and crushed into all that acephalous clockwork.

He recovered his mental health by an emphatic effort, and said to Flambeau, "Well, there it is. The poor fellow has evaporated like a cloud and left a red streak on the floor. The tale does not belong to this world."

"There is only one thing to be done," said Flambeau, "whether it belongs to this world or the other, I must go down and talk to my friend."

They descended, passing the man with the pail, who again asseverated that he had let no intruder pass, down to the commissionaire and the hovering chestnut man, who rigidly reasserted their own watchfulness. But when Angus looked round for his fourth confirmation he could not see it, and called out with some nervousness, "Where is the policeman?"

"I beg your pardon," said Father Brown; "that is my fault. I just sent him down the road to investigate something—that I just thought worth investigating."

"Well, we want him back pretty soon," said Angus abruptly, "for the wretched man upstairs has not only been murdered, but wiped out."

"How?" asked the priest.

"Father," said Flambeau, after a pause, "upon my soul I believe it is more in your department than mine. No friend or foe has entered the house, but Smythe is gone, as if stolen by the fairies. If that is not supernatural, I—"

As he spoke they were all checked by an unusual sight; the big blue policeman came round the corner of the crescent, running. He came straight up to Brown.

"You're right, sir," he panted, "they've just found poor Mr. Smythe's body in the canal down below."

Angus put his hand wildly to his head. "Did he run down and drown himself?" he asked.

"He never came down, I'll swear," said the constable, "and he wasn't drowned either, for he died of a great stab over the heart."

"And yet you saw no one enter?" said Flambeau in a grave voice.

"Let us walk down the road a little," said the priest.

As they reached the other end of the crescent he observed abruptly, "Stupid of me! I forgot to ask the policeman something. I wonder if they found a light brown sack."

"Why a light brown sack?" asked Angus, astonished.

"Because if it was any other coloured sack, the case must begin over again," said Father Brown; "but if it was a light brown sack, why, the case is finished."

"I am pleased to hear it," said Angus with hearty irony. "It hasn't begun, so far as I am concerned."

"You must tell us all about it," said Flambeau with a strange heavy simplicity, like a child.

Unconsciously they were walking with quickening steps down the long sweep of road on the other side of the high crescent, Father Brown leading briskly, though in silence. At last he said with an almost touching vagueness, "Well, I'm afraid you'll think it so prosy. We always begin at the abstract end of things, and you can't begin this story anywhere else.

"Have you ever noticed this—that people never answer what you say? They answer what you mean—or what they think you mean. Suppose one lady says to another in a country house, 'Is anybody staying with you?' the lady doesn't answer 'Yes; the butler, the three footmen, the parlourmaid, and so on,' though the parlourmaid may be in the room, or the butler behind her chair. She says 'There is *nobody* staying with us,' meaning nobody of the sort you mean. But suppose a doctor inquiring into an epidemic asks, 'Who is staying in the house?' then the lady will remember the butler, parlourmaid, and the rest. All language is used like that; you never get a question answered literally, even when you get it answered truly. When those four quite honest men said that no man had gone into the Mansions, they did not really mean that *no man* had gone into them They meant no man whom they could suspect of being your man. A man did go into the house, and did come out of it, but they never noticed him."

"An invisible man?" inquired Angus, raising his red eyebrows.

"A mentally invisible man," said Father Brown.

A minute or two after he resumed in the same unassuming voice, like a man thinking his way. "Of course you can't think of such a man, until you do think of him. That's where his cleverness comes in. But I came to think of him through two or three little things in the tale Mr. Angus told us. First, there was the fact that this Welkin went for long walks. And then there was the vast lot of stamp paper on the window. And then, most of all, there were the two things the young lady said—things that couldn't be true. Don't get annoyed," he added hastily, noting a sudden movement of the Scotchman's head; "she thought they were true. A person *can't* be quite alone in a street a second before she receives a letter. She can't be quite alone in a street when she starts reading a letter just received. There must be somebody pretty near her; he must be mentally invisible."

"Why must there be somebody near her?" asked Angus.

"Because," said Father Brown, "barring carrier-pigeons, somebody must have brought her the letter."

"Do you really mean to say," asked Flambeau, with energy, "that Welkin carried his rival's letters to his lady?"

"Yes," said the priest. "Welkin carried his rival's letters to his lady. You see, he had to."

"Oh, I can't stand much more of this," exploded Flambeau. "Who is this fellow? What does he look like? What is the usual get-up of a mentally invisible man?"

"He is dressed rather handsomely in red, blue and gold," replied the priest promptly with precision, "and in this striking, and even showy, costume he entered Himylaya Mansions under eight human eyes; he killed Smythe in cold blood, and came down into the street again carrying the dead body in his arms—"

"Reverend sir," cried Angus, standing still, "are you raving mad, or am I?"

"You are not mad," said Brown, "only a little unobservant. You have not noticed such a man as this, for example."

He took three quick strides forward, and put his hand on the shoulder of an ordinary passing postman who had bustled by them unnoticed under the shade of the trees.

"Nobody ever notices postmen somehow," he said thoughtfully; "yet they have passions like other men, and even carry large bags where a small corpse can be stowed quite easily."

The postman, instead of turning naturally, had ducked and tumbled against the garden fence. He was a lean fair-bearded man of very ordinary appearance, but as he turned an alarmed face over his shoulder, all three men were fixed with an almost fiendish squint.

Flambeau went back to his sabres, purple rugs and Persian cat, having many things to attend to. John Turnbull Angus went back to the lady at the shop, with whom that imprudent young man contrives to be extremely comfortable. But Father Brown walked those snow-covered hills under the stars for many hours with a murderer, and what they said to each other will never be known.

THE MURDER OF BENNETT SANDMAN

Edgar Wallace

Y. SYMON SWUNG HIS PYJAMA'D LEGS CLEAR OF THE BED, SWITCHED ON the light and blinked at the telephone stupidly. Then he picked it up, and with the intonation of a lioness robbed of her young demanded:

"Hel-lo!"

"You Y.?"

"Yuh—who do you think it is?"

"There's a good murder at Tilson's Mansions—No. 74."

"Wise Symon" was the pleasantest-mannered police reporter that ever took note, and to be called from his sleep at 3 A.M. for lesser happenings than murders (and "good murders" at that) was no novel experience.

Nevertheless was he annoyed, for he was working on a forged War Bond case which promised to be full of interest, and he had been in bed exactly forty minutes.

"Can't you put one of the other fellows on it? I don't want to miss this bond story. Issenheim is the crook, and a county bank manager is in it up to his neck."

"I'll put Stern on that story," said the night editor's voice. "He can pick it up from the notes of yours we already have. Get up to Tilson's Mansions like a good little sportsman. There is a hidden hand end to it."

"Who's the corpse?" asked Y.

"Bennett Sandman," replied the voice, and Y. jumped.

"Bennett Sandman!"

Wise Symon was justified in his surprise. He expected many things to happen to Mr. Bennett Sandman, but that he should be murdered was not one of these. He would not have been surprised, for example, to hear that the junior member of the some-time firm of Messrs. Griffith & Sandman, Solicitors, had been arrested for fraud. There was once a great advertising scheme for selling land, which Wise Symon had been instrumental in exposing. Sandman was in that undoubtedly—though his outraged partner was innocent. Much that was unpleasant might have happened to Bennett Sandman but for the outbreak of war and the departure of his partner for France.

"You're sure you said 'murdered'?" asked Y.

"Yes—we just had it in over the 'phone." Symon grunted.

"All right," he complained; "but if ever a son of mine shows the slightest inclination to take up journalism, we'll go to the mat on it; Mr. Oliver, it's a dog's life. I'd sooner sweep a road, or work in a bone factory where you can sleep o' nights. I'd sooner—"

But the night editor had rung off at the word "right," and it was the operator who interrupted him with a weary "Finished?" He put his notebook and pencil in his pocket and went out into the sharp morning air with a shudder and a long-drawn "br-r-r!" There was a policeman in the vestibule of Tilson's Mansions, and the policeman knew Y.

"Roon's in charge of the case," he said. "You'll find him upstairs."

"Roon," said Y. bitterly, "is the one man in the C.I.D. who can turn a murder into a tragedy. Have you sent for anyone who understands real detective work?"

The man grinned.

"The divisional surgeon is up there now," he said. "We're expecting the ambulance any minute."

Wise Symon paused with one foot on the marble stairs leading to the upper floors.

"I suppose you won't know anything about this murder till you read about it in the papers?" he said. "In other words you have no first-hand information as to how he was killed?"

"Roon says he was stabbed by a woman," said the officer.

Mr. Symon gave a despairing groan.

"That means he was shot by a man," he said, and mounted the stairs.

Roon himself answered the door and offered the police reporter a welcome, which made up in chilliness all that it lacked in cordiality.

"Hello!" he said, barring the entrance. "Sorry Symon, but you can't come in. The police surgeon's here, and he's death on reporters."

"Ah, come off, Roon," wheedled the wise man. "I'm running this story in the *Sunday Special*—are you going to let somebody else get all the credit for your work?"

Roon hesitated.

"The Commissioner doesn't like our men figuring in the papers," he said. "Do you know Dr. Trowburn?"

"He's my own cousin's uncle," replied Wise Symon promptly, and was admitted.

Though he might not in truth claim so close a connection, or indeed any relationship at all, he knew and was known to the doctor.

"They got you out too, did they?" he growled. "Well, you ought to be feeling pretty foolish."

"Where is the 'respected deceased?'" asked Symon looking round.

"There isn't any 'respected deceased,'" replied the coroner.

Mr. Symon looked from the coroner to Roon.

"If you will forgive the following extract from my biography, I would like to say that in all my long and grisly experiences I have never yet written up a good murder that hadn't a 'respected deceased'—sometimes lamented by the community, but more often not."

The police surgeon nodded.

"That is my experience, too; perhaps Roon will tell you."

"Well, Y., it's like this," began Roon, "and is it asking you too much not to pull my leg over this story which, in my judgment, is the story of a murder."

Detective Roon was a stout man, with a coppery skin and a black moustache waxed at the ends. The hair he possessed was employed to hide the site of the hair he did not possess. He wore a diamond ring on his little finger, and used scent. From which may be gathered this outstanding fact, that Roon did not hate himself.

"In my judgment," said Roon, "there is a terrible mystery here."

"You've been reading detective stories," said the exasperated Symon. "What the devil do you mean by springing a murder on us without a corpse?"

"It's like this," said Roon. "Mr. Bennett Sandman has been receiving threatening letters, and I've had the case in hand. In fact I've been shadowing him. To-night he dined at the Astoria, and ordinarily I would have picked him up after he was through and come home with him in his car. But to-night he was unusually nervous and asked me if I'd mind hanging round the hotel whilst he was dining, and keeping a sharp look-out for a girl with red hair. That is all the description I got—she would have red hair. Well, I sat about in the lounge and watched the people coming and going. The only red-haired girl I saw was the lady's-maid of Lillie Bertino, the dancer, at the Hippoceum—I know her pretty well."

"And when you saw the lady what were you supposed to do—arrest her for having red hair?" asked Wise Symon.

"If you'll let me go on," said Roon aggrieved, "I'd be obliged. As I was saying, I saw nobody. At ten minutes after twelve, Mr. Sandman came downstairs from the private dining-room, where his party had been, and he was accompanied by a young lady."

"By 'young lady' do you mean a youthful person of quality or a well-dressed chorus girl?" asked Mr. Symon brutally.

"She might have been either," said the cautious Roon. "Mr. Sandman asked me to take a taxi and follow him. He and the young lady went alone."

"To the flat?"

"No, they parted at the street entrance. The young lady went on in the car. I came up just as she was driving off."

Wise Symon closed his eyes and conjured up the topography.

"She went round the block to the right, of course," he said.

"Yes, I think she did," said Roon in surprise. "How did you know that?"

"This building runs through to a narrow street if I remember aright," said Wise Symon. "You can reach that street by the fire escape. That leads to a bedroom," he pointed to an open doorway, "and to another room and to the fire escape, so that if the murdered man felt in need of a little fresh air he could stroll through an open window and descend at his leisure into the back street, being picked up by the car round the corner—but I am anticipating. What happened after you had seen the lady off?"

"I went upstairs," said Roon, "to see Mr. Sandman before I left for the night. My hand was on the knocker when the door opened, and there was Mr. Sandman—a terrible sight!" He paused.

"Go on, we're not thrilled!" said Mr. Symon wearily. "In what way was he terrible?"

"His shirt-front was streaming with blood," said Roon, swallowing hard. "He said to me with a sort of gasp, 'Roon! Roon! The woman has knifed me! Quick, catch her!' and he pointed to the door. I flew down the stairs and flew out through the front lobby, but there was nobody in sight."

Again he paused impressively.

"Except yourself, my aviator," said Wise Symon, whose stock of patience was becoming rapidly exhausted. "Obviously you are the murderer. Then what did you do? You flew back, I suppose, like a blinking canary and perched on the gas bracket and saw everything?"

"The door was closed when I got back," said Roon gruffly. "I knocked, but there was no answer. I tried to smash in the door, but I couldn't. Then I tried to force the fanlight."

"In fact, you couldn't get in, so you 'phoned the office?"

"I found a policeman and posted him here," said Roon, "and 'phoned to the office. When I got back, to my surprise, the door was open."

"And there was no body?"

"No: there was no body," reluctantly admitted Roon.

"So in addition to your own fancy flights the other bird had flown."

"Well, I don't think it's a laughing matter," said the offended Roon.

"Neither do I. I think it's a very serious matter. You have got the divisional surgeon out of bed; you've got me out of bed. By-the-way, did you call up the office?"

"No: I did not," said Roon, and he obviously spoke the truth.

"I will use the late Mr. Sandman's 'phone and find out who did," said Mr. Symon.

The office could tell him nothing except that somebody had called through purporting to be Roon, and had offered the information that the tragedy had been committed and that Mr. Bennett Sandman was the victim.

"Well, I'm not staying any longer," said the doctor. "I think we can leave Roon to clear up this little mystery, Symon."

"I think so," said Wise Symon. He turned to Roon as he left. "Unless you want to be the hero of the most comical story that has ever been published in the *Telephone-Herald*, Roon, you had better supply me with early news of anything that turns up."

"You can't intimidate me," said Roon stoutly, but Wise Symon waved a warning finger as he disappeared in the wake of the coroner.

"It is a curious thing it should happen to Sandman," said the doctor as they descended the stairs. "There doesn't seem any money in it, and I can't imagine Sandman doing a thing like this for the sheer love of adventure. Besides which he has made a great deal of money lately."

"I don't know much about him," said Symon; "but I do know this, that he's not the kind of fellow that would allow himself to be murdered unless there was money in it."

"That just about describes him," said the doctor grimly. "He was the partner of one of the whitest men that I have ever met, young Jack Griffith."

"Oh, yes, Griffith was all right," nodded Y. "I've got nothing against Griffith. He was well out of that land swindle. By the way, is that partnership dissolved?—I haven't observed that Sandman has been struck off the Rolls?"

"I believe it was dissolved a few days before Griffith went to France. He has been a prisoner in Germany, you know, and has just been released. Of course, nobody knows why they split. Jack isn't the sort of boy to advertise his troubles, but I guess, rather than know, that Sandman had been up to some sort of shady business, and Jack found it out. Sandman was pretty hard hit just about then and in need of money. He has made a small fortune during the war, by the way. The fact beyond dispute is that the partnership is dissolved, though I believe there are still certain details of the dissolution to be settled when Jack comes back."

They walked along the deserted street in silence which Symon broke.

"That doesn't seem a very adequate reason for getting oneself murdered," he said.

"Roon seems to think there's some political reason."

"That's the truest thing you have ever said, doctor."

"What?" asked the doctor in surprise.

"That Roon seems to think," said Wise Symon with an angelic smile.

He parted from the coroner and went to the office to report. There was nothing fresh to be learnt, and Wise Symon showed his wisdom by returning home and going to bed.

He was awakened at 10:30 in the morning by the appearance at his bedside of Mr. Roon.

"Ugh!" shuddered Mr. Symon, "I thought you were real."

"I'm doing you a favour, Symon, that I wouldn't do for any other man on the Press," said Roon as he sat on the edge of the bed.

"Then you are real," said Symon; "nobody else in the world would talk like that. What's the favour—do you mind not sitting on my feet?"

"We've found something!"

He took out his pocket-book and selected, with that fussy care which the owners of congested pocket-books display, a folded paper.

"I found it at four o'clock this morning," said Roon; "when I say 'it' this is only a copy," he shook the paper. "I had made a very careful examination of every room and suddenly it occurred to me that perhaps there was a secret drawer to the writing bureau. The idea grew on me."

"Unless you want me to go to sleep again," interrupted Wise Symon, "turn your serial into a short paragraph. Of course, there's a secret drawer in all bureaux. It's the first thing you look for anyway. Well, you found the bureau and you found a paper."

"If you don't want to hear the story—" said Mr. Roon annoyed.

"I don't, I want the facts," said Symon; "let's have a look at that paper."

He took the document, unfolded it and read:

"In the event of anything happening to me I most earnestly request that the officer in charge of any inquiry which may attend my death shall take from Locker 69 in the International Safe Deposit a sealed envelope inscribed: 'In the matter of Bennett Sandman' and shall deliver that envelope without delay to the Chief Constable of Dublin. The envelope must not be opened under any circumstances except by him, since it contains information of vital national importance in relation to Ireland."

"There you are," said Mr. Roon in triumph.

"Where am I?" demanded Symon.

"Politics! I knew there was politics in this business."

Mr. Symon read the document again.

"Has the Chief seen this?"

"Yes, and he's rattled; in fact, everybody at the office is rattled," said Roon with satisfaction. "They have been on the 'phone to the Home Office, and orders have been given that the envelope is to be sent forward—I am to take it."

Wise Symon was sitting up in bed, his arms folded, his head bent in thought.

"And you'll take it," he repeated mechanically.

"I thought perhaps you'd like to be present when the envelope is handed over. We are going down to the deposit at 11:30."

"I should very much like to be present, Roon," said Wise Symon, mildly for him. "Will you tell me this, is it a crime to hoax Scotland Yard?"

Roon thought.

"No; I don't think so. You wouldn't be very popular, you know."

"And I suppose it isn't even a crime to hoax you," said Wise Symon slowly. "Of course, he's got nothing to lose."

"Who's got nothing to lose?" asked Roon.

"Mr. Bennett Sandman," replied Mr. Symon.

At 11:30 he formed one of the little group which stood contemplating the banked rows of tiny steel doors which constituted the furniture and decoration of No. 5 vault. He, with the Chief Inspector of X Branch C.I.D. and Roon, had been escorted to the deposit by the manager, who very reluctantly lent his assistance at all.

"The proceedings are most irregular, and of course I should not open this locker at all but for the police order."

"I think you could very well open it on the instructions left by Mr. Bennett Sandman," said the inspector.

"That's where you are wrong, inspector," replied the manager; "this doesn't happen to be Mr. Sandman's locker at all. Mr. Sandman held it in conjunction with his partner, Mr. Griffith, when Sandman and Griffith were in partnership."

"Have you ever been notified that Mr. Sandman was not to use this locker?"

The manager hesitated.

"I won't go so far as saying that," he said; "but I do know that Mr. Griffith insisted upon Sandman surrendering his key. Why not wait till Mr. Griffith comes back? He'll be home in a week or two."

The police chief shook his head.

"We have our instructions to forward the envelope to Dublin, and there's nothing else to be done."

The manager nodded. With his precious passkey he opened the locker, thrust in his hand and pulled out a number of fat envelopes which were tied together with tape.

"Here is the thing you want," he drew from the bundle a sealed packet.

The officer took it.

"Relating to Mr. Bennett Sandman," he read.

He turned it over. It was heavily sealed.

"You will give me a receipt for it, of course," said the manager, relocking the little steel safe.

"Certainly," said the chief; "here you are, Roon, put that in your inside pocket. You will take the afternoon train to Fishguard, and, you will allow nobody to touch that packet until you place it in the hands of Mr. Kennedy."

Never did little Roon behave so importantly as he did at that moment. Solemnly he unbuttoned his coat and thrust the packet away in his inside pocket, and. as solemnly buttoned his great-coat over that.

"That concludes our business for the morning, Symon. What do you think of it?"

"I think it is very funny," said Wise Symon.

"I don't see any humorous side to it," demurred the inspector; "but they say you're a whale for wisdom, Mr. Symon."

"The owl is the fish you're thinking of, Chief," said Wise Symon.

Outside in the street the little group split up, Roon strutting (there is no other word for it) homeward to prepare for his journey. Wise Symon watched him, and stopped the chief of police who was taking his departure.

"One moment," he said, "I don't know how wise I really am, but it seems to me that if I took this extraordinary adventure at its face value, I should be the biggest fool in this town."

"What does that mean?" asked the policeman.

"Doesn't it occur to you that all the circumstances are very remarkable? Bennett Sandman, a man who has been fired by his partner for crooked work—"

"How did you know that?" asked the Chief quickly.

"I guessed it," said Wise Symon grimly: "there are some things you've got to guess, and whilst young Griffith is in Germany, or at any rate out of touch, we must confine ourselves to guessing. Griffith is one of those loyal idiots who would never give away a defaulting partner, but I would recall to your memory the fact that just before the outbreak of war there was a big land swindle with which the name of Griffith & Sandman was associated—they acted as solicitors for the crooks. The issue of that case was rather obscured by the outbreak of war."

"I remember," nodded the Chief. "There was a settlement and the case was kept out of court."

"And Griffith did the settling, I'll bet," said Wise Symon. "Sandman remains behind, makes a lot of money, probably by some new swindle—"

"What are you driving at?" interrupted the police chief curiously.

"Nothing, only I want you to watch Roon. Don't let him out of sight till those papers are delivered in Dublin."

The chief of police smiled.

"You must think I'm a child. Of course he's watched. Two of my men picked him up the moment he left here, and will shadow him to Dublin. Roon doesn't know—he would feel sore if he did. There's no foolish modesty about Roon."

Roon had rooms at Merville Hotel, an economical hostel in Bloomsbury, and this obviated any necessity for taking a cab. Incidentally it enabled the shadowing police to keep some distance from him and save him the humiliating knowledge that his Chief had answered the question *quis custodiet ipsos custodes?* by placing him under the watchful care of two of his comrades.

So Roon went back to the hotel alone, passed straight up to his room and locked the door. This was a quarter after noon, and the train for Fishguard was due to leave at two.

True to his instructions he avoided crowds and ordered his lunch in his room.

At a quarter to one a telegraph messenger arrived at the little hotel. Because of Roon's peculiar work, it was the practice to send all telegrams direct to his room, and not, as is the usual case, to put them into the hotel box or to "page" them.

The messenger who called went up to Roon's room, knocked at the door which Roon opened cautiously.

"Roon!" said the messenger.

"That's me," said the detective and took the envelope from the messenger's hand.

"There's a reply," said the messenger gruffly.

The detective turned away to the window to read the message.

The telegraph messenger strode quickly along the main street. He was evidently in a hurry and on most important business, for he beckoned two taxis before he found one which was disengaged. An energetic telegraph boy was, under any circumstance, a phenomenon which appealed to Wise Symon, but this messenger was not returning to the Central Telegraph Office at all. He was hastening in the opposite direction and was, moreover, employing the services of a taxi-cab to increase that haste. Nor, thought Wise Symon, as he brought his little two-seater car in the track of the taxi, do messenger boys take a cab to go home to their meals.

He knew nothing of Roon and the telegram, was wholly unconscious of the fact that Roon lay insensible in his room with a bloody head, breathing stertorously, and that the messenger (who in real life was aged twenty-four, and an expert user of what is called a "cosh") was carrying in his pocket a sealed envelope inscribed: "In the matter of Mr. Bennett Sandman," though he guessed something had happened. He was in the vestibule when the telegraph boy had arrived, so also was an intelligent officer of the detective service, whilst another detective was before the building and a third was at the side under Roon's window.

He was acting on impulse when he followed the messenger into the street, and now, as the taxi-cab gathered speed, Wise Symon knew that his impulse was right.

The cars passed beyond the line where town merges into country, where the serried blocks of dwelling-houses part into little villas standing in their tiny grounds, and these in turn give way to green fields and tree-shaded lanes. The taxi-cab stopped at a small railway station and the messenger jumped out and passed into the station building.

Wise Symon checked his car, descended and followed at leisure. He found the messenger pacing the platform. A train was signalled and the hum of its wheels was faintly audible. Presently, with a roar and a clatter, it pulled into the station and stopped, and a man jumped out. He was the only passenger to alight. Until the train pulled out the messenger did not approach him, but as the last car cleared the man came forward and the two were engaged in earnest conversation before they walked from the platform into the road towards the waiting taxi.

The door of the taxi-cab had been opened by the messenger and the passenger had one foot upon the step when Wise Symon intervened.

"I hate to interrupt your joy-ride, Mr. Bennett Sandman," he said; "but last night there was a murder committed in town, in which you are considerably interested."

"I don't know what you mean," said the passenger. "Who are you?"

"If you take off your blue spectacles, you will probably recognize me," said Wise Symon coolly. "You are not so dead that you can't see."

Bennett Sandman took off his spectacles with a little nervous laugh.

"Well, I fooled you fellows anyway. It was a little practical joke of mine. Nobody can charge me with that you know, Symon."

"Excuse me," said Symon.

The wind had flapped open Sandman's overcoat and he had seen the end of a sealed envelope stuck away in the inside pocket. With a lightning dive he snatched it.

"You're both going back with me to Scotland Yard," said Wise Symon. "I have no authority for using this gun," he said, caressing the Browning he had slipped from his pocket; "but I think I could explain the shooting to everybody's satisfaction."

He looked over his shoulder to the taxi-cab driver who was watching the proceedings with interest.

"Cannon Row Station," he said—and then to the two men sharply: "get in!"

"In that," said Wise Symon pointing to the envelope on the Assistant Commissioner's table, "you will probably find a full statement of Sandman's swindle, and likely as not, a confession signed by him. As I read the case, young Griffith only discovered how deeply his partner was involved just before he joined up."

"You're quite right," said the Commissioner, "we have had a cable from Mr. Griffith. Sandman signed a confession, which is in that envelope, and which was placed with Mr. Griffith's documents in the safe deposit. I have since learnt that Sandman has made several attempts to get access to the safe."

"So he thought out this great murder scheme to avoid exposure and disgrace—he would certainly have been struck off the Rolls when Griffith came back," said Wise Symon. "On the excuse of having received threatening letters, he got Roon appointed to shadow him, knowing that Roon would be in charge of the 'murder case' and would be the man to whom the packet would be handed if the authorities believed his story. He kept Roon close to him on the night of the murder by putting him in the vestibule of the Astoria to watch for a red-haired girl who had no existence. It was he who telephoned my office to get the publicity he wanted."

"But why Dublin?" asked the Commissioner.

"It was necessary that Roon should be the custodian of the packet for just so long as would give Sandman a chance to take it from him. Roon was his trump card. He was determined to ensure having him on the spot when the 'murder' was committed. He hired the thug, just as he hired the girl who accompanied him home that night."

The Commissioner nodded.

"You're rather rough on poor Roon," he said, "his head will be in bandages for weeks."

"What use has he got for a head anyway?" demanded Wise Symon unpleasantly.

THE S. S.

M. P. Shiel

Well-made, healthy children bring much into the world along with
them. . . . When Nature abhors, she speaks it aloud: the creature
that lives with a false life is soon destroyed. Unfruitfulness, painful
existence, early destruction, these are her curses, the tokens of her
displeasure.

GOETHE

And Argos was so depleted of Men (i.e. *after the battle with Cleomenes*)
that the slaves usurped everything—ruling and disposing—until
such time as the sons of the slain were grown up.

HERODOTUS

T O SAY THAT THERE ARE EPIDEMICS OF SUICIDE IS TO GIVE EXPRESSION TO
what is now a mere commonplace of knowledge. And so far are they from
being of rare occurrence, that it has even been affirmed that every sensational case of *felo de se* published in the newspapers is sure to be followed by some
others more obscure: their frequency, indeed, is out of all proportion with the *extent* of
each particular outbreak. Sometimes, however, especially in villages and small town-
ships, the wildfire madness becomes an all-involving passion, emulating in its fury the
great plagues of history. Of such kind was the craze in Versailles in 1793, when about
a quarter of the whole population perished by the scourge; while that at the *Hôtel des
Invalides* in Paris was only a notable one of the many which have occurred during
the present century. At such times it is as if the optic nerve of the mind throughout
whole communities became distorted, till in the noseless and black-robed Reaper it
discerned an angel of very loveliness. As a brimming maiden, out-worn by her virgin-
ity, yields half-fainting to the dear sick stress of her desire—with just such faintings,
wanton fires, does the soul, over-taxed by the continence of living, yield voluntary to
the grave, and adulterously make of Death its paramour.

When she sees a bank
Stuck full of flowers, she, with a sigh, will tell
Her servants, what a pretty place it were
To bury lovers in; and make her maids
Pluck 'em, and strew her over like a corse.

The *mode* spreads—then rushes into rage: to breathe is to be obsolete: to wear the shroud becomes *comme il faut*, this cerecloth acquiring all the attractiveness and *éclat* of a wedding-garment. The coffin is not too strait for lawless nuptial bed; and the sweet clods of the valley will prove no barren bridegroom of a writhing progeny. There is, however, nothing specially mysterious in the operation of a pestilence of this nature: it is as conceivable, if not yet as explicable, as the contagion of cholera, mind being at least as sensitive to the touch of mind as body to that of body.

It was during the ever-memorable outbreak of this obscure malady in the year 1875 that I ventured to break in on the calm of that deep Silence in which, as in a mantle, my friend Prince Zaleski had wrapped himself. I wrote, in fact, to ask him what he thought of the epidemic. His answer was in the laconic words addressed to the Master in the house of woe at Bethany:

"Come and see."

To this, however, he added in postscript: "But what epidemic?"

I had momentarily lost sight of the fact that Zaleski had so absolutely cut himself off from the world, that he was not in the least likely to know anything even of the appalling series of events to which I had referred. And yet it is no exaggeration to say that those events had thrown the greater part of Europe into a state of consternation, and even confusion. In London, Manchester, Paris, and Berlin, especially the excitement was intense. On the Sunday preceding the writing of my note to Zaleski, I was present at a monster demonstration held in Hyde Park, in which the Government was held up on all hands to the popular derision and censure—for it will be remembered that to many minds the mysterious accompaniments of some of the deaths daily occurring conveyed a still darker significance than that implied in mere self-destruction, and seemed to point to a succession of purposeless and hideous murders. The demagogues, I must say, spoke with some wildness and incoherence. Many laid the blame at the door of the police, and urged that things would be different were *they* but placed under municipal, instead of under imperial, control. A thousand panaceas were invented, a thousand aimless censures passed. But the people listened with vacant ear. Never have I seen the populace so agitated, and yet so subdued, as with the sense of some impending doom. The glittering eye betrayed the excitement, the pallor of the cheek the doubt, the haunting *fear*. None felt himself quite safe; men recognized shuddering the grin of death in the air. To tingle with affright, and to know not why—that is the transcendentalism of terror. The threat of the cannon's mouth is trivial in its effect on the mind in comparison with the menace of a Shadow. It is the pestilence that walketh *by night* that is intolerable. As for myself, I confess to being pervaded with a nameless and numbing awe during all those weeks. And this feeling appeared to be general in the land. The journals had but one topic; the party organs threw politics to the winds. I heard that on the Stock Exchange, as in the Paris *Bourse*, business decreased to a minimum. In Parliament the work of law-threshing practically ceased, and the time of Ministers was nightly spent in answering volumes of angry "Questions," and in facing motion after motion for the "adjournment" of the House.

It was in the midst of all this commotion that I received Prince Zaleski's brief "Come and see." I was flattered and pleased: flattered, because I suspected that to me alone, of all men, would such an invitation, coming from him, be addressed; and pleased, because many a time in the midst of the noisy city street and the garish, dusty world, had the thought of that vast mansion, that dim and silent chamber, flooded my mind with a drowsy sense of the romantic, till, from very excess of melancholy sweetness in the picture, I was fain to close my eyes. I avow that that lonesome room—gloomy in its lunar bath of soft perfumed light—shrouded in the sullen voluptuousness of plushy, narcotic-breathing draperies—pervaded by the mysterious spirit of its brooding occupant—grew more and more on my fantasy, till the remembrance had for me all the cool refreshment shed by a midsummer-night's dream in the dewy deeps of some Perrhaebian grove of cornel and lotos and ruby stars of the asphodel. It was, therefore, in all haste that I set out to share for a time in the solitude of my friend.

Zaleski's reception of me was most cordial; immediately on my entrance into his sanctum he broke into a perfect torrent of wild, enthusiastic words, telling me with a kind of rapture, that he was just then laboriously engaged in co-ordinating to one of the calculi certain new properties he had discovered in the parabola, adding with infinite gusto his "firm" belief that the ancient Assyrians were acquainted with all our modern notions respecting the parabola itself, the projection of bodies in general, and of the heavenly bodies in particular; and must, moreover, from certain inferences of his own in connection with the Winged Circle, have been conversant with the fact that light is not an ether, but only the vibration of an ether. He then galloped on to suggest that I should at once take part with him in his investigations, and commented on the timeliness of my visit. I, on my part, was anxious for his opinion on other and far weightier matters than the concerns of the Assyrians, and intimated as much to him. But for two days he was firm in his tacit refusal to listen to my story; and, concluding that he was disinclined to undergo the agony of unrest with which he was always tormented by any mystery which momentarily baffled him, I was, of course, forced to hold my peace. On the third day, however, of his own accord he asked me to what epidemic I had referred. I then detailed to him some of the strange events which were agitating the mind of the outside world. From the very first he was interested: later on that interest grew into a passion, a greedy soul-consuming quest after the truth, the intensity of which was such at last as to move me even to pity.

I may as well here restate the facts as I communicated them to Zaleski. The concatenation of incidents, it will be remembered, started with the extraordinary death of that eminent man of science, Professor Schleschinger, consulting laryngologist to the *Charité* Hospital in Berlin. The professor, a man of great age, was on the point of contracting his third marriage with the beautiful and accomplished daughter of the Herr Geheimrath Otto von Friedrich. The contemplated union, which was entirely one of those *mariages de convenance* so common in good society, sprang out of the professor's ardent desire to leave behind him a direct heir to his very considerable wealth. By his first two marriages, indeed, he had had large families, and was at this very time surrounded by quite an army of little grandchildren, from whom (all his direct descendants being dead) he might have been content to select his heir; but the old German prejudices in these matters are strong, and he still hoped to be represented on his decease by a son of his own. To this whim the charming Ottilie was marked by her parents as the victim. The wedding, however, had been postponed owing to a slight illness of the veteran scientist, and just as he was on the point of final recovery from it, death intervened to prevent altogether the execution of his design. Never did death of man create a profounder sensation; *never was death of man followed by consequences more terrible.* The *Residenz* of the scientist was a stately mansion near the University in the *Unter den Linden* boulevard, that is to say, in the most fashionable *Quartier* of Berlin. His bedroom from a considerable height looked out on a small back garden, and in this room he had been engaged in conversation with his colleague and medical attendant, Dr. Johann Hofmeier, to a late hour of the night. During all this time he seemed cheerful, and spoke quite lucidly on various topics. In particular, he exhibited to his colleague a curious strip of what looked like ancient papyrus, on which were traced certain grotesque and apparently meaningless figures. This, he said, he had found some days before on the bed of a poor woman in one of the horribly low quarters that surround Berlin, on whom he had had occasion to make a *post-mortem* examination. The woman had suffered from partial paralysis. She had a small young family, none of whom, however, could give any account of the slip, except one little girl, who declared that she had taken it "from her mother's mouth" after death. The slip was soiled, and had a fragrant smell, as though it had been smeared with honey. The professor added that all through his illness he had been employing himself by examining these figures. He was convinced, he said, that they contained some archaeological significance; but, in any case, he ceased not to ask himself how came a slip of papyrus to be found in such a situation—on the bed of a dead Berlinerin of the poorest class? The story of its being taken from the *mouth* of the woman was, of course, unbelievable. The whole incident seemed to puzzle, while it amused him; seemed to appeal to the instinct—so strong in him—to investigate, to probe. For days, he declared, he had been endeavoring, in vain, to make anything of the figures. Dr. Hofmeier, too, examined the slip, but inclined to believe that the figures—rude and uncouth as they were—were only such as might be drawn by any schoolboy in an idle moment. They consisted merely of a man and a woman seated on a bench, with what looked like an ornamental border running round them. After a pleasant evening's scientific gossip, Dr. Hofmeier, a little after midnight, took his departure from the bed-side. An hour later the servants were roused from sleep by one deep, raucous cry proceeding from the professor's room. They hastened to his door; it was locked on the inside; all was still within. No answer coming to their calls, the door was broken in. They found their master lying calm and dead on his bed. A window of the room was open, but there was nothing to show that anyone had entered it. Dr. Hofmeier was sent for, and was soon on the scene. After examining the body, he failed to find anything to account for the sudden demise of his old friend and chief. One observation, however, had the effect of causing him to tingle with horror. On his entrance he had noticed, lying on the side of the bed, the piece of papyrus with which the professor had been toying in the earlier part of the day, and had removed it. But, as he was on the point of leaving the room, he happened to approach the corpse once more, and bending over it, noticed that the lips and teeth were slightly parted. Drawing open the now stiffened jaws, he found—to his amazement, to his stupefaction—that, neatly folded beneath the dead tongue, lay just such another piece of papyrus as that which he had removed from the bed. He drew it out—it was clammy. He put it to his nose—it exhaled the fragrance of honey. He opened it—it was covered by figures. He compared them with the figures on the other slip—they were just so similar as two draftsmen hastily copying from a common model would make them. The doctor was unnerved: he hurried homeward, and immediately submitted the honey on the papyrus to a rigorous chemical analysis: he suspected poison—a subtle poison—as the means of a suicide, grotesquely, insanely accomplished. He found the fluid to be perfectly innocuous—pure honey, and nothing more.

The next day Germany thrilled with the news that Professor Schleschinger had destroyed himself. For suicide, however, some of the papers substituted murder, though of neither was there an atom of actual proof. On the day following, three persons died by their own hands in Berlin, of whom two were young members of the medical profession; on the day following that, the number rose to nineteen, Hamburg, Dresden, and Aachen joining in the frenzied death-dance; within three weeks from the night on which Professor Schleschinger met his unaccountable end, eight thousand persons in Germany, France, and Great Britain, died in that startlingly sudden and secret manner which we call "tragic," many of them obviously by their own hands, many, in what seemed the servility of a fatal imitativeness, with figured, honey-smeared slips of papyrus beneath their tongues. Even now—now, after years—I thrill intensely to recall the dread remembrance; but to live through it, to breathe daily the mawkish, miasmatic atmosphere, all vapid with the suffocating death—ah, it was terror too deep, nausea too foul, for mortal bearing. Novalis has somewhere hinted at the possibility (or the desirability) of a simultaneous suicide and voluntary return by the whole human family into the sweet bosom of our ancient Father—I half expected it was coming, had come, *then*. It was as if the old, good-easy, meek-eyed man of science, dying, had left his effectual curse on all the world, and had thereby converted civilization into one omnivorous grave, one universal charnel-house.

I spent several days in reading out to Zaleski accounts of particular deaths as they had occurred. He seemed never to tire of listening, lying back for the most part on the silver-cushioned couch, and wearing an inscrutable mask. Sometimes he rose and paced the carpet with noiseless footfall, his steps increasing to the swaying, uneven velocity of an animal in confinement as a passage here or there attracted him, and then subsiding into their slow regularity again. At any interruption in the reading, he would instantly turn to me with a certain impatience, and implore me to proceed; and when our stock of matter failed, he broke out into actual anger that I had not brought more with me. Henceforth the negro, Ham, using my trap, daily took a double journey—one before sunrise, and one at dusk—to the nearest townlet, from which he would return loaded with newspapers. With unimaginable eagerness did both Zaleski and I seize, morning after morning, and evening after evening, on these budgets, to gloat for long hours over the ever-lengthening tale of death. As for him, sleep forsook him. He was a man of small reasonableness, scorning the limitations of human capacity; his palate brooked no meat when his brain was headlong in the chase; even the mild narcotics which were now his food and drink seemed to lose something of their power to mollify, to curb him. Often rising from slumber in what I took to be the dead of night—though of day or night there could be small certainty in that dim dwelling—I would peep into the domed chamber, and see him there under the livid-green light of the censer, the leaden smoke issuing from his lips, his eyes fixed unweariedly on a square piece of ebony which rested on the coffin of the mummy near him. On this ebony he had pasted side by side several woodcuts—snipped from the newspapers—of the figures traced on the pieces of papyrus found in the mouths of the dead. I could see, as time passed, that he was concentrating all his powers on these figures; for the details of the deaths themselves were all of a dreary sameness, offering few salient points for investigation. In those cases where the suicide had left behind him clear evidence of the means by which he had committed the act, there was nothing to investigate; the others—rich and poor alike, peer and peasant—trooped out by thousands on the far journey, without leaving the faintest footprint to mark the road by which they had gone.

This was perhaps the reason that, after a time, Zaleski discarded the newspapers, leaving their perusal to me, and turned his attention exclusively to the ebon tablet. Knowing as I full well did the daring and success of his past spiritual adventures—the subtlety, the imagination, the imperial grip of his intellect—I did not at all doubt that his choice was wise, and would in the end be justified. These woodcuts—now so notorious—were all exactly similar in design, though minutely differing here and there in drawing. The following is a facsimile of one of them taken by me at random:

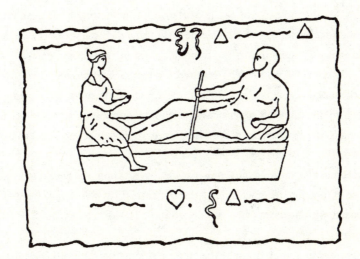

The time passed. It now began to be a grief to me to see the turgid pallor that gradually overspread the always ashen countenance of Zaleski; I grew to consider the ravaging life that glared and blazed in his sunken eye as too volcanic, demonic, to be canny: the mystery, I decided at last—if mystery there were—was too deep, too dark, for him. Hence perhaps it was, that I now absented myself more and more from him in the adjoining room in which I slept. There one day I sat reading over the latest list of horrors, when I heard a loud cry from the vaulted chamber. I rushed to the door and beheld him standing, gazing with wild eyes at the ebon tablet held straight out in front of him.

"By Heaven!" he cried, stamping savagely with his foot. "By Heaven! Then I certainly *am* a fool! *It is the staff of Phoebus in the hand of Hermes!*"

I hastened to him. "Tell me," I said, "have you discovered anything?"

"It is possible."

"And has there really been foul play—murder—in any of these deaths?"

"Of that, at least, I was certain from the first."

"Great God!" I exclaimed, "could any son of man so convert himself into a fiend, a beast of the wilderness—"

"You judge precisely in the manner of the multitude," he answered somewhat petulantly. "Illegal murder is always a mistake, but not necessarily a crime. Remember Corday. But in cases where the murder of one is really fiendish, why is it qualitatively less fiendish than the murder of many? On the other hand, had Brutus slain a thousand Caesars—each act involving an additional exhibition of the sublimest self-suppression—he might well have taken rank as a saint in heaven."

Failing for the moment to see the drift or the connection of the argument, I contented myself with waiting events. For the rest of that day and the next Zaleski seemed to have dismissed the matter of the tragedies from his mind, and entered calmly on his former studies. He no longer consulted the news, or examined the figures on the tablet. The papers, however, still arrived daily, and of these he soon afterwards laid several before me, pointing, with a curious smile, to a small paragraph in each. These all appeared in the advertisement columns, were worded alike, and read as follows:

A true son of Lycurgus, *having news,* desires to know the *time* and *place* of the next meeting of his Phyle. Address Zaleski, at R—— Abbey, in the county of M——.

I gazed in mute alternation at the advertisement and at him. I may here stop to make mention of a very remarkable sensation which my association with him occasionally produced in me. I felt it with intense, with unpleasant, with irritating keenness at this moment. It was the sensation of being borne aloft—aloft—by a force external to myself—such a sensation as might possibly tingle through an earthworm when lifted into illimitable airy heights by the strongly-daring pinions of an eagle. It was the feeling of being hurried out beyond one's depth—caught and whiffed away by the all-compelling sweep of some rabid vigor into a new, foreign element. Something akin I have experienced in an "express" as it raged with me—winged, rocking, ecstatic, shrilling a dragon Aha!—round a too narrow curve. It was a sensation very far from agreeable.

"To that," he said, pointing to the paragraph, "we may, I think, shortly expect an answer. Let us only hope that when it comes it may be immediately intelligible."

We waited throughout the whole of that day and night, hiding our eagerness under the pretense of absorption in our books. If by chance I fell into an uneasy doze, I found him on waking ever watchful, and poring over the great tome before him. About the time, however, when, could we have seen it, the first grey of dawn must have been peeping over the land, his impatience again became painful to witness; he rose and paced the room, muttering occasionally to himself. This only ceased, when, hours later, Ham entered the room with an envelope in his hand. Zaleski seized it—tore it open—ran his eye over the contents—and dashed *it* to the ground with an oath.

"Curse it!" he groaned. "Ah, curse it! unintelligible—every syllable of it!"

I picked up the missive and examined it. It was a slip of papyrus covered with the design now so hideously familiar, except only that the two central figures were wanting. At the bottom was written the date of the fifteenth of November—it was then the morning of the twelfth—and the name "Morris." The whole, therefore, presented the following appearance:

My eyes were now heavy with sleep, every sense half-drunken with the vaporlike atmosphere of the room, so that, having abandoned something of hope, I tottered willingly to my bed, and fell into a profound slumber, which lasted till what must have been the time of the gathering in of the shades of night. I then rose. Missing Zaleski, I sought through all the chambers for him. He was nowhere to be seen. The negro informed me with an affectionate and anxious tremor in the voice that his master had left the rooms some hours before, but had said nothing to him. I ordered the man to descend and look into the sacristy of the small chapel wherein I had deposited my *calèche*, and in the field behind, where my horse should be. He returned with the news that both had disappeared. Zaleski, I then concluded, had undoubtedly departed on a journey.

I was deeply touched by the demeanor of Ham as the hours went by. He wandered stealthily about the rooms like a lost being. It was like matter sighing after, weeping over, spirit. Prince Zaleski had never before withdrawn himself from the *surveillance* of this sturdy watchman, and his disappearance now was like a convulsion in their little cosmos. Ham implored me repeatedly, if I could, to throw some light on the meaning of this catastrophe. But I too was in the dark. The Titanic frame of the Ethiopian trembled with emotion as in broken, childish words he told me that he felt instinctively the approach of some great danger to the person of his master. So a day passed away, and then another. On the next he roused me from sleep to hand me a letter which, on opening, I found to be from Zaleski. It was hastily scribbled in pencil, dated "London, Nov. 14th," and ran thus:

> For my body—should I not return by Friday night—you will, no doubt, be good enough to make search. *Descend* the river, keeping constantly to the left; consult the papyrus; and stop at the *Descensus AEsopi*. Seek diligently, and you will find. For the rest, you know my fancy for cremation: take me, if you will, to the crematorium of *Père-Lachaise*. My whole fortune I decree to Ham, the Lybian.

Ham was all for knowing the contents of this letter, but I refused to communicate a word of it. I was dazed, I was more than ever perplexed, I was appalled by the frenzy of Zaleski. Friday night! It was then Thursday morning. And I was expected to wait through the dreary interval uncertain, agonized, inactive! I was offended with my friend; his conduct bore the interpretation of mental distraction. The leaden hours passed all oppressively while I sought to appease the keenness of my unrest with the anodyne of drugged sleep. On the next morning, however, another letter—a rather massive one—reached me. The covering was directed in the writing of Zaleski, but on it he had scribbled the words: "This need not be opened unless I fail to reappear before Saturday." I therefore laid the packet aside unread.

I waited all through Friday, resolved that at six o'clock, if nothing happened, I should make some sort of effort. But from six I remained, with eyes strained towards the doorway, until ten. I was so utterly at a loss, my ingenuity was so entirely baffled by the situation, that I could devise no course of action which did not immediately appear absurd. But at midnight I sprang up—no longer would I endure the carking suspense. I seized a taper, and passed through the doorway. I had not proceeded far, however, when my light was extinguished. Then I remembered with a shudder that I should have to pass through the whole vast length of the building in order to gain an exit. It was an all but hopeless task in the profound darkness to thread my way through the labyrinth of halls and corridors, of tumble-down stairs, of bat-haunted vaults, of purposeless angles and involutions; but I proceeded with something of a blind obstinacy, groping my way with arms held out before me. In this manner I had wandered on for perhaps a quarter of an hour, when my fingers came into distinct momentary contact with what felt like cold and humid human flesh. I shrank back, unnerved as I already was, with a murmur of affright.

"Zaleski?" I whispered with bated breath.

Intently as I strained my ears, I could detect no reply. The hairs of my head, catching terror from my fancies, erected themselves.

Again I advanced, and again I became aware of the sensation of contact. With a quick movement I passed my hand upward and downward.

It was indeed he. He was half-reclining, half-standing against a wall of the chamber: that he was not dead, I at once knew by his uneasy breathing. Indeed, when, having chafed his hands for some time, I tried to rouse him, he quickly recovered himself, and muttered: "I fainted; I want sleep—only sleep." I bore him back to the lighted room, assisted by Ham in the latter part of the journey. Ham's ecstasies were infinite; he had hardly hoped to see his master's face again. His garments being wet and soiled, the negro divested him of them, and dressed him in a tightly-fitting scarlet robe of Babylonish pattern, reaching to the feet, but leaving the lower neck and forearm bare, and girt round the stomach by a broad gold-orphreyed *ceinture*. With all the tenderness of a woman, the man stretched his master thus arrayed on the couch. Here he kept an Argus guard while Zaleski, in one deep unbroken slumber of a night and a day, reposed before him. When at last the sleeper woke, in his eye—full of divine instinct—flitted the wonted falchion-flash of the whetted, two-edged intellect; the secret, austere, self-conscious smile of triumph curved his lip; not a trace of pain or fatigue remained. After a substantial meal on nuts, autumn fruits, and wine of Samos, he resumed his place on the couch; and I sat by his side to hear the story of his wandering. He said:

"We have, Shiel, had before us a very remarkable series of murders, and a very remarkable series of suicides. Were they in any way connected? To this extent, I think—that the mysterious, the unparalleled nature of the murders gave rise to a morbid condition in the public mind, which in turn resulted in the epidemic of suicide. But though such an epidemic has its origin in the instinct of imitation so common in men, you must not suppose that the mental process is a *conscious* one. A person feels an impulse to go and do, and is not aware that at bottom it is only an impulse to go and do *likewise*. He would indeed repudiate such an assumption. Thus one man destroys himself, and another imitates him—but whereas the former uses a pistol, the latter uses a rope. It is rather absurd, therefore, to imagine that in any of those cases in which the slip of papyrus has been found in the mouth after death, the cause of death has been the slavish imitativeness of the suicidal mania—for this, as I say, is never *slavish*. The papyrus then—quite apart from the unmistakable evidences of suicide invariably left by each self-destroyer—affords us definite and certain means by which we can distinguish the two classes of deaths; and we are thus able to divide the total number into two nearly equal halves.

"But you start—you are troubled—you never heard or read of murder such as this, the simultaneous murder of thousands over wide areas of the face of the globe; here you feel is something outside your experience, deeper than your profoundest imaginings. To the question 'by whom committed?' and 'with what motive?' your mind can conceive no possible answer. And yet the answer must be, 'by man, and for human motives,'—for the Angel of Death with flashing eye and flaming sword is himself long dead; and again we can say at once, by no *one* man, but by many, a cohort, an army of men; and again, by no *common* men, but by men hellish (or heavenly) in cunning, in resource, in strength and unity of purpose; men laughing to scorn the flimsy prophylactics of society, separated by an infinity of self-confidence and spiritual integrity from the ordinary easily-crushed criminal of our days.

"This much at least I was able to discover from the first; and immediately I set myself to the detection of motive by a careful study of each case. This, too, in due time, became clear to me—but to motive it may perhaps be more convenient to refer later on. What next engaged my attention was the figures on the papyrus, and devoutly did I hope that by their solution I might be able to arrive at some more exact knowledge of the mystery.

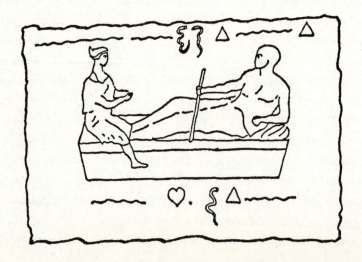

"The figures round the border first attracted me, and the mere *reading* of them gave me very little trouble. But I was convinced that behind their meaning thus read lay some deep esoteric significance; and this, almost to the last, I was utterly unable to fathom. You perceive that these border figures consist of waved lines of two different lengths, drawings of snakes, triangles looking like the Greek delta, and a heart-shaped object with a dot following it. These succeed one another in a certain definite order on all the slips. What, I asked myself, were these drawings meant to represent—letters, numbers, things, or abstractions? This I was the more readily able to determine because I have often, in thinking over the shape of the Roman letter *S*, wondered whether it did not owe its convolute form to an attempt on the part of its inventor to make a picture of the *serpent*; *S* being the sibilant or hissing letter, and the serpent the hissing animal. This view, I fancy (though I am not sure), has escaped the philologists, but of course you know that all letters were originally *pictures of things*, and of what was *S* a picture, if not of the serpent? I therefore assumed, by way of trial, that the snakes in the diagram stood for a sibilant letter, that is, either *C* or *S*. And thence, supposing this to be the case, I deduced: firstly, that all the other figures stood for letters; and secondly, that they all appeared in the form of pictures of the things of which those letters were originally meant to be pictures. Thus the letter 'm,' one of the four '*liquid*' consonants, is, as we now write it, only a shortened form of a waved line; and as a waved line it was originally written, and was the character by which *a stream of running water* was represented in writing; indeed it only owes its name to the fact that when the lips are pressed together, and 'm' uttered by a continuous effort, a certain resemblance to the murmur of running water is produced. The longer waved line in the diagram I therefore took to represent 'm'; and it at once followed that the shorter meant 'n,' for no two letters of the commoner European alphabets differ only in length (as distinct from shape) except 'm' and 'n,' and 'w' and 'v'; indeed, just as the French call 'w' 'double-ve,' so very properly might 'm' be called 'double-en'. But, in this case, the longer not being 'w,' the shorter could not be 'v': it was therefore 'n.' And now there only remained the heart and the triangle. I was unable to think of any letter that could ever have been intended for the picture of a heart, but the triangle I knew to be the letter *A*. This was originally written without the cross-bar from prop to prop, and the two feet at the bottom of the props were not separated as now, but joined; so that the letter formed a true triangle. It was meant by the primitive man to be a picture of his primitive house, this house being, of course, hut-shaped, and consisting of a conical roof without walls. I had thus, with the exception of the heart, disentangled the whole, which then (leaving a space for the heart) read as follows:

$$mn \ \Big\{ \ \begin{matrix} ss \\ \\ cc \end{matrix} \qquad anan \ldots san.$$

"But 'c' before 'a' being never a sibilant (except in some few so-called 'Romance' languages), but a guttural, it was for the moment discarded; also as no word begins with the letters 'mn'—except 'mnemonics' and its fellows—I concluded that a vowel must be omitted between these letters, and thence that all vowels (except 'a') were omitted; again, as the double 's' can never come after 'n' I saw that either a vowel was omitted between the two 's's,' or that the first word ended after the first 's.' Thus I got

$$m \ ns \ sanan \ldots san,$$

or, supplying the now quite obvious vowels,

$$mens \ sana \ in \ldots sano.$$

"The heart I now knew represented the word 'corpore,' the Latin word for 'heart' being 'cor,' and the dot—showing that the word as it stood was an abbreviation—conclusively proved every one of my deductions.

"So far all had gone flowingly. It was only when I came to consider the central figures that for many days I spent my strength in vain. You heard my exclamation of delight and astonishment when at last a ray of light pierced the gloom. At no time, indeed, was I wholly in the dark as to the *general* significance of these figures, for I saw at once their resemblance to the sepulchral reliefs of classical times. In case you are not minutely acquainted with the technique of these stones, I may as well show you one, which I myself removed from an old grave in Tarentum."

He took from a niche a small piece of close-grained marble, about a foot square, and laid it before me. On one side it was exquisitely sculptured in relief.

"This," he continued, "is a typical example of the Greek grave-stone, and having seen one specimen you may be said to have seen almost all, for there is surprisingly little variety in the class. You will observe that the scene represents a man reclining on a couch; in his hand he holds a *patera*, or dish, filled with grapes and pomegranates, and beside him is a tripod bearing the viands from which he is banqueting. At his feet sits a woman—for the Greek lady never reclined at table. In addition to these two figures a horse's head, a dog, or a serpent may sometimes be seen; and these forms comprise the almost invariable pattern of all grave reliefs. Now, that this was the real model from which the figures on the papyrus were taken I could not doubt, when I considered the seemingly absurd fidelity with which in each murder the papyrus, smeared with honey, was placed under the tongue of the victim. I said to myself: it can only be that the assassins have bound themselves to the observance of a strict and narrow ritual from which no departure is under any circumstances permitted—perhaps for the sake of signalling the course of events to others at a distance. But what ritual? That question I was able to answer when I knew the answer to these others—why *under the tongue*, and why *smeared with honey*? For no reason, except that the Greeks (not the Romans till very late in their history) always placed an *obolos*, or penny, beneath the tongue of the dead to pay his passage across the Stygian river of ghosts; for no reason, except that to these same Greeks honey was a sacred fluid, intimately associated in their minds with the mournful subject of Death; a fluid with which the bodies of the deceased were anointed, and sometimes—especially in Sparta and the Pelasgic South—embalmed; with which libations were poured to Hermes Psuchopompos, conductor of the dead to the regions of shade; with which offerings were made to all the chthonic deities, and the souls of the departed in general. You remember, for instance, the melancholy words of Helen addressed to Hermione in *Orestes*:

Καὶ λαβὲ χοὰς τάσδ' ἐν χεροῖν κόμας τ' εμὰς. ἐλθοῦσα
δ' ἀμφὶ τὸν Κλυταιμνήστρας τάφον μελίκρατ' ἄφες
γάλακτος οἰνωπόν τ' ἄχνην.

"And so everywhere. The ritual then of the murderers was a *Greek* ritual, their cult a Greek cult—preferably, perhaps, a South Greek one, a Spartan one, for it was here that the highly conservative peoples of that region clung longest and fondliest to this semi-barbarous worship. This then being so, I was made all the more certain of my conjecture that the central figures on the papyrus were drawn from a Greek model.

"Here, however, I came to a standstill. I was infinitely puzzled by the rod in the man's hand. In none of the Greek grave-reliefs does any such thing as a rod make an appearance, except in one well-known example where the god Hermes—generally represented as carrying the *caduceus*, or staff, given him by Phoebus—appears leading a dead maiden to the land of night. But in every other example of which I am aware the sculpture represents a man *living*, not dead, banqueting *on earth*, not in Hades, by the side of his living companion. What then could be the significance of the staff in the hand of this living man? It was only after days of the hardest struggle, the cruellest suspense, that the thought flashed on me that the idea of Hermes leading away the dead female might, in this case, have been carried one step farther; that the male figure might be no living man, no man at all, but *Hermes himself* actually banqueting in Hades with the soul of his disembodied *protégée*! The thought filled me with a rapture I cannot describe, and you witnessed my excitement. But, at all events, I saw that this was a truly tremendous departure from Greek art and thought, to which in general the copyists seemed to cling so religiously. There must therefore be a reason, a strong reason, for vandalism such as this. And that, at any rate, it was no longer difficult to discover; for now I knew that the male figure was no mortal, but a god, a spirit, a DAEMON (in the Greek sense of the word); and the female figure I saw by the marked shortness of her drapery to be no Athenian, but a Spartan; no matron either, but a maiden, a lass, a lassie; and now I had forced on me lassie daemon, *Lacedaemon.*

"This then was the badge, the so carefully-buried badge, of this society of men. The only thing which still puzzled and confounded me at this stage was the startling circumstance that a *Greek* society should make use of a *Latin* motto. It was clear that either all my conclusions were totally wrong, or else the motto *mens sana in corpore sano* contained wrapped up in itself some acroamatic meaning which I found myself unable to penetrate, and which the authors had found no Greek motto capable of conveying. But at any rate, having found this much, my knowledge led me of itself one step further; for I perceived that, widely extended as were their operations, the society was necessarily in the main an *English*, or at least an English-speaking one—for of this the word 'lassie' was plainly indicative: it was easy now to conjecture London, the monster-city in which all things lose themselves, as their headquarters; and at this point in my investigations I despatched to the papers the advertisement you have seen."

"But," I exclaimed, "even now I utterly fail to see by what mysterious processes of thought you arrived at the wording of the advertisement; even now it conveys no meaning to my mind."

"That," he replied," will grow clear when we come to a right understanding of the baleful *motive* which inspired these men. I have already said that I was not long in discovering it. There was only one possible method of doing so—and that was, by all means, by any means, to find out some condition or other common to every one of the victims before death. It is true that I was unable to do this in some few cases, but where I failed, I was convinced that my failure was due to the insufficiency of the evidence at my disposal, rather than to the actual absence of the condition. Now, let us take almost any two cases you will, and seek for this common condition: let us take, for example, the first two that attracted the attention of the world—the poor woman of the slums of Berlin, and the celebrated man of science. Separated by as wide an interval as they are, we shall yet find, if we look closely, in each case the same pathetic tokens of the still uneliminated *striae* of our poor humanity. The woman is not an old woman, for she has a 'small young' family, which, had she lived, might have been increased: notwithstanding which, she has suffered from hemiplegia, 'partial paralysis.' The professor, too, has had not one, but two, large families, and an 'army of grand-children': but note well the startling, the hideous fact, that *every one of his children is dead!* The crude grave has gaped before the cock to suck in *every one* of those shrunk forms, so indigent of vital impulse, so pauper of civism, lust, so drafty, so vague, so lean—but not before they have had time to dower with the ah and wo of their infirmity a whole wretched 'army of grand-children.' And yet this man of wisdom is on the point, in his old age, of marrying once again, of producing for the good of his race still more of this poor human stuff. You see the lurid significance, the point of resemblance—you see it? And, O heaven, is it not too sad? For me, I tell you, the whole business has a tragic pitifulness too deep for words. But this brings me to the discussion of a large matter. It would, for instance, be interesting to me to hear what you, a modern European, saturated with all the notions of your little day, what *you* consider the supreme, the all-important question for the nations of Europe at this moment. Am I far wrong in assuming that you would rattle off half a dozen of the moot points agitating rival factions in your own land, select one of them, and call that 'the question of the hour'? I wish I could see as you see; I wish to God I did not see deeper. In order to lead you to my point, what, let me ask you, what *precisely* was it that ruined the old nations—that brought, say Rome, to her knees at last? Centralization, you say, top-heavy imperialism, dilettante pessimism, the love of luxury. At bottom, believe me, it was not one of these high-sounding things—it was simply war; the sum total of the battles of centuries. But let me explain myself: this is a novel view to you, and you are perhaps unable to conceive how or why war was so fatal to the old world, because you see how little harmful it is to the new. If you collected in a promiscuous way a few millions of modern Englishmen and slew them all simultaneously, what, think you, would be the effect from the point of view of the State? The effect, I conceive, would be indefinitely small, wonderfully transitory; there would, of course, be a momentary lacuna in the boiling surge: yet the womb of humanity is full of sap, and uberant; Ocean-tide, wooed of that Ilithyia whose breasts are many, would flow on, and the void would soon be filled. But the effect would only be thus insignificant, if, as I said, your millions were taken promiscuously (as in the modern army), not if they were *picked* men—in *that* case the loss (or gain) would be excessive, and permanent for all time. Now, the war-hosts of the ancient commonwealths—not dependent on the mechanical contrivances of the modern army—were necessarily composed of the very best men: the strong-boned, the heart-stout, the sound in wind and limb. Under these conditions the State shuddered through all her frame, thrilled adown every filament, at the death of a single one of her sons in the field. As only the feeble, the aged, bided at home, their number after each battle became larger *in proportion to the whole* than before. Thus the nation, more and more, with ever-increasing rapidity, declined in bodily, and of course spiritual, quality, until the *end* was reached, and Nature swallowed up the weaklings whole; and thus war, which to the modern state is at worst the blockhead and indecent *affaires d'honneur* of persons in office—and which, surely, before you and I die will cease altogether—was to the ancient a genuine and remorselessly fatal scourge.

"And now let me apply these facts to the Europe of our own time. We no longer have world-serious war—but in its place we have a scourge, the effect of which on the modern state is *precisely the same* as the effect of war on the ancient, only—in the end—far more destructive, far more subtle, sure, horrible, disgusting. The name of this pestilence is Medical Science. Yes, it is most true, shudder —shudder—as you will! Man's best friend turns to an asp in his bosom to sting him to the basest of deaths. The devastating growth of medical, and especially surgical, science—that, if you like, for us all, is 'the question of the hour'! And what a question! of what surpassing importance, in the presence of which all other 'questions' whatever dwindle into mere academic triviality. For just as the ancient State was wounded to the heart through the death of her healthy sons in the field, just so slowly, just so silently, is the modern receiving deadly hurt by the botching and tinkering of her unhealthy children. The net result is in each case the same—the altered ratio of the total amount of reproductive health to the total amount of reproductive disease. They recklessly spent their best; we sedulously conserve our worst; and as they pined and died of anaemia, so we, unless we repent, must perish in a paroxysm of black-blood apoplexy. And this prospect becomes more certain, when you reflect that the physician as we know him is not, like other men and things, a being of gradual growth, of slow evolution: from Adam to the middle of the last century the world saw nothing even in the least resembling him. No son of Paian *he*, but a fatherless, full-grown birth from the incessant matrix of Modern Time, so motherly of monstrous litters of Gorgon and Hydra and Chimaeras dire'; you will understand what I mean when you consider the quite recent date of, say, the introduction of anaesthetics or antiseptics, the discovery of the knee-jerk, bacteriology, or even of such a doctrine as the circulation of the blood. We are at this very time, if I mistake not, on the verge of new insights which will enable man to laugh at disease—laugh at it in the sense of overruling its natural tendency to produce death, not by any means in the sense of destroying its ever-expanding *existence*. Do you know that at this moment your hospitals are crammed with beings in human likeness suffering from a thousand obscure and subtly-ineradicable ills, all of whom, if left alone, would die almost at once, but ninety in the hundred of whom will, as it is, be sent forth 'cured,' like missionaries of hell, and the horrent shapes of Night and Acheron, to mingle in the pure river of humanity the poison-taint of their protean vileness? Do you know that in your schools one-quarter of the children are already purblind? Have you gauged the importance of your tremendous consumption of quack catholicons, of the fortunes derived from their sale, of the spread of modern nervous disorders, of toothless youth and thrice loathsome age among the helot-classes? Do you know that in the course of my late journey to London, I walked from Piccadilly Circus to Hyde Park Corner, during which time I observed some five hundred people, of whom twenty-seven only were perfectly healthy, well-formed men, and eighteen healthy, beautiful women? On every hand—with a thrill of intensest joy, I say it!—is to be seen, if not yet commencing civilization, then progress, progress—wide as the world—toward it: only here—at the heart—is there decadence, fatty degeneration. Brain-evolution—and favoring airs—and the ripening time—and the silent Will of God, of God—all these in conspiracy seem to be behind, urging the whole ship's company of us to some undreamable luxury of glory—when lo, this check, artificial, evitable. Less death, more disease—that is the sad, the unnatural record; children especially—so sensitive to the physician's art—living on by hundreds of thousands, bearing within them the germs of wide-spreading sorrow, who in former times would have died. And if you consider that the proper function of the doctor is the strictly limited one of curing the curable, rather than of self-gloriously perpetuating the incurable, you may find it difficult to give a quite rational answer to this simple question: *why?* Nothing is so sure as that to the unit it is a cruelty; nothing so certain as that to humanity it is a wrong; to say that such and such an one was sent by the All Wise, and must *therefore* be not merely permitted, but elaborately coaxed and forced, to live, is to utter a blasphemy against Man at which even the ribald tongue of a priest might falter; and as a matter of fact, society, in just contempt for this species of argument, never hesitates to hang, for its own imagined good, its heaven-sent catholics, protestants, sheep, sheep-stealers, etc. What then, you ask, would I do with these unholy ones? To save the State would I pierce them with a sword, or leave them to the slow throes of their agonies? Ah, do not expect me to answer that question—I do not know what to answer. The whole spirit of the present is one of a broad and beautiful, if quite thoughtless, humanism, and I, a child of the present, cannot but be borne along by it, coerced into sympathy with it. 'Beautiful' I say: for if anywhere in the world you have seen a sight more beautiful than a group of hospital *savants* bending with endless scrupulousness over a little pauper child, concentering upon its frailty the whole human skill and wisdom of ages, so have not I. Here have you the full realization of a parable diviner than that of the man who went down from Jerusalem to Jericho. Beautiful then; with at least surface beauty, like the serpent *lachesis mutus*; but, like many beautiful things, deadly too, *in*human. And, on the whole, an answer will have to be found. As for me, it is a doubt which has often agitated me, whether the central dogma of Judaism and Christianity alike can, after all, be really one of the inner verities of this our earthly being—the dogma, that by the shedding of the innocent blood, and by that alone, shall the race of man find cleansing and salvation. Will no agony of reluctance overcome the necessity that one man die, 'so that the whole people perish not'? Can it be true that by nothing less than the 'three days of pestilence' shall the land be purged of its stain, and is this old divine alternative about to confront us in new, modern form? Does the inscrutable Artemis indeed demand offerings of human blood to suage her anger? Most sad that man should ever need, should ever have needed, to foul his hand in the μυσαϱὸν αἷμα of his own veins! But what is, is. And can it be fated that the most advanced civilization of the future shall needs have in it, as the first and chief element of its glory, the most barbarous of all the rituals of barbarism—the immolation of hecatombs which wail a muling human wail? Is it indeed part of man's strange destiny through the deeps of Time that he one day bow his back to the duty of pruning himself as a garden, so that he run not to a waste wilderness? Shall the physician, the *accoucheur*, of the time to come be expected, and commanded, to do on the ephod and breast-plate, anoint his head with the oil of gladness, and add to the function of healer the function of Sacrificial Priest? These you say, are wild, dark questions. Wild enough, dark enough. We know how Sparta—the 'man-taming Sparta' Simonides calls her—answered them. Here was the complete subordination of all unit-life to the well-being of the Whole. The child, immediately on his entry into the world, fell under the control of the State: it was not left to the judgment of his parents, as elsewhere, whether he should be brought up or not, but a commission of the Phyle in which he was born decided the question. If he was weakly, if he had any bodily unsightliness, he was exposed on a place called Taygetus, and so perished. It was a consequence of this that never did the sun in his course light on man half so godly stalwart, on woman half so houri-lovely, as in stern and stout old Sparta. Death, like all mortal, they must bear; disease, once and for all, they were resolved to have done with. The word which they used to express the idea 'ugly,' meant also 'hateful,' 'vile,' 'disgraceful'—and I need hardly point out to you the significance of that fact alone; for they considered—and rightly—that there is no sort of natural reason why every denizen of earth should not be perfectly hale, integral, sane, beautiful—if only very moderate pains be taken to procure this divine result. One fellow, indeed, called Nancleidas, grew a little too fat to please the sensitive eyes of the Spartans: I believe he was periodically whipped. Under a system so very barbarous, the supersweet, egoistic voice of the club-footed poet Byron would, of course, never have been heard: one brief egoistic 'lament' on Taygetus, and so an end. It is not, however, certain that the world could not have managed very well without Lord Byron. The one thing that admits of no contradiction is that it cannot manage without the holy citizen, and that disease, to men and to nations, can have but one meaning, annihilation near or ultimate. At any rate, from these remarks, you will now very likely be able to arrive at some understanding of the wording of the advertisements which I sent to the papers."

Zaleski, having delivered himself of this singular *tirade*, paused: replaced the sepulchral relief in its niche: drew a drapery of silver cloth over his bare feet and the hem of his antique garment of Babylon: and then continued:

"After some time the answer to the advertisement at length arrived; but what was my disgust to find that it was perfectly unintelligible to me. I had asked for a date and an address: the reply came giving a date, and an address, too—but an address wrapped up in cypher, which, of course, I, as a supposed member of the society, was expected to be able to read. At any rate, I now knew the significance of the incongruous circumstance that the Latin proverb *mens sana etc.* should be adopted as the motto of a Greek society; the significance lay in this, that the motto *contained an address*—the address of their meeting-place, or at least, of their chief meeting-place. I was now confronted with the task of solving—and of solving quickly, without the loss of an hour—this enigma; and I confess that it was only by the most violent and extraordinary concentration of what I may call the dissecting faculty, that I was able to do so in good time. And yet there was no special difficulty in the matter. For looking at the motto as it stood in cypher, the first thing I perceived was that, in order to read the secret, the heart-shaped figure must be left out of consideration, if there was any *consistency* in the system of cyphers at all, for it belonged to a class of symbols quite distinct from that of all the others, not being, like them, a picture-letter. Omitting this, therefore, and taking all the other vowels and consonants whether actually represented in the device or not, I now got the proverb in the form *mens sana in . . . pore sano*. I wrote this down, and what instantly struck me was the immense, the altogether unusual, number of *liquids* in the motto—six in all, amounting to no less than one-third of the total number of letters! Putting these all together you get *mnnnnr*, and you can see that the very appearance of the 'm's' and 'n's' (especially when *written*) running into one another, of itself suggests a stream of water. Having previously arrived at the conclusion of London as the meeting-place, I could not now fail to go on to the inference of *the Thames*; there, or near there, would I find those whom I sought. The letters 'mnnnnr,' then, meant the Thames: what did the still remaining letters mean? I now took these remaining letters, placing them side by side: I got aaa, sss, ee, oo, p, and i. Juxtaposing these nearly in the order indicated by the frequency of their occurrence, and their place in the Roman alphabet, you at once and inevitably get the word *AEsopi*. And now I was fairly startled by this symmetrical proof of the exactness of my own deductions in other respects, but, above all, far above all, by the occurrence of that word '*AEsopi.*' For who was AEsopus? He was a slave who was freed for his wise and witful sallies: he is therefore typical of the liberty of the wise—their moral manumission from temporary and narrow law; he was also a close friend of Croesus: he is typical, then, of the union of wisdom with wealth—true wisdom with real wealth; lastly, and above all, he was thrown by the Delphians from a rock on account of his wit: he is typical, therefore, of death—the shedding of blood—as a result of wisdom, this thought being an elaboration of Solomon's great maxim, 'in much wisdom is much sorrow.' But how accurately all this fitted in with what would naturally be the doctrines of the men on whose track I was! I could no longer doubt the justness of my reasonings, and immediately, while you slept, I set off for London.

"Of my haps in London I need not give you a very particular account. The meeting was to be held on the fifteenth, and by the morning of the thirteenth I had reached a place called Wargrave, on the Thames. There I hired a light canoe, and thence proceeded down the river in a somewhat zig-zag manner, narrowly examining the banks on either side, and keeping a sharp out-look for some board, or sign, or house, that would seem to betoken any sort of connection with the word 'AEsopi.' In this way I passed a fruitless day, and having reached the shipping region, made fast my craft, and in a spirit of *diablerie* spent the night in a common lodging-house, in the company of the most remarkable human beings, characterized by an odor of alcohol, and a certain obtrusive *bonne camaraderie* which the prevailing fear of death could not altogether repress. By dawn of the fourteenth I was on my journey again—on, and ever on. Eagerly I longed for a sight of the word I sought: but I had misjudged the men against whose cunning I had measured my own. I should have remembered more consistently that they were no ordinary men. As I was destined to find, there lay a deeper, more cabalistic meaning in the motto than any I had been able to dream of. I had proceeded on my pilgrimage down the river a long way past Greenwich, and had now reached a desolate and level reach of land stretching away on either hand. Paddling my boat from the right to the left bank, I came to a spot where a little arm of the river ran up some few yards into the land. The place wore a specially dreary and deserted aspect: the land was flat, and covered with low shrubs. I rowed into this arm of shallow water and rested on my oar, wearily bethinking myself what was next to be done. Looking round, however, I saw to my surprise that at the end of this arm there was a short narrow pathway—a winding road—leading from the riverbank. I stood up in the boat and followed its course with my eyes. It was met by another road also winding among the bushes, but in a slightly different direction. At the end of this was a little, low, high-roofed, round house, without doors or windows. And then—and then—tingling now with a thousand raptures—I beheld a pool of water near this structure, and then another low house, a counterpart of the first—and then, still leading on in the same direction, another pool—and then a great rock, heart-shaped—and then another winding road—and then another pool of water. All was a model—*exact to the minutest particular*—of the device on the papyrus! The first long-waved line was the river itself; the three short-waved lines were the arm of the river and the two pools; the three snakes were the three winding roads; the two triangles representing the letter *A* were the two high-roofed round houses; the heart was the rock! I sprang, now thoroughly excited, from the boat, and ran in headlong haste to the end of the last lake. Here there was a rather thick and high growth of bushes, but peering among them, my eye at once caught a white oblong board supported on a stake: on this, in black letters, was marked the words, 'Descensus Aesopi.' It was necessary, therefore, to go *down*: the meeting-place was subterranean. It was without difficulty that I discovered a small opening in the ground, half hidden by the underwood; from the orifice I found that a series of wooden steps led directly downwards, and I at once boldly descended. No sooner, however, had I touched the bottom than I was confronted by an ancient man in Hellenic apparel, armed with the Greek *ʒiphos* and *peltè*. His eyes, accustomed to the gloom, pierced me long with an earnest scrutiny.

" 'You are a Spartan?' he asked at length.

" 'Yes,' I answered promptly.

" 'Then how is it you do not know that I am stone deaf?'

"I shrugged, indicating that for the moment I had forgotten the fact.

" 'You *are* a Spartan?' he repeated.

"I nodded with emphasis.

" 'Then, how is it you omit to make the sign?'

"Now, you must not suppose that at this point I was nonplussed, for in that case you would not give due weight to the strange inherent power of the mind to rise to the occasion of a sudden emergency—to stretch itself long to the length of an event; I do not hesitate to say that *no* combination of circumstances can defeat a vigorous brain fully alert, and in possession of itself. With a quickness to which the lightning-flash is tardy, I remembered that this was a spot indicated by the symbols on the papyrus: I remembered that this same papyrus was always placed under the *tongue* of the dead; I remembered, too, that among that very nation whose language had afforded the motto, to 'turn up the *thumb*' (*pollicem vertere*) was a symbol significant of death. I touched the under surface of my tongue with the tip of my thumb. The aged man was appeased. I passed on, and examined the place.

"It was simply a vast circular hall, the arched roof of which was supported on colonnades of what I took to be pillars of porphyry. Down the middle and round the sides ran tables of the same material; the walls were clothed in hangings of sable velvet, on which, in infinite reproduction, was embroidered in cypher the motto of the society. The chairs were cushioned in the same stuff. Near the center of the circle stood a huge statue, of what really seemed to me to be pure beaten gold. On the great ebon base was inscribed the word ΛΥΚΥΡΓΟΣ. From the roof swung by brazen chains a single misty lamp.

"Having seen this much I reascended to the land of light, and being fully resolved on attending the meeting on the next day or night, and not knowing what my fate might then be, I wrote to inform you of the means by which my body might be traced.

"But on the next day a new thought occurred to me: I reasoned thus: 'these men are not common assassins; they wage a too rash warfare against diseased life, but not against life in general. In all probability they have a quite immoderate, quite morbid reverence for the sanctity of healthy life. They will not therefore take mine, *unless* they suppose me to be the only living outsider who has a knowledge of their secret, and therefore think it absolutely necessary for the carrying out of their beneficent designs that my life should be sacrificed. I will therefore prevent such a motive from occurring to them by communicating to another their whole secret, and—if the necessity should arise—*letting them know* that I have done so, without telling them who that other is. Thus my life will be assured.' I therefore wrote to you on that day a full account of all I had discovered, giving you to understand, however, on the envelope, that you need not examine the contents for some little time.

"I waited in the subterranean vault during the greater part of the next day; but not till midnight did the confederates gather. What happened at that meeting I shall not disclose, even to you. All was sacred—solemn—full of awe. Of the choral hymns there sung, the hierophantic ritual, liturgies, paeans, the gorgeous symbolisms—of the wealth there represented, the culture, art, self-sacrifice—of the mingling of all the tongues of Europe—I shall not speak; nor shall I repeat names which you would at once recognize as familiar to you—though I may, perhaps, mention that the 'Morris,' whose name appears on the papyrus sent to me is a well-known *littérateur* of that name. But this in confidence, for some years at least.

"Let me, however, hurry to a conclusion. My turn came to speak. I rose undaunted, and calmly disclosed myself; during the moment of hush, of wide-eyed paralysis that ensued, I declared that fully as I coincided with their views in general,

I found myself unable to regard their methods with approval—these I could not but consider too rash, too harsh, too premature. My voice was suddenly drowned by one universal, earth-shaking roar of rage and contempt, during which I was surrounded on all sides, seized, pinioned, and dashed on the central table. All this time, in the hope and love of life, I passionately shouted that I was not the only living being who shared in their secret. But my voice was drowned, and drowned again, in the whirling tumult. None heard me. A powerful and little-known anaesthetic—the means by which all their murders have been accomplished—was now produced. A cloth, saturated with the fluid, was placed on my mouth and nostrils. I was stifled. Sense failed. The incubus of the universe blackened down upon my brain. How I tugged at the mandrakes of speech! was a locked pugilist with language! In the depth of my extremity the half-thought, I remember, floated, like a mist, through my fading consciousness, that now perhaps—now—there was silence around me; that *now*, could my palsied lips find dialect, I should be heard, and understood. My whole soul rose focussed to the effort—my body jerked itself upwards. At that moment I knew my spirit truly great, genuinely sublime. For I *did* utter something—my dead and shuddering tongue *did* babble forth some coherency. Then I fell back, and all was once more the ancient Dark. On the next day when I woke, I was lying on my back in my little boat, placed there by God knows whose hands. At all events, one thing was clear—I *had* uttered something—I was saved. With what of strength remained to me I reached the place where I had left your *calèche*, and started on my homeward way. The necessity to sleep was strong upon me, for the fumes of the anaesthetic still clung about my brain; hence, after my long journey, I fainted on my passage through the house, and in this condition you found me.

"Such then is the history of my thinkings and doings in connection with this ill-advised confraternity: and now that their cabala is known to others—to how many others *they* cannot guess—I think it is not unlikely that we shall hear little more of the Society of Sparta."

THE MYSTERIOUS CARD

Cleveland Moffett

RICHARD BURWELL, OF NEW YORK, WILL NEVER CEASE TO REGRET THAT THE French language was not made a part of his education. This is why:

On the second evening after Burwell arrived in Paris, feeling lonely without his wife and daughter, who were still visiting a friend in London, his mind naturally turned to the theater. So, after consulting the daily amusement calendar, he decided to visit the *Folies Bergère*, which he had heard of as one of the notable sights. During an intermission he went into the beautiful garden, where gay crowds were strolling among the flowers, and lights, and fountains. He had just seated himself at a little three-legged table, with a view to enjoying the novel scene, when his attention was attracted by a lovely woman, gowned strikingly, though in perfect taste, who passed near him, leaning on the arm of a gentleman. The only thing that he noticed about this gentleman was that he wore eye-glasses.

Now Burwell had never posed as a captivator of the fair sex, and could scarcely credit his eyes when the lady left the side of her escort and, turning back as if she had forgotten something, passed close by him, and deftly placed a card on his table. The card bore some French words written in purple ink, but, not knowing that language, he was unable to make out their meaning. The lady paid no further heed to him, but, rejoining the gentleman with the eye-glasses, swept out of the place with the grace and dignity of a princess. Burwell remained staring at the card.

Needless to say, he thought no more of the performance or of the other attractions about him. Everything seemed flat and tawdry compared with the radiant vision that had appeared and disappeared so mysteriously. His one desire now was to discover the meaning of the words written on the card.

Calling a fiacre, he drove to the Hôtel Continental, where he was staying. Proceeding directly to the office and taking the manager aside, Burwell asked if he would be kind enough to translate a few words of French into English. There were no more than twenty words in all.

"Why, certainly," said the manager, with French politeness, and cast his eyes over the card. As he read, his face grew rigid with astonishment, and, looking at his questioner sharply, he exclaimed: "Where did you get this, monsieur?"

Burwell started to explain, but was interrupted by: "That will do, that will do. You must leave the hotel."

"What do you mean?" asked the man from New York, in amazement.

"You must leave the hotel now—to-night—without fail," commanded the manager excitedly.

Now it was Burwell's turn to grow angry, and he declared heatedly that if he wasn't wanted in this hotel there were plenty of others in Paris where he would be welcome. And, with an assumption of dignity, but piqued at heart, he settled his bill, sent for his belongings, and drove up the Rue de la Paix to the Hôtel Bellevue, where he spent the night.

The next morning he met the proprietor, who seemed to be a good fellow, and, being inclined now to view the incident of the previous evening from its ridiculous side, Burwell explained what had befallen him, and was pleased to find a sympathetic listener.

"Why, the man was a fool," declared the proprietor. "Let me see the card; I will tell you what it means." But as he read, his face and manner changed instantly.

"This is a serious matter," he said sternly. "Now I understand why my confrère refused to entertain you. I regret, monsieur, but I shall be obliged to do as he did."

"What do you mean?"

"Simply that you cannot remain here."

With that he turned on his heel, and the indignant guest could not prevail upon him to give any explanation.

"We'll see about this," said Burwell, thoroughly angered.

It was now nearly noon, and the New Yorker remembered an engagement to lunch with a friend from Boston, who, with his family, was stopping at the Hôtel de l'Alma. With his luggage on the carriage, he ordered the *cocher* to drive directly there, determined to take counsel with his countryman before selecting new quarters. His friend was highly indignant when he heard the story—a fact that gave Burwell no little comfort, knowing, as he did, that the man was accustomed to foreign ways from long residence abroad.

"It is some silly mistake, my dear fellow; I wouldn't pay any attention to it. Just have your luggage taken down and stay here. It is a nice, homelike place, and it will be very jolly, all being together. But, first, let me prepare a little 'nerve settler' for you."

After the two had lingered a moment over their Manhattan cocktails, Burwell's friend excused himself to call the ladies. He had proceeded only two or three steps when he turned, and said: "Let's see that mysterious card that has raised all this row."

He had scarcely withdrawn it from Burwell's hand when he started back, and exclaimed:—

"Great God, man! Do you mean to say—this is simply—"

Then, with a sudden movement of his hand to his head, he left the room.

He was gone perhaps five minutes, and when he returned his face was white.

"I am awfully sorry," he said nervously; "but the ladies tell me they—that is, my wife—she has a frightful headache. You will have to excuse us from the lunch."

Instantly realizing that this was only a flimsy pretense, and deeply hurt by his friend's behavior, the mystified man arose at once and left without another word. He was now determined to solve this mystery at any cost. What could be the meaning of the words on that infernal piece of pasteboard?

Profiting by his humiliating experiences, he took good care not to show the card to any one at the hotel where he now established himself,—a comfortable little place near the Grand Opera House.

All through the afternoon he thought of nothing but the card, and turned over in his mind various ways of learning its meaning without getting himself into further trouble. That evening he went again to the *Folies Bergère* in the hope of finding the mysterious woman, for he was now more than ever anxious to discover who she was. It even occurred to him that she might be one of those beautiful Nihilist conspirators, or, perhaps, a Russian spy, such as he had read of in novels. But he failed to find her, either then or on the three subsequent evenings which he passed in the same place. Meanwhile the card was burning in his pocket like a hot coal. He dreaded the thought of meeting any one that he knew, while this horrible cloud hung over him. He bought a French-English dictionary and tried to pick out the meaning word by word, but failed. It was all Greek to him. For the first time in his life, Burwell regretted that he had not studied French at college.

After various vain attempts to either solve or forget the torturing riddle, he saw no other course than to lay the problem before a detective agency. He accordingly put his case in the hands of an *agent de la sûreté* who was recommended as a competent and trustworthy man. They had a talk together in a private room, and, of course, Burwell showed the card. To his relief, his adviser at least showed no sign of taking offense. Only he did not and would not explain what the words meant.

"It is better," he said, "that monsieur should not know the nature of this document for the present. I will do myself the honor to call upon monsieur to-morrow at his hotel, and then monsieur shall know everything."

"Then it is really serious?" asked the unfortunate man.

"Very serious," was the answer.

The next twenty-four hours Burwell passed in a fever of anxiety. As his mind conjured up one fearful possibility after another he deeply regretted that he had not torn up the miserable card at the start. He even seized it,—prepared to strip it into fragments, and so end the whole affair. And then his Yankee stubbornness again asserted itself, and he determined to see the thing out, come what might.

"After all," he reasoned, "it is no crime for a man to pick up a card that a lady drops on his table."

Crime or no crime, however, it looked very much as if he had committed some grave offense when, the next day, his detective drove up in a carriage, accompanied by a uniformed official, and requested the astounded American to accompany them to the police headquarters.

"What for?" he asked.

"It is only a formality," said the detective; and when Burwell still protested the man in uniform remarked: "You 'd better come quietly, monsieur; you will have to come, anyway."

An hour later, after severe cross-examination by another official, who demanded many facts about the New Yorker's age, place of birth, residence, occupation, etc., the bewildered man found himself in the Conciergerie prison. Why he was there or what was about to befall him Burwell had no means of knowing; but before the day was over he succeeded in having a message sent to the American Legation, where he demanded immediate protection as a citizen of the United States. It was not until evening, however, that the Secretary of Legation, a consequential person, called at the prison. There followed a stormy interview, in which the prisoner used some strong language, the French officers gesticulated violently and talked very fast, and the Secretary calmly listened to both sides, said little, and smoked a good cigar.

"I will lay your case before the American minister," he said as he rose to go, "and let you know the result to-morrow."

"But this is an outrage. Do you mean to say—" Before he could finish, however, the Secretary, with a strangely suspicious glance, turned and left the room.

That night Burwell slept in a cell.

The next morning he received another visit from the non-committal Secretary, who informed him that matters had been arranged, and that he would be set at liberty forthwith.

"I must tell you, though," he said, "that I have had great difficulty in accomplishing this, and your liberty is granted only on condition that you leave the country within twenty-four hours, and never under any conditions return."

Burwell stormed, raged, and pleaded; but it availed nothing. The Secretary was inexorable, and yet he positively refused to throw any light upon the causes of this monstrous injustice.

"Here is your card," he said, handing him a large envelope closed with the seal of Legation. "I advise you to burn it and never refer to the matter again."

That night the ill-fated man took the train for London, his heart consumed by hatred for the whole French nation, together with a burning desire for vengeance. He wired his wife to meet him at the station, and for a long time debated with himself whether he should at once tell her the sickening truth. In the end he decided that it was better to keep silent. No sooner, however, had she seen him than her woman's instinct told her that he was laboring under some mental strain. And he saw in a moment that to withhold from her his burning secret was impossible, especially when she began to talk of the trip they had planned through France. Of course no trivial reason would satisfy her for his refusal to make this trip, since they had been looking forward to it for years; and yet it was impossible now for him to set foot on French soil.

So he finally told her the whole story, she laughing and weeping in turn. To her, as to him, it seemed incredible that such overwhelming disasters could have grown out of so small a cause, and, being a fluent French scholar, she demanded a sight of the fatal piece of pasteboard. In vain her husband tried to divert her by proposing a trip through Italy. She would consent to nothing until she had seen the mysterious card which Burwell was now convinced he ought long ago to have destroyed. After refusing for awhile to let her see it, he finally yielded. But, although he had learned to dread the consequences of showing that cursed card, he was little prepared for what followed. She read it, turned pale, gasped for breath, and nearly fell to the floor.

"I told you not to read it," he said; and then, growing tender at the sight of her distress, he took her hand in his and begged her to be calm. "At least tell me what the thing means," he said. "We can bear it together; you surely can trust me."

But she, as if stung by rage, pushed him from her and declared, in a tone such as he had never heard from her before, that never, never again would she live with him. "You are a monster!" she exclaimed. And those were the last words he heard from her lips.

Failing utterly in all efforts at reconciliation, the half-crazed man took the first steamer for New York, having suffered in scarcely a fortnight more than in all his previous life. His whole pleasure trip had been ruined, he had failed to consummate important business arrangements, and now he saw his home broken up and his happiness ruined. During the voyage he scarcely left his stateroom, but lay there prostrated with agony. In this black despondency the one thing that sustained him was the thought

of meeting his partner, Jack Evelyth, the friend of his boyhood, the sharer of his success, the bravest, most loyal fellow in the world. In the face of even the most damning
circumstances, he felt that Evelyth's rugged common sense would evolve some way of
escape from this hideous nightmare. Upon landing at New York he hardly waited for
the gang-plank to be lowered before he rushed on shore and grasped the hand of his
partner, who was waiting on the wharf.

"Jack," was his first word, "I am in dreadful trouble, and you are the only man in
the world who can help me."

An hour later Burwell sat at his friend's dinner table, talking over the situation.

Evelyth was all kindness, and several times as he listened to Burwell's story his
eyes filled with tears.

"It does not seem possible, Richard," he said, "that such things can be; but I will
stand by you; we will fight it out together. But we cannot strike in the dark. Let me see
this card."

"There is the damned thing," Burwell said, throwing it on the table.

Evelyth opened the envelope, took out the card, and fixed his eyes on the sprawl-
ing purple characters.

"Can you read it?" Burwell asked excitedly.

"Perfectly," his partner said. The next moment he turned pale, and his voice
broke. Then he clasped the tortured man's hand in his with a strong grip. "Richard,"
he said slowly, "if my only child had been brought here dead it would not have caused
me more sorrow than this does. You have brought me the worst news one man could
bring another."

His agitation and genuine suffering affected Burwell like a death sentence.

"Speak, man," he cried; "do not spare me. I can bear anything rather than this
awful uncertainty. Tell me what the card means."

Evelyth took a swallow of brandy and sat with head bent on his clasped hands.

"No, I can't do it; there are some things a man must not do."

Then he was silent again, his brows knitted. Finally he said solemnly:—

"No, I can't see any other way out of it. We have been true to each other all our
lives; we have worked together and looked forward to never separating. I would rather
fail and die than see this happen. But we have got to separate, old friend; we have got
to separate."

They sat there talking until late into the night. But nothing that Burwell could do
or say availed against his friend's decision. There was nothing for it but that Evelyth
should buy his partner's share of the business or that Burwell buy out the other. The
man was more than fair in the financial proposition he made; he was generous, as he

always had been, but his determination was inflexible; the two must separate. And they did.

With his old partner's desertion, it seemed to Burwell that the world was leagued against him. It was only three weeks from the day on which he had received the mysterious card; yet in that time he had lost all that he valued in the world,—wife, friends, and business. What next to do with the fatal card was the sickening problem that now possessed him.

He dared not show it; yet he dared not destroy it. He loathed it; yet he could not let it go from his possession. Upon returning to his house he locked the accursed thing away in his safe as if it had been a package of dynamite or a bottle of deadly poison. Yet not a day passed that he did not open the drawer where the thing was kept and scan with loathing the mysterious purple scrawl.

In desperation he finally made up his mind to take up the study of the language in which the hateful thing was written. And still he dreaded the approach of the day when he should decipher its awful meaning.

One afternoon, less than a week after his arrival in New York, as he was crossing Twenty-third Street on the way to his French teacher, he saw a carriage rolling up Broadway. In the carriage was a face that caught his attention like a flash. As he looked again he recognized the woman who had been the cause of his undoing. Instantly he sprang into another cab and ordered the driver to follow after. He found the house where she was living. He called there several times; but always received the same reply, that she was too much engaged to see any one. Next he was told that she was ill, and on the following day the servant said she was much worse. Three physicians had been summoned in consultation. He sought out one of these and told him it was a matter of life or death that he see this woman. The doctor was a kindly man and promised to assist him. Through his influence, it came about that on that very night Burwell stood by the bedside of this mysterious woman. She was beautiful still, though her face was worn with illness.

"Do you recognize me?" he asked tremblingly, as he leaned over the bed, clutching in one hand an envelope containing the mysterious card. "Do you remember seeing me at the *Folies Bergère* a month ago?"

"Yes," she murmured, after a moment's study of his face; and he noted with relief that she spoke English.

"Then, for God's sake, tell me, what does it all mean?" he gasped, quivering with excitement.

"I gave you the card because I wanted you to—to—"

Here a terrible spasm of coughing shook her whole body, and she fell back exhausted.

An agonizing despair tugged at Burwell's heart. Frantically snatching the card from its envelope, he held it close to the woman's face.

"Tell me! Tell me!"

With a supreme effort, the pale figure slowly raised itself on the pillow, its fingers clutching at the counterpane.

Then the sunken eyes fluttered—forced themselves open—and stared in stony amazement upon the fatal card, while the trembling lips moved noiselessly, as if in an attempt to speak. As Burwell, choking with eagerness, bent his head slowly to hers, a suggestion of a smile flickered across the woman's face. Again the mouth quivered, the man's head bent nearer and nearer to hers, his eyes riveted upon the lips. Then, as if to aid her in deciphering the mystery, he turned his eyes to the card.

With a cry of horror he sprang to his feet, his eyeballs starting from their sockets. Almost at the same moment the woman fell heavily upon the pillow.

Every vestige of the writing had faded! The card was blank!

The woman lay there dead.

THE MYSTERIOUS CARD UNVEILED

No physician was ever more scrupulous than I have been, during my thirty years of practice, in observing the code of professional secrecy; and it is only for grave reasons, partly in the interests of medical science, largely as a warning to intelligent people, that I place upon record the following statements.

One morning a gentleman called at my offices to consult me about some nervous trouble. From the moment I saw him, the man made a deep impression on me, not so much by the pallor and worn look of his face as by a certain intense sadness in his eyes, as if all hope had gone out of his life. I wrote a prescription for him, and advised him to try the benefits of an ocean voyage. He seemed to shiver at the idea, and said that he had been abroad too much, already.

As he handed me my fee, my eye fell upon the palm of his hand, and I saw there, plainly marked on the Mount of Saturn, a cross surrounded by two circles. I should explain that for the greater part of my life I have been a constant and enthusiastic student of palmistry. During my travels in the Orient, after taking my degree, I spent months studying this fascinating art at the best sources of information in the world. I have read everything published on palmistry in every known language, and my library on the subject is perhaps the most complete in existence. In my time I have examined at least fourteen thousand palms, and taken casts of many of the more interesting of them. But I had never seen such a palm as this; at least, never but once, and the horror of the case was so great that I shudder even now when I call it to mind.

"Pardon me," I said, keeping the patient's hand in mine, "would you let me look at your palm?"

I tried to speak indifferently, as if the matter were of small consequence, and for some moments I bent over the hand in silence. Then, taking a magnifying glass from my desk, I looked at it still more closely. I was not mistaken; here was indeed the sinister double circle on Saturn's mount, with the cross inside,—a marking so rare as to portend some stupendous destiny of good or evil, more probably the latter.

I saw that the man was uneasy under my scrutiny, and, presently, with some hesitation, as if mustering courage, he asked: "Is there anything remarkable about my hand?"

"Yes," I said, "there is. Tell me, did not something very unusual, something very horrible, happen to you about ten or eleven years ago?'

I saw by the way the man started that I had struck near the mark, and, studying the stream of fine lines that crossed his lifeline from the Mount of Venus, I added: "Were you not in some foreign country at that time?"

The man's face blanched, but he only looked at me steadily out of those mournful eyes. Now I took his other hand, and compared the two, line by line, mount by mount, noting the short square fingers, the heavy thumb, with amazing willpower in its upper joint, and gazing again and again at that ominous sign on Saturn.

"Your life has been strangely unhappy, your years have been clouded by some evil influence."

"My God," he said weakly, sinking into a chair, "how can you know these things?"

"It is easy to know what one sees," I said, and tried to draw him out about his past, but the words seemed to stick in his throat.

"I will come back and talk to you again," he said, and he went away without giving me his name or any revelation of his life.

Several times he called during subsequent weeks, and gradually seemed to take on a measure of confidence in my presence. He would talk freely of his physical condition, which seemed to cause him much anxiety. He even insisted upon my making the most careful examination of all his organs, especially of his eyes, which, he said, had troubled him at various times. Upon making the usual tests, I found that he was suffering from a most uncommon form of color blindness, that seemed to vary in its manifestations, and to be connected with certain hallucinations or abnormal mental states which recurred periodically, and about which I had great difficulty in persuading him to speak. At each visit I took occasion to study his hand anew, and each reading of the palm gave me stronger conviction that here was a life mystery that would abundantly repay any pains taken in unraveling it.

While I was in this state of mind, consumed with a desire to know more of my unhappy acquaintance and yet not daring to press him with questions, there came a tragic happening that revealed to me with startling suddenness the secret I was bent on knowing. One night, very late,—in fact it was about four o'clock in the morning,—I received an urgent summons to the bedside of a man who had been shot. As I bent over him I saw that it was my friend, and for the first time I realized that he was a man of wealth and position, for he lived in a beautifully furnished house filled with art treasures and looked after by a retinue of servants. From one of these I learned that he was Richard Burwell, one of New York's most respected citizens—in fact, one of her best-known philanthropists, a man who for years had devoted his life and fortune to good works among the poor.

But what most excited my surprise was the presence in the house of two officers, who informed me that Mr. Burwell was under arrest, charged with murder. The officers assured me that it was only out of deference to his well-known standing in the community that the prisoner had been allowed the privilege of receiving medical treatment in his own home; their orders were peremptory to keep him under close surveillance.

Giving no time to further questionings, I at once proceeded to examine the injured man, and found that he was suffering from a bullet wound in the back at about the height of the fifth rib. On probing for the bullet, I found that it had lodged near the heart, and decided that it would be exceedingly dangerous to try to remove it immediately. So I contented myself with administering a sleeping potion.

As soon as I was free to leave Burwell's bedside I returned to the officers and obtained from them details of what had happened. A woman's body had been found a few hours before, shockingly mutilated, on Water Street, one of the dark ways in the swarming region along the river front. It had been found at about two o'clock in the morning by some printers from the office of the *Courier des Etats Unis*, who, in coming from their work, had heard cries of distress and hurried to the rescue. As they drew near they saw a man spring away from something huddled on the sidewalk, and plunge into the shadows of the night, running from them at full speed.

Suspecting at once that here was the mysterious assassin so long vainly sought for many similar crimes, they dashed after the fleeing man, who darted right and left through the maze of dark streets, giving out little cries like a squirrel as he ran. Seeing that they were losing ground, one of the printers fired at the fleeing shadow, his shot being followed by a scream of pain, and hurrying up they found a man writhing on the ground. The man was Richard Burwell.

The news that my sad-faced friend had been implicated in such a revolting occurrence shocked me inexpressibly, and I was greatly relieved the next day to learn from the papers that a most unfortunate mistake had been made. The evidence given before the coroner's jury was such as to abundantly exonerate Burwell from all shadow of guilt. The man's own testimony, taken at his bedside, was in itself almost conclusive in his favor. When asked to explain his presence so late at night in such a part of the city, Burwell stated that he had spent the evening at the Florence Mission, where he had made an address to some unfortunates gathered there, and that later he had gone with a young missionary worker to visit a woman living on Frankfort Street, who was dying of consumption. This statement was borne out by the missionary worker himself, who testified that Burwell had been most tender in his ministrations to the poor woman and had not left her until death had relieved her sufferings.

Another point which made it plain that the printers had mistaken their man in the darkness, was the statement made by all of them that, as they came running up, they had overheard some words spoken by the murderer, and that these words were in their own language, French. Now it was shown conclusively that Burwell did not know the French language, that indeed he had not even an elementary knowledge of it.

Another point in his favor was a discovery made at the spot where the body was found. Some profane and ribald words, also in French, had been scrawled in chalk on the door and doorsill, being in the nature of a coarse defiance to the police to find the assassin, and experts in handwriting who were called testified unanimously that Burwell, who wrote a refined, scholarly hand, could never have formed those misshapen words.

Furthermore, at the time of his arrest no evidence was found on the clothes or person of Burwell, nothing in the nature of bruises or bloodstains that would tend to implicate him in the crime. The outcome of the matter was that he was honorably discharged by the coroner's jury, who were unanimous in declaring him innocent, and who brought in a verdict that the unfortunate woman had come to her death at the hand of some person or persons unknown.

On visiting my patient late on the afternoon of the second day I saw that his case was very grave, and I at once instructed the nurses and attendants to prepare for an operation. The man's life depended upon my being able to extract the bullet, and the chance of doing this was very small. Mr. Burwell realized that his condition was critical, and, beckoning me to him, told me that he wished to make a statement he felt might be his last. He spoke with agitation which was increased by an unforeseen happening. For just then a servant entered the room and whispered to me that there was a gentleman downstairs who insisted upon seeing me, and who urged business of great importance. This message the sick man overheard, and lifting himself with an effort, he said excitedly: "Tell me, is he a tall man with glasses?"

The servant hesitated.

"I knew it; you cannot deceive me; that man will haunt me to my grave. Send him away, doctor; I beg of you not to see him."

Humoring my patient, I sent word to the stranger that I could not see him, but, in an undertone, instructed the servant to say that the man might call at my office the next morning. Then, turning to Burwell, I begged him to compose himself and save his strength for the ordeal awaiting him.

"No, no," he said, "I need my strength now to tell you what you must know to find the truth. You are the only man who has understood that there has been some terrible influence at work in my life. You are the only man competent to study out what that influence is, and I have made provision in my will that you shall do so after I am gone. I know that you will heed my wishes?"

The intense sadness of his eyes made my heart sink; I could only grip his hand and remain silent.

"Thank you; I was sure I might count on your devotion. Now, tell me, doctor, you have examined me carefully, have you not?"

I nodded.

"In every way known to medical science?"

I nodded again.

"And have you found anything wrong with me,—I mean, besides this bullet, anything abnormal?"

"As I have told you, your eyesight is defective; I should like to examine your eyes more thoroughly when you are better."

"I shall never be better; besides it isn't my eyes; I mean myself, my soul,—you haven't found anything wrong there?"

"Certainly not; the whole city knows the beauty of your character and your life."

"Tut, tut; the city knows nothing. For ten years I have lived so much with the poor that people have almost forgotten my previous active life when I was busy with moneymaking and happy in my home. But there is a man out West, whose head is white and whose heart is heavy, who has not forgotten, and there is a woman in London, a silent, lonely woman, who has not forgotten. The man was my partner, poor Jack Evelyth; the woman was my wife. How can a man be so cursed, doctor, that his love and friendship bring only misery to those who share it? How can it be that one who has in his heart only good thoughts can be constantly under the shadow of evil? This charge of murder is only one of several cases in my life where, through no fault of mine, the shadow of guilt has been cast upon me.

"Years ago, when my wife and I were perfectly happy, a child was born to us, and a few months later, when it was only a tender, helpless little thing that its mother loved with all her heart, it was strangled in its cradle, and we never knew who strangled it, for the deed was done one night when there was absolutely no one in the house but my wife and myself. There was no doubt about the crime, for there on the tiny neck were the finger marks where some cruel hand had closed until life went.

"Then a few years later, when my partner and I were on the eve of fortune, our advance was set back by the robbery of our safe. Some one opened it in the night, some one who knew the combination, for it was the work of no burglar, and yet there were only two persons in the world who knew that combination, my partner and myself. I tried to be brave when these things happened, but as my life went on it seemed more and more as if some curse were on me.

"Eleven years ago I went abroad with my wife and daughter. Business took me to Paris, and I left the ladies in London, expecting to have them join me in a few days. But they never did join me, for the curse was on me still, and before I had been forty-eight hours in the French capital something happened that completed the wreck of my life. It doesn't seem possible, does it, that a simple white card with some words scrawled on it in purple ink could effect a man's undoing? And yet that was my fate. The card was given me by a beautiful woman with eyes like stars. She is dead long ago, and why she wished to harm me I never knew. You must find that out.

"You see I did not know the language of the country, and, wishing to have the words translated,—surely that was natural enough,—I showed the card to others. But no one would tell me what it meant. And, worse than that, wherever I showed it, and to whatever person, there evil came upon me quickly. I was driven from one hotel after another; an old acquaintance turned his back on me; I was arrested and thrown into prison; I was ordered to leave the country."

The sick man paused for a moment in his weakness, but with an effort forced himself to continue:—

"When I went back to London, sure of comfort in the love of my wife, she too, on seeing the card, drove me from her with cruel words. And when finally, in deepest despair, I returned to New York, dear old Jack, the friend of a lifetime, broke with me when I showed him what was written. What the words were I do not know, and suppose no one will ever know, for the ink has faded these many years. You will find the card in my safe with other papers. But I want you, when I am gone, to find out the mystery of my life; and—and—about my fortune, that must be held until you have decided. There is no one who needs my money as much as the poor in this city, and I have bequeathed it to them unless—"

In an agony of mind, Mr. Burwell struggled to go on, I soothing and encouraging him.

"Unless you find what I am afraid to think, but—but—yes, I must say it,—that I have not been a good man, as the world thinks, but have—O doctor, if you find that I have unknowingly harmed any human being, I want that person, or these persons to have my fortune. Promise that."

Seeing the wild light in Burwell's eyes, and the fever that was burning him, I gave the promise asked of me, and the sick man sank back calmer.

A little later, the nurse and attendants came for the operation. As they were about to administer the ether, Burwell pushed them from him, and insisted on having brought to his bedside an iron box from the safe.

"The card is here," he said, laying his trembling hand upon the box, "you will remember your promise!"

Those were his last words, for he did not survive the operation.

Early the next morning I received this message: "The stranger of yesterday begs to see you"; and presently a gentleman of fine presence and strength of face, a tall, dark-complexioned man wearing glasses, was shown into the room.

"Mr. Burwell is dead, is he not?" were his first words.

"Who told you?"

"No one told me, but I know it, and I thank God for it."

There was something in the stranger's intense earnestness that convinced me of his right to speak thus, and I listened attentively.

"That you may have confidence in the statement I am about to make, I will first tell you who I am"; and he handed me a card that caused me to lift my eyes in wonder, for it bore a very great name, that of one of Europe's most famous savants.

"You have done me much honor, sir," I said with respectful inclination.

"On the contrary you will oblige me by considering me in your debt, and by never revealing my connection with this wretched man. I am moved to speak partly from considerations of human justice, largely in the interest of medical science. It is right for me to tell you, doctor, that your patient was beyond question the Water Street assassin."

"Impossible!" I cried.

"You will not say so when I have finished my story, which takes me back to Paris, to the time, eleven years ago, when this man was making his first visit to the French capital."

"The mysterious card!" I exclaimed.

"Ah, he has told you of his experience, but not of what befell the night before, when he first met my sister."

"Your sister?"

"Yes, it was she who gave him the card, and, in trying to befriend him, made him suffer. She was in ill health at the time, so much so that we had left our native India for extended journeyings. Alas! we delayed too long, for my sister died in New York, only a few weeks later, and I honestly believe her taking off was hastened by anxiety inspired by this man."

"Strange," I murmured, "how the life of a simple New York merchant could become entangled with that of a great lady of the East."

"Yet so it was. You must know that my sister's condition was due mainly to an over fondness for certain occult investigations, from which I had vainly tried to dissuade her. She had once befriended some adepts, who, in return, had taught her things about the souls he had better have left unlearned. At various times while with her I had seen strange things happen, but I never realized what unearthly powers were in her until that night in Paris. We were returning from a drive in the Bois; it was about ten o'clock, and the city lay beautiful around us as Paris looks on a perfect summer's night. Suddenly my sister gave a cry of pain and put her hand to her heart. Then, changing from French to the language of our country, she explained to me quickly that something frightful was taking place there, where she pointed her finger across the river, that we must go to the place at once—the driver must lash his horses—every second was precious.

"So affected was I by her intense conviction, and such confidence had I in my sister's wisdom, that I did not oppose her, but told the man to drive as she directed. The carriage fairly flew across the bridge, down the Boulevard St. Germain, then to the left, threading its way through the narrow streets that lie along the Seine. This way and that, straight ahead here, a turn there, she directing our course, never hesitating, as if drawn by some unseen power, and always urging the driver on to greater speed. Finally, we came to a black-mouthed, evil-looking alley, so narrow and roughly paved that the carriage could scarcely advance.

"'Come on!' my sister cried, springing to the ground; 'we will go on foot, we are nearly there. Thank God, we may yet be in time.'

"No one was in sight as we hurried along the dark alley, and scarcely a light was visible, but presently a smothered scream broke the silence, and, touching my arm, my sister exclaimed:—

"'There, draw your weapon, quick, and take the man at any cost!'

"So swiftly did everything happen after that that I hardly know my actions, but a few minutes later I held pinioned in my arms a man whose blows and writhings had been all in vain; for you must know that much exercise in the jungle had made me strong of limb. As soon as I had made the fellow fast I looked down and found moaning on the ground a poor woman, who explained with tears and broken words that the man had been in the very act of strangling her. Searching him I found a long-bladed knife of curious shape, and keen as a razor, which had been brought for what horrible purpose you may perhaps divine.

"Imagine my surprise, on dragging the man back to the carriage, to find, instead of the ruffianly assassin I expected, a gentleman as far as could be judged from face and manner. Fine eyes, white hands, careful speech, all the signs of refinement, and the dress of a man of means.

"'How can this be?' I said to my sister in our own tongue as we drove away, I holding my prisoner on the opposite seat where he sat silent.

"'It is a *kulos-man*,' she said, shivering, 'it is a fiend-soul. There are a few such in the whole world, perhaps two or three in all.'

"'But he has a good face.'

"'You have not seen his real face yet; I will show it to you, presently.'

"In the strangeness of these happenings and the still greater strangeness of my sister's words, I had all but lost the power of wonder. So we sat without further word until the carriage stopped at the little chateau we had taken near the Pare Monteau.

"I could never properly describe what happened that night; my knowledge of these things is too limited. I simply obeyed my sister in all that she directed, and kept my eyes on this man as no hawk ever watched its prey. She began by questioning him, speaking in a kindly tone which I could ill understand. He seemed embarrassed, dazed, and professed to have no knowledge of what had occurred, or how he had come where we found him. To all my inquiries as to the woman or the crime he shook his head blankly, and thus aroused my wrath.

"'Be not angry with him, brother; he is not lying, it is the other soul.'

"She asked him about his name and country, and he replied without hesitation that he was Richard Burwell, a merchant from New York, just arrived in Paris, traveling for pleasure in Europe with his wife and daughter. This seemed reasonable, for the man spoke English, and, strangely enough, seemed to have no knowledge of French, although we both remembered hearing him speak French to the woman.

"'There is no doubt,' my sister said, 'It is indeed a *kulos*-man; It knows that I am here, that I am Its master. Look, look!' she cried sharply, at the same time putting her eyes so close to the man's face that their fierce light seemed to burn into him. What power she exercised I do not know, nor whether some words she spoke, unintelligible to me, had to do with what followed, but instantly there came over this man, this pleasant-looking, respectable American citizen, such a change as is not made by death worms gnawing in a grave. Now there was a fiend groveling at her feet, a foul, sin-stained fiend.

"'Now you see the demon-soul,' said my sister. 'Watch It writhe and struggle; it has served me well, brother, sayest thou not so, the lore I gained from our wise men?'

"The horror of what followed chilled my blood; nor would I trust my memory were it not that there remained and still remains plain proof of all that I affirm. This hideous creature, dwarfed, crouching, devoid of all resemblance to the man we had but now beheld, chattering to us in curious old-time French, poured out such horrid blasphemy as would have blanched the cheek of Satan, and made recital of such evil deeds as never mortal ear gave heed to. And as she willed my sister checked It or allowed It to go on. What it all meant was more than I could tell. To me it seemed as if these tales of wickedness had no connection with our modern life, or with the world around us, and so I judged presently from what my sister said.

"'Speak of the later time, since thou wast in this clay.'

"Then I perceived that the creature came to things of which I knew: It spoke of New York, of a wife, a child, a friend. It told of strangling the child, of robbing the friend; and was going on to tell God knows what other horrid deeds when my sister stopped It.

"'Stand as thou didst in killing the little babe, stand, stand!' and once more she spoke some words unknown to me. Instantly the demon sprang forward, and, bending Its clawlike hands, clutched them around some little throat that was not there,—but I could see it in my mind. And the look on its face was a blackest glimpse of hell.

"'And now stand as thou didst in robbing the friend, stand, stand'; and again came the unknown words, and again the fiend obeyed.

"'These we will take for future use,' said my sister. And bidding me watch the creature carefully until she should return, she left the room, and, after none too short an absence, returned bearing a black box that was an apparatus for photography, and something more besides,—some newer, stranger kind of photography that she had learned. Then, on a strangely fashioned card, a transparent white card, composed of many layers of finest Oriental paper, she took the pictures of the creature in those two creeping poses. And when it all was done, the card seemed as white as before, and empty of all meaning until one held it up and examined it intently. Then the pictures showed. And between the two there was a third picture, which somehow seemed to show, at the same time, two faces in one, two souls, my sister said, the kindly visaged man we first had seen, and then the fiend.

"Now my sister asked for pen and ink and I gave her my pocket pen which was filled with purple ink. Handing this to the *kulos*-man she bade him write under the first picture: 'Thus I killed my babe.' And under the second picture: 'Thus I robbed my friend.' And under the third, the one that was between the other two: 'This is the soul of Richard Burwell.' An odd thing about this writing was that it was in the same old French the creature had used in speech, and yet Burwell knew no French.

"My sister was about to finish with the creature when a new idea took her, and she said, looking at It as before:—'Of all thy crimes which one is the worst? Speak, I command thee!'

"Then the fiend told how once It had killed every soul in a house of holy women and buried the bodies in a cellar under a heavy door.

" 'Where was the house?'

" 'At No. 19 Rue Picpus, next to the old graveyard.'

" 'And when was this?'

"Here the fiend seemed to break into fierce rebellion, writhing on the floor with hideous contortions, and pouring forth words that meant nothing to me, but seemed to reach my sister's understanding, for she interrupted from time to time, with quick, stern words that finally brought it to subjection.

" 'Enough,' she said, 'I know all,' and then she spoke some words again, her eyes fixed as before, and the reverse change came. Before us stood once more the honest-looking, fine-appearing gentleman, Richard Burwell, of New York.

" 'Excuse me, madame,' he said, awkwardly, but with deference; 'I must have dosed a little. I am not myself to-night.'

" 'No,' said my sister, 'you have not been yourself to-night.'

"A little later I accompanied the man to the Continental Hotel, where he was stopping, and, returning to my sister, I talked with her until late into the night. I was alarmed to see that she was wrought to a nervous tension that augured ill for her health. I urged her to sleep, but she would not.

" 'No,' she said, 'think of the awful responsibility that rests upon me.' And then she went on with her strange theories and explanations, of which I understood only that here was a power for evil more terrible than a pestilence, menacing all humanity.

"Once in many cycles it happens,' she said, 'that a *kulos-soul* pushes itself within the body of a new-born child, when the pure soul waiting to enter is delayed. Then the two live together through that life, and this hideous principle of evil has a chance upon the earth. It is my will, as I feel it my duty, to see this poor man again. The chances are that he will never know us, for the shock of this night to his normal soul is so great as to wipe out memory.'

"The next evening, about the same hour, my sister insisted that I should go with her to the *Folies Bergère*, a concert garden, none too well frequented, and when I remonstrated, she said: 'I must go,—It is there,' and the words sent a shiver through me.

"We drove to this place, and passing into the garden, presently discovered Richard Burwell seated at a little table, enjoying the scene of pleasure, which was plainly new to him. My sister hesitated a moment what to do, and then, leaving my arm, she advanced to the table and dropped before Burwell's eyes the card she had prepared. A moment later, with a look of pity on her beautiful face, she rejoined me and we went away. It was plain he did not know us."

To so much of the savant's strange recital I had listened with absorbed interest, though without a word, but now I burst in with questions.

"What was your sister's idea in giving Burwell the card?" I asked.

"It was in the hope that she might make the man understand his terrible condition, that is, teach the pure soul to know its loathsome companion."

"And did her effort succeed?"

"Alas! it did not; my sister's purpose was defeated by the man's inability to see the pictures that were plain to every other eye. It is impossible for the *kulos-man* to know his own degradation."

"And yet this man has for years been leading a most exemplary life?"

My visitor shook his head. "I grant you there has been improvement, due largely to experiments I have conducted upon him according to my sister's wishes. But the fiend soul was never driven out. It grieves me to tell you, doctor, that not only was this man the Water Street assassin, but he was the mysterious murderer, the long-sought-for mutilator of women, whose red crimes have baffled the police of Europe and America for the past ten years."

"You know this," said I, starting up, "and yet did not denounce him?"

"It would have been impossible to prove such a charge, and besides, I had made oath to my sister that I would use the man only for these soul-experiments. What are his crimes compared with the great secret of knowledge I am now able to give the world?"

"A secret of knowledge?"

"Yes," said the savant, with intense earnestness, "I may tell you now, doctor, what the whole world will know, ere long, that it is possible to compel every living person to reveal the innermost secrets of his or her life, so long as memory remains, for memory is only the power of producing in the brain material pictures that may be projected externally by the thought rays and made to impress themselves upon the photographic plate, precisely as ordinary pictures do."

"You mean," I exclaimed, "that you can photograph the two principles of good and evil that exist in us?"

"Exactly that. The great truth of a dual soul existence, that was dimly apprehended by one of your Western novelists, has been demonstrated by me in the laboratory with my camera. It is my purpose, at the proper time, to entrust this precious knowledge to a chosen few who will perpetuate it and use it worthily."

"Wonderful, wonderful!" I cried, "and now tell me, if you will, about the house on the Rue Picpus. Did you ever visit the place?"

"We did, and found that no buildings had stood there for fifty years, so we did not pursue the search."*

"And the writing on the card, have you any memory of it, for Burwell told me that the words have faded?"

"I have something better than that; I have a photograph of both card and writing, which my sister was careful to take. I had a notion that the ink in my pocket pen would fade, for it was a poor affair. This photograph I will bring you to-morrow."

"Bring it to Burwell's house," I said.

The next morning the stranger called as agreed upon.

"Here is the photograph of the card," he said.

"And here is the original card," I answered, breaking the seal of the envelope I had taken from Burwell's iron box. "I have waited for your arrival to look at it. Yes, the writing has indeed vanished; the card seems quite blank."

"Not when you hold it this way," said the stranger, and as he tipped the card I saw such a horrid revelation as I can never forget. In an instant I realized how the shock of seeing that card had been too great for the soul of wife or friend to bear. In these pictures was the secret of a cursed life. The resemblance to Burwell was unmistakable, the proof against him was overwhelming. In looking upon that piece of pasteboard the wife had seen a crime which the mother could never forgive, the partner had seen

---

* Years later, some workmen in Paris, making excavations in the Rue Picpus, came upon a heavy door buried under a mass of debris, under an old cemetery. On lifting the door they found a vaultlike chamber in which were a number of female skeletons, and graven on the walls were blasphemous words written in French, which experts declared dated from fully two hundred years before. They also declared this handwriting identical with that found on the door at the Water Street murder in New York. Thus we may deduce a theory of fiend reincarnation; for it would seem clear, almost to the point of demonstration, that this murder of the seventeenth century was the work of the same evil soul that killed the poor woman on Water Street towards the end of the nineteenth century.

a crime which the friend could never forgive. Think of a loved face suddenly melting before your eyes into a grinning skull, then into a mass of putrefaction, then into the ugliest fiend of hell, leering at you, distorted with all the marks of vice and shame. That is what I saw, that is what they had seen!

"Let us lay these two cards in the coffin," said my companion impressively, "we have done what we could."

Eager to be rid of the hateful piece of pasteboard (for who could say that the curse was not still clinging about it?), I took the strange man's arm, and together we advanced into the adjoining room where the body lay. I had seen Burwell as he breathed his last, and knew that there had been a peaceful look on his face as he died. But now, as we laid the two white cards on the still breast, the savant suddenly touched my arm, and pointing to the dead man's face, now frightfully distorted, whispered:— "See, even in death It followed him. Let us close the coffin quickly."

THE HOUND OF
THE BASKERVILLES

Arthur Conan Doyle

I. MR. SHERLOCK HOLMES

Mr. Sherlock Holmes, who was usually very late in the mornings, save upon those not infrequent occasions when he stayed up all night, was seated at the break-fast table. I stood upon the hearth-rug and picked up the stick which our visitor had left behind him the night before. It was a fine, thick piece of wood, bulbous-headed, of the sort which is known as a "Penang lawyer." Just under the head was a broad silver band, nearly an inch across. "To James Mortimer, MRCS, from his friends of the CCH," was engraved upon it, with the date "1884." It was just such a stick as the old-fashioned family practitioner used to carry—dignified, solid, and reassuring.

"Well, Watson, what do you make of it?"

Holmes was sitting with his back to me, and I had given him no sign of my occupation.

"How did you know what I was doing? I believe you have eyes in the back of your head."

"I have, at least, a well-polished, silver-plated coffee-pot in front of me," said he. "But, tell me, Watson, what do you make of our visitor's stick? Since we have been so unfortunate as to miss him and have no notion of his errand, this accidental souvenir becomes of importance. Let me hear you reconstruct the man by an examination of it."

"I think," said I, following so far as I could the methods of my companion, "that Dr. Mortimer is a successful elderly medical man, well-esteemed, since those who know him give him this mark of their appreciation."

"Good!" said Holmes. "Excellent!"

"I think also that the probability is in favour of his being a country practitioner who does a great deal of his visiting on foot."

"Why so?"

"Because this stick, though originally a very handsome one, has been so knocked about that I can hardly imagine a town practitioner carrying it. The thick iron ferrule is worn down, so it is evident that he has done a great amount of walking with it."

"Perfectly sound!" said Holmes.

"And then again, there is the 'friends of the CCH.' I should guess that to be the Something Hunt, the local hunt to whose members he has possibly given some surgical assistance, and which has made him a small presentation in return."

"Really, Watson, you excel yourself," said Holmes, pushing back his chair and lighting a cigarette. "I am bound to say that in all the accounts which you have been so good as to give of my own small achievements you have habitually underrated your own abilities. It may be that you are not yourself luminous, but you are a conductor of light. Some people without possessing genius have a remarkable power of stimulating it. I confess, my dear fellow, that I am very much in your debt."

He had never said as much before, and I must admit that his words gave me keen pleasure, for I had often been piqued by his indifference to my admiration and to the attempts which I had made to give publicity to his methods. I was proud, too, to think that I had so far mastered his system as to apply it in a way which earned his approval. He now took the stick from my hands and examined it for a few minutes with his naked eyes. Then, with an expression of interest, he laid down his cigarette, and, carrying the cane to the window, he looked over it again with a convex lens.

"Interesting, though elementary," said he, as he returned to his favourite corner of the settee. "There are certainly one or two indications upon the stick. It gives us the basis for several deductions."

"Has anything escaped me?" I asked, with some self-importance. "I trust that there is nothing of consequence which I have overlooked?"

"I am afraid, my dear Watson, that most of your conclusions were erroneous. When I said that you stimulated me I meant, to be frank, that in noting your fallacies I was occasionally guided towards the truth. Not that you are entirely wrong in this instance. The man is certainly a country practitioner. And he walks a good deal."

"Then I was right."

"To that extent."

"But that was all."

"No, no, my dear Watson, not all—by no means all. I would suggest, for example, that a presentation to a doctor is more likely to come from a hospital than from a hunt, and that when the initials 'CC' are placed before that hospital the words 'Charing Cross' very naturally suggest themselves."

"You may be right."

"The probability lies in that direction. And if we take this as a working hypothesis we have a fresh basis from which to start our construction of this unknown visitor."

"Well, then, supposing that 'CCH' does stand for 'Charing Cross Hospital,' what further inferences may we draw?"

"Do none suggest themselves? You know my methods. Apply them!"

"I can only think of the obvious conclusion that the man has practised in town before going to the country."

"I think that we might venture a little farther than this. Look at it in this light. On what occasion would it be most probable that such a presentation would be made? When would his friends unite to give him a pledge of their good will? Obviously at the moment when Dr. Mortimer withdrew from the service of the hospital in order to start in practice for himself. We know there has been a presentation. We believe there has been a change from a town hospital to a country practice. Is it, then, stretching our inference too far to say that the presentation was on the occasion of the change?"

"It certainly seems probable."

"Now, you will observe that he could not have been on the *staff* of the hospital, since only a man well-established in a London practice could hold such a position, and such a one would not drift into the country. What was he, then? If he was in the hospital and yet not on the staff, he could only have been a house-surgeon or a house-physician—little more than a senior student. And he left five years ago—the date is on the stick. So your grave, middle-aged family practitioner vanishes into thin air, my dear Watson, and there emerges a young fellow under thirty, amiable, unambitious, absent-minded, and the possessor of a favourite dog, which I should describe roughly as being larger than a terrier and smaller than a mastiff."

I laughed incredulously as Sherlock Holmes leaned back in his settee and blew little wavering rings of smoke up to the ceiling.

"As to the latter part, I have no means of checking you," said I, "but at least it is not difficult to find out a few particulars about the man's age and professional career."

From my small medical shelf I took down the Medical Directory and turned up the name. There were several Mortimers, but only one who could be our visitor. I read his record aloud.

"Mortimer, James, MRCS, 1882, Grimpen, Dartmoor, Devon, House-surgeon, from 1882 to 1884, at Charing Cross Hospital. Winner of the Jackson Prize for Comparative Pathology, with essay entitled 'Is Disease a Reversion?' Corresponding member of the Swedish Pathological Society. Author of 'Some Freaks of Atavism' (*Lancet*, 1882), 'Do We Progress?' (*Journal of Psychology*, March, 1883). Medical Officer for the parishes of Grimpen, Thorsley, and High Barrow."

"No mention of that local hunt, Watson," said Holmes, with a mischievous smile, "but a country doctor, as you very astutely observed. I think that I am fairly justified in my inferences. As to the adjectives, I said, if I remember right, amiable, unambitious, and absent-minded. It is my experience that it is only an amiable man in this world who receives testimonials, only an unambitious one who abandons a London career for the country, and only an absent-minded one who leaves his stick and not his visiting-card after waiting an hour in your room."

"And the dog?"

"Has been in the habit of carrying this stick behind his master. Being a heavy stick the dog has held it tightly by the middle, and the marks of his teeth are very plainly visible. The dog's jaw, as shown in the space between these marks, is too broad in my opinion for a terrier and not broad enough for a mastiff. It may have been—yes, by Jove, it *is* a curly-haired spaniel."

He had risen and paced the room as he spoke. Now he halted in the recess of the window. There was such a ring of conviction in his voice that I glanced up in surprise.

"My dear fellow, how can you possibly be so sure of that?"

"For the very simple reason that I see the dog himself on our very doorstep, and there is the ring of its owner. Don't move, I beg you, Watson. He is a professional brother of yours, and your presence may be of assistance to me. Now is the dramatic moment of fate, Watson, when you hear a step upon the stair which is walking into your life, and you know not whether for good or ill. What does Dr. James Mortimer, the man of science, ask of Sherlock Holmes, the specialist in crime? Come in!"

The appearance of our visitor was a surprise to me since I had expected a typical country practitioner. He was a very tall, thin man, with a long nose like a beak, which shot out between two keen, grey eyes, set closely together and sparkling brightly from behind a pair of gold-rimmed glasses. He was clad in a professional but rather slovenly fashion, for his frock-coat was dingy and his trousers frayed. Though young, his long back was already bowed, and he walked with a forward thrust of his head and a general air of peering benevolence. As he entered his eyes fell upon the stick in Holmes's hand, and he ran towards it with an exclamation of joy.

"I am so very glad," said he. "I was not sure whether I had left it here or in the Shipping Office. I would not lose that stick for the world."

"A presentation, I see," said Holmes.

"Yes, sir."

"From Charing Cross Hospital?"

"From one or two friends there on the occasion of my marriage."

"Dear, dear, that's bad!" said Holmes, shaking his head.

Dr. Mortimer blinked through his glasses in mild astonishment.

"Why was it bad?"

"Only that you have disarranged our little deductions. Your marriage, you say?"

"Yes, sir. I married, and so left the hospital, and with it all hopes of a consulting practice. It was necessary to make a home of my own."

"Come, come, we are not so far wrong after all," said Holmes. "And now, Dr. James Mortimer—"

"Mister, sir, Mister—a humble MRCS."

"And a man of precise mind, evidently."

"A dabbler in science, Mr. Holmes, a picker up of shells on the shores of the great unknown ocean. I presume that it is Mr. Sherlock Holmes whom I am addressing and not—"

"No, this is my friend Dr. Watson."

"Glad to meet you, sir. I have heard your name mentioned in connection with that of your friend. You interest me very much, Mr. Holmes. I had hardly expected so dolichocephalic a skull or such well-marked supra-orbital development. Would you have any objection to my running my finger along your parietal fissure? A cast of your skull, sir, until the original is available, would be an ornament to any anthropological museum. It is not my intention to be fulsome, but I confess that I covet your skull."

Sherlock Holmes waved our strange visitor into a chair.

"You are an enthusiast in your line of thought, I perceive, sir, as I am in mine," said he. "I observe from your forefinger that you make your own cigarettes. Have no hesitation in lighting one."

The man drew out paper and tobacco and twirled the one up in the other with surprising dexterity. He had long, quivering fingers as agile and restless as the antennae of an insect.

Holmes was silent, but his little darting glances showed me the interest which he took in our curious companion.

"I presume, sir," said he at last, "that it was not merely for the purpose of examining my skull that you have done me the honour to call here last night and again to-day?"

"No, sir, no; though I am happy to have had the opportunity of doing that as well. I came to you, Mr. Holmes, because I recognised that I am myself an unpractical man, and because I am suddenly confronted with a most serious and extraordinary problem. Recognizing, as I do, that you are the second highest expert in Europe—"

"Indeed, sir! May I inquire who has the honour to be the first?" asked Holmes, with some asperity.

"To the man of precisely scientific mind the work of Monsieur Bertillon must always appeal strongly."

"Then had you not better consult him?"

"I said, sir, to the precisely scientific mind. But as a practical man of affairs it is acknowledged that you stand alone. I trust, sir, that I have not inadvertently—"

"Just a little," said Holmes. "I think, Dr. Mortimer, you would do wisely if without more ado you would kindly tell me plainly what the exact nature of the problem is in which you demand my assistance."

II. The Curse of the Baskervilles

"I have in my pocket a manuscript," said Dr. James Mortimer.

"I observed it as you entered the room," said Holmes.

"It is an old manuscript."

"Early eighteenth century, unless it is a forgery."

"How can you say that, sir?"

"You have presented an inch or two of it to my examination all the time that you have been talking. It would be a poor expert who could not give the date of a document within a decade or so. You may possibly have read my little monograph upon the subject. I put that at 1730."

"The exact date is 1742." Dr. Mortimer drew it from his breast-pocket. "This family paper was committed to my care by Sir Charles Baskerville, whose sudden and tragic death some three months ago created so much excitement in Devonshire. I may say that I was his personal friend as well as his medical attendant. He was a strong-minded man, sir, shrewd, practical, and as unimaginative as I am myself. Yet he took this document very seriously, and his mind was prepared for just such an end as did eventually overtake him."

Holmes stretched out his hand for the manuscript and flattened it upon his knee.

"You will observe, Watson, the alternative use of the long *s* and the short. It is one of several indications which enabled me to fix the date."

I looked over his shoulder at the yellow paper and the faded script. At the head was written: "Baskerville Hall," and below, in large, scrawling figures: "1742."

"It appears to be a statement of some sort."

"Yes, it is a statement of a certain legend which runs in the Baskerville family."

"But I understand that it is something more modern and practical upon which you wish to consult me?"

"Most modern. A most practical, pressing matter, which must be decided within twenty-four hours. But the manuscript is short and is intimately connected with the affair. With your permission I will read it to you."

Holmes leaned back in his chair, placed his finger-tips together, and closed his eyes, with an air of resignation. Dr. Mortimer turned the manuscript to the light, and read in a high, crackling voice the following curious, old-world narrative.

"Of the origin of the Hound of the Baskervilles there have been many state-ments, yet as I come in a direct line from Hugo Baskerville, and as I had the story from my father, who also had it from his, I have set it down with all belief that it occurred even as is here set forth. And I would have you believe, my sons, that the same Justice which punishes sin may also most graciously forgive it, and that no ban is so heavy but that by prayer and repentance it may be removed. Learn then from this story not to fear the fruits of the past, but rather to be circumspect in the future, that those foul passions whereby our family has suffered so grievously may not again be loosed to our undoing.

"Know then that in the time of the Great Rebellion (the history of which by the learned Lord Clarendon I most earnestly commend to your attention) this Manor of Baskerville was held by Hugo of that name, nor can it be gain-said that he was a most wild, profane, and godless man. This, in truth, his neighbours might have pardoned, seeing that saints have never flourished in those parts, but there was in him a certain wanton and cruel humour which made his name a by-word through the West. It chanced that this Hugo came to love (if, indeed, so dark a passion may be known under so bright a name) the daughter of a yeoman who held lands near the Baskerville estate. But the young maiden, being discreet and of good repute, would ever avoid him, for she feared his evil name. So it came to pass that one Michaelmas this Hugo, with five or six of his idle and wicked companions, stole down upon the farm and carried off the maiden, her father and brothers being from home, as he well knew. When they had brought her to the Hall the maiden was placed in an upper chamber, while Hugo and his friends sat down to a long carouse, as was their nightly custom. Now, the poor lass upstairs was like to have her wits turned at the singing and shouting and terrible oaths which came up to her from below, for they say that the words used by Hugo Baskerville, when he was in wine, were such as might blast the man who said them. At last in the stress of her fear she did that which might have daunted the bravest or most active man, for by the aid of the growth of ivy which covered (and still covers) the south wall, she came down from under the eaves, and so homeward across the moor, there being three leagues betwixt the Hall and her father's farm.

"It chanced that some little time later Hugo left his guests to carry food and drink—with other worse things, perchance—to his captive, and so found the cage empty and the bird escaped. Then, as it would seem, he became as one that hath a devil, for, rushing down the stairs into the dining-hall, he sprang upon the great table, flagons and trenchers flying before him, and he cried aloud before all the company that he would that very night render his body and soul to the Powers of Evil if he might but overtake the wench. And while the revellers stood aghast at the fury of the man, one more wicked or, it may be, more drunken than the rest, cried out that they should put the hounds upon her. Whereat Hugo ran from the house, crying to his grooms that they should saddle his mare and unkennel the pack, and giving the hounds a kerchief of the maid's he swung them to the line, and so off full cry in the moonlight over the moor.

"Now, for some space the revellers stood agape, unable to understand all that had been done in such haste. But anon their bemused wits awoke to the nature of the deed which was like to be done upon the moorlands. Everything was now in an uproar, some calling for their pistols, some for their horses, and some for another flask of wine. But at length some sense came back to their crazed minds, and the whole of them, thirteen in number, took horse and started in pursuit. The moon shone clear above them, and they rode swiftly abreast, taking that course which the maid must needs have taken if she were to reach her own home.

"They had gone a mile or two when they passed one of the night shepherds upon the moorlands, and they cried to him to know if he had seen the hunt. And the man, as the story goes, was so crazed with fear that he could scarce speak, but at last he said that he had indeed seen the unhappy maiden, with the hounds upon her track. 'But I have seen more than that,' said he, 'for Hugo Baskerville passed me upon his black mare, and there ran mute behind him such a hound of hell as God forbid should ever be at my heels.'

"So the drunken squires cursed the shepherd and rode onwards. But soon their skins turned cold, for there came a sound of galloping across the moor, and the black mare, dabbled with white froth, went past with trailing bridle and empty saddle. Then the revellers rode close together, for a great fear was on them, but they still followed over the moor, though each, had he been alone, would have been right glad to have turned his horse's head. Riding slowly in this fashion, they came at last upon the hounds. These, though known for their valour and their breed, were whimpering in a cluster at the head of a deep dip or goyal, as we call it, upon the moor, some slinking away and some, with starting hackles and staring eyes, gazing down the narrow valley before them.

"The company had come to a halt, more sober men, as you may guess, than when they started. The most of them would by no means advance, but three of them, the boldest, or, it may be the most drunken, rode forward down the goyal. Now it opened into a broad space in which stood two of those great stones, still to be seen there, which were set by certain forgotten peoples in the days of old. The moon was shining bright upon the clearing, and there in the centre lay the unhappy maid where she had fallen, dead of fear and of fatigue. But it was not the sight of her body, nor yet was it that of the body of Hugo Baskerville lying near her, which raised the hair upon the heads of these three dare-devil roisterers, but it was that, standing over Hugo, and plucking at his throat, there stood a foul thing, a great, black beast, shaped like a hound, yet larger than any hound that ever mortal eye has rested upon. And even as they looked the thing tore the throat out of Hugo Baskerville, on which, as it turned its blazing eyes and dripping jaws upon them, the three shrieked with fear and rode for dear life, still scream-ing, across the moor. One, it is said, died that very night of what he had seen, and the other twain were but broken men for the rest of their days.

"Such is the tale, my sons, of the coming of the hound which is said to have plagued the family so sorely ever since. If I have set it down it is because that which is clearly known hath less terror than that which is but hinted at and guessed. Nor can it be denied that many of the family have been unhappy in their deaths, which have been sudden, bloody, and mysteri-ous. Yet may we shelter ourselves in the infinite goodness of Providence, which would not forever punish the innocent beyond that third or fourth generation which is threatened in Holy Writ. To that Providence, my sons, I hereby commend you, and I counsel you by way of caution to forbear from crossing the moor in those dark hours when the powers of evil are exalted.

"(This from Hugo Baskerville to his sons Rodger and John, with instruc-tions that they say nothing thereof to their sister Elizabeth.)"

When Dr. Mortimer had finished reading this singular narrative he pushed his spectacles up on his forehead and stared across at Mr. Sherlock Holmes. The latter yawned and tossed the end of his cigarette into the fire.

"Well?" said he.

"Do you find it interesting?"

"To a collector of fairy-tales."

Dr. Mortimer drew a folded newspaper out of his pocket.

"Now, Mr. Holmes, we will give you something a little more recent. This is the *Devon County Chronicle* of June 14th of this year. It is a short account of the facts elicited at the death of Sir Charles Baskerville which occurred a few days before that date."

My friend leaned a little forward and his expression became intent. Our visitor readjusted his glasses and began:

"The recent sudden death of Sir Charles Baskerville, whose name has been mentioned as the probable Liberal candidate for Mid-Devon at the next election, has cast a gloom over the county. Though Sir Charles had resided at Baskerville Hall for a comparatively short period his amiability of character and extreme generosity had won the affection and respect of all who had been brought into contact with him. In these days of *nouveaux riches* it is refreshing to find a case where the scion of an old county family which has fallen upon evil days is able to make his own fortune and to bring it back with him to restore the fallen grandeur of his line. Sir Charles, as is well known, made large sums of money in South African speculation. More wise than those who go on until the wheel turns against them, he realized his gains and returned to England with them. It is only two years since he took up his residence at Baskerville Hall, and it is common talk how large were those schemes of reconstruction and improvement which have been interrupted by his death. Being himself childless, it was his openly expressed desire that the whole country-side should, within his own lifetime, profit by his good fortune, and many will have personal reasons for bewailing his untimely end. His generous donations to local and county charities have been frequently chronicled in these columns.

"The circumstances connected with the death of Sir Charles cannot be said to have been entirely cleared up by the inquest, but at least enough has been done to dispose of those rumours to which local superstition has given rise. There is no reason whatever to suspect foul play, or to imagine that death could be from any but natural causes. Sir Charles was a widower, and a man who may be said to have been in some ways of an eccentric habit of mind. In spite of his considerable wealth he was simple in his personal tastes, and his indoor servants at Baskerville Hall consisted of a married couple named Barrymore, the husband acting as butler and the wife as housekeeper. Their evidence, corroborated by that of several friends, tends to show that Sir Charles's health has for some time been impaired, and points especially to some affection of the heart, manifesting itself in changes of colour, breathlessness, and acute attacks of nervous depression.

Dr. James Mortimer, the friend and medical attendant of the deceased, has given evidence to the same effect.

"The facts of the case are simple. Sir Charles Baskerville was in the habit every night before going to bed of walking down the famous Yew Alley of Baskerville Hall. The evidence of the Barrymores shows that this had been his custom. On the 4th of June Sir Charles had declared his intention of starting next day for London, and had ordered Barrymore to prepare his luggage. That night he went out as usual for his nocturnal walk, in the course of which he was in the habit of smoking a cigar. He never returned. At twelve o'clock Barrymore, finding the hall door still open, became alarmed and, lighting a lantern, went in search of his master. The day had been wet, and Sir Charles's footmarks were easily traced down the Alley. Half-way down this walk there is a gate which leads out on to the moor. There were indications that Sir Charles had stood for some little time here. He then proceeded down the Alley, and it was at the far end of it that his body was discovered. One fact which has not been explained is the statement of Barrymore that his master's footprints altered their character from the time he passed the moor-gate, and that he appeared from thence onwards to have been walking upon his toes. One Murphy, a gipsy horse-dealer, was on the moor at no great distance at the time, but he appears by his own confession to have been the worse for drink. He declares that he heard cries, but is unable to state from what direction they came. No signs of violence were to be discovered upon Sir Charles's person, and though the doctor's evidence pointed to an almost incredible facial distortion—so great that Dr. Mortimer refused at first to believe that it was indeed his friend and patient who lay before him—it was explained that that is a symptom which is not unusual in cases of dyspnoea and death from cardiac exhaustion. This explanation was borne out by the post-mortem examination, which showed long-standing organic disease, and the coroner's jury returned a verdict in accordance with the medical evidence. It is well that this is so, for it is obviously of the utmost importance that Sir Charles's heir should settle at the Hall, and continue the good work which has been so sadly interrupted. Had the prosaic finding of the coroner not finally put an end to the romantic stories which have been whispered in connection with the affair, it might have been difficult to find a tenant for Baskerville Hall. It is understood that the next-of-kin is Mr. Henry Baskerville, if he be still alive, the son of Sir Charles Baskerville's younger brother. The young man, when last heard of, was in America, and inquiries are being instituted with a view to informing him of his good fortune."

Dr. Mortimer refolded his paper and replaced it in his pocket.

"Those are the public facts, Mr. Holmes, in connection with the death of Sir Charles Baskerville."

"I must thank you," said Sherlock Holmes, "for calling my attention to a case which certainly presents some features of interest. I had observed some newspaper comment at the time, but I was exceedingly preoccupied by that little affair of the Vatican cameos, and in my anxiety to oblige the Pope I lost touch with several interesting English cases. This article, you say, contains all the public facts?"

"It does."

"Then let me have the private ones." He leaned back, put his finger-tips together, and assumed his most impassive and judicial expression.

"In doing so," said Dr. Mortimer, who had begun to show signs of some strong emotion, "I am telling that which I have not confided to anyone. My motive for withholding it from the coroner's inquiry is that a man of science shrinks from placing himself in the public position of seeming to endorse a popular superstition. I had the further motive that Baskerville Hall, as the paper says, would certainly remain untenanted if anything were done to increase its already rather grim reputation. For both these reasons I thought that I was justified in telling rather less than I knew, since no practical good could result from it, but with you there is no reason why I should not be perfectly frank.

"The moor is very sparsely inhabited, and those who live near each other are thrown very much together. For this reason I saw a good deal of Sir Charles Baskerville. With the exception of Mr. Frankland, of Lafter Hall, and Mr. Stapleton, the naturalist, there are no other men of education within many miles. Sir Charles was a retiring man, but the chance of his illness brought us together, and a community of interests in science kept us so. He had brought back much scientific information from South Africa, and many a charming evening we have spent together discussing the comparative anatomy of the Bushman and the Hottentot.

"Within the last few months it became increasingly plain to me that Sir Charles's nervous system was strained to the breaking point. He had taken this legend which I have read you exceedingly to heart—so much so that, although he would walk in his own grounds, nothing would induce him to go out upon the moor at night. Incredible as it may appear to you, Mr. Holmes, he was honestly convinced that a dreadful fate overhung his family, and certainly the records which he was able to give of his ancestors were not encouraging. The idea of some ghastly presence constantly haunted him, and on more than one occasion he has asked me whether I had on my medical journeys at night ever seen any strange creature or heard the baying of a hound. The latter question he put to me several times, and always with a voice which vibrated with excitement.

"I can well remember driving up to his house in the evening, some three weeks before the fatal event. He chanced to be at his hall door. I had descended from my gig and was standing in front of him, when I saw his eyes fix themselves over my shoulder, and stare past me with an expression of the most dreadful horror. I whisked round and had just time to catch a glimpse of something which I took to be a large black calf passing at the head of the drive. So excited and alarmed was he that I was compelled to go down to the spot where the animal had been and look around for it. It was gone, however, and the incident appeared to make the worst impression upon his mind. I stayed with him all the evening, and it was on that occasion, to explain the emotion which he had shown, that he confided to my keeping that narrative which I read to you when first I came. I mention this small episode because it assumes some importance in view of the tragedy which followed, but I was convinced at the time that the matter was entirely trivial and that his excitement had no justification.

"It was at my advice that Sir Charles was about to go to London. His heart was, I knew, affected, and the constant anxiety in which he lived, however chimerical the cause of it might be, was evidently having a serious effect upon his health. I thought that a few months among the distractions of town would send him back a new man. Mr. Stapleton, a mutual friend who was much concerned at his state of health, was of the same opinion. At the last instant came this terrible catastrophe.

"On the night of Sir Charles's death Barrymore the butler, who made the discovery, sent Perkins the groom on horseback to me, and as I was sitting up late I was able to reach Baskerville Hall within an hour of the event. I checked and corroborated all the facts which were mentioned at the inquest. I followed the footsteps down the Yew Alley, I saw the spot at the moor-gate where he seemed to have waited. I remarked the change in the shape of the prints after that point, I noted that there were no other footsteps save those of Barrymore on the soft gravel, and finally I carefully examined the body, which had not been touched until my arrival. Sir Charles lay on his face, his arms out, his fingers dug into the ground, and his features convulsed with some strong emotion to such an extent that I could hardly have sworn to his identity. There was certainly no physical injury of any kind. But one false statement was made by Barrymore at the inquest. He said that there were no traces upon the ground round the body. He did not observe any. But I did—some little distance off, but fresh and clear."

"Footprints?"

"Footprints."

"A man's or a woman's?"

Dr. Mortimer looked strangely at us for an instant, and his voice sank almost to a whisper as he answered:

"Mr. Holmes, they were the footprints of a gigantic hound!"

III. The Problem

I confess that at these words a shudder passed through me. There was a thrill in the doctor's voice which showed that he was himself deeply moved by that which he told us. Holmes leaned forward in his excitement, and his eyes had the hard, dry glitter which shot from them when he was keenly interested.

"You saw this?"

"As clearly as I see you."

"And you said nothing?"

"What was the use?"

"How was it that no one else saw it?"

"The marks were some twenty yards from the body, and no one gave them a thought. I don't suppose I should have done so had I not known this legend."

"There are many sheep-dogs on the moor?"

"No doubt, but this was no sheep-dog."

"You say it was large?"

"Enormous."

"But it had not approached the body?"

"No."

"What sort of night was it?'

"Damp and raw."

"But not actually raining?"

"No."

"What is the alley like?"

"There are two lines of old yew hedge, twelve feet high and impenetrable. The walk in the centre is about eight feet across."

"Is there anything between the hedges and the walk?"

"Yes, there is a strip of grass about six feet broad on either side."

"I understand that the yew hedge is penetrated at one point by a gate?"

"Yes, the wicket-gate which leads on to the moor."

"Is there any other opening?"

"None."

"So that to reach the Yew Alley one either has to come down it from the house or else to enter it by the moor-gate?"

"There is an exit through a summer-house at the far end."

"Had Sir Charles reached this?"

"No; he lay about fifty yards from it."

"Now, tell me, Dr. Mortimer—and this is important—the marks which you saw were on the path and not on the grass?"

"No marks could show on the grass."

"Were they on the same side of the path as the moor-gate?"

"Yes; they were on the edge of the path on the same side as the moor-gate."

"You interest me exceedingly. Another point. Was the wicket-gate closed?"

"Closed and padlocked."

"How high was it?"

"About four feet high."

"Then anyone could have got over it?"

"Yes."

"And what marks did you see by the wicket-gate?"

"None in particular."

"Good Heaven! Did no one examine?"

"Yes, I examined myself."

"And found nothing?"

"It was all very confused. Sir Charles had evidently stood there for five or ten minutes."

"How do you know that?"

"Because the ash had twice dropped from his cigar."

"Excellent! This is a colleague, Watson, after our own heart. But the marks?"

"He had left his own marks all over that small patch of gravel. I could discern no others."

Sherlock Holmes struck his hand against his knee with an impatient gesture.

"If I had only been there!" he cried. "It is evidently a case of extraordinary interest, and one which presented immense opportunities to the scientific expert. That gravel page upon which I might have read so much has been long ere this smudged by the rain and defaced by the clogs of curious peasants. Oh, Dr. Mortimer, Dr. Mortimer, to think that you should not have called me in! You have indeed much to answer for."

"I could not call you in, Mr. Holmes, without disclosing these facts to the world, and I have already given my reasons for not wishing to do so. Besides, besides—"

"Why do you hesitate?"

"There is a realm in which the most acute and most experienced of detectives is helpless."

"You mean that the thing is supernatural?"

"I did not positively say so."

"No, but you evidently think it."

"Since the tragedy, Mr. Holmes, there have come to my ears several incidents which are hard to reconcile with the settled order of Nature."

"For example?"

"I find that before the terrible event occurred several people had seen a creature upon the moor which corresponds with this Baskerville demon, and which could not possibly be any animal known to science. They all agreed that it was a huge creature, luminous, ghastly, and spectral. I have cross-examined these men, one of them a hard-headed countryman, one a farrier, and one a moorland farmer, who all tell the same story of this dreadful apparition, exactly corresponding to the hell-hound of the legend. I assure you that there is a reign of terror in the district, and that it is a hardy man who will cross the moor at night."

"And you, a trained man of science, believe it to be supernatural?"

"I do not know what to believe."

Holmes shrugged his shoulders. "I have hitherto confined my investigations to this world," said he. "In a modest way I have combated evil, but to take on the Father of Evil himself would, perhaps, be too ambitious a task. Yet you must admit that the footmark is material."

"The original hound was material enough to tug a man's throat out, and yet he was diabolical as well."

"I see that you have quite gone over to the supernaturalists. But now, Dr. Mortimer, tell me this. If you hold these views, why have you come to consult me at all? You tell me in the same breath that it is useless to investigate Sir Charles's death, and that you desire me to do it."

"I did not say that I desired you to do it."

"Then, how can I assist you?"

"By advising me as to what I should do with Sir Henry Baskerville, who arrives at Waterloo Station"—Dr. Mortimer looked at his watch—"in exactly one hour and a quarter."

"He being the heir?"

"Yes. On the death of Sir Charles we inquired for this young gentleman, and found that he had been farming in Canada. From the accounts which have reached us he is an excellent fellow in every way. I speak now not as a medical man but as a trustee and executor of Sir Charles's will."

"There is no other claimant, I presume?"

"None. The only other kinsman whom we have been able to trace was Rodger Baskerville, the youngest of three brothers of whom poor Sir Charles was the elder. The second brother, who died young, is the father of this lad Henry. The third, Rodger, was the black sheep of the family. He came of the old masterful Baskerville strain, and was the very image, they tell me, of the family picture of old Hugo. He made England too hot to hold him, fled to Central America, and died there in 1876 of yellow fever. Henry is the last of the Baskervilles. In one hour and five minutes I meet him at Waterloo Station. I have had a wire that he arrived at Southampton this morning. Now, Mr. Holmes, what would you advise me to do with him?"

"Why should he not go to the home of his fathers?"

"It seems natural, does it not? And yet, consider that every Baskerville who goes there meets with an evil fate. I feel sure that if Sir Charles could have spoken with me before his death he would have warned me against bringing this the last of the old race, and the heir to great wealth, to that deadly place. And yet it cannot be denied that the prosperity of the whole poor, bleak country-side depends upon his presence. All the good work which has been done by Sir Charles will crash to the ground if there is no tenant of the Hall. I fear lest I should be swayed too much by my own obvious interest in the matter, and that is why I bring the case before you and ask for your advice."

Holmes considered for a little time. "Put into plain words, the matter is this," said he. "In your opinion there is a diabolical agency which makes Dartmoor an unsafe abode for a Baskerville—that is your opinion?"

"At least I might go the length of saying that there is some evidence that this may be so."

"Exactly. But surely if your supernatural theory be correct, it could work the young man evil in London as easily as in Devonshire. A devil with merely local powers like a parish vestry would be too inconceivable a thing."

"You put the matter more flippantly, Mr. Holmes, than you would probably do if you were brought into personal contact with these things. Your advice, then, as I understand it, is that the young man will be as safe in Devonshire as in London. He comes in fifty minutes. What would you recommend?"

"I recommend, sir, that you take a cab, call off your spaniel, who is scratching at my front door, and proceed to Waterloo to meet Sir Henry Baskerville."

"And then?"

"And then you will say nothing to him at all until I have made up my mind about the matter."

"How long will it take you to make up your mind?"

"Twenty-four hours. At ten o'clock to-morrow, Dr. Mortimer, I will be much obliged to you if you will call upon me here, and it will be of help to me in my plans for the future if you will bring Sir Henry Baskerville with you."

"I will do so, Mr. Holmes."

He scribbled the appointment on his shirt-cuff and hurried off in his strange, peering, absent-minded fashion. Holmes stopped him at the head of the stair.

"Only one more question, Dr. Mortimer. You say that before Sir Charles Baskerville's death several people saw this apparition upon the moor?"

"Three people did."

"Did any see it after?"

"I have not heard of any."

"Thank you. Good morning."

Holmes returned to his seat with that quiet look of inward satisfaction which meant that he had a congenial task before him.

"Going out, Watson?"

"Unless I can help you."

"No, my dear fellow, it is at the hour of action that I turn to you for aid. But this is splendid, really unique from some points of view. When you pass Bradley's, would you ask him to send up a pound of the strongest shag tobacco? Thank you. It would be as well if you could make it convenient not to return before evening. Then I should be very glad to compare impressions as to this most interesting problem which has been submitted to us this morning."

I knew that seclusion and solitude were very necessary for my friend in those hours of intense mental concentration during which he weighed every particle of evidence, constructed alternative theories, balanced one against the other, and made up his mind as to which points were essential and which immaterial. I therefore spent the day at my club, and did not return to Baker Street until evening. It was nearly nine o'clock when I found myself in the sitting-room once more.

My first impression as I opened the door was that a fire had broken out, for the room was so filled with smoke that the light of the lamp upon the table was blurred by it. As I entered, however, my fears were set at rest, for it was the acrid fumes of strong, coarse tobacco, which took me by the throat and set me coughing. Through the haze I had a vague vision of Holmes in his dressing-gown coiled up in an armchair with his black clay pipe between his lips. Several rolls of paper lay around him.

"Caught cold, Watson?" said he.

"No, it's this poisonous atmosphere."

"I suppose it *is* pretty thick, now that you mention it."

"Thick! It is intolerable."

"Open the window, then! You have been at your club all day, I perceive."

"My dear Holmes!"

"Am I right?"

"Certainly, but how——?"

He laughed at my bewildered expression.

"There is a delightful freshness about you, Watson, which makes it a pleasure to exercise any small powers which I possess at your expense. A gentleman goes forth on a showery and miry day. He returns immaculate in the evening with the gloss still on his hat and his boots. He has been a fixture therefore all day. He is not a man with intimate friends. Where, then, could he have been? Is it not obvious?"

"Well, it is rather obvious."

"The world is full of obvious things which nobody by any chance ever observes. Where do you think that I have been?"

"A fixture also."

"On the contrary, I have been to Devonshire."

"In spirit?"

"Exactly. My body has remained in this arm-chair, and has, I regret to observe, consumed in my absence two large pots of coffee and an incredible amount of tobacco. After you left I sent down to Stanford's for the Ordnance map of this portion of the moor, and my spirit has hovered over it all day. I flatter myself that I could find my way about."

"A large scale map, I presume?"

"Very large." He unrolled one section and held it over his knee. "Here you have the particular district which concerns us. That is Baskerville Hall in the middle."

"With a wood round it?"

"Exactly. I fancy the Yew Alley, though not marked under that name, must stretch along this line, with the moor, as you perceive, upon the right of it. This small clump of buildings here is the hamlet of Grimpen, where our friend Dr. Mortimer has his headquarters. Within a radius of five miles there are, as you see, only a very few scattered dwellings. Here is Lafter Hall, which was mentioned in the narrative. There is a house indicated here which may be the residence of the naturalist—Stapleton, if I remember right, was his name. Here are two moorland farmhouses, High Tor and Foulmire. Then fourteen miles away the great convict prison of Princetown. Between and around these scattered points extends the desolate, lifeless moor. This, then, is the stage upon which tragedy has been played, and upon which we may help to play it again."

"It must be a wild place."

"Yes, the setting is a worthy one. If the devil did desire to have a hand in the affairs of men—"

"Then you are yourself inclining to the supernatural explanation."

"The devil's agents may be of flesh and blood, may they not? There are two questions waiting for us at the outset. The one is whether any crime has been committed at all; the second is, what is the crime and how was it committed? Of course, if Dr. Mortimer's surmise should be correct, and we are dealing with forces outside the ordinary laws of Nature, there is an end of our investigation. But we are bound to exhaust all other hypotheses before falling back upon this one. I think we'll shut that window again, if you don't mind. It is a singular thing, but I find that a concentrated atmosphere helps a concentration of thought. I have not pushed it to the length of getting into a box to think, but that is the logical outcome of my convictions. Have you turned the case over in your mind?"

"Yes, I have thought a good deal of it in the course of the day."

"What do you make of it?"

"It is very bewildering."

"It has certainly a character of its own. There are points of distinction about it. That change in the footprints, for example. What do you make of that?"

"Mortimer said that the man had walked on tiptoe down that portion of the alley."

"He only repeated what some fool had said at the inquest. Why should a man walk on tiptoe down the alley?"

"What then?"

"He was running, Watson—running desperately, running for his life, running until he burst his heart and fell dead upon his face."

"Running from what?"

"There lies our problem. There are indications that the man was crazed with fear before ever he began to run."

"How can you say that?"

"I am presuming that the cause of his fears came to him across the moor. If that were so, and it seems most probable, only a man who had lost his wits would have run from the house instead of towards it. If the gipsy's evidence may be taken as true, he ran with cries for help in the direction where help was least likely to be. Then again, whom was he waiting for that night, and why was he waiting for him in the Yew Alley rather than in his own house?"

"You think that he was waiting for someone?"

"The man was elderly and infirm. We can understand his taking an evening stroll, but the ground was damp and the night inclement. Is it natural that he should stand for five or ten minutes, as Dr. Mortimer, with more practical sense than I should have given him credit for, deduced from the cigar ash?"

"But he went out every evening."

"I think it unlikely that he waited at the moor-gate every evening. On the contrary, the evidence is that he avoided the moor. That night he waited there. It was the night before he was to take his departure for London. The thing takes shape, Watson. It becomes coherent. Might I ask you to hand me my violin, and we will postpone all further thought upon this business until we have had the advantage of meeting Dr. Mortimer and Sir Henry Baskerville in the morning."

IV. SIR HENRY BASKERVILLE

Our breakfast-table was cleared early, and Holmes waited in his dressing-gown for the promised interview. Our clients were punctual to their appointment, for the clock had just struck ten when Dr. Mortimer was shown up, followed by the young Baronet. The latter was a small, alert, dark-eyed man about thirty years of age, very sturdily built, with thick black eyebrows and a strong, pugnacious face. He wore a ruddy-tinted tweed suit, and had the weather-beaten appearance of one who has spent most of his time in the open air, and yet there was something in his steady eye and the quiet assurance of his bearing which indicated the gentleman.

"This is Sir Henry Baskerville," said Dr. Mortimer.

"Why, yes," said he, "and the strange thing is, Mr. Sherlock Holmes, that if my friend here had not proposed coming round to you this morning I should have come on my own. I understand that you think out little puzzles, and I've had one this morning which wants more thinking out than I am able to give it."

"Pray take a seat, Sir Henry. Do I understand you to say that you have yourself had some remarkable experience since you arrived in London?"

"Nothing of much importance, Mr. Holmes. Only a joke, as like as not. It was this letter, if you can call it a letter, which reached me this morning."

He laid an envelope upon the table, and we all bent over it. It was of common quality, greyish in colour. The address, "Sir Henry Baskerville, Northumberland Hotel," was printed in rough characters; the post-mark "Charing Cross," and the date of posting the preceding evening.

"Who knew that you were going to the Northumberland Hotel?" asked Holmes, glancing keenly across at our visitor.

"No one could have known. We only decided after I met Dr. Mortimer."

"But Dr. Mortimer was, no doubt, already stopping there?"

"No, I had been staying with a friend," said the doctor. "There was no possible indication that we intended to go to this hotel."

"Hum! Someone seems to be very deeply interested in your movements." Out of the envelope he took a half-sheet of foolscap paper folded into four. This he opened and spread flat upon the table. Across the middle of it a single sentence had been formed by the expedient of pasting printed words upon it. It ran: "As you value your life or your reason keep away from the moor." The word "moor" only was printed in ink.

"Now," said Sir Henry Baskerville, "perhaps you will tell me, Mr. Holmes, what in thunder is the meaning of that, and who it is that takes so much interest in my affairs?"

"What do you make of it, Dr. Mortimer? You must allow that there is nothing supernatural about this, at any rate?"

"No, sir, but it might very well come from someone who was convinced that the business is supernatural."

"What business?" asked Sir Henry, sharply. "It seems to me that all you gentlemen know a great deal more than I do about my own affairs."

"You shall share our knowledge before you leave this room, Sir Henry. I promise you that," said Sherlock Holmes. "We will confine ourselves for the present, with your permission, to this very interesting document, which must have been put together and posted yesterday evening. Have you yesterday's *Times*, Watson?"

"It is here in the corner."

"Might I trouble you for it—the inside page, please, with the leading articles?" He glanced swiftly over it, running his eyes up and down the columns. "Capital article this on Free Trade. Permit me to give you an extract from it. 'You may be cajoled into imagining that your own special trade or your own industry will be encouraged by a protective tariff, but it stands to reason that such legislation must in the long run keep away wealth from the country, diminish the value of our imports, and lower the general conditions of life in this island.' What do you think of that, Watson?" cried Holmes, in high glee, rubbing his hands together with satisfaction. "Don't you think that is an admirable sentiment?"

Dr. Mortimer looked at Holmes with an air of professional interest, and Sir Henry Baskerville turned a pair of puzzled dark eyes upon me.

"I don't know much about the tariff and things of that kind," said he; "but it seems to me we've got a bit off the trail so far as that note is concerned."

"On the contrary, I think we are particularly hot upon the trail, Sir Henry. Watson here knows more about my methods than you do, but I fear that even he has not quite grasped the significance of this sentence."

"No, I confess that I see no connection."

"And yet, my dear Watson, there is so very close a connection that the one is extracted out of the other. 'You,' 'your,' 'your,' 'life,' 'reason,' 'value,' 'keep away,' 'from the.' Don't you see now whence these words have been taken?"

"By thunder, you're right! Well, if that isn't smart!" cried Sir Henry.

"If any possible doubt remained it is settled by the fact that 'keep away' and 'from the' are cut out in one piece."

"Well, now—so it is!"

"Really, Mr. Holmes, this exceeds anything which I could have imagined," said Dr. Mortimer, gazing at my friend in amazement. "I could understand anyone saying that the words were from a newspaper; but that you should name which, and add that it came from the leading article, is really one of the most remarkable things which I have ever known. How did you do it?"

"I presume, Doctor, that you could tell the skull of a Negro from that of an Esquimaux?"

"Most certainly."

"But how?"

"Because that is my special hobby. The differences are obvious. The supra-orbital crest, the facial angle, the maxillary curve, the—"

"But this is my special hobby, and the differences are equally obvious. There is as much difference to my eyes between the leaded bourgeois type of a *Times* article and the slovenly print of an evening halfpenny paper as there could be between your Negro and your Esquimaux. The detection of types is one of the most elementary branches of knowledge to the special expert in crime, though I confess that once when I was very young I confused the *Leeds Mercury with the Western Morning News. But a Times leader is* entirely distinctive, and these words could have been taken from nothing else. As it was done yesterday the strong probability was that we should find the words in yesterday's issue."

"So far as I can follow you, then, Mr. Holmes," said Sir Henry Baskerville, "someone cut out this message with a scissors—"

"Nail-scissors," said Holmes. "You can see that it was a very short-bladed scissors, since the cutter had to take two snips over 'keep away.'"

"That is so. Someone, then, cut out the message with a pair of short-bladed scissors, pasted it with paste—"

"Gum," said Holmes.

"With gum on to the paper. But I want to know why the word 'moor' should have been written?"

"Because he could not find it in print. The other words were all simple, and might be found in any issue, but 'moor' would be less common."

"Why, of course, that would explain it. Have you read anything else in this message, Mr. Holmes?"

"There are one or two indications, and yet the utmost pains have been taken to remove all clues. The address, you observe, is printed in rough characters. But *The Times* is a paper which is seldom found in any hands but those of the highly educated. We may take it, therefore, that the letter was composed by an educated man who wished to pose as an uneducated one, and his effort to conceal his own writing suggests that that writing might be known, or come to be known, by you. Again, you will observe that the words are not gummed on in an accurate line, but that some are much higher than others. 'Life,' for example, is quite out of its proper place. That may point to carelessness or it may point to agitation and hurry upon the part of the cutter. On the whole I incline to the latter view, since the matter was evidently important, and it is unlikely that the composer of such a letter would be careless. If he were in a hurry it opens up the interesting question why he should be in a hurry, since any letter posted up to early morning would reach Sir Henry before he would leave his hotel. Did the composer fear an interruption—and from whom?"

"We are coming now rather into the region of guesswork," said Dr. Mortimer.

"Say, rather, into the region where we balance probabilities and choose the most likely. It is the scientific use of the imagination, but we have always some material basis on which to start our speculations. Now, you would call it a guess, no doubt, but I am almost certain that this address has been written in an hotel."

"How in the world can you say that?"

"If you examine it carefully you will see that both the pen and the ink have given the writer trouble. The pen has spluttered twice in a single word, and has run dry three times in a short address, showing that there was very little ink in the bottle. Now, a private pen or ink-bottle is seldom allowed to be in such a state, and the combination of the two must be quite rare. But you know the hotel ink and the hotel pen, where it is rare to get anything else. Yes, I have very little hesitation in saying that could we examine the waste-paper baskets of the hotels around Charing Cross until we found the remains of the mutilated *Times leader we could lay* our hands straight upon the person who sent this singular message. Hullo! Hullo! What's this?"

He was carefully examining the foolscap, upon which the words were pasted, holding it only an inch or two from his eyes.

"Well?"

"Nothing," said he, throwing it down. "It is a blank half-sheet of paper, without even a water-mark upon it. I think we have drawn as much as we can from this curious letter; and now, Sir Henry, has anything else of interest happened to you since you have been in London?"

"Why, no, Mr. Holmes. I think not."

"You have not observed anyone follow or watch you?"

"I seem to have walked right into the thick of a dime novel," said our visitor. "Why in thunder should anyone follow or watch me?"

"We are coming to that. You have nothing else to report to us before we go into this matter?"

"Well, it depends upon what you think worth reporting."

"I think anything out of the ordinary routine of life well worth reporting."

Sir Henry smiled. "I don't know much of British life yet, for I have spent nearly all my time in the States and in Canada. But I hope that to lose one of your boots is not part of the ordinary routine of life over here."

"You have lost one of your boots?"

"My dear sir," cried Dr. Mortimer, "it is only mislaid. You will find it when you return to the hotel. What is the use of troubling Mr. Holmes with trifles of this kind?"

"Well, he asked me for anything outside the ordinary routine."

"Exactly," said Holmes, "however foolish the incident may seem. You have lost one of your boots, you say?"

"Well, mislaid it, anyhow. I put them both outside my door last night, and there was only one in the morning. I could get no sense out of the chap who cleans them. The worst of it is that I only bought the pair last night in the Strand, and I have never had them on."

"If you have never worn them, why did you put them out to be cleaned?"

"They were tan boots, and had never been varnished. That was why I put them out."

"Then I understand that on your arrival in London yesterday you went out at once and bought a pair of boots?"

"I did a good deal of shopping. Dr. Mortimer here went round with me. You see, if I am to be squire down there I must dress the part, and it may be that I have got a little careless in my ways out West. Among other things I bought these brown boots—gave six dollars for them—and had one stolen before ever I had them on my feet."

"It seems a singularly useless thing to steal," said Sherlock Holmes. "I confess that I share Dr. Mortimer's belief that it will not be long before the missing boot is found."

"And, now, gentlemen," said the Baronet, with decision, "it seems to me that I have spoken quite enough about the little that I know. It is time that you kept your promise, and gave me a full account of what we are all driving at."

"Your request is a very reasonable one," Holmes answered. "Dr. Mortimer, I think you could not do better than to tell your story as you told it to us."

Thus encouraged, our scientific friend drew his papers from his pocket, and presented the whole case as he had done upon the morning before. Sir Henry Baskerville listened with the deepest attention and with an occasional exclamation of surprise.

"Well, I seem to have come into an inheritance with a vengeance," said he, when the long narrative was finished. "Of course, I've heard of the hound ever since I was in the nursery. It's the pet story of the family, though I never thought of taking it seriously before. But as to my uncle's death—well, it all seems boiling up in my head, and I can't get it clear yet. You don't seem quite to have made up your mind whether it's a case for a policeman or a clergyman."

"Precisely."

"And now there's this affair of the letter to me at the hotel. I suppose that fits into its place."

"It seems to show that someone knows more than we do about what goes on upon the moor," said Dr. Mortimer.

"And also," said Holmes, "that someone is not ill-disposed towards you, since they warn you of danger."

"Or it may be that they wish for their own purposes to scare me away."

"Well, of course, that is possible also. I am very much indebted to you, Dr. Mortimer, for introducing me to a problem which presents several interesting alternatives. But the practical point which we now have to decide, Sir Henry, is whether it is or is not advisable for you to go to Baskerville Hall."

"Why should I not go?"

"There seems to be danger."

"Do you mean danger from this family fiend or do you mean danger from human beings?"

"Well, that is what we have to find out."

"Whichever it is, my answer is fixed. There is no devil in hell, Mr. Holmes, and there is no man upon earth who can prevent me from going to the home of my own people, and you may take that to be my final answer." His dark brows knitted and his face flushed to a dusky red as he spoke. It was evident that the fiery temper of the Baskervilles was not extinct in this their last representative. "Meanwhile," said he, "I have hardly had time to think over all that you have told me. It's a big thing for a man to have to understand and to decide at one sitting. I should like to have a quiet hour by myself to make up my mind. Now, look here, Mr. Holmes, it's half-past eleven now, and I am going back right away to my hotel. Suppose you and your friend, Dr. Watson, come round and lunch with us at two? I'll be able to tell you more clearly then how this thing strikes me."

"Is that convenient to you, Watson?"

"Perfectly."

"Then you may expect us. Shall I have a cab called?"

"I'd prefer to walk, for this affair has flurried me rather."

"I'll join you in a walk, with pleasure," said his companion.

"Then we meet again at two o'clock. Au revoir, and good morning!"

We heard the steps of our visitors descend the stair and the bang of the front door. In an instant Holmes had changed from the languid dreamer to the man of action.

"Your hat and boots, Watson, quick! Not a moment to lose!" He rushed into his room in his dressing-gown, and was back again in a few seconds in a frock-coat. We hurried together down the stairs and into the street. Dr. Mortimer and Baskerville were still visible about two hundred yards ahead of us in the direction of Oxford Street.

"Shall I run on and stop them?"

"Not for the world, my dear Watson. I am perfectly satisfied with your company, if you will tolerate mine. Our friends are wise, for it is certainly a very fine morning for a walk."

He quickened his pace until we had decreased the distance which divided us by about half. Then, still keeping a hundred yards behind, we followed into Oxford Street and so down Regent Street. Once our friends stopped and stared into a shop window, upon which Holmes did the same. An instant afterwards he gave a little cry of satisfaction, and, following the direction of his eager eyes, I saw that a hansom cab with a man inside which had halted on the other side of the street was now walking slowly onwards again.

"There's our man, Watson! Come along! We'll have a good look at him, if we can do no more."

At that instant I was aware of a bushy black beard and a pair of piercing eyes turned upon us through the side window of the cab. Instantly the trap-door at the top flew up, something was screamed to the driver, and the cab flew madly off down Regent Street. Holmes looked eagerly round for another, but no empty one was in sight. Then he dashed in wild pursuit amid the stream of the traffic, but the start was too great, and already the cab was out of sight.

"There now!" said Holmes, bitterly, as he emerged panting and white with vexation from the tide of vehicles. "Was ever such bad luck and such bad management, too? Watson, Watson, if you are an honest man you will record this also and set it against my successes!"

"Who was the man?"

"I have not an idea."

"A spy?"

"Well, it was evident from what we have heard that Baskerville has been very closely shadowed by someone since he has been in town. How else could it be known so quickly that it was the Northumberland Hotel which he had chosen? If they had followed him the first day I argued that they would follow him also the second. You may have observed that I twice strolled over to the window while Dr. Mortimer was reading his legend."

"Yes, I remember."

"I was looking out for loiterers in the street, but I saw none. We are dealing with a clever man, Watson. This matter cuts very deep, and though I have not finally made up my mind whether it is a benevolent or a malevolent agency which is in touch with us, I am conscious always of power and design. When our friends left I at once followed them in the hopes of marking down their invisible attendant. So wily was he that he had not trusted himself upon foot, but he had availed himself of a cab, so that he could loiter behind or dash past them and so escape their notice. His method had the additional advantage that if they were to take a cab he was all ready to follow them. It has, however, one obvious disadvantage."

"It puts him in the power of the cabman."

"Exactly."

"What a pity we did not get the number!"

"My dear Watson, clumsy as I have been, you surely do not seriously imagine that I neglected to get the number? 2704 is our man. But that is no use to us for the moment."

"I fail to see how you could have done more."

"On observing the cab I should have instantly turned and walked in the other direction. I should then at my leisure have hired a second cab and followed the first at a respectful distance, or, better still, have driven to the Northumberland Hotel and waited there. When our unknown had followed Baskerville home we should have had the opportunity of playing his own game upon himself, and seeing where he made for. As it is, by an indiscreet eagerness, which was taken advantage of with extraordinary quickness and energy by our opponent, we have betrayed ourselves and lost our man."

We had been sauntering slowly down Regent Street during this conversation, and Dr. Mortimer, with his companion, had long vanished in front of us.

"There is no object in our following them," said Holmes. "The shadow has departed and will not return. We must see what further cards we have in our hands, and play them with decision. Could you swear to that man's face within the cab?"

"I could swear only to the beard."

"And so could I—from which I gather that in all probability it was a false one. A clever man upon so delicate an errand has no use for a beard save to conceal his features. Come in here, Watson!"

He turned into one of the district messenger offices, where he was warmly greeted by the manager.

"Ah, Wilson, I see you have not forgotten the little case in which I had the good fortune to help you?"

"No, sir, indeed I have not. You saved my good name, and perhaps my life."

"My dear fellow, you exaggerate. I have some recollection, Wilson, that you had among your boys a lad named Cartwright, who showed some ability during the investigation."

"Yes, sir, he is still with us."

"Could you ring him up? Thank you! And I should be glad to have change of this five-pound note."

A lad of fourteen, with a bright, keen face, had obeyed the summons of the manager. He stood now gazing with great reverence at the famous detective.

"Let me have the Hotel Directory," said Holmes. "Thank you! Now, Cartwright, there are the names of twenty-three hotels here, all in the immediate neighbourhood of Charing Cross. Do you see?"

"Yes, sir."

"You will visit each of these in turn."

"Yes, sir."

"You will begin in each case by giving the outside porter one shilling. Here are twenty-three shillings."

"Yes, sir."

"You will tell him that you want to see the waste paper of yesterday. You will say that an important telegram has miscarried, and that you are looking for it. You understand?"

"Yes, sir."

"But what you are really looking for is the centre page of *The Times* with some holes cut in it with scissors. Here is a copy of *The Times*. It is this page. You could easily recognize it, could you not?"

"Yes, sir."

"In each case the outside porter will send for the hall porter, to whom also you will give a shilling. Here are twenty-three shillings. You will then learn in possibly twenty cases out of the twenty-three that the waste of the day before has been burned or removed. In the three other cases you will be shown a heap of paper, and will look for this page of *The Times* among it. The odds are enormously against your finding it. There are ten shillings over in case of emergencies. Let me have a report by wire at Baker Street before evening. And now, Watson, it only remains for us to find out by wire the identity of the cabman, No. 2704, and then we will drop into one of the Bond Street picture-galleries and fill in the time until we are due at the hotel."

V. THREE BROKEN THREADS

Sherlock Holmes had, in a very remarkable degree, the power of detaching his mind at will. For two hours the strange business in which we had been involved appeared to be forgotten, and he was entirely absorbed in the pictures of the modern Belgian masters. He would talk of nothing but art, of which he had the crudest ideas, from our leaving the gallery until we found ourselves at the Northumberland Hotel.

"Sir Henry Baskerville is upstairs expecting you," said the clerk. "He asked me to show you up at once when you came."

"Have you any objection to my looking at your register?" said Holmes.

"Not in the least."

The book showed that two names had been added after that of Baskerville. One was Theophilus Johnson and family, of Newcastle; the other Mrs. Oldmore and maid, of High Lodge, Alton.

"Surely that must be the same Johnson whom I used to know," said Holmes to the porter. "A lawyer, is he not, grey-headed, and walks with a limp?"

"No, sir, this is Mr. Johnson the coal-owner, a very active gentleman, not older than yourself."

"Surely you are mistaken about his trade?"

"No, sir; he has used this hotel for many years, and he is very well known to us."

"Ah, that settles it. Mrs. Oldmore, too; I seem to remember the name. Excuse my curiosity, but often in calling upon one friend one finds another."

"She is an invalid lady, sir. Her husband was once mayor of Gloucester. She always comes to us when she is in town."

"Thank you; I am afraid I cannot claim her acquaintance. We have established a most important fact by these questions, Watson," he continued, in a low voice, as we went upstairs together. "We know now that the people who are so interested in our friend have not settled down in his own hotel. That means that while they are, as we have seen, very anxious to watch him, they are equally anxious that he should not see them. Now, this is a most suggestive fact."

"What does it suggest?"

"It suggests—hullo, my dear fellow, what on earth is the matter?"

As we came round the top of the stairs we had run up against Sir Henry Baskerville himself. His face was flushed with anger, and he held an old and dusty boot in one of his hands. So furious was he that he was hardly articulate, and when he did speak it was in a much broader and more Western dialect than any which we had heard from him in the morning.

"Seems to me they are playing me for a sucker in this hotel," he cried. "They'll find they've started in to monkey with the wrong man unless they are careful. By thunder, if that chap can't find my missing boot there will be trouble. I can take a joke with the best, Mr. Holmes, but they've got a bit over the mark this time."

"Still looking for your boot?"

"Yes, sir, and mean to find it."

"But, surely, you said that it was a new brown boot?"

"So it was, sir. And now it's an old black one."

"What! you don't mean to say—?"

"That's just what I do mean to say. I only had three pairs in the world—the new brown, the old black, and the patent leathers, which I am wearing. Last night they took one of my brown ones, and to-day they have sneaked one of the black. Well, have you got it? Speak out, man, and don't stand staring!"

An agitated German waiter had appeared upon the scene.

"No, sir; I have made inquiry all over the hotel, but I can hear no word of it."

"Well, either that boot comes back before sundown or I'll see the manager and tell him that I go right straight out of this hotel."

"It shall be found, sir—I promise you that if you will have a little patience it will be found."

"Mind it is, for it's the last thing of mine that I'll lose in this den of thieves. Well, well, Mr. Holmes, you'll excuse my troubling you about such a trifle—"

"I think it's well worth troubling about."

"Why, you look very serious over it."

"How do you explain it?"

"I just don't attempt to explain it. It seems the very maddest, queerest thing that ever happened to me."

"The queerest, perhaps," said Holmes, thoughtfully.

"What do you make of it yourself?"

"Well, I don't profess to understand it yet. This case of yours is very complex, Sir Henry. When taken in conjunction with your uncle's death I am not sure that of all the five hundred cases of capital importance which I have handled there is one which cuts so deep. But we hold several threads in our hands, and the odds are that one or other of them guides us to the truth. We may waste time in following the wrong one, but sooner or later we must come upon the right."

We had a pleasant luncheon in which little was said of the business which had brought us together. It was in the private sitting-room to which we afterwards repaired that Holmes asked Baskerville what were his intentions.

"To go to Baskerville Hall."

"And when?"

"At the end of the week."

"On the whole," said Holmes, "I think that your decision is a wise one. I have ample evidence that you are being dogged in London, and amid the millions of this great city it is difficult to discover who these people are or what their object can be. If their intentions are evil they might do you a mischief, and we should be powerless to prevent it. You did not know, Dr. Mortimer, that you were followed this morning from my house?"

Dr. Mortimer started violently. "Followed! By whom?"

"That, unfortunately, is what I cannot tell you. Have you among your neighbours or acquaintances on Dartmoor any man with a black, full beard?"

"No—or, let me see—why, yes. Barrymore, Sir Charles's butler, is a man with a full, black beard."

"Ha! Where is Barrymore?"

"He is in charge of the Hall."

"We had best ascertain if he is really there, or if by any possibility he might be in London."

"How can you do that?"

"Give me a telegraph form. 'Is all ready for Sir Henry?' That will do. Address to Mr. Barrymore, Baskerville Hall. Which is the nearest telegraph-office? Grimpen. Very good, we will send a second wire to the postmaster, Grimpen: 'Telegram to

Mr. Barrymore, to be delivered into his own hand. If absent, please return wire to Sir Henry Baskerville, Northumberland Hotel.' That should let us know before evening whether Barrymore is at his post in Devonshire or not."

"That's so," said Baskerville. "By the way, Dr. Mortimer, who is this Barrymore, anyhow?"

"He is the son of the old caretaker, who is dead. They have looked after the Hall for four generations now. So far as I know, he and his wife are as respectable a couple as any in the county."

"At the same time," said Baskerville, "it's clear enough that so long as there are none of the family at the Hall these people have a mighty fine home and nothing to do."

"That is true."

"Did Barrymore profit at all by Sir Charles's will?" asked Holmes.

"He and his wife had five hundred pounds each."

"Ha! Did they know that they would receive this?"

"Yes; Sir Charles was very fond of talking about the provisions of his will."

"That is very interesting."

"I hope," said Dr. Mortimer, "that you do not look with suspicious eyes upon everyone who received a legacy from Sir Charles, for I also had a thousand pounds left to me."

"Indeed! And anyone else?"

"There were many insignificant sums to individuals and a large number of public charities. The residue all went to Sir Henry."

"And how much was the residue?"

"Seven hundred and forty thousand pounds."

Holmes raised his eyebrows in surprise. "I had no idea that so gigantic a sum was involved," said he.

"Sir Charles had the reputation of being rich, but we did not know how very rich he was until we came to examine his securities. The total value of the estate was close on to a million."

"Dear me! It is a stake for which a man might well play a desperate game. And one more question, Dr. Mortimer. Supposing that anything happened to our young friend here—you will forgive the unpleasant hypothesis!—who would inherit the estate?"

"Since Rodger Baskerville, Sir Charles's younger brother, died unmarried, the estate would descend to the Desmonds, who are distant cousins. James Desmond is an elderly clergyman in Westmorland."

"Thank you. These details are all of great interest. Have you met Mr. James Desmond?"

"Yes; he once came down to visit Sir Charles. He is a man of venerable appearance and of saintly life. I remember that he refused to accept any settlement from Sir Charles, though he pressed it upon him."

"And this man of simple tastes would be the heir to Sir Charles's thousands?"

"He would be the heir to the estate, because that is entailed. He would also be the heir to the money unless it were willed otherwise by the present owner, who can, of course, do what he likes with it."

"And have you made your will, Sir Henry?"

"No, Mr. Holmes, I have not. I've had no time, for it was only yesterday that I learned how matters stood. But in any case I feel that the money should go with the title and estate. That was my poor uncle's idea. How is the owner going to restore the glories of the Baskervilles if he has not money enough to keep up the property? House, land, and dollars must go together."

"Quite so. Well, Sir Henry, I am of one mind with you as to the advisability of your going down to Devonshire without delay. There is only one provision which I must make. You certainly must not go alone."

"Dr. Mortimer returns with me."

"But Dr. Mortimer has his practice to attend to, and his house is miles away from yours. With all the good will in the world, he may be unable to help you. No, Sir Henry, you must take with you someone, a trusty man, who will be always by your side."

"Is it possible that you could come yourself, Mr. Holmes?"

"If matters came to a crisis I should endeavour to be present in person; but you can understand that, with my extensive consulting practice and with the constant appeals which reach me from many quarters, it is impossible for me to be absent from London for an indefinite time. At the present instant one of the most revered names in England is being besmirched by a blackmailer, and only I can stop a disastrous scandal. You will see how impossible it is for me to go to Dartmoor."

"Whom would you recommend, then?"

Holmes laid his hand upon my arm.

"If my friend would undertake it there is no man who is better worth having at your side when you are in a tight place. No one can say so more confidently than I."

The proposition took me completely by surprise, but before I had time to answer Baskerville seized me by the hand and wrung it heartily.

"Well, now, that is real kind of you, Dr. Watson," said he. "You see how it is with me, and you know just as much about the matter as I do. If you will come down to Baskerville Hall and see me through I'll never forget it."

The promise of adventure had always a fascination for me, and I was complimented by the words of Holmes and by the eagerness with which the Baronet hailed me as a companion.

"I will come with pleasure," said I. "I do not know how I could employ my time better."

"And you will report very carefully to me," said Holmes. "When a crisis comes, as it will do, I will direct how you shall act. I suppose that by Saturday all might be ready?"

"Would that suit Dr. Watson?"

"Perfectly."

"Then on Saturday, unless you hear to the contrary, we shall meet at the 10:30 train from Paddington."

We had risen to depart when Baskerville gave a cry of triumph, and diving into one of the corners of the room he drew a brown boot from under a cabinet.

"My missing boot!" he cried.

"May all our difficulties vanish as easily!" said Sherlock Holmes.

"But it is a very singular thing," Dr. Mortimer remarked. "I searched this room carefully before lunch."

"And so did I," said Baskerville. "Every inch of it."

"There was certainly no boot in it then."

"In that case the waiter must have placed it there while we were lunching."

The German was sent for, but professed to know nothing of the matter, nor could any inquiry clear it up. Another item had been added to that constant and apparently purposeless series of small mysteries which had succeeded each other so rapidly. Setting aside the whole grim story of Sir Charles's death, we had a line of inexplicable incidents all within the limits of two days, which included the receipt of the printed letter, the black-bearded spy in the hansom, the loss of the new brown boot, the loss of the old black boot, and now the return of the new brown boot. Holmes sat in silence in the cab as we drove back to Baker Street, and I knew from his drawn brows and keen face that his mind, like my own, was busy in endeavouring to frame some scheme into which all these strange and apparently disconnected episodes could be fitted. All afternoon and late into the evening he sat lost in tobacco and thought.

Just before dinner two telegrams were handed in. The first ran:

Have just heard that Barrymore is at the Hall.—BASKERVILLE

The second:

Visited twenty-three hotels as directed, but sorry to report unable to trace cut sheet of *Times*.—CARTWRIGHT

"There go two of my threads, Watson. There is nothing more stimulating than a case where everything goes against you. We must cast round for another scent."

"We have still the cabman who drove the spy."

"Exactly. I have wired to get his name and address from the Official Registry. I should not be surprised if this were an answer to my question."

The ring at the bell proved to be something even more satisfactory than an answer, however, for the door opened and a rough-looking fellow entered who was evidently the man himself.

"I got a message from the head office that a gent at this address had been inquiring for 2704," said he. "I've driven my cab this seven years and never a word of complaint. I came here straight from the Yard to ask you to your face what you had against me."

"I have nothing in the world against you, my good man," said Holmes. "On the contrary, I have half a sovereign for you if you will give me a clear answer to my questions."

"Well, I've had a good day and no mistake," said the cabman, with a grin. "What was it you wanted to ask, sir?"

"First of all your name and address, in case I want you again."

"John Clayton, 3, Turpey Street, the Borough. My cab is out of Shipley's Yard, near Waterloo Station."

Sherlock Holmes made a note of it.

"Now, Clayton, tell me all about the fare who came and watched this house at ten o'clock this morning and afterwards followed the two gentlemen down Regent Street."

The man looked surprised and a little embarrassed.

"Why, there's no good my telling you things, for you seem to know as much as I do already," said he. "The truth is that the gentleman told me that he was a detective, and that I was to say nothing about him to anyone."

"My good fellow, this is a very serious business, and you may find yourself in a pretty bad position if you try to hide anything from me. You say that your fare told you that he was a detective?"

"Yes, he did."

"When did he say this?"

"When he left me."

"Did he say anything more?"

"He mentioned his name."

Holmes cast a swift glance of triumph at me.

"Oh, he mentioned his name, did he? That was imprudent. What was the name that he mentioned?"

"His name," said the cabman, "was Mr. Sherlock Holmes."

Never have I seen my friend more completely taken aback than by the cabman's reply. For an instant he sat in silent amazement. Then he burst into a hearty laugh.

"A touch, Watson—an undeniable touch!" said he. "I feel a foil as quick and supple as my own. He got home upon me very prettily that time. So his name was Sherlock Holmes, was it?"

"Yes, sir, that was the gentleman's name."

"Excellent! Tell me where you picked him up and all that occurred."

"He hailed me at half-past nine in Trafalgar Square. He said that he was a detective, and he offered me two guineas if I would do exactly what he wanted all day and ask no questions. I was glad enough to agree. First we drove down to the Northumberland Hotel and waited there until two gentlemen came out and took a cab from the rank. We followed their cab until it pulled up somewhere near here."

"This very door," said Holmes.

"Well, I couldn't be sure of that, but I dare say my fare knew all about it. We pulled up half-way down the street and waited an hour and a half. Then the two gentlemen passed us, walking, and we followed down Baker Street and along—"

"I know," said Holmes.

"Until we got three-quarters down Regent Street. Then my gentleman threw up the trap, and he cried that I should drive right away to Waterloo Station as hard as I could go. I whipped up the mare and we were there under the ten minutes. Then he paid up his two guineas, like a good one, and away he went into the station. Only just as he was leaving he turned round and said: 'It might interest you to know that you have been driving Mr. Sherlock Holmes.' That's how I came to know the name."

"I see. And you saw no more of him?"

"Not after he went into the station."

"And how would you describe Mr. Sherlock Holmes?"

The cabman scratched his head. "Well, he wasn't altogether such an easy gentleman to describe. I'd put him at forty years of age, and he was of a middle height, two or three inches shorter than you, sir. He was dressed like a toff, and he had a black beard, cut square at the end, and a pale face. I don't know as I could say more than that."

"Colour of his eyes?"

"No, I can't say that."

"Nothing more that you can remember?"

"No, sir; nothing."

"Well, then, here is your half-sovereign. There's another one waiting for you if you can bring any more information. Good-night!"

"Good-night, sir, and 'hank you!"

John Clayton departed, chuckling, and Holmes turned to me with a shrug of the shoulders and a rueful smile.

"Snap goes our third thread, and we end where we began," said he. "The cunning rascal! He knew our number, knew that Sir Henry Baskerville had consulted me, spotted who I was in Regent Street, conjectured that I had got the number of the cab and would lay my hands on the driver, and so sent back this audacious message. I tell you, Watson, this time we have got a foeman who is worthy of our steel. I've been checkmated in London. I can only wish you better luck in Devonshire. But I'm not easy in my mind about it."

"About what?"

"About sending you. It's an ugly business, Watson, an ugly, dangerous business, and the more I see of it the less I like it. Yes, my dear fellow, you may laugh, but I give you my word that I shall be very glad to have you back safe and sound in Baker Street once more."

VI. BASKERVILLE HALL

Sir Henry Baskerville and Dr. Mortimer were ready upon the appointed day, and we started as arranged for Devonshire. Mr. Sherlock Holmes drove with me to the station, and gave me his last parting injunctions and advice.

"I will not bias your mind by suggesting theories or suspicions, Watson," said he; "I wish you simply to report facts in the fullest possible manner to me, and you can leave me to do the theorizing."

"What sort of facts?" I asked.

"Anything which may seem to have a bearing, however indirect, upon the case, and especially the relations between young Baskerville and his neighbours, or any fresh particulars concerning the death of Sir Charles. I have made some inquiries myself in the last few days, but the results have, I fear, been negative. One thing only appears to be certain, and that is that Mr. James Desmond, who is the next heir, is an elderly gentleman of a very amiable disposition, so that this persecution does not arise from him. I really think that we may eliminate him entirely from our calculations. There remain the people who will actually surround Sir Henry Baskerville upon the moor."

"Would it not be well in the first place to get rid of this Barrymore couple?"

"By no means. You could not make a greater mistake. If they are innocent it would be a cruel injustice, and if they are guilty we should be giving up all chance of bringing it home to them. No, no, we will preserve them upon our list of suspects. Then there is a groom at the Hall, if I remember right. There are two moorland farmers. There is our friend Dr. Mortimer, whom I believe to be entirely honest, and there is his wife, of whom we know nothing. There is this naturalist Stapleton, and there is his sister, who is said to be a young lady of attractions. There is Mr. Frankland, of Lafter Hall, who is also an unknown factor, and there are one or two other neighbours. These are the folk who must be your very special study."

"I will do my best."

"You have arms, I suppose?"

"Yes, I thought it as well to take them."

"Most certainly. Keep your revolver near you night and day, and never relax your precautions."

Our friends had already secured a first-class carriage, and were waiting for us upon the platform.

"No, we have no news of any kind," said Dr. Mortimer, in answer to my friend's questions. "I can swear to one thing, and that is that we have not been shadowed during the last two days. We have never gone out without keeping a sharp watch, and no one could have escaped our notice."

"You have always kept together, I presume?"

"Except yesterday afternoon. I usually give up one day to pure amusement when I come to town, so I spent it at the Museum of the College of Surgeons."

"And I went to look at the folk in the park," said Baskerville. "But we had no trouble of any kind."

"It was imprudent, all the same," said Holmes, shaking his head and looking very grave. "I beg, Sir Henry, that you will not go about alone. Some great misfortune will befall you if you do. Did you get your other boot?"

"No, sir, it is gone forever."

"Indeed. That is very interesting. Well, good-bye," he added, as the train began to glide down the platform. "Bear in mind, Sir Henry, one of the phrases in that queer old legend which Dr. Mortimer has read to us, and avoid the moor in those hours of darkness when the powers of evil are exalted."

I looked back at the platform when we had left it far behind, and saw the tall, austere figure of Holmes standing motionless and gazing after us.

The journey was a swift and pleasant one, and I spent it in making the more intimate acquaintance of my two companions, and in playing with Dr. Mortimer's spaniel. In a very few hours the brown earth had become ruddy, the brick had changed to granite, and red cows grazed in well-hedged fields where the lush grasses and more luxuriant vegetation spoke of a richer, if a damper, climate. Young Baskerville stared eagerly out of the window, and cried aloud with delight as he recognized the familiar features of the Devon scenery.

"I've been over a good part of the world since I left it, Dr. Watson," said he; "but I have never seen a place to compare with it."

"I never saw a Devonshire man who did not swear by his county," I remarked.

"It depends upon the breed of men quite as much as on the county," said Dr. Mortimer. "A glance at our friend here reveals the rounded head of the Celt, which carries inside it the Celtic enthusiasm and power of attachment. Poor Sir Charles's head was of a very rare type, half Gaelic, half Ivernian in its characteristics. But you were very young when you last saw Baskerville Hall, were you not?"

"I was a boy in my teens at the time of my father's death, and had never seen the Hall, for he lived in a little cottage on the south coast. Thence I went straight to a friend in America. I tell you it is all as new to me as it is to Dr. Watson, and I'm as keen as possible to see the moor."

"Are you? Then your wish is easily granted, for there is your first sight of the moor," said Dr. Mortimer, pointing out of the carriage window.

Over the green squares of the fields and the low curve of a wood there rose in the distance a grey, melancholy hill, with a strange jagged summit, dim and vague in the distance, like some fantastic landscape in a dream. Baskerville sat for a long time, his eyes fixed upon it, and I read upon his eager face how much it meant to him, this first sight of that strange spot where the men of his blood had held sway so long and left their mark so deep. There he sat, with his tweed suit and his American accent, in the corner of a prosaic railway-carriage, and yet as I looked at his dark and expressive face I felt more than ever how true a descendant he was of that long line of high-blooded, fiery, and masterful men. There were pride, valour, and strength in his thick brows, his sensitive nostrils, and his large hazel eyes. If on that forbidding moor a difficult and dangerous quest should lie before us, this was at least a comrade for whom one might venture to take a risk with the certainty that he would bravely share it.

The train pulled up at a small wayside station, and we all descended. Outside, beyond the low, white fence, a wagonette with a pair of cobs was waiting. Our coming was evidently a great event, for station-master and porters clustered round us to carry out our luggage. It was a sweet, simple country spot, but I was surprised to observe that by the gate there stood two soldierly men in dark uniforms, who leaned upon their short rifles and glanced keenly at us as we passed. The coachman, a hard-faced, gnarled little fellow, saluted Sir Henry Baskerville, and in a few minutes we were flying swiftly down the broad, white road. Rolling pasture lands curved upwards on either side of us, and old gabled houses peeped out from amid the thick green foliage, but behind the peaceful and sunlit country-side there rose ever, dark against the evening sky, the long, gloomy curve of the moor, broken by the jagged and sinister hills.

The wagonette swung round into a side road, and we curved upwards through deep lanes worn by centuries of wheels, high banks on either side, heavy with dripping moss and fleshy hart's-tongue ferns. Bronzing bracken and mottled bramble gleamed in the light of the sinking sun. Still steadily rising, we passed over a narrow granite bridge, and skirted a noisy stream, which gushed swiftly down, foaming and roaring amid the grey boulders. Both road and stream wound up through a valley dense with scrub oak and fir. At every turning Baskerville gave an exclamation of delight, looking eagerly about him and asking countless questions. To his eyes all seemed beautiful, but to me a tinge of melancholy lay upon the country-side, which bore so clearly the mark of the waning year. Yellow leaves carpeted the lanes and fluttered down upon us as we passed. The rattle of our wheels died away as we drove through drifts of rotting vegetation—sad gifts, as it seemed to me, for Nature to throw before the carriage of the returning heir of the Baskervilles.

"Hullo!" cried Dr. Mortimer, "what is this?"

A steep curve of heath-clad land, an outlying spur of the moor, lay in front of us. On the summit, hard and clear like an equestrian statue upon its pedestal, was a mounted soldier, dark and stern, his rifle poised ready over his forearm. He was watching the road along which we travelled.

"What is this, Perkins?" asked Dr. Mortimer.

Our driver half turned in his seat.

"There's a convict escaped from Princetown, sir. He's been out three days now, and the warders watch every road and every station, but they've had no sight of him yet. The farmers about here don't like it, sir, and that's a fact."

"Well, I understand that they get five pounds if they can give information."

"Yes, sir, but the chance of five pounds is but a poor thing compared to the chance of having your throat cut. You see, it isn't like any ordinary convict. This is a man that would stick at nothing."

"Who is he, then?"

"It is Selden, the Notting Hill murderer."

I remembered the case well, for it was one in which Holmes had taken an interest on account of the peculiar ferocity of the crime and the wanton brutality which had marked all the actions of the assassin. The commutation of his death sentence had been due to some doubts as to his complete sanity, so atrocious was his conduct. Our wagonette had topped a rise and in front of us rose the huge expanse of the moor, mottled with gnarled and craggy cairns and tors. A cold wind swept down from it and set us shivering. Somewhere there, on that desolate plain, was lurking this fiendish man, hiding in a burrow like a wild beast, his heart full of malignancy against the whole race which had cast him out. It needed but this to complete the grim suggestiveness of the barren waste, the chilling wind, and the darkling sky. Even Baskerville fell silent and pulled his overcoat more closely around him.

We had left the fertile country behind and beneath us. We looked back on it now, the slanting rays of a low sun turning the streams to threads of gold and glowing on the red earth new turned by the plough and the broad tangle of the woodlands. The road in front of us grew bleaker and wilder over huge russet and olive slopes, sprinkled with giant boulders. Now and then we passed a moorland cottage, walled and roofed with stone, with no creeper to break its harsh outline. Suddenly we looked down into a cup-like depression, patched with stunted oaks and firs which had been twisted and bent by the fury of years of storm. Two high, narrow towers rose over the trees. The driver pointed with his whip.

"Baskerville Hall," said he.

Its master had risen, and was staring with flushed cheeks and shining eyes. A few minutes later we had reached the lodge-gates, a maze of fantastic tracery in wrought iron, with weather-bitten pillars on either side, blotched with lichens, and surmounted by the boars' heads of the Baskervilles. The lodge was a ruin of black granite and bared ribs of rafters, but facing it was a new building, half constructed, the first fruit of Sir Charles's South African gold.

Through the gateway we passed into the avenue, where the wheels were again hushed amid the leaves, and the old trees shot their branches in a sombre tunnel over our heads. Baskerville shuddered as he looked up the long, dark drive to where the house glimmered like a ghost at the farther end.

"Was it here?" he asked, in a low voice.

"No, no, the Yew Alley is on the other side."

The young heir glanced round with a gloomy face.

"It's no wonder my uncle felt as if trouble here coming on him in such a place as this," said he. "It's enough to scare any man. I'll have a row of electric lamps up here inside of six months, and you won't know it again with a thousand-candle-power Swan and Edison right here in front of the hall door."

The avenue opened into a broad expanse of turf, and the house lay before us. In the fading light I could see that the centre was a heavy block of building from which a porch projected. The whole front was draped in ivy, with a patch clipped bare here and there where a window or a coat-of-arms broke through the dark veil. From this central block rose the twin towers, ancient, crenellated, and pierced with many loopholes. To right and left of the turrets were more modern wings of black granite. A dull light shone through heavy mullioned windows, and from the high chimneys which rose from the steep, high-angled roof there sprang a single black column of smoke.

"Welcome, Sir Henry! Welcome, to Baskerville Hall!"

A tall man had stepped from the shadow of the porch to open the door of the wagonette. The figure of a woman was silhouetted against the yellow light of the hall. She came out and helped the man to hand down our bags.

"You don't mind my driving straight home, Sir Henry?" said Dr. Mortimer. "My wife is expecting me."

"Surely you will stay and have some dinner?"

"No, I must go. I shall probably find some work awaiting me. I would stay to show you over the house, but Barrymore will be a better guide than I. Good-bye, and never hesitate night or day to send for me if I can be of service."

The wheels died away down the drive while Sir Henry and I turned into the hall, and the door clanged heavily behind us. It was a fine apartment in which we found ourselves, large, lofty, and heavily raftered with huge balks of age-blackened oak. In the great old-fashioned fireplace behind the high iron dogs a log-fire crackled and snapped. Sir Henry and I held out our hands to it, for we were numb from our long drive. Then we gazed round us at the high, thin window of old stained glass, the oak panelling, the stags' heads, the coats-of-arms upon the walls, all dim and sombre in the subdued light of the central lamp.

"It's just as I imagined it," said Sir Henry. "Is it not the very picture of an old family home? To think that this should be the same hall in which for five hundred years my people have lived! It strikes me solemn to think of it."

I saw his dark face lit up with a boyish enthusiasm as he gazed about him. The light beat upon him where he stood, but long shadows trailed down the walls and hung like a black canopy above him. Barrymore had returned from taking our luggage to our rooms. He stood in front of us now with the subdued manner of a well-trained servant. He was a remarkable-looking man, tall, handsome, with a square black beard, and pale, distinguished features.

"Would you wish dinner to be served at once, sir?"

"Is it ready?"

"In a very few minutes, sir. You will find hot water in your rooms. My wife and I will be happy, Sir Henry, to stay with you until you have made your fresh arrangements, but you will understand that under the new conditions this house will require a considerable staff."

"What new conditions?"

"I only meant, sir, that Sir Charles led a very retired life, and we were able to look after his wants. You would, naturally, wish to have more company, and so you will need changes in your household."

"Do you mean that your wife and you wish to leave?"

"Only when it is quite convenient to you, sir."

"But your family have been with us for several generations, have they not? I should be sorry to begin my life here by breaking an old family connection."

I seemed to discern some signs of emotion upon the butler's white face.

"I feel that also, sir, and so does my wife. But to tell the truth, sir, we were both very much attached to Sir Charles, and his death gave us a shock and made these surroundings very painful to us. I fear that we shall never again be easy in our minds at Baskerville Hall."

"But what do you intend to do?"

"I have no doubt, sir, that we shall succeed in establishing ourselves in some business. Sir Charles's generosity has given us the means to do so. And now, sir, perhaps I had best show you to your rooms."

A square balustraded gallery ran round the top of the old hall, approached by a double stair. From this central point two long corridors extended the whole length of the building, from which all the bedrooms opened. My own was in the same wing as Baskerville's and almost next door to it. These rooms appeared to be much more modern than the central part of the house, and the bright paper and numerous candles did something to remove the sombre impression which our arrival had left upon my mind.

But the dining-room which opened out of the hall was a place of shadow and gloom. It was a long chamber with a step separating the dais where the family sat from the lower portion reserved for their dependents. At one end a minstrels' gallery overlooked it. Black beams shot across above our heads, with a smoke-darkened ceiling beyond them. With rows of flaring torches to light it up, and the colour and rude hilarity of an old-time banquet, it might have softened; but now, when two black-clothed gentlemen sat in the little circle of light thrown by a shaded lamp, one's voice became hushed and one's spirit subdued. A dim line of ancestors, in every variety of dress, from the Elizabethan knight to the buck of the Regency, stared down upon us and daunted us by their silent company. We talked little, and I for one was glad when the meal was over and we were able to retire into the modern billiard-room and smoke a cigarette.

"My word, it isn't a very cheerful place," said Sir Henry. "I suppose one can tone down to it, but I feel a bit out of the picture at present. I don't wonder that my uncle got a little jumpy if he lived all alone in such a house as this. However, if it suits you, we will retire early tonight, and perhaps things may seem more cheerful in the morning."

I drew aside my curtains before I went to bed and looked out from my window. It opened upon the grassy space which lay in front of the hall door. Beyond, two copses of trees moaned and swung in a rising wind. A half moon broke through the rifts of racing clouds. In its cold light I saw beyond the trees a broken fringe of rocks and the long, low curve of the melancholy moor. I closed the curtain, feeling that my last impression was in keeping with the rest.

And yet it was not quite the last. I found myself weary and yet wakeful, tossing restlessly from side to side, seeking for the sleep which would not come. Far away a chiming clock struck out the quarters of the hours, but otherwise a deathly silence lay upon the old house. And then suddenly, in the very dead of the night, there came a sound to my ears, clear, resonant, and unmistakable. It was the sob of a woman, the muffled, strangling gasp of one who is torn by an uncontrollable sorrow. I sat up in bed and listened intently. The noise could not have been far away, and was certainly in the house. For half an hour I waited with every nerve on the alert, but there came no other sound save the chiming clock and the rustle of the ivy on the wall.

VII. THE STAPLETONS OF MERRIPIT HOUSE

The fresh beauty of the following morning did something to efface from our minds the grim and grey impression which had been left upon both of us by our first experience at Baskerville Hall. As Sir Henry and I sat at breakfast the sunlight flooded in through the high mullioned windows, throwing watery patches of colour from the coats-of-arms which covered them. The dark panelling glowed like bronze in the golden rays, and it was hard to realize that this was indeed the chamber which had struck such a gloom into our souls upon the evening before.

"I guess it is ourselves and not the house that we have to blame!" said the Baronet. "We were tired with our journey and chilled by our drive, so we took a grey view of the place. Now we are fresh and well, so it is all cheerful once more."

"And yet it was not entirely a question of imagination," I answered. "Did you, for example, happen to hear someone, a woman I think, sobbing in the night?"

"That is curious, for I did when I was half asleep fancy that I heard something of the sort. I waited quite a time, but there was no more of it, so I concluded that it was all a dream."

"I heard it distinctly, and I am sure that it was really the sob of a woman."

"We must ask about this right away."

He rang the bell and asked Barrymore whether he could account for our experience. It seemed to me that the pallid features of the butler turned a shade paler still as he listened to his master's question.

"There are only two women in the house, Sir Henry," he answered. "One is the scullery-maid, who sleeps in the other wing. The other is my wife, and I can answer for it that the sound could not have come from her."

And yet he lied as he said it, for it chanced that after breakfast I met Mrs. Barrymore in the long corridor with the sun full upon her face. She was a large, impassive, heavy-featured woman with a stern, set expression of mouth. But her tell-tale eyes were red and glanced at me from between swollen lids. It was she, then, who wept in the night, and if she did so her husband must know it. Yet he had taken the obvious risk of dis-covery in declaring that it was not so. Why had he done this? And why did she weep so bitterly? Already round this pale-faced, handsome, black-bearded man there was gathering an atmosphere of mystery and of gloom. It was he who had been the first to discover the body of Sir Charles, and we had only his word for all the circumstances which led up to the old man's death. Was it possible that it was Barrymore, after all, whom we had seen in the cab in Regent Street? The beard might well have been the same. The cabman had described a somewhat shorter man, but such an impression might easily have been erroneous. How could I settle the point forever? Obviously the first thing to do was to see the Grimpen postmaster, and find whether the test tele-gram had really been placed in Barrymore's own hands. Be the answer what it might, I should at least have something to report to Sherlock Holmes.

Sir Henry had numerous papers to examine after breakfast, so that the time was propitious for my excursion. It was a pleasant walk of four miles along the edge of the moor, leading me at last to a small grey hamlet, in which two larger buildings, which proved to be the inn and the house of Dr. Mortimer, stood high above the rest. The postmaster, who was also the village grocer, had a clear recollection of the telegram.

"Certainly, sir," said he, "I had the telegram delivered to Mr. Barrymore exactly as directed."

"Who delivered it?"

"My boy here. James, you delivered that telegram to Mr. Barrymore at the Hall last week, did you not?"

"Yes, father, I delivered it."

"Into his own hands?" I asked.

"Well, he was up in the loft at the time, so that I could not put it into his own hands, but I gave it into Mrs. Barrymore's hands, and she promised to deliver it at once."

"Did you see Mr. Barrymore?"

"No, sir; I tell you he was in the loft."

"If you didn't see him, how do you know he was in the loft?"

"Well, surely his own wife ought to know where he is," said the postmaster, testily. "Didn't he get the telegram? If there is any mistake it is for Mr. Barrymore himself to complain."

It seemed hopeless to pursue the inquiry any further, but it was clear that in spite of Holmes's ruse we had no proof that Barrymore had not been in London all the time. Suppose that it were so—suppose that the same man had been the last who had seen Sir Charles alive, and the first to dog the new heir when he returned to England. What then? Was he the agent of others, or had he some sinister design of his own? What interest could he have in persecuting the Baskerville family? I thought of the strange warning clipped out of the leading article of *The Times*. Was that his work or was it possibly the doing of someone who was bent upon counteracting his schemes? The only conceivable motive was that which had been suggested by Sir Henry, that if the family could be scared away a comfortable and permanent home would be secured for the Barrymores. But surely such an explanation as that would be quite inadequate to account for the deep and subtle scheming which seemed to be weaving an invisible net round the young baronet. Holmes himself had said that no more complex case had come to him in all the long series of his sensational investigations. I prayed, as I walked back along the grey, lonely road, that my friend might soon be freed from his preoccupations and able to come down to take this heavy burden of responsibility from my shoulders.

Suddenly my thoughts were interrupted by the sound of running feet behind me and by a voice which called me by name. I turned, expecting to see Dr. Mortimer, but to my surprise it was a stranger who was pursuing me. He was a small, slim, clean-shaven, prim-faced man, flaxen-haired and lean-jawed, between thirty and forty years of age, dressed in a grey suit and wearing a straw hat. A tin box for botanical specimens hung over his shoulder, and he carried a green butterfly-net in one of his hands.

"You will, I am sure, excuse my presumption, Dr. Watson," said he, as he came panting up to where I stood. "Here on the moor we are homely folk, and do not wait for formal introductions. You may possibly have heard my name from our mutual friend, Mortimer. I am Stapleton, of Merripit House."

"Your net and box would have told me as much," said I, "for I knew that Mr. Stapleton was a naturalist. But how did you know me?"

"I have been calling on Mortimer, and he pointed you out to me from the window of his surgery as you passed. As our road lay the same way I thought that I would overtake you and introduce myself. I trust that Sir Henry is none the worse for his journey?"

"He is very well, thank you."

"We were all rather afraid that after the sad death of Sir Charles the new baronet might refuse to live here. It is asking much of a wealthy man to come down and bury himself in a place of this kind, but I need not tell you that it means a very great deal to the country-side. Sir Henry has, I suppose, no superstitious fears in the matter?"

"I do not think that it is likely."

"Of course you know the legend of the fiend dog which haunts the family?"

"I have heard it."

"It is extraordinary how credulous the peasants are about here! Any number of them are ready to swear that they have seen such a creature upon the moor." He spoke with a smile, but I seemed to read in his eyes that he took the matter more seriously. "The story took a great hold upon the imagination of Sir Charles, and I have no doubt that it led to his tragic end."

"But how?"

"His nerves were so worked up that the appearance of any dog might have had a fatal effect upon his diseased heart. I fancy that he really did see something of the kind upon that last night in the Yew Alley. I feared that some disaster might occur, for I was very fond of the old man, and I knew that his heart was weak."

"How did you know that?"

"My friend Mortimer told me."

"You think then, that some dog pursued Sir Charles, and that he died of fright in consequence?"

"Have you any better explanation?"

"I have not come to any conclusion."

"Has Mr. Sherlock Holmes?"

The words took away my breath for an instant, but a glance at the placid face and steadfast eyes of my companion showed that no surprise was intended.

"It is useless for us to pretend that we do not know you, Dr. Watson," said he. "The records of your detective have reached us here, and you could not celebrate him without being known yourself. When Mortimer told me your name he could not deny your identity. If you are here, then it follows that Mr. Sherlock Holmes is interesting himself in the matter, and I am naturally curious to know what view he may take."

"I am afraid that I cannot answer that question."

"May I ask if he is going to honour us with a visit himself?"

"He cannot leave town at present. He has other cases which engage his attention."

"What a pity! He might throw some light on that which is so dark to us. But as to your own researches, if there is any possible way in which I can be of service to you,

I trust that you will command me. If I had any indication of the nature of your suspicions, or how you propose to investigate the case, I might perhaps even now give you some aid or advice."

"I assure you that I am simply here upon a visit to my friend Sir Henry, and that I need no help of any kind."

"Excellent!" said Stapleton. "You are perfectly right to be wary and discreet. I am justly reproved for what I feel was an unjustifiable intrusion, and I promise you that I will not mention the matter again."

We had come to a point where a narrow grassy path struck off from the road and wound away across the moor. A steep, boulder-sprinkled hill lay upon the right which had in bygone days been cut into a granite quarry. The face which was turned towards us formed a dark cliff, with ferns and brambles growing in its niches. From over a distant rise there floated a grey plume of smoke.

"A moderate walk along this moor-path brings us to Merripit House," said he. "Perhaps you will spare an hour that I may have the pleasure of introducing you to my sister."

My first thought was that I should be by Sir Henry's side. But then I remembered the pile of papers and bills with which his study table was littered. It was certain that I could not help him with those. And Holmes had expressly said that I should study the neighbours upon the moor. I accepted Stapleton's invitation, and we turned together down the path.

"It is a wonderful place, the moor," said he, looking round over the undulating downs, long green rollers, with crests of jagged granite foaming up into fantastic surges. "You never tire of the moor. You cannot think the wonderful secrets which it contains. It is so vast, and so barren, and so mysterious."

"You know it well, then?"

"I have only been here two years. The residents would call me a new-comer. We came shortly after Sir Charles settled. But my tastes led me to explore every part of the country round, and I should think that there are few men who know it better than I do."

"Is it so hard to know?"

"Very hard. You see, for example, this great plain to the north here, with the queer hills breaking out of it. Do you observe anything remarkable about that?"

"It would be a rare place for a gallop."

"You would naturally think so, and the thought has cost folk their lives before now. You notice those bright green spots scattered thickly over it?"

"Yes, they seem more fertile than the rest."

Stapleton laughed. "That is the great Grimpen Mire," said he. "A false step yonder means death to man or beast. Only yesterday I saw one of the moor ponies wander into it. He never came out. I saw his head for quite a long time craning out of the bog-hole, but it sucked him down at last. Even in dry seasons it is a danger to cross it, but after these autumn rains it is an awful place. And yet I can find my way to the very heart of it and return alive. By George, there is another of those miserable ponies!"

Something brown was rolling and tossing among the green sedges. Then a long, agonized, writhing neck shot upwards and a dreadful cry echoed over the moor. It turned me cold with horror, but my companion's nerves seemed to be stronger than mine.

"It's gone!" said he. "The Mire has him. Two in two days, and many more, perhaps, for they get in the way of going there in the dry weather, and never know the difference until the Mire has them in its clutch. It's a bad place, the great Grimpen Mire."

"And you say you can penetrate it?"

"Yes, there are one or two paths which a very active man can take. I have found them out."

"But why should you wish to go into so horrible a place?"

"Well, you see the hills beyond? They are really islands cut off on all sides by the impassable Mire, which has crawled round them in the course of years. That is where the rare plants and the butterflies are, if you have the wit to reach them."

"I shall try my luck some day."

He looked at me with a surprised face. "For God's sake put such an idea out of your mind," said he. "Your blood would be upon my head. I assure you that there would not be the least chance of your coming back alive. It is only by remembering certain complex landmarks that I am able to do it."

"Hullo," I cried. "What is that?"

A long, low moan, indescribably sad, swept over the moor. It filled the whole air, and yet it was impossible to say whence it came. From a dull murmur it swelled into a deep roar and then sank back into a melancholy, throbbing murmur once again. Stapleton looked at me with a curious expression in his face.

"Queer place, the moor!" said he.

"But what is it?"

"The peasants say it is the Hound of the Baskervilles calling for its prey. I've heard it once or twice before, but never quite so loud."

I looked round, with a chill of fear in my heart, at the huge swelling plain, mottled with the green patches of rushes. Nothing stirred over the vast expanse save a pair of ravens, which croaked loudly from a tor behind us.

"You are an educated man. You don't believe such nonsense as that?" said I. "What do you think is the cause of so strange a sound?"

"Bogs make queer noises sometimes. It's the mud settling, or the water rising, or something."

"No, no, that was a living voice."

"Well, perhaps it was. Did you ever hear a bittern booming?"

"No, I never did."

"It's a very rare bird—practically extinct—in England now, but all things are possible upon the moor. Yes, I should not be surprised to learn that what we have heard is the cry of the last of the bitterns."

"It's the weirdest, strangest thing that ever I heard in my life."

"Yes, it's rather an uncanny place altogether. Look at the hillside yonder. What do you make of those?"

The whole steep slope was covered with grey circular rings of stone, a score of them at least.

"What are they? Sheep-pens?"

"No, they are the homes of our worthy ancestors. Prehistoric man lived thickly on the moor, and as no one in particular has lived there since, we find all his little arrangements exactly as he left them. These are his wigwams with the roofs off. You can even see his hearth and his couch if you have the curiosity to go inside."

"But it is quite a town. When was it inhabited?"

"Neolithic man—no date."

"What did he do?"

"He grazed his cattle on these slopes, and he learned to dig for tin when the bronze sword began to supersede the stone axe. Look at the great trench in the opposite hill. That is his mark. Yes, you will find some very singular points about the moor, Dr. Watson. Oh, excuse me an instant! It is surely Cyclopides."

A small fly or moth had fluttered across our path, and in an instant Stapleton was rushing with extraordinary energy and speed in pursuit of it. To my dismay the creature flew straight for the great Mire, but my acquaintance never paused for an instant, bounding from tuft to tuft behind it, his green net waving in the air. His grey clothes and jerky, zigzag, irregular progress made him not unlike some huge moth himself. I was standing watching his pursuit with a mixture of admiration for his extraordinary activity and fear lest he should lose his footing in the treacherous Mire, when I heard the sound of steps, and, turning round, found a woman near me upon the path. She had come from the direction in which the plume of smoke indicated the position of Merripit House, but the dip of the moor had hid her until she was quite close.

I could not doubt that this was the Miss Stapleton of whom I had been told, since ladies of any sort must be few upon the moor, and I remembered that I had heard someone describe her as being a beauty. The woman who approached me was certainly that, and of a most uncommon type. There could not have been a greater contrast between brother and sister, for Stapleton was neutral tinted, with light hair and grey eyes, while she was darker than any brunette whom I have seen in England—slim, elegant, and tall. She had a proud, finely cut face, so regular that it might have seemed impassive were it not for the sensitive mouth and the beautiful dark, eager eyes. With her perfect figure and elegant dress she was, indeed, a strange apparition upon a lonely moorland path. Her eyes were on her brother as I turned, and then she quickened her pace towards me. I had raised my hat, and was about to make some explanatory remark, when her own words turned all my thoughts into a new channel.

"Go back!" she said. "Go straight back to London, instantly."

I could only stare at her in stupid surprise. Her eyes blazed at me, and she tapped the ground impatiently with her foot.

"Why should I go back?" I asked.

"I cannot explain." She spoke in a low, eager voice, with a curious lisp in her utterance. "But for God's sake do what I ask you. Go back and never set foot upon the moor again."

"But I have only just come."

"Man, man!" she cried. "Can you not tell when a warning is for your own good? Go back to London! Start to-night! Get away from this place at all costs! Hush, my brother is coming! Not a word of what I have said. Would you mind getting that orchid for me among the mare's-tails yonder? We are very rich in orchids on the moor, though, of course, you are rather late to see the beauties of the place."

Stapleton had abandoned the chase and came back to us breathing hard and flushed with his exertions.

"Hullo, Beryl!" said he, and it seemed to me that the tone of his greeting was not altogether a cordial one.

"Well, Jack, you are very hot."

"Yes, I was chasing a Cyclopides. He is very rare, and seldom found in the late autumn. What a pity that I should have missed him!"

He spoke unconcernedly, but his small light eyes glanced incessantly from the girl to me.

"You have introduced yourselves, I can see."

"Yes. I was telling Sir Henry that it was rather late for him to see the true beauties of the moor."

"Why, who do you think this is?"

"I imagine that it must be Sir Henry Baskerville."

"No, no," said I. "Only a humble commoner, but his friend. My name is Dr. Watson."

A flush of vexation passed over her expressive face.

"We have been talking at cross purposes," said she.

"Why, you had not very much time for talk," her brother remarked, with the same questioning eyes.

"I talked as if Dr. Watson were a resident instead of being merely a visitor," said she. "It cannot much matter to him whether it is early or late for the orchids. But you will come on, will you not, and see Merripit House?"

A short walk brought us to it, a bleak moorland house, once the farm of some grazier in the old prosperous days, but now put into repair and turned into a modern dwelling. An orchard surrounded it, but the trees, as is usual upon the moor, were stunted and nipped, and the effect of the whole place was mean and melancholy. We were admitted by a strange, wizened, rusty-coated old manservant, who seemed in keeping with the house. Inside, however, there were large rooms furnished with an elegance in which I seemed to recognize the taste of the lady. As I looked from their windows at the interminable granite-flecked moor rolling unbroken to the farthest horizon I could not but marvel at what could have brought this highly educated man and this beautiful woman to live in such a place.

"Queer spot to choose, is it not?" said he, as if in answer to my thought. "And yet we manage to make ourselves fairly happy, do we not, Beryl?"

"Quite happy," said she, but there was no ring of conviction in her words.

"I had a school," said Stapleton. "It was in the north country. The work to a man of my temperament was mechanical and uninteresting, but the privilege of living with youth, of helping to mould those young minds and of impressing them with one's own character and ideals, was very dear to me. However, the fates were against us. A serious epidemic broke out in the school, and three of the boys died. It never recovered from the blow, and much of my capital was irretrievably swallowed up. And yet, if it were not for the loss of the charming companionship of the boys, I could rejoice over my own misfortune, for, with my strong tastes for botany and zoology, I find an unlimited field of work here, and my sister is as devoted to Nature as I am. All this, Dr. Watson, has been brought upon your head by your expression as you surveyed the moor out of our window."

"It certainly did cross my mind that it might be a little dull—less for you, perhaps, than for your sister."

"No, no, I am never dull," said she quickly.

"We have books, we have our studies, and we have interesting neighbours. Dr. Mortimer is a most learned man in his own line. Poor Sir Charles was also an admirable companion. We knew him well, and miss him more than I can tell. Do you think that I should intrude if I were to call this afternoon and make the acquaintance of Sir Henry?"

"I am sure that he would be delighted."

"Then perhaps you would mention that I propose to do so. We may in our humble way do something to make things more easy for him until he becomes accustomed to his new surroundings. Will you come upstairs, Dr. Watson, and inspect my collection of Lepidoptera? I think it is the most complete one in the south-west of England. By the time that you have looked through them lunch will be almost ready."

But I was eager to get back to my charge. The melancholy of the moor, the death of the unfortunate pony, the weird sound which had been associated with the grim legend of the Baskervilles—all these things tinged my thoughts with sadness. Then on the top of these more or less vague impressions there had come the definite and distinct warning of Miss Stapleton, delivered with such intense earnestness that I could not doubt that some grave and deep reason lay behind it. I resisted all pressure to stay for lunch, and I set off at once upon my return journey, taking the grass-grown path by which we had come.

It seems, however, that there must have been some short cut for those who knew it, for before I had reached the road I was astounded to see Miss Stapleton sitting upon a rock by the side of the track. Her face was beautifully flushed with her exertions, and she held her hand to her side.

"I have run all the way in order to cut you off, Dr. Watson," said she. "I had not even time to put on my hat. I must not stop, or my brother may miss me. I wanted to say to you how sorry I am about the stupid mistake I made in thinking that you were Sir Henry. Please forget the words I said, which have no application whatever to you."

"But I can't forget them, Miss Stapleton," said I. "I am Sir Henry's friend, and his welfare is a very close concern of mine. Tell me why it was that you were so eager that Sir Henry should return to London."

"A woman's whim, Dr. Watson. When you know me better you will understand that I cannot always give reasons for what I say or do."

"No, no. I remember the thrill in your voice. I remember the look in your eyes. Please, please, be frank with me, Miss Stapleton, for ever since I have been here I have been conscious of shadows all round me. Life has become like that great Grimpen Mire, with little green patches everywhere into which one may sink and with no guide to point the track. Tell me, then, what it was that you meant, and I will promise to convey your warning to Sir Henry."

An expression of irresolution passed for an instant over her face, but her eyes had hardened again when she answered me.

"You make too much of it, Dr. Watson," said she. "My brother and I were very much shocked by the death of Sir Charles. We knew him very intimately, for his favourite walk was over the moor to our house. He was deeply impressed with the curse which hung over his family, and when this tragedy came I naturally felt that there must be some grounds for the fears which he had expressed. I was distressed, therefore, when another member of the family came down to live here, and I felt that he should be warned of the danger which he will run. That was all which I intended to convey."

"But what is the danger?"

"You know the story of the hound?"

"I do not believe in such nonsense."

"But I do. If you have any influence with Sir Henry, take him away from a place which has always been fatal to his family. The world is wide. Why should he wish to live at the place of danger?"

"Because it *is* the place of danger. That is Sir Henry's nature. I fear that unless you can give me some more definite information than this it would be impossible to get him to move."

"I cannot say anything definite, for I do not know anything definite."

"I would ask you one more question, Miss Stapleton. If you meant no more than this when you first spoke to me, why should you not wish your brother to overhear what you said? There is nothing to which he, or anyone else, could object."

"My brother is very anxious to have the Hall inhabited, for he thinks it is for the good of the poor folk upon the moor. He would be very angry if he knew that I had said anything which might induce Sir Henry to go away. But I have done my duty now and I will say no more. I must get back, or he will miss me and suspect that I have seen you. Good-bye!"

She turned, and had disappeared in a few minutes among the scattered boulders, while I, with my soul full of vague fears, pursued my way to Baskerville Hall.

VIII. First Report of Dr. Watson

From this point onwards I will follow the course of events by transcribing my own letters to Mr. Sherlock Holmes which lie before me on the table. One page is missing, but otherwise they are exactly as written, and show my feelings and suspicions of the moment more accurately than my memory, clear as it is upon these tragic events, can possibly do.

Baskerville Hall, Oct. 13th

My Dear Holmes,

My previous letters and telegrams have kept you pretty well up-to-date as to all that has occurred in this most God-forsaken corner of the world. The longer one stays here the more does the spirit of the moor sink into one's soul, its vastness, and also its grim charm. When you are once out upon its bosom you have left all traces of modern England behind you, but on the other hand you are conscious everywhere of the homes and the work of prehistoric people. On all sides of you as you walk are the houses of these forgotten folk, with their graves and the huge monoliths which are supposed to have marked their temples. As you look at their grey stone huts against the scarred hillsides you leave your own age behind you, and if you were to see a skin-clad, hairy man crawl out from the low door, fitting a flint-tipped arrow on to the string of his bow, you would feel that his presence there was more natural than your own. The strange thing is that they should have lived so thickly on what must always have been most unfruitful soil. I am no antiquarian, but I could imagine that they were some unwarlike and harried race who were forced to accept that which none other would occupy.

All this, however, is foreign to the mission on which you sent me, and will probably be very uninteresting to your severely practical mind. I can still remember your complete indifference as to whether the sun moved round the earth or the earth round the sun. Let me, therefore, return to the facts concerning Sir Henry Baskerville.

If you have not had any report within the last few days it is because up till today there was nothing of importance to relate. Then a very surprising circumstance occurred, which I shall tell you in due course. But, first of all, I must keep you in touch with some of the other factors in the situation.

One of these, concerning which I have said little, is the escaped convict upon the moor. There is strong reason now to believe that he has got right away, which is a considerable relief to the lonely householders of this district. A fortnight has passed since his flight, during which he has not been seen and nothing has been heard of him. It is surely inconceivable that he could have held out upon the moor during all that time. Of course, so far as his concealment goes there is no difficulty at all. Any one of these stone huts would give him a hiding-place. But there is nothing to eat unless he were to catch and slaughter one of the moor sheep. We think, therefore, that he has gone, and the outlying farmers sleep the better in consequence.

We are four able-bodied men in this household, so that we could take good care of ourselves, but I confess that I have had uneasy moments when I have thought of the Stapletons. They live miles from any help. There are one maid, an old man-servant, the sister, and the brother, the latter not a very strong man. They would be helpless in the hands of a desperate fellow like this Notting Hill criminal, if he could once effect an entrance. Both Sir Henry and I were concerned at their situation, and it was suggested that Perkins the groom should go over to sleep there, but Stapleton would not hear of it.

The fact is that our friend the baronet begins to display a considerable interest in our fair neighbour. It is not to be wondered at, for time hangs heavily in this lonely spot to an active man like him, and she is a very fascinating and beautiful woman. There is something tropical and exotic about her which forms a singular contrast to her cool and unemotional brother. Yet he also gives the idea of hidden fires. He has certainly a very marked influence over her, for I have seen her continually glance at him as she talked as if seeking approbation for what she said. I trust that he is kind to her. There is a dry glitter in his eyes, and a firm set of his thin lips, which go with a positive and possibly a harsh nature. You would find him an interesting study.

He came over to call upon Baskerville on that first day, and the very next morning he took us both to show us the spot where the legend of the wicked Hugo is supposed to have had its origin. It was an excursion of some miles across the moor to a place which is so dismal that it might have suggested the story. We found a short valley between rugged tors which led to an open, grassy space flecked over with the white cotton grass. In the middle of it rose two great stones, worn and sharpened at the upper end, until they looked like the huge, corroding fangs of some monstrous beast. In every way it corresponded with the scene of the old tragedy. Sir Henry was much interested, and asked Stapleton more than once whether he did really believe in the possibility of the interference of the supernatural in the affairs of men. He spoke lightly, but it was evident that he was very much in earnest. Stapleton was guarded in his replies, but it was easy to see that he said less than he might, and that he would not express his whole opinion out of consideration for the feelings of the Baronet. He told us of similar cases where families had suffered from some evil influence, and he left us with the impression that he shared the popular view upon the matter.

On our way back we stayed for lunch at Merripit House, and it was there that Sir Henry made the acquaintance of Miss Stapleton. From the first moment that he saw her he appeared to be strongly attracted by her, and I am much mistaken if the feeling was not mutual. He referred to her again and again on our walk home, and since then hardly a day has passed that we have not seen something of the brother and sister. They dine here to-night, and there is some talk of our going to them next week. One would imagine that such a match would be very welcome to Stapleton, and yet I have more than once caught a look of the strongest disapprobation in his face when Sir Henry has been paying some attention to his sister. He is much attached to her, no doubt, and would lead a lonely life without her, but it would seem the height of selfishness, if he were to stand in the way of her making so brilliant a marriage. Yet I am certain that he does not wish their intimacy to ripen into love, and I have several times observed that he has taken pains to prevent them from being *tête-à-tête*. By the way, your instructions to me never to allow Sir Henry to go out alone will become very much more onerous if a love affair were to be added to our other difficulties. My popularity would soon suffer if I were to carry out your orders to the letter.

The other day—Thursday, to be more exact—Dr. Mortimer lunched with us. He has been excavating a barrow at Long Down, and has got a prehistoric skull which fills him with great joy. Never was there such a single-minded enthusiast as he! The Stapletons came in afterwards, and the good doctor took us all to the Yew Alley, at Sir Henry's request, to show us exactly how everything occurred upon that fatal night. It is a long, dismal walk, the Yew Alley, between two high walls of clipped hedge, with a narrow band of grass upon either side. At the far end is an old, tumble-down summer-house. Half-way down is the moor-gate, where the old gentleman left his cigar ash. It is a white wooden gate with a latch. Beyond it lies the wide moor. I remembered your theory of the affair and tried to picture all that had occurred. As the old man stood there he saw something coming across the moor, something which terrified him so that he lost his wits, and ran and ran until he died of sheer horror and exhaustion. There was the long, gloomy tunnel down which he fled. And from what? A sheep-dog of the moor? Or a spectral hound, black, silent, and monstrous? Was there a human agency in the matter? Did the pale, watchful Barrymore know more than he cared to say? It was all dim and vague, but always there is the dark shadow of crime behind it.

One other neighbour I have met since I wrote last. This is Mr. Frankland, of Lafter Hall, who lives some four miles to the south of us. He is an elderly man, red-faced, white-haired, and choleric. His passion is for the British law, and he has spent a large fortune in litigation. He fights for the mere pleasure of fighting, and is equally ready to take up either side of a question, so that it is no wonder that he has found it a costly amusement. Sometimes he will shut up a right of way and defy the parish to make him open it. At others he will with his own hands tear down some other man's gate and declare that a path has existed there from time immemorial, defying the owner to prosecute him for trespass. He is learned in old manorial and communal rights, and he applies his knowledge sometimes in favour of the villagers of Fernworthy and sometimes against them, so that he is periodically either carried in triumph down the village street or else burned in effigy, according to his latest exploit. He is said to have about seven lawsuits upon his hands at present, which will probably swallow up the remainder of his fortune, and so draw his sting and leave him harmless for the future. Apart from the law he seems a kindly, good-natured person, and I only mention him because you were particular that I should send some description of the people who surround us. He is curiously employed at present, for, being an amateur astronomer, he has an excellent telescope, with which he lies upon the roof of his own house and sweeps the moor all day in the hope of catching a glimpse of the escaped convict. If he would confine his energies to this all would be well, but there are rumours that he intends to prosecute Dr. Mortimer for opening a grave without the consent of the next-of-kin, because he dug up the neolithic skull in the barrow on Long Down. He helps to keep our lives from being monotonous and gives a little comic relief where it is badly needed.

And now, having brought you up to date on the escaped convict, the Stapletons, Dr. Mortimer, and Frankland of Lafter Hall, let me end on that which is most important and tell you more about the Barrymores, and especially about the surprising development of last night.

First of all about the test telegram, which you sent from London in order to make sure that Barrymore was really here. I have already explained that the testimony of the postmaster shows that the test was worthless and that we have no proof one way or the other. I told Sir Henry how the matter stood, and he at once, in his downright fashion, had Barrymore up and asked him whether he had received the telegram himself. Barrymore said that he had.

"Did the boy deliver it into your own hands?" asked Sir Henry.

Barrymore looked surprised, and considered for a little time.

"No," said he, "I was in the box-room at the time, and my wife brought it up to me."

"Did you answer it yourself?"

"No; I told my wife what to answer, and she went down to write it."

In the evening he returned to the subject of his own accord.

"I could not quite understand the object of your questions this morning, Sir Henry," said he. "I trust that they do not mean that I have done anything to forfeit your confidence?"

Sir Henry had to assure him that it was not so and pacify him by giving him a considerable part of his old wardrobe, the London outfit having now all arrived.

Mrs. Barrymore is of interest to me. She is a heavy, solid person, very limited, intensely respectable, and inclined to be puritanical. You could hardly conceive a less emotional subject. Yet I have told you how, on the first night here, I heard her sobbing bitterly, and since then I have more than once observed traces of tears upon her face. Some deep sorrow gnaws ever at her heart. Sometimes I wonder if she has a guilty memory which haunts her, and sometimes I suspect Barrymore of being a domestic tyrant. I have always felt that there was something singular and questionable in this man's character, but the adventure of last night brings all my suspicions to a head.

And yet it may seem a small matter in itself. You are aware that I am not a very sound sleeper, and since I have been on guard in this house my slumbers have been lighter than ever. Last night, about two in the morning, I was aroused by a stealthy step passing my room. I rose, opened my door, and peeped out. A long black shadow was trailing down the corridor. It was thrown by a man who walked softly down the passage with a candle held in his hand. He was in shirt and trousers, with no covering to his feet. I could merely see the outline, but his height told me that it was Barrymore. He walked very slowly and circumspectly, and there was something indescribably guilty and furtive in his whole appearance.

I have told you that the corridor is broken by the balcony which runs round the hall, but that it is resumed upon the farther side. I waited until he had passed out of sight, and then I followed him. When I came round the balcony he had reached the end of the farther corridor, and I could see from the glimmer of light through an open door that he had entered one of the rooms. Now, all these rooms are unfurnished and unoccupied, so that his expedition became more mysterious than ever. The light shone steadily, as if he were standing motionless. I crept down the passage as noiselessly as I could and peeped round the corner of the door.

Barrymore was crouching at the window with the candle held against the glass. His profile was half turned towards me, and his face seemed to be rigid with expectation as he stared out into the blackness of the moor. For some minutes he stood watching intently. Then he gave a deep groan and with an impatient gesture he put out the light. Instantly I made my way back to my room, and very shortly came the stealthy steps passing once more upon their return journey. Long afterwards when I had fallen into a light sleep I heard a key turn somewhere in a lock, but I could not tell whence the sound came. What it all means I cannot guess, but there is some secret business going on in this house of gloom which sooner or later we shall get to the bottom of. I do not trouble you with my theories, for you asked me to furnish you only with facts. I have had a long talk with Sir Henry this morning, and we have made a plan of campaign founded upon my observations of last night. I will not speak about it just now, but it should make my next report interesting reading.

IX. THE LIGHT UPON THE MOOR
[Second report of Dr. Watson]

Baskerville Hall, Oct. 15th

My Dear Holmes,

If I was compelled to leave you without much news during the early days of my mission you must acknowledge that I am making up for lost time, and that events are now crowding thick and fast upon us. In my last report I ended upon my top note with Barrymore at the window, and now I have quite a budget already which will, unless I am much mistaken, considerably surprise you. Things have taken a turn which I could not have anticipated. In some ways they have within the last forty-eight hours become much clearer and in some ways they have become more complicated. But I will tell you all and you shall judge for yourself.

Before breakfast on the morning following my adventure I went down the corridor and examined the room in which Barrymore had been on the night before. The western window through which he had stared so intently has, I noticed, one peculiarity above all other windows in the house—it commands the nearest out-look on to the moor. There is an opening between two trees which enables one from this point of view to look right down upon it, while from all the other windows it is only a distant glimpse which can be obtained. It follows, therefore, that Barrymore, since only this window would serve his purpose, must have been looking out for something or somebody upon the moor. The night was very dark, so that I can hardly imagine how he could have hoped to see anyone. It had struck me that it was possible that some love intrigue was on foot. That would have accounted for his stealthy movements and also for the uneasiness of his wife. The man is a striking-looking fellow, very well equipped to steal the heart of a country girl, so that this theory seemed to have something to support it. That opening of the door which I had heard after I had returned to my room might mean that he had gone out to keep some clandestine appointment. So I reasoned with myself in the morning, and I tell you the direction of my suspicions, however much the result may have shown that they were unfounded.

But whatever the true explanation of Barrymore's movements might be, I felt that the responsibility of keeping them to myself until I could explain them was more than I could bear. I had an interview with the baronet in his study after breakfast, and I told him all that I had seen. He was less surprised than I had expected.

"I knew that Barrymore walked about nights, and I had a mind to speak to him about it," said he. "Two or three times I have heard his steps in the passage, coming and going, just about the hour you name."

"Perhaps, then, he pays a visit every night to that particular window," I suggested.

"Perhaps he does. If so, we should be able to shadow him, and see what it is that he is after. I wonder what your friend Holmes would do if he were here?"

"I believe that he would do exactly what you now suggest," said I. "He would follow Barrymore and see what he did."

"Then we shall do it together."

"But surely he would hear us."

"The man is rather deaf, and in any case we must take our chance of that. We'll sit up in my room to-night, and wait until he passes." Sir Henry rubbed his hands with pleasure, and it was evident that he hailed the adventure as a relief to his somewhat quiet life upon the moor.

The baronet has been in communication with the architect who prepared the plans for Sir Charles, and with a contractor from London, so that we may expect great changes to begin here soon. There have been decorators and furnishers up from Plymouth, and it is evident that our friend has large ideas, and means to spare no pains or expense to restore the grandeur of his family. When the house is renovated and refurnished, all that he will need will be a wife to make it complete. Between ourselves, there are pretty clear signs that this will not be wanting if the lady is willing, for I have seldom seen a man more infatuated with a woman than he is with our beautiful neighbour, Miss Stapleton. And yet the course of true love does not run quite as smoothly as one would under the circumstances expect. To-day, for example, its surface was broken by a very unexpected ripple, which has caused our friend considerable perplexity and annoyance.

After the conversation which I have quoted about Barrymore, Sir Henry put on his hat and prepared to go out. As a matter of course I did the same.

"What, are *you* coming, Watson?" he asked, looking at me in a curious way.

"That depends on whether you are going on the moor," said I.

"Yes, I am."

"Well, you know what my instructions are. I am sorry to intrude, but you heard how earnestly Holmes insisted that I should not leave you, and especially that you should not go alone upon the moor."

Sir Henry put his hand upon my shoulder, with a pleasant smile.

"My dear fellow," said he, "Holmes, with all his wisdom, did not foresee some things which have happened since I have been on the moor. You understand me? I am sure that you are the last man in the world who would wish to be a spoil-sport. I must go out alone."

It put me in a most awkward position. I was at a loss what to say or what to do, and before I had made up my mind he picked up his cane and was gone.

But when I came to think the matter over my conscience reproached me bitterly for having on any pretext allowed him to go out of my sight. I imagined what my feelings would be if I had to return to you and to confess that some misfortune had occurred through my disregard for your instructions. I assure you my cheeks flushed at the very thought. It might not even now be too late to overtake him, so I set off at once in the direction of Merripit House.

I hurried along the road at the top of my speed without seeing anything of Sir Henry, until I came to the point where the moor path branches off. There, fearing that perhaps I had come in the wrong direction, after all, I mounted a hill from which I could command a view—the same hill which is cut into the dark quarry. Then I saw him at once. He was on the moor path, about a quarter of a mile off, and a lady was by his side who could only be Miss Stapleton. It was clear that there was already an understanding between them and that they had met by appointment. They were walking slowly along in deep conversation, and I saw her making quick little movements of her hands as if she were very earnest in what she was saying, while he listened intently, and once or twice shook his head in strong dissent. I stood among the rocks watching them, very much puzzled as to what I should do next. To follow them and break into their intimate conversation seemed to be an outrage, and yet my clear duty was never for an instant to let him out of my sight. To act the spy upon a friend was a hateful task. Still, I could see no better course than to observe him from the hill, and to clear my conscience by confessing to him afterwards what I had done. It is true that if any sudden danger had threatened him I was too far away to be of use, and yet I am sure that you will agree with me that the position was very difficult, and that there was nothing more which I could do.

Our friend, Sir Henry, and the lady had halted on the path and were standing deeply absorbed in their conversation, when I was suddenly aware that I was not the only witness of their interview. A wisp of green floating in the air caught my eye, and another glance showed me that it was carried on a stick by a man who was moving among the broken ground. It was Stapleton with his butterfly-net. He was very much closer to the pair than I was, and he appeared to be moving in their direction. At this instant Sir Henry suddenly drew Miss Stapleton to his side. His arm was round her, but it seemed to me that she was straining away from him with her face averted. He stooped his head to hers, and she raised one hand as if in protest. Next moment I saw them spring apart and turn hurriedly round. Stapleton was the cause of the interruption. He was running wildly towards them, his absurd net dangling behind him. He gesticulated and almost danced with excitement in front of the lovers. What the scene meant I could not imagine, but it seemed to me that Stapleton was abusing Sir Henry, who offered explanations, which became more angry as the other refused to accept them. The lady stood by in haughty silence. Finally Stapleton turned upon his heel and beckoned in a peremptory way to his sister, who, after an irresolute glance at Sir Henry, walked off by the side of her brother. The naturalist's angry gestures showed that the lady was included in his displeasure. The baronet stood for a minute looking after them, and then he walked slowly back the way that he had come, his head hanging, the very picture of dejection.

What all this meant I could not imagine, but I was deeply ashamed to have witnessed so intimate a scene without my friend's knowledge. I ran down the hill, therefore, and met the baronet at the bottom. His face was flushed with anger and his brows were wrinkled, like one who is at his wits' ends what to do.

"Hullo, Watson! Where have you dropped from?" said he. "You don't mean to say that you came after me in spite of all?"

I explained everything to him: how I had found it impossible to remain behind, how I had followed him, and how I had witnessed all that had occurred. For an instant his eyes blazed at me, but my frankness disarmed his anger, and he broke at last into a rather rueful laugh.

"You would have thought the middle of that prairie a fairly safe place for a man to be private," said he, "but, by thunder, the whole country-side seems to have been out to see me do my wooing—and a mighty poor wooing at that! Where had you engaged a seat?"

"I was on that hill."

"Quite in the back row, eh? But her brother was well up to the front. Did you see him come out on us?"

"Yes, I did."

"Did he ever strike you as being crazy—this brother of hers?"

"I can't say that he ever did."

"I dare say not. I always thought him sane enough until to-day, but you can take it from me that either he or I ought to be in a strait-jacket. What's the matter with me, anyhow? You've lived near me for some weeks, Watson. Tell me straight, now! Is there anything that would prevent me from making a good husband to a woman that I loved?"

"I should say not."

"He can't object to my worldly position, so it must be myself that he has this down on. What has he against me? I never hurt man or woman in my life that I know of. And yet he would not so much as let me touch the tips of her fingers."

"Did he say so?"

"That, and a deal more. I tell you, Watson, I've only known her these few weeks, but from the first I just felt that she was made for me, and she, too—she was happy when she was with me, and that I'll swear. There's a light in a woman's eyes that speaks louder than words. But he has never let us get together, and it was only to-day for the first time that I saw a chance of having a few words with her alone. She was glad to meet me, but when she did it was not love that she would talk about, and she wouldn't let me talk about it either if she could have stopped it. She kept coming back to it that this was a place of danger, and that she would never be happy until I had left it. I told her that since I had seen her I was in no hurry to leave it, and that if she really wanted me to go, the only way to work it was for her to arrange to go with me. With that I offered in as many words to marry her, but before she could answer down came this brother of hers, running at us with a face on him like a madman. He was just white with rage, and those light eyes of his were blazing with fury. What was I doing with the lady? How dared I offer her attentions which were distasteful to her? Did I think that because I was a baronet I could do what I liked? If he had not been her brother I should have known better how to answer him. As it was I told him that my feelings towards his sister were such as I was not ashamed of, and that I hoped that she might honour me by becoming my wife. That seemed to make the matter no better, so then I lost my temper too, and I answered him rather more hotly than I should, perhaps, considering that she was standing by. So it ended by his going off with her, as you saw, and here am I as badly puzzled a man as any in this county. Just tell me what it all means, Watson, and I'll owe you more than ever I can hope to pay."

I tried one or two explanations, but, indeed, I was completely puzzled myself. Our friend's title, his fortune, his age, his character, and his appearance are all in his favour, and I know nothing against him, unless it be this dark fate which runs in his family. That his advances should be rejected so brusquely without any reference to the lady's own wishes, and that the lady should accept the situation without protest, is very amazing. However, our conjectures were set at rest by a visit from Stapleton himself that very afternoon. He had come to offer apologies for his rudeness of the morning, and after a long private interview with Sir Henry in his study the upshot of their conversation was that the breach is quite healed, and that we are to dine at Merripit House next Friday as a sign of it.

"I don't say now that he isn't a crazy man," said Sir Henry; "I can't forget the look in his eyes when he ran at me this morning, but I must allow that no man could make a more handsome apology than he has done."

"Did he give any explanation of his conduct?"

"His sister is everything in his life, he says. That is natural enough, and I am glad that he should understand her value. They have always been together, and according to his account he has been a very lonely man with only her as a companion, so that the thought of losing her was really terrible to him. He had not understood, he said, that I was becoming attached to her, but when he saw with his own eyes that it was really so, and that she might be taken away from him, it gave him such a shock that for a time he was not responsible for what he said or did. He was very sorry for all that had passed, and he recognized how foolish and how selfish it was that he should imagine that he could hold a beautiful woman like his sister to himself for her whole life. If she had to leave him he had rather it was to a neighbour like myself than to anyone else. But in any case it was a blow to him, and it would take him some time before he could prepare himself to meet it. He would withdraw all opposition upon his part if I would promise for three months to let the matter rest, and to be content with cultivating the lady's friendship during that time without claiming her love. This I promised, and so the matter rests."

So there is one of our small mysteries cleared up. It is something to have touched bottom anywhere in this bog in which we are floundering. We know now why Stapleton looked with disfavour upon his sister's suitor—even when that suitor was so eligible a one as Sir Henry. And now I pass on to another thread which I have extricated out of the tangled skein, the mystery of the sobs in the night, of the tear-stained face of Mrs. Barrymore, of the secret journey of the butler to the western lattice-window. Congratulate me, my dear Holmes, and tell me that I have not disappointed you as an agent—that you do not regret the confidence which you showed in me when you sent me down. All these things have by one night's work been thoroughly cleared.

I have said "by one night's work," but, in truth, it was by two nights' work, for on the first we drew entirely blank. I sat up with Sir Henry in his room until nearly three o'clock in the morning, but no sound of any sort did we hear except the chiming clock upon the stairs. It was a most melancholy vigil, and ended by each of us falling asleep in our chairs. Fortunately we were not discouraged, and we determined to try again. The next night we lowered the lamp and sat smoking cigarettes, without making the least sound. It was incredible how slowly the hours crawled by, and yet we were helped through it by the same sort of patient interest which the hunter must feel as he watches the trap into which he hopes the game may wander. One struck, and two, and we had almost for the second time given it up in despair, when in an instant we both sat bolt upright in our chairs, with all our weary senses keenly on the alert once more. We had heard the creak of a step in the passage.

Very stealthily we heard it pass along until it died away in the distance. Then the baronet gently opened his door, and we set out in pursuit. Already our man had gone round the gallery, and the corridor was all in darkness. Softly we stole along until we had come into the other wing. We were just in time to catch a glimpse of the tall, black-bearded figure, his shoulders rounded, as he tip-toed down the passage. Then he passed through the same door as before, and the light of the candle framed it in the darkness and shot one single yellow beam across the gloom of the corridor. We shuffled cautiously towards it, trying every plank before we dared to put our whole weight upon it. We had taken the precaution of leaving our boots behind us, but, even so, the old boards snapped and creaked beneath our tread. Sometimes it seemed impossible that he should fail to hear our approach. However, the man is fortunately rather deaf, and he was entirely preoccupied in that which he was doing. When at last we reached the door and peeped through we found him crouching at the window, candle in hand, his white, intent face pressed against the pane, exactly as I had seen him two nights before.

We had arranged no plan of campaign, but the baronet is a man to whom the most direct way is always the most natural. He walked into the room, and as he did so Barrymore sprang up from the window with a sharp hiss of his breath, and stood, livid and trembling, before us. His dark eyes, glaring out of the white mask of his face, were full of horror and astonishment as he gazed from Sir Henry to me.

"What are you doing here, Barrymore?"

"Nothing, sir." His agitation was so great that he could hardly speak, and the shadows sprang up and down from the shaking of his candle. "It was the window, sir. I go round at night to see that they are fastened."

"On the second floor?"

"Yes, sir, all the windows."

"Look here, Barrymore," said Sir Henry, sternly, "we have made up our minds to have the truth out of you, so it will save you trouble to tell it sooner rather than later. Come, now! No lies! What were you doing at that window?"

The fellow looked at us in a helpless way, and he wrung his hands together like one who is in the last extremity of doubt and misery.

"I was doing no harm, sir. I was holding a candle to the window."

"And why were you holding a candle to the window?"

"Don't ask me, Sir Henry—don't ask me! I give you my word , sir, that it is not my secret, and that I cannot tell it. If it concerned no one but myself I would not try to keep it from you."

A sudden idea occurred to me, and I took the candle from the window-sill, where the butler had placed it.

"He must have been holding it as a signal," said I. "Let us see if there is any answer."

I held it as he had done, and stared out into the darkness of the night. Vaguely I could discern the black bank of the trees and the lighter expanse of the moor, for the moon was behind the clouds. And then I gave a cry of exultation, for a tiny pin-point of yellow light had suddenly transfixed the dark veil, and glowed steadily in the centre of the black square framed by the window.

"There it is!" I cried.

"No, no, sir, it is nothing—nothing at all," the butler broke in; "I assure you, sir—"

"Move your light across the window, Watson!" cried the baronet. "See, the other moves also! Now, you rascal, do you deny that it is a signal? Come, speak up! Who is your confederate out yonder, and what is this conspiracy that is going on?"

The man's face became openly defiant.

"It is my business, and not yours. I will not tell."

"Then you leave my employment right away."

"Very good, sir. If I must, I must."

"And you go in disgrace. By thunder, you may well be ashamed of yourself. Your family has lived with mine for over a hundred years under this roof, and here I find you deep in some dark plot against me."

"No, no, sir; no, not against you!"

It was a woman's voice, and Mrs. Barrymore, paler and more horror-struck than her husband, was standing at the door. Her bulky figure in a shawl and skirt might have been comic were it not for the intensity of feeling upon her face.

"We have to go, Eliza. This is the end of it. You can pack our things," said the butler.

"Oh, John, John, have I brought you to this? It is my doing, Sir Henry—all mine. He has done nothing except for my sake, and because I asked him."

"Speak out, then! What does it mean?"

"My unhappy brother is starving on the moor. We cannot let him perish at our very gates. The light is a signal to him that food is ready for him, and his light out yonder is to show the spot to which to bring it."

"Then your brother is—"

"The escaped convict, sir—Selden, the criminal."

"That's the truth, sir," said Barrymore. "I said that it was not my secret, and that I could not tell it to you. But now you have heard it, and you will see that if there was a plot it was not against you."

This, then, was the explanation of the stealthy expeditions at night and the light at the window. Sir Henry and I both stared at the woman in amazement. Was it possible that this stolidly respectable person was of the same blood as one of the most notorious criminals in the country?

"Yes, sir, my name was Selden, and he is my younger brother. We humoured him too much when he was a lad, and gave him his own way in everything, until he came to think that the world was made for his pleasure, and that he could do what he liked in it. Then, as he grew older, he met wicked companions, and the devil entered into him until he broke my mother's heart and dragged our name in the dirt. From crime to crime he sank lower and lower, until it is only the mercy of God which has snatched him from the scaffold; but to me, sir, he was always the little curly-headed boy that I had nursed and played with, as an elder sister would. That was why he broke prison, sir. He knew that I was here, and that we could not refuse to help him. When he dragged himself here one night, weary and starving, with the warders hard at his heels, what could we do? We took him in and fed him and cared for him. Then you returned, sir, and my brother thought he would be safer on the moor than anywhere else until the hue and cry was over, so he lay in hiding there. But every second night we made sure if he was still there by putting a light in the window, and if there was an answer my husband took out some bread and meat to him. Every day we hoped that he was gone, but as long as he was there we could not desert him. That is the whole truth, as I am an honest Christian woman, and you will see that if there is blame in the matter it does not lie with my husband, but with me, for whose sake he has done all that he has."

The woman's words came with an intense earnestness which carried conviction with them.

"Is this true, Barrymore?"

"Yes, Sir Henry. Every word of it."

"Well, I cannot blame you for standing by your own wife. Forget what I have said. Go to your room, you two, and we shall talk further about this matter in the morning."

When they were gone we looked out of the window again. Sir Henry had flung it open, and the cold night wind beat in upon our faces. Far away in the black distance there still glowed that one tiny point of yellow light.

"I wonder he dares," said Sir Henry.

"It may be so placed as to be only visible from here."

"Very likely. How far do you think it is?"

"Out by the Cleft Tor, I think."

"Not more than a mile or two off."

"Hardly that."

"Well, it cannot be far if Barrymore had to carry out the food to it. And he is waiting, this villain, beside that candle. By thunder, Watson, I am going out to take that man!"

The same thought had crossed my own mind. It was not as if the Barrymores had taken us into their confidence. Their secret had been forced from them. The man was a danger to the community, an unmitigated scoundrel for whom there was neither pity nor excuse. We were only doing our duty in taking this chance of putting him back where he could do no harm. With his brutal and violent nature, others would have to pay the price if we held our hands. Any night, for example, our neighbours the Stapletons might be attacked by him, and it may have been the thought of this which made Sir Henry so keen upon the adventure.

"I will come," said I.

"Then get your revolver and put on your boots. The sooner we start the better, as the fellow may put out his light and be off."

In five minutes we were outside the door, starting upon our expedition. We hurried through the dark shrubbery, amid the dull moaning of the autumn wind and the rustle of the falling leaves. The night-air was heavy with the smell of damp and decay. Now and again the moon peeped out for an instant, but clouds were driving over the face of the sky, and just as we came out on the moor a thin rain began to fall. The light still burned steadily in front.

"Are you armed?" I asked.

"I have a hunting-crop."

"We must close in on him rapidly, for he is said to be a desperate fellow. We shall take him by surprise and have him at our mercy before he can resist."

"I say, Watson," said the baronet, "what would Holmes say to this? How about that hour of darkness in which the power of evil is exalted?"

As if in answer to his words there rose suddenly out of the vast gloom of the moor that strange cry which I had already heard upon the borders of the great Grimpen Mire. It came with the wind through the silence of the night, a long, deep mutter, then a rising howl, and then the sad moan in which it died away. Again and again it sounded, the whole air throbbing with it, strident, wild, and menacing. The baronet caught my sleeve, and his face glimmered white through the darkness.

"Good heavens, what's that, Watson?"

"I don't know. It's a sound they have on the moor. I heard it once before."

It died away, and an absolute silence closed in upon us. We stood straining our ears, but nothing came.

"Watson," said the baronet, "it was the cry of a hound."

My blood ran cold in my veins, for there was a break in his voice which told of the sudden horror which had seized him.

"What do they call this sound?" he asked.

"Who?"

"The folk on the country-side."

"Oh, they are ignorant people. Why should you mind what they call it?"

"Tell me, Watson. What do they say of it?"

I hesitated, but could not escape the question.

"They say it is the cry of the Hound of the Baskervilles."

He groaned, and was silent for a few moments.

"A hound it was," he said at last, "but it seemed to come from miles away over yonder, I think."

"It was hard to say whence it came."

"It rose and fell with the wind. Isn't that the direction of the great Grimpen Mire?"

"Yes, it is."

"Well, it was up there. Come now, Watson, didn't you think yourself that it was the cry of a hound? I am not a child. You need not fear to speak the truth."

"Stapleton was with me when I heard it last. He said that it might be the calling of a strange bird."

"No, no, it was a hound. My God, can there be some truth in all these stories? Is it possible that I am really in danger from so dark a cause? You don't believe it, do you, Watson?"

"No, no."

"And yet it was one thing to laugh about it in London, and it is another to stand out here in the darkness of the moor and to hear such a cry as that. And my uncle! There was the footprint of the hound beside him as he lay. It all fits together. I don't think that I am a coward, Watson, but that sound seemed to freeze my very blood. Feel my hand!"

It was as cold as a block of marble.

"You'll be all right to-morrow."

"I don't think I'll get that cry out of my head. What do you advise that we do now?"

"Shall we turn back?"

"No, by thunder; we have come out to get our man, and we will do it. We are after the convict, and a hell-hound, as likely as not, after us. Come on. We'll see it through if all the fiends of the pit were loose upon the moor."

We stumbled slowly along in the darkness, with the black loom of the craggy hills around us, and the yellow speck of light burning steadily in front. There is nothing so deceptive as the distance of a light upon a pitch-dark night, and sometimes the glimmer seemed to be far away upon the horizon and sometimes it might have been within a few yards of us. But at last we could see whence it came, and then we knew that we were indeed very close. A guttering candle was stuck in a crevice of the rocks which flanked it on each side so as to keep the wind from it, and also to prevent it from being visible, save in the direction of Baskerville Hall. A boulder of granite concealed our approach, and crouching behind it we gazed over it at the signal light. It was strange to see this single candle burning there in the middle of the moor, with no sign of life near it—just the one straight yellow flame and the gleam of the rock on each side of it.

"What shall we do now?" whispered Sir Henry.

"Wait here. He must be near his light. Let us see if we can get a glimpse of him."

The words were hardly out of my mouth when we both saw him. Over the rocks, in the crevice of which the candle burned, there was thrust out an evil yellow face, a terrible animal face, all seamed and scored with vile passions. Foul with mire, with a bristling beard, and hung with matted hair, it might well have belonged to one of those old savages who dwelt in the burrows on the hill-sides. The light beneath him was reflected in his small, cunning eyes, which peered fiercely to right and left through the darkness, like a crafty and savage animal who has heard the steps of the hunters.

Something had evidently aroused his suspicions. It may have been that Barrymore had some private signal which we had neglected to give, or the fellow may have had some other reason for thinking that all was not well, but I could read his fears upon his wicked face. Any instant he might dash out the light and vanish in the darkness. I sprang forward, therefore, and Sir Henry did the same. At the same moment the convict screamed out a curse at us and hurled a rock which splintered up against the boulder which had sheltered us. I caught one glimpse of his short, squat, strongly-built figure as he sprang to his feet and turned to run. At the same moment by a lucky chance the moon broke through the clouds. We rushed over the brow of the hill, and there was our man running with great speed down the other side, springing over the stones in his way with the activity of a mountain goat. A lucky long shot of my revolver might have crippled him, but I had brought it only to defend myself if attacked, and not to shoot an unarmed man who was running away.

We were both fair runners and in good condition, but we soon found that we had no chance of overtaking him. We saw him for a long time in the moonlight until he was only a small speck moving swiftly among the boulders upon the side of a distant hill. We ran and ran until we were completely blown, but the space between us grew ever wider. Finally we stopped and sat panting on two rocks, while we watched him disappearing in the distance.

And it was at this moment that there occurred a most strange and unexpected thing. We had risen from our rocks and were turning to go home, having abandoned the hopeless chase. The moon was low upon the right, and the jagged pinnacle of a granite tor stood up against the lower curve of its silver disc. There, outlined as black as an ebony statue on that shining background, I saw the figure of a man upon the tor. Do not think that it was a delusion, Holmes. I assure you that I have never in my life seen anything more clearly. As far as I could judge, the figure was that of a tall, thin man. He stood with his legs a little separated, his arms folded, his head bowed, as if he were brooding over that enormous wilderness of peat and granite which lay before him. He might have been the very spirit of that terrible place. It was not the convict. This man was far from the place where the latter had disappeared. Besides, he was a much taller man. With a cry of surprise I pointed him out to the baronet, but in the instant during which I had turned to grasp his arm the man was gone. There was the sharp pinnacle of granite still cutting the lower edge of the moon, but its peak bore no trace of that silent and motionless figure.

I wished to go in that direction and to search the tor, but it was some distance away. The Baronet's nerves were still quivering from that cry, which recalled the dark story of his family, and he was not in the mood for fresh adventures. He had not seen this lonely man upon the tor, and could not feel the thrill which his strange presence and his commanding attitude had given to me. "A warder, no doubt," said he. "The moor has been thick with them since this fellow escaped." Well, perhaps his explanation may be the right one, but I should like to have some further proof of it. To-day we mean to communicate to the Princetown people where they should look for their missing man, but it is hard lines that we have not actually had the triumph of bringing him back as our own prisoner. Such are the adventures of last night, and you must acknowledge, my dear Holmes, that I have done you very well in the matter of a report. Much of what I tell you is no doubt quite irrelevant, but still I feel that it is best that I should let you have all the facts and leave you to select for yourself those which will be of most service to you in helping you to your conclusions. We are certainly making some progress. So far as the Barrymores go, we have found the motive of their actions, and that has cleared up the situation very much. But the moor with its mysteries and its strange inhabitants remains as inscrutable as ever. Perhaps in my next I may be able to throw some light upon this also. Best of all would it be if you could come down to us. [In any case you will hear from me again in the course of the next few days.]

X. Extract from the Diary of Dr. Watson

So far I have been able to quote from the reports which I have forwarded during these early days to Sherlock Holmes. Now, however, I have arrived at a point in my narrative where I am compelled to abandon this method and to trust once more to my recollections, aided by the diary which I kept at the time. A few extracts from the latter will carry me on to those scenes which are indelibly fixed in every detail upon my memory. I proceed, then, from the morning which followed our abortive chase of the convict and our other strange experiences upon the moor.

October 16th—A dull and foggy day, with a drizzle of rain. The house is banked in with rolling clouds, which rise now and then to show the dreary curves of the moor, with thin, silver veins upon the sides of the hills, and the distant boulders gleaming where the light strikes upon their wet faces. It is melancholy outside and in. The baronet is in a black reaction after the excitements of the night. I am conscious myself of a weight at my heart and a feeling of impending danger—ever-present, which is the more terrible because I am unable to define it.

And have I not cause for such a feeling? Consider the long sequence of incidents which have all pointed to some sinister influence which is at work around us. There is the death of the last occupant of the Hall, fulfilling so exactly the conditions of the family legend, and there are the repeated reports from peasants of the appearance of a strange creature upon the moor. Twice I have with my own ears heard the sound which resembled the distant baying of a hound. It is incredible, impossible, that it should really be outside the ordinary laws of Nature. A spectral hound which leaves material footmarks and fills the air with its howling is surely not to be thought of. Stapleton may fall in with such a superstition, and Mortimer also; but if I have one quality upon earth it is common sense, and nothing will persuade me to believe in such a thing. To do so would be to descend to the level of these poor peasants who are not content with a mere fiend-dog, but must needs describe him with hell-fire shooting from his mouth and eyes. Holmes would not listen to such fancies, and I am his agent. But facts are facts, and I have twice heard this crying upon the moor. Suppose that there were really some huge hound loose upon it; that would go far to explain everything. But where could such a hound lie concealed, where did it get its food, where did it come from, how was it that no one saw it by day?

It must be confessed that the natural explanation offers almost as many difficulties as the other. And always, apart from the hound, there was the fact of the human agency in London, the man in the cab, and the letter which warned Sir Henry against the moor. This at least was real, but it might have been the work of a protecting friend as easily as an enemy. Where was that friend or enemy now? Had he remained in London, or had he followed us down here? Could he—could he be the stranger whom I had seen upon the Tor?

It is true that I have had only the one glance at him, and yet there are some things to which I am ready to swear. He is no one whom I have seen down here, and I have now met all the neighbours. The figure was far taller than that of Stapleton, far thinner than that of Frankland. Barrymore it might possibly have been, but we had left him behind us, and I am certain that he could not have followed us. A stranger then is still dogging us, just as a stranger had dogged us in London. We have never shaken him off. If I could lay my hands upon that man, then at last we might find ourselves at the end of all our difficulties. To this one purpose I must now devote all my energies.

My first impulse was to tell Sir Henry all my plans. My second and wisest one is to play my own game and speak as little as possible to anyone. He is silent and distrait. His nerves have been strangely shaken by that sound upon the moor. I will say nothing to add to his anxieties, but I will take my own steps to attain my own end.

We had a small scene this morning after breakfast. Barrymore asked leave to speak with Sir Henry, and they were closeted in his study some little time. Sitting in the billiard-room, I more than once heard the sound of voices raised, and I had a pretty good idea what the point was which was under discussion. After a time the Baronet opened his door and called for me.

"Barrymore considers that he has a grievance," he said. "He thinks that it was unfair on our part to hunt his brother-in-law down when he, of his own free will, had told us the secret."

The butler was standing, very pale but very collected, before us.

"I may have spoken too warmly, sir," said he, "and if I have I am sure that I beg your pardon. At the same time, I was very much surprised when I heard you two gentlemen come back this morning and learned that you had been chasing Selden. The poor fellow has enough to fight against without my putting more upon his track."

"If you had told us of your own free will it would have been a different thing," said the baronet. "You only told us, or rather your wife only told us, when it was forced from you and you could not help yourself."

"I didn't think you would have taken advantage of it, Sir Henry—indeed I didn't."

"The man is a public danger. There are lonely houses scattered over the moor, and he is a fellow who would stick at nothing. You only want to get a glimpse of his face to see that. Look at Mr. Stapleton's house, for example, with no one but himself to defend it. There's no safety for anyone until he is under lock and key."

"He'll break into no house, sir. I give you my solemn word upon that. And he will never trouble anyone in this country again. I assure you, Sir Henry, that in a very few days the necessary arrangements will have been made and he will be on his way to South America. For God's sake, sir, I beg of you not to let the police know that he is still on the moor. They have given up the chase there, and he can lie quiet until the ship is ready for him. You can't tell on him without getting my wife and me into trouble. I beg you, sir, to say nothing to the police."

"What do you say, Watson?"

I shrugged my shoulders. "If he were safely out of the country it would relieve the taxpayer of a burden."

"But how about the chance of his holding someone up before he goes?"

"He would not do anything so mad, sir. We have provided him with all that he can want. To commit a crime would be to show where he was hiding."

"That is true," said Sir Henry. "Well, Barrymore——"

"God bless you, sir, and thank you from my heart! It would have killed my poor wife had he been taken again."

"I guess we are aiding and abetting a felony, Watson? But, after what we have heard, I don't feel as if I could give the man up, so there is an end of it. All right, Barrymore, you can go."

With a few broken words of gratitude the man turned, but he hesitated and then came back.

"You've been so kind to us, sir, that I should like to do the best I can for you in return. I know something, Sir Henry, and perhaps I should have said it before, but it was long after the inquest that I found it out. I've never breathed a word about it yet to a mortal man. It's about poor Sir Charles's death."

The baronet and I were both upon our feet.

"Do you know how he died?"

"No, sir, I don't know that."

"What, then?"

"I know why he was at the gate at that hour. It was to meet a woman."

"To meet a woman! He?"

"Yes, sir."

"And the woman's name?"

"I can't give you the name, sir, but I can give you the initials. Her initials were L.L."

"How do you know this, Barrymore?"

"Well, Sir Henry, your uncle had a letter that morning. He had usually a great many letters, for he was a public man and well known for his kind heart, so that everyone who was in trouble was glad to turn to him. But that morning, as it chanced, there was only this one letter, so I took the more notice of it. It was from Coombe Tracey, and it was addressed in a woman's hand."

"Well?"

"Well, sir, I thought no more of the matter, and never would have done had it not been for my wife. Only a few weeks ago she was cleaning out Sir Charles's study—it had never been touched since his death—and she found the ashes of a burned letter in the back of the grate. The greater part of it was charred to pieces, but one little slip, the end of a page, hung together, and the writing could still be read, though it was grey on a black ground. It seemed to us to be a postscript at the end of the letter, and it said: 'Please, please, as you are a gentleman, burn this letter, and be at the gate by ten o'clock.' Beneath it were signed the initials L.L."

"Have you got that slip?"

"No, sir, it crumbled all to bits after we moved it."

"Had Sir Charles received any other letters in the same writing?"

"Well, sir, I took no particular notice of his letters. I should not have noticed this one only it happened to come alone."

"And you have no idea who L.L. is?"

"No, sir. No more than you have. But I expect if we could lay our hands upon that lady we should know more about Sir Charles's death."

"I cannot understand, Barrymore, how you came to conceal this important information."

"Well, sir, it was immediately after that our own trouble came to us. And then again, sir, we were both of us very fond of Sir Charles, as we well might be considering all that he has done for us. To rake this up couldn't help our poor master, and it's well to go carefully when there's a lady in the case. Even the best of us—"

"You thought it might injure his reputation?"

"Well, sir, I thought no good could come of it. But now you have been kind to us, and I feel as if it would be treating you unfairly not to tell you all that I know about the matter."

"Very good, Barrymore; you can go."

When the butler had left us, Sir Henry turned to me. "Well, Watson, what do you think of this new light?"

"It seems to leave the darkness rather blacker than before."

"So I think. But if we can only trace L.L. it should clear up the whole business. We have gained that much. We know that there is someone who has the facts if we can only find her. What do you think we should do?"

"Let Holmes know all about it at once. It will give him the clue for which he has been seeking. I am much mistaken if it does not bring him down."

I went at once to my room and drew up my report of the morning's conversation for Holmes. It was evident to me that he had been very busy of late, for the notes which I had from Baker Street were few and short, with no comments upon the information which I had supplied, and hardly any reference to my mission. No doubt his blackmailing case is absorbing all his faculties. And yet this new factor must surely arrest his attention and renew his interest. I wish that he were here.

October 17th—All day to-day the rain poured down, rustling on the ivy and dripping from the eaves. I thought of the convict out upon the bleak, cold, shelterless moor. Poor fellow! Whatever his crimes, he has suffered something to atone for them. And then I thought of that other one—the face in the cab, the figure against the moon. Was he also out in that deluge—the unseen watcher, the man of darkness? In the evening I put on my waterproof and I walked far upon the sodden moor, full of dark imaginings, the rain beating upon my face and the wind whistling about my ears. God help those who wander into the Great Mire now, for even the firm uplands are becoming a morass. I found the Black Tor upon which I had seen the solitary watcher, and from its craggy summit I looked out myself across the melancholy downs. Rain squalls drifted across their russet face, and the heavy, slate-coloured clouds hung low over the landscape, trailing in grey wreaths down the sides of the fantastic hills. In the distant hollow on the left, half hidden by the mist, the two thin towers of Baskerville Hall rose above the trees. They were the only signs of human life which I could see, save only those prehistoric huts which lay thickly upon the slopes of the hills. Nowhere was there any trace of that lonely man whom I had seen on the same spot two nights before.

As I walked back I was overtaken by Dr. Mortimer driving in his dog-cart over a rough moorland track, which led from the outlying farmhouse of Foulmire. He has been very attentive to us, and hardly a day has passed that he has not called at the Hall to see how we were getting on. He insisted upon my climbing into his dog-cart and he gave me a lift homewards. I found him much troubled over the disappearance of his little spaniel. It had wandered on to the moor and had never come back. I gave him such consolation as I might, but I thought of the pony on the Grimpen Mire, and I do not fancy that he will see his little dog again.

"By the way, Mortimer," said I, as we jolted along the rough road, "I suppose there are few people living within driving distance of this whom you do not know?"

"Hardly any, I think."

"Can you, then, tell me the name of any woman whose initials are L.L.?"

He thought for a few minutes. "No," said he. "There are a few gipsies and labouring folk for whom I can't answer, but among the farmers or gentry there is no one
whose initials are those. Wait a bit, though," he added, after a pause. "There is Laura
Lyons—her initials are L.L.—but she lives in Coombe Tracey."

"Who is she?" I asked.

"She is Frankland's daughter."

"What? Old Frankland the crank?"

"Exactly. She married an artist named Lyons, who came sketching on the moor.
He proved to be a blackguard and deserted her. The fault, from what I hear, may not
have been entirely on one side. Her father refused to have anything to do with her,
because she had married without his consent, and perhaps for one or two other reasons as well. So, between the old sinner and the young one the girl has had a pretty
bad time."

"How does she live?"

"I fancy old Frankland allows her a pittance, but it cannot be more, for his
own affairs are considerably involved. Whatever she may have deserved one could
not allow her to go hopelessly to the bad. Her story got about, and several of the
people here did something to enable her to earn an honest living. Stapleton did for
one, and Sir Charles for another. I gave a trifle myself. It was to set her up in a typewriting business."

He wanted to know the object of my inquiries, but I managed to satisfy his curiosity without telling him too much, for there is no reason why we should take anyone
into our confidence. To-morrow morning I shall find my way to Coombe Tracey,
and if I can see this Mrs. Laura Lyons, of equivocal reputation, a long step will have
been made towards clearing one incident in this chain of mysteries. I am certainly
developing the wisdom of the serpent, for when Mortimer pressed his questions to an
inconvenient extent I asked him casually to what type Frankland's skull belonged, and
so heard nothing but craniology for the rest of our drive. I have not lived for years
with Sherlock Holmes for nothing.

I have only one other incident to record upon this tempestuous and melancholy
day. This was my conversation with Barrymore just now, which gives me one more
strong card which I can play in due time.

Mortimer had stayed to dinner, and he and the Baronet played écarté afterwards.
The butler brought me my coffee into the library, and I took the chance to ask him a
few questions.

"Well," said I, "has this precious relation of yours departed, or is he still lurking
out yonder?"

"I don't know, sir. I hope to Heaven that he has gone, for he has brought nothing but trouble here! I've not heard of him since I left out food for him last, and that was three days ago."

"Did you see him then?"

"No, sir; but the food was gone when next I went that way."

"Then he was certainly there?"

"So you would think, sir, unless it was the other man who took it."

I sat with my coffee-cup half-way to my lips, and stared at Barrymore.

"You know that there is another man, then?"

"Yes, sir; there is another man upon the moor."

"Have you seen him?"

"No, sir."

"How do you know of him, then?"

"Selden told me of him, sir, a week ago or more. He's in hiding, too, but he's not a convict, so far as I can make out. I don't like it, Dr. Watson—I tell you straight, sir, that I don't like it." He spoke with a sudden passion of earnestness.

"Now, listen to me, Barrymore! I have no interest in this matter but that of your master. I have come here with no object except to help him. Tell me, frankly, what it is that you don't like."

Barrymore hesitated for a moment, as if he regretted his outburst, or found it difficult to express his own feelings in words.

"It's all these goings-on, sir," he cried, at last, waving his hand towards the rain-lashed window which faced the moor. "There's foul play somewhere, and there's black villainy brewing, to that I'll swear! Very glad I should be, sir, to see Sir Henry on his way back to London again!"

"But what is it that alarms you?"

"Look at Sir Charles's death! That was bad enough, for all that the coroner said. Look at the noises on the moor at night. There's not a man would cross it after sun-down if he was paid for it. Look at this stranger hiding out yonder, and watching and waiting! What's he waiting for? What does it mean? It means no good to anyone of the name of Baskerville, and very glad I shall be to be quit of it all on the day that Sir Henry's new servants are ready to take over the Hall."

"But about this stranger," said I. "Can you tell me anything about him? What did Selden say? Did he find out where he hid or what he was doing?"

"He saw him once or twice, but he is a deep one, and gives nothing away. At first he thought that he was the police, but soon he found that he had some lay of his own.

A kind of gentleman he was, as far as he could see, but what he was doing he could not make out."

"And where did he say that he lived?"

"Among the old houses on the hillside—the stone huts where the old folk used to live."

"But how about his food?"

"Selden found out that he has got a lad who works for him and brings him all he needs. I dare say he goes to Coombe Tracey for what he wants."

"Very good, Barrymore. We may talk further of this some other time."

When the butler had gone I walked over to the black window, and I looked through a blurred pane at the driving clouds and at the tossing outline of the wind-swept trees. It is a wild night indoors, and what must it be in a stone hut upon the moor? What passion of hatred can it be which leads a man to lurk in such a place at such a time? And what deep and earnest purpose can he have which calls for such a trial? There, in that hut upon the moor, seems to lie the very centre of that problem which has vexed me so sorely. I swear that another day shall not have passed before I have done all that man can do to reach the heart of the mystery.

XI. THE MAN ON THE TOR

The extract from my private diary which forms the last chapter has brought my narrative up to the 18th of October, a time when these strange events began to move swiftly towards their terrible conclusion. The incidents of the next few days are indelibly graven upon my recollection, and I can tell them without reference to the notes made at the time. I start, then, from the day which succeeded that upon which I had established two facts of great importance, the one that Mrs. Laura Lyons of Coombe Tracey had written to Sir Charles Baskerville and made an appointment with him at the very place and hour that he met his death, the other that the lurking man upon the moor was to be found among the stone huts upon the hillside. With these two facts in my possession I felt that either my intelligence or my courage must be deficient if I could not throw some further light upon these dark places.

I had no opportunity to tell the baronet what I had learned about Mrs. Lyons upon the evening before, for Dr. Mortimer remained with him at cards until it was very late. At breakfast, however, I informed him about my discovery, and asked him whether he would care to accompany me to Coombe Tracey. At first he was very eager to come, but on second thoughts it seemed to both of us that if I went alone the results might be better. The more formal we made the visit the less information we might obtain. I left

Sir Henry behind, therefore, not without some prickings of conscience, and drove off upon my new quest.

When I reached Coombe Tracey I told Perkins to put up the horses, and I made inquiries for the lady whom I had come to interrogate. I had no difficulty in finding her rooms, which were central and well appointed. A maid showed me in without ceremony, and as I entered the sitting-room a lady who was sitting before a Remington typewriter sprang up with a pleasant smile of welcome. Her face fell, however, when she saw that I was a stranger, and she sat down again and asked me the object of my visit.

The first impression left by Mrs. Lyons was one of extreme beauty. Her eyes and hair were of the same rich hazel colour, and her cheeks, though considerably freckled, were flushed with the exquisite bloom of the brunette, the dainty pink which lurks at the heart of the sulphur rose. Admiration was, I repeat, the first impression. But the second was criticism. There was something subtly wrong with the face, some coarseness of expression, some hardness, perhaps, of eye, some looseness of lip which marred its perfect beauty. But these, of course, are after-thoughts. At the moment I was simply conscious that I was in the presence of a very handsome woman, and that she was asking me the reasons for my visit. I had not quite understood until that instant how delicate my mission was.

"I have the pleasure," said I, "of knowing your father."

It was a clumsy introduction, and the lady made me feel it.

"There is nothing in common between my father and me," she said. "I owe him nothing, and his friends are not mine. If it were not for the late Sir Charles Baskerville and some other kind hearts I might have starved for all that my father cared."

"It was about the late Sir Charles Baskerville that I have come here to see you."

The freckles started out on the lady's face.

"What can I tell you about him?" she asked, and her fingers played nervously over the stops of her typewriter.

"You knew him, did you not?"

"I have already said that I owe a great deal to his kindness. If I am able to support myself it is largely due to the interest which he took in my unhappy situation."

"Did you correspond with him?"

The lady looked quickly up, with an angry gleam in her hazel eyes.

"What is the object of these questions?" she asked, sharply.

"The object is to avoid a public scandal. It is better that I should ask them here than that the matter should pass outside our control."

She was silent and her face was very pale. At last she looked up with something reckless and defiant in her manner.

"Well, I'll answer," she said. "What are your questions?"

"Did you correspond with Sir Charles?"

"I certainly wrote to him once or twice to acknowledge his delicacy and his generosity."

"Have you the dates of those letters?"

"No."

"Have you ever met him?"

"Yes, once or twice, when he came into Coombe Tracey. He was a very retiring man, and he preferred to do good by stealth."

"But if you saw him so seldom and wrote so seldom, how did he know enough about your affairs to be able to help you, as you say that he has done?"

She met my difficulty with the utmost readiness.

"There were several gentlemen who knew my sad history and united to help me. One was Mr. Stapleton, a neighbour and intimate friend of Sir Charles. He was exceedingly kind, and it was through him that Sir Charles learned about my affairs."

I knew already that Sir Charles Baskerville had made Stapleton his almoner upon several occasions, so the lady's statement bore the impress of truth upon it.

"Did you ever write to Sir Charles asking him to meet you?" I continued.

Mrs. Lyons flushed with anger again.

"Really, sir, this is a very extraordinary question."

"I am sorry, madam, but I must repeat it."

"Then I answer—certainly not."

"Not on the very day of Sir Charles's death?"

The flush had faded in an instant, and a deathly face was before me. Her dry lips could not speak the "No" which I saw rather than heard.

"Surely your memory deceives you," said I. "I could even quote a passage of your letter. It ran 'Please, please, as you are a gentleman, burn this letter, and be at the gate by ten o'clock.'"

I thought that she had fainted, but she recovered herself by a supreme effort.

"Is there no such thing as a gentleman?" she gasped.

"You do Sir charles an injustice. He *did* burn the letter. But sometimes a letter may be legible even when burned. You acknowledge now that you wrote it?"

"Yes, I did write it," she cried, pouring out her soul in a torrent of words. "I did write it. Why should I deny it? I have no reason to be ashamed of it. I wished him to help me. I believed that if I had an interview I could gain his help, so I asked him to meet me."

"But why at such an hour?"

"Because I had only just learned that he was going to London next day and might be away for months. There were reasons why I could not get there earlier."

"But why a rendezvous in the garden instead of a visit to the house?"

"Do you think a woman could go alone at that hour to a bachelor's house?"

"Well, what happened when you did get there?"

"I never went."

"Mrs. Lyons!"

"No, I swear it to you on all I hold sacred. I never went. Something intervened to prevent my going."

"What was that?"

"That is a private matter. I cannot tell it."

"You acknowledge then, that you made an appointment with Sir Charles at the very hour and place at which he met his death, but you deny that you kept the appointment?"

"That is the truth."

Again and again I cross-questioned her, but I could never get past that point.

"Mrs. Lyons," said I, as I rose from this long and inconclusive interview, "you are taking a very great responsibility and putting yourself in a very false position by not making an absolutely clean breast of all that you know. If I have to call in the aid of the police you will find how seriously you are compromised. If your position is innocent, why did you in the first instance deny having written to Sir Charles upon that date?"

"Because I feared that some false conclusion might be drawn from it, and that I might find myself involved in a scandal."

"And why were you so pressing that Sir Charles should destroy your letter?"

"If you have read the letter you will know."

"I did not say that I had read all the letter."

"You quoted some of it."

"I quoted the postscript. The letter had, as I said, been burned, and it was not all legible. I ask you once again why it was that you were so pressing that Sir Charles should destroy this letter which he received on the day of his death."

"The matter is a very private one."

"The more reason why you should avoid a public investigation."

"I will tell you, then. If you have heard anything of my unhappy history you will know that I made a rash marriage and had reason to regret it."

"I have heard so much."

"My life has been one incessant persecution from a husband whom I abhor. The law is upon his side, and every day I am faced by the possibility that he may force me to live with him. At the time that I wrote this letter to Sir Charles I had learned that there was a prospect of my regaining my freedom if certain expenses could be met. It meant everything to me—peace of mind, happiness, self-respect—everything. I knew Sir Charles's generosity, and I thought that if he heard the story from my own lips he would help me."

"Then how is it that you did not go?"

"Because I received help in the interval from another source."

"Why, then, did you not write to Sir Charles and explain this?"

"So I should have done had I not seen his death in the paper next morning."

The woman's story hung coherently together, and all my questions were unable to shake it. I could only check it by finding if she had, indeed, instituted divorce proceedings against her husband at or about the time of the tragedy.

It was unlikely that she would dare to say that she had not been to Baskerville Hall if she really had been, for a trap would be necessary to take her there, and could not have returned to Coombe Tracey until the early hours of the morning. Such an excursion could not be kept secret. The probability was, therefore, that she was telling the truth, or, at least, a part of the truth. I came away baffled and disheartened. Once again I had reached that dead wall which seemed to be built across every path by which I tried to get at the object of my mission. And yet the more I thought of the lady's face and of her manner the more I felt that something was being held back from me. Why should she turn so pale? Why should she fight against every admission until it was forced from her? Why should she have been so reticent at the time of the tragedy? Surely the explanation of all this could not be as innocent as she would have me believe. For the moment I could proceed no farther in that direction, but must turn back to that other clue which was to be sought for among the stone huts upon the moor.

And that was a most vague direction. I realized it as I drove back and noted how hill after hill showed traces of the ancient people. Barrymore's only indication had been that the stranger lived in one of these abandoned huts, and many hundreds of them are scattered throughout the length and breadth of the moor. But I had my own experience for a guide, since it had shown me the man himself standing upon the summit of the Black Tor. That, then, should be the centre of my search. From there I should explore every hut upon the moor until I lighted upon the right one. If this man were inside it I should find out from his own lips, at the point of my revolver if necessary, who he was and why he had dogged us so long. He might slip away from us in the crowd of Regent Street, but it would puzzle him to do so upon the lonely moor. On the other hand, if I should find the hut, and its tenant should not be within it, I must remain there, however long the vigil, until he returned. Holmes had missed him in London. It would indeed be a triumph for me if I could run him to earth where my master had failed.

Luck had been against us again and again in this inquiry, but now at last it came to my aid. And the messenger of good fortune was none other than Mr. Frankland, who was standing, grey-whiskered and red-faced, outside the gate of his garden, which opened on to the high road along which I travelled.

"Good-day, Dr. Watson," cried he, with unwonted good humour, "you must really give your horses a rest, and come in to have a glass of wine and to congratulate me."

My feelings towards him were very far from being friendly after what I had heard of his treatment of his daughter, but I was anxious to send Perkins and the wagonette home, and the opportunity was a good one. I alighted and sent a message to Sir Henry that I should walk over in time for dinner. Then I followed Frankland into his dining-room.

"It is a great day for me, sir—one of the red-letter days of my life," he cried with many chuckles. "I have brought off a double event. I mean to teach them in these parts that law is law, and that there is a man here who does not fear to invoke it. I have established a right of way through the centre of old Middleton's park, slap across it, sir, within a hundred yards of his own front door. What do you think of that? We'll teach these magnates that they cannot ride rough-shod over the rights of the commoners, confound them! And I've closed the wood where the Fernworthy folk used to picnic. These infernal people seem to think that there are no rights of property, and that they can swarm where they like with their papers and their bottles. Both cases decided, Dr. Watson, and both in my favour. I haven't had such a day since I had Sir John Morland for trespass, because he shot in his own warren."

"How on earth did you do that?"

"Look it up in the books, sir. It will repay reading—Frankland v. Morland, Court of Queen's Bench. It cost me £200, but I got my verdict."

"Did it do you any good?"

"None, sir, none. I am proud to say that I had no interest in the matter. I act entirely from a sense of public duty. I have no doubt, for example, that the Fernworthy people will burn me in effigy to-night. I told the police last time they did it that they should stop these disgraceful exhibitions. The county constabulary is in a scandalous state, sir, and it has not afforded me the protection to which I am entitled. The case of Frankland v. Regina will bring the matter before the attention of the public. I told them that they would have occasion to regret their treatment of me, and already my words have come true."

"How so?" I asked.

The old man put on a very knowing expression.

"Because I could tell them what they are dying to know; but nothing would induce me to help the rascals in any way."

I had been casting round for some excuse by which I could get away from his gossip, but now I began to wish to hear more of it. I had seen enough of the contrary nature of the old sinner to understand that any strong sign of interest would be the surest way to stop his confidences.

"Some poaching case, no doubt?" said I, with an indifferent manner.

"Ha, ha, my boy, a very much more important matter than that! What about the convict on the moor?"

I started. "You don't mean that you know where he is?" said I.

"I may not know exactly where he is, but I am quite sure that I could help the police to lay their hands on him. Has it never struck you that the way to catch that man was to find out where he got his food, and so trace it to him?"

He certainly seemed to be getting uncomfortably near the truth. "No doubt," said I; "but how do you know that he is anywhere upon the moor?"

"I know it because I have seen with my own eyes the messenger who takes him his food."

My heart sank for Barrymore. It was a serious thing to be in the power of this spiteful old busybody. But his next remark took a weight from my mind.

"You'll be surprised to hear that his food is taken to him by a child. I see him every day through my telescope upon the roof. He passes along the same path at the same hour, and to whom should he be going except to the convict?"

Here was luck indeed! And yet I suppressed all appearance of interest. A child! Barrymore had said that our unknown was supplied by a boy. It was on his track, and not upon the convict's, that Frankland had stumbled. If I could get his knowledge it might save me a long and weary hunt. But incredulity and indifference were evidently my strongest cards.

"I should say that it was much more likely that it was the son of one of the moor-land shepherds taking out his father's dinner."

The least appearance of opposition struck fire out of the old autocrat. His eyes looked malignantly at me, and his grey whiskers bristled like those of an angry cat.

"Indeed, sir!" said he, pointing out over the wide-stretching moor. "Do you see that Black Tor over yonder? Well, do you see the low hill beyond with the thorn-bush upon it? It is the stoniest part of the whole moor. Is that a place where a shepherd would be likely to take his station? Your suggestion, sir, is a most absurd one."

I meekly answered that I had spoken without knowing all the facts. My submission pleased him and led him to further confidences.

"You may be sure, sir, that I have very good grounds before I come to an opinion. I have seen the boy again and again with his bundle. Every day, and sometimes twice a day, I have been able—but wait a moment, Dr. Watson. Do my eyes deceive me, or is there at the present moment something moving upon that hillside?"

It was several miles off, but I could distinctly see a small dark dot against the dull green and grey.

"Come, sir, come!" cried Frankland, rushing upstairs. "You will see with your own eyes and judge for yourself."

The telescope, a formidable instrument mounted upon a tripod, stood upon the flat leads of the house. Frankland clapped his eye to it and gave a cry of satisfaction.

"Quick, Dr. Watson, quick, before he passes over the hill!"

There he was, sure enough, a small urchin with a little bundle upon his shoulder, toiling slowly up the hill. When he reached the crest I saw the ragged, uncouth figure outlined for an instant against the cold blue sky. He looked round him, with a furtive and stealthy air, as one who dreads pursuit. Then he vanished over the hill.

"Well! Am I right?"

"Certainly, there is a boy who seems to have some secret errand."

"And what the errand is even a county constable could guess. But not one word shall they have from me, and I bind you to secrecy also, Dr. Watson. Not a word! You understand?"

"Just as you wish."

"They have treated me shamefully—shamefully. When the facts come out in Frankland *v.* Regina I venture to think that a thrill of indignation will run through the country. Nothing would induce me to help the police in any way. For all they cared it might have been me, instead of my effigy, which these rascals burned at the stake. Surely you are not going! You will help me to empty the decanter in honour of this great occasion!"

But I resisted all his solicitations and succeeded in dissuading him from his announced intention of walking home with me. I kept the road as long as his eye was on me, and then I struck off across the moor and made for the stony hill over which the boy had disappeared. Everything was working in my favour, and I swore that it should not be through lack of energy or perseverance that I should miss the chance which Fortune had thrown in my way.

The sun was already sinking when I reached the summit of the hill, and the long slopes beneath me were all golden-green on one side and grey shadow on the other.

A haze lay low upon the farthest sky-line, out of which jutted the fantastic shapes of Belliver and Vixen Tor. Over the wide expanse there was no sound and no movement. One great grey bird, a gull or curlew, soared aloft in the blue heaven. He and I seemed to be the only living things between the huge arch of the sky and the desert beneath it. The barren scene, the sense of loneliness, and the mystery and urgency of my task all struck a chill into my heart. The boy was nowhere to be seen. But down beneath me in a cleft of the hills there was a circle of the old stone huts, and in the middle of them there was one which retained sufficient roof to act as a screen against the weather. My heart leaped within me as I saw it. This must be the burrow where the stranger lurked. At last my foot was on the threshold of his hiding-place—his secret was within my grasp.

As I approached the hut, walking as warily as Stapleton would do when with poised net he drew near the settled butterfly, I satisfied myself that the place had indeed been used as a habitation. A vague pathway among the boulders led to the dilapidated opening which served as a door. All was silent within. The unknown might be lurking there, or he might be prowling on the moor. My nerves tingled with the sense of adventure. Throwing aside my cigarette, I closed my hand upon the butt of my revolver, and, walking swiftly up to the door, I looked in. The place was empty.

But there were ample signs that I had not come upon a false scent. This was certainly where the man lived. Some blankets rolled in a waterproof lay upon that very stone slab upon which neolithic man had once slumbered. The ashes of a fire were heaped in a rude grate. Beside it lay some cooking utensils and a bucket half-full of water. A litter of empty tins showed that the place had been occupied for some time, and I saw, as my eyes became accustomed to the chequered light, a pannikin and a half-full bottle of spirits standing in the corner. In the middle of the hut a flat stone served the purpose of a table, and upon this stood a small cloth bundle—the same, no doubt, which I had seen through the telescope upon the shoulder of the boy. It contained a loaf of bread, a tinned tongue, and two tins of preserved peaches. As I set it down again, after having examined it, my heart leaped to see that beneath it there lay a sheet of paper with writing upon it. I raised it, and this was what I read, roughly scrawled in pencil:

Dr. Watson has gone to Coombe Tracey.

For a minute I stood there with the paper in my hands thinking out the meaning of this curt message. It was I, then, and not Sir Henry, who was being dogged by this secret man. He had not followed me himself, but he had set an agent—the boy, perhaps—upon my track, and this was his report. Possibly I had taken no step since I had been upon the moor which had not been observed and repeated. Always there was this feeling of an unseen force, a fine net drawn round us with infinite skill and delicacy, holding us so lightly that it was only at some supreme moment that one realized that one was indeed entangled in its meshes.

If there was one report there might be others, so I looked round the hut in search of them. There was no trace, however, of anything of the kind, nor could I discover any sign which might indicate the character or intentions of the man who lived in this singular place, save that he must be of Spartan habits, and cared little for the comforts of life. When I thought of the heavy rains and looked at the gaping roof I understood how strong and immutable must be the purpose which had kept him in that inhospitable abode. Was he our malignant enemy, or was he by chance our guardian angel? I swore that I would not leave the hut until I knew.

Outside the sun was sinking low and the west was blazing with scarlet and gold. Its reflection was shot back in ruddy patches by the distant pools which lay amid the Great Grimpen Mire. There were the two towers of Baskerville Hall, and there a distant blur of smoke which marked the village of Grimpen. Between the two, behind the hill, was the house of the Stapletons. All was sweet and mellow and peaceful in the golden evening light, and yet as I looked at them my soul shared none of the peace of Nature, but quivered at the vagueness and the terror of that interview which every instant was bringing nearer. With tingling nerves, but a fixed purpose, I sat in the dark recess of the hut and waited with sombre patience for the coming of its tenant.

And then at last I heard him. Far away came the sharp clink of a boot striking upon a stone. Then another and yet another, coming nearer and nearer. I shrank back into the darkest corner, and cocked the pistol in my pocket, determined not to discover myself until I had an opportunity of seeing something of the stranger. There was a long pause, which showed that he had stopped. Then once more the footsteps approached and a shadow fell across the opening of the hut.

"It is a lovely evening, my dear Watson," said a well-known voice. "I really think that you will be more comfortable outside than in."

XII. Death on the Moor

For a moment or two I sat breathless, hardly able to believe my ears. Then my senses and my voice came back to me, while a crushing weight of responsibility seemed in an instant to be lifted from my soul. That cold, incisive, ironical voice could belong to but one man in all the world.

"Holmes!" I cried—"Holmes!"

"Come out," said he, "and please be careful with the revolver."

I stooped under the rude lintel, and there he sat upon a stone outside, his grey eyes dancing with amusement as they fell upon my astonished features. He was thin and worn, but clear and alert, his keen face bronzed by the sun and roughened by the wind. In his tweed suit and cloth cap he looked like any other tourist upon the moor, and he had contrived, with that cat-like love of personal cleanliness which was one of his characteristics, that his chin should be as smooth and his linen as perfect as if he were in Baker Street.

"I never was more glad to see anyone in my life," said I, as I wrung him by the hand.

"Or more astonished, eh?"

"Well, I must confess to it."

"The surprise was not all on one side, I assure you. I had no idea that you had found my occasional retreat, still less that you were inside it, until I was within twenty paces of the door."

"My footprint, I presume?"

"No, Watson; I fear that I could not undertake to recognize your footprint amid all the footprints of the world. If you seriously desire to deceive me you must change your tobacconist; for when I see the stub of a cigarette marked Bradley, Oxford Street, I know that my friend Watson is in the neighbourhood. You will see it there beside the path. You threw it down, no doubt, at that supreme moment when you charged into the empty hut."

"Exactly."

"I thought as much—and knowing your admirable tenacity, I was convinced that you were sitting in ambush, a weapon within reach, waiting for the tenant to return. So you actually thought that I was the criminal?"

"I did not know who you were, but I was determined to find out."

"Excellent, Watson! And how did you localize me? You saw me, perhaps, on the night of the convict hunt, when I was so imprudent as to allow the moon to rise behind me?"

"Yes, I saw you then."

"And have, no doubt, searched all the huts until you came to this one?"

"No, your boy had been observed, and that gave me a guide where to look."

"The old gentleman with the telescope, no doubt. I could not make it out when first I saw the light flashing upon the lens." He rose and peeped into the hut. "Ha, I see that Cartwright has brought up some supplies. What's this paper? So you have been to Coombe Tracey, have you?"

"Yes."

"To see Mrs. Laura Lyons?"

"Exactly."

"Well done! Our researches have evidently been running on parallel lines, and when we unite our results I expect we shall have a fairly full knowledge of the case."

"Well, I am glad from my heart that you are here, for indeed the responsibility and the mystery were both becoming too much for my nerves. But how in the name of wonder did you come here, and what have you been doing? I thought that you were in Baker Street working out that case of blackmailing."

"That was what I wished you to think."

"Then you use me, and yet do not trust me!" I cried, with some bitterness. "I think that I have deserved better at your hands, Holmes."

"My dear fellow, you have been invaluable to me in this as in many other cases, and I beg that you will forgive me if I have seemed to play a trick upon you. In truth, it was partly for your own sake that I did it, and it was my appreciation of the danger which you ran which led me to come down and examine the matter for myself. Had I been with Sir Henry and you it is evident that my point of view would have been the same as yours, and my presence would have warned our very formidable opponents to be on their guard. As it is, I have been able to get about as I could not possibly have done had I been living in the Hall, and I remain an unknown factor in the business, ready to throw in all my weight at a critical moment."

"But why keep me in the dark?"

"For you to know could not have helped us, and might possibly have led to my discovery. You would have wished to tell me something, or in your kindness you would have brought me out some comfort or other, and so an unnecessary risk would be run. I brought Cartwright down with me—you remember the little chap at the Express office—and he has seen after my simple wants: a loaf of bread and a clean collar. What does man want more? He has given me an extra pair of eyes upon a very active pair of feet, and both have been invaluable."

"Then my reports have all been wasted!" My voice trembled as I recalled the pains and the pride with which I had composed them.

Holmes took a bundle of papers from his pocket.

"Here are your reports, my dear fellow, and very well thumbed, I assure you. I made excellent arrangements, and they are only delayed one day upon their way. I must compliment you exceedingly upon the zeal and the intelligence which you have shown over an extraordinarily difficult case."

I was still rather raw over the deception which had been practised upon me, but the warmth of Holmes's praise drove my anger from my mind. I felt also in my heart that he was right in what he said, and that it was really best for our purpose that I should not have known that he was upon the moor.

"That's better," said he, seeing the shadow rise from my face. "And now tell me the result of your visit to Mrs. Laura Lyons—it was not difficult for me to guess that it was to see her that you had gone, for I am already aware that she is the one person in Coombe Tracey who might be of service to us in the matter. In fact, if you had not gone to-day it is exceedingly probable that I should have gone to-morrow."

The sun had set and dusk was settling over the moor. The air had turned chill, and we withdrew into the hut for warmth. There, sitting together in the twilight, I told Holmes of my conversation with the lady. So interested was he that I had to repeat some of it twice before he was satisfied.

"This is most important," said he, when I had concluded. "It fills up a gap which I had been unable to bridge, in this most complex affair. You are aware, perhaps, that a close intimacy exists between this lady and the man Stapleton?"

"I did not know of a close intimacy."

"There can be no doubt about the matter. They meet, they write, there is a complete understanding between them. Now, this puts a very powerful weapon into our hands. If I could use it to detach his wife—"

"His wife?"

"I am giving you some information now, in return for all that you have given me. The lady who has passed here as Miss Stapleton is in reality his wife."

"Good heavens, Holmes! Are you sure of what you say? How could he have permitted Sir Henry to fall in love with her?"

"Sir Henry's falling in love could do no harm to anyone except Sir Henry. He took particular care that Sir Henry did not *make* love to her, as you have yourself observed. I repeat that the lady is his wife and not his sister."

"But why this elaborate deception?"

"Because he foresaw that she would be very much more useful to him in the character of a free woman."

All my unspoken instincts, my vague suspicions, suddenly took shape and centred upon the naturalist. In that impassive, colourless man, with his straw hat and his butterfly-net, I seemed to see something terrible—a creature of infinite patience and craft, with a smiling face and a murderous heart.

"It is he, then, who is our enemy—it is he who dogged us in London?"

"So I read the riddle."

"And the warning—it must have come from her!"

"Exactly."

The shape of some monstrous villainy, half seen, half guessed, loomed through the darkness which had girt me so long.

"But are you sure of this, Holmes? How do you know that the woman is his wife?"

"Because he so far forgot himself as to tell you a true piece of autobiography upon the occasion when he first met you, and I dare say he has many a time regretted it since. He *was* once a schoolmaster in the North of England. Now, there is no one more easy to trace than a schoolmaster. There are scholastic agencies by which one may identify any man who has been in the profession. A little investigation showed me that a school had come to grief under atrocious circumstances, and that the man who had owned it—the name was different—had disappeared with his wife. The description agreed. When I learned that the missing man was devoted to entomology the identification was complete."

The darkness was rising, but much was still hidden by the shadows.

"If this woman is in truth his wife, where does Mrs. Laura Lyons come in?" I asked.

"That is one of the points upon which your own researches have shed a light. Your interview with the lady has cleared the situation very much. I did not know about a projected divorce between herself and her husband. In that case, regarding Stapleton as an unmarried man, she counted no doubt upon becoming his wife."

"And when she is undeceived?"

"Why, then we may find the lady of service. It must be our first duty to see her—both of us—to-morrow. Don't you think, Watson, that you are away from your charge rather long? Your place should be at Baskerville Hall."

The last red streaks had faded away in the west and night had settled upon the moor. A few faint stars were gleaming in a violet sky.

"One last question, Holmes," I said, as I rose. "Surely there is no need of secrecy between you and me. What is the meaning of it all? What is he after?"

Holmes's voice sank as he answered—"It is murder, Watson—refined, cold-blooded, deliberate murder. Do not ask me for particulars. My nets are closing upon him, even as his are upon Sir Henry, and with your help he is already almost at my mercy. There is but one danger which can threaten us. It is that he should strike before we are ready to do so. Another day—two at the most—and I have my case complete, but until then guard your charge as closely as ever a fond mother watched her ailing child. Your mission to-day has justified itself, and yet I could almost wish that you had not left his side—Hark!"

A terrible scream—a prolonged yell of horror and anguish burst out of the silence of the moor. That frightful cry turned the blood to ice in my veins.

"Oh, my God!" I gasped. "What is it? What does it mean?"

Holmes had sprung to his feet, and I saw his dark, athletic outline at the door of the hut, his shoulders stooping, his head thrust forward, his face peering into the darkness.

"Hush!" he whispered. "Hush!"

The cry had been loud on account of its vehemence, but it had pealed out from somewhere far off on the shadowy plain. Now it burst upon our ears, nearer, louder, more urgent than before.

"Where is it?" Holmes whispered; and I knew from the thrill of his voice that he, the man of iron, was shaken to the soul. "Where is it, Watson?"

"There, I think." I pointed into the darkness.

"No, there!"

Again the agonized cry swept through the silent night, louder and much nearer than ever. And a new sound mingled with it, a deep, muttered rumble, musical and yet menacing, rising and falling like the low, constant murmur of the sea.

"The hound!" cried Holmes. "Come, Watson, come! Great heavens, if we are too late!"

He had started running swiftly over the moor, and I had followed at his heels. But now from somewhere among the broken ground immediately in front of us there came one last despairing yell, and then a dull, heavy thud. We halted and listened. Not another sound broke the heavy silence of the windless night.

I saw Holmes put his hand to his forehead, like a man distracted. He stamped his feet upon the ground.

"He has beaten us, Watson. We are too late."

"No, no, surely not!"

"Fool that I was to hold my hand. And you, Watson, see what comes of abandoning your charge! But, by Heaven, if the worst has happened, we'll avenge him!"

Blindly we ran through the gloom, blundering against boulders, forcing our way through gorse bushes, panting up hills and rushing down slopes, heading always in the direction whence those dreadful sounds had come. At every rise Holmes looked eagerly round him, but the shadows were thick upon the moor and nothing moved upon its dreary face.

"Can you see anything?"

"Nothing."

"But hark, what is that?"

A low moan had fallen upon our ears. There it was again upon our left! On that side a ridge of rocks ended in a sheer cliff, which overlooked a stone-strewn slope.

On its jagged face was spread-eagled some dark, irregular object. As we ran towards it the vague outline hardened into a definite shape. It was a prostrate man face downwards upon the ground, the head doubled under him at a horrible angle, the shoulders rounded and the body hunched together as if in the act of throwing a somersault. So grotesque was the attitude that I could not for the instant realize that that moan had been the passing of his soul. Not a whisper, not a rustle, rose now from the dark figure over which we stooped. Holmes laid his hand upon him, and held it up again, with an exclamation of horror. The gleam of the match which he struck shone upon his clotted fingers and upon the ghastly pool which widened slowly from the crushed skull of the victim. And it shone upon something else which turned our hearts sick and faint within us—the body of Sir Henry Baskerville!

There was no chance of either of us forgetting that peculiar ruddy tweed suit—the very one which he had worn on the first morning that we had seen him in Baker Street. We caught the one clear glimpse of it, and then the match flickered and went out, even as the hope had gone out of our souls. Holmes groaned, and his face glimmered white through the darkness.

"The brute! the brute!" I cried, with clenched hands. "Oh, Holmes, I shall never forgive myself for having left him to his fate."

"I am more to blame than you, Watson. In order to have my case well rounded and complete, I have thrown away the life of my client. It is the greatest blow which has befallen me in my career. But how could I know—how *could* I know—that he would risk his life alone upon the moor in the face of all my warnings?"

"That we should have heard his screams—my God, those screams!—and yet have been unable to save him! Where is this brute of a hound which drove him to his death? It may be lurking among these rocks at this instant. And Stapleton, where is he? He shall answer for this deed."

"He shall. I will see to that. Uncle and nephew have been murdered—the one frightened to death by the very sight of a beast which he thought to be supernatural, the other driven to his end in his wild flight to escape from it. But now we have to prove the connection between the man and the beast. Save from what we heard, we cannot even swear to the existence of the latter, since Sir Henry has evidently died from the fall. But, by heavens, cunning as he is, the fellow shall be in my power before another day is past!"

We stood with bitter hearts on either side of the mangled body, overwhelmed by this sudden and irrevocable disaster which had brought all our long and weary labours to so piteous an end. Then, as the moon rose, we climbed to the top of the rocks over which our poor friend had fallen, and from the summit we gazed out over the shadowy moor, half silver and half gloom. Far away, miles off, in the direction of Grimpen, a single steady yellow light was shining. It could only come from the lonely abode of the Stapletons. With a bitter curse I shook my fist at it as I gazed.

"Why should we not seize him at once?"

"Our case is not complete. The fellow is wary and cunning to the last degree. It is not what we know, but what we can prove. If we make one false move the villain may escape us yet."

"What can we do?"

"There will be plenty for us to do to-morrow. To-night we can only perform the last offices to our poor friend."

Together we made our way down the precipitous slope and approached the body, black and clear against the silver stones. The agony of those contorted limbs struck me with a spasm of pain and blurred my eyes with tears.

"We must send for help, Holmes! We cannot carry him all the way to the Hall. Good heavens, are you mad?"

He had uttered a cry and bent over the body. Now he was dancing and laughing and wringing my hand. Could this be my stern, self-contained friend? These were hidden fires, indeed!

"A beard! A beard! The man has a beard!"

"A beard?"

"It is not the Baronet—it is—why, it is my neighbour, the convict!"

With feverish haste we had turned the body over, and that dripping beard was pointing up to the cold, clear moon. There could be no doubt about the beetling forehead, the sunken animal eyes. It was indeed the same face which had glared upon me in the light of the candle from over the rock—the face of Selden, the criminal.

Then in an instant it was all clear to me. I remembered how the Baronet had told me that he had handed his old wardrobe to Barrymore. Barrymore had passed it on in order to help Selden in his escape. Boots, shirt, cap—it was all Sir Henry's. The tragedy was still black enough, but this man had at least deserved death by the laws of his country. I told Holmes how the matter stood, my heart bubbling over with thankfulness and joy.

"Then the clothes have been the poor fellow's death," said he. "It is clear enough that the hound has been laid on from some article of Sir Henry's—the boot which was abstracted in the hotel, in all probability—and so ran this man down. There is one very singular thing, however: How came Selden, in the darkness, to know that the hound was on his trail?"

"He heard him."

"To hear a hound upon the moor would not work a hard man like this convict into such a paroxysm of terror that he would risk recapture by screaming wildly for help. By his cries he must have run a long way after he knew the animal was on his track. How did he know?"

"A greater mystery to me is why this hound, presuming that all our conjectures are correct—"

"I presume nothing."

"Well, then, why this hound should be loose to-night. I suppose that it does not always run loose upon the moor. Stapleton would not let it go unless he had reason to think that Sir Henry would be there."

"My difficulty is the more formidable of the two, for I think that we shall very shortly get an explanation of yours, while mine may remain forever a mystery. The question now is, what shall we do with this poor wretch's body? We cannot leave it here to the foxes and the ravens."

"I suggest that we put it in one of the huts until we can communicate with the police."

"Exactly. I have no doubt that you and I could carry it so far. Hullo, Watson, what's this? It's the man himself, by all that's wonderful and audacious! Not a word to show your suspicions—not a word, or my plans crumble to the ground."

A figure was approaching us over the moor, and I saw the dull red glow of a cigar. The moon shone upon him, and I could distinguish the dapper shape and jaunty walk of the naturalist. He stopped when he saw us, and then came on again.

"Why, Dr. Watson, that's not you, is it? You are the last man that I should have expected to see out on the moor at this time of night. But, dear me, what's this? Somebody hurt? Not—don't tell me that it is our friend Sir Henry!"

He hurried past me and stooped over the dead man. I heard a sharp intake of his breath and the cigar fell from his fingers.

"Who—who's this?" he stammered.

"It is Selden, the man who escaped from Princetown."

Stapleton turned a ghastly face upon us, but by a supreme effort he had overcome his amazement and his disappointment. He looked sharply from Holmes to me.

"Dear me! What a very shocking affair! How did he die?"

"He appears to have broken his neck by falling over these rocks. My friend and I were strolling on the moor when we heard a cry."

"I heard a cry also. That was what brought me out. I was uneasy about Sir Henry."

"Why about Sir Henry in particular?" I could not help asking.

"Because I had suggested that he should come over. When he did not come I was surprised, and I naturally became alarmed for his safety when I heard cries upon the moor. By the way"—his eyes darted again from my face to Holmes's—"did you hear anything else besides a cry?"

"No," said Holmes; "did you?"

"No."

"What do you mean then?"

"Oh, you know the stories that the peasants tell about a phantom hound, and so on. It is said to be heard at night upon the moor. I was wondering if there were any evidence of such a sound to-night."

"We heard nothing of the kind," said I.

"And what is your theory of this poor fellow's death?"

"I have no doubt that anxiety and exposure have driven him off his head. He has rushed about the moor in a crazy state and eventually fallen over here and broken his neck."

"That seems the most reasonable theory," said Stapleton, and he gave a sigh which I took to indicate his relief. "What do you think about it, Mr. Sherlock Holmes?"

My friend bowed his compliments.

"You are quick at identification," said he.

"We have been expecting you in these parts since Dr. Watson came down. You are in time to see a tragedy."

"Yes, indeed. I have no doubt that my friend's explanation will cover the facts. I will take an unpleasant remembrance back to London with me to-morrow."

"Oh, you return to-morrow?"

"That is my intention."

"I hope your visit has cast some light upon those occurrences which have puzzled us?"

Holmes shrugged his shoulders. "One cannot always have the success for which one hopes. An investigator needs facts, and not legends or rumours. It has not been a satisfactory case."

My friend spoke in his frankest and most unconcerned manner. Stapleton still looked hard at him. Then he turned to me.

"I would suggest carrying this poor fellow to my house, but it would give my sister such a fright that I do not feel justified in doing it. I think that if we put something over his face he will be safe until morning."

And so it was arranged. Resisting Stapleton's offer of hospitality, Holmes and I set off to Baskerville Hall, leaving the naturalist to return alone. Looking back we saw the figure moving slowly away over the broad moor, and behind him that one black smudge on the silvered slope which showed where the man was lying who had come so horribly to his end.

"We're at close grips at last," said Holmes, as we walked together across the moor. "What a nerve the fellow has! How he pulled himself together in the face of what must have been a paralysing shock when he found that the wrong man had fallen a victim to his plot. I told you in London, Watson, and I tell you now again, that we have never had a foeman more worthy of our steel."

"I am sorry that he has seen you."

"And so was I at first. But there was no getting out of it."

"What effect do you think it will have upon his plans, now that he knows you are here?"

"It may cause him to be more cautious, or it may drive him to desperate measures at once. Like most clever criminals, he may be too confident in his own cleverness and imagine that he has completely deceived us."

"Why should we not arrest him at once?"

"My dear Watson, you were born to be a man of action. Your instinct is always to do something energetic. But supposing, for argument's sake, that we had him arrested to-night, what on earth the better off should we be for that? We could prove nothing against him. There's the devilish cunning of it! If he were acting through a human agent we could get some evidence, but if we were to drag this great dog to the light of day it would not help in putting a rope round the neck of its master."

"Surely we have a case."

"Not a shadow of one—only surmise and conjecture. We should be laughed out of court if we came with such a story and such evidence."

"There is Sir Charles's death."

"Found dead without a mark upon him. You and I know that he died of sheer fright, and we know also what frightened him; but how are we to get twelve stolid jurymen to know it? What signs are there of a hound? Where are the marks of its fangs? Of course, we know that a hound does not bite a dead body, and that Sir Charles was dead before ever the brute overtook him. But we have to *prove* all this, and we are not in a position to do it."

"Well, then, to-night?"

"We are not much better off to-night. Again, there was no direct connection between the hound and the man's death. We never saw the hound. We heard it; but we could not prove that it was running upon this man's trail. There is a complete absence of motive. No, my dear fellow; we must reconcile ourselves to the fact that we have no case at present, and that it is worth our while to run any risk in order to establish one."

"And how do you propose to do so?"

"I have great hopes of what Mrs. Laura Lyons may do for us when the position of affairs is made clear to her. And I have my own plan as well. Sufficient for to-morrow is the evil thereof; but I hope before the day is past to have the upper hand at last."

I could draw nothing further from him, and he walked, lost in thought, as far as the Baskerville gates.

"Are you coming up?"

"Yes; I see no reason for further concealment. But one last word, Watson. Say nothing of the hound to Sir Henry. Let him think that Selden's death was as Stapleton would have us believe. He will have a better nerve for the ordeal which he will have to undergo to-morrow, when he is engaged, if I remember your report aright, to dine with these people."

"And so am I."

"Then you must excuse yourself, and he must go alone. That will be easily arranged. And now, if we are too late for dinner, I think that we are both ready for our suppers."

XIII. Fixing the Nets

Sir Henry was more pleased than surprised to see Sherlock Holmes, for he had for some days been expecting that recent events would bring him down from London. He did raise his eyebrows, however, when he found that my friend had neither any luggage nor any explanations for its absence. Between us we soon supplied his wants, and then over a belated supper we explained to the Baronet as much of our experience as it seemed desirable that he should know. But first I had the unpleasant duty of breaking the news of Selden's death to Barrymore and his wife. To him it may have been an unmitigated relief, but she wept bitterly in her apron. To all the world he was the man of violence, half animal and half demon; but to her he always remained the little wilful boy of her own girlhood, the child who had clung to her hand. Evil indeed is the man who has not one woman to mourn him.

"I've been moping in the house all day since Watson went off in the morning," said the baronet. "I guess I should have some credit, for I have kept my promise. If I hadn't sworn not to go about alone I might have had a more lively evening, for I had a message from Stapleton asking me over there."

"I have no doubt that you would have had a more lively evening," said Holmes, drily. "By the way, I don't suppose you appreciate that we have been mourning over you as having broken your neck?"

Sir Henry opened his eyes. "How was that?"

"This poor wretch was dressed in your clothes. I fear your servant who gave them to him may get into trouble with the police."

"That is unlikely. There was no mark on any of them, as far as I know."

"That's lucky for him—in fact, it's lucky for all of you, since you are all on the wrong side of the law in this matter. I am not sure that as a conscientious detective my first duty is not to arrest the whole household. Watson's reports are most incriminating documents."

"But how about the case?" asked the baronet. "Have you made anything out of the tangle? I don't know that Watson and I are much the wiser since we came down."

"I think that I shall be in a position to make the situation rather more clear to you before long. It has been an exceedingly difficult and most complicated business. There are several points upon which we still want light—but it is coming, all the same."

"We've had one experience, as Watson has no doubt told you. We heard the hound on the moor, so I can swear that it is not all empty superstition. I had something to do with dogs when I was out West, and I know one when I hear one. If you can muzzle that one and put him on a chain I'll be ready to swear you are the greatest detective of all time."

"I think I will muzzle him and chain him all right if you will give me your help."

"Whatever you tell me to do I will do."

"Very good; and I will ask you also to do it blindly, without always asking the reason."

"Just as you like."

"If you will do this I think the chances are that our little problem will soon be solved. I have no doubt—"

He stopped suddenly and stared fixedly up over my head into the air. The lamp beat upon his face, and so intent was it and so still that it might have been that of a clear-cut classical statue, a personification of alertness and expectation.

"What is it?" we both cried.

I could see as he looked down that he was repressing some internal emotion. His features were still composed, but his eyes shone with amused exultation.

"Excuse the admiration of a connoisseur," said he, as he waved his hand towards the line of portraits which covered the opposite wall. "Watson won't allow that I know anything of art, but that is mere jealousy, because our views upon the subject differ. Now, these are a really very fine series of portraits."

"Well, I'm glad to hear you say so," said Sir Henry, glancing with some surprise at my friend. "I don't pretend to know much about these things, and I'd be a better judge of a horse or a steer than of a picture. I didn't know that you found time for such things."

"I know what is good when I see it, and I see it now. That's a Kneller, I'll swear, that lady in the blue silk over yonder, and the stout gentleman with the wig ought to be a Reynolds. They are all family portraits, I presume?"

"Every one."

"Do you know the names?"

"Barrymore has been coaching me in them, and I think I can say my lessons fairly well."

"Who is the gentleman with the telescope?"

"That is Rear-Admiral Baskerville, who served under Rodney in the West Indies. The man with the blue coat and the roll of paper is Sir William Baskerville, who was Chairman of Committees of the House of Commons under Pitt."

"And this Cavalier opposite to me—the one with the black velvet and the lace?"

"Ah, you have a right to know about him. That is the cause of all the mischief, the wicked Hugo, who started the Hound of the Baskervilles. We're not likely to forget him."

I gazed with interest and some surprise upon the portrait.

"Dear me!" said Holmes, "he seems a quiet, meek-mannered man enough, but I dare say that there was a lurking devil in his eyes. I had pictured him as a more robust and ruffianly person."

"There's no doubt about the authenticity, for the name and the date, 1647, are on the back of the canvas."

Holmes said little more, but the picture of the old roysterer seemed to have a fascination for him, and his eyes were continually fixed upon it during supper. It was not until later, when Sir Henry had gone to his room, that I was able to follow the trend of his thoughts. He led me back into the banqueting-hall, his bedroom candle in his hand, and he held it up against the time-stained portrait on the wall.

"Do you see anything there?"

I looked at the broad plumed hat, the curling love-locks, the white lace collar, and the straight severe face which was framed between them. It was not a brutal countenance, but it was prim, hard, and stern, with a firm-set, thin-lipped mouth, and a coldly intolerant eye.

"Is it like anyone you know?"

"There is something of Sir Henry about the jaw."

"Just a suggestion, perhaps. But wait an instant!"

He stood upon a chair, and holding up the light in his left hand, he curved his right arm over the broad hat and round the long ringlets.

"Good heavens!" I cried, in amazement.

The face of Stapleton had sprung out of the canvas.

"Ha, you see it now. My eyes have been trained to examine faces and not their trimmings. It is the first quality of a criminal investigator that he should see through a disguise."

"But this is marvellous. It might be his portrait."

"Yes, it is an interesting instance of a throw-back, which appears to be both physical and spiritual. A study of family portraits is enough to convert a man to the doctrine of reincarnation. The fellow is a Baskerville—that is evident."

"With designs upon the succession."

"Exactly. This chance of the picture has supplied us with one of our most obvious missing links. We have him, Watson, we have him, and I dare swear that before to-morrow night he will be fluttering in our net as helpless as one of his own butterflies. A pin, a cork, and a card, and we add him to the Baker Street collection!" He burst into one of his rare fits of laughter as he turned away from the picture. I have not heard him laugh often, and it has always boded ill to somebody.

I was up betimes in the morning, but Holmes was afoot earlier still, for I saw him as I dressed coming up the drive.

"Yes, we should have a full day to-day," he remarked, and he rubbed his hands with the joy of action. "The nets are all in place, and the drag is about to begin. We'll know before the day is out whether we have caught our big, lean-jawed pike, or whether he has got through the meshes."

"Have you been on the moor already?"

"I have sent a report from Grimpen to Princetown as to the death of Selden. I think I can promise that none of you will be troubled in the matter. And I have also communicated with my faithful Cartwright, who would certainly have pined away at the door of my hut as a dog does at his master's grave if I had not set his mind at rest about my safety."

"What is the next move?"

"To see Sir Henry. Ah, here he is!"

"Good morning, Holmes," said the baronet. "You look like a general who is planning a battle with his chief of the staff."

"That is the exact situation. Watson was asking for orders."

"And so do I."

"Very good. You are engaged, as I understand, to dine with our friends the Stapletons to-night."

"I hope that you will come also. They are very hospitable people, and I am sure that they would be very glad to see you."

"I fear that Watson and I must go to London."

"To London?"

"Yes, I think that we should be more useful there at the present juncture."

The baronet's face perceptibly lengthened. "I hoped that you were going to see me through this business. The Hall and the moor are not very pleasant places when one is alone."

"My dear fellow, you must trust me implicitly and do exactly what I tell you. You can tell your friends that we should have been happy to have come with you, but that urgent business required us to be in town. We hope very soon to return to Devonshire. Will you remember to give them that message?"

"If you insist upon it."

"There is no alternative, I assure you."

I saw by the Baronet's clouded brow that he was deeply hurt by what he regarded as our desertion.

"When do you desire to go?" he asked, coldly.

"Immediately after breakfast. We will drive in to Coombe Tracey, but Watson will leave his things as a pledge that he will come back to you. Watson, you will send a note to Stapleton to tell him that you regret that you cannot come."

"I have a good mind to go to London with you," said the Baronet. "Why should I stay here alone?"

"Because it is your post of duty. Because you gave me your word that you would do as you were told, and I tell you to stay."

"All right, then, I'll stay."

"One more direction! I wish you to drive to Merripit House. Send back your trap, however, and let them know that you intend to walk home."

"To walk across the moor?"

"Yes."

"But that is the very thing which you have so often cautioned me not to do."

"This time you may do it with safety. If I had not every confidence in your nerve and courage I would not suggest it, but it is essential that you should do it."

"Then I will do it."

"And as you value your life do not go across the moor in any direction save along the straight path which leads from Merripit House to the Grimpen Road, and is your natural way home."

"I will do just what you say."

"Very good. I should be glad to get away as soon after breakfast as possible, so as to reach London in the afternoon."

I was much astounded by this programme, though I remembered that Holmes had said to Stapleton on the night before that his visit would terminate next day. It had not crossed my mind, however, that he would wish me to go with him, nor could I understand how we could both be absent at a moment which he himself declared to be critical. There was nothing for it, however, but implicit obedience; so we bade good-bye to our rueful friend, and a couple of hours afterwards we were at the station of Coombe Tracey and had dispatched the trap upon its return journey. A small boy was waiting upon the platform.

"Any orders, sir?"

"You will take this train to town, Cartwright. The moment you arrive you will send a wire to Sir Henry Baskerville, in my name, to say that if he finds the pocket-book which I have dropped he is to send it by registered post to Baker Street."

"Yes, sir."

"And ask at the station office if there is a message for me."

The boy returned with a telegram, which Holmes handed to me. It ran:

Wire received. Coming down with unsigned warrant. Arrive five-forty.

—Lestrade

"That is in answer to mine of this morning. He is the best of the professionals, I think, and we may need his assistance. Now, Watson, I think that we cannot employ our time better than by calling upon your acquaintance, Mrs. Laura Lyons."

His plan of campaign was beginning to be evident. He would use the Baronet in order to convince the Stapletons that we were really gone, while we would actually return at the instant when we were likely to be needed. That telegram from London, if mentioned by Sir Henry to the Stapletons, must remove the last suspicions from their minds. Already I seemed to see our nets drawing close round that lean-jawed pike.

Mrs. Laura Lyons was in her office, and Sherlock Holmes opened his interview with a frankness and directness which considerably amazed her.

"I am investigating the circumstances which attended the death of the late Sir Charles Baskerville," said he. "My friend here, Dr. Watson, has informed me of what you have communicated, and also of what you have withheld in connection with that matter."

"What have I withheld?" she asked defiantly.

"You have confessed that you asked Sir Charles to be at the gate at ten o'clock. We know that that was the place and hour of his death. You have withheld what the connection is between these events."

"There is no connection."

"In that case the coincidence must indeed be an extraordinary one. But I think that we shall succeed in establishing a connection after all. I wish to be perfectly frank with you, Mrs. Lyons. We regard this case as one of murder, and the evidence may implicate not only your friend Mr. Stapleton, but his wife as well."

The lady sprang from her chair. "His wife!" she cried.

"The fact is no longer a secret. The person who has passed for his sister is really his wife."

Mrs. Lyons had resumed her seat. Her hands were grasping the arms of her chair, and I saw that the pink nails had turned white with the pressure of her grip.

"His wife!" she said, again. "His wife! He was not a married man."

Sherlock Holmes shrugged his shoulders.

"Prove it to me! Prove it to me! And if you can do so——!" The fierce flash of her eyes said more than any words.

"I have come prepared to do so," said Holmes, drawing several papers from his pocket. "Here is a photograph of the couple taken in York four years ago. It is endorsed 'Mr. and Mrs. Vandeleur,' but you will have no difficulty in recognizing him, and her also, if you know her by sight. Here are three written descriptions by trustworthy witnesses of Mr. and Mrs. Vandeleur, who at that time kept St. Oliver's private school. Read them, and see if you can doubt the identity of these people."

She glanced at them, and then looked up at us with the set, rigid face of a desperate woman.

"Mr. Holmes," she said, "this man had offered me marriage on condition that I could get a divorce from my husband. He has lied to me, the villain, in every conceivable way. Not one word of truth has he ever told me. And why—why? I imagined that all was for my own sake. But now I see that I was never anything but a tool in his hands. Why should I preserve faith with him who never kept any with me? Why should I try to shield him from the consequences of his own wicked acts? Ask me what you like, and there is nothing which I shall hold back. One thing I swear to you, and that is, that when I wrote the letter I never dreamed of any harm to the old gentleman, who had been my kindest friend."

"I entirely believe you, madam," said Sherlock Holmes. "The recital of these events must be very painful to you, and perhaps it will make it easier if I tell you what occurred, and you can check me if I make any material mistake. The sending of this letter was suggested to you by Stapleton?"

"He dictated it."

"I presume that the reason he gave was that you would receive help from Sir Charles for the legal expenses connected with your divorce?"

"Exactly."

"And then after you had sent the letter he dissuaded you from keeping the appointment?"

"He told me that it would hurt his self-respect that any other man should find the money for such an object, and that though he was a poor man himself he would devote his last penny to removing the obstacles which divided us."

"He appears to be a very consistent character. And then you heard nothing until you read the reports of the death in the paper?"

"No."

"And he made you swear to say nothing about your appointment with Sir Charles?"

"He did. He said that the death was a very mysterious one, and that I should certainly be suspected if the facts came out. He frightened me into remaining silent."

"Quite so. But you had your suspicions?"

She hesitated and looked down.

"I knew him," she said. "But if he had kept faith with me I should always have done so with him."

"I think that on the whole you have had a fortunate escape," said Sherlock Holmes. "You have had him in your power and he knew it, and yet you are alive. You have been walking for some months very near to the edge of a precipice. We must wish you good morning now, Mrs. Lyons, and it is probable that you will very shortly hear from us again."

"Our case becomes rounded off, and difficulty after difficulty thins away in front of us," said Holmes as we stood waiting for the arrival of the express from town. "I shall soon be in the position of being able to put into a single connected narrative one of the most singular and sensational crimes of modern times. Students of criminology will remember the analogous incidents in Grodno, in Little Russia, in the year '66, and of course there are the Anderson murders in North Carolina, but this case possesses some features which are entirely its own. Even now we have no clear case against this very wily man. But I shall be very much surprised if it is not clear enough before we go to bed this night."

The London express came roaring into the station, and a small, wiry bulldog of a man had sprung from a first-class carriage. We all three shook hands, and I saw at once from the reverential way in which Lestrade gazed at my companion that he had learned a good deal since the days when they had first worked together. I could well remember the scorn which the theories of the reasoner used then to excite in the practical man.

"Anything good?" he asked.

"The biggest thing for years," said Holmes. "We have two hours before we need think of starting. I think we might employ it in getting some dinner, and then, Lestrade, we will take the London fog out of your throat by giving you a breath of the pure night air of Dartmoor. Never been there? Ah, well, I don't suppose you will forget your first visit."

XIV. The Hound of the Baskervilles

One of Sherlock Holmes's defects—if, indeed, one may call it a defect—was that he was exceedingly loth to communicate his full plans to any other person until the instant of their fulfilment. Partly it came no doubt from his own masterful nature, which loved to dominate and surprise those who were around him. Partly also from his professional caution, which urged him never to take any chances. The result, however, was very trying for those who were acting as his agents and assistants. I had often suffered under it, but never more so than during that long drive in the darkness. The great ordeal was in front of us; at last we were about to make our final effort, and yet Holmes had said nothing, and I could only surmise what his course of action would be. My nerves thrilled with anticipation when at last the cold wind upon our faces and the dark, void spaces on either side of the narrow road told me that we were back upon the moor once again. Every stride of the horses and every turn of the wheels was taking us nearer to our supreme adventure.

Our conversation was hampered by the presence of the driver of the hired wagonette, so that we were forced to talk of trivial matters when our nerves were tense with emotion and anticipation. It was a relief to me, after that unnatural restraint, when we at last passed Frankland's house and knew that we were drawing near to the Hall and to the scene of action. We did not drive up to the door, but got down near the gate of the avenue. The wagonette was paid off and ordered to return to Coombe Tracey forthwith, while we started to walk to Merripit House.

"Are you armed, Lestrade?"

The little detective smiled. "As long as I have my trousers I have a hip-pocket, and as long as I have my hip-pocket I have something in it."

"Good! My friend and I are also ready for emergencies."

"You're mighty close about this affair, Mr. Holmes. What's the game now?"

"A waiting game."

"My word, it does not seem a very cheerful place," said the detective, with a shiver, glancing round him at the gloomy slopes of the hill and at the huge lake of fog which lay over the Grimpen Mire. "I see the lights of a house ahead of us."

"That is Merripit House and the end of our journey. I must request you to walk on tip-toe and not to talk above a whisper."

We moved cautiously along the track as if we were bound for the house, but Holmes halted us when we were about two hundred yards from it.

"This will do," said he. "These rocks upon the right make an admirable screen."

"We are to wait here?"

"Yes, we shall make our little ambush here. Get into this hollow, Lestrade. You have been inside the house, have you not, Watson? Can you tell the position of the rooms? What are those latticed windows at this end?"

"I think they are the kitchen windows."

"And the one beyond, which shines so brightly?"

"That is certainly the dining-room."

"The blinds are up. You know the lie of the land best. Creep forward quietly and see what they are doing—but for Heaven's sake don't let them know that they are watched!"

I tip-toed down the path and stooped behind the low wall which surrounded the stunted orchard. Creeping in its shadow, I reached a point whence I could look straight through the uncurtained window.

There were only two men in the room, Sir Henry and Stapleton. They sat with their profiles towards me on either side of the round table. Both of them were smoking cigars, and coffee and wine were in front of them. Stapleton was talking with animation, but the Baronet looked pale and distrait. Perhaps the thought of that lonely walk across the ill-omened moor was weighing heavily upon his mind.

As I watched them Stapleton rose and left the room, while Sir Henry filled his glass again and leaned back in his chair, puffing at his cigar. I heard the creak of a door and the crisp sound of boots upon gravel. The steps passed along the path on the other side of the wall under which I crouched. Looking over, I saw the naturalist pause at the door of an outhouse in the corner of the orchard. A key turned in a lock, and as he passed in there was a curious scuffling noise from within. He was only a minute or so inside, and then I heard the key turn once more, and he passed me and re-entered the house. I saw him rejoin his guest and I crept quietly back to where my companions were waiting to tell them what I had seen.

"You say, Watson, that the lady is not there?" Holmes asked, when I had finished my report.

"No."

"Where can she be, then, since there is no light in any other room except the kitchen?"

"I cannot think where she is."

I have said that over the great Grimpen Mire there hung a dense, white fog. It was drifting slowly in our direction and banked itself up like a wall on that side of us, low, but thick and well defined. The moon shone on it, and it looked like a great shimmering ice-field, with the heads of the distant tors as rocks borne upon its surface. Holmes's face was turned towards it, and he muttered impatiently as he watched its sluggish drift.

"It's moving towards us, Watson."

"Is that serious?"

"Very serious, indeed—the one thing upon earth which could have disarranged my plans. He can't be very long now. It is already ten o'clock. Our success and even his life may depend upon his coming out before the fog is over the path."

The night was clear and fine above us. The stars shone cold and bright, while a half-moon bathed the whole scene in a soft, uncertain light. Before us lay the dark bulk of the house, its serrated roof and bristling chimneys hard outlined against the silver-spangled sky. Broad bars of golden light from the lower windows stretched across the orchard and the moor. One of them was suddenly shut off. The servants had left the kitchen. There only remained the lamp in the dining-room where the two men, the murderous host and the unconscious guest, still chatted over their cigars.

Every minute that white woolly plain which covered one half of the moor was drifting closer and closer to the house. Already the first thin wisps of it were curling across the golden square of the lighted window. The farther wall of the orchard was already invisible, and the trees were standing out of a swirl of white vapour. As we watched it the fog-wreaths came crawling round both corners of the house and rolled slowly into one dense bank, on which the upper floor and the roof floated like a strange ship upon a shadowy sea. Holmes struck his hand passionately upon the rock in front of us, and stamped his feet in his impatience.

"If he isn't out in a quarter of an hour the path will be covered. In half an hour we won't be able to see our hands in front of us."

"Shall we move farther back upon higher ground?"

"Yes, I think it would be as well."

So as the fog-bank flowed onwards, we fell back before it until we were half a mile from the house, and still that dense white sea, with the moon silvering its upper edge, swept slowly and inexorably on.

"We are going too far," said Holmes. "We dare not take the chance of his being overtaken before he can reach us. At all costs we must hold our ground where we are." He dropped on his knees and clapped his ear to the ground. "Thank God, I think that I hear him coming."

A sound of quick steps broke the silence of the moor. Crouching among the stones, we stared intently at the silver-tipped bank in front of us. The steps grew louder, and through the fog, as through a curtain, there stepped the man whom we were awaiting. He looked round him in surprise as he emerged into the clear, star-lit night. Then he came swiftly along the path, passed close to where we lay, and went on up the long slope behind us. As he walked he glanced continually over either shoulder, like a man who is ill at ease.

"Hist!" cried Holmes, and I heard the sharp click of a cocking pistol. "Look out! It's coming!"

There was a thin, crisp, continuous patter from somewhere in the heart of that crawling bank. The cloud was within fifty yards of where we lay, and we glared at it, all three, uncertain what horror was about to break from the heart of it. I was at Holmes's elbow, and I glanced for an instant at his face. It was pale and exultant, his eyes shining brightly in the moonlight. But suddenly they started forward in a rigid, fixed stare, and his lips parted in amazement. At the same instant Lestrade gave a yell of terror and threw himself face downwards upon the ground. I sprang to my feet, my inert hand grasping my pistol, my mind paralysed by the dreadful shape which had sprung out upon us from the shadows of the fog. A hound it was, an enormous coal-black hound, but not such a hound as mortal eyes have ever seen. Fire burst from its open mouth, its eyes glowed with a smouldering glare, its muzzle and hackles and dewlap were outlined in flickering flame. Never in the delirious dream of a disordered brain could anything more savage, more appalling, more hellish, be conceived than that dark form and savage face which broke upon us out of the wall of fog.

With long bounds the huge black creature was leaping down the track, following hard upon the footsteps of our friend. So paralysed were we by the apparition that we allowed him to pass before we had recovered our nerve. Then Holmes and I both fired together, and the creature gave a hideous howl, which showed that one at least had hit him. He did not pause, however, but bounded onwards. Far away on the path we saw Sir Henry looking back, his face white in the moonlight, his hands raised in horror, glaring helplessly at the frightful thing which was hunting him down.

But that cry of pain from the hound had blown all our fears to the winds. If he was vulnerable he was mortal, and if we could wound him we could kill him. Never have I seen a man run as Holmes ran that night. I am reckoned fleet of foot, but he outpaced me as much as I outpaced the little professional. In front of us as we flew up the track we heard scream after scream from Sir Henry and the deep roar of the hound. I was in time to see the beast spring upon its victim, hurl him to the ground and worry at his throat. But the next instant Holmes had emptied five barrels of his revolver into the creature's flank. With a last howl of agony and a vicious snap in the air it rolled upon its back, four feet pawing furiously, and then fell limp upon its side. I stooped, panting, and pressed my pistol to the dreadful, shimmering head, but it was useless to press the trigger. The giant hound was dead.

Sir Henry lay insensible where he had fallen. We tore away his collar, and Holmes breathed a prayer of gratitude when we saw that there was no sign of a wound and that the rescue had been in time. Already our friend's eyelids shivered and he made a feeble effort to move. Lestrade thrust his brandy-flask between the Baronet's teeth, and two frightened eyes were looking up at us.

"My God!" he whispered. "What was it? What, in Heaven's name, was it?"

"It's dead, whatever it is," said Holmes. "We've laid the family ghost once and forever."

In mere size and strength it was a terrible creature which was lying stretched before us. It was not a pure bloodhound and it was not a pure mastiff; but it appeared to be a combination of the two—gaunt, savage, and as large as a small lioness. Even now, in the stillness of death, the huge jaws seemed to be dripping with a bluish flame, and the small, deep-set, cruel eyes were ringed with fire. I placed my hand upon the glowing muzzle, and as I held them up my own fingers smouldered and gleamed in the darkness.

"Phosphorus," I said.

"A cunning preparation of it," said Holmes, sniffing at the dead animal. "There is no smell which might have interfered with his power of scent. We owe you a deep apology, Sir Henry, for having exposed you to this fright. I was prepared for a hound, but not for such a creature as this. And the fog gave us little time to receive him."

"You have saved my life."

"Having first endangered it. Are you strong enough to stand?"

"Give me another mouthful of that brandy, and I shall be ready for anything. So! Now, if you will help me up. What do you propose to do?"

"To leave you here. You are not fit for further adventures to-night. If you will wait, one or other of us will go back with you to the Hall."

He tried to stagger to his feet; but he was still ghastly pale and trembling in every limb. We helped him to a rock, where he sat shivering with his face buried in his hands.

"We must leave you now," said Holmes. "The rest of our work must be done, and every moment is of importance. We have our case, and now we only want our man.

"It's a thousand to one against our finding him at the house," he continued, as we retraced our steps swiftly down the path. "Those shots must have told him that the game was up."

"We were some distance off, and this fog may have deadened them."

"He followed the hound to call him off—of that you may be certain. No, no, he's gone by this time! But we'll search the house and make sure."

The front door was open, so we rushed in and hurried from room to room, to the amazement of a doddering old manservant, who met us in the passage. There was no light save in the dining-room, but Holmes caught up the lamp, and left no corner of the house unexplored. No sign could we see of the man whom we were chasing. On the upper floor, however, one of the bedroom doors was locked.

"There's someone in here!" cried Lestrade. "I can hear a movement. Open this door!"

A faint moaning and rustling came from within. Holmes struck the door just over the lock with the flat of his foot, and it flew open. Pistol in hand, we all three rushed into the room.

But there was no sign within it of that desperate and defiant villain whom we expected to see. Instead we were faced by an object so strange and so unexpected that we stood for a moment staring at it in amazement.

The room had been fashioned into a small museum, and the walls were lined by a number of glass-topped cases full of that collection of butterflies and moths the formation of which had been the relaxation of this complex and dangerous man. In the centre of this room there was an upright beam, which had been placed at some period as a support for the old worm-eaten balk of timber which spanned the roof. To this post a figure was tied, so swathed and muffled in the sheets which had been used to secure it that one could not for the moment tell whether it was that of a man or a woman. One towel passed round the throat, and was secured at the back of the pillar. Another covered the lower part of the face and over it two dark eyes—eyes full of grief and shame and a dreadful questioning—stared back at us. In a minute we had torn off the gag, unswathed the bonds, and Mrs. Stapleton sank upon the floor in front of us. As her beautiful head fell upon her chest I saw the clear red weal of a whiplash across her neck.

"The brute!" cried Holmes. "Here, Lestrade, your brandy-bottle! Put her in the chair! She has fainted from ill-usage and exhaustion."

She opened her eyes again. "Is he safe?" she asked. "Has he escaped?"

"He cannot escape us, madam."

"No, no, I did not mean my husband. Sir Henry? Is he safe?"

"Yes."

"And the hound?"

"It is dead."

She gave a long sigh of satisfaction. "Thank God! Thank God! Oh, this villain! See how he has treated me!" She shot her arms out from her sleeves, and we saw with horror that they were all mottled with bruises. "But this is nothing—nothing! It is my mind and soul that he has tortured and defiled. I could endure it all, ill-usage, solitude, a life of deception, everything, as long as I could still cling to the hope that I had his love, but now I know that in this also I have been his dupe and his tool." She broke into passionate sobbing as she spoke.

"You bear him no good will, madam," said Holmes. "Tell us, then, where we shall find him. If you have ever aided him in evil, help us now and so atone."

"There is but one place where he can have fled," she answered. "There is an old tin mine on an island in the heart of the Mire. It was there that he kept his hound and there also he had made preparations so that he might have a refuge. That is where he would fly."

The fog-bank lay like white wool against the window. Holmes held the lamp towards it.

"See," said he. "No one could find his way into the Grimpen Mire tonight."

She laughed and clapped her hands. Her eyes and teeth gleamed with fierce merriment.

"He may find his way in, but never out," she cried. "How can he see the guiding wands to-night? We planted them together, he and I, to mark the pathway through the Mire. Oh, if I could only have plucked them out to-day! Then indeed you would have had him at your mercy!"

It was evident to us that all pursuit was in vain until the fog had lifted. Meanwhile we left Lestrade in possession of the house, while Holmes and I went back with the baronet to Baskerville Hall. The story of the Stapletons could no longer be withheld from him, but he took the blow bravely when he learned the truth about the woman whom he had loved. But the shock of the night's adventures had shattered his nerves, and before morning he lay delirious in a high fever, under the care of Dr. Mortimer. The two of them were destined to travel together round the world before Sir Henry had become once more the hale, hearty man that he had been before he became master of that ill-omened estate.

And now I come rapidly to the conclusion of this singular narrative, in which I have tried to make the reader share those dark fears and vague surmises which clouded our lives so long, and ended in so tragic a manner. On the morning after the death of the hound the fog had lifted and we were guided by Mrs. Stapleton to the point where they had found a pathway through the bog. It helped us to realize the horror of this woman's life when we saw the eagerness and joy with which she laid us on her husband's track. We left her standing upon the thin peninsula of firm, peaty soil which tapered out into the widespread bog. From the end of it a small wand planted here and there showed where the path zig-zagged from tuft to tuft of rushes among those green-scummed pits and foul quagmires which barred the way to the stranger. Rank reeds and lush, slimy water-plants sent an odour of decay and a heavy miasmatic vapour into our faces, while a false step plunged us more than once thigh-deep into the dark, quivering mire, which shook for yards in soft undulations around our feet. Its tenacious grip plucked at our heels as we walked, and when we sank into it it was as if some malignant hand was tugging us down into those obscene depths, so grim and purposeful was the clutch in which it held us. Once only we saw a trace that someone had passed that perilous way before us. From amid a tuft of cotton-grass which bore it up out of the slime some dark thing was projecting. Holmes sank to his waist as he stepped from the path to seize it, and had we not been there to drag him out he could never have set his foot upon firm land again. He held an old black boot in the air. "Meyers, Toronto," was printed on the leather inside.

"It is worth a mud bath," said he. "It is our friend Sir Henry's missing boot."

"Thrown there by Stapleton in his flight."

"Exactly. He retained it in his hand after using it to set the hound upon his track. He fled when he knew the game was up, still clutching it. And he hurled it away at this point of his flight. We know at least that he came so far in safety."

But more than that we were never destined to know, though there was much which we might surmise. There was no chance of finding footsteps in the mire, for the rising mud oozed swiftly in upon them, but as we at last reached firmer ground beyond the morass we all looked eagerly for them. But no slightest sign of them ever met our eyes. If the earth told a true story, then Stapleton never reached that island of refuge towards which he struggled through the fog upon that last night. Somewhere in the heart of the great Grimpen Mire, down in the foul slime of the huge morass which had sucked him in, this cold and cruel-hearted man is forever buried.

Many traces we found of him in the bog-girt island where he had hid his savage ally. A huge driving-wheel and a shaft half-filled with rubbish showed the position of an abandoned mine. Beside it were the crumbling remains of the cottages of the miners, driven away, no doubt, by the foul reek of the surrounding swamp. In one of these a staple and chain, with a quantity of gnawed bones, showed where the animal had been confined. A skeleton with a tangle of brown hair adhering to it lay among the *débris*.

"A dog!" said Holmes. "By Jove, a curly-haired spaniel. Poor Mortimer will never see his pet again. Well, I do not know that this place contains any secret which we have not already fathomed. He could hide his hound, but he could not hush its voice, and hence came those cries which even in daylight were not pleasant to hear. On an emergency he could keep the hound in the outhouse at Merripit, but it was always a risk, and it was only on the supreme day, which he regarded as the end of all his efforts, that he dared do it. This paste in the tin is no doubt the luminous mixture with which the creature was daubed. It was suggested, of course, by the story of the family hell-hound, and by the desire to frighten old Sir Charles to death. No wonder the poor devil of a convict ran and screamed, even as our friend did, and as we ourselves might have done, when he saw such a creature bounding through the darkness of the moor upon his track. It was a cunning device, for, apart from the chance of driving your victim to his death, what peasant would venture to inquire too closely into such a creature should he get sight of it, as many have done, upon the moor? I said it in London, Watson, and I say it again now, that never yet have we helped to hunt down a more dangerous man than he who is lying yonder"—he swept his long arm towards the huge mottled expanse of green-splotched bog which stretched away until it merged into the russet slopes of the moor.

XV. A Retrospection

It was the end of November, and Holmes and I sat, upon a raw and foggy night, on either side of a blazing fire in our sitting-room in Baker Street. Since the tragic upshot of our visit to Devonshire he had been engaged in two affairs of the utmost importance, in the first of which he had exposed the atrocious conduct of Colonel Upwood in connection with the famous card scandal of the Nonpareil Club, while in the second he had defended the unfortunate Mme. Montpensier from the charge of murder, which hung over her in connection with the death of her step-daughter, Mlle. Carère, the young lady who, as it will be remembered, was found six months later alive and married in New York. My friend was in excellent spirits over the success which had attended a succession of difficult and important cases, so that I was able to induce him to discuss the details of the Baskerville mystery. I had waited patiently for the opportunity, for I was aware that he would never permit cases to overlap, and that his clear and logical mind would not be drawn from its present work to dwell upon memories of the past. Sir Henry and Dr. Mortimer were, however, in London, on their way to that long voyage which had been recommended for the restoration of his shattered nerves. They had called upon us that very afternoon, so that it was natural that the subject should come up for discussion.

"The whole course of events," said Holmes, "from the point of view of the man who called himself Stapleton, was simple and direct, although to us, who had no means in the beginning of knowing the motives of his actions and could only learn part of the facts, it all appeared exceedingly complex. I have had the advantage of two conversations with Mrs. Stapleton, and the case has now been so entirely cleared up that I am not aware that there is anything which has remained a secret to us. You will find a few notes upon the matter under the heading B in my indexed list of cases."

"Perhaps you would kindly give me a sketch of the course of events from memory."

"Certainly, though I cannot guarantee that I carry all the facts in my mind. Intense mental concentration has a curious way of blotting out what has passed. The barrister who has his case at his fingers' end, and is able to argue with an expert upon his own subject, finds that a week or two of the courts will drive it all out of his head once more. So each of my cases displaces the last, and Mlle. Carère has blurred my recollection of Baskerville Hall. To-morrow some other little problem may be submitted to my notice, which will in turn dispossess the fair French lady and the infamous Upwood. So far as the case of the Hound goes, however, I will give you the course of events as nearly as I can, and you will suggest anything which I may have forgotten.

"My inquiries show beyond all question that the family portrait did not lie, and that this fellow was indeed a Baskerville. He was a son of that Rodger Baskerville, the younger brother of Sir Charles, who fled with a sinister reputation to South America, where he was said to have died unmarried. He did, as a matter of fact, marry, and had one child, this fellow, whose real name is the same as his father. He married Beryl Garcia, one of the beauties of Costa Rica, and, having purloined a considerable sum of public money, he changed his name to Vandeleur and fled to England, where he established a school in the east of Yorkshire. His reason for attempting this special line of business was that he had struck up an acquaintance with a consumptive tutor upon the voyage home, and that he had used this man's ability to make the undertaking a success. Fraser, the tutor, died, however, and the school which had begun well, sank from disrepute into infamy. The Vandeleurs found it convenient to change their name to Stapleton, and he brought the remains of his fortune, his schemes for the future, and his taste for entomology to the south of England. I learned at the British Museum that he was a recognized authority upon the subject, and that the name of Vandeleur has been permanently attached to a certain moth which he had, in his Yorkshire days, been the first to describe.

"We now come to that portion of his life which has proved to be of such intense interest to us. The fellow had evidently made inquiry, and found that only two lives intervened between him and a valuable estate. When he went to Devonshire his plans were, I believe, exceedingly hazy, but that he meant mischief from the first is evident from the way in which he took his wife with him in the character of his sister. The idea of using her as a decoy was clearly already in his mind, though he may not have been certain how the details of his plot were to be arranged. He meant in the end to have the estate, and he was ready to use any tool or run any risk for that end. His first act was to establish himself as near to his ancestral home as he could, and his second was to cultivate a friendship with Sir Charles Baskerville and with the neighbours.

"The Baronet himself told him about the family hound, and so prepared the way for his own death. Stapleton, as I will continue to call him, knew that the old man's heart was weak and that a shock would kill him. So much he had learned from Dr. Mortimer. He had heard also that Sir Charles was superstitious and had taken this grim legend very seriously. His ingenious mind instantly suggested a way by which the Baronet could be done to death, and yet it would be hardly possible to bring home the guilt to the real murderer.

"Having conceived the idea, he proceeded to carry it out with considerable finesse. An ordinary schemer would have been content to work with a savage hound. The use of artificial means to make the creature diabolical was a flash of genius upon his part. The dog he bought in London from Ross and Mangles the dealers in Fulham Road. It was the strongest and most savage in their possession. He brought it down by the North Devon line, and walked a great distance over the moor, so as to get it home without exciting any remarks. He had already on his insect hunts learned to penetrate the Grimpen Mire, and so had found a safe hiding-place for the creature. Here he kennelled it and waited his chance.

"But it was some time coming. The old gentleman could not be decoyed outside of his grounds at night. Several times Stapleton lurked about with his hound, but without avail. It was during these fruitless quests that he, or rather his ally, was seen by peasants, and that the legend of the demon dog received a new confirmation. He had hoped that his wife might lure Sir Charles to his ruin, but here she proved unexpectedly independent. She would not endeavour to entangle the old gentleman in a sentimental attachment which might deliver him over to his enemy. Threats and even, I am sorry to say, blows failed to move her. She would have nothing to do with it, and for a time Stapleton was at a deadlock.

"He found a way out of his difficulties through the chance that Sir Charles, who had conceived a friendship with him, made him the minister of his charity in the case of this unfortunate woman, Mrs. Laura Lyons. By representing himself as a single man, he acquired complete influence over her, and he gave her to understand that in the event of her obtaining a divorce from her husband he would marry her. His plans were suddenly brought to a head by his knowledge that Sir Charles was about to leave the Hall on the advice of Dr. Mortimer, with whose opinion he himself pretended to coincide. He must act at once, or his victim might get beyond his power. He therefore put pressure upon Mrs. Lyons to write this letter, imploring the old man to give her an interview on the evening before his departure for London. He then, by a specious argument, prevented her from going, and so had the chance for which he had waited.

"Driving back in the evening from Coombe Tracey, he was in time to get his hound, to treat it with his infernal paint, and to bring the beast round to the gate at which he had reason to expect that he would find the old gentleman waiting. The dog, incited by its master, sprang over the wicket-gate and pursued the unfortunate Baronet, who fled screaming down the Yew Alley. In that gloomy tunnel it must indeed have been a dreadful sight to see that huge black creature, with its flaming jaws and blazing eyes, bounding after its victim. He fell dead at the end of the alley from heart disease and terror. The hound had kept upon the grassy border while the baronet had run down the path, so that no track but the man's was visible. On seeing him lying still the creature had probably approached to sniff at him, but, finding him dead, had turned away again. It was then that it left the print which was actually observed by Dr. Mortimer. The hound was called off and hurried away to its lair in the Grimpen Mire, and a mystery was left which puzzled the authorities, alarmed the country-side, and finally brought the case within the scope of our observation.

"So much for the death of Sir Charles Baskerville. You perceive the devilish cunning of it, for really it would be almost impossible to make a case against the real murderer. His only accomplice was one who could never give him away, and the grotesque, inconceivable nature of the device only served to make it more effective. Both of the women concerned in the case, Mrs. Stapleton and Mrs. Laura Lyons, were left with a strong suspicion against Stapleton. Mrs. Stapleton knew that he had designs upon the old man, and also of the existence of the hound. Mrs. Lyons knew neither of these things, but had been impressed by the death occurring at the time of an uncancelled appointment which was only known to him. However, both of them were under his influence, and he had nothing to fear from them. The first half of his task was successfully accomplished, but the more difficult still remained.

"It is possible that Stapleton did not know of the existence of an heir in Canada. In any case he would very soon learn it from his friend Dr. Mortimer, and he was told by the latter all details about the arrival of Henry Baskerville. Stapleton's first idea was that this young stranger from Canada might possibly be done to death in London without coming down to Devonshire at all. He distrusted his wife ever since she had refused to help him in laying a trap for the old man, and he dared not leave her long out of his sight for fear he should lose his influence over her. It was for this reason that he took her to London with him. They lodged, I find, at the Mexborough Private Hotel, in Craven Street, which was actually one of those called upon by my agent in search of evidence. Here he kept his wife imprisoned in her room while he, disguised in a beard, followed Dr. Mortimer to Baker Street, and afterwards to the station and to the Northumberland Hotel. His wife had some inkling of his plans; but she had such a fear of her husband—a fear founded upon brutal ill-treatment—that she dare not write to warn the man whom she knew to be in danger. If the letter should fall into Stapleton's hands her own life would not be safe. Eventually, as we know, she adopted the expedient of cutting out the words which would form the message, and addressing the letter in a disguised hand. It reached the Baronet, and gave him the first warning of his danger.

"It was very essential for Stapleton to get some article of Sir Henry's attire, so that, in case he was driven to use the dog, he might always have the means of setting him upon his track. With characteristic promptness and audacity he set about this at once, and we cannot doubt that the boots or chambermaid of the hotel was well bribed to help him in his design. By chance, however, the first boot which was procured for him was a new one, and, therefore, useless for his purpose. He then had it returned and obtained another—a most instructive incident, since it proved conclusively to my mind that we were dealing with a real hound, as no other supposition could explain this anxiety to obtain an old boot and this indifference to a new one. The more *outré* and grotesque an incident is the more carefully it deserves to be examined, and the very point which appears to complicate a case is, when duly considered and scientifically handled, the one which is most likely to elucidate it.

"Then we had the visit from our friends next morning, shadowed always by Stapleton in the cab. From his knowledge of our rooms and of my appearance, as well as from his general conduct, I am inclined to think that Stapleton's career of crime has been by no means limited to this single Baskerville affair. It is suggestive that during the last three years there have been four considerable burglaries in the West Country, for none of which was any criminal ever arrested. The last of these, at Folkestone Court, in May, was remarkable for the cold-blooded pistolling of the page, who surprised the masked and solitary burglar. I cannot doubt that Stapleton recruited his waning resources in this fashion, and that for years he has been a desperate and dangerous man.

"We had an example of his readiness of resource that morning when he got away from us so successfully, and also of his audacity in sending back my own name to me through the cabman. From that moment he understood that I had taken over the case in London, and that therefore there was no chance for him there. He returned to Dartmoor and awaited the arrival of the Baronet."

"One moment!" said I. "You have, no doubt, described the sequence of events correctly, but there is one point which you have left unexplained. What became of the hound when its master was in London?"

"I have given some attention to this matter, and it is undoubtedly of importance. There can be no question that Stapleton had a confidant, though it is unlikely that he ever placed himself in his power by sharing all his plans with him. There was an old manservant at Merripit House, whose name was Anthony. His connection with the Stapletons can be traced for several years, as far back as the schoolmastering days, so that he must have been aware that his master and mistress were really husband and wife. This man has disappeared and has escaped from the country. It is suggestive that Anthony is not a common name in England, while Antonio is so in all Spanish or Spanish-American countries. The man, like Mrs. Stapleton herself, spoke good English, but with a curious lisping accent. I have myself seen this old man cross the Grimpen Mire by the path which Stapleton had marked out. It is very probable, therefore, that in the absence of his master it was he who cared for the hound, though he may never have known the purpose for which the beast was used.

"The Stapletons then went down to Devonshire, whither they were soon followed by Sir Henry and you. One word now as to how I stood myself at that time. It may possibly recur to your memory that when I examined the paper upon which the printed words were fastened I made a close inspection for the water-mark. In doing so I held it within a few inches of my eyes, and was conscious of a faint smell of the scent known as white jessamine. There are seventy-five perfumes, which it is very necessary that the criminal expert should be able to distinguish from each other, and cases have more than once within my own experience depended upon their prompt recognition. The scent suggested the presence of a lady, and already my thoughts began to turn towards the Stapletons. Thus I had made certain of the hound, and had guessed at the criminal before ever we went to the West Country.

"It was my game to watch Stapleton. It was evident, however, that I could not do this if I were with you, since he would be keenly on his guard. I deceived everybody, therefore, yourself included, and I came down secretly when I was supposed to be in London. My hardships were not so great as you imagine, though such trifling details must never interfere with the investigation of a case. I stayed for the most part at Coombe Tracey, and only used the hut upon the moor when it was necessary to be near the scene of action. Cartwright had come down with me, and in his disguise as a country boy he was of great assistance to me. I was dependent upon him for food and clean linen. When I was watching Stapleton, Cartwright was frequently watching you, so that I was able to keep my hand upon all the strings.

"I have already told you that your reports reached me rapidly, being forwarded instantly from Baker Street to Coombe Tracey. They were of great service to me, and especially that one incidentally truthful piece of biography of Stapleton's. I was able to establish the identity of the man and the woman, and knew at last exactly how I stood. The case had been considerably complicated through the incident of the escaped convict and the relations between him and the Barrymores. This also you cleared up in a very effective way, though I had already come to the same conclusions from my own observations.

"By the time that you discovered me upon the moor I had a complete knowledge of the whole business, but I had not a case which could go to a jury. Even Stapleton's attempt upon Sir Henry that night, which ended in the death of the unfortunate convict, did not help us much in proving murder against our man. There seemed to be no alternative but to catch him red-handed, and to do so we had to use Sir Henry, alone and apparently unprotected, as a bait. We did so, and at the cost of a severe shock to our client we succeeded in completing our case and driving Stapleton to his destruction. That Sir Henry should have been exposed to this is, I must confess, a reproach to my management of the case, but we had no means of foreseeing the terrible and paralysing spectacle which the beast presented, nor could we predict the fog which enabled him to burst upon us at such short notice. We succeeded in our object at a cost which both the specialist and Dr. Mortimer assure me will be a temporary one. A long journey may enable our friend to recover not only from his shattered nerves but also from his wounded feelings. His love for the lady was deep and sincere, and to him the saddest part of all this black business was that he should have been deceived by her.

"It only remains now to indicate the part which she had played throughout. There can be no doubt that Stapleton exercised an influence over her which may have been love or may have been fear, or very possibly both, since they are by no means incompatible emotions. It was, at least, absolutely effective. At his command she consented to pass as his sister, though he found the limits of his power over her when he endeavoured to make her the direct accessory to murder. She was ready to warn Sir Henry so far as she could without implicating her husband, and again and again she tried to do so. Stapleton himself seems to have been capable of jealousy, and when he saw the baronet paying court to the lady, even though it was part of his own plan, still he could not help interrupting with a passionate outburst which revealed the fiery soul which his self-contained manner so cleverly concealed. By encouraging the intimacy he made it certain that Sir Henry would frequently come to Merripit House, and that he would sooner or later get the opportunity which he desired. On the day of the crisis, however, his wife turned suddenly against him. She had learned something of the death of the convict, and she knew that the hound was being kept in the out-house on the evening that Sir Henry was coming to dinner. She taxed her husband with his intended crime and a furious scene followed, in which he showed her for the first time that she had a rival in his love. Her fidelity turned in an instant to bitter hatred, and he saw that she would betray him. He tied her up, therefore, that she might have no chance of warning Sir Henry, and he hoped, no doubt, that when the whole country-side put down the baronet's death to the curse of his family, as they certainly would do, he could win his wife back to accept an accomplished fact, and to keep silent upon what she knew. In this I fancy that in any case he made a miscalculation, and that, if we had not been there, his doom would none the less have been sealed. A woman of Spanish blood does not condone such an injury so lightly. And now, my dear Watson, without referring to my notes, I cannot give you a more detailed account of this curious case. I do not know that anything essential has been left unexplained."

"He could not hope to frighten Sir Henry to death, as he had done the old uncle, with his bogie hound."

"The beast was savage and half-starved. If its appearance did not frighten its victim to death, at least it would paralyse the resistance which might be offered."

"No doubt. There only remains one difficulty. If Stapleton came into the succession, how could he explain the fact that he, the heir, had been living unannounced under another name so close to the property? How could he claim it without causing suspicion and inquiry?"

"It is a formidable difficulty, and I fear that you ask too much when you expect me to solve it. The past and the present are within the field of my inquiry, but what a man may do in the future is a hard question to answer. Mrs. Stapleton has heard her husband discuss the problem on several occasions. There were three possible courses. He might claim the property from South America, establish his identity before the British authorities there, and so obtain the fortune without ever coming to England at all; or he might adopt an elaborate disguise during the short time that he need be in London; or, again, he might furnish an accomplice with the proofs and papers, putting him in as heir, and retaining a claim upon some proportion of his income. We cannot doubt, from what we know of him, that he would have found some way out of the difficulty. And now, my dear Watson, we have had some weeks of severe work, and for one evening, I think, we may turn our thoughts into more pleasant channels. I have a box for *Les Huguenots*. Have you heard the De Reszkes? Might I trouble you then to be ready in half an hour, and we can stop at Marcini's for a little dinner on the way?"

THE IVY COTTAGE MYSTERY

Arthur Morrison

I HAD BEEN WORKING DOUBLE TIDES FOR A MONTH: AT NIGHT ON MY MORNING paper, as usual; and in the morning on an evening paper as *locum tenens* for another man who was taking a holiday. This was an exhausting plan of work, although it only actually involved some six hours' attendance a day, or less, at the two offices. I turned up at the head-quarters of my own paper at ten in the evening, and by the time I had seen the editor, selected a subject, written my leader, corrected the slips, chatted, smoked, and so on, and cleared off, it was very usually one o'clock. This meant bed at two, or even three, after supper at the club.

This was all very well at ordinary periods, when any time in the morning would do for rising, but when I had to be up again soon after seven, and round at the evening paper office by eight, I naturally felt a little worn and disgusted with things by midday, after a sharp couple of hours' leaderette scribbling and paragraphing, with attendant sundries.

But the strain was over, and on the first day of comparative comfort I indulged in a midday breakfast and the first undisgusted glance at a morning paper for a month. I felt rather interested in an inquest, begun the day before, on the body of a man whom I had known very slightly before I took to living in chambers.

His name was Gavin Kingscote, and he was an artist of a casual and desultory sort, having, I believe, some small private means of his own. As a matter of fact, he had boarded in the same house in which I had lodged myself for a while, but as I was at the time a late homer and a fairly early riser, taking no regular board in the house, we never became much acquainted. He had since, I understood, made some judicious Stock Exchange speculations, and had set up house in Finchley.

Now the news was that he had been found one morning murdered in his smoking-room, while the room itself, with others, was in a state of confusion. His pockets had been rifled, and his watch and chain were gone, with one or two other small articles of value. On the night of the tragedy a friend had sat smoking with him in the room where the murder took place, and he had been the last person to see Mr. Kingscote alive. A jobbing gardener, who kept the garden in order by casual work from time to time, had been arrested in consequence of footprints exactly corresponding with his boots, having been found on the garden beds near the French window of the smoking-room.

I finished my breakfast and my paper, and Mrs. Clayton, the housekeeper, came to clear my table. She was sister of my late landlady of the house where Kingscote had lodged, and it was by this connection that I had found my chambers. I had not seen the housekeeper since the crime was first reported, so I now said:

"This is shocking news of Mr. Kingscote, Mrs. Clayton. Did you know him yourself?"

She had apparently only been waiting for some such remark to burst out with whatever information she possessed.

"Yes, sir," she exclaimed: "shocking indeed. Pore young feller! I see him often when I was at my sister's, and he was always a nice, quiet gentleman, so different from some. My sister, she's awful cut up, sir, I assure you. And what d'you think 'appened, sir, only last Tuesday? You remember Mr. Kingscote's room where he painted the woodwork so beautiful with gold flowers, and blue, and pink? He used to tell my sister she'd always have something to remember him by. Well, two young fellers, gentlemen I can't call them, come and took that room (it being to let), and went and scratched off all the paint in mere wicked mischief, and then chopped up all the panels into sticks and bits! Nice sort o' gentlemen them! And then they bolted in the morning, being afraid, I s'pose, of being made to pay after treating a pore widder's property like that. That was only Tuesday, and the very next day the pore young gentleman himself's dead, murdered in his own 'ouse, and him going to be married an' all! Dear, dear! I remember once he said—"

Mrs. Clayton was a good soul, but once she began to talk some one else had to stop her. I let her run on for a reasonable time, and then rose and prepared to go out. I remembered very well the panels that had been so mischievously destroyed. They made the room the show-room of the house, which was an old one. They were indeed less than half finished when I came away, and Mrs. Lamb, the landlady, had shown them to me one day when Kingscote was out. All the walls of the room were panelled and painted white, and Kingscote had put upon them an eccentric but charming decoration, obviously suggested by some of the work of Mr. Whistler. Tendrils, flowers, and butterflies in a quaint convention wandered thinly from panel to panel, giving the otherwise rather uninteresting room an unwonted atmosphere of richness and elegance. The lamentable jackasses who had destroyed this had certainly selected the best feature of the room whereon to inflict their senseless mischief.

I strolled idly downstairs, with no particular plan for the afternoon in my mind, and looked in at Hewitt's offices. Hewitt was reading a note, and after a little chat he informed me that it had been left an hour ago, in his absence, by the brother of the man I had just been speaking of.

"He isn't quite satisfied," Hewitt said, "with the way the police are investigating the case, and asks me to run down to Finchley and look round. Yesterday I should have refused, because I have five cases in progress already, but to-day I find that circumstances have given me a day or two. Didn't you say you knew the man?"

"Scarcely more than by sight. He was a boarder in the house at Chelsea where I stayed before I started chambers."

"Ah, well; I think I shall look into the thing. Do you feel particularly interested in the case? I mean, if you've nothing better to do, would you come with me?"

"I shall be very glad," I said. "I was in some doubt what to do with myself. Shall you start at once?"

"I think so. Kerrett, just call a cab. By the way, Brett, which paper has the fullest report of the inquest yesterday? I'll run over it as we go down."

As I had only seen one paper that morning, I could not answer Hewitt's question. So we bought various papers as we went along in the cab, and I found the reports while Martin Hewitt studied them. Summarised, this was the evidence given—

Sarah Dodson, general servant, deposed that she had been in service at Ivy Cottage, the residence of the deceased, for five months, the only other regular servant being the housekeeper and cook. On the evening of the previous Tuesday both servants retired a little before eleven, leaving Mr. Kingscote with a friend in the smoking or sitting room. She never saw her master again alive. On coming downstairs the following morning and going to open the smoking-room windows, she was horrified to discover the body of Mr. Kingscote lying on the floor of the room with blood about the head. She at once raised an alarm, and, on the instructions of the housekeeper, fetched a doctor, and gave information to the police. In answer to questions, witness stated she had heard no noise of any sort during the night, nor had anything suspicious occurred.

Hannah Carr, housekeeper and cook, deposed that she had been in the late Mr. Kingscote's service since he had first taken Ivy Cottage—a period of rather more than a year. She had last seen the deceased alive on the evening of the previous Tuesday, at half-past ten, when she knocked at the door of the smoking-room, where Mr. Kingscote was sitting with a friend, to ask if he would require anything more. Nothing was required, so witness shortly after went to bed. In the morning she was called by the previous witness, who had just gone downstairs, and found the body of deceased lying as described. Deceased's watch and chain were gone, as also was a ring he usually wore, and his pockets appeared to have been turned out. All the ground floor of the house was in confusion, and a bureau, a writing-table, and various drawers were open—a bunch of keys usually carried by deceased being left hanging at one keyhole. Deceased had drawn some money from the bank on the Tuesday, for current expenses; how much she did not know. She had not heard or seen anything suspicious during the night. Besides Dodson and herself, there were no regular servants; there was a charwoman, who came occasionally, and a jobbing gardener, living near, who was called in as required.

Mr. James Vidler, surgeon, had been called by the first witness between seven and eight on Wednesday morning. He found the deceased lying on his face on the floor of the smoking-room, his feet being about eighteen inches from the window, and his head lying in the direction of the fireplace. He found three large contused wounds on the head, any one of which would probably have caused death. The wounds had all been inflicted, apparently, with the same blunt instrument—probably a club or life preserver, or other similar weapon. They could not have been done with the poker. Death was due to concussion of the brain, and deceased had probably been dead seven or eight hours when witness saw him. He had since examined the body more closely, but found no marks at all indicative of a struggle having taken place; indeed, from the position of the wounds and their severity, he should judge that the deceased had been attacked unawares from behind, and had died at once. The body appeared to be perfectly healthy.

Then there was police evidence, which showed that all the doors and windows were found shut and completely fastened, except the front door, which, although shut, was not bolted. There were shutters behind the French windows in the smoking-room, and these were found fastened. No money was found in the bureau, nor in any of the opened drawers, so that if any had been there, it had been stolen. The pockets were entirely empty, except for a small pair of nail scissors, and there was no watch upon the body, nor a ring. Certain footprints were found on the garden beds, which had led the police to take certain steps. No footprints were to be seen on the garden path, which was hard gravel.

Mr. Alexander Campbell, stockbroker, stated that he had known deceased for some few years, and had done business for him. He and Mr. Kingscote frequently called on one another, and on Tuesday evening they dined together at Ivy Cottage. They sat smoking and chatting till nearly twelve o'clock, when Mr. Kingscote himself let him out, the servants having gone to bed. Here the witness proceeded rather excitedly: "That is all I know of this horrible business, and I can say nothing else. What the police mean by following and watching me—"

The Coroner: "Pray be calm, Mr. Campbell. The police must do what seems best to them in a case of this sort. I am sure you would not have them neglect any means of getting at the truth."

Witness: "Certainly not. But if they suspect me, why don't they say so? It is intolerable that I should be—"

The Coroner: "Order, order, Mr. Campbell. You are here to give evidence."

The witness then, in answer to questions, stated that the French windows of the smoking-room had been left open during the evening, the weather being very warm. He could not recollect whether or not deceased closed them before he left, but he certainly did not close the shutters. Witness saw nobody near the house when he left.

Mr. Douglas Kingscote, architect, said deceased was his brother. He had not seen him for some months, living as he did in another part of the country. He believed his brother was fairly well off, and he knew that he had made a good amount by speculation in the last year or two. Knew of no person who would be likely to owe his brother a grudge, and could suggest no motive for the crime except ordinary robbery. His brother was to have been married in a few weeks. Questioned further on this point, witness said that the marriage was to have taken place a year ago, and it was with that view that Ivy Cottage, deceased's residence, was taken. The lady, however, sustained a domestic bereavement, and afterwards went abroad with her family: she was, witness believed, shortly expected back to England.

William Bales, jobbing gardener, who was brought up in custody, was cautioned, but elected to give evidence. Witness, who appeared to be much agitated, admitted having been in the garden of Ivy Cottage at four in the morning, but said that he had only gone to attend to certain plants, and knew absolutely nothing of the murder. He however admitted that he had no order for work beyond what he had done the day before. Being further pressed, witness made various contradictory statements, and finally said that he had gone to take certain plants away.

The inquest was then adjourned.

This was the case as it stood—apparently not a case presenting any very striking feature, although there seemed to me to be doubtful peculiarities in many parts of it. I asked Hewitt what he thought.

"Quite impossible to think anything, my boy, just yet; wait till we see the place. There are any number of possibilities. Kingscote's friend, Campbell, may have come in again, you know, by way of the window—or he may not. Campbell may have owed him money or something—or he may not. The anticipated wedding may have something to do with it—or, again, *that* may not. There is no limit to the possibilities, as far as we can see from this report—a mere dry husk of the affair. When we get closer we shall examine the possibilities by the light of more detailed information. One *probability* is that the wretched gardener is innocent. It seems to me that his was only a comparatively blameless manoeuvre not unheard of at other times in his trade. He came at four in the morning to steal away the flowers he had planted the day before, and felt rather bashful when questioned on the point. Why should he trample on the beds, else? I wonder if the police thought to examine the beds for traces of rooting up, or questioned the housekeeper as to any plants being missing? But we shall see."

We chatted at random as the train drew near Finchley, and I mentioned *inter alia* the wanton piece of destruction perpetrated at Kingscote's late lodgings. Hewitt was interested.

"That was curious," he said, "very curious. Was anything else damaged? Furniture and so forth?"

"I don't know. Mrs. Clayton said nothing of it, and I didn't ask her. But it was quite bad enough as it was. The decoration was really good, and I can't conceive a meaner piece of tomfoolery than such an attack on a decent woman's property."

Then Hewitt talked of other cases of similar stupid damage by creatures inspired by a defective sense of humour, or mere love of mischief. He had several curious and sometimes funny anecdotes of such affairs at museums and picture exhibitions, where the damage had been so great as to induce the authorities to call him in to discover the offender. The work was not always easy, chiefly from the mere absence of intelligible motive; nor, indeed, always successful. One of the anecdotes related to a case of malicious damage to a picture—the outcome of blind artistic jealousy—a case which had been hushed up by a large expenditure in compensation. It would considerably startle most people, could it be printed here, with the actual names of the parties concerned.

Ivy Cottage, Finchley, was a compact little house, standing in a compact little square of garden, little more than a third of an acre, or perhaps no more at all. The front door was but a dozen yards or so back from the road, but the intervening space was well treed and shrubbed. Mr. Douglas Kingscote had not yet returned from town, but the housekeeper, an intelligent, matronly woman, who knew of his intention to call in Martin Hewitt, was ready to show us the house.

"*First*," Hewitt said, when we stood in the smoking-room, "I observe that somebody has shut the drawers and the bureau. That is unfortunate. Also, the floor has been washed and the carpet taken up, which is much worse. That, I suppose, was because the police had finished their examination, but it doesn't help me to make one at all. Has *anything*—anything *at all*—been left as it was on Tuesday morning?"

"Well, sir, you see everything was in such a muddle," the housekeeper began, "and when the police had done—"

"Just so. I know. You 'set it to rights,' eh? Oh, that setting to rights! It has lost me a fortune at one time and another. As to the other rooms, now, have they been set to rights?"

"Such as was disturbed have been put right, sir, of course."

"Which were disturbed? Let me see them. But wait a moment."

He opened the French windows, and closely examined the catch and bolts. He knelt and inspected the holes whereinto the bolts fell, and then glanced casually at the folding shutters. He opened a drawer or two, and tried the working of the locks with the keys the housekeeper carried. They were, the housekeeper explained, Mr. Kingscote's own keys. All through the lower floors Hewitt examined some things attentively and closely, and others with scarcely a glance, on a system unaccountable to me. Presently, he asked to be shown Mr. Kingscote's bedroom, which had not been disturbed, "set to rights," or slept in since the crime. Here, the housekeeper said, all drawers were kept unlocked but two—one in the wardrobe and one in the dressing-table, which Mr. Kingscote had always been careful to keep locked. Hewitt immediately pulled both drawers open without difficulty. Within, in addition to a few odds and ends, were papers. All the contents of these drawers had been turned over confusedly, while those of the unlocked drawers were in perfect order.

"The police," Hewitt remarked, "may not have observed these matters. Any more than such an ordinary thing as *this*," he added, picking up a bent nail lying at the edge of a rug.

The housekeeper doubtless took the remark as a reference to the entire unimportance of a bent nail, but I noticed that Hewitt dropped the article quietly into his pocket.

We came away. At the front gate we met Mr. Douglas Kingscote, who had just returned from town. He introduced himself, and expressed surprise at our promptitude both of coming and going.

"You can't have got anything like a clue in this short time, Mr. Hewitt?" he asked.

"Well, no," Hewitt replied, with a certain dryness, "perhaps not. But I doubt whether a month's visit would have helped me to get anything very striking out of a washed floor and a houseful of carefully cleaned-up and 'set-to-rights' rooms. Candidly, I don't think you can reasonably expect much of me. The police have a much better chance—they had the scene of the crime to examine. I have seen just such a few rooms as any one might see in the first well-furnished house he might enter. The trail of the housemaid has overlaid all the others."

"I'm very sorry for that; the fact was, I expected rather more of the police; and, indeed, I wasn't here in time entirely to prevent the clearing up. But still, I thought your well-known powers—"

"My dear sir, my 'well-known powers' are nothing but common sense assiduously applied and made quick by habit. That won't enable me to see the invisible."

"But can't we have the rooms put back into something of the state they were in? The cook will remember—"

"No, no. That would be worse and worse; that would only be the housemaid's trail in turn overlaid by the cook's. You must leave things with me for a little, I think."

"Then you don't give the case up?" Mr. Kingscote asked anxiously.

"Oh, no! I don't give it up just yet. Do you know anything of your brother's private papers—as they were before his death?"

"I never knew anything till after that. I have gone over them, but they are all very ordinary letters. Do you suspect a theft of papers?"

Martin Hewitt, with his hands on his stick behind him, looked sharply at the other, and shook his head. "No," he said, "I can't quite say that."

We bade Mr. Douglas Kingscote good-day, and walked towards the station. "Great nuisance, that setting to rights," Hewitt observed, on the way. "If the place had been left alone, the job might have been settled one way or another by this time. As it is, we shall have to run over to your old lodgings."

"My old lodgings?" I repeated, amazed. "Why my old lodgings?"

Hewitt turned to me with a chuckle and a wide smile. "Because we can't see the broken panelwork anywhere else," he said. "Let's see—Chelsea, isn't it?"

"Yes, Chelsea. But why—you don't suppose the people who defaced the panels also murdered the man who painted them?"

"Well," Hewitt replied, with another smile, "that would be carrying a practical joke rather far, wouldn't it? Even for the ordinary picture damager."

"You mean you *don't* think they did it, then? But what *do* you mean?"

"My dear fellow, I don't mean anything but what I say. Come now, this is rather an interesting case despite appearances, and it *has* interested me: so much, in fact, that I really think I forgot to offer Mr. Douglas Kingscote my condolence on his bereavement. You see a problem is a problem, whether of theft, assassination, intrigue, or anything else, and I only think of it as one. The work very often makes me forget merely human sympathies. Now, you have often been good enough to express a very flattering interest in my work, and you shall have an opportunity of exercising your own common sense in the way I am always having to exercise mine. You shall see all my evidence (if I'm lucky enough to get any) as I collect it, and you shall make your own inferences. That will be a little exercise for you; the sort of exercise I should give a pupil if I had one. But I will give you what information I have, and you shall start fairly from this moment. You know the inquest evidence, such as it was, and you saw everything I did in Ivy Cottage?"

"Yes; I think so. But I'm not much the wiser."

"Very well. Now I will tell you. What does the whole case look like? How would you class the crime?"

"I suppose as the police do. An ordinary case of murder with the object of robbery."

"It is *not* an ordinary case. If it were, I shouldn't know as much as I do, little as that is; the ordinary cases are always difficult. The assailant did not come to commit a burglary, although he was a skilled burglar, or one of them was, if more than one were concerned. The affair has, I think, nothing to do with the expected wedding, nor had Mr. Campbell anything to do in it—at any rate, personally—nor the gardener. The criminal (or one of them) was known personally to the dead man, and was well-dressed: he (or again one of them, and I think there were two) even had a chat with Mr. Kingscote before the murder took place. He came to ask for something which Mr. Kingscote was unwilling to part with,—perhaps hadn't got. It was not a bulky thing. Now you have all my materials before you."

"But all this doesn't look like the result of the blind spite that would ruin a man's work first and attack him bodily afterwards."

"Spite isn't always blind, and there are other blind things besides spite; people with good eyes in their heads are blind sometimes, even detectives."

"But where did you get all this information? What makes you suppose that this was a burglar who didn't want to burgle, and a well-dressed man, and so on?"

Hewitt chuckled and smiled again.

"I saw it—saw it, my boy, that's all," he said. "But here comes the train."

On the way back to town, after I had rather minutely described Kingscote's work on the boarding-house panels, Hewitt asked me for the names and professions of such fellow lodgers in that house as I might remember. "When did you leave yourself?" he ended.

"Three years ago, or rather more. I can remember Kingscote himself; Turner, a medical student—James Turner, I think; Harvey Challitt, diamond merchant's articled pupil—he was a bad egg entirely, he's doing five years for forgery now; by the bye he had the room we are going to see till he was marched off, and Kingscote took it—a year before I left; there was Norton—don't know what he was; 'something in the City,' I think; and Carter Paget, in the Admiralty Office. I don't remember any more at this moment; there were pretty frequent changes. But you can get it all from Mrs. Lamb, of course."

"Of course; and Mrs. Lamb's exact address is—what?"

I gave him the address, and the conversation became disjointed. At Farringdon station, where we alighted, Hewitt called two hansoms. Preparing to enter one, he motioned me to the other, saying, "You get straight away to Mrs. Lamb's at once. She may be going to burn that splintered wood, or to set things to rights, after the manner of her kind, and you can stop her. I must make one or two small inquiries, but I shall be there half an hour after you."

"Shall I tell her our object?"

"Only that I may be able to catch her mischievous lodgers—nothing else yet." He jumped into the hansom and was gone.

I found Mrs. Lamb still in a state of indignant perturbation over the trick served her four days before. Fortunately, she had left everything in the panelled room exactly as she had found it, with an idea of the being better able to demand or enforce reparation should her lodgers return. "The room's theirs, you see, sir," she said, "till the end of the week, since they paid in advance, and they may come back and offer to make amends, although I doubt it. As pleasant-spoken a young chap as you might wish, he seemed, him as come to take the rooms. 'My cousin,' says he, 'is rather an invalid, havin' only just got over congestion of the lungs, and he won't be in London till this evening late. He's comin' up from Birmingham,' he ses, 'and I hope he won't catch a fresh cold on the way, although of course we've got him muffled up plenty.' He took the rooms, sir, like a gentleman, and mentioned several gentlemen's names I knew well, as had lodged here before; and then he put down on that there very table, sir"—Mrs. Lamb indicated the exact spot with her hand, as though that made the whole thing much more wonderful—"he put down on that very table a week's rent in advance, and ses, 'That's always the best sort of reference, Mrs. Lamb, I think,' as kind-mannered as anything—and never 'aggled about the amount nor nothing. He only had a little black bag, but he said his cousin had all the luggage coming in the train, and as there was so much p'r'aps they wouldn't get it here till next day. Then he went out and came in with his cousin at eleven that night—Sarah let 'em in her own self—and in the morning they was gone—and this!" Poor Mrs. Lamb, plaintively indignant, stretched her arm towards the wrecked panels.

"If the gentleman as you say is comin' on, sir," she pursued, "can do anything to find 'em, I'll prosecute 'em, that I will, if it costs me ten pound. I spoke to the constable on the beat, but he only looked like a fool, and said if I knew where they were I might charge 'em with wilful damage, or county court 'em. Of course I know I can do that if I knew where they were, but how can I find 'em? Mr. Jones he said his name was; but how many Joneses is there in London, sir?"

I couldn't imagine any answer to a question like this, but I condoled with Mrs. Lamb as well as I could. She afterwards went on to express herself much as her sister had done with regard to Kingscote's death, only as the destruction of her panels loomed larger in her mind, she dwelt primarily on that. "It might almost seem," she said, "that somebody had a deadly spite on the pore young gentleman, and went breakin' up his paintin' one night, and murderin' him the next!"

I examined the broken panels with some care, having half a notion to attempt to deduce something from them myself, if possible. But I could deduce nothing. The beading had been taken out, and the panels, which were thick in the centre but bevelled at the edges, had been removed and split up literally into thin firewood, which lay in a tumbled heap on the hearth and about the floor. Every panel in the room had been treated in the same way, and the result was a pretty large heap of sticks, with nothing whatever about them to distinguish them from other sticks, except the paint on one face, which I observed in many cases had been scratched and scraped away. The rug was drawn half across the hearth, and had evidently been used to deaden the sound of chopping. But mischief—wanton and stupid mischief—was all I could deduce from it all.

Mr. Jones's cousin, it seemed, only Sarah had seen, as she admitted him in the evening, and then he was so heavily muffled that she could not distinguish his features, and would never be able to identify him. But as for the other one, Mrs. Lamb was ready to swear to him anywhere.

Hewitt was long in coming, and internal symptoms of the approach of dinner-time (we had had no lunch) had made themselves felt before a sharp ring at the door-bell foretold his arrival. "I have had to wait for answers to a telegram," he said in explanation, "but at any rate I have the information I wanted. And these are the mysterious panels, are they?"

Mrs. Lamb's true opinion of Martin Hewitt's behaviour as it proceeded would have been amusing to know. She watched in amazement the antics of a man who purposed finding out who had been splitting sticks by dint of picking up each separate stick and staring at it. In the end he collected a small handful of sticks by themselves and handed them to me, saying, "Just put these together on the table, Brett, and see what you make of them."

I turned the pieces painted side up, and fitted them together into a complete panel, joining up the painted design accurately. "It is an entire panel," I said.

"Good. Now look at the sticks a little more closely, and tell me if you notice anything peculiar about them—any particular in which they differ from all the others."

I looked. "Two adjoining sticks," I said, "have each a small semi-circular cavity stuffed with what seems to be putty. Put together it would mean a small circular hole, perhaps a knot-hole, half an inch or so in diameter, in the panel, filled in with putty, or whatever it is."

"A *knot-hole*?" Hewitt asked, with particular emphasis.

"Well, no, not a knot-hole, of course, because that would go right through, and this doesn't. It is probably less than half an inch deep from the front surface."

"Anything else? Look at the whole appearance of the wood itself. Colour, for instance."

"It is certainly darker than the rest."

"So it is." He took the two pieces carrying the puttied hole, threw the rest on the heap, and addressed the landlady. "The Mr. Harvey Challitt who occupied this room before Mr. Kingscote, and who got into trouble for forgery, was the Mr. Harvey Challitt who was himself robbed of diamonds a few months before on a staircase, wasn't he?"

"Yes, sir," Mrs. Lamb replied in some bewilderment. "He certainly was that, on his own office stairs, chloroformed."

"Just so, and when they marched him away because of the forgery, Mr. Kingscote changed into his rooms?"

"Yes, and very glad I was. It was bad enough to have the disgrace brought into the house, without the trouble of trying to get people to take his very rooms, and I thought—"

"Yes, yes, very awkward, very awkward!" Hewitt interrupted rather impatiently. "The man who took the rooms on Monday, now—you'd never seen him before, had you?"

"No, sir."

"Then is *that* anything like him?" Hewitt held a cabinet photograph before her.

"Why—why—law, yes, that's *him*!"

Hewitt dropped the photograph back into his breast pocket with a contented "Um," and picked up his hat. "I think we may soon be able to find that young gentleman for you, Mrs. Lamb. He is not a very respectable young gentleman, and perhaps you are well rid of him, even as it is. Come, Brett," he added, "the day hasn't been wasted, after all."

We made towards the nearest telegraph office. On the way I said, "That puttied-up hole in the piece of wood seems to have influenced you: Is it an important link?"

"Well—yes," Hewitt answered, "it is. But all those other pieces are important, too."

"But why?"

"Because there are no holes in them." He looked quizzically at my wondering face, and laughed aloud. "Come," he said, "I won't puzzle you much longer. Here is the post-office. I'll send my wire, and then we'll go and dine at Luzatti's."

He sent his telegram, and we cabbed it to Luzatti's. Among actors, journalists, and others who know town and like a good dinner, Luzatti's is well known. We went upstairs for the sake of quietness, and took a table standing alone in a recess just inside the door. We ordered our dinner, and then Hewitt began:

"Now tell me what *your* conclusion is in this matter of the Ivy Cottage murder."

"Mine? I haven't one. I'm sorry I'm so very dull, but I really haven't."

"Come, I'll give you a point. Here is the newspaper account (torn sacrilegiously from my scrapbook for your benefit) of the robbery perpetrated on Harvey Challitt a few months before his forgery. Read it."

"Oh, but I remember the circumstances very well. He was carrying two packets of diamonds belonging to his firm downstairs to the office of another firm of diamond merchants on the ground floor. It was a quiet time in the day, and half-way down he was seized on a dark landing, made insensible by chloroform, and robbed of the diamonds—five or six thousand pounds' worth altogether, of stones of various smallish individual values up to thirty pounds or so. He lay unconscious on the landing till one of the partners, noticing that he had been rather long gone, followed and found him. That's all, I think."

"Yes, that's all. Well, what do you make of it?"

"I'm afraid I don't quite see the connection with this case."

"Well, then, I'll give you another point. The telegram I've just sent releases information to the police, in consequence of which they will probably apprehend Harvey Challitt and his confederate, Henry Gillard, *alias* Jones, for the murder of Gavin Kingscote. Now, then."

"Challitt! But he's in gaol already."

"Tut, tut, consider. Five years' penal was his dose, although for the first offence, because the forgery was of an extremely dangerous sort. You left Chelsea over three years ago yourself, and you told me that his difficulty occurred a year before. That makes four years, at least. Good conduct in prison brings a man out of a five years' sentence in that time or a little less, and, as a matter of fact, Challitt was released rather more than a week ago."

"Still, I'm afraid I don't see what you are driving at."

"Whose story is this about the diamond robbery from Harvey Challitt?"

"His own."

"Exactly. His own. Does his subsequent record make him look like a person whose stories are to be accepted without doubt or question?"

"Why, no. I think I see—no, I don't. You mean he stole them himself? I've a sort of dim perception of your drift now, but still I can't fix it. The whole thing's too complicated."

"It is a little complicated for a first effort, I admit, so I will tell you. This is the story. Harvey Challitt is an artful young man, and decides on a theft of his firm's diamonds. He first prepares a hiding-place somewhere near the stairs of his office, and when the opportunity arrives he puts the stones away, spills his chloroform, and makes a smell—possibly sniffs some, and actually goes off on the stairs, and the whole thing's done. He is carried into the office—the diamonds are gone. He tells of the attack on the stairs, as we have heard, and he is believed. At a suitable opportunity he takes his plunder from the hiding-place, and goes home to his lodgings. What is he to do with those diamonds? He can't sell them yet, because the robbery is publicly notorious, and all the regular jewel buyers know him.

"Being a criminal novice, he doesn't know any regular receiver of stolen goods, and if he did would prefer to wait and get full value by an ordinary sale. There will always be a danger of detection so long as the stones are not securely hidden, so he proceeds to hide them. He knows that if any suspicion were aroused his rooms would be searched in every likely place, so he looks for an unlikely place. Of course, he thinks of taking out a panel and hiding them behind that. But the idea is so obvious that it won't do; the police would certainly take those panels out to look behind them. Therefore he determines to hide them in the panels. See here"—he took the two pieces of wood with the filled hole from his tail pocket and opened his penknife—"the putty near the surface is softer than that near the bottom of the hole; two different lots of putty, differently mixed, perhaps, have been used, therefore, presumably, at different times.

"But to return to Challitt. He makes holes with a centre-bit in different places on the panels, and in each hole he places a diamond, embedding it carefully in putty. He smooths the surface carefully flush with the wood, and then very carefully paints the place over, shading off the paint at the edges so as to leave no signs of a patch. He doesn't do the whole job at once, creating a noise and a smell of paint, but keeps on steadily, a few holes at a time, till in a little while the whole wainscoting is set with hidden diamonds, and every panel is apparently sound and whole."

"But, then—there was only one such hole in the whole lot."

"Just so, and that very circumstance tells us the whole truth. Let me tell the story first—I'll explain the clue after. The diamonds lie hidden for a few months—he grows impatient. He wants the money, and he can't see a way of getting it. At last he determines to make a bolt and go abroad to sell his plunder. He knows he will want money for expenses, and that he may not be able to get rid of his diamonds at once. He also expects that his suddenly going abroad while the robbery is still in people's minds will bring suspicion on him in any case, so, in for a penny in for a pound, he commits a bold forgery, which, had it been successful, would have put him in funds and enabled him to leave the country with the stones. But the forgery is detected, and he is haled to prison, leaving the diamonds in their wainscot setting.

"Now we come to Gavin Kingscote. He must have been a shrewd fellow—the sort of man that good detectives are made of. Also he must have been pretty unscrupulous. He had his suspicions about the genuineness of the diamond robbery, and kept his eyes open. What indications he had to guide him we don't know, but living in the same house a sharp fellow on the look-out would probably see enough. At any rate, they led him to the belief that the diamonds were in the thief's rooms, but not among his movables, or they would have been found after the arrest. Here was his chance. Challitt was out of the way for years, and there was plenty of time to take the house to pieces if it were necessary. So he changed into Challitt's rooms.

"How long it took him to find the stones we shall never know. He probably tried many other places first, and, I expect, found the diamonds at last by pricking over the panels with a needle. Then came the problem of getting them out without attracting attention. He decided not to trust to the needle, which might possibly leave a stone or two undiscovered, but to split up each panel carefully into splinters so as to leave no part unexamined. Therefore he took measurements, and had a number of panels made by a joiner of the exact size and pattern of those in the room, and announced to his landlady his intention of painting her panels with a pretty design. This to account for the wet paint, and even for the fact of a panel being out of the wall, should she chance to bounce into the room at an awkward moment. All very clever, eh?"

"Very."

"Ah, he was a smart man, no doubt. Well, he went to work, taking out a panel, substituting a new one, painting it over, and chopping up the old one on the quiet, getting rid of the splinters out of doors when the booty had been extracted. The decoration progressed and the little heap of diamonds grew. Finally, he came to the last panel, but found that he had used all his new panels and hadn't one left for a substitute. It must have been at some time when it was difficult to get hold of the joiner—Bank Holiday, perhaps, or Sunday, and he was impatient. So he scraped the paint off, and went carefully over every part of the surface—experience had taught him by this that all the holes were of the same sort—and found one diamond. He took it out, refilled the hole with putty, painted the old panel and put it back. *These* are pieces of that old panel—the only old one of the lot.

"Nine men out of ten would have got out of the house as soon as possible after the thing was done, but he was a cool hand and stayed. That made the whole thing look a deal more genuine than if he had unaccountably cleared out as soon as he had got his room nicely decorated. I expect the original capital for those Stock Exchange operations we heard of came out of those diamonds. He stayed as long as suited him, and left when he set up housekeeping with a view to his wedding. The rest of the story is pretty plain. You guess it, of course?"

"Yes," I said, "I think I can guess the rest, in a general sort of way—except as to one or two points." "It's all plain—perfectly. See here! Challitt, in gaol, determines to get those diamonds when he comes out. To do that without being suspected it will be necessary to hire the room. But he knows that he won't be able to do that himself, because the landlady, of course, knows him, and won't have an ex-convict in the house. There is no help for it; he must have a confederate, and share the spoil. So he makes the acquaintance of another convict, who seems a likely man for the job, and whose sentence expires about the same time as his own. When they come out, he arranges the matter with this confederate, who is a well-mannered (and pretty well-known) housebreaker, and the latter calls at Mrs. Lamb's house to look for rooms. The very room itself happens to be to let, and of course it is taken, and Challitt (who is the invalid cousin) comes in at night muffled and unrecognisable.

"The decoration on the panel does not alarm them, because, of course, they suppose it to have been done on the old panels and over the old paint. Challitt tries the spots where diamonds were left—there are none—there is no putty even. Perhaps, think they, the panels have been shifted and interchanged in the painting, so they set to work and split them all up as we have seen, getting more desperate as they go on. Finally they realize that they are done, and clear out, leaving Mrs. Lamb to mourn over their mischief.

"They know that Kingscote is the man who has forestalled them, because Gillard (or Jones), in his chat with the landlady, has heard all about him and his painting of the panels. So the next night they set off for Finchley. They get into Kingscote's garden and watch him let Campbell out. While he is gone, Challitt quietly steps through the French window into the smoking-room, and waits for him, Gillard remaining outside.

"Kingscote returns, and Challitt accuses him of taking the stones. Kingscote is contemptuous—doesn't care for Challitt, because he knows he is powerless, being the original thief himself; besides, knows there is no evidence, since the diamonds are sold and dispersed long ago. Challitt offers to divide the plunder with him—Kingscote laughs and tells him to go; probably threatens to throw him out, Challitt being the smaller man. Gillard, at the open window, hears this, steps in behind, and quietly knocks him on the head. The rest follows as a matter of course. They fasten the window and shutters, to exclude observation; turn over all the drawers, etc., in case the jewels are there; go to the best bedroom and try there, and so on. Failing (and possibly being disturbed after a few hours' search by the noise of the acquisitive gardener), Gillard, with the instinct of an old thief, determines they shan't go away with nothing, so empties Kingscote's pockets and takes his watch and chain and so on. They go out by the front door and shut it after them. *Voilà tout.*"

I was filled with wonder at the prompt ingenuity of the man who in these few hours of hurried inquiry could piece together so accurately all the materials of an intricate and mysterious affair such as this; but more, I wondered where and how he had collected those materials.

"There is no doubt, Hewitt," I said, "that the accurate and minute application of what you are pleased to call your common sense has become something very like an instinct with you. What did you deduce from? You told me your conclusions from the examination of Ivy Cottage, but not how you arrived at them."

"They didn't leave me much material downstairs, did they? But in the bedroom, the two drawers which the thieves found locked were ransacked—opened probably with keys taken from the dead man. On the floor I saw a bent French nail; here it is. You see, it is twice bent at right angles, near the head and near the point, and there is the faint mark of the pliers that were used to bend it. It is a very usual burglars' tool, and handy in experienced hands to open ordinary drawer locks. Therefore, I knew that a professional burglar had been at work. He had probably fiddled at the drawers with the nail first, and then had thrown it down to try the dead man's keys.

"But I knew this professional burglar didn't come for a burglary, from several indications. There was no attempt to take plate, the first thing a burglar looks for. Valuable clocks were left on mantelpieces, and other things that usually go in an ordinary burglary were not disturbed. Notably, it was to be observed that no doors or windows were broken, or had been forcibly opened; therefore, it was plain that the thieves had come in by the French window of the smoking-room, the only entrance left open at the last thing. *Therefore*, they came in, or one did, knowing that Mr. Kingscote was up, and being quite willing—presumably anxious—to see him. Ordinary burglars would have waited till he had retired, and then could have got through the closed French window as easily almost as if it were open, notwithstanding the thin wooden shutters, which would never stop a burglar for more than five minutes. Being anxious to see him, they—or again, *one* of them—presumably knew him. That they had come to *get* something was plain, from the ransacking. As, in the end, they *did* steal his money and watch, but did *not* take larger valuables, it was plain that they had no bag with them—which proves not only that they had not come to burgle, for every burglar takes his bag, but that the thing they came to get was not bulky. Still, they could easily have removed plate or clocks by rolling them up in a table-cover or other wrapper, but such a bundle, carried by well-dressed men, would attract attention—therefore it was probable that they were well dressed. Do I make it clear?"

"Quite—nothing seems simpler now it is explained—that's the way with difficult puzzles."

"There was nothing more to be got at the house. I had already in my mind the curious coincidence that the panels at Chelsea had been broken the very night before that of the murder, and determined to look at them in any case. I got from you the name of the man who had lived in the panelled room before Kingscote, and at once remembered it (although I said nothing about it) as that of the young man who had been chloroformed for his employer's diamonds. I keep things of that sort in my mind, you see—and, indeed, in my scrap-book. You told me yourself about his imprisonment, and there I was with what seemed now a hopeful case getting into a promising shape.

"You went on to prevent any setting to rights at Chelsea, and I made enquiries as to Challitt. I found he had been released only a few days before all this trouble arose, and I also found the name of another man who was released from the same establishment only a few days earlier. I knew this man (Gillard) well, and knew that nobody was a more likely rascal for such a crime as that at Finchley. On my way to Chelsea I called at my office, gave my clerk certain instructions, and looked up my scrap-book. I found the newspaper account of the chloroform business, and also a photograph of Gillard—I keep as many of these things as I can collect. What I did at Chelsea you know. I saw that one panel was of old wood and the rest new. I saw the hole in the old panel, and I asked one or two questions. The case was complete."

We proceeded with our dinner. Presently I said: "It all rests with the police now, of course?"

"Of course. I should think it very probable that Challitt and Gillard will be caught. Gillard, at any rate, is pretty well known. It will be rather hard on the surviving Kingscote, after engaging me, to have his dead brother's diamond transactions publicly exposed as a result, won't it? But it can't be helped. *Fiat justitia*, of course."

"How will the police feel over this?" I asked. "You've rather cut them out, eh?"

"Oh, the police are all right. They had not the information I had, you see; they knew nothing of the panel business. If Mrs. Lamb had gone to Scotland Yard instead of to the policeman on the beat, perhaps I should never have been sent for."

The same quality that caused Martin Hewitt to rank as mere "common-sense" his extraordinary power of almost instinctive deduction, kept his respect for the abilities of the police at perhaps a higher level than some might have considered justified.

We sat some little while over our dessert, talking as we sat, when there occurred one of those curious conjunctions of circumstances that we notice again and again in ordinary life, and forget as often, unless the importance of the occasion fixes the matter in the memory. A young man had entered the dining-room, and had taken his seat at a corner table near the back window. He had been sitting there for some little time before I particularly observed him. At last he happened to turn his thin, pale face in my direction, and our eyes met. It was Challitt—the man we had been talking of!

I sprang to my feet in some excitement.

"That's the man!" I cried. "Challitt!"

Hewitt rose at my words, and at first attempted to pull me back. Challitt, in guilty terror, saw that we were between him and the door, and turning, leaped upon the sill of the open window, and dropped out. There was a fearful crash of broken glass below, and everybody rushed to the window.

Hewitt drew me through the door, and we ran downstairs. "Pity you let out like that," he said, as he went. "If you'd kept quiet we could have sent out for the police with no trouble. Never mind—can't help it."

Below, Challitt was lying in a broken heap in the midst of a crowd of waiters. He had crashed through a thick glass skylight and fallen, back downward, across the back of a lounge. He was taken away on a stretcher unconscious, and, in fact, died in a week in hospital from injuries to the spine.

During his periods of consciousness he made a detailed statement, bearing out the conclusions of Martin Hewitt with the most surprising exactness, down to the smallest particulars. He and Gillard had parted immediately after the crime, judging it safer not to be seen together. He had, be affirmed, endured agonies of fear and remorse in the few days since the fatal night at Finchley, and had even once or twice thought of giving himself up. When I so excitedly pointed him out, he knew at once that the game was up, and took the one desperate chance of escape that offered. But to the end he persistently denied that he had himself committed the murder, or had even thought of it till he saw it accomplished. That had been wholly the work of Gillard, who, listening at the window and perceiving the drift of the conversation, suddenly beat down Kingscote from behind with a life-preserver. And so Harvey Challitt ended his life at the age of twenty-six.

Gillard was never taken. He doubtless left the country, and has probably since that time become "known to the police" under another name abroad. Perhaps he has even been hanged, and if he has been, there was no miscarriage of justice, no matter what the charge against him may have been.

THE TRAGEDY AT
BROOKBEND COTTAGE

Ernest Bramah

Max," said Mr. Carlyle, when Parkinson had closed the door behind him, "this is Lieutenant Hollyer, whom you consented to see."

"To hear," corrected Carrados, smiling straight into the healthy and rather embarrassed face of the stranger before him. "Mr. Hollyer knows of my disability?"

"Mr. Carlyle told me," said the young man, "but, as a matter of fact, I had heard of you before, Mr. Carrados, from one of our men. It was in connexion with the foundering of the *Ivan Saratov*."

Carrados wagged his head in good-humoured resignation.

"And the owners were sworn to inviolable secrecy!" he exclaimed. "Well, it is inevitable, I suppose. Not another scuttling case, Mr. Hollyer?"

"No, mine is quite a private matter," replied the lieutenant. "My sister, Mrs. Creake—but Mr. Carlyle would tell you better than I can. He knows all about it."

"No, no; Carlyle is a professional. Let me have it in the rough, Mr. Hollyer. My ears are my eyes, you know."

"Very well, sir. I can tell you what there is to tell, right enough, but I feel that when all's said and done it must sound very little to another, although it seems important enough to me."

"We have occasionally found trifles of significance ourselves," said Carrados encouragingly. "Don't let that deter you."

This was the essence of Lieutenant Hollyer's narrative:

"I have a sister, Millicent, who is married to a man called Creake. She is about twenty-eight now and he is at least fifteen years older. Neither my mother (who has since died), nor I, cared very much about Creake. We had nothing particular against him, except, perhaps, the moderate disparity of age, but none of us appeared to have anything in common. He was a dark, taciturn man, and his moody silence froze up conversation. As a result, of course, we didn't see much of each other."

"This, you must understand, was four or five years ago, Max," interposed Mr. Carlyle officiously.

Carrados maintained an uncompromising silence. Mr. Carlyle blew his nose and contrived to impart a hurt significance into the operation. Then Lieutenant Hollyer continued:

"Millicent married Creake after a very short engagement. It was a frightfully subdued wedding—more like a funeral to me. The man professed to have no relations and apparently he had scarcely any friends or business acquaintances. He was an agent for something or other and had an office off Holborn. I suppose he made a living out of it then, although we knew practically nothing of his private affairs, but I gather that it has been going down since, and I suspect that for the past few years they have been getting along almost entirely on Millicent's little income. You would like the particulars of that?"

"Please," assented Carrados.

"When our father died about seven years ago, he left three thousand pounds. It was invested in Canadian stock and brought in a little over a hundred a year. By his will my mother was to have the income of that for life and on her death it was to pass to Millicent, subject to the payment of a lump sum of five hundred pounds to me. But my father privately suggested to me that if I should have no particular use for the money at the time, he would propose my letting Millicent have the income of it until I did want it, as she would not be particularly well off. You see, Mr. Carrados, a great deal more had been spent on my education and advancement than on her; I had my pay, and, of course, I could look out for myself better than a girl could."

"Quite so," agreed Carrados.

"Therefore I did nothing about that," continued the lieutenant. "Three years ago I was over again but I did not see much of them. They were living in lodgings. That was the only time since the marriage that I have seen them until last week. In the meanwhile our mother had died and Millicent had been receiving her income. She wrote me several letters at the time. Otherwise we did not correspond much, but about a year ago she sent me their new address—Brookbend Cottage, Mulling Common—a house that they had taken. When I got two months' leave I invited myself there as a matter of course, fully expecting to stay most of my time with them, but I made an excuse to get away after a week. The place was dismal and unendurable, the whole life and atmosphere indescribably depressing." He looked round with an instinct of caution, leaned forward earnestly, and dropped his voice. "Mr. Carrados, it is my absolute conviction that Creake is only waiting for a favourable opportunity to murder Millicent."

"Go on," said Carrados quietly. "A week of the depressing surroundings of Brookbend Cottage would not alone convince you of that, Mr. Hollyer."

"I am not so sure," declared Hollyer doubtfully. "There was a feeling of suspicion and—before me—polite hatred that would have gone a good way towards it.

All the same there *was* something more definite. Millicent told me this the day after I went there. There is no doubt that a few months ago Creake deliberately planned to poison her with some weed-killer. She told me the circumstances in a rather distressed moment, but afterwards she refused to speak of it again—even weakly denied it—and, as a matter of fact, it was with the greatest difficulty that I could get her at any time to talk about her husband or his affairs. The gist of it was that she had the strongest suspicion that Creake doctored a bottle of stout which he expected she would drink for her supper when she was alone. The weed-killer, properly labelled, but also in a beer bottle, was kept with other miscellaneous liquids in the same cupboard as the beer but on a high shelf. When he found that it had miscarried he poured away the mixture, washed out the bottle and put in the dregs from another. There is no doubt in my mind that if he had come back and found Millicent dead or dying he would have contrived it to appear that she had made a mistake in the dark and drunk some of the poison before she found out."

"Yes," assented Carrados. "The open way; the safe way."

"You must understand that they live in a very small style, Mr. Carrados, and Millicent is almost entirely in the man's power. The only servant they have is a woman who comes in for a few hours every day. The house is lonely and secluded. Creake is sometimes away for days and nights at a time, and Millicent, either through pride or indifference, seems to have dropped off all her old friends and to have made no others. He might poison her, bury the body in the garden, and be a thousand miles away before anyone began even to inquire about her. What am I to do, Mr. Carrados?"

"He is less likely to try poison than some other means now," pondered Carrados. "That having failed, his wife will always be on her guard. He may know, or at least suspect, that others know. No. . . . The common-sense precaution would be for your sister to leave the man, Mr. Hollyer. She will not?"

"No," admitted Hollyer, "she will not. I at once urged that." The young man struggled with some hesitation for a moment and then blurted out: "The fact is, Mr. Carrados, I don't understand Millicent. She is not the girl she was. She hates Creake and treats him with a silent contempt that eats into their lives like acid, and yet she is so jealous of him that she will let nothing short of death part them. It is a horrible life they lead. I stood it for a week and I must say, much as I dislike my brother-in-law, that he has something to put up with. If only he got into a passion like a man and killed her it wouldn't be altogether incomprehensible."

"That does not concern us," said Carrados. "In a game of this kind one has to take sides and we have taken ours. It remains for us to see that our side wins. You mentioned jealousy, Mr. Hollyer. Have you any idea whether Mrs. Creake has real ground for it?"

"I should have told you that," replied Lieutenant Hollyer, "I happened to strike up with a newspaper man whose office is in the same block as Creake's. When I mentioned the name he grinned. 'Creake,' he said, 'oh, he's the man with the romantic typist, isn't he?' 'Well, he's my brother-in-law,' I replied. 'What about the typist?' Then the chap shut up like a knife. 'No, no,' he said, 'I didn't know he was married. I don't want to get mixed up in anything of that sort. I only said that he had a typist. Well, what of that? So have we; so has everyone.' There was nothing more to be got out of him, but the remark and the grin meant—well, about as usual, Mr. Carrados."

Carrados turned to his friend.

"I suppose you know all about the typist by now, Louis?"

"We have had her under efficient observation, Max," replied Mr. Carlyle, with severe dignity.

"Is she unmarried?"

"Yes; so far as ordinary repute goes, she is."

"That is all that is essential for the moment. Mr. Hollyer opens up three excellent reasons why this man might wish to dispose of his wife. If we accept the suggestion of poisoning—though we have only a jealous woman's suspicion for it—we add to the wish the determination. Well, we will go forward on that. Have you got a photograph of Mr. Creake?"

The lieutenant took out his pocket-book.

"Mr. Carlyle asked me for one. Here is the best I could get."

Carrados rang the bell.

"This, Parkinson," he said, when the man appeared, "is a photograph of a Mr.— What first name, by the way?"

"Austin," put in Hollyer, who was following everything with a boyish mixture of excitement and subdued importance.

"—of a Mr. Austin Creake. I may require you to recognize him."

Parkinson glanced at the print and returned it to his master's hand.

"May I inquire if it is a recent photograph of the gentleman, sir?" he asked.

"About six years ago," said the lieutenant, taking in this new actor in the drama with frank curiosity. "But he is very little changed."

"Thank you, sir. I will endeavour to remember Mr. Creake, sir."

Lieutenant Hollyer stood up as Parkinson left the room. The interview seemed to be at an end.

"Oh, there's one other matter," he remarked. "I am afraid that I did rather an unfortunate thing while I was at Brookbend. It seemed to me that as all Millicent's money would probably pass into Creake's hands sooner or later I might as well have my five hundred pounds, if only to help her with afterwards. So I broached the subject and said that I should like to have it now as I had an opportunity for investing."

"And you think?"

"It may possibly influence Creake to act sooner than he otherwise might have done. He may have got possession of the principal even and find it very awkward to replace it."

"So much the better. If your sister is going to be murdered it may as well be done next week as next year so far as I am concerned. Excuse my brutality, Mr. Hollyer, but this is simply a case to me and I regard it strategically. Now Mr. Carlyle's organization can look after Mrs. Creake for a few weeks but it cannot look after her for ever. By increasing the immediate risk we diminish the permanent risk."

"I see," agreed Hollyer. "I'm awfully uneasy but I'm entirely in your hands."

"Then we will give Mr. Creake every inducement and every opportunity to get to work. Where are you staying now?"

"Just now with some friends at St. Albans."

"That is too far." The inscrutable eyes retained their tranquil depth but a new quality of quickening interest in the voice made Mr. Carlyle forget the weight and burden of his ruffled dignity. "Give me a few minutes, please. The cigarettes are behind you, Mr. Hollyer." The blind man walked to the window and seemed to look out over the cypress-shaded lawn. The lieutenant lit a cigarette and Mr. Carlyle picked up *Punch*. Then Carrados turned round again.

"You are prepared to put your own arrangements aside?" he demanded of his visitor.

"Certainly."

"Very well. I want you to go down now—straight from here—to Brookbend Cottage. Tell your sister that your leave is unexpectedly cut short and that you sail to-morrow."

"The *Martian*?"

"No, no; the *Martian* doesn't sail. Look up the movements on your way there and pick out a boat that does. Say you are transferred. Add that you expect to be away only two or three months and that you really want the five hundred pounds by the time of your return. Don't stay in the house long, please."

"I understand, sir."

"St. Albans is too far. Make your excuse and get away from there to-day. Put up somewhere in town, where you will be in reach of the telephone. Let Mr. Carlyle and myself know where you are. Keep out of Creake's way. I don't want actually to tie you down to the house, but we may require your services. We will let you know at the first sign of anything doing and if there is nothing to be done we must release you."

"I don't mind that. Is there nothing more that I can do now?"

"Nothing. In going to Mr. Carlyle you have done the best thing possible; you have put your sister into the care of the shrewdest man in London." Whereat the object of this quite unexpected eulogy found himself becoming covered with modest confusion.

"Well, Max?" remarked Mr. Carlyle tentatively when they were alone.

"Well, Louis?"

"Of course it wasn't worth while rubbing it in before young Hollyer, but, as a matter of fact, every single man carries the life of any other man—only one, mind you—in his hands, do what you will."

"Provided he doesn't bungle," acquiesced Carrados.

"Quite so."

"And also that he is absolutely reckless of the consequences."

"Of course."

"Two rather large provisos. Creake is obviously susceptible to both. Have you seen him?"

"No. As I told you, I put a man on to report his habits in town. Then, two days ago, as the case seemed to promise some interest—for he certainly is deeply involved with the typist, Max, and the thing might take a sensational turn any time—I went down to Mulling Common myself. Although the house is lonely it is on the electric tram route. You know the sort of market garden rurality that about a dozen miles out of London offers—alternate bricks and cabbages. It was easy enough to get to know about Creake locally. He mixes with no one there, goes into town at irregular times but generally every day, and is reputed to be devilish hard to get money out of. Finally I made the acquaintance of an old fellow who used to do a day's gardening at Brookbend occasionally. He has a cottage and a garden of his own with a greenhouse, and the business cost me the price of a pound of tomatoes."

"Was it—a profitable investment?"

"As tomatoes, yes; as information, no. The old fellow had the fatal disadvantage from our point of view of labouring under a grievance. A few weeks ago Creake told him that he would not require him again as he was going to do his own gardening in future."

"That is something, Louis."

"If only Creake was going to poison his wife with hyoscyamine and bury her, instead of blowing her up with a dynamite cartridge and claiming that it came in among the coal."

"True, true. Still——"

"However, the chatty old soul had a simple explanation for everything that Creake did. Creake was mad. He had even seen him flying a kite in his garden where it was bound to get wrecked among the trees. 'A lad of ten would have known better,' he declared. And certainly the kite did get wrecked, for I saw it hanging over the road myself. But that a sane man should spend his time 'playing with a toy' was beyond him."

"A good many men have been flying kites of various kinds lately," said Carrados. "Is he interested in aviation?"

"I dare say. He appears to have some knowledge of scientific subjects. Now what do you want me to do, Max?"

"Will you do it?"

"Implicitly—subject to the usual reservations."

"Keep your man on Creake in town and let me have his reports after you have seen them. Lunch with me here now. 'Phone up to your office that you are detained on unpleasant business and then give the deserving Parkinson an afternoon off by looking after me while we take a motor run round Mulling Common. If we have time we might go on to Brighton, feed at the 'Ship,' and come back in the cool."

"Amiable and thrice lucky mortal," sighed Mr. Carlyle, his glance wandering round the room.

But, as it happened, Brighton did not figure in that day's itinerary. It had been Carrados's intention merely to pass Brookbend Cottage on this occasion, relying on his highly developed faculties, aided by Mr. Carlyle's description, to inform him of the surroundings. A hundred yards before they reached the house he had given an order to his chauffeur to drop into the lowest speed and they were leisurely drawing past when a discovery by Mr. Carlyle modified their plans.

"By Jupiter!" that gentleman suddenly exclaimed, "there's a board up, Max. The place is to be let."

Carrados picked up the tube again. A couple of sentences passed and the car stopped by the roadside, a score of paces past the limit of the garden. Mr. Carlyle took out his notebook and wrote down the address of a firm of house agents.

"You might raise the bonnet and have a look at the engines, Harris," said Carrados. "We want to be occupied here for a few minutes."

"This is sudden; Hollyer knew nothing of their leaving," remarked Mr. Carlyle.

"Probably not for three months yet. All the same, Louis, we will go on to the agents and get a card to view, whether we use it to-day or not."

A thick hedge, in its summer dress effectively screening the house beyond from public view, lay between the garden and the road. Above the hedge showed an occasional shrub; at the corner nearest to the car a chestnut flourished. The wooden gate, once white, which they had passed, was grimed and rickety. The road itself was still the unpretentious country lane that the advent of the electric car had found it. When Carrados had taken in these details there seemed little else to notice. He was on the point of giving Harris the order to go on when his ear caught a trivial sound.

"Someone is coming out of the house, Louis," he warned his friend. "It may be Hollyer, but he ought to have gone by this time."

"I don't hear anyone," replied the other, but as he spoke a door banged noisily and Mr. Carlyle slipped into another seat and ensconced himself behind a copy of *The Globe*.

"Creake himself," he whispered across the car, as a man appeared at the gate. "Hollyer was right; he is hardly changed. Waiting for a car, I suppose."

But a car very soon swung past them from the direction in which Mr. Creake was looking and it did not interest him. For a minute or two longer he continued to look expectantly along the road. Then he walked slowly up the drive back to the house.

"We will give him five or ten minutes," decided Carrados. "Harris is behaving very naturally."

Before even the shorter period had run out they were repaid. A telegraph-boy cycled leisurely along the road, and, leaving his machine at the gate, went up to the cottage. Evidently there was no reply, for in less than a minute he was trundling past them back again. Round the bend an approaching tram clanged its bell noisily, and, quickened by the warning sound, Mr. Creake again appeared, this time with a small portmanteau in his hand. With a backward glance he hurried on towards the next stopping-place, and, boarding the car as it slackened down, he was carried out of their knowledge.

"Very convenient of Mr. Creake," remarked Carrados, with quiet satisfaction. "We will now get the order and go over the house in his absence. It might be useful to have a look at the wire as well."

"It might, Max," acquiesced Mr. Carlyle a little dryly. "But if it is, as it probably is, in Creake's pocket, how do you propose to get it?"

"By going to the post office, Louis."

"Quite so. Have you ever tried to see a copy of a telegram addressed to someone else?"

"I don't think I have ever had occasion yet," admitted Carrados. "Have you?"

"In one or two cases I have perhaps been an accessory to the act. It is generally a matter either of extreme delicacy or considerable expenditure."

"Then for Hollyer's sake we will hope for the former here." And Mr. Carlyle smiled darkly and hinted that he was content to wait for a friendly revenge.

A little later, having left the car at the beginning of the straggling High Street, the two men called at the village post office. They had already visited the house agent and obtained an order to view Brookbend Cottage, declining, with some difficulty, the clerk's persistent offer to accompany them. The reason was soon forthcoming. "As a matter of fact," explained the young man, "the present tenant is under *our* notice to leave."

"Unsatisfactory, eh?" said Carrados encouragingly.

"He's a corker," admitted the clerk, responding to the friendly tone. "Fifteen months and not a doit of rent have we had. That's why I should have liked—"

"We will make every allowance," replied Carrados.

The post office occupied one side of a stationer's shop. It was not without some inward trepidation that Mr. Carlyle found himself committed to the adventure. Carrados, on the other hand, was the personification of bland unconcern.

"You have just sent a telegram to Brookbend Cottage," he said to the young lady behind the brass-work lattice. "We think it may have come inaccurately and should like a repeat." He took out his purse. "What is the fee?"

The request was evidently not a common one. "Oh," said the girl uncertainly, "wait a minute, please." She turned to a pile of telegram duplicates behind the desk and ran a doubtful finger along the upper sheets. "I think this is all right. You want it repeated?"

"Please." Just a tinge of questioning surprise gave point to the courteous tone.

"It will be fourpence. If there is an error the amount will be refunded."

Carrados put down a coin and received his change.

"Will it take long?" he inquired carelessly, as he pulled on his glove.

"You will most likely get it within a quarter of an hour," she replied.

"Now you've done it," commented Mr. Carlyle, as they walked back to their car. "How do you propose to get that telegram, Max?"

"Ask for it," was the laconic explanation.

And, stripping the artifice of any elaboration, he simply asked for it and got it. The car, posted at a convenient bend in the road, gave him a warning note as the telegraph-boy approached. Then Carrados took up a convincing attitude with his hand on the gate while Mr. Carlyle lent himself to the semblance of a departing friend. That was the inevitable impression when the boy rode up.

"Creake, Brookbend Cottage?" inquired Carrados, holding out his hand, and without a second thought the boy gave him the envelope and rode away on the assurance that there would be no reply.

"Some day, my friend," remarked Mr. Carlyle, looking nervously towards the unseen house, "your ingenuity will get you into a tight corner."

"Then my ingenuity must get me out again," was the retort. "Let us have our 'view' now. The telegram can wait."

An untidy workwoman took their order and left them standing at the door. Presently a lady whom they both knew to be Mrs. Creake appeared.

"You wish to see over the house?" she said, in a voice that was utterly devoid of any interest. Then, without waiting for a reply, she turned to the nearest door and threw it open.

"This is the drawing-room," she said, standing aside. They walked into a sparsely furnished, damp-smelling room and made a pretence of looking round, while Mrs. Creake remained silent and aloof.

"The dining-room," she continued, crossing the narrow hall and opening another door.

Mr. Carlyle ventured a genial commonplace in the hope of inducing conversation. The result was not encouraging. Doubtless they would have gone through the house under the same frigid guidance had not Carrados been at fault in a way that Mr. Carlyle had never known him fail before. In crossing the hall he stumbled over a mat and almost fell.

"Pardon my clumsiness," he said to the lady. "I am, unfortunately, quite blind. But," he added, with a smile, to turn off the mishap, "even a blind man must have a house."

The man who had eyes was surprised to see a flood of colour rush into Mrs. Creake's face.

"Blind!" she exclaimed, "oh, I beg your pardon. Why did you not tell me? You might have fallen."

"I generally manage fairly well," he replied. "But, of course, in a strange house—"

She put her hand on his arm very lightly.

"You must let me guide you, just a little," she said.

The house, without being large, was full of passages and inconvenient turnings. Carrados asked an occasional question and found Mrs. Creake quite amiable without effusion. Mr. Carlyle followed them from room to room in the hope, though scarcely the expectation, of learning something that might be useful.

"This is the last one. It is the largest bedroom," said their guide. Only two of the upper rooms were fully furnished and Mr. Carlyle at once saw, as Carrados knew without seeing, that this was the one which the Creakes occupied.

"A very pleasant outlook," declared Mr. Carlyle.

"Oh, I suppose so," admitted the lady vaguely. The room, in fact, looked over the leafy garden and the road beyond. It had a French window opening on to a small balcony, and to this, under the strange influence that always attracted him to light, Carrados walked.

"I expect that there is a certain amount of repair needed?" he said, after standing there a moment.

"I am afraid there would be," she confessed.

"I ask because there is a sheet of metal on the floor here," he continued. "Now that, in an old house, spells dry rot to the wary observer."

"My husband said that the rain, which comes in a little under the window, was rotting the boards there," she replied. "He put that down recently. I had not noticed anything myself."

It was the first time she had mentioned her husband; Mr. Carlyle pricked up his ears.

"Ah, that is a less serious matter," said Carrados. "May I step out on to the balcony?"

"Oh yes, if you like to." Then, as he appeared to be fumbling at the catch, "Let me open it for you."

But the window was already open, and Carrados, facing the various points of the compass, took in the bearings.

"A sunny, sheltered corner," he remarked. "An ideal spot for a deck-chair and a book."

She shrugged her shoulders half contemptuously.

"I dare say," she replied, "but I never use it."

"Sometimes, surely," he persisted mildly. "It would be my favourite retreat. But then—"

"I was going to say that I had never even been out on it, but that would not be quite true. It has two uses for me, both equally romantic; I occasionally shake a duster from it, and when my husband returns late without his latchkey he wakes me up and I come out here and drop him mine."

Further revelation of Mr. Creake's nocturnal habits was cut off, greatly to Mr. Carlyle's annoyance, by a cough of unmistakable significance from the foot of the stairs. They had heard a trade cart drive up to the gate, a knock at the door, and the heavy-footed woman tramp along the hall.

"Excuse me a minute, please," said Mrs. Creake.

"Louis," said Carrados, in a sharp whisper, the moment they were alone, "stand against the door."

With extreme plausibility Mr. Carlyle began to admire a picture so situated that while he was there it was impossible to open the door more than a few inches.

From that position he observed his confederate go through the curious procedure of kneeling down on the bedroom floor and for a full minute pressing his ear to the sheet of metal that had already engaged his attention. Then he rose to his feet, nodded, dusted his trousers, and Mr. Carlyle moved to a less equivocal position.

"What a beautiful rose-tree grows up your balcony," remarked Carrados, stepping into the room as Mrs. Creake returned. "I suppose you are very fond of gardening?"

"I detest it," she replied.

"But this *Glorie*, so carefully trained——?"

"Is it?" she replied. "I think my husband was nailing it up recently." By some strange fatality Carrados's most aimless remarks seemed to involve the absent Mr. Creake. "Do you care to see the garden?"

The garden proved to be extensive and neglected. Behind the house was chiefly orchard. In front, some semblance of order had been kept up; here it was lawn and shrubbery, and the drive they had walked along. Two things interested Carrados: the soil at the foot of the balcony, which he declared on examination to be particularly suitable for roses, and the fine chestnut-tree in the corner by the road.

As they walked back to the car Mr. Carlyle lamented that they had learned so little of Creake's movements.

"Perhaps the telegram will tell us something," suggested Carrados. "Read it, Louis."

Mr. Carlyle cut open the envelope, glanced at the enclosure, and in spite of his disappointment could not restrain a chuckle.

"My poor Max," he explained, "you have put yourself to an amount of ingenious trouble for nothing. Creake is evidently taking a few days' holiday and prudently availed himself of the Meteorological Office forecast before going. Listen: *'Immediate prospect for London warm and settled. Further outlook cooler but fine.'* Well, well; I did get a pound of tomatoes for *my* fourpence."

"You certainly scored there, Louis," admitted Carrados, with humorous appreciation. "I wonder," he added speculatively, "whether it is Creake's peculiar taste usually to spend his week-end holiday in London."

"Eh?" exclaimed Mr. Carlyle, looking at the words again, "by gad, that's rum, Max. They go to Weston-super-Mare. Why on earth should he want to know about London?"

"I can make a guess, but before we are satisfied I must come here again. Take another look at that kite, Louis. Are there a few yards of string hanging loose from it?"

"Yes, there are."

"Rather thick string—unusually thick for the purpose?"

"Yes; but how do you know?"

As they drove home again Carrados explained, and Mr. Carlyle sat aghast, saying incredulously: "Good God, Max, is it possible?"

An hour later he was satisfied that it was possible. In reply to his inquiry someone in his office telephoned him the information that "they" had left Paddington by the four-thirty for Weston.

It was more than a week after his introduction to Carrados that Lieutenant Hollyer had a summons to present himself at The Turrets again. He found Mr. Carlyle already there and the two friends awaiting his arrival.

"I stayed in all day after hearing from you this morning, Mr. Carrados," he said, shaking hands. "When I got your second message I was all ready to walk straight out of the house. That's how I did it in the time. I hope everything is all right?"

"Excellent," replied Carrados. "You'd better have something before we start. We probably have a long and perhaps an exciting night before us."

"And certainly a wet one," assented the lieutenant. "It was thundering over Mulling way as I came along."

"That is why you are here," said his host. "We are waiting for a certain message before we start, and in meantime you may as well understand what we expect to happen. As you saw, there is a thunderstorm coming on. The Meteorological Office morning forecast predicted it for the whole of London if the conditions remained. That was why I kept you in readiness. Within an hour it is now inevitable that we shall experience a deluge. Here and there damage will be done to trees and buildings; here and there a person will probably be struck and killed."

"Yes."

"It is Mr. Creake's intention that his wife should be among the victims."

"I don't exactly follow," said Hollyer, looking from one man to the other. "I quite admit that Creake would be immensely relieved if such a thing did happen, but the chance is surely an absurdly remote one."

"Yet unless we intervene it is precisely what a coroner's jury will decide has happened. Do you know whether your brother-in-law has any practical knowledge of electricity, Mr. Hollyer?"

"I cannot say. He was so reserved, and we really knew so little of him—"

"Yet in 1896 an Austin Creake contributed an article on 'Alternating Currents' to the American *Scientific World*. That would argue a fairly intimate acquaintanceship."

"But do you mean that he is going to direct a flash of lightning?"

"Only into the minds of the doctor who conducts the post-mortem, and the coroner. This storm, the opportunity for which he has been waiting for weeks, is merely the cloak to his act. The weapon which he has planned to use—scarcely less powerful than lightning but much more tractable—is the high voltage current of electricity that flows along the tram wire at his gate."

"Oh!" exclaimed Lieutenant Hollyer, as the sudden revelation struck him.

"Some time between eleven o'clock to-night—about the hour when your sister goes to bed—and one-thirty in the morning—the time up to which he can rely on the current—Creake will throw a stone up at the balcony window. Most of his preparation has long been made; it only remains for him to connect up a short length to the window handle and a longer one at the other end to tap the live wire. That done, he will wake his wife in the way I have said. The moment she moves the catch of the window—and he has carefully filed its parts to ensure perfect contact—she will be electrocuted as effectually as if she sat in the executioner's chair in Sing Sing prison."

"But what are we doing here!" exclaimed Hollyer, starting to his feet, pale and horrified. "It is past ten now and anything may happen."

"Quite natural, Mr. Hollyer," said Carrados reassuringly, "but you need have no anxiety. Creake is being watched, the house is being watched, and your sister is as safe as if she slept to-night in Windsor Castle. Be assured that whatever happens he will not be allowed to complete his scheme; but it is desirable to let him implicate himself to the fullest limit. Your brother-in-law, Mr. Hollyer, is a man with a peculiar capacity for taking pains."

"He is a damned cold-blooded scoundrel!" exclaimed the young officer fiercely. "When I think of Millicent five years ago—"

"Well, for that matter, an enlightened nation has decided that electrocution is the most humane way of removing its superfluous citizens," suggested Carrados mildly. "He is certainly an ingenious-minded gentleman. It is his misfortune that in Mr. Carlyle he was fated to be opposed by an even subtler brain—"

"No, no! Really, Max!" protested the embarrassed gentleman.

"Mr. Hollyer will be able to judge for himself when I tell him that it was Mr. Carlyle who first drew attention to the significance of the abandoned kite," insisted Carrados firmly. "Then, of course, its object became plain to me—as indeed to any-one. For ten minutes, perhaps, a wire must be carried from the overhead line to the chestnut-tree. Creake has everything in his favour, but it is just within possibility that the driver of an inopportune tram might notice the appendage. What of that? Why, for more than a week he has seen a derelict kite with its yards of trailing string hang-ing in the tree. A very calculating mind, Mr. Hollyer. It would be interesting to know what line of action Mr. Creake has mapped out for himself afterwards. I expect he has half-a-dozen artistic little touches up his sleeve. Possibly he would merely singe his wife's hair, burn her feet with a red-hot poker, shiver the glass of the French window, and be content with that to let well alone. You see, lightning is so varied in its effects that whatever he did or did not do would be right. He is in the impregnable position of the body showing all the symptoms of death by lightning shock and nothing else but lightning to account for it—a dilated eye, heart contracted in systole, bloodless lungs shrunk to a third the normal weight, and all the rest of it. When he has removed a few outward traces of his work Creake might quite safely 'discover' his dead wife and rush off for the nearest doctor. Or he may have decided to arrange a convincing alibi, and creep away, leaving the discovery to another. We shall never know; he will make no confession."

"I wish it was well over," admitted Hollyer. "I'm not particularly jumpy, but this gives me a touch of the creeps."

"Three more hours at the worst, Lieutenant," said Carrados cheerfully. "Ah-ha, something is coming through now."

He went to the telephone and received a message from one quarter; then made another connection and talked for a few minutes with someone else.

"Everything working smoothly," he remarked between times over his shoulder. "Your sister has gone to bed, Mr. Hollyer."

Then he turned to the house telephone and distributed his orders.

"So we," he concluded, "must get up."

By the time they were ready a large closed motor car was waiting. The lieutenant thought he recognized Parkinson in the well-swathed form beside the driver, but there was no temptation to linger for a second on the steps. Already the stinging rain had lashed the drive into the semblance of a frothy estuary; all round the lightning jagged its course through the incessant tremulous glow of more distant lightning, while the thunder only ceased its muttering to turn at close quarters and crackle viciously.

"One of the few things I regret missing," remarked Carrados tranquilly; "but I hear a good deal of colour in it."

The car slushed its way down to the gate, lurched a little heavily across the dip into the road, and, steadying as it came upon the straight, began to hum contentedly along the deserted highway.

"We are not going direct?" suddenly inquired Hollyer, after they had travelled perhaps half-a-dozen miles. The night was bewildering enough but he had the sailor's gift for location.

"No; through Hunscott Green and then by a field-path to the orchard at the back," replied Carrados. "Keep a sharp look out for the man with the lantern about here, Harris," he called through the tube.

"Something flashing just ahead, sir," came the reply, and the car slowed down and stopped.

Carrados dropped the near window as a man in glistening waterproof stepped from the shelter of a lich-gate and approached.

"Inspector Beedel, sir," said the stranger, looking into the car.

"Quite right, Inspector," said Carrados. "Get in."

"I have a man with me, sir."

"We can find room for him as well."

"We are very wet."

"So shall we all be soon."

The lieutenant changed his seat and the two burly forms took places side by side. In less than five minutes the car stopped again, this time in a grassy country lane.

"Now we have to face it," announced Carrados. "The inspector will show us the way."

The car slid round and disappeared into the night, while Beedel led the party to a stile in the hedge. A couple of fields brought them to the Brookbend boundary. There a figure stood out of the black foliage, exchanged a few words with their guide and piloted them along the shadows of the orchard to the back door of the house.

"You will find a broken pane near the catch of the scullery window," said the blind man.

"Right, sir," replied the inspector. "I have it. Now who goes through?"

"Mr. Hollyer will open the door for us. I'm afraid you must take off your boots and all wet things, Lieutenant. We cannot risk a single spot inside."

They waited until the back door opened, then each one divested himself in a similar manner and passed into the kitchen, where the remains of a fire still burned. The man from the orchard gathered together the discarded garments and disappeared again.

Carrados turned to the lieutenant.

"A rather delicate job for you now, Mr. Hollyer. I want you to go up to your sister, wake her, and get her into another room with as little fuss as possible. Tell her as much as you think fit and let her understand that her very life depends on absolute stillness when she is alone. Don't be unduly hurried, but not a glimmer of a light, please."

Ten minutes passed by the measure of the battered old alarum on the dresser shelf before the young man returned.

"I've had rather a time of it," he reported, with a nervous laugh, "but I think it will be all right now. She is in the spare room."

"Then we will take our places. You and Parkinson come with me to the bedroom. Inspector, you have your own arrangements. Mr. Carlyle will be with you."

They dispersed silently about the house. Hollyer glanced apprehensively at the door of the spare room as they passed it but within was as quiet as the grave. Their room lay at the other end of the passage.

"You may as well take your place in the bed now, Hollyer," directed Carrados when they were inside and the door closed. "Keep well down among the clothes. Creake has to get up on the balcony, you know, and he will probably peep through the window, but he dare come no farther. Then when he begins to throw up stones slip on this dressing-gown of your sister's. I'll tell you what to do after."

The next sixty minutes drew out into the longest hour that the lieutenant had ever known. Occasionally he heard a whisper pass between the two men who stood behind the window curtains, but he could see nothing. Then Carrados threw a guarded remark in his direction.

"He is in the garden now."

Something scraped slightly against the outer wall. But the night was full of wilder sounds, and in the house the furniture and the boards creaked and sprung between the yawling of the wind among the chimneys, the rattle of the thunder and the pelting of the rain. It was a time to quicken the steadiest pulse, and when the crucial moment came, when a pebble suddenly rang against the pane with a sound that the tense waiting magnified into a shivering crash, Hollyer leapt from the bed on the instant.

"Easy, easy," warned Carrados feelingly. "We will wait for another knock." He passed something across. "Here is a rubber glove. I have cut the wire but you had better put it on. Stand just for a moment at the window, move the catch so that it can blow open a little, and drop immediately. Now."

Another stone had rattled against the glass. For Hollyer to go through his part was the work merely of seconds, and with a few touches Carrados spread the dressing-gown to more effective disguise about the extended form. But an unforeseen and in the circumstances rather horrible interval followed, for Creake, in accordance with some detail of his never-revealed plan, continued to shower missile after missile against the panes until even the unimpressionable Parkinson shivered.

"The last act," whispered Carrados, a moment after the throwing had ceased. "He has gone round to the back. Keep as you are. We take cover now." He pressed behind the arras of an extemporized wardrobe, and the spirit of emptiness and desolation seemed once more to reign over the lonely house.

From half-a-dozen places of concealment ears were straining to catch the first guiding sound. He moved very stealthily, burdened, perhaps, by some strange scruple in the presence of the tragedy that he had not feared to contrive, paused for a moment at the bedroom door, then opened it very quietly, and in the fickle light read the consummation of his hopes.

"At last!" they heard the sharp whisper drawn from his relief. "At last!"

He took another step and two shadows seemed to fall upon him from behind, one on either side. With primitive instinct a cry of terror and surprise escaped him as he made a desperate movement to wrench himself free, and for a short second he almost succeeded in dragging one hand into a pocket. Then his wrists slowly came together and the handcuffs closed.

"I am Inspector Beedel," said the man on his right side. "You are charged with the attempted murder of your wife, Millicent Creake."

"You are mad," retorted the miserable creature, falling into a desperate calmness. "She has been struck by lightning."

"No, you blackguard, she hasn't," wrathfully exclaimed his brother-in-law, jumping up. "Would you like to see her?"

"I also have to warn you," continued the inspector impassively, "that anything you say may be used as evidence against you."

A startled cry from the farther end of the passage arrested their attention.

"Mr. Carrados," called Hollyer, "oh, come at once."

At the open door of the other bedroom stood the lieutenant, his eyes still turned towards something in the room beyond, a little empty bottle in his hand.

"Dead!" he exclaimed tragically, with a sob, "with this beside her. Dead just when she would have been free of the brute."

The blind man passed into the room, sniffed the air, and laid a gentle hand on the pulseless heart.

"Yes," he replied. "That, Hollyer, does not always appeal to the woman, strange to say."

A CASE OF PREMEDITATION

R. Austin Freeman

Mr. Rufus Pembury was not pleased when, as the train was about to move out of Maidstone (East) Station, a coarse and burly man (clearly a denizen of the third class) was ushered into his compartment by the guard. His resentment deepened as the stranger sat down and fixed upon Mr. Pembury a gaze of impertinent intensity.

Mr. Pembury fidgeted in his seat, looked into his pocket-book, and even thought of opening his umbrella. Finally he turned to the stranger with frosty remonstrance:

"I imagine, sir, that you will have no difficulty in recognizing me, should we ever meet again—which God forbid."

"I should reckernize you among ten thousand," was the reply, so unexpected as to leave Mr. Pembury speechless.

"You see," the stranger continued impressively, "I've got the gift of faces. I never forget."

"That must be a great consolation," said Pembury.

"It's very useful to me," said the stranger; "at least, it used to be, when I was a warder at Portland. You remember me, I dare say. My name is Pratt. I was assistant warder in your time. God-forsaken hole, Portland!"

Pembury pulled himself together.

"I think," said he, "you must be mistaking me for some one else."

"I don't," replied Pratt. "You're Francis Dobbs. Slipped away from Portland one evening about twelve years ago. Clothes washed up on the Bill next day. As neat a mizzle as ever I heard of. But there are a couple of photographs and a set of finger-prints at the Habitual Criminals Register. P'r'aps you'd like to come and see 'em?"

"Why should I go to the Habitual Criminals Register?" Pembury demanded faintly.

"Ah! Exactly. Why should you?—when you are a man of means and a little judiciously invested capital would render it unnecessary."

Pembury looked out of the window, and for a minute or more preserved a stony silence. At length he turned to Pratt. "How much?"

"I shouldn't think a couple of hundred a year would hurt you," was the calm reply.

Pembury reflected. "What makes you think I am a man of means?" he asked presently.

Pratt smiled grimly. "Bless you, Mr. Pembury," said he, "I know all about you. Why, for the last six months I have been living within half a mile of your house."

"The devil you have!"

"Yes. When I retired from the service, General O'Gorman engaged me as caretaker of his place at Baysford, and the very day after I came down I met you, but, naturally, I kept out of sight. Thought I'd find out whether you were good for anything before I spoke, so I've been keeping my ears open, and I find you are good for a couple of hundred."

There was an interval of silence, and then the ex-warder resumed:

"That's what comes of having a memory for faces. Now, there's Jack Ellis, on the other hand. He must have had you under his nose for a couple of years, and yet he's never twigged—he never will, either," added Pratt, already regretting the confidence into which his vanity had led him.

"Who is Jack Ellis?" Pembury demanded.

"Why, he's a sort of supenum'ary at the Baysford police station. He was in the Civil Guard at Portland in your time, but he got his left forefinger chopped off, so they pensioned him, and he got this billet. But he'll never reckernize you."

"Who is this General O'Gorman? I seem to know the name."

"I expect you do," said Pratt. "He was governor of Dartmoor when I was there, and, let me tell you, if he'd been at Portland in your time, you'd never have got away. The General is a great man on bloodhounds. He kept a pack at Dartmoor, and there were no attempted escapes in those days."

"Has he the pack still?" asked Pembury.

"Rather. He's always hoping there'll be a burglary or a murder in the neighborhood, so as he can try 'em. But, to come back to our little arrangement, what do you say to a couple of hundred, paid quarterly, if you like?"

"I can't settle the matter offhand," said Pembury. "You must give me time to think it over."

"Very well," said Pratt. "I shall be back at Baysford to-morrow. Shall I look in at your place to-morrow night?"

"No," replied Pembury; "you'd better not be seen at my house, nor I at yours. If I meet you at some quiet spot, we can settle our business without any one knowing that we have met. It won't take long, and we can't be too careful."

"That's true," agreed Pratt. "Well, I'll tell you what. There's an avenue leading up to our house—you know it, I expect. The gates are always ajar, excepting at night.

Now, I'll be down by the six thirty at Baysford. Our place is a quarter of an hour from the station. Say you meet me in the avenue at a quarter to seven. How will that do?"

"That will suit me," answered Pembury.

"Hallo!" said Pratt, suddenly. "This'll be Swanley, I expect. So long. To-morrow evening, in the avenue, at a quarter to seven."

"Very well," said Mr. Pembury. He spoke coldly enough, but there was a flush on his cheeks and an angry light in his eyes, which, perhaps, the ex-warder noticed; for, when he had stepped out and shut the door, he thrust his head in at the window and said threateningly:

"One more word, Mr. Pembury-Dobbs. No hanky-panky, you know. I'm an old hand, and pretty fly, I am. So don't you try any chickery-pokery on me. That's all!"

He withdrew his head and disappeared, leaving Pembury to his reflections.

Rufus Pembury, to give him his real name, was a man of strong character and intelligence. So much so that, having tried the criminal career and found it not worth pursuing, he had definitely abandoned it. When the cattle-boat that had picked him up off Portland Bill landed him at an American port, he brought all his ability and energy to bear on legitimate commercial pursuits, with such success that at the end of ten years he was able to return to England with a moderate competence. Then he had taken a modest house near the little town of Baysford, and here he might have lived out the rest of his life in peace but for the unlucky chance that brought Pratt into the neighborhood.

There is something eminently unsatisfactory about a blackmailer. No arrangement with him has any permanent validity. The thing that he has sold remains in his possession to sell over again. He pockets the price of emancipation, but retains the key of the fetters. In short, the blackmailer is a totally impossible person.

Such were Rufus Pembury's reflections, even while Pratt was making his proposals, which he had never for an instant entertained. Pratt must be eliminated: it was a logical consequence. The profound meditations, therefore, in which Pembury remained immersed for the remainder of the journey had nothing whatever to do with the quarterly allowance; they were concerned exclusively with the elimination of ex-warder Pratt.

When Pembury alighted at Charing Cross, he directed his steps toward a quiet private hotel. The woman manager greeted him by his name as she handed him his key. "Are you staying in town, Mr. Pembury?" she asked.

"No," was the reply; "I go back to-morrow morning. But I may be coming up again shortly. By the way, you used to have an Encyclopaedia. Could I see it for a moment?"

That a gentleman from the country should desire to look up the subject of *bounds* would not, to a casual observer, have seemed unnatural. But when from *bounds* he proceeded to the article on *blood*, and thence to one devoted to *perfumes*, the observer might reasonably have felt some surprise; and this surprise might have been augmented if he had followed Mr. Pembury's subsequent proceedings, and especially if he had considered them as the actions of a man whose immediate aim was the removal of a superfluous unit of the population.

Having deposited his bag and umbrella in his room, Pembury set forth from the hotel as one with a definite purpose; and his footsteps led, in the first place, to an umbrella shop in the Strand, where he selected a thick rattan cane. There was nothing remarkable in this, perhaps; but the cane was of an uncomely thickness, and the salesman protested.

"I like a thick cane," said Pembury.

"Yes, sir; but for a gentleman of your height" (Pembury was a small, slightly built man), "I would venture to suggest—"

"I like a thick cane," repeated Pembury. "Cut it down to the proper length, and don't rivet the ferrule on."

His next investment would have seemed more to the purpose, though suggestive of unexpected crudity of method. It was a large Norwegian knife. Not content with this, he went on to a second cutler's, and purchased another knife, the exact duplicate of the first.

Shopping appeared to be a positive mania with Rufus Pembury. In the course of the next half hour he acquired a cheap hand-bag, an artist's japanned brush-case, a three-cornered file, a stick of elastic glue, and a pair of iron crucible-tongs. Still insatiable, he repaired to a chemist's shop, where he further enriched himself with a packet of absorbent cotton-wool and an ounce of permanganate of potash; and, as the chemist wrapped up these articles, Pembury watched him impassively.

"I suppose you don't keep musk?" he asked.

The chemist paused in the act of heating a stick of sealing-wax. "No, sir, not the solid musk; it's so very costly. But I have the essence."

"That isn't as strong as the pure stuff, I suppose?"

"No," replied the chemist, with a smile, "not *so* strong, but strong enough. These animal perfumes are so very penetrating, you know, and so lasting. Why, I venture to say that if you were to sprinkle a table-spoonful of the essence in the middle of St. Paul's, the place would smell of it six months hence."

"You don't say so!" said Pembury. "Well, that ought to be enough for anybody. I'll take a small quantity, please, and, for goodness' sake, see that there isn't any on the outside of the bottle. The stuff isn't for myself, and I don't want to go about smelling like a civet-cat."

"Naturally you don't," agreed the chemist. "There, sir," said he, when the musk was ready, "there is not a drop on the outside of the bottle, and, if I fit it with a rubber cork, you will be quite secure."

Pembury's dislike of musk appeared to be excessive, for, when the chemist had retired to change half a crown, he took the brush-case from the hand-bag, pulled off its lid, and then, with the crucible-tongs, daintily lifted the bottle off the counter, slid it softly into the brush-case, and, replacing the lid, returned the case and tongs to the bag. The other two packets he took from the counter and dropped into his pocket; and, having received his change, left the shop and walked thoughtfully back toward the Strand. Suddenly a new idea seemed to strike him. He halted, and then strode away northward to make the oddest of all his purchases.

The transaction took place in a shop in the Seven Dials whose strange stock in trade ranged from water-snails to Angora cats. Pembury looked at a cage of guinea-pigs in the window, and entered the shop.

"Do you happen to have a dead guinea-pig?" he asked.

"No; mine are all alive," replied the man, adding, with a sinister grin: "but they're not immortal, you know."

Pembury looked at the man distastefully. There is an appreciable difference between a guinea-pig and a blackmailer. "Any small mammal would do," he said.

"There's a dead rat in that cage, if he's any good," said the man. "Died this morning."

"I'll take the rat," said Pembury; "he'll do quite well."

Accordingly the little corpse was wrapped up in a parcel and deposited in the bag, and Pembury made his way back to the hotel. After a modest lunch he spent the remainder of the day transacting the business that had originally brought him to town. He did not return to his hotel until ten o'clock, when he went immediately to his room. But before undressing (and after locking his door) he did a very strange and unaccountable thing. Having pulled off the loose ferrule from his newly purchased cane, he bored a hole in the bottom of it with the spike end of the file. Then, with the file, he enlarged the hole until only a narrow rim of the bottom was left. He next rolled up a small ball of cotton-wool and pushed it into the ferrule; and, having smeared the end of the cane with elastic glue, he replaced the ferrule, warming it over the gas to make the glue stick.

When he had finished with the cane, he turned his attention to one of the Norwegian knives. First, with the file, he carefully removed most of the bright yellow varnish from the wooden handle, and laid the knife down, open. Then he unwrapped the dead rat which he had bought at the zoölogist's. Laying the animal on a sheet of paper, he cut off its head, and, holding it up by the tail, allowed the blood to drop on the knife, spreading it over both sides of the blade and handle.

Then he laid the knife on the paper, and softly opened the window. From the darkness below came the voice of a cat, and in its direction Pembury flung the body of the rat, and closed the window. Finally, having washed his hands and stuffed the paper from the parcel into the fireplace, he went to bed.

His proceedings in the morning were equally mysterious. Having breakfasted betimes, he returned to his bedroom and locked himself in. Then he tied his new cane, handle downward, to the leg of the dressing-table. Next, with the crucible-tongs, he drew the little bottle of musk from the brush-case, and, having assured himself, by sniffing at it, that the exterior was really free from odor, he withdrew the rubber cork. Then, slowly and with infinite care, he poured perhaps half a teaspoonful of the essence on the cotton-wool that bulged from the hole in the ferrule. When it was saturated, he proceeded to treat the knife in the same fashion, letting a little of the essence fall on the wooden handle, which soaked it up readily. This done, he opened the window and looked out. The body of the rat had disappeared. Holding out the musk-bottle, he dropped it into some laurel bushes that grew in the yard below, flinging the rubber cork after it.

His next proceeding was to squeeze a small quantity of vaseline on his fingers, and thoroughly to smear the shoulder of the brush-case and the inside of the lid, so as to insure an air-tight joint. Having wiped his fingers, he picked up the knife with the crucible-tongs, and, dropping it into the brush-case, immediately pushed on the lid. Then he heated the tips of the tongs in the gas flame, to destroy the scent, packed the tongs and brush-case in his bag, untied the cane,—carefully avoiding contact with the ferrule,—and, taking up the two bags, went out, holding the cane by its middle.

There was no difficulty in finding an empty compartment, for first-class passengers were few at that time in the morning. Pembury waited on the platform until the guard's whistle sounded; then he stepped into the compartment, shut the door, and laid the cane on the seat, with its ferrule projecting out of the offside window; in which position it remained until the train drew into Baysford Station.

Pembury left his dressing-bag in the cloak-room, and, again grasping the cane by its middle, and carrying the smaller hand-bag, he sallied forth. The town of Baysford lay about half a mile to the east of the station; his own house was a mile along the road to the west; and half way between his house and the station was the residence of General O'Gorman. Pembury knew the place well. It stood on the edge of a great expanse of flat meadows, and communicated with the road by an avenue, nearly three hundred yards long, of ancient trees. The avenue was shut off from the road by a pair of iron gates; but these were merely ornamental, for the place was accessible from the surrounding meadows—indeed, an indistinct foot-path crossed the meadows and intersected the avenue about half way up.

Pembury approached the avenue by the footpath, and, as he entered it, examined the adjacent trees with more than a casual interest. The two between which he had entered were an elm and a great pollard oak, the latter being an immense tree whose huge, warty bole divided, about seven feet from the ground, into three limbs, each as large as a fair-sized tree, of which the largest swept outward in a great curve half way across the avenue. On this patriarch Pembury bestowed special attention, walking completely around it, and finally laying down his bag and cane (the latter resting on the bag, with the ferrule off the ground), that he might climb up, by the aid of the warty outgrowths, to examine the crown.

Apparently the oak did not meet his requirements, for he climbed down again. Then, beyond the elm, he caught sight of an ancient pollard hornbeam—a strange, fantastic tree whose trunk widened out trumpetlike, above, into a broad crown, from the edge of which multitudinous branches uprose like the limbs of some weird hamadryad.

The crown of the trunk was barely six feet from the ground, and he found that he could reach it easily. Standing the cane against the tree,—ferrule down this time,—he took the brush-case from his bag, pulled off the lid, and, with the crucible-tongs, lifted out the knife and laid it on the crown of the tree, just out of sight, leaving the tongs, also invisible, still grasping the knife. He was about to replace the brush-case in the bag, when he appeared to alter his mind. Sniffing at it, and finding it reeking with the sickly perfume, he pushed the lid on again, and threw the case up into the tree, where he heard it roll down into the central hollow of the crown. Then he closed the bag, and, taking the cane by its handle, moved slowly away in the direction whence he had come, passing out of the avenue between the elm and the oak.

His mode of progress was certainly peculiar. He walked very slowly, trailing the cane along the ground, and every few paces he stopped and pressed the ferrule firmly against the earth. To any one observing him, he would have appeared wrapped in an absorbing reverie. In this manner he moved across the fields, not returning to the highroad until he came to a narrow lane that led out into High Street. Immediately opposite the lane was the police station, distinguished from the adjacent cottages only by its lamp, its open door, and the notices posted up outside. Straight across the road Pembury walked, still trailing the cane, and halted at the station door to read the notices, resting his cane on the door-step as he did so. Through the open doorway he could see a man writing at a desk. The man's back was toward him, but presently a movement brought his left hand into view, and Pembury noted that the forefinger was missing. This, then, was Jack Ellis, late of the Civil Guard at Portland.

Even while he was looking, the man turned his head, and Pembury recognized him at once. He had frequently met him on the road between Baysford and the adjoining village of Thorpe, and always at the same time. Apparently Ellis paid a daily visit to Thorpe,—perhaps to receive a report from the rural constable,—starting between three and four and returning at seven or a quarter past.

Pembury looked at his watch. It was fifteen minutes after three. He moved away thoughtfully (holding his cane by the middle now), and began to walk slowly in the direction of Thorpe. For a while he was deeply meditative and his face wore a puzzled frown. Then it suddenly cleared, and he strode forward at a brisker pace. Presently he passed through a gap in the hedge, and, walking in a field parallel with the road, took out his purse—a small pigskin pouch. Having frugally emptied it of its contents, excepting a few shillings, he thrust the ferrule of his cane into the small compartment ordinarily reserved for gold or notes. And thus he continued to walk on slowly, carrying the cane by the middle, with the purse jammed on the end.

At length he reached a sharp double curve in the road, whence he could see back for a considerable distance, and here, opposite a small opening, he sat down to wait. The hedge would screen him effectually from the gaze of passersby without interfering with his view.

A quarter of an hour passed. He began to be uneasy. Had he been mistaken? Were Ellis' visits only occasional instead of daily, as he had thought? That would be tiresome, though not actually disastrous. But at this point in his reflections a figure came into view, advancing along the road with a steady swing. He recognized the figure as Ellis. But there was another person advancing from the opposite direction, apparently a laborer. Pembury prepared to shift his ground, but another glance showed him that the laborer would pass first. He waited. The laborer came on, and at length passed the opening. After the laborer had gone on, Ellis disappeared for a moment in a bend of the road. Instantly Pembury passed his cane through the opening in the hedge, shook off the purse, and pushed it into the middle of the footway. Then he crept forward behind the hedge toward the approaching officer, and again sat down to wait. On came the steady tramp of the unsuspecting Ellis, and, as the sound passed, Pembury drew aside an obstructing branch and peered out at the retreating figure. Would Ellis see the purse? It was not a conspicuous object.

The footsteps stopped abruptly. Looking out, Pembury saw the police official stoop, pick up the purse, examine its contents, and finally stow it in his trousers pocket. Pembury heaved a sigh of relief, and, as the figure passed out of sight round a curve in the road, he rose, stretched himself, and strode briskly away.

A group of ricks suggested a fresh idea. Walking to the farther side of one of the ricks, and thrusting his cane deeply into it, he pushed it home with a piece of stick until the handle was lost in the straw. The hand-bag was now all that was left. He opened it and smelled of its interior, but, though he could detect no odor, he resolved to be rid of it.

As he emerged from the gap, a wagon jogged slowly by. Stepping into the road, Pembury quickly overtook the wagon, and, having glanced around, laid the bag lightly on the tail-board. Then he set off for the station to get his dressing-bag.

On arriving home, he went straight up to his bedroom, and, ringing for the house-keeper, ordered a substantial meal. Then he took off his clothes, and deposited them, even to the shirt, socks, and necktie, in a trunk in which his summer clothing was stored, with a plentiful sprinkling of naphthol to preserve it from moths. Taking the packet of permanganate of potash from his dressing-bag, he passed into the adjoining bath-room, and, tipping the crystals into the bath, turned on the water. Soon the bath was filled with a pink solution of the salt, and into this Pembury plunged, immersing his entire body and thoroughly soaking his hair. Then he emptied the bath, rinsed himself in clear water, and dressed in fresh clothing. Finally he ate a hearty meal, and then lay down to rest until it should be time to start for the rendezvous.

Half past six found him lurking in the shadow by the station approach, within sight of the solitary lamp. He heard the train come in, saw the stream of passengers emerge, and noted one figure detach itself from the throng and turn into the Thorpe road. It was Pratt, as the lamplight showed him—Pratt striding forward to the meet-ing-place with an air of jaunty satisfaction and an uncommonly creaky pair of boots.

Pembury followed him at a distance, until he was well past the stile at the entrance to the foot-path. Evidently he was going on to the gates. Then Pembury vaulted over the stile and strode swiftly across the dark meadows.

When he plunged into the deep gloom of the avenue, his first act was to grope his way to the hornbeam, and slip his hand up to the crown to satisfy himself that the tongs were as he had left them. Reassured by the touch of his fingers on the iron loops, he turned and walked slowly down the avenue. The duplicate knife, ready opened, was in his left inside breast pocket, and he fingered its handle as he walked.

Presently the iron gate squeaked mournfully, and then the rhythmical creak of a pair of boots coming up the avenue was audible. Pembury walked forward slowly until a darker smear emerged from the surrounding gloom, when he called out:

"Is that you, Pratt?"

"That's me," was the cheerful response, and, as he drew nearer, the ex-warder asked:

"Have you brought the rhino, old man?"

The insolent familiarity of the man's tone strengthened Pembury's nerve and hardened his heart. "Of course," he replied; "but we must have a definite understanding, you know."

"Look here," said Pratt. "I've got no time for jaw. The General will be here presently; he's riding over from Bingfield with a friend. You hand over the dibbs, and we'll talk some other time."

"That is all very well," said Pembury, "but you must understand—" He paused abruptly, and stood still. They were now close to the hornbeam, and, as he stood, he stared up into the dark mass of foliage.

"What's the matter?" demanded Pratt. "What are you staring at?"

He, too, had halted, and now stood gazing intently into the darkness.

Then, in an instant, Pembury whipped out the knife, and drove it, with all his strength, into the broad back of the ex-warder, below the left shoulder-blade.

With a hideous yell, Pratt turned and grappled with his assailant. A powerful man, and a competent wrestler, he was far more than a match for Pembury unarmed, and in a moment he had him by the throat. But Pembury clung to him tightly, and, as they trampled to and fro, round and round, he stabbed again and again, with the viciousness of a scorpion, while Pratt's cries grew gurgling and husky. Then they fell heavily to the ground, Pembury underneath. Pratt relaxed his hold, and in a moment grew limp and inert. Pembury pushed him off and rose, breathing heavily.

But he wasted no time. There had been more noise than he had bargained for. Quickly stepping to the hornbeam, he reached up for the tongs. His fingers slid into the looped handles of the tongs that grasped the knife, and he lifted it out from its hiding-place and deposited it on the ground a few feet from the body. Then he went back to the tree and carefully pushed the tongs over into the hollow of the crown.

At this moment a woman's voice sounded shrilly from the top of the avenue.

"Is that you, Mr. Pratt?" it called.

Pembury started, and then stepped back quickly, on tiptoe, to the body. For there was the duplicate knife. He must take that away at all costs.

The corpse was lying on its back. The knife was underneath it, driven into the very haft. Pembury had to use both hands to lift the body, and even then he had some difficulty in disengaging the weapon. And, meanwhile, the voice, repeating its question, came nearer.

At last he succeeded in drawing out the knife, and thrust it into his breast pocket. The corpse fell back, and he stood up, gasping.

"Mr. Pratt! Are you there?"

The nearness of the voice startled Pembury, and, turning sharply, he saw a light twinkling between the trees. And then the gates creaked loudly, and he heard the crunch of a horse's hoofs on the gravel.

He stood for an instant, bewildered, utterly taken by surprise. He had not reckoned on a horse. His intended flight across the meadows toward Thorpe was now impossible. If he were overtaken he would be lost; for he knew there was blood on his clothes and hands, to say nothing of the knife in his pocket.

But his confusion lasted only for an instant. He remembered the oak tree, and ran to it. Touching it as little as possible with his bloody hands, he climbed quickly up into the crown. The great horizontal limb was nearly three feet in diameter, and, as he lay out on it, gathering his coat closely about him, he was quite invisible from below.

He had hardly settled himself when the light that he had seen came into full view, revealing a woman advancing with a stable lantern in her hand. And, almost at the same moment, a streak of brighter light burst from the opposite direction. The horseman was accompanied by a man on a bicycle.

The two men came on apace, and the horseman, sighting the woman, called out: "Anything the matter, Mrs. Parton?"

But at that moment the light of the bicycle lamp fell full on the prostrate corpse. The two men uttered a simultaneous cry of horror, the woman shrieked aloud; and then the horseman sprang from the saddle and ran toward the body.

"Why," he exclaimed, stooping over it, "it's Pratt!" And, as the cyclist came up, and his lamp shone on a great pool of blood, he added:

"There's been foul play here, Hanford."

Hanford flashed his lamp around the body, lighting up the ground for several yards.

"What is that behind you, O'Gorman?" he said suddenly. "Isn't it a knife?"

He was moving quickly toward it, when O'Gorman held up his hand.

"Don't touch it!" he exclaimed. "We'll put the hounds on to it. They'll soon track the scoundrel, whoever he is. Hanford, this fellow has fairly delivered himself into our hands!"

He stood looking down at the knife with something uncommonly like exultation, and then, turning quickly to his friend, said:

"Look here, Hanford, you ride off to the police station as hard as you can pelt. Send or bring an officer, and I'll scour the meadows meanwhile. If I haven't got the scoundrel when you come back, we'll put the hounds on to his knife and run the beggar down."

"Right!" replied Hanford, and rode away into the darkness.

"Mrs. Parton," said O'Gorman, "watch that knife. See that nobody touches it, while I go and search the meadows."

Pembury's position was cramped and uncomfortable; but he hardly dared to breathe, for the woman below him was not a dozen yards away. It was with mingled feelings of relief and apprehension that he presently saw a group of lights approaching rapidly along the road from Baysford. For a time they were hidden by the trees, and then, the whir of wheels sounded on the drive, and streaks of light on the tree-trunks announced the new arrivals. There were three bicycles, ridden by Mr. Hanford, a police inspector, and a sergeant; and, as they drew up, the General came thundering back into the avenue.

"Is Ellis with you?" he asked, as he pulled up.

"No, sir," was the reply. "He hadn't come in from Thorpe when we left. He's late."

"Have you sent for a doctor?"

"Yes, sir; I've sent for Dr. Hills," said the inspector. "Is Pratt dead?"

"Seems to be," replied O'Gorrnan, "but we'd better leave that to the doctor. There's the murderer's knife. Nobody has touched it. I'm going to fetch the blood-hounds now."

"Ah, that's the thing!" said the inspector. "The man can't be far away." He rubbed his hands with a satisfied air as O'Gorman cantered away up the avenue.

In less than a minute there came out of the darkness the deep baying of hounds. Then into the circle of light emerged three sinister shapes, loose-limbed and gaunt, in charge of the General and a man.

"Here, inspector," shouted the General, "you take one; I can't hold 'em both."

The inspector ran forward and seized one of the leashes, and the General led his hound up to the knife on the ground. Pembury watched the great brute with almost impersonal curiosity.

For some minutes the hound stood motionless, sniffing at the knife; then it turned away, and walked to and fro with its muzzle to the ground. Suddenly it lifted its head, bayed loudly, lowered its muzzle, and started forward between the oak and the elm, dragging the General after it at a run.

Then the inspector brought his hound to the knife, and was soon bounding away to the tug of the leash in the General's wake.

"They don't make no mistakes, they don't," said the man Bailey, addressing the gratified sergeant, as he brought forward the third hound; "you'll see—"

But his remark was cut short by a violent jerk of the leash, and the next minute he was flying after the others, followed by Mr. Hanford.

The sergeant daintily picked up the knife by its ring, wrapped it in his handkerchief, and bestowed it in his pocket. Then he ran off after the hounds.

Pembury smiled grimly. His scheme was working out admirably, in spite of the unforeseen difficulties. If that confounded woman would only go away, he could climb down and take himself off while the course was clear. He listened to the baying of the hounds gradually growing fainter, and cursed the dilatoriness of the doctor. Confound the fellow! Didn't he realize that this was a case of life or death? Those infernal doctors had no sense of responsibility.

Suddenly a fresh light appeared coming up the avenue, and then a bicycle swept up to the scene of the tragedy, and a small, elderly man jumped down beside the body. He stooped over the dead man, felt the wrist, pushed back an eyelid, held a match to the eye, and rose.

"This is a shocking affair, Mrs. Parton," said he. "The poor fellow is quite dead. You had better help me carry him to the house."

Pembury watched them raise the body and stagger away with it up the avenue. He heard their shuffling steps die away, and the door of the house shut. And still he listened. From far away in the meadows came, at intervals, the baying of the hounds. Other sound there was none. Presently the doctor would come back for his bicycle, but for the moment the coast was clear. Pembury rose stiffly. His hands had stuck to the tree where they had pressed against it, and they were still sticky and damp. Quickly he let himself down to the ground, listened again for a moment, and then, making a small circuit to avoid the lamplight, crossed the avenue and stole away across the meadows.

The night was intensely dark, and not a soul was stirring. He strode forward quickly, peering into the darkness, and stopping now and again to listen; but no sound came to his ears save the now faint baying of the distant hounds. Not far from his house, he remembered, was a deep ditch spanned by a wooden bridge, and toward this he now made his way; for he knew that his appearance would convict him at a glance. Arrived at the ditch, he stooped to wash his hands and wrists; and, as he bent forward, the knife fell from his breast pocket into the shallow water. He groped for it, found it, and drove it deep into the mud as far out as he could reach. Then he wiped his hands on some water-weed, crossed the bridge, and started homeward.

He approached his house from the rear, satisfied himself that his housekeeper was in the kitchen, and, letting himself in very quietly with his key, went quickly up to his bedroom. Here be washed thoroughly,—in the bath, so he could get rid of the discolored water,—changed his clothes, and packed those that he took off in a portmanteau.

By the time he had done this the supper gong sounded. As he took his seat at the table, spruce and fresh in appearance, quietly cheerful in manner, he addressed his housekeeper. "I wasn't able to finish my business in London," he said. "I shall have to go up again to-morrow."

"Shall you come back the same day?" asked the housekeeper.

"Perhaps," was the reply, "and perhaps not. It will depend on circumstances."

He did not say what the circumstances might be, nor did the housekeeper ask. Mr. Pembury was not addicted to confidences. He was an eminently discreet man; and discreet men say little.

II. JERVIS SPEAKS

The autumn morning was cool, the fire roared jovially. I thrust my slippered feet toward the blaze, and meditated on nothing in particular, with catlike enjoyment. Presently a disapproving grunt from Thorndyke attracted my attention, and I looked round lazily. With the shears he was extracting the readable portions of the morning paper, and had paused with a small cutting between his finger and thumb.

"Bloodhounds again," said he. "We shall be hearing presently of the revival of the ordeal by fire."

"And a deuced comfortable ordeal, too, on a morning like this," I said. "What is the case?"

He was about to reply, when a sharp rat-tat from the little brass knocker announced a disturber of our peace. Thorndyke admitted a police inspector in uniform.

"I believe I am speaking to Dr. Thorndyke?" said the officer; and, as Thorndyke nodded, he went on:

"My name, sir, is Fox—Inspector Fox of the Baysford police. Perhaps you've seen by the morning paper that we have had to arrest one of our own men? That's rather awkward, you know, sir."

"Very," agreed Thorndyke.

"Yes, it's bad; but we had to do it. There was no way out, that we could see. Still, we want the accused to have every chance, both for our sake and for his own, so the chief constable thought he'd like to have your opinion on the case."

"Let us have the particulars," said Thorndyke, taking a writing-pad from a drawer. "Begin at the beginning," he added, "and tell us all you know."

"Well," said the inspector, after a preliminary cough, "to begin with the murdered man, his name is Pratt. He was a retired prison warder, and was employed as steward by General O'Gorman, who is a retired prison governor—you may have heard of him in connection with his pack of bloodhounds.

"Well, Pratt came down from London yesterday evening by a train arriving at Baysford at six thirty. He was seen by the guard, the ticket collector, and the outside porter. The porter saw him leave the station at six thirty-seven. General O'Gorman's house is about half a mile from the station.

"At five minutes to seven, the General and a gentleman named Hanford, and the General's housekeeper, a Mrs. Parton, found Pratt lying dead in the avenue that leads up to the house. Apparently he had been stabbed, for there was a lot of blood about, and a knife—a Norwegian knife—was lying on the ground near the body. Mrs. Parton had thought she heard some one in the avenue calling out for help, and she came out with a lantern. She met the General and Mr. Hanford, and all three seem to have caught sight of the body at the same moment.

"Mr. Hanford cycled down to us at once with the news. We sent for a doctor, and I went back with Mr. Hanford, and took a sergeant with me. Then the General, who had galloped his horse over the meadows each side of the avenue without having seen anybody, fetched out his bloodhounds and led them up to the knife. All three hounds took up the scent at once,—I held the leash of one of them,—and they took us across the meadows without a pause or a falter, over stiles and fences, along a lane, out into the town, and then, one after the other, they crossed the road in a bee-line to the police station, bolted in at the door, which stood open, and made straight for the desk, where a supernumerary officer named Ellis was writing. They made a rare to-do, struggling to get at him, and it was as much as we could do to hold them back. As for Ellis, he turned as pale as a ghost."

"Was any one else in the room?" asked Thorndyke.

"Oh, yes; there were two constables and a messenger. We led the hounds up to them, but the brutes wouldn't take any notice of them. They wanted Ellis."

"And what did you do?"

"Why, we arrested Ellis, of course. Couldn't do anything else."

"Is there anything against the accused man?"

"Yes, there is. He and Pratt were on distinctly unfriendly terms. They were old comrades, for Ellis was in the Civil Guard at Portland when Pratt was warder there— he was pensioned off from the service because he got his left forefinger chopped off. But lately they had had some unpleasantness about a woman."

"And what sort of a man is Ellis?"

"A remarkably decent fellow, he always seemed, quiet, steady, good-natured; I should have said he wouldn't hurt a fly. We all liked him—better than we liked Pratt, in fact, for poor Pratt was what you'd call an old soldier—sly, you know, sir, and a bit of a sneak."

"You searched and examined Ellis, course?"

"Yes. There was nothing suspicious about him, except that he had two purses. But he says he picked up one of them—a small pigskin pouch—on the foot-path of the Thorpe road yesterday afternoon. At any rate, the purse was not Pratt's."

Thorndyke made a note on his pad, and then asked: "There were no bloodstains or marks on his clothing?"

"No; his clothing was not marked or disarranged in any way." '

"Any cuts, scratches, or bruises on his person?"

"None whatever," replied the inspector.

"At what time did you arrest Ellis?"

"Half past seven exactly."

"Have you ascertained what his movements were? Had he been near the scene of the murder?"

"Yes; he had been to Thorpe, and would pass the gates of the avenue on his way back. And he was later than usual in returning, though not later than he has often been before."

"And now, as to the murdered man. Has the body been examined?"

"Yes; I had Dr. Hills' report before I left. There were no less than seven deep knife-wounds, all on the left side of the back. The knife, covered with blood, was found near the body."

"What has been done with it, by the way?" asked Thorndyke.

"The sergeant who was with me picked it up and rolled it in his handkerchief to carry in his pocket. I took it from him just as it was, and locked it in a despatch-box, handkerchief and all."

"Has the knife been recognized as Ellis' property?"

"No, sir; it has not."

"Were there any recognizable footprints or marks of a struggle?" Thorndyke asked.

The inspector grinned sheepishly. "I haven't examined the spot, of course, sir," said he; "but, after the General's horse and the bloodhounds and Mr. Hanford had been over it twice, going and returning, why, you see, sir—"

"Exactly, exactly," said Thorndyke. "Well, inspector, I shall be pleased to act for the defense. It seems to me that the case against Ellis is, in some respects, rather inconclusive."

The inspector was frankly amazed. "It hadn't struck me in that light, sir," he said.

"No? Well, that is my view; and I think the best plan will be for me to come down with you and investigate matters on the spot."

The inspector assented cheerfully, and we withdrew to prepare for the expedition.

"You are coming, I suppose, Jervis?" said Thorndyke.

"If I shall be of any use," I replied.

"Of course you will," said he. "Two heads are better than one, and, by the look of things, ours will be the only ones with any sense in them. We will take the research case, of course, and we may as well have a camera with us."

The corpse had been laid on a billiard-table on a pair of horse-cloths covered with a waterproof sheet, and the dead man's clothes were on a side-table. Thorndyke first directed his attention to the former, and we stooped together over the gaping wounds. Then, turning to the table, Thorndyke held up the coat, waistcoat, and shirt, and, having examined the holes in them through a lens, handed them to me without comment. Neither the wounds nor the clothes presented anything particularly suggestive. Evidently the weapon used had been a thick-backed, single-edged knife like the one described, and the discoloration around the wounds indicated that the weapon had a definite shoulder, like that of a Norwegian knife, and that it had been driven in with savage violence. These proceedings the General viewed wit h evident impatience, and presently he withdrew.

"Do you find anything that throws any light on the case?" the inspector asked, when the examination was concluded.

"That is impossible to say until we have seen the knife," replied Thorndyke; "but, while we are waiting for it, we may as well go and look at the scene of the tragedy. These are Pratt's boots. I think?" He lifted a pair of stout laced boots from the table, and inspected the soles.

"Yes," replied Fox, "and pretty easy they'd have been to track, if the case had been the other way about. Those protectors are as good as a trade-mark."

"We'll take the boots, at any rate," said Thorndyke; and we went out and walked down the avenue.

The place where the murder had been committed was easily identified by a large dark stain on the gravel at one side of the drive, half way between two trees—an ancient pollard hornbeam and an elm. Next to the elm was a pollard oak with a squat, warty bole about seven feet high, and three enormous limbs, of which one slanted half way across the avenue; and between these two trees the ground was covered with the tracks of men and hounds superimposed upon the hoof-prints of a horse.

"Where was the knife found?" Thorndyke asked.

The inspector indicated a spot near the middle of the drive, almost opposite the hornbeam, and Thorndyke, picking up a large stone, laid it on the spot. Then he sur-

veyed the scene thoughtfully, looking up and down the drive, and at the trees that
bordered it, and finally walked slowly to the space between the elm and the oak, scan-
ning the ground as he went. "There is no dearth of footprints," he remarked grimly, as
he looked down at the trampled earth.

"No; but the question is, whose are they?" said the inspector.

"Yes, that is the question," agreed Thorndyke; "and we will begin the solution by
identifying those of Pratt."

"I don't see how that will help us," said the inspector. "We know he was here."

"The hue-and-cry procession," remarked Thorndyke, "seems to have passed out
between the elm and the oak; elsewhere the ground seems pretty clear."

He walked around the elm, still looking earnestly at the ground, and presently
continued:

"Now, here, in the soft earth bordering the turf, are the prints of a pair of smallish feet wearing pointed boots—a rather short man, evidently, by the size of foot and
length of stride, and he doesn't seem to have belonged to the procession. But I don't
see Pratt's; he doesn't seem to have come off the hard gravel."

He continued to walk slowly toward the hornbeam, with his eyes fixed on the
ground. Suddenly he halted, and stooped with an eager look at the earth; and, as Fox
and I approached, he stood up and pointed.

"Pratt's footprints—faint and fragmentary, but unmistakable. And now, inspector, you see their importance. They furnish the time factor in respect to the other
footprints. Look at this one, and then look at that."

He pointed from one to another of the faint impressions of the dead man's foot.

"You mean that there are signs of a struggle?" said Fox.

"I mean more than that," replied Thorndyke. "Here is one of Pratt's footprints
treading into the print of a small, pointed foot; and there, at the edge of the gravel, is
another of Pratt's, nearly obliterated by the tread of a pointed foot. Obviously, the
first footprint was made before Pratt's, and the second one after his; and the necessary
inference is that the owner of the pointed foot was here at the same time as Pratt."

"Then he must have been the murderer!" exclaimed Fox.

"Presumably," answered Thorndyke; "but let us see whither he went."

"You notice, in the first place, that the man stood close to this tree,"—he indicated
the hornbeam,—"and that he went toward the elm. Let us follow him. He passes the
elm, you see, and you will observe that these tracks form a regular series, leading from
the hornbeam and not mixed up with the marks of the struggle. They were, therefore,
probably made after the murder. You will also notice that they pass along the backs of
the trees—outside the avenue, that is. What does that suggest to you?"

"It suggests to me," I said, when the inspector had shaken his head hopelessly, "that there was possibly some one in the avenue when the man was stealing off."

"Precisely," said Thorndyke. "The body was found not more than nine minutes after Pratt arrived here. But the murder must have taken some time. Let us follow the tracks. They pass the elm, and go behind the next tree. But wait! there is something odd here."

He passed behind the great pollard oak, and looked down at the soft earth at its roots.

"Here is a pair of impressions much deeper than the rest, and they are not a part of the track, since their toes point toward the tree. What do you make of that?"

Without waiting for an answer, he began closely to scan the bole of the tree, and especially a large, warty protuberance about three feet from the ground. On the bark above this was a vertical mark, as if something had scraped down the tree, and from the wart itself a dead twig had been newly broken off and lay upon the ground. Thorndyke set his foot on the protuberance, and, springing up, brought his eye above the level of the crown, from which the great boughs branched out.

"Ah!" he exclaimed. "Here is something much more definite."

He scrambled up into the crown of the tree, and, having glanced quickly around, beckoned to us. I stepped upon the projecting stump, and, as my eyes rose above the crown, I perceived the brown, shiny impression of a hand on the edge. Climbing into the crown, I was quickly followed by the inspector, and we both stood up by Thorndyke between the three boughs. From where we stood we looked on the upper side of the great limb that swept out across the avenue; and there, on its lichen-covered surface, we saw the imprints, in reddish-brown, of a pair of open hands.

"You notice," said Thorndyke, leaning out upon the bough, "that he is a short man—I cannot conveniently place my hands so low. You also note that he has both forefingers intact, and so is certainly not Ellis."

"If you mean to say, sir, that these marks were made by the murderer," said Fox, "I say it is impossible. Why, that would mean that he was here looking down at us when we were searching for him with the hounds! The presence of the hounds proves that this man could not have been the murderer."

"On the contrary," said Thorndyke, "the presence of this man with bloody hands confirms the other evidence, which all indicates that the hounds were never on the murderer's trail at all. Come, now, inspector, I put it to you: Here is a murdered man. The murderer almost certainly has blood upon his hands. And here is a man with bloody hands lurking in a tree within a few feet of the corpse, and within a few minutes of its discovery—as is shown by the footprints. What are the reasonable probabilities?"

"But you are forgetting the bloodhounds, sir, and the murderer's knife," urged the inspector.

"Tut, tut, man!" exclaimed Thorndyke. "Those bloodhounds are a positive obsession. But I see a sergeant coming up the drive—with the knife, I hope. Perhaps that will solve the riddle for us."

The sergeant, who carried a small despatch-box, halted opposite the tree in some surprise while we descended, when he came forward, with a military salute, and handed the box to the inspector; who forthwith unlocked it, and, lifting the lid, displayed an object wrapped in a pocket handkerchief.

"There is the knife, sir," said he, "just as I received it. The handkerchief is the sergeant's."

Thorndyke unrolled the handkerchief, and took from it a large-sized Norwegian knife, which he looked at critically and handed to me. While I was inspecting the blade, he shook out the handkerchief, and, having looked it over on both sides, turned to the sergeant and asked:

"At what time did you pick up this knife?"

"About seven fifteen, sir, directly after the hounds had started. I was careful to pick it up by the ring, and I wrapped it in the handkerchief at once."

"Seven fifteen," said Thorndyke—"less than half an hour after the murder. That is very singular. Do you observe the state of this handkerchief? There is not a mark on it, not a trace of any bloodstain, which shows that when the knife was picked up the blood on it was dry. Things dry slowly, if they dry at all, in the air of an autumn evening. The appearances seem to suggest that the blood on the knife was dry when it was thrown down. By the way, sergeant, what do you scent your handkerchief with?"

"Scent, sir!" exclaimed the astonished officer. "Me scent my handkerchief! No, sir, certainly not. Never used scent in my life, sir."

Thorndyke held out the handkerchief, and the sergeant sniffed at it incredulously.

"It certainly does seem to smell of scent," he admitted, "but it must be the knife."

The same idea having occurred to me, I applied the handle of the knife to my nose, and instantly detected the sickly sweet odor of musk.

"The question is," said the inspector, when the two articles had been tested by us all, "was it the knife that scented the handkerchief or the handkerchief that scented the knife?"

"You heard what the sergeant said," replied Thorndyke. "There was no scent on the handkerchief when the knife was wrapped in it. Do you know, inspector, this scent seems to me to offer a very curious suggestion. Consider the facts of the case: the distinct trail leading straight to Ellis, who is nevertheless found to be without a scratch or a spot of blood; the obvious inconsistencies in the case; and now this knife, apparently dropped with dried blood on it, and scented with musk. To me it suggests a carefully planned, coolly premeditated crime. The murderer knew about the General's blood-hounds, and made use of them as a blind. He left this knife, smeared with blood and tainted with musk, to furnish a scent. No doubt some object also scented with musk would be drawn over the ground to give the trail. It is only a suggestion, of course, but it is worth considering."

"But, sir," the inspector objected eagerly, "if the murderer had handled the knife, it would haves scented him too."

"Exactly; so, as the man is evidently not a fool, we may assume that he did not handle it. He will have left it here in readiness, hidden in some place whence he could knock it down, say with a stick, without touching it."

"Perhaps in this very tree, sir," suggested the sergeant, pointing to the oak.

"No," said Thorndyke; "he would hardly have hidden in the tree where the knife had been. The hounds might have scented the place instead of following the trail at once. The most likely hiding-place for the knife would be nearest the spot where it was found."

He walked over to the stone that marked the spot, and, looking round, continued: "You see, that hornbeam is much the nearest, and its flat crown would be very convenient for the purpose—easily reached even by a short man, as he appears to be. Let us see if there are any traces of it. Perhaps you will give me a 'back up,' sergeant, as we haven't a ladder."

The sergeant assented with a faint grin, and, stooping beside the tree in an attitude suggesting the game of leap-frog, placed his hands firmly on his knees. Grasping a stout branch, Thorndyke swung himself up on the sergeant's broad back, whence he looked down into the crown of the tree. Then, parting the branches, he stepped on to the ledge and disappeared into the central hollow.

When he reappeared, he held in his hands two very singular objects: a pair of iron crucible-tongs and an artist's brush-case of black-japanned tin. The former article he handed down to me, but the brush-case he held carefully by its wire handle as he dropped to the ground.

"The significance of these things is, I think, obvious," he said. "The tongs were used to handle the knife with, and the case to carry it in, so that it should not scent the murderer's clothes or bag. It was very carefully planned."

"If that is so," said the inspector, "the inside of the case ought to smell of musk."

"No doubt," said Thorndyke. "But, before we open it, there is a rather important matter to be attended to. Will you give me the vitogen powder, Jervis?"

I opened the canvas-covered "research case," and took from it an object like a diminutive pepper-caster—an iodoform dredger, in fact—and handed it to him. Grasping the brush-case by its wire handle, he freely sprinkled the pale yellow powder from the dredger all around the pull-off lid, tapping the top with his knuckles to make the fine particles spread. Then he blew off the superfluous powder, and the two police officers gave a gasp of joy; for now, on the black background, there stood out plainly a number of finger-prints, so clear and distinct that the ridge-pattern could easily be made out.

"These will probably be his right hand," said Thorndyke. "Now for the left." He treated the body of the case in the same way, and the entire surface was spotted with oval white impressions. "Now, Jervis," said he, "if you will put on a glove and pull off the lid, we can test the inside."

The lid came off without difficulty, and, as it separated with a hollow sound, a faint, musky odor exhaled from its interior.

"The remainder of the inquiry," said Thorndyke, "will be best conducted at the police station, where, also, we can photograph these finger-prints. That is where the value of the finger-prints comes in. If he is an old 'lag,' his prints will be at Scotland Yard."

"That's true, sir," said the inspector. "I suppose you want to see Ellis."

"I want to see that purse," replied Thorndyke. "That is probably the other end of the clue."

As soon as we arrived at the station, the inspector unlocked a safe and brought out a parcel. "These are Ellis' things," said he, as he opened it, "and that is the purse."

He handed Thorndyke a small pigskin pouch, which my colleague opened, and, having smelled of the inside, passed to me. The odor of musk was plainly perceptible.

"It has probably tainted the other contents of the parcel," said Thorndyke, sniffing at each article in turn; "but they all seem odorless to me, whereas the purse smells quite distinctly."

Having taken the finger-prints of the accused man, Ellis, and made several photographs of the strange finger-prints, we returned to town that evening. Thorndyke gave a few parting injunctions to the inspector.

"Remember," he said, "that the man must have washed his hands before he could appear in public. Search the banks of every pond, ditch, and stream in the neighborhood for footprints like those in the avenue, and, if you find any, search the bottom of the water thoroughly, for he is quite likely to have dropped the knife into the mud."

The photographs that we handed in at Scotland Yard that night enabled the experts to identify the finger-prints as those of Francis Dobbs, an escaped convict. The two photographs, profile and full-face, which were attached to his record, were sent down to Baysford, with a description of the man, and were in due course identified with a somewhat mysterious individual who passed by the name of Rufus Pembury, and who had lived in the neighborhood as a private gentleman for about two years. But Rufus Pembury was not to be found, either at his genteel house or elsewhere. All that was known was that, on the day after the murder, he had converted his entire "personalty" into "bearer securities," and had vanished from mortal ken. Nor has he ever been heard of to this day.

THE SCARLET THREAD

Jacques Futrelle

I

The Thinking Machine—Professor Augustus S. F. X. Van Dusen, Ph.D., LL.D., F.R.S., M.D., etc., scientist and logician—listened intently and without comment to a weird, seemingly inexplicable story. Hutchinson Hatch, reporter, was telling it. The bowed figure of the savant lay at ease in a large chair. The enormous head with its bushy yellow hair was thrown back, the thin, white fingers were pressed tip to tip and the blue eyes, narrowed to mere slits, squinted aggressively upward. The scientist was in a receptive mood.

"From the beginning, every fact you know," he had requested.

"It's all out in the Back Bay," the reporter explained. "There is a big apartment house there, a fashionable establishment, in a side street, just off Commonwealth Avenue. It is five stories in all, and is cut up into small suites, of two and three rooms with bath. These suites are handsomely, even luxuriously furnished, and are occupied by people who can afford to pay big rents. Generally these are young unmarried men, although in several cases they are husband and wife. It is a house of every modern improvement, elevator service, hall boys, liveried door men, spacious corridors and all that. It has both the gas and electric systems of lighting. Tenants are at liberty to use either or both.

"A young broker, Weldon Henley, occupies one of the handsomest of these suites, being on the second floor, in front. He has met with considerable success in the Street. He is a bachelor and lives there alone. There is no personal servant. He dabbles in photography as a hobby, and is said to be remarkably expert.

"Recently there was a report that he was to be married this Winter to a beautiful Virginia girl who has been visiting Boston from time to time, a Miss Lipscomb— Charlotte Lipscomb, of Richmond. Henley has never denied or affirmed this rumor, although he has been asked about it often. Miss Lipscomb is impossible of access even when she visits Boston. Now she is in Virginia, I understand, but will return to Boston later in the season."

The reporter paused, lighted a cigarette and leaned forward in his chair, gazing steadily into the inscrutable eyes of the scientist.

"When Henley took the suite he requested that all the electric lighting apparatus be removed from his apartments," he went on. "He had taken a long lease of the place, and this was done. Therefore he uses only gas for lighting purposes, and he usually keeps one of his gas jets burning low all night."

"Bad, bad for his health," commented the scientist.

"Now comes the mystery of the affair," the reporter went on. "It was five weeks or so ago Henley retired as usual—about midnight. He locked his door on the inside—he is positive of that—and awoke about four o'clock in the morning nearly asphyxiated by gas. He was barely able to get up and open the window to let in the fresh air. The gas jet he had left burning was out, and the suite was full of gas."

"Accident, possibly," said The Thinking Machine. "A draught through the apartments; a slight diminution of gas pressure; a hundred possibilities."

"So it was presumed," said the reporter. "Of course it would have been impossible for—"

"Nothing is impossible," said the other, tartly. "Don't say that. It annoys me exceedingly."

"Well, then, it seems highly improbable that the door had been opened or that anyone came into the room and did this deliberately," the newspaper man went on, with a slight smile. "So Henley said nothing about this; attributed it to accident. The next night he lighted his gas as usual, but he left it burning a little brighter. The same thing happened again."

"Ah," and The Thinking Machine changed his position a little. "The second time."

"And again he awoke just in time to save himself," said Hatch. "Still he attributed the affair to accident, and determined to avoid a recurrence of the affair by doing away with the gas at night. Then he got a small night lamp and used this for a week or more."

"Why does he have a light at all?" asked the scientist, testily.

"I can hardly answer that," replied Hatch. "I may say, however, that he is of a very nervous temperament, and gets up frequently during the night. He reads occasionally when he can't sleep. In addition to that he has slept with a light going all his life; it's a habit."

"Go on."

"One night he looked for the night lamp, but it had disappeared—at least he couldn't find it—so he lighted the gas again. The fact of the gas having twice before gone out had been dismissed as a serious possibility. Next morning at five o'clock a bell boy, passing through the hall, smelled gas and made a quick investigation. He decided it came from Henley's place, and rapped on the door. There was no answer. It ultimately developed that it was necessary to smash in the door. There on the bed they found Henley unconscious with the gas pouring into the room from the jet which he had left lighted. He was revived in the air, but for several hours was deathly sick."

"Why was the door smashed in?" asked The Thinking Machine. "Why not unlocked?"

"It was done because Henley had firmly barred it," Hatch explained. "He had become suspicious, I suppose, and after the second time he always barred his door and fastened every window before he went to sleep. There may have been a fear that some one used a key to enter."

"Well?" asked the scientist. "After that?"

"Three weeks or so elapsed, bringing the affair down to this morning," Hatch went on. "Then the same thing happened a little differently. For instance, after the third time the gas went out Henley decided to find out for himself what caused it, and so expressed himself to a few friends who knew of the mystery. Then, night after night, he lighted the gas as usual and kept watch. It was never disturbed during all that time, burning steadily all night. What sleep he got was in daytime.

"Last night Henley lay awake for a time; then, exhausted and tired, fell asleep. This morning early he awoke; the room was filled with gas again. In some way my city editor heard of it and asked me to look into the mystery."

That was all. The two men were silent for a long time, and finally The Thinking Machine turned to the reporter.

"Does anyone else in the house keep gas going all night?" he asked.

"I don't know," was the reply. "Most of them, I know, use electricity."

"Nobody else has been overcome as he has been?"

"No. Plumbers have minutely examined the lighting system all over the house and found nothing wrong."

"Does the gas in the house all come through the same meter?"

"Yes, so the manager told me. This meter, a big one, is just off the engine room. I supposed it possible that some one shut it off there on these nights long enough to extinguish the lights all over the house, then turned it on again. That is, presuming that it was done purposely. Do you think it was an attempt to kill Henley?"

"It might be," was the reply. "Find out for me just who in the house uses gas; also if anyone else leaves a light burning all night; also what opportunity anyone would have to get at the meter, and then something about Henley's love affair with Miss Lipscomb. Is there anyone else? If so, who? Where does he live? When you find out these things come back here."

• • •

That afternoon at one o'clock Hatch returned to the apartments of The Thinking Machine, with excitement plainly apparent on his face.

"Well? "asked the scientist.

"A French girl, Louise Regnier, employed as a maid by Mrs. Standing in the house, was found dead in her room on the third floor to-day at noon," Hatch explained quickly. "It looks like suicide."

"How?" asked The Thinking Machine.

"The people who employed her—husband and wife—have been away for a couple of days," Hatch rushed on. "She was in the suite alone. This noon she had not appeared, there was an odor of gas and the door was broken in. Then she was found dead."

"With the gas turned on?"

"With the gas turned on. She was asphyxiated."

"Dear me, dear me," exclaimed the scientist. He arose and took up his hat. "Let's go see what this is all about."

II

When Professor Van Dusen and Hatch arrived at the apartment house they had been preceded by the Medical Examiner and the police. Detective Mallory, whom both knew, was moving about in the apartment where the girl had been found dead. The body had been removed and a telegram sent to her employers in New York.

"Too late," said Mallory, as they entered.

"What was it, Mr. Mallory?" asked the scientist.

"Suicide," was the reply. "No question of it. It happened in this room," and he led the way into the third room of the suite. "The maid, Miss Regnier, occupied this, and was here alone last night. Mr. and Mrs. Standing, her employers, have gone to New York for a few days. She was left alone, and killed herself."

Without further questioning The Thinking Machine went over to the bed, from which the girl's body had been taken, and, stooping beside it, picked up a book. It was a novel by "The Duchess." He examined this critically, then, standing on a chair, he examined the gas jet. This done, he stepped down and went to the window of the little room. Finally The Thinking Machine turned to the detective.

"Just how much was the gas turned on?" he asked.

"Turned on full," was the reply.

"Were both the doors of the room closed?"

"Both, yes."

"Any cotton, or cloth, or anything of the sort stuffed in the cracks of the window?"

"No. It's a tight-fitting window, anyway. Are you trying to make a mystery out of this?"

"Cracks in the doors stuffed?" The Thinking Machine went on.

"No." There was a smile about the detective's lips.

The Thinking Machine, on his knees, examined the bottom of one of the doors, that which led into the hall. The lock of this door had been broken when employees burst into the room. Having satisfied himself here and at the bottom of the other door, which connected with the bedroom adjoining, The Thinking Machine again climbed on a chair and examined the doors at the top.

"Both transoms closed, I suppose?" he asked.

"Yes," was the reply. "You can't make anything but suicide out of it," explained the detective. "The Medical Examiner has given that as his opinion—and everything I find indicates it."

"All right," broke in The Thinking Machine abruptly. "Don't let us keep you."

After awhile Detective Mallory went away. Hatch and the scientist went down to the office floor, where they saw the manager. He seemed to be greatly distressed, but was willing to do anything he could in the matter.

"Is your night engineer perfectly trustworthy?" asked The Thinking Machine.

"Perfectly," was the reply. "One of the best and most reliable men I ever met. Alert and wide-awake."

"Can I see him a moment? The night man, I mean?"

"Certainly," was the reply. "He's downstairs. He sleeps there. He's probably up by this time. He sleeps usually till one o'clock in the daytime, being up all night."

"Do you supply gas for your tenants?"

"Both gas and electricity are included in the rent of the suites. Tenants may use one or both."

"And the gas all comes through one meter?"

"Yes, one meter. It's just off the engine room."

"I suppose there's no way of telling just who in the house uses gas?"

"No. Some do and some don't. I don't know."

This was what Hatch had told the scientist. Now together they went to the basement, and there met the night engineer, Charles Burlingame, a tall, powerful, clean-cut man, of alert manner and positive speech. He gazed with a little amusement at the slender, almost childish figure of The Thinking Machine and the grotesquely large head.

"You are in the engine room or near it all night every night?" began The Thinking Machine.

"I haven't missed a night in four years," was the reply.

"Anybody ever come here to see you at night?"

"Never. It's against the rules."

"The manager or a hall boy?"

"Never."

"In the last two months?" The Thinking Machine persisted.

"Not in the last two years," was the positive reply. "I go on duty every night at seven o'clock, and I am on duty until seven in the morning. I don't believe I've seen anybody in the basement here with me between those hours for a year at least."

The Thinking Machine was squinting steadily into the eyes of the engineer, and for a time both were silent. Hatch moved about the scrupulously clean engine room and nodded to the day engineer, who sat leaning back against the wall. Directly in front of him was the steam gauge.

"Have you a fireman?" was The Thinking Machine's next question.

"No. I fire myself," said the night man. "Here's the coal," and he indicated a bin within half a dozen feet of the mouth of the boiler.

"I don't suppose you ever had occasion to handle the gas meter?" insisted The Thinking Machine.

"Never touched it in my life," said the other. "I don't know anything about meters, anyway."

"And you never drop off to sleep at night for a few minutes when you get lonely? Doze, I mean?"

The engineer grinned good-naturedly.

"Never had any desire to, and besides I wouldn't have the chance," he explained. "There's a time check here,"—and he indicated it. "I have to punch that every half hour all night to prove that I have been awake."

"Dear me, dear me," exclaimed The Thinking Machine, irritably. He went over and examined the time check—a revolving paper disk with hours marked on it, made to move by the action of a clock, the face of which showed in the middle.

"Besides there's the steam gauge to watch," went on the engineer. "No engineer would dare go to sleep. There might be an explosion."

"Do you know Mr. Weldon Henley?" suddenly asked The Thinking Machine.

"Who?" asked Burlingame.

"Weldon Henley?"

"No-o," was the slow response. "Never heard of him. Who is he?"

"One of the tenants, on the second floor, I think."

"Lord, I don't know any of the tenants. What about him?"

"When does the inspector come here to read the meter?"

"I never saw him. I presume in daytime, eh Bill?" and he turned to the day engineer.

"Always in daytime—usually about noon," Bill from his corner.

"Any other entrance to the basement except this way—and you could see anyone coming here this way I suppose?"

"Sure I could see 'em. There's no other entrance to the cellar except the coal hole in the sidewalk in front."

"Two big electric lights in front of the building, aren't there?"

"Yes. They go all night."

A slightly puzzled expression crept into the eyes of The Thinking Machine. Hatch knew from the persistency of the questions that he was not satisfied; yet he was not able to fathom or to understand all the queries. In some way they had to do with the possibility of some one having access to the meter.

"Where do you usually sit at night here?" was the next question.

"Over there where Bill's sitting. I always sit there."

The Thinking Machine crossed the room to Bill, a typical, grimy-handed man of his class.

"May I sit there a moment?" he asked.

Bill arose lazily, and The Thinking Machine sank down into the chair. From this point he could see plainly through the opening into the basement proper—there was no door—the gas meter of enormous proportions through which all the gas in the house passed. An electric light in the door made it bright as daylight. The Thinking Machine noted these things, arose, nodded his thanks to the two men and, still with the puzzled expression on his face, led the way upstairs. There the manager was still in his office.

"I presume you examine and know that the time check in the engineer's room is properly punched every half-hour during the night?" he asked.

"Yes. I examine the dial every day—have them here, in fact, each with the date on it."

"May I see them?"

Now the manager was puzzled. He produced the cards, one for each day, and for half an hour The Thinking Machine studied them minutely. At the end of that time, when he arose and Hatch looked at him inquiringly, he saw still the perplexed expression.

After urgent solicitation, the manager admitted them to the apartments of Weldon Henley. Mr. Henley himself had gone to his office in State Street. Here The Thinking Machine did several things which aroused the curiosity of the manager, one of which was to minutely study the gas jets. Then The Thinking Machine opened one of the front windows and glanced out into the street. Below fifteen feet was the sidewalk; above was the solid front of the building, broken only by a flagpole which, properly roped, extended from the hall window of the next floor above out over the sidewalk a distance of twelve feet or so.

"Ever use that flagpole?" he asked the manager.

"Rarely," said the manager. "On holidays sometimes—Fourth of July and such times. We have a big flag for it."

From the apartments The Thinking Machine led the way to the hall, up the stairs and to the flagpole. Leaning out of this window, he looked down toward the window of the apartments he had just left. Then he inspected the rope of the flagpole, drawing it through his slender hands slowly and carefully. At last he picked off a slender thread of scarlet and examined it.

"Ah," he exclaimed. Then to Hatch: "Let's go, Mr. Hatch. Thank you," this last to the manager, who had been a puzzled witness.

Once on the street, side by side with The Thinking Machine, Hatch was bursting with questions, but he didn't ask them. He knew it would be useless. At last The Thinking Machine broke the silence.

"That girl, Miss Regnier, *was murdered*," he said suddenly, positively. "There have been four attempts to murder Henley."

"How?" asked Hatch, startled.

"By a scheme so simple that neither you nor I nor the police have ever heard of it being employed," was the astonishing reply. "*It is perfectly horrible in its simplicity.*"

"What was it?" Hatch insisted, eagerly.

"It would be futile to discuss that now," was the rejoinder. "There has been murder. We know how. Now the question is—who? What person would have a motive to kill Henley?"

III

There was a pause as they walked on.

"Where are we going?" asked Hatch finally.

"Come up to my place and let's consider this matter a bit further," replied The Thinking Machine.

Not another word was spoken by either until half an hour later, in the small laboratory. For a long time the scientist was thoughtful—deeply thoughtful. Once he took down a volume from a shelf and Hatch glanced at the title. It was "Gases: Their Properties." After awhile he returned this to the shelf and took down another, on which the reporter caught the title, "Anatomy."

"Now, Mr. Hatch," said The Thinking Machine in his perpetually crabbed voice, "we have a most remarkable riddle. It gains this remarkable aspect from its very simplicity. It is not, however, necessary to go into that now. I will make it clear to you when we know the motives.

"As a general rule, the greatest crimes never come to light because the greatest criminals, their perpetrators, are too clever to be caught. Here we have what I might call a great crime committed with a subtle simplicity that is wholly disarming, and a greater crime even than this was planned. This was to murder Weldon Henley. The first thing for you to do is to see Mr. Henley and warn him of his danger. Asphyxiation will not be attempted again, but there is a possibility of poison, a pistol shot, a knife, anything almost. As a matter of fact, he is in great peril.

"Superficially, the death of Miss Regnier, the maid, looks to be suicide. Instead it is the fruition of a plan which has been tried time and again against Henley. There is a possibility that Miss Regnier was not an intentional victim of the plot, but the fact remains that she was murdered. Why? Find the motive for the plot to murder Mr. Henley and you will know why."

The Thinking Machine reached over to the shelf, took a book, looked at it a moment, then went on:

"The first question to determine positively is: Who hated Weldon Henley sufficiently to desire his death? You say he is a successful man in the Street. Therefore there is a possibility that some enemy there is at the bottom of the affair, yet it seems hardly probable. If by his operations Mr. Henley ever happened to wreck another man's fortune find this man and find out all about him. He may be the man. There will be innumerable questions arising from this line of inquiry to a man of your resources. Leave none of them unanswered.

"On the other hand there is Henley's love affair. Had he a rival who might desire his death? Had he any rival? If so, find out all about him. He may be the man who planned all this. Here, too, there will be questions arising which demand answers. Answer them—all of them—fully and clearly before you see me again.

"Was Henley ever a party to a liaison of any kind? Find that out, too. A vengeful woman or a discarded sweetheart of a vengeful woman, you know, will go to any extreme. The rumor of his engagement to Miss—Miss—"

"Miss Lipscomb," Hatch supplied.

"The rumor of his engagement to Miss Lipscomb might have caused a woman whom he had once been interested in or who was once interested in him to attempt his life. The subtler murders—that is, the ones which are most attractive as problems—are nearly always the work of a cunning woman. I know nothing about women myself," he hastened to explain; "but Lombroso has taken that attitude. Therefore, see if there is a woman."

Most of these points Hatch had previously seen—seen with the unerring eye of a clever newspaper reporter—yet there were several which had not occurred to him. He nodded his understanding.

"Now the center of the affair, of course," The Thinking Machine continued, "is the apartment house where Henley lives. The person who attempted his life either lives there or has ready access to the place, and frequently spends the night there. This is a vital question for you to answer. I am leaving all this to you because you know better how to do these things than I do. That's all, I think. When these things are all learned come back to me."

The Thinking Machine arose as if the interview were at an end, and Hatch also arose, reluctantly. An idea was beginning to dawn in his mind.

"Does it occur to you that there is any connection whatever between Henley and Miss Regnier?" he asked.

"It is possible," was the reply. "I had thought of that. If there is a connection it is not apparent yet."

"Then how—how was it she—she was killed, or killed herself, whichever may be true, and—"

"The attempt to kill Henley killed her. That's all I can say now."

"That all?" asked Hatch, after a pause.

"No. Warn Mr. Henley immediately that he is in grave danger. Remember the person who has planned this will probably go to any extreme. I don't know Mr. Henley, of course, but from the fact that he always had a light at night I gather that he is a timid sort of man—not necessarily a coward, but a man lacking in stamina—therefore, one who might better disappear for a week or so until the mystery is cleared up. Above all, impress upon him the importance of the warning."

The Thinking Machine opened his pocketbook and took from it the scarlet thread which he had picked from the rope of the flagpole.

"Here, I believe, is the real clew to the problem," he explained to Hatch. "What does it seem to be?"

Hatch examined it closely.

"I should say a strand from a Turkish bath robe," was his final judgment.

"Possibly. Ask some cloth expert what he makes of it, then if it sounds promising look into it. Find out if by any possibility it can be any part of any garment worn by any person in the apartment house."

"But it's so slight—" Hatch began.

"I know," the other interrupted, tartly. "It's slight, but I believe it is a part of the wearing apparel of the person, man or woman, who has four times attempted to kill Mr. Henley and who did kill the girl. Therefore, it is important."

Hatch looked at him quickly.

"Well, how—in what manner—did it come where you found it?"

"Simple enough," said the scientist. "It is a wonder that there were not more pieces of it—that's all."

Perplexed by his instructions, but confident of results, Hatch left The Thinking Machine. What possible connection could this tiny bit of scarlet thread, found on a flagpole, have with some one shutting off the gas in Henley's rooms? How did any one go into Henley's rooms to shut off the gas? How was it Miss Regnier was dead? What was the manner of her death?

A cloth expert in a great department store turned his knowledge on the tiny bit of scarlet for the illumination of Hatch, but he could go no further than to say that it seemed to be part of a Turkish bath robe.

"Man or woman's?" asked Hatch.

"The material from which bath robes are made is the same for both men and women," was the reply. "I can say nothing else. Of course there's not enough of it to even guess at the pattern of the robe."

Then Hatch went to the financial district and was ushered into the office of Weldon Henley, a slender, handsome man of thirty-two or three years, pallid of face and nervous in manner. He still showed the effect of the gas poisoning, and there was even a trace of a furtive fear—fear of something, he himself didn't know what—in his actions.

Henley talked freely to the newspaper man of certain things, but of other things was resentfully reticent. He admitted his engagement to Miss Lipscomb, and finally even admitted that Miss Lipscomb's hand had been sought by another man, Regnault Cabell, formerly of Virginia.

"Could you give me his address?" asked Hatch.

"He lives in the same apartment house with me—two floors above," was the reply.

Hatch was startled; startled more than he would have cared to admit.

"Are you on friendly terms with him?" he asked.

"Certainly," said Henley. "I won't say anything further about this matter. It would be unwise for obvious reasons."

"I suppose you consider that this turning on of the gas was an attempt on your life?"

"I can't suppose anything else."

Hatch studied the pallid face closely as he asked the next question.

"Do you know Miss Regnier was found dead to-day?"

"Dead?" exclaimed the other, and he arose. "Who—what—who is she?"

It seemed a distinct effort for him to regain control of himself.

The reporter detailed then the circumstances of the finding of the girl's body, and the broker listened without comment. From that time forward all the reporter's questions were either parried or else met with a flat refusal to answer. Finally Hatch repeated to him the warning which he had from The Thinking Machine, and feeling that he had accomplished little, went away.

At eight o'clock that night—a night of complete darkness—Henley was found unconscious, lying in a little used walk in the Common. There was a bullet hole through his left shoulder, and he was bleeding profusely. He was removed to the hospital, where he regained consciousness for just a moment.

"Who shot you?" he was asked.

"None of your business," he replied, and lapsed into unconsciousness.

IV

Entirely unaware of this latest attempt on the life of the broker, Hutchinson Hatch steadily pursued his investigations. They finally led him to an intimate friend of Regnault Cabell. The young Southerner had apartments on the fourth floor of the big house off Commonwealth Avenue, directly over those Henley occupied, but two flights higher up. This friend was a figure in the social set of the Back Bay. He talked to Hatch freely of Cabell.

"He's a good fellow," he explained, "one of the best I ever met, and comes of one of the best families Virginia ever had—a true F. F. V. He's pretty quick tempered and all that, but an excellent chap, and everywhere he has gone here he has made friends."

"He used to be in love with Miss Lipscomb of Virginia, didn't he?" asked Hatch, casually.

"Used to be?" the other repeated with a laugh. "He *is* in love with her. But recently he understood that she was engaged to Weldon Henley, a broker—you may have heard of him?—and that, I suppose, has dampened his ardor considerably. As a matter of fact, Cabell took the thing to heart. He used to know Miss Lipscomb in Virginia—she comes from another famous family there—and he seemed to think he had a prior claim on her."

Hatch heard all these things as any man might listen to gossip, but each additional fact was sinking into his mind, and each additional fact led his suspicions on deeper into the channel they had chosen.

"Cabell is pretty well to do," his informant went on, "not rich as we count riches in the North, but pretty well to do, and I believe he came to Boston because Miss Lipscomb spent so much of her time here. She is a beautiful young woman of twenty-two and extremely popular in the social world everywhere, particularly in Boston. Then there was the additional fact that Henley was here."

"No chance at all for Cabell?" Hatch suggested.

"Not the slightest," was the reply. "Yet despite the heartbreak he had, he was the first to congratulate Henley on winning her love. And he meant it, too."

"What's his attitude toward Henley now?" asked Hatch. His voice was calm, but there was an underlying tense note imperceptible to the other.

"They meet and speak and move in the same set. There's no love lost on either side, I don't suppose, but there is no trace of any ill feeling."

"Cabell doesn't happen to be a vindictive sort of man?"

"Vindictive?" and the other laughed. "No. He's like a big boy, forgiving, and all that; hot-tempered, though. I could imagine him in a fit of anger making a personal matter of it with Henley, but I don't think he ever did."

The mind of the newspaper man was rapidly focusing on one point; the rush of thoughts, questions and doubts silenced him for a moment. Then:

"How long has Cabell been in Boston?"

"Seven or eight months—that is, he has had apartments here for that long—but he has made several visits South. I suppose it's South. He has a trick of dropping out of sight occasionally. I understand that he intends to go South for good very soon. If I'm not mistaken, he is trying now to rent his suite."

Hatch looked suddenly at his informant; an idea of seeing Cabell and having a legitimate excuse for talking to him had occurred to him.

"I'm looking for a suite," he volunteered at last. "I wonder if you would give me a card of introduction to him? We might get together on it."

Thus it happened that half an hour later, about ten minutes past nine o'clock, Hatch was on his way to the big apartment house. In the office he saw the manager.

"Heard the news?" asked the manager.

"No," Hatch replied. "What is it?"

"Somebody's shot Mr. Henley as he was passing through the Common early to-night."

Hatch whistled his amazement.

"Is he dead?"

"No, but he is unconscious. The hospital doctors say it is a nasty wound, but not necessarily dangerous."

"Who shot him? Do they know?"

"He knows, but he won't say."

Amazed and alarmed by this latest development, an accurate fulfillment of The Thinking Machine's prophecy, Hatch stood thoughtful for a moment, then recovering his composure a little asked for Cabell.

"I don't think there's much chance of seeing him," said the manager. "He's going away on the midnight train—going South, to Virginia."

"Going away to-night?" Hatch gasped.

"Yes; it seems to have been rather a sudden determination. He was talking to me here half an hour or so ago, and said something about going away. While he was here the telephone boy told me that Henley had been shot; they had 'phoned from the hospital to inform us. Then Cabell seemed greatly agitated. He said he was going away to-night, if he could catch the midnight train, and now he's packing."

"I suppose the shooting of Henley upset him considerably?" the reporter suggested.

"Yes, I guess it did," was the reply. "They moved in the same set and belonged to the same clubs."

The manager sent Hatch's card of introduction to Cabell's apartments. Hatch went up and was ushered into a suite identical with that of Henley's in every respect save in minor details of furnishings. Cabell stood in the middle of the floor, with his personal belongings scattered about the room; his valet, evidently a Frenchman, was busily engaged in packing.

Cabell's greeting was perfunctorily cordial; he seemed agitated. His face was flushed and from time to time he ran his fingers through his long, brown hair. He stared at Hatch in a preoccupied fashion, then they fell into conversation about the rent of the apartments.

"I'll take almost anything reasonable," Cabell said hurriedly. "You see, I am going away to-night, rather more suddenly than I had intended, and I am anxious to get the lease off my hands. I pay two hundred dollars a month for these just as they are."

"May I look them over?" asked Hatch.

He passed from the front room into the next. Here, on a bed, was piled a huge lot of clothing, and the valet, with cleft fingers, was brushing and folding, preparatory to packing. Cabell was directly behind him.

"Quite comfortable, you see," he explained. "There's room enough if you are alone. Are you?"

"Oh, yes," Hatch replied.

"This other room here," Cabell explained, "is not in very tidy shape now. I have been out of the city for several weeks, and— What's the matter?" he demanded suddenly.

Hatch had turned quickly at the words and stared at him, then recovered himself with a start.

"I beg your pardon," he stammered. "I rather thought I saw you in town here a week or so ago—of course I didn't know you—and I was wondering if I could have been mistaken."

"Must have been," said the other easily. "During the time I was away a Miss ——, a friend of my sister's, occupied the suite. I'm afraid some of her things are here. She hasn't sent for them as yet. She occupied this room, I think; when I came back a few days ago she took another place and all her things haven't been removed."

"I see," remarked Hatch, casually. "I don't suppose there's any chance of her returning here unexpectedly if I should happen to take her apartments?"

"Not the slightest. She knows I am back, and thinks I am to remain. She was to send for these things."

Hatch gazed about the room ostentatiously. Across a trunk lay a Turkish bath robe with a scarlet stripe in it. He was anxious to get hold of it, to examine it closely. But he didn't dare to, then. Together they returned to the front room.

"I rather like the place," he said, after a pause, "but the price is—"

"Just a moment," Cabell interrupted. "Jean, before you finish packing that suit case be sure to put my bath robe in it. It's in the far room."

Then one question was settled for Hatch. After a moment the valet returned with the bath robe, which had been in the far room. It was Cabell's bath robe. As Jean passed the reporter an end of the robe caught on a corner of the trunk, and, stopping, the reporter unfastened it. A tiny strand of thread clung to the metal; Hatch detached it and stood idly twirling it in his fingers.

"As I was saying," he resumed, "I rather like the place, but the price is too much. Suppose you leave it in the hands of the manager of the house—"

"I had intended doing that," the Southerner interrupted.

"Well, I'll see him about it later," Hatch added.

With a cordial, albeit pre-occupied, handshake, Cabell ushered him out. Hatch went down in the elevator with a feeling of elation; a feeling that he had accomplished something. The manager was waiting to get into the lift.

"Do you happen to remember the name of the young lady who occupied Mr. Cabell's suite while he was away?" he asked.

"Miss Austin," said the manager, "but she's not young. She was about forty-five years old, I should judge."

"Did Mr. Cabell have his servant Jean with him?"

"Oh, no," said the manager. "The valet gave up the suite to Miss Austin entirely, and until Mr. Cabell returned occupied a room in the quarters we have for our own employees."

"Was Miss Austin ailing any way?" asked Hatch. "I saw a large number of medicine bottles upstairs."

"I don't know what was the matter with her," replied the manager, with a little puzzled frown. "She certainly was not a woman of sound mental balance—that is, she was eccentric, and all that. I think rather it was an act of charity for Mr. Cabell to let her have the suite in his absence. Certainly we didn't want her."

Hatch passed out and burst in eagerly upon The Thinking Machine in his laboratory. .

"Here," he said, and triumphantly he extended the tiny scarlet strand which he had received from The Thinking Machine, and the other of the identical color which came from Cabell's bath robe. "Is that the same?"

The Thinking Machine placed them under the microscope and examined them immediately. Later he submitted them to a chemical test.

"*It is the same*," he said, finally.

"Then the mystery is solved," said Hatch, conclusively.

V

The Thinking Machine stared steadily into the eager, exultant eyes of the newspaper man until Hatch at last began to fear that he had been precipitate. After awhile, under close scrutiny, the reporter began to feel convinced that he had made a mistake—he didn't quite see where, but it must be there, and the exultant manner passed. The voice of The Thinking Machine was like a cold shower.

"Remember, Mr. Hatch," he said, critically, "that unless every possible question has been considered one cannot boast of a solution. Is there any possible question lingering yet in your mind?"

The reporter silently considered that for a moment, then:

"Well, I have the main facts, anyway. There may be one or two minor questions left, but the principal ones are answered."

"Then tell me, to the minutest detail, what you have learned, what has happened."

Professor Van Dusen sank back in his old, familiar pose in the large arm chair and Hatch related what he had learned and what he surmised. He related, too, the peculiar circumstances surrounding the wounding of Henley, and right on down to the beginning and end of the interview with Cabell in the latter's apartments. The Thinking Machine was silent for a time, then there came a host of questions.

"Do you know where the woman—Miss Austin—is now?" was the first.

"No," Hatch had to admit.

"Or her precise mental condition?"

"No."

"Or her exact relationship to Cabell?"

"No."

"Do you know, then, what the valet, Jean, knows of the affair?"

"No, not that," said the reporter, and his face flushed under the close questioning. "He was out of the suite every night."

"Therefore might have been the very one who turned on the gas," the other put in testily.

"So far as I can learn, nobody could have gone into that room and turned on the gas," said the reporter, somewhat aggressively. "Henley barred the doors and windows and kept watch, night after night."

"Yet the moment he was exhausted and fell asleep the gas was turned on to kill him," said The Thinking Machine; "thus we see that *he was watched more closely than he watched.*"

"I see what you mean now," said Hatch, after a long pause.

"I should like to know what Henley and Cabell and the valet knew of the girl who was found dead," The Thinking Machine suggested. "Further, I should like to know if there was a good-sized mirror—not one set in a bureau or dresser—either in Henley's room or the apartments where the girl was found. Find out this for me and—never mind. I'll go with you."

The scientist left the room. When he returned he wore his coat and hat. Hatch arose mechanically to follow. For a block or more they walked along, neither speaking. The Thinking Machine was the first to break the silence:

"You believe Cabell is the man who attempted to kill Henley?"

"Frankly, yes," replied the newspaper man.

"Why?"

"Because he had the motive—disappointed love."

"How?"

"I don't know," Hatch confessed. "The doors of the Henley suite were closed. I don't see how anybody passed them."

"And the girl? Who killed her? How? Why?"

Disconsolately Hatch shook his head as he walked on. The Thinking Machine interpreted his silence aright.

"Don't jump at conclusions," he advised sharply. "You are confident Cabell was to blame for this—and he might have been, I don't know yet—but you can suggest nothing to show how he did it. I have told you before that imagination is half of logic."

At last the lights of the big apartment house where Henley lived came in sight. Hatch shrugged his shoulders. He had grave doubts—based on what he knew—whether The Thinking Machine would be able to see Cabell. It was nearly eleven o'clock and Cabell was to leave for the South at midnight.

"Is Mr. Cabell here?" asked the scientist of the elevator boy.

"Yes, just about to go, though. He won't see anyone."

"Hand him this note," instructed The Thinking Machine, and he scribbled something on a piece of paper. "He'll see us."

The boy took the paper and the elevator shot up to the fourth floor. After awhile he returned.

"He'll see you," he said.

"Is he unpacking?"

"After he read your note twice he told his valet to unpack," the boy replied.

"Ah, I thought so," said The Thinking Machine.

With Hatch, mystified and puzzled, following, The Thinking Machine entered the elevator to step out a second or so later on the fourth floor. As they left the car they saw the door of Cabell's apartment standing open; Cabell was in the door. Hatch traced a glimmer of anxiety in the eyes of the young man.

"Professor Van Dusen?" Cabell inquired.

"Yes," said the scientist. "It was of the utmost importance that I should see you, otherwise I should not have come at this time of night."

With a wave of his hand Cabell passed that detail.

"I was anxious to get away at midnight," he explained, "but, of course, now I shan't go, in view of your note. I have ordered my valet to unpack my things, at least until to-morrow."

The reporter and the scientist passed into the luxuriously furnished apartments. Jean, the valet, was bending over a suit case as they entered, removing some things he had been carefully placing there. He didn't look back or pay the least attention to the visitors.

"This is your valet?" asked The Thinking Machine.

"Yes," said the young man.

"French, isn't he?"

"Yes."

"Speak English at all?"

"Very badly," said Cabell. "I use French when I talk to him."

"Does he know that you are accused of murder?" asked The Thinking Machine, in a quiet, conversational tone.

The effect of the remark on Cabell was startling. He staggered back a step or so as if he had been struck in the face, and a crimson flush overspread his brow. Jean, the valet, straightened up suddenly and looked around. There was a queer expression, too, in his eyes; an expression which Hatch could not fathom.

"Murder?" gasped Cabell, at last.

"Yes, he speaks English all right," remarked The Thinking Machine. "Now, Mr. Cabell, will you please tell me just who Miss Austin is, and where she is, and her mental condition? Believe me, it may save you a great deal of trouble. What I said in the note is not exaggerated."

The young man turned suddenly and began to pace back and forth across the room. After a few minutes he paused before The Thinking Machine, who stood impatiently waiting for an answer.

"I'll tell you, yes," said Cabell, firmly. "Miss Austin is a middle-aged woman whom my sister befriended several times—was, in fact, my sister's governess when she was a child. Of late years she has not been wholly right mentally, and has suffered a great deal of privation. I had about concluded arrangements to put her in a private sanitarium. I permitted her to remain in these rooms in my absence, South. I did not take Jean—he lived in the quarters of the other employees of the place, and gave the apartment entirely to Miss Austin. It was simply an act of charity."

"What was the cause of your sudden determination to go South to-night?" asked the scientist.

"I won't answer that question," was the sullen reply.

There was a long, tense silence. Jean, the valet, came and went several times.

"How long has Miss Austin known Mr. Henley?"

"Presumably since she has been in these apartments," was the reply.

"Are you sure *you* are not Miss Austin?" demanded the scientist.

The question was almost staggering, not only to Cabell, but to Hatch. Suddenly, with flaming face, the young Southerner leaped forward as if to strike down The Thinking Machine.

"That won't do any good," said the scientist, coldly. "Are you sure you are not Miss Austin?" he repeated.

"Certainly I am not Miss Austin," responded Cabell, fiercely.

"Have you a mirror in these apartments about twelve inches by twelve inches?" asked The Thinking Machine, irrelevantly.

"I—I don't know," stammered the young man. "I—have we, Jean?"

"*Oui*," replied the valet.

"Yes," snapped The Thinking Machine. "Talk English, please. May I see it?"

The valet, without a word but with a sullen glance at the questioner, turned and left the room. He returned after a moment with the mirror. The Thinking Machine carefully examined the frame, top and bottom and on both sides. At last he looked up; again the valet was bending over a suit case.

"Do you use gas in these apartments?" the scientist asked suddenly.

"No," was the bewildered response. "What is all this, anyway?"

Without answering, The Thinking Machine drew a chair up under the chandelier where the gas and electric fixtures were and began to finger the gas tips. After awhile he climbed down and passed into the next room, with Hatch and Cabell, both hopelessly mystified, following. There the scientist went through the same process of fingering the gas jets. Finally, one of the gas tips came out in his hand.

"Ah," he exclaimed, suddenly, and Hatch knew the note of triumph in it. The jet from which the tip came was just on a level with his shoulder, set between a dressing table and a window. He leaned over and squinted at the gas pipe closely. Then he returned to the room where the valet was.

"Now, Jean," he began, in an even, calm voice, "please tell me *if you did or did not kill Miss Regnier purposely?*"

"I don't know what you mean," said the servant sullenly, angrily, as he turned on the scientist.

"You speak very good English now," was The Thinking Machine's terse comment. "Mr. Hatch, lock the door and use this 'phone to call the police."

Hatch turned to do as he was bid and saw a flash of steel in young Cabell's hand, which was drawn suddenly from a hip pocket. It was a revolver. The weapon glittered in the light, and Hatch flung himself forward. There was a sharp report, and a bullet was buried in the floor.

VI

Then came a fierce, hard fight for possession of the revolver. It ended with the weapon in Hatch's hand, and both he and Cabell blowing from the effort they had expended. Jean, the valet, had turned at the sound of the shot and started toward the door leading into the hall. The Thinking Machine had stepped in front of him, and now stood there with his back to the door. Physically he would have been a child in the hands of the valet, yet there was a look in his eyes which stopped him.

"Now, Mr. Hatch," said the scientist quietly, a touch of irony in his voice, "hand me the revolver, then 'phone for Detective Mallory to come here immediately. Tell him we have a murderer—and if he can't come at once get some other detective whom you know."

"Murderer!" gasped Cabell.

Uncontrollable rage was blazing in the eyes of the valet, and he made as if to throw The Thinking Machine aside, despite the revolver, when Hatch was at the telephone. As Jean started forward, however, Cabell stopped him with a quick, stern gesture. Suddenly the young Southerner turned on The Thinking Machine; but it was with a question.

"What does it all mean?" he asked, bewildered.

"It means that that man there," and The Thinking Machine indicated the valet by a nod of his head, "is a murderer—that he killed Louise Regnier; that he shot Weldon Henley on Boston Common, and that, with the aid of Miss Regnier, he had four times previously attempted to kill Mr. Henley. Is he coming, Mr. Hatch?"

"Yes," was the reply. "He says he'll be here directly."

"Do you deny it?" demanded The Thinking Machine of the valet.

"I've done nothing," said the valet sullenly. "I'm going out of here."

Like an infuriated animal he rushed forward. Hatch and Cabell seized him and bore him to the floor. There, after a frantic struggle, he was bound and the other three men sat down to wait for Detective Mallory. Cabell sank back in his chair with a perplexed frown on his face. From time to time he glanced at Jean. The flush of anger which had been on the valet's face was gone now; instead there was the pallor of fear.

"Won't you tell us?" pleaded Cabell impatiently.

"When Detective Mallory comes and takes his prisoner," said The Thinking Machine.

Ten minutes later they heard a quick step in the hall outside and Hatch opened the door. Detective Mallory entered and looked from one to another inquiringly.

"That's your prisoner, Mr. Mallory," said the scientist, coldly. "I charge him with the murder of Miss Regnier, whom you were so confident committed suicide; I charge him with five attempts on the life of Weldon Henley, four times by gas poisoning, in which Miss Regnier was his accomplice, and once by shooting. He is the man who shot Mr. Henley."

The Thinking Machine arose and walked over to the prostrate man, handing the revolver to Hatch. He glared down at Jean fiercely.

"Will you tell how you did it or shall I?" he demanded.

His answer was a sullen, defiant glare. He turned and picked up the square mirror which the valet had produced previously.

"That's where the screw was, isn't it?" he asked, as he indicated a small hole in the frame of the mirror. Jean stared at it and his head sank forward hopelessly. "And this is the bath robe you wore, isn't it?" he demanded again, and from the suit case he pulled out the garment with the scarlet stripe.

"I guess you got me all right," was the sullen reply.

"It might be better for you if you told the story then?" suggested The Thinking Machine.

"You know so much about it, tell it yourself."

"Very well," was the calm rejoinder. "I will. If I make any mistake you will correct me."

For a long time no one spoke. The Thinking Machine had dropped back into a chair and was staring through his thick glasses at the ceiling; his finger tips were pressed tightly together. At last he began:

"There are certain trivial gaps which only the imagination can supply until the matter is gone into more fully. I should have supplied these myself, but the arrest of this man, Jean, was precipitated by the attempted hurried departure of Mr. Cabell for the South to-night, and I did not have time to go into the case to the fullest extent.

"Thus, we begin with the fact that there were several clever attempts made to murder Mr. Henley. This was by putting out the gas which he habitually left burning in his room. It happened four times in all; thus proving that it was an attempt to kill him. If it had been only once it might have been accident, even twice it might have been accident, but the same accident does not happen four times at the same time of night.

"Mr. Henley finally grew to regard the strange extinguishing of the gas as an effort to kill him, and carefully locked and barred his door and windows each night. He believed that some one came into his apartments and put out the light, leaving the gas flow. This, of course, was not true. Yet the gas was put out. How? My first idea, a natural one, was that it was turned off for an instant at the meter, when the light would go out, then turned on again. This, I convinced myself, was not true. Therefore still the question—how?

"It is a fact—I don't know how widely known it is—but it is a fact that every gas light in this house might be extinguished at the same time from this room without leaving it. How? Simply by removing the gas jet tip and blowing into the gas pipe. It would not leave a jet in the building burning. It is due to the fact that the lung power is greater than the pressure of the gas in the pipes, and forces it out.

"Thus we have the method employed to extinguish the light in Mr. Henley's rooms, and all the barred and locked doors and windows would not stop it. At the same time it threatened the life of every other person in the house—that is, every other person who used gas. It was probably for this reason that the attempt was always made late at night, I should say three or four o'clock. That's when it was done, isn't it?" he asked suddenly of the valet.

Staring at The Thinking Machine in open-mouthed astonishment the valet nodded his acquiescence before he was fully aware of it.

"Yes, that's right," The Thinking Machine resumed complacently. "This was easily found out—comparatively. The next question was how was a watch kept on Mr. Henley? It would have done no good to extinguish the gas before he was asleep, or to have turned it on when he was not in his rooms. It might have led to a speedy discovery of just how the thing was done.

"There's a spring lock on the door of Mr. Henley's apartment. Therefore it would have been impossible for anyone to peep through the keyhole. There are no cracks through which one might see. How was this watch kept? How was the plotter to satisfy himself positively of the time when Mr. Henley was asleep? How was it the gas was put out at no time of the score or more nights Mr. Henley himself kept watch? Obviously he was watched through a window.

"No one could climb out on the window ledge and look into Mr. Henley's apartments. No one could see into that apartment from the street—that is, could see whether Mr. Henley was asleep or even in bed. They could see the light. Watch was kept with the aid offered by the flagpole, supplemented with a mirror—this mirror. A screw was driven into the frame—it has been removed now—it was swung on the flagpole rope and pulled out to the end of the pole, facing the building. To a man standing in the hall window of the third floor it offered precisely the angle necessary to reflect the interior of Mr. Henley's suite, possibly even showed him in bed through a narrow opening in the curtain. There is no shade on the windows of that suite; heavy curtains instead. Is that right?"

Again the prisoner was surprised into a mute acquiescence.

"I saw the possibility of these things, and I saw, too, that at three or four o'clock in the morning it would be perfectly possible for a person to move about the upper halls of this house without being seen. If he wore a heavy bath robe, with a hood, say, no one would recognize him even if he were seen, and besides the garb would not cause suspicion. This bath robe has a hood.

"Now, in working the mirror back and forth on the flagpole at night a tiny scarlet thread was pulled out of the robe and clung to the rope. I found this thread; later

Mr. Hatch found an identical thread in these apartments. Both came from that bath robe. Plain logic shows that the person who blew down the gas pipes worked the mirror trick; the person who worked the mirror trick left the thread; the thread comes back to the bath robe—that bath robe there," he pointed dramatically. "Thus the person who desired Henley's death was in these apartments, or had easy access to them."

He paused a moment and there was a tense silence. A great light was coming to Hatch, slowly but surely. The brain that had followed all this was unlimited in possibilities.

"Even before we traced the origin of the crime to this room," went on the scientist, quietly now, "attention had been attracted here, particularly to you, Mr. Cabell. It was through the love affair, of which Miss Lipscomb was the center. Mr. Hatch learned that you and Henley had been rivals for her hand. It was that, even before this scarlet thread was found, which indicated that you might have some knowledge of the affair, directly or indirectly.

"You are not a malicious or revengeful man, Mr. Cabell. But you are hot-tempered—extremely so. You demonstrated that just now, when, angry and not understanding, but feeling that your honor was at stake, you shot a hole in the floor."

"What?" asked Detective Mallory.

"A little accident," explained The Thinking Machine quickly. "Not being a malicious or revengeful man, you are not the man to deliberately go ahead and make elaborate plans for the murder of Henley. In a moment of passion you might have killed him—but never deliberately as the result of premeditation. Besides you were out of town. Who was then in these apartments? Who had access to these apartments? Who might have used your bath robe? Your valet, possibly Miss Austin. Which? Now, let's see how we reached this conclusion which led to the valet.

"Miss Regnier was found dead. It was not suicide. How did I know? Because she had been reading with the gas light at its full. If she had been reading by the gas light, how was it then that it went out and suffocated her before she could arise and shut it off? Obviously she must have fallen asleep over her book and left the light burning.

"If she was in this plot to kill Henley, why did she light the jet in her room? There might have been some slight defect in the electric bulb in her room which she had just discovered. Therefore she lighted the gas, intending to extinguish it—turn it off entirely—later. But she fell asleep. Therefore when the valet here blew into the pipe, intending to kill Mr. Henley, he unwittingly killed the woman he loved—Miss Regnier. It was perfectly possible, meanwhile, that she did not know of the attempt to be made that particular night, although she had participated in the others, knowing that Henley had night after night sat up to watch the light in his rooms.

"The facts, as I knew them, showed no connection between Miss Regnier and this man at that time—nor any connection between Miss Regnier and Henley. It might have been that the person who blew the gas out of the pipe from these rooms knew nothing whatever of Miss Regnier, just as he didn't know who else he might have killed in the building.

"But I had her death and the manner of it. I had eliminated you, Mr. Cabell. Therefore there remained Miss Austin and the valet. Miss Austin was eccentric—insane, if you will. Would she have any motive for killing Henley? I could imagine none. Love? Probably not. Money? They had nothing in common on that ground. What? Nothing that I could see. Therefore, for the moment, I passed Miss Austin by, after asking you, Mr. Cabell, if you were Miss Austin.

"What remained? The valet. Motive? Several possible ones, one or two probable. He is French, or says he is. Miss Regnier is French. Therefore I had arrived at the conclusion that they knew each other as people of the same nationality will in a house of this sort. And remember, I had passed by Mr. Cabell and Miss Austin, so the valet was the only one left; he could use the bath robe.

"Well, the motive. Frankly that was the only difficult point in the entire problem—difficult because there were so many possibilities. And each possibility that suggested itself suggested also a woman. Jealousy? There must be a woman. Hate? Probably a woman. Attempted extortion? With the aid of a woman. No other motive which would lead to so elaborate a plot of murder would come forward. Who was the woman? Miss Regnier.

"Did Miss Regnier know Henley? Mr. Hatch had reason to believe he knew her because of his actions when informed of her death. Knew her how? People of such relatively different planes of life can know each other—or do know each other—only on one plane. Henley is a typical young man, fast, I dare say, and liberal. Perhaps, then, there had been a liason. When I saw this possibility I had my motives—all of them—jealousy, hate and possibly attempted extortion as well.

"What was more possible than Mr. Henley and Miss Regnier had been acquainted? All liasons are secret ones. Suppose she had been cast off because of the engagement to a young woman of Henley's own level? Suppose she had confided in the valet here? Do you see? Motives enough for any crime, however diabolical. The attempts on Henley's life possibly followed an attempted extortion of money. The shot which wounded Henley was fired by this man, Jean. Why? Because the woman who had cause to hate Henley was dead. Then the man? He was alive and vindictive. Henley knew who shot him, and knew why, but he'll never say it publicly. He can't afford to. It would ruin him. I think probably that's all. Do you want to add anything?" he asked of the valet.

"No," was the fierce reply. "I'm sorry I didn't kill him, that's all. It was all about as you said, though God knows how you found it out," he added, desperately.

"Are you a Frenchman?"

"I was born in New York, but lived in France for eleven years. I first knew Louise there."

Silence fell upon the little group. Then Hatch asked a question:

"You told me, Professor, that there would be no other attempt to kill Henley by extinguishing the gas. How did you know that?"

"Because one person—the wrong person—had been killed that way," was the reply. "For this reason it was hardly likely that another attempt of that sort would be made. You had no intention of killing Louise Regnier, had you, Jean?"

"No, God help me, no."

"It was all done in these apartments," The Thinking Machine added, turning to Cabell, "at the gas jet from which I took the tip. It had been only loosely replaced and the metal was tarnished where the lips had dampened it."

"It must take great lung power to do a thing like that," remarked Detective Mallory.

"You would be amazed to know how easily it is done," said the scientist. "Try it some time."

The Thinking Machine arose and picked up his hat; Hatch did the same. Then the reporter turned to Cabell.

"Would you mind telling me why you were so anxious to get away to-night?" he asked.

"Well, no," Cabell explained, and there was a rush of red to his face. "It's because I received a telegram from Virginia—Miss Lipscomb, in fact. Some of Henley's past had come to her knowledge and the telegram told me that the engagement was broken. On top of this came the information that Henley had been shot and—I was considerably agitated."

The Thinking Machine and Hatch were walking along the street.

"What did you write in the note you sent to Cabell that made him start to unpack?" asked the reporter, curiously.

"There are some things that it wouldn't be well for everyone to know," was the enigmatic response. "Perhaps it would be just as well for you to overlook this little omission."

"Of course, of course," replied the reporter, wonderingly.

THE RED SILK SCARF

Maurice Leblanc

O N LEAVING HIS HOUSE ONE MORNING, AT HIS USUAL EARLY HOUR FOR
going to the Law Courts, Chief-inspector Ganimard noticed the curious
behaviour of an individual who was walking along the Rue Pergolèse in
front of him. Shabbily dressed and wearing a straw hat, though the day was the first
of December, the man stooped at every thirty or forty yards to fasten his boot-lace,
or pick up his stick, or for some other reason. And, each time, he took a little piece of
orange-peel from his pocket and laid it stealthily on the curb of the pavement. It was
probably a mere display of eccentricity, a childish amusement to which no one else
would have paid attention; but Ganimard was one of those shrewd observers who
are indifferent to nothing that strikes their eyes and who are never satisfied until they
know the secret cause of things. He therefore began to follow the man.

Now, at the moment when the fellow was turning to the right, into the Avenue
de la Grande-Armée, the inspector caught him exchanging signals with a boy of
twelve or thirteen, who was walking along the houses on the left-hand side. Twenty
yards farther, the man stooped and turned up the bottom of his trousers legs. A bit
of orange-peel marked the place. At the same moment, the boy stopped and, with a
piece of chalk, drew a white cross, surrounded by a circle, on the wall of the house
next to him.

The two continued on their way. A minute later, a fresh halt. The strange individual picked up a pin and dropped a piece of orange-peel; and the boy at once made a
second cross on the wall and again drew a white circle round it.

"By Jove!" thought the chief-inspector, with a grunt of satisfaction. "This is
rather promising. . . . What on earth can those two merchants be plotting?"

The two "merchants" went down the Avenue Friedland and the Rue du Faubourg-
Saint-Honoré, but nothing occurred that was worthy of special mention. The double
performance was repeated at almost regular intervals and, so to speak, mechanically.
Nevertheless, it was obvious, on the one hand, that the man with the orange-peel did
not do his part of the business until after he had picked out with a glance the house
that was to be marked and, on the other hand, that the boy did not mark that particular
house until after he had observed his companion's signal. It was certain, therefore,

that there was an agreement between the two; and the proceedings presented no small interest in the chief-inspector's eyes.

At the Place Beauveau the man hesitated. Then, apparently making up his mind, he twice turned up and twice turned down the bottom of his trousers legs. Hereupon, the boy sat down on the curb, opposite the sentry who was mounting guard outside the Ministry of the Interior, and marked the flagstone with two little crosses contained within two circles. The same ceremony was gone through a little further on, when they reached the Elysée. Only, on the pavement where the President's sentry was marching up and down, there were three signs instead of two.

"Hang it all!" muttered Ganimard, pale with excitement and thinking, in spite of himself, of his inveterate enemy, Lupin, whose name came to his mind whenever a mysterious circumstance presented itself. "Hang it all, what does it mean?"

He was nearly collaring and questioning the two "merchants." But he was too clever to commit so gross a blunder. The man with the orange-peel had now lit a cigarette; and the boy, also placing a cigarette-end between his lips, had gone up to him, apparently with the object of asking for a light.

They exchanged a few words. Quick as thought, the boy handed his companion an object which looked—at least, so the inspector believed—like a revolver. They both bent over this object; and the man, standing with his face to the wall, put his hand six times in his pocket and made a movement as though he were loading a weapon.

As soon as this was done, they walked briskly to the Rue de Suréne; and the inspector, who followed them as closely as he was able to do without attracting their attention, saw them enter the gateway of an old house of which all the shutters were closed, with the exception of those on the third or top floor.

He hurried in after them. At the end of the carriage-entrance he saw a large court-yard, with a house-painter's sign at the back and a staircase on the left.

He went up the stairs and, as soon as he reached the first floor, ran still faster, because he heard, right up at the top, a din as of a free-fight.

When he came to the last landing he found the door open. He entered, listened for a second, caught the sound of a struggle, rushed to the room from which the sound appeared to proceed and remained standing on the threshold, very much out of breath and greatly surprised to see the man of the orange-peel and the boy banging the floor with chairs.

At that moment a third person walked out of an adjoining room. It was a young man of twenty-eight or thirty, wearing a pair of short whiskers in addition to his moustache, spectacles, and a smoking-jacket with an astrakhan collar and looking like a foreigner, a Russian.

"Good morning, Ganimard," he said. And turning to the two companions, "Thank you, my friends, and all my congratulations on the successful result. Here's the reward I promised you."

He gave them a hundred-franc note, pushed them outside and shut both doors.

"I am sorry, old chap," he said to Ganimard. "I wanted to talk to you . . . wanted to talk to you badly."

He offered him his hand and, seeing that the inspector remained flabbergasted and that his face was still distorted with anger, he exclaimed:

"Why, you don't seem to understand! . . . And yet it's clear enough. . . . I wanted to see you particularly. . . . So what could I do?" And, pretending to reply to an objection, "No, no, old chap," he continued. "You're quite wrong. If I had written or telephoned, you would not have come . . . or else you would have come with a regiment. Now I wanted to see you all alone; and I thought the best thing was to send those two decent fellows to meet you, with orders to scatter bits of orange-peel and draw crosses and circles, in short, to mark out your road to this place. . . . Why, you look quite bewildered! What is it? Perhaps you don't recognize me? Lupin. . . . Arsène Lupin. . . . Ransack your memory. . . . Doesn't the name remind you of anything?"

"You dirty scoundrel!" Ganimard snarled between his teeth.

Lupin seemed greatly distressed and, in an affectionate voice:

"Are you vexed? Yes, I can see it in your eyes. . . . The Dugrival business, I suppose? I ought to have waited for you to come and take me in charge? . . . There now, the thought never occurred to me! I promise you, next time. . . ."

"You scum of the earth!" growled Ganimard.

"And I thinking I was giving you a treat! Upon my word, I did. I said to myself, 'That dear old Ganimard! We haven't met for an age. He'll simply rush at me when he sees me!'"

Ganimard, who had not yet stirred a limb, seemed to be waking from his stupor. He looked around him, looked at Lupin, visibly asked himself whether he would not do well to rush at him in reality and then, controlling himself, took hold of a chair and settled himself in it, as though he had suddenly made up his mind to listen to his enemy:

"Speak," he said. "And don't waste my time with any nonsense. I'm in a hurry."

"That's it," said Lupin, "let's talk. You can't imagine a quieter place than this. It's an old manor-house, which once stood in the open country, and it belongs to the Duc de Rochelaure. The duke, who has never lived in it, lets this floor to me and the outhouses to a painter and decorator. I always keep up a few establishments of this kind: it's a sound, practical plan. Here, in spite of my looking like a Russian nobleman,

I am M. Daubreuil, an ex-cabinet-minister. . . . You understand, I had to select a rather overstocked profession, so as not to attract attention. . . ."

"Do you think I care a hang about all this?" said Ganimard, interrupting him.

"Quite right, I'm wasting words and you're in a hurry. Forgive me. I sha'n't be long now. . . . Five minutes, that's all . . . I'll start at once. . . Have a cigar? No? Very well, no more will I."

He sat down also, drummed his fingers on the table, while thinking, and began in this fashion:

"On the 17th of October, 1599, on a warm and sunny autumn day . . . Do you follow me? . . But, now that I come to think of it, is it really necessary to go back to the reign of Henry IV, and tell you all about the building of the Pont-Neuf? No, I don't suppose you are very well up in French history; and I should only end by muddling you. Suffice it, then, for you to know that, last night, at one o'clock in the morning, a boatman passing under the last arch of the Pont-Neuf aforesaid, along the left bank of the river, heard something drop into the front part of his barge. The thing had been flung from the bridge and its evident destination was the bottom of the Seine. The bargee's dog rushed forward, barking, and, when the man reached the end of his craft, he saw the animal worrying a piece of newspaper that had served to wrap up a number of objects. He took from the dog such of the contents as had not fallen into the water, went to his cabin and examined them carefully. The result struck him as interesting; and, as the man is connected with one of my friends, he sent to let me know. This morning I was waked up and placed in possession of the facts and of the objects which the man had collected. Here they are."

He pointed to them, spread out on a table. There were, first of all, the torn pieces of a newspaper. Next came a large cut-glass inkstand, with a long piece of string fastened to the lid. There was a bit of broken glass and a sort of flexible cardboard, reduced to shreds. Lastly, there was a piece of bright scarlet silk, ending in a tassel of the same material and colour.

"You see our exhibits, friend of my youth," said Lupin. "No doubt, the problem would be more easily solved if we had the other objects which went overboard owing to the stupidity of the dog. But it seems to me, all the same, that we ought to be able to manage, with a little reflection and intelligence. And those are just your great qualities. How does the business strike you?'

Ganimard did not move a muscle. He was willing to stand Lupin's chaff, but his dignity commanded him not to speak a single word in answer nor even to give a nod or shake of the head that might have been taken to express approval or criticism.

"I see that we are entirely of one mind," continued Lupin, without appearing to remark the chief-inspector's silence. "And I can sum up the matter briefly, as told us by these exhibits. Yesterday evening, between nine and twelve o'clock, a showily dressed young woman was wounded with a knife and then caught round the throat and choked to death by a well-dressed gentleman, wearing a single eyeglass and interested in racing, with whom the aforesaid showily dressed young lady had been eating three meringues and a coffee éclair."

Lupin lit a cigarette and, taking Ganimard by the sleeve:

"Aha, that's up against you, chief-inspector! You thought that, in the domain of police deductions, such feats as those were prohibited to outsiders! Wrong, sir! Lupin juggles with inferences and deductions for all the world like a detective in a novel. My proofs are dazzling and absolutely simple."

And, pointing to the objects one by one, as he demonstrated his statement, he resumed:

"I said, after nine o'clock yesterday evening. This scrap of newspaper bears yesterday's date, with the words, 'Evening edition.' Also, you will see here, pasted to the paper, a bit of one of those yellow wrappers in which the subscribers' copies are sent out. These copies are always delivered by the nine o'clock post. Therefore, it was after nine o'clock. I said, a well-dressed man. Please observe that this tiny piece of glass has the round hole of a single eyeglass at one of the edges and that the single eyeglass is an essentially aristocratic article of wear. This well-dressed man walked into a pastry-cook's shop. Here is the very thin cardboard, shaped like a box, and still showing a little of the cream of the meringues and éclairs which were packed in it in the usual way. Having got his parcel, the gentleman with the eyeglass joined a young person whose eccentricity in the matter of dress is pretty clearly indicated by this bright-red silk scarf. Having joined her, for some reason as yet unknown he first stabbed her with a knife and then strangled her with the help of this same scarf. Take your magnifying glass, chief-inspector, and you will see, on the silk, stains of a darker red which are, here, the marks of a knife wiped on the scarf and, there, the marks of a hand, covered with blood, clutching the material. Having committed the murder, his next business is to leave no trace behind him. So he takes from his pocket, first, the newspaper to which he subscribes—a racing-paper, as you will see by glancing at the contents of this scrap; and you will have no difficulty in discovering the title—and, secondly, a cord, which, on inspection, turns out to be a length of whip-cord. These two details prove—do they not?—that our man is interested in racing and that he himself rides. Next, he picks up the fragments of his eyeglass, the cord of which has been broken in the struggle. He takes a pair of scissors—observe the hacking of the scissors—and cuts off the stained part of the scarf, leaving the other end, no doubt, in his victim's clenched hands. He makes a ball of the confectioner's cardboard box. He also puts in certain things that would have betrayed him, such as the knife, which must have slipped into the Seine. He wraps everything in the newspaper, ties it with the cord and fastens this cut-glass inkstand to it, as a make-weight. Then he makes himself scarce. A little later, the parcel falls into the waterman's barge. And there you are. Oof, it's hot work! . . . What do you say to the story?"

He looked at Ganimard to see what impression his speech had produced on the inspector. Ganimard did not depart from his attitude of silence.

Lupin began to laugh:

"As a matter of fact, you're annoyed and surprised. But you're suspicious as well: 'Why should that confounded Lupin hand the business over to me,' say you, 'instead of keeping it for himself, hunting down the murderer and rifling his pockets, if there was a robbery?' The question is quite logical, of course. But—there is a 'but'—I have no time, you see. I am full up with work at the present moment: a burglary in London, another at Lausanne, an exchange of children at Marseilles, to say nothing of having to save a young girl who is at this moment shadowed by death. That's always the way: it never rains but it pours. So I said to myself, 'Suppose I handed the business over to my dear old Ganimard? Now that it is half-solved for him, he is quite capable of succeeding. And what a service I shall be doing him! How magnificently he will be able to distinguish himself!' No sooner said than done. At eight o'clock in the morning, I sent the joker with the orange-peel to meet you. You swallowed the bait; and you were here by nine, all on edge and eager for the fray."

Lupin rose from his chair. He went over to the inspector and, with his eyes in Ganimard's, said:

"That's all. You now know the whole story. Presently, you will know the victim: some ballet-dancer, probably, some singer at a music-hall. On the other hand, the chances are that the criminal lives near the Pont-Neuf, most likely on the left bank. Lastly, here are all the exhibits. I make you a present of them. Set to work. I shall only keep this end of the scarf. If ever you want to piece the scarf together, bring me the other end, the one which the police will find round the victim's neck. Bring it me in four weeks from now to the day, that is to say, on the 29th of December, at ten o'clock in the morning. You can be sure of finding me here. And don't be afraid: this is all perfectly serious, friend of my youth; I swear it is. No humbug, honour bright. You can go straight ahead. Oh, by the way, when you arrest the fellow with the eyeglass, be a bit careful: he is left-handed! Good-bye, old dear, and good luck to you!"

Lupin spun round on his heel, went to the door, opened it and disappeared before Ganimard had even thought of taking a decision. The inspector rushed after him, but at once found that the handle of the door, by some trick of mechanism which he did not know, refused to turn. It took him ten minutes to unscrew the lock and ten minutes more to unscrew the lock of the hall-door. By the time that he had scrambled down the three flights of stairs, Ganimard had given up all hope of catching Arsène Lupin.

Besides, he was not thinking of it. Lupin inspired him with a queer, complex feeling, made up of fear, hatred, involuntary admiration and also the vague instinct that he, Ganimard, in spite of all his efforts, in spite of the persistency of his endeavours, would never get the better of this particular adversary. He pursued him from a sense of duty and pride, but with the continual dread of being taken in by that formidable hoaxer and scouted and fooled in the face of a public that was always only too willing to laugh at the chief-inspector's mishaps.

This business of the red scarf, in particular, struck him as most suspicious. It was interesting, certainly, in more ways than one, but so very improbable! And Lupin's explanation, apparently so logical, would never stand the test of a severe examination!

"No," said Ganimard, "this is all swank: a parcel of suppositions and guesswork based upon nothing at all. I'm not to be caught with chaff."

When he reached the headquarters of police, at 36 Quai des Orfèvres, he had quite made up his mind to treat the incident as though it had never happened.

He went up to the Criminal Investigation Department. Here, one of his fellow-inspectors said:

"Seen the chief?"

"No."

"He was asking for you just now."

"Oh, was he?"

"Yes, you had better go after him."

"Where?"

"To the Rue de Berne . . . there was a murder there last night."

"Oh! Who's the victim?"

"I don't know exactly . . . a music-hall singer, I believe."

Ganimard simply muttered:

"By Jove!"

Twenty minutes later he stepped out of the underground railway-station and made for the Rue de Berne.

The victim, who was known in the theatrical world by her stage-name of Jenny Saphir, occupied a small flat on the second floor of one of the houses. A policeman took the chief-inspector upstairs and showed him the way, through two sitting-rooms, to a bedroom, where he found the magistrates in charge of the inquiry, together with the divisional surgeon and M. Dudouis, the head of the detective-service.

Ganimard started at the first glance which he gave into the room. He saw, lying on a sofa, the corpse of a young woman whose hands clutched a strip of red silk! One of the shoulders, which appeared above the low-cut bodice, bore the marks of two wounds surrounded with clotted blood. The distorted and almost blackened features still bore an expression of frenzied terror.

The divisional surgeon, who had just finished his examination, said:

"My first conclusions are very clear. The victim was twice stabbed with a dagger and afterward strangled. The immediate cause of death was asphyxia."

"By Jove!" thought Ganimard again, remembering Lupin's words and the picture which he had drawn of the crime.

The examining-magistrate objected:

"But the neck shows no discoloration."

"She may have been strangled with a napkin or a handkerchief," said the doctor.

"Most probably," said the chief detective, "with this silk scarf, which the victim was wearing and a piece of which remains, as though she had clung to it with her two hands to protect herself."

"But why does only that piece remain?" asked the magistrate. "What has become of the other?"

"The other may have been stained with blood and carried off by the murderer. You can plainly distinguish the hurried slashing of the scissors."

"By Jove!" said Ganimard, between his teeth, for the third time. "That brute of a Lupin saw everything without seeing a thing!"

"And what about the motive of the murder?" asked the magistrate. "The locks have been forced, the cupboards turned upside down. Have you anything to tell me, M. Dudouis?"

The chief of the detective-service replied:

"I can at least suggest a supposition, derived from the statements made by the servant. The victim, who enjoyed a greater reputation on account of her looks than through her talent as a singer, went to Russia, two years ago, and brought back with her a magnificent sapphire, which she appears to have received from some person of importance at the court. Since then, she went by the name of Jenny Saphir and seems generally to have been very proud of that present, although, for prudence sake, she never wore it. I daresay that we shall not be far out if we presume the theft of the sapphire to have been the cause of the crime."

"But did the maid know where the stone was?"

"No, nobody did. And the disorder of the room would tend to prove that the murderer did not know either."

"We will question the maid," said the examining-magistrate.

M. Dudouis took the chief-inspector aside and said:

"You're looking very old-fashioned, Ganimard. What's the matter? Do you suspect anything?"

"Nothing at all, chief."

"That's a pity. We could do with a bit of showy work in the department. This is one of a number of crimes, all of the same class, of which we have failed to discover the perpetrator. This time we want the criminal . . . and quickly!"

"A difficult job, chief."

"It's got to be done. Listen to me, Ganimard. According to what the maid says, Jenny Saphir led a very regular life. For a month past she was in the habit of frequently receiving visits, on her return from the music-hall, that is to say, at about half-past ten, from a man who would stay until midnight or so. 'He's a society man,' Jenny Saphir used to say, 'and he wants to marry me.' This society man took every precaution to avoid being seen, such as turning up his coat-collar and lowering the brim of his hat when he passed the porter's box. And Jenny Saphir always made a point of sending away her maid, even before he came. This is the man whom we have to find."

"Has he left no traces?"

"None at all. It is obvious that we have to deal with a very clever scoundrel, who prepared his crime beforehand and committed it with every possible chance of escaping unpunished. His arrest would be a great feather in our cap. I rely on you, Ganimard."

"Ah, you rely on me, chief?" replied the inspector. "Well, we shall see . . . we shall see. . . . I don't say no. . . . Only . . ."

He seemed in a very nervous condition, and his agitation struck M. Dudouis.

"Only," continued Ganimard, "only I swear . . . do you hear, chief? I swear. . . ."

"What do you swear?"

"Nothing. . . . We shall see, chief . . . we shall see. . . ."

Ganimard did not finish his sentence until he was outside, alone. And he finished it aloud, stamping his foot, in a tone of the most violent anger:

"Only, I swear to Heaven that the arrest shall be effected by my own means, without my employing a single one of the clues with which that villain has supplied me. Ah, no! Ah, no! . . ."

Railing against Lupin, furious at being mixed up in this business and resolved, nevertheless, to get to the bottom of it, he wandered aimlessly about the streets. His brain was seething with irritation; and he tried to adjust his ideas a little and to discover, among the chaotic facts, some trifling detail, unperceived by all, unsuspected by Lupin himself, that might lead him to success.

He lunched hurriedly at a bar, resumed his stroll and suddenly stopped, petrified, astounded and confused. He was walking under the gateway of the very house in the Rue de Surène to which Lupin had enticed him a few hours earlier! A force stronger than his own will was drawing him there once more. The solution of the problem lay there. There and there alone were all the elements of the truth. Do and say what he would, Lupin's assertions were so precise, his calculations so accurate, that, worried to the innermost recesses of his being by so prodigious a display of perspicacity, he could not do other than take up the work at the point where his enemy had left it.

Abandoning all further resistance, he climbed the three flights of stairs. The door of the flat was open. No one had touched the exhibits. He put them in his pocket and walked away.

From that moment, he reasoned and acted, so to speak, mechanically, under the influence of the master whom he could not choose but obey.

Admitting that the unknown person whom he was seeking lived in the neighbourhood of the Pont-Neuf, it became necessary to discover, somewhere between that bridge and the Rue de Berne, the first-class confectioner's shop, open in the evenings, at which the cakes were bought. This did not take long to find. A pastry-cook near the Gare Saint-Lazare showed him some little cardboard boxes, identical in material and shape with the one in Ganimard's possession. Moreover, one of the shop-girls remembered having served, on the previous evening, a gentleman whose face was almost concealed in the collar of his fur coat, but whose eyeglass she had happened to notice.

"That's one clue checked," thought the inspector. "Our man wears an eyeglass."

He next collected the pieces of the racing-paper and showed them to a newsvendor, who easily recognized the *Turf Illustré*. Ganimard at once went to the offices of the *Turf* and asked to see the list of subscribers. Going through the list, he jotted down the names and addresses of all those who lived anywhere near the Pont-Neuf and principally—because Lupin had said so—those on the left bank of the river.

He then went back to the Criminal Investigation Department, took half a dozen men and packed them off with the necessary instructions.

At seven o'clock in the evening, the last of these men returned and brought good news with him. A certain M. Prévailles, a subscriber to the *Turf*, occupied an entresol flat on the Quai des Augustins. On the previous evening, he left his place, wearing a fur coat, took his letters and his paper, the *Turf lllustré*, from the porter's wife, walked away and returned home at midnight. This M. Prévailles wore a single eyeglass. He was a regular race-goer and himself owned several hacks which he either rode himself or jobbed out.

The inquiry had taken so short a time and the results obtained were so exactly in accordance with Lupin's predictions that Ganimard felt quite overcome on hearing the detective's report. Once more he was measuring the prodigious extent of the resources at Lupin's disposal. Never in the course of his life—and Ganimard was already well-advanced in years—had he come across such perspicacity, such a quick and far-seeing mind.

He went in search of M. Dudouis.

"Everything's ready, chief. Have you a warrant?"

"Eh?"

"I said, everything is ready for the arrest, chief."

"You know the name of Jenny Saphir's murderer?"

"Yes."

"But how? Explain yourself."

Ganimard had a sort of scruple of conscience, blushed a little and nevertheless replied:

"An accident, chief. The murderer threw everything that was likely to compromise him into the Seine. Part of the parcel was picked up and handed to me."

"By whom?"

"A boatman who refused to give his name, for fear of getting into trouble. But I had all the clues I wanted. It was not so difficult as I expected."

And the inspector described how he had gone to work.

"And you call that an accident!" cried M. Dudouis. "And you say that it was not difficult! Why, it's one of your finest performances! Finish it yourself, Ganimard, and be prudent."

Ganimard was eager to get the business done. He went to the Quai des Augustins with his men and distributed them around the house. He questioned the portress, who said that her tenant took his meals out of doors, but made a point of looking in after dinner.

A little before nine o'clock, in fact, leaning out of her window, she warned Ganimard, who at once gave a low whistle. A gentleman in a tall hat and a fur coat was coming along the pavement beside the Seine. He crossed the road and walked up to the house.

Ganimard stepped forward:

"M. Prévailles, I believe?"

"Yes, but who are you?"

"I have a commission to . . ."

He had not time to finish his sentence. At the sight of the men appearing out of the shadow, Prévailles quickly retreated to the wall and faced his adversaries, with his back to the door of a shop on the ground-floor, the shutters of which were closed.

"Stand back!" he cried. "I don't know you!"

His right hand brandished a heavy stick, while his left was slipped behind him and seemed to be trying to open the door.

Ganimard had an impression that the man might escape through this way and through some secret outlet:

"None of this nonsense," he said, moving closer to him. "You're caught. . . . You had better come quietly."

But, just as he was laying hold of Prévailles' stick, Ganimard remembered the warning which Lupin gave him: Prévailles was left-handed; and it was his revolver for which he was feeling behind his back.

The inspector ducked his head. He had noticed the man's sudden movement. Two reports rang out. No one was hit.

A second later, Prévailles received a blow under the chin from the butt-end of a revolver, which brought him down where he stood. He was entered at the Dépôt soon after nine o'clock.

Ganimard enjoyed a great reputation even at that time. But this capture, so quickly effected, by such very simple means, and at once made public by the police, won him a sudden celebrity. Prévailles was forthwith saddled with all the murders that had remained unpunished; and the newspapers vied with one another in extolling Ganimard's prowess.

The case was conducted briskly at the start. It was first of all ascertained that Prévailles, whose real name was Thomas Derocq, had already been in trouble. Moreover, the search instituted in his rooms, while not supplying any fresh proofs, at least led to the discovery of a ball of whip-cord similar to the cord used for doing up the parcel and also to the discovery of daggers which would have produced a wound similar to the wounds on the victim.

But, on the eighth day, everything was changed. Until then Prévailles had refused to reply to the questions put to him; but now, assisted by his counsel, he pleaded a circumstantial alibi and maintained that he was at the Folies-Bergère on the night of the murder.

As a matter of fact, the pockets of his dinner-jacket contained the counterfoil of a stall-ticket and a programme of the performance, both bearing the date of that evening.

"An alibi prepared in advance," objected the examining-magistrate.

"Prove it," said Prévailles.

The prisoner was confronted with the witnesses for the prosecution. The young lady from the confectioner's "thought she knew" the gentleman with the eyeglass. The hall-porter in the Rue de Berne "thought he knew" the gentleman who used to come to see Jenny Saphir. But nobody dared to make a more definite statement.

The examination, therefore, led to nothing of a precise character, provided no solid basis whereon to found a serious accusation.

The judge sent for Ganimard and told him of his difficulty.

"I can't possibly persist, at this rate. There is no evidence to support the charge."

"But surely you are convinced in your own mind, monsieur le juge d'instruction! Prévailles would never have resisted his arrest unless he was guilty."

"He says that he thought he was being assaulted. He also says that he never set eyes on Jenny Saphir; and, as a matter of fact, we can find no one to contradict his assertion. Then again, admitting that the sapphire has been stolen, we have not been able to find it at his flat."

"Nor anywhere else," suggested Ganimard.

"Quite true, but that is no evidence against him. I'll tell you what we shall want, M. Ganimard, and that very soon: the other end of this red scarf."

"The other end?"

"Yes, for it is obvious that, if the murderer took it away with him, the reason was that the stuff is stained with the marks of the blood on his fingers."

Ganimard made no reply. For several days he had felt that the whole business was tending to this conclusion. There was no other proof possible. Given the silk scarf—and in no other circumstances—Prévailles' guilt was certain. Now Ganimard's position required that Prévailles' guilt should be established. He was responsible for the arrest, it had cast a glamour around him, he had been praised to the skies as the most formidable adversary of criminals; and he would look absolutely ridiculous if Prévailles were released.

Unfortunately, the one and only indispensable proof was in Lupin's pocket. How was he to get hold of it?

Ganimard cast about, exhausted himself with fresh investigations, went over the inquiry from start to finish, spent sleepless nights in turning over the mystery of the Rue de Berne, studied the records of Prévailles' life, sent ten men hunting after the invisible sapphire. Everything was useless.

On the 28th of December, the examining-magistrate stopped him in one of the passages of the Law Courts:

"Well, M. Ganimard, any news?"

"No, monsieur le juge d'instruction."

"Then I shall dismiss the case."

"Wait one day longer."

"What's the use? We want the other end of the scarf; have you got it?"

"I shall have it to-morrow."

"To-morrow!"

"Yes, but please lend me the piece in your possession."

"What if I do?"

"If you do, I promise to let you have the whole scarf complete."

"Very well, that's understood."

Ganimard followed the examining-magistrate to his room and came out with the piece of silk:

"Hang it all!" he growled. "Yes, I will go and fetch the proof and I shall have it too . . . always presuming that Master Lupin has the courage to keep the appointment."

In point of fact, he did not doubt for a moment that Master Lupin would have this courage, and that was just what exasperated him. Why had Lupin insisted on this meeting? What was his object, in the circumstances?

Anxious, furious and full of hatred, he resolved to take every precaution necessary not only to prevent his falling into a trap himself, but to make his enemy fall into one, now that the opportunity offered. And, on the next day, which was the 29th of December, the date fixed by Lupin, after spending the night in studying the old manor-house in the Rue de Surène and convincing himself that there was no other outlet than the front door, he warned his men that he was going on a dangerous expedition and arrived with them on the field of battle.

He posted them in a café and gave them formal instructions: if he showed himself at one of the third-floor windows, or if he failed to return within an hour, the detectives were to enter the house and arrest any one who tried to leave it.

The chief-inspector made sure that his revolver was in working order and that he could take it from his pocket easily. Then he went upstairs.

He was surprised to find things as he had left them, the doors open and the locks broken. After ascertaining that the windows of the principal room looked out on the street, he visited the three other rooms that made up the flat. There was no one there.

"Master Lupin was afraid," he muttered, not without a certain satisfaction.

"Don't be silly," said a voice behind him.

Turning round, he saw an old workman, wearing a house-painter's long smock, standing in the doorway.

"You needn't bother your head," said the man. "It's I, Lupin. I have been working in the painter's shop since early morning. This is when we knock off for breakfast. So I came upstairs."

He looked at Ganimard with a quizzing smile and cried:

"'Pon my word, this is a gorgeous moment I owe you, old chap! I wouldn't sell it for ten years of your life; and yet you know how I love you! What do you think of it, artist? Wasn't it well thought out and well foreseen? Foreseen from alpha to omega? Did I understand the business? Did I penetrate the mystery of the scarf? I'm not saying that there were no holes in my argument, no links missing in the chain . . . But what a masterpiece of intelligence! Ganimard, what a reconstruction of events! What an intuition of everything that had taken place and of everything that was going to take place, from the discovery of the crime to your arrival here in search of a proof! What really marvellous divination! Have you the scarf?"

"Yes, half of it. Have you the other?"

"Here it is. Let's compare."

They spread the two pieces of silk on the table. The cuts made by the scissors corresponded exactly. Moreover, the colours were identical.

"But I presume," said Lupin, "that this was not the only thing you came for. What you are interested in seeing is the marks of the blood. Come with me, Ganimard: it's rather dark in here."

They moved into the next room, which, though it overlooked the courtyard, was lighter; and Lupin held his piece of silk against the windowpane:

"Look," he said, making room for Ganimard.

The inspector gave a start of delight. The marks of the five fingers and the print of the palm were distinctly visible. The evidence was undeniable. The murderer had seized the stuff in his blood-stained hand, in the same hand that had stabbed Jenny Saphir, and tied the scarf round her neck.

"And it is the print of a left hand," observed Lupin. "Hence my warning, which had nothing miraculous about it, you see. For, though I admit, friend of my youth, that you may look upon me as a superior intelligence, I won't have you treat me as a wizard."

Ganimard had quickly pocketed the piece of silk. Lupin nodded his head in approval:

"Quite right, old boy, it's for you. I'm so glad you're glad! And, you see, there was no trap about all this . . . only the wish to oblige . . . a service between friends, between pals. . . . And also, I confess, a little curiosity. . . . Yes, I wanted to examine this other piece of silk, the one the police had. . . . Don't be afraid: I'll give it back to you. . . . Just a second. . . ."

Lupin, with a careless movement, played with the tassel at the end of this half of the scarf, while Ganimard listened to him in spite of himself:

"How ingenious these little bits of women's work are! Did you notice one detail in the maid's evidence? Jenny Saphir was very handy with her needle and used to make all her own hats and frocks. It is obvious that she made this scarf herself. . . . Besides, I noticed that from the first. I am naturally curious, as I have already told you, and I made a thorough examination of the piece of silk which you have just put in your pocket. Inside the tassel, I found a little sacred medal, which the poor girl had stitched into it to bring her luck. Touching, isn't it, Ganimard? A little medal of Our Lady of Good Succour."

The inspector felt greatly puzzled and did not take his eyes off the other. And Lupin continued:

"Then I said to myself, 'How interesting it would be to explore the other half of the scarf, the one which the police will find round the victim's neck!' For this other half, which I hold in my hands at last, is finished off in the same way . . . so I shall be able to see if it has a hiding-place too and what's inside it. . . . But look, my friend, isn't it cleverly made? And so simple! All you have to do is to take a skein of red cord and braid it round a wooden cup, leaving a little recess, a little empty space in the middle, very small, of course, but large enough to hold a medal of a saint. . . or anything. . . . A precious stone, for instance. . . . Such as a sapphire. . . ."

At that moment he finished pushing back the silk cord and, from the hollow of a cup he took between his thumb and forefinger a wonderful blue stone, perfect in respect of size and purity.

"Ha! What did I tell you, friend of my youth?"

He raised his head. The inspector had turned livid and was staring wild-eyed, as though fascinated by the stone that sparkled before him. He at last realized the whole plot:

"You dirty scoundrel!" he muttered, repeating the insults which he had used at the first interview. "You scum of the earth!"

The two men were standing one against the other.

"Give me back that," said the inspector.

Lupin held out the piece of silk.

"And the sapphire," said Ganimard, in a peremptory tone.

"Don't be silly."

"Give it back, or . . ."

"Or what, you idiot!" cried Lupin. "Look here, do you think I put you on to this soft thing for nothing?"

"Give it back!"

"You haven't noticed what I've been about, that's plain! What! For four weeks I've kept you on the move like a deer; and you want to . . . ! Come, Ganimard, old chap, pull yourself together! . . . Don't you see that you've been playing the good dog for four weeks on end? . . . Fetch it, Rover! . . . There's a nice blue pebble over there, which master can't get at. Hunt it, Ganimard, fetch it . . . bring it to master. . . . Ah, he's his master's own good little dog! . . . Sit up! Beg! . . . Does'ms want a bit of sugar, then? . . ."

Ganimard, containing the anger that seethed within him, thought only of one thing, summoning his detectives. And, as the room in which he now was looked out on the courtyard, he tried gradually to work his way round to the communicating door. He would then run to the window and break one of the panes.

"All the same," continued Lupin, "what a pack of dunderheads you and the rest must be! You've had the silk all this time and not one of you ever thought of feeling it, not one of you ever asked himself the reason why the poor girl hung on to her scarf. Not one of you! You just acted at haphazard, without reflecting, without foreseeing anything. . . ."

The inspector had attained his object. Taking advantage of a second when Lupin had turned away from him, he suddenly wheeled round and grasped the door-handle. But an oath escaped him: the handle did not budge.

Lupin burst into a fit of laughing:

"Not even that! You did not even foresee that! You lay a trap for me and you won't admit that I may perhaps smell the thing out beforehand. . . . And you allow yourself to be brought into this room without asking whether I am not bringing you here for a particular reason and without remembering that the locks are fitted with a special mechanism. Come now, speaking frankly, what do you think of it yourself?"

"What do I think of it?" roared Ganimard, beside himself with rage.

He had drawn his revolver and was pointing it straight at Lupin's face.

"Hands up!" he cried. "That's what I think of it!"

Lupin placed himself in front of him and shrugged his shoulders:

"Sold again!" he said.

"Hands up, I say, once more!"

"And sold again, say I. Your deadly weapon won't go off."

"What?"

"Old Catherine, your housekeeper, is in my service. She damped the charges this morning while you were having your breakfast coffee."

Ganimard made a furious gesture, pocketed the revolver and rushed at Lupin.

"Well?" said Lupin, stopping him short with a well-aimed kick on the shin.

Their clothes were almost touching. They exchanged defiant glances, the glances of two adversaries who mean to come to blows. Nevertheless, there was no fight. The recollection of the earlier struggles made any present struggle useless. And Ganimard, who remembered all his past failures, his vain attacks, Lupin's crushing reprisals, did not lift a limb. There was nothing to be done. He felt it. Lupin had forces at his command against which any individual force simply broke to pieces. So what was the good?

"I agree," said Lupin, in a friendly voice, as though answering Ganimard's unspoken thought, "you would do better to let things be as they are. Besides, friend of my youth, think of all that this incident has brought you: fame, the certainty of quick promotion and, thanks to that, the prospect of a happy and comfortable old age! Surely, you don't want the discovery of the sapphire and the head of poor Arsène Lupin in addition! It wouldn't be fair. To say nothing of the fact that poor Arsène Lupin saved your life. . . . Yes, sir! Who warned you, at this very spot, that Prévailles was left-handed? . . . And is this the way you thank me? It's not pretty of you, Ganimard. Upon my word, you make me blush for you!"

While chattering, Lupin had gone through the same preformance as Ganimard and was now near the door. Ganimard saw that his foe was about to escape him. Forgetting all prudence, he tried to block his way and received a tremendous butt in the stomach, which sent him rolling to the opposite wall.

Lupin dexterously touched a spring, turned the handle, opened the door and slipped away, roaring with laughter as he went.

Twenty minutes later, when Ganimard at last succeeded in joining his men, one of them said to him:

"A house-painter left the house, as his mates were coming back from breakfast, and put a letter in my hand. 'Give that to your governor,' he said. 'Which governor?' I asked; but he was gone. I suppose it's meant for you."

"Let's have it."

Ganimard opened the letter. It was hurriedly scribbled in pencil and contained these words:

This is to warn you, friend of my youth, against excessive credulity. When a fellow tells you that the cartridges in your revolver are damp, however great your confidence in that fellow may be, even though his name be Arsène Lupin, never allow yourself to be taken in. Fire first; and, if the fellow hops the twig, you will have acquired the proof (1) that the cartridges are not damp; and (2) that old Catherine is the most honest and respectable of housekeepers.

One of these days, I hope to have the pleasure of making her acquaintance.

Meanwhile, friend of my youth, believe me always affectionately and sincerely yours,

ARSÈNE LUPIN.

THE BUSINESS MINISTER

H. C. Bailey

PHASE I: THE SCANDAL

"Oh, to be in England now that April's here,'" said Reggie Fortune as, trying to hide himself in his coat, he slipped and slid down the gangway to his native land. The Boulogne boat behind him, lost in driving snow, could be inferred from escaping steam and the glimmer of a rosette of lights. "The Flying Dutchman's new packet," Reggie muttered, and hummed the helmsman's song from the opera, till a squall coming round the corner stung what of his face he could not bury like small shot.

He continued to suffer. The heat in the Pullman was tinned. He did not like the toast. The train ran slow, and whenever he wiped the steamy window he saw white-blanketed country and fresh swirls of snow. So he came into Charing Cross some seven hours late, and it had no taxi. He said what he could. You imagine him, balanced by the two suitcases which he could not bear to part with, wading through deep snow from the Tube station at Oxford Circus to Wimpole Street, and subsiding limp but still fluent into the arms of Sam his factotum. And the snow went on falling.

It was about this time, in his judgment, 11 P.M. on 15th April, that a man fell from the top story of Montmorency House, the hugest and newest of the new blocks of flats thereabouts. He fell down the well which lights the inner rooms and, I suppose, made something of a thud as his body passed through the cushion of snow and hit the concrete below. But in the howl of the wind and the rattle of windows it would have been extraordinary if any one had heard him or taken him for something more than a slate or a chimney pot. He was not in a condition to explain himself. And the snow went on falling.

Mr. Fortune, though free from his coat and his hat and his scarf and his gloves, though scorching both hands and one foot at the hall fire, was still telling Sam his troubles when the Hon. Stanley Lomas came downstairs. Mr. Fortune said, "Help!"

"Had a good time?" said Lomas cheerily. "Did you get to Seville?"

"Oh, Peter, don't say things like that. I can't bear it. Have the feelings of a man. Be a brother, Lomas. I've been in nice, kind countries with a well-bred climate, and I come back to this epileptic blizzard, and here's Lomas pale and perky waiting for me on the mat. And then you're civil! Oh, Sophonisba! Sophonisba, oh!"

"I did rather want to see you," Lomas explained.

"I hate seeing you. I hate seeing anything raw and alive. If you talk to me I shall cry. My dear man, have you had dinner?"

"Hours ago."

"That wasn't quite nice of you, you know. When you come to see me, you shouldn't dine first. It makes me suspect your taste. Well, well! Come and see me eat. That is a sight which has moved strong men to tears, the pure ecstasy of joy, Lomas. The sublime and the beautiful, by R. Fortune. And Sam says Elise has a *timbale de foie gras* and her very own *entrecôte*. Dine again, Whittington. And we will look upon the wine when it is red. My Chambertin is strongly indicated. And then I will fall asleep for a thousand years, same like the Sleeping Beauty."

"I wish I could."

"Lomas, old dear!" Reggie turned and looked him over. "Yes, you have been going it. You ought to get away."

"I dare say I shall. That is one of the things I'm going to ask you—what you think about resignation."

"Oh, Peter! As bad as that?" Reggie whistled. "Sorry I was futile. But I couldn't know. There's been nothing in the papers."

"Only innuendoes. Damme, you can't get away from it in the clubs."

They had it out over dinner.

Some months before a new Government had been formed, which was advertised to bring heaven down to earth without delay. And the first outward sign of its inward and spiritual grace was the Great Coal Ramp. Some folks in the City began to buy the shares of certain coal companies. Some folks in the City began to spread rumours that the Government was going to nationalize mines district by district—those districts first in which the shares had been bought. The shares then went to a vast price.

"All the usual nauseating features of a Stock Exchange boom," said Reggie. "No. This is founded on fact," said Lomas. "That's the distinguishing feature. It was worked on the truth, the whole truth, and nothing but the truth. Whoever started the game had exact and precise information. They only touched those companies which the Government meant to take over; they knew everything and they knew it right. Somebody of the inner circle gave the plan away."

"'Politics is a cursed profession,'" said Reggie.

Lomas looked gloomily at his Burgundy. "Politicians are almost the lowest of God's creatures," he agreed. "I know that. I'm a Civil servant. But I don't see how any of them can have had a finger in this pie. The scheme hadn't come before the Cabinet. Everybody knew, of course, that something was going to be done. But the whole point is the particular companies concerned in this primary provisional scheme. And nobody knew which they were but the President of the Board of Trade and his private secretary."

"The President—that's Horace Kimball."

"Yes. No politics about him. He's the rubber king, you know. He was brought in on the business men for a business Cabinet cry. He was really put there to get these nationalization schemes through."

"And he begins by arousing city scandal. Business men and business methods. Well, well! Give me the politicians after all. I was born respectable. I would rather be swindled in the quiet, old-fashioned way. I like a sense of style."

"Quite—quite," said Lomas heartily. "But I must say I have nothing against Kimball. He is the usual thing. Thinks he is like Napoleon—pathetically anxious you should suppose he has been educated. But he really is quite an able fellow, and he means to be civil. Only he's mad to catch the fellow who gave his scheme away. I don't blame him. But it's damned awkward."

"If only Kimball and his private secretary knew, either Kimball or the private secretary gave it away."

"My dear Fortune, if you say things like that, I shall break down. That is the hopeless sort of jingle I say in my sleep. I believe Kimball's honest. That's his reputation. As keen as they make 'em, but absolutely straight. And why should he play double? He is ridiculously rich. If he wanted money it was idiotic to go into the Government. He would do much better for himself in business. No; he must have gone into politics for power and position and so on. And then at the start his career is mucked by a financial scandal. You can't suppose he had a hand in it. It's too mad."

"Remains the private secretary. Don't Mr. Kimball like his private secretary?"

"Oh yes. Kimball thinks very well of him. I pointed out to Kimball that on the facts we were bound to suspect Sandford, and he was quite huffy about it—said he had the highest opinion of Sandford, asked what evidence I had, and so on."

"Very good and proper, and even intelligent. My respects to H. Kimball. What evidence have you, Lomas, old thing?"

"You just put the case yourself," said Lomas, with some irritation. "Only Kimball and Sandford were in the secret. It's impossible in the nature of things Kimball should have sold it. Remains Sandford."

"Oh, Peter! That's not evidence, that's an argument."

"I know, confound you. But there is evidence of a sort. One of Sandford's friends is a young fellow called Walkden, and he's in one of the firms which have been running the Stock Exchange boom."

"It's queer," said Reggie, and lit a pipe. "But it wouldn't hang a yellow dog."

"Do you think I don't know that?" Lomas cried. "We have nothing to act on, and they're all cursing me because we haven't!"

"Meaning Kimball?"

"Kimball—Kimball's calling twice a day to know how the case is going on, please. But the whole Government's on it now. Minutes from the Home Secretary—bitter mems. from the Prime Minister. They want a scapegoat, of course. Governments do."

"Find us some one to hang or we'll hang you?"

"I told you I was thinking of resigning."

"Because they want to bully you into making a case against the private secretary—and you have a conscience?"

"Lord, no. I'd convict him to-day if I could. I don't like the fellow. He's a young prig. But I can't convict him. No; I don't think they want to hang anybody in particular. But they must have somebody to hang, and I can't find him."

"It isn't much in my way," Reggie murmured. "The Civil Service frightens me. I have a brother-in-law in the Treasury. Sometimes he lets me dine with him. Meditations among the Tombs for Reginald. No. It isn't much in my way. I want passion and gore. But you intrigue me, Lomas, you do indeed. I would know more of H. Kimball and Secretary Sandford. They worry me."

"My God, they worry me," said Lomas heartily.

"They are too good to be true. I wonder if there's any other nigger in the wood pile?"

"Well, I can't find him."

"Hope on, hope ever. Don't you remember it was the dowager popped the Bohun sapphires? And don't you resign. If the Prime Minister sends you another nasty mem., say you have your eye on his golf pro. A man who putts like that must have something on his conscience. And don't you resign for all the politicians outside hell. It may be they want to get rid of you. I'll come and see you tomorrow."

"I wish you would," said Lomas. "You have a mighty good eye for a face."

"My dear old thing! I never believe in faces, that's all. The only one I ever liked was that girl who broke her sister-in-law's nose. But I'll come round."

Comforted by wine and sympathy, Lomas was sent away to trudge home through a foot of snow. And the snow went on falling.

PHASE II: THE PRIVATE SECRETARY

The snow lingered. Though hoses washed it out of the highways, in every side street great mounds lay unmelted, and the park was dingily white. Reggie shivered as he got out of his car in Scotland Yard, and he scurried upstairs and put himself as close as he could to Lomas's fire—ousting Superintendent Bell.

"I'm waiting for you," said Lomas quietly. "There's a new fact. Three thousand pounds has been paid into Sandford's account. It was handed in over the counter in notes of small amounts yesterday morning. Cashier fancies it was paid in by a stoutish man in glasses—couldn't undertake to identify."

"It's a wicked world, Lomas. That wouldn't matter so much if it was sensible. Some day I will take to crime, just to show you how to do it. Who is Sandford, what is he, that such queer things happen round him?"

"I don't know so much about queer, sir," said Superintendent Bell. "I suppose this three thousand is his share of the swag."

"That's what we're meant to suppose," Reggie agreed. "That's what I resent."

"You mean, why the devil should he have it put in the bank? He must know his account would be watched. That's the point I took," said Lomas wearily.

"Well, sir, as I was saying, it's the usual sort of thing," Superintendent Bell protested. "When a city gang has bought a fellow in a good position and got all they can get out of him, it often happens they don't care any more about him. They'd rather break him than not. It happened in the Bewick affair, the Grantley deal—" He reeled off a string of cases. "What I mean to say, sir, there isn't honour among thieves. When they see one of themselves in a decent position, they'll do him in if they can. Envy, that's what it is. I suppose we're all envious. But in my experience, when a fellow isn't straight he gets a double go of envy in him. I mean to say, for sheer spiteful envy the crooks beat the band."

Reggie nodded. "Do you know, Bell, I don't ever remember your being wrong, when you had given an opinion. By the way, what is your opinion?"

Superintendent Bell smiled slowly. "We do have to be so careful, sir. Would you believe it, I don't so much as know who did the open-air work in the Coal Ramp. There was half a dozen firms in the boom, quite respectable firms. But who had the tip first, and who was doing the big business, I know no more than the babe in arms."

"Yes, there's some brains about," Lomas agreed.

But Reggie, who was watching the Superintendent, said, "What's up your sleeve, Bell?"

The Superintendent laughed. "You do have a way of putting things, Mr. Fortune." He lit a cigarette and looked at his chief. "I don't know what you thought of Mr. Sandford, Mr. Lomas?"

"More do I, Bell," said Lomas. "I only know he's not a man and a brother."

"What I should describe as a lonely cove, sir," Bell suggested. "Chiefly interested in himself, you might say."

"He's a climber," said Lomas.

"Well, well! Who is Sandford—what is he, that all the world don't love him?" Reggie asked. "Who was his papa? What was his school?"

"Well, now, it's rather odd you should ask that, sir," said Superintendent Bell.

"He didn't have a school. He didn't have a father," said Lomas. "First he knows he was living with his widowed mother, an only child, in a little village in North Wales— Llan something. He went to the local grammar-school. He was a kind of prize boy. He got a scholarship at Pembroke, Oxford. Then Mrs. Sandford died, leaving him about a pound a week. He got firsts at Oxford, and came into the Home Civil pretty high. He's done well in his Department, and they can't stand him."

"Good brain, no geniality, if you take my meaning," said the Superintendent.

"I hate him already," Reggie murmured.

"That's quite easy," said Lomas. "Well, he's a clever second-rater, that's what it comes to."

"Poor devil," Reggie murmured.

"There's swarms of them in the service. The only odd thing about Sandford is that he don't seem to have any origins. Like that fellow in the Bible who had no ancestors—Melchizedek, was it? Well, Mrs. Sandford had no beginning either. She wasn't native to Llanfairfechan—that's the place. She came there when Sandford was a small kid. Nobody there knows where from. He says he don't know where from. Nobody knows who his father was. He says he don't know. He says she left no papers of any sort. She had an annuity, and the fifty pounds a year she left him was in Consols. He never knew of any relations. Nobody in Llanwhat's-its-name can remember anybody ever coming to see her. And she died ten years ago."

"You might say it looked as if she wanted to hide," said Superintendent Bell. "But, Lord, you can't tell. Might be just a sorrowful widow. It takes 'em that way sometimes."

"Has anybody ever shown any interest in Melchizedek?" said Reggie.

"O Lord, no! Nobody ever heard of him out of his Department. And there they all hate him. But he's the sort of fellow you can't keep down."

"Poor devil," Reggie murmured again.

"You won't be so damned sympathetic when you've met him," Lomas said. A slip of paper was presented to him. "Hallo! Here's Kimball. I thought he was leaving me alone too long. Well, we've got something for him to-day."

"He has a large fat head": thus some perky journalist began a sketch of the Rt. Hon. Horace Kimball. And he faithfully reported the first elementary effect of seeing Mr. Kimball, who looked a heavy fellow, with the bulk of his head and neck supported on a sturdy frame. But on further acquaintance people discovered a vivacity of movement and a keenness of expression which made them uncomfortable. Yet he had, as I intend you to observe, a bluff, genial manner, and his cruellest critics were always those who had not met him. For the rest, he aimed at a beautiful neatness in his clothes, and succeeded.

He rushed in. "Well, Lomas, if we don't make an end of this business, it'll make an end of us," he announced, and flung himself at a chair. "Anything new?"

"I have just been discussing it with Mr. Fortune."

"That's right. Want the best brains we can get." He nodded his heavy head at Reggie. "What do you make of it?"

"I don't wonder you find it harassing," Reggie said.

"Harassing! That's putting it mildly. I've lost more sleep over it than I want to think about." He became aware that Reggie was studying him. "Doctor, aren't you?" he laughed ruefully. "I'm not a case, you know."

"I apologize for the professional instinct," Reggie said. "But it does make me say you ought to see your doctor, sir."

"My doctor can't tell me anything I don't know. It's this scandal that's the matter with me. You wouldn't say I was sentimental, would you? You wouldn't take me for an innocent? Well, do you know, I've been in business thirty years, and I've never had one of my own people break faith with me. That's what irritates me. Somebody in my own office, somebody close to me, selling me. By God, it's maddening!"

"Whom do you suspect?" said Reggie.

Kimball flung himself about, and the chair creaked. "Damn it, man, we've had all that out over and over again. I can't suspect any one. I won't suspect any one. But the thing's been done."

"As I understand, the only people who knew the scheme were yourself and Sandford, your secretary?"

"I'd as soon suspect myself as Sandford."

"Yesterday three thousand pounds in notes was paid by somebody, who didn't give his name, into Sandford's account," said Lomas.

"Great God!" said Kimball, and rolled back in his chair, breathing heavily. "That's what I wouldn't let myself believe."

"Have you got any brandy, Lomas?" said Reggie, watching his pallor professionally. Lomas started up. Reggie reached out and began to feel Kimball's pulse.

"Don't do that," said Kimball sharply, and dragged his hand away. "Good Lord, man, I'm not ill! No, thanks, Lomas, nothing, nothing. I never touch spirits. I'll be all right in a moment. But it does rather knock me over to find I've got to believe it was Sandford." He struggled out of his chair, walked to the window, and flung it up and dabbed at his forehead. He stood there a moment in the raw air, took a pinch of snuff, and turned on them vigorously. "There's no doubt about this evidence, eh? We can't get away from it?"

"I'm afraid we must ask Sandford for an explanation," said Lomas.

"Most unpleasant thing I ever did in my life," Kimball said. "Well, there's no help for it, I suppose. Still, he may have a perfectly good explanation. Damn it, I won't make up my mind till I must. I've always found him quite straight—and very efficient too. Cleverest fellow I ever had about me. Send for him then; say I'll be glad to see him here. Come now, Lomas, what do you think yourself? He may be able to account for it quite naturally, eh?"

"He may. But I can't see how," Lomas said gloomily. "Can you?"

"I suppose you think I'm a fool, but I like to believe in my fellows," said Kimball, and they passed an awkward five minutes till Sandford came.

He looked a good young man. He was rather small, he was very lean, he wore eyeglasses. Everything about him was correct and restrained. But there was an oddity of structure about his face: it seemed to come to a point at the end of his nose, and yet his lower jaw looked heavy.

He made graded salutations to Kimball his chief and to Lomas. He looked at Reggie and Superintendent Bell as though he expected them to retreat from his presence. And he turned upon Kimball a glance that bade him lose no time.

Kimball seemed to find some difficulty in beginning. He cleared his throat, blew his nose, and took another pinch of snuff. "I don't know if you guess why I sent for you," he broke out.

"I infer that it is on this matter of the gamble in coal shares," said Sandford precisely.

"Yes. Do you know of any new fact?"

"Nothing has come before me."

"Well, there's something I want you to explain. I dare say you have a satisfactory explanation. But I'm bound to ask for it."

"I have nothing to explain that I know of."

"It's been brought to my knowledge that yesterday three thousand pounds in notes was paid into your account. Where did it come from?"

Sandford took off his eyeglasses and cleaned them, and put them on again. "I have no information," he said in the most correct official manner.

"Good God, man, you must see what it means!" Kimball cried.

"I beg your pardon, sir. I have no notion of what it means. I find it difficult to believe that you have been correctly informed."

"You don't suppose I should take up a charge like this unless I was compelled to."

"There's no doubt of the fact, Mr. Sandford," said Lomas gloomily.

"Indeed! Then I have only to say that no one has any authority to make payments into my account. As you have gone into the affair so carefully, I suppose you have found out who did."

"He didn't give his name, you see. Can you tell us who he was?" Lomas said.

"I repeat, sir, I know nothing about the transaction."

"And that's all you say?"

"I need hardly add that I shall not accept the money."

"You know the matter can't end there!" Kimball cried. "Come, man, you're not doing yourself justice. Nothing could be worse for you than this tone, can't you see that?"

"I beg your pardon, sir. I do not see what you wish me to say. You spoke of making a charge. Will you be so good as to state it?"

"If you must have it! This boom was begun on information which only you had besides myself. And immediately after the boom this large sum is paid secretly into your account. You must see what everybody will say—what I should say myself if I didn't know you—that you sold the plan, and this money is your price. Come, you must have some explanation for us—some defence, at least."

"I say again, sir, I know nothing of the matter. I should hope that what scandal may say will have no influence upon any one who knows my character and my career."

"Good God, man, we're dealing with facts! Where did that three thousand pounds come from?"

"I have no information. I have no idea."

For the first time Reggie spoke. "I wonder if you have a theory?"

"I don't consider it is my duty to imagine theories."

"Do you know any one who wants to ruin you? Or why any one should?"

"I beg your pardon. I must decline to be led into wild speculations of that kind."

Kimball started up. "You make it impossible to do anything for you. I have given you every chance, remember that—every chance. It's beyond me now. I can only advise you to consider your position. I don't know whether your resignation will save you from worse consequences. I'll do what I can. But you make it very hard. Good morning. You had better not go back to the office."

"I deny every imputation," said Sandford. "Good morning, sir."

Half apologetically Kimball turned to the others. "There's nothing for it, I suppose. We'll have to go through with it now. You'll let me have an official report. The fellow's hopeless. Poor devil!"

"I can't say he touches my heart," said Lomas.

Kimball laughed without mirth. "He can't help himself," he said, and went out.

"I shouldn't have thought Kimball was so human," said Lomas.

"Well, sir, he always has stuck to his men, I must say," said Superintendent Bell.

"I wonder he could stick to Sandford for a day."

"That Mr. Sandford, he is what you might call a superior person," Bell chuckled. "Funny how they brazen it out, that kind."

"Yes, I don't doubt he thinks he was most impressive. Well, Fortune, there's not much here for you, I'm afraid."

Reggie had gone to the window and was fidgeting there. "I say, the wind's changed," said he. "That's something, anyway."

Phase III: The Man Under the Snow

The porter of Montmorency House, awaking next morning, discovered that even in the well of his flats, where the air is ever the most stagnant in London, the snow was melting fast. After breakfast he saw some clothes emerging from the slush. This annoyed him, for he cherished that little court. The tenants, he remarked to his wife, were always doing something messy, but dropping their trousers down the well was the limit. He splashed out into the slush and found a corpse.

After lunch Reggie Fortune, drowsing over the last published play of Herr Wedekind, was roused by the telephone, which, speaking with the voice of Superintendent Bell, urged him to come at once to the mortuary.

"Who's dead?" he asked. "Sandford hanged himself in red tape? Kimball had a stroke?"

"It's what you might call anonymous," said the voice of the Superintendent. "Just the sort of case you like."

"I never like a case," said Reggie, with indignation, and rang off.

At the door of the mortuary Superintendent Bell appeared as his car stopped.

"You're damned mysterious," Reggie complained.

"Not me, sir. If you can tell me who the fellow is, I'll be obliged. But what I want to know first is, what was the cause of death. You'll excuse me, I won't tell you how he was found till you've formed your opinion."

"What the devil do you mean by that?"

"I don't want you to be prejudiced in any way, sir, if you take my meaning."

"Damn your impudence. When did you ever see me prejudiced?"

"Dear me, Mr. Fortune, I never heard you swear so much," said Bell sadly. "Don't be hasty, sir. I have my reasons. I have, really."

He led the way into the room where the dead man lay. He pulled back the sheet which covered the body. "Well, well!" said Reggie Fortune. For the dead man's face was not there.

"You'll excuse me. I shouldn't be any good to you," said the Superintendent thickly, and made for the door.

Reggie did not look round. "Send Sam in with my things," he said.

It was a long time afterwards when, rather pale for him, his round and comfortable face veiled in an uncommon gravity, he came out.

Superintendent Bell threw away his cigarette. "Ghastly, isn't it?" he said with sympathy.

"Mad," said Reggie. "Come on." A shower of warm rain was being driven before the west wind, but he opened everything in his car that would open, and told the chauffeur to drive round Regent's Park. "Come on, Bell. The rain won't hurt you."

"I don't wonder you want a blow. Poor chap! As ugly a mess as ever I saw."

"I suppose I'm afraid," said Reggie slowly. "It's unusual and annoying. I suppose the only thing that does make you afraid is what's mad. Not the altogether crazy—that's only a nuisance—but what's damned clever and yet mad. An able fellow with a mania on one point. I suppose that's what the devil is, Bell."

"Good Lord, sir," said Superintendent Bell.

"What I want is muffins," said Reggie—"several muffins and a little tea and my domestic hearth. Then I'll feel safe."

He spread himself out, sitting on the small of his back before his study fire, and in that position contrived to eat and drink with freedom.

"In another world, Bell," he said dreamily—"in another and a gayer world it seems to me you wanted to know the cause of death. And you didn't want me to be prejudiced. Kindly fellow. But there's no prejudice about. It's quite a plain case."

"Is it indeed, sir? You surprise me."

"The dead man was killed by a blow on the left temple, from some heavy, blunt weapon—a life-preserver, perhaps, a stick, a poker. At the same time, or immediately after death, his face was battered in by the same or a similar weapon. Death probably occurred some days ago. After death, but not long after death, the body received other injuries, a broken rib and left shoulder-blade, probably by a fall from some height. That's the medical evidence. There are other curious circumstances."

"Just a few!" said Bell, with a grim chuckle. "You're very definite, sir, if I might say so. I suppose he couldn't have been killed and had his face smashed like—like he did—by the fall?"

"You can cut that right out. He was killed by a blow and blows smashed his face in. Where did you find him?"

"He was found when the snow melted this morning in the well at Montmorency House."

"Under the snow? That puts the murder on the night of the fifteenth. Yes, that fits; that accounts for his sodden clothes."

"There's a good deal it don't account for," said Bell gloomily.

"I saw him just as he was found?" Bell nodded. "Somebody took a lot of pains with him. He was fully dressed—collar and tie, boots. But a lot of his internal buttons were undone. And there's not a name, not even a maker's name, on any of his clothes. His linen's new and don't show a laundry mark. Yes, somebody took a lot of pains we shouldn't know him."

"I don't know what you're getting at, sir."

"Don't you? Is it likely a man wearing decent clothes would not have his linen marked and his tailor's name somewhere? Is it likely a man who had his tie and collar on wouldn't do up his undershirt? No. The beggar's clothes were changed after he was killed. That must have been a grisly business too. He's not a tender-hearted fellow who did this job. Valet the body you've killed and then bash its face in! Well, well! Have some more tea?"

"Not me," said Bell, with a gulp. "You talked about a madman, sir, didn't you?"

"Oh no, no, no. Not the kind of mad that runs amuck. Not homicidal mania. This isn't just smashing up a chap's body for the sake of smashing. There's lot of purpose here. This is damned cold, calculating crime. That kind of mad. Some fellow's got an object that makes it worth while to him to do any beastliness. That's the worst kind of mad, Bell. Not homicidal mania—that only makes a man a beast. What's here is the sort of thing that makes a man a devil."

"You're going a bit beyond me, sir. It's a bloody murder, and that's all I want."

"Yes, that's our job," said Reggie thoughtfully. Together they went off to Montmorency House.

"How would you describe deceased, sir?" said Bell.

"Man of about fifty, under middle height, inclined to be stout, unusual bald."

"It ain't much to go by, is it?" Bell sighed. "We don't so much as know if he was clean shaved or not."

"He was, I think. I saw no trace of facial hair. But it's rash to argue from not finding things. And he might have been shaved after he was killed."

"And then smashed? My Lord! And they smashed him thorough too, didn't they?"

"Very logical bit of crime, Bell."

"Logical! God bless my soul! But I mean to say, sir, we haven't got much to go on. Suppose I advertise there's a man of fifty missing, rather short and stout and bald, I shall look a bit of an ass."

"Well, I wouldn't advertise. He'd had an operation, by the way—on the ear. But I wouldn't say that either. In fact, I wouldn't say anything about him just yet. Hold your trumps."

"Trumps? What is trumps then, Mr. Fortune?"

"Anything you know is always trumps."

"You'll excuse me, but it's not my experience, sir."

They came to Montmorency House, where detectives were already domesticated with the porter, and had done the obvious things. The body, it was to be presumed, had fallen from one of the windows opening on the well. The men who had flats round the well were all accounted for, save one. Mr. Rand, tenant of a flat on the top story, had not been seen for some days. Ringing at Mr. Rand's door had produced no reply.

"Well, we do seem to be getting a bit warmer," said Superintendent Bell. And his subordinate in charge of the inquiries at the flats beamed and rubbed his hands, and remarked that Rand seemed to have been a mysterious chap—only had his flat a few weeks, not used it regularly, not by any means; no visitors to speak of, civil but distant. "That sounds all right," said Bell, and looked at Reggie.

"What was he like?" said Reggie.

"Middle size to biggish, wore glasses, well dressed, brown hair, which he wore rather long, they say," the inspector reeled off glibly.

"That's put the lid on," said Bell. "Won't do for the corpse, Warren. Not a bit like it. Well, sir, where are we now?" He turned to Reggie.

"You will go so fast," Reggie complained, and sat down. "I'm pantin' after you in vain. What's the primary hypothesis, Bell?"

"Sir?"

"Do we assume the corpse is Rand, or that Rand chucked the corpse out of window?"

"Ah, there's that," said the inspector eagerly. "We hadn't worked on that."

"We haven't worked on anything, if you ask me," said Bell gloomily. "What's your opinion then, Mr. Fortune?"

"The primary hypothesis is that we're looking for an able, masterful madman. Therefore my opinion is that the whole thing will look perfectly rational when we've got it all combed out—grantin' the madman's original mad idea."

"Am I to go round London looking for a rational madman?" Bell protested.

"My dear chap, you could catch 'em by the thousand. There's nobody so damned rational as the lunatic. That's where he falls down. Do not be discouraged. He's logical. He don't keep his eye on the facts. That is where we come in."

"We've come in all right, but we don't seem like getting out," Bell grumbled. "I'm keeping my eye on the facts all right. But they won't fit."

"You're very hasty to-day, Bell," said Reggie mildly. "Why is this?"

"I can see that fellow's face," Bell muttered.

"Well, well! He's told us all he can, poor devil. We'll get on, if you please. Because Rand's away, it don't follow that Rand's the corpse. It might have come out of some other tenant's window. Know anything about the other tenants?"

"All most respectable, sir," said the inspector.

"My dear man, the whole affair is most respectable. Do get that into your head. I dare say we'll find the corpse was a conveyancer murdered by a civil servant. A crime of quiet, middle-class taste. What sort of fellows are the other fellows?"

"Well, sir, there's a retired engineer, and a young chap, just married, in the Rimington firm, and a naval officer, and several young doctors with consulting-rooms in Harley Street, and one of the Maynards, the Devonshire family. That's all with any rooms on the well. I've seen 'em all, and, if you ask me, they're right out of it; they're not the sort, not one of them."

"I dare say," said Reggie. "They don't sound as if they would fit. None of them heard anything?"

"No, sir; that's queer, to be sure."

"It happened the night of the blizzard. You wouldn't have noticed a bomb. Well, who was Rand?"

"That's what no one knows, sir. He'd only been here a few weeks. They're service flats, you know, and furnished. He gave a banker's reference. Bank says he has no money reason to be missing. Quiet, stable account. Income from investments. Balance three hundred odd. But the bank don't know anything about him. He's had an account for years. He used to live off Jermyn Street, apartment-house. The landlady died last year."

"And the landlady died last year," Reggie repeated. "He's elusive, is Mr. Rand. Same like our corpse. But is Rand missing, Bell? He's not been seen for a few days. There's not much in that. He never used his flat regularly."

"And, so far as we know, deceased isn't Rand."

"Well, I don't know quite as far as that," said Reggie.

"Good Lord, the porter who found him didn't recognize the body."

"Remember his face."

"My God, don't talk about his face."

"Sorry, sorry. Well, I dare say the porter was upset too."

"Yes, but the porter said Rand was biggish, and the body's on the small side. The porter said he had a lot of hair, and the body's absolutely bald."

"My dear chap, give a man a straight back and a bit of manner and lots of fellows think he's biggish—while he's alive. And a man that's absolutely bald is just the man to wear a wig."

"I thought we were to go by facts," Bell said gloomily.

"And so we are, Bell. Just a-going to begin, Mr. Snodgrass, sir. No rash haste."

"Have you got something up your sleeve?"

"Not one little trump. Oh, my dear Bell, how can you? Did I ever? My simple open heart is broken."

"You're damned cheerful, aren't you?"

"My dear man, I never made you swear before. My dear Bell! Sorry. Let's get on. Let's get on. I want to call on the elusive Rand."

There was nothing individual about the rooms of Mr. Rand. He had been content with the furniture supplied by the owners of the place, which was of the usual wholesale dullness. Reggie turned to the manager of the flats. "I suppose there's nothing in the place Mr. Rand owns? Not even the pictures?"

"The pictures were supplied by the contractors for the furniture, sir. So—"

"The Lord have mercy on their souls," said Reggie.

"So there is nothing of the tenant's personal property except his clothes."

"He is elusive, our friend Rand," Reggie murmured, wandering about the room. "Smoked rather a showy cigar. Drank a fair whisky. Doesn't tell us much about him. Do the servants come here every day?"

The manager was embarrassed. "Well, sir, in point of fact, we're short-handed just now. Not unless they're rung for. Not unless we know the tenant's using the rooms."

"Don't apologize, don't apologize. In point of fact, they haven't been here since"—he looked critically at some dust upon a grim bronze—"since when?"

"I should say some days," said the manager, with diffidence.

"I should say a week. No matter. Many thanks."

Superintendent Bell with some urgency ushered the manager out. When he had done that he turned upon his inspector. "Confound you, Warren, what do you want to stare at the waste-paper basket for? That chap would have seen it if Mr. Fortune hadn't got interested in the smokes and drinks."

Reggie laughed and the inspector abased himself. "Very sorry, sir. Didn't know I stared. But it is so blooming odd."

Bell snorted and lifted the basket on to the table. It was nearly full of black burnt paper. "Why did they burn it in the basket?" said the inspector.

"Because the fireplaces are all gas stoves, I suppose," said Bell. "But I don't know why they couldn't leave the stuff on the hearth."

"Because this is a tidy crime," said Reggie. "Nice, quiet, middle-class crime. No ugly mess. I told you that."

The Superintendent gazed at him. "Now what can you know, you know?"

"I don't know. I feel. I feel the kind of man that did it. Don't you? I'll lay you odds he came of a neat, virtuous, middle-class home."

The Superintendent started. "Who are you thinking of?"

"You are so hasty to-day, Bell. I haven't got a 'who.' Still anonymous is the slayer. But I'll swear I've got his character."

"Have you, though!" said Bell. "Tidy fellow! Don't make a mess! Remember that face?"

"Oh, I said he was mad."

"Well, I'm not yet. I'm only feeling what I can feel." He began to examine the burnt paper. "Letters mostly. Some stoutish paper. Some stuff looks a bit like a note-book. That's all we'll get out of that."

"Well, except the one thing. Whoever did that was clearing up. Clearing up something that might have left traces that might have been dangerous. Same like he cleared up the dead man's face. Don't you see? Somebody and some affair had to be absolutely abolished."

"Yes. What was it?"

"We mayn't ever know that," said Reggie slowly.

"I believe you," said Bell, and laughed. "I feel that, sir."

The inspector and he began to examine the room in detail, opening drawers and cupboards. But except for tobacco and spirits they found no trace of Mr. Rand. Nothing had been broken open, but nothing was locked. "No keys on the deceased were there, Mr. Fortune?" said Bell suddenly. "And that's a point, too. Very few men go about without any keys."

"Well, hang it, very few men go about without any money," Reggie expostulated. "The corpse hadn't a copper. You can take it the way we found him wasn't the way he used to go about. He'd do his vest up, for instance."

"Ah," said Bell sagely. "You've got it all in your head, I must say. That's the thing about you, Mr. Fortune, if you don't mind my saying so. You've always got a whole case in your mind at once; there's some of us only see it in bits, so to speak."

Reggie smiled. He understood that Superintendent Bell was repenting of having lost his temper, and was anxious to make it up. "I never found so good a fellow to work with as you, Bell," he said. "You always keep a level head."

Superintendent Bell shook it and stared at Reggie. "Not to-day. As you know very well, Mr. Fortune, begging your pardon. I've been rattled, and that's the truth. Ought to know better at my time of life, to be sure. I've seen a good deal, too, you might say. But there's some things I'll never get used to. And that chap's face upset me."

Reggie nodded. "Yes. I was sayin'—the only things that make you afraid are the mad things. And the only thing that does you good is to fight 'em. That's why I've cheered up."

"That's right, sir. Well, now, these facts of yours. There's no papers anywhere. All burnt in that basket. Rather odd there is not so much as a book."

"I don't think he was a man of culture, the elusive Rand. But you've missed something, haven't you?"

"I dare say," Bell grinned. "I generally do when you're about."

"There's not a sign the murder was done in this room."

"Oh, I saw that all right. But we hadn't any reason to think it was."

"No," Reggie sighed, "no. So tidy. So tidy." And they went into Mr. Rand's bedroom.

That also was tidy. No trace of a struggle, of blood. That also had no papers, no books, nothing personal but clothes.

"Spent a good deal at his tailor's," said Bell, looking into a well-filled wardrobe, and read out the name of a man in Savile Row. "Hallo. They're not all the same make. Some cheaper stuff. Why, what's the matter with his boots, sir?" For Reggie was taking up one pair after another.

"Nothing. All quite satisfactory. About a nine and rather broad. The corpse wore about a nine and had a broad foot. What's that about his clothes? Different tailors? Are the clothes all the same size? All made for the same man?" Suit after suit was spread out on the bed. They were to the same measure; they all were marked "W. H. Rand." "Quite satisfactory," Reggie purred. "They'd fit the corpse all right. Pretty different styles, though. He dressed to look different different times. He is elusive, is W. H. Rand."

They began to open drawers. There was the same abundance, the same variety of styles in Mr. Rand's hosiery. "Yes, he meant to be elusive," Reggie murmured.

"Anything from a bookmaker to a church-warden at a funeral. 16½ collars, though. And that's the measure of the corpse. Is all the linen marked?"

It was, and with ink, so that the mark could only be removed by taking out a piece of the stuff. "If the corpse is Rand, where the devil did his shirt come from?" said Reggie. "The slayer unpicked the name from his coat. That was one of the Savile Row suits. But the shirt? Did the slayer bring a change of linen with him? Provident fellow, very provident."

Bell, on his knees by a chest of drawers, gave a grunt. "Lord, here's a drawer tumbled. And that's the first yet. It's new stuff, too—not worn."

Reggie bent over him and whistled. "Not marked. Same sort of stuff as the corpse wears. And the drawer's left untidy. The first untidy drawer. Well, well. Everybody breaks down somewhere. He began to be untidy then. When he got to the shirt and the vest." He shivered and turned away to the window. "This damned place looks out on the well," he cried out, and turned back and sat down. "Bah! The slayer did that, I suppose," he muttered, and sprang up. "Believe in ghosts, you men?"

"Good Lord, sir, don't you start giving us the jumps!" said Bell.

Reggie was at the dressing-table. "Sorry, sorry," he said over his shoulder, opening and shutting drawers. Then he turned with something in his hands. "That wasn't such a bad shot of mine, Bell. Here's a wig. The corpse is uncommon bald. The elusive Rand had lots of brown hair. Here's a nice brown wig."

"There's no blood on it!" Bell cried.

"No. I guess this is Mr. Rand's second best. The one he had on when he was killed wouldn't look nice now."

"That about settles it," Bell said slowly.

"We haven't seen the bathroom," said Reggie.

Bell looked at him and shrugged.

"Not likely to be much there, sir," said the inspector.

"There could be," said Reggie gravely, and led the way.

It was a bathroom of some size but no luxury. Only the sheer necessities of bathing were provided. The lower half of the walls was tiled, the floor of linoleum. Reggie stopped in the doorway. "Anything strike you about it, Bell?"

"Looks new, sir."

"Yes. Nice and clean. Tidy, don't you know. But there's no towels and no sponge. Yet in the bedroom everything was ready for Rand to sleep there to-night— pyjamas, brushes and comb, everything. Didn't he use towels? Didn't he have a sponge?"

"What do you mean, sir?"

"This is where the slayer cleared up after the murder. And he took the dirty towels and the bloody sponge away with him. Tidy fellow—always tidy. Just wait, will you?" And he went into the bathroom on all fours. About the middle of the room he stopped, and pored over the linoleum, and felt it with the tips of his fingers. Then he stood up and went to the window, opened it, and looked out. He examined the sill, and then sat himself on it in the manner of a window cleaner, and began to study the window frame. After a minute or two he pulled out a pocket-knife, and with great care cut a piece of wood. He put this down on the edge of the porcelain basin, and resumed his study. When he had finished he went down again on his hands and knees, and wandered over the floor. He made an exclamation, he lay down on his stomach, and stretched underneath the bath. When he stood up he had in his hand something that glittered. He held it out on his palm to Bell.

"What's that, sir? A match-box?"

"It might be. A gold match-box—provisionally. No name. No initials. On opening—we find inside—a little white powder"—he smelt it, put a fragment on the tip of his finger and tasted—"which is cocaine. Well, come in, Bell, come in. See what you can make of the place. I can't find a fingerprint anywhere." He slipped the gold box into his pocket.

The two detectives came in, and went over the room even more minutely than he. "There's nothing that tells me anything," said Bell.

Reggie sat on the edge of the bath. "Well, well, I wouldn't say that," he said mildly. "It's not what we could wish, Bell. But there are points—there are points."

"All right, sir. Call Mr. Fortune," Bell grinned.

"I don't say it'll ever go into court. But some things we do know. The dead man is Rand, the elusive Rand. He had papers worth burning. He was killed by a powerful man with one or two blows, probably in the sitting-room. After death he was stripped and dressed in the unmarked clothes, probably here. For his body was brought where a mess could be cleaned up, to have the face smashed in. You can see the dents in the linoleum where his head lay. And then he was pitched out by that window. There's a bit of animal matter, probably human tissue, on that scrap of wood. Then the slayer packed up everything that was bloody and went off; and one of 'em—the tidy slayer or the elusive Rand—one of 'em used cocaine."

Superintendent Bell shrugged his shoulders. "It don't take us very far, sir, does it? It don't amount to so much. What I should call a baffling case. I mean to say, we don't seem to get near anybody."

Reggie grunted, got off the bath, and taking with him his bit of wood, went back to the sitting-room, the two detectives in silent attendance. There he tumbled Mr. Rand's cigarettes out of their box, and put his bit of wood in it.

"I suppose there's nothing more here," he murmured, his eyes wandering round the room. "Try it with the lights on. Switch on, inspector. . . . No. Ah, what's that?" He went to the gas fire and picked out of its lumps of sham coal a scrap of gleaming metal. The next moment he was down on his knees, pulling the fire to pieces. "Give me an envelope, will you?" he said over his shoulder, and they saw he was collecting scraps of broken glass.

"What is it, sir?"

"That's the bridge of a pair of rimless eyeglasses. And if we're lucky we can reconstruct the lenses. When Rand was hit, his glasses jumped off and smashed themselves. That's the fourth thing the slayer didn't think of."

"You don't miss much, Mr. Fortune. Still, it is baffling, very baffling. Even now, we don't know anybody, so to speak. We don't even know Rand. What was Rand, would you say? It was worth somebody's while to do him in. I suppose he knew something. But what did he know? Who was Rand?"

Reggie was putting on his overcoat. He collected his envelope and his cigarette box and put them away, looking the while with dreamy eyes at Superintendent Bell. "Yes," he said; "yes, there's a lot of unknown quantities about just now. Who the devil was Rand? Well, well! I think that finishes us here. Will you ring for the lift, inspector?" When he was left alone with Bell, he still gazed dreamily at that plump, stolid face. "Yes. Who the devil was Rand? And if you come to that, who the devil is Sandford?"

"Good Lord, Mr. Fortune, do you mean this business is that business?"

"Well, there's a lot of unknown quantities about," said Reggie.

PHASE IV: THE CHARGE

When they talked about the case afterwards, Reggie and Lomas used to agree that it was a piece of pure art. "Crime unstained by any vulgar greed or sentiment; sheer crime; iniquity neat. An impressive thing, Lomas, old dear."

"So it is," Lomas nodded. "One meets cases of the kind, but never quite of so pure a style. Upon my soul, Fortune, it has a sort of grandeur—the intensity of purpose, the contempt for ordinary values, the absolute uselessness of it. And it was damned clever."

Reggie chose a cigar. "Great work," he sighed. "All the marks of the real great man, if it wasn't diabolical. He was a great man, but for the hate in him. Just like the devil."

"You're so moral," Lomas protested. "Don't you feel the beauty of it?"

"Of course I'm moral. I'm sane. Oh, so sane, Lomas, old thing. That's why I beat the wily criminal. And the devil, God help him."

"Yes, you're as sane as a boy," Lomas nodded.

But all that was afterwards.

Everything that was done in the case is not (though you may have feared so) written here. We take it in the critical, significant scenes, and the next of them arrived some days after the discovery of the corpse.

Lomas was in his room with Superintendent Bell, when Kimball came to them. He was brisker than ever. "Anything new, is there? Have you hit on anything? I came round at once, you see, when I got your note. Delighted to get it. Much better to have all the details cleared up. Well, what is it?"

"I'm afraid I've nothing for you myself," said Lomas. "The fact is, Fortune thought you might be able to give him some information on one or two points."

"I? God bless me, you know all that I know. Where is he, then, if he wants me?"

And Reggie came. "Have you been waitin'?" he said, with his airiest manner. "So sorry. Things are really rollin' up, you know. New facts by every post. Well, well." He dropped into a chair and blinked at the party. "What are we all doin' here? Oh, ah! I remember." He smiled and nodded at Kimball. "It was that fellow I wanted to ask you about."

Kimball, as was natural, did not relish this sort of thing. "I understood you had something important on hand. I've no time to waste."

"Why, it's so jolly hard to understand what's important and what isn't, don't you know? But it all comes out in the end."

"You think so, do you? This is the coal affair?"

"I wouldn't say that," Reggie answered thoughtfully. "No, I wouldn't say that. After all, the Coal Ramp isn't the only pebble on the beach."

"Then why the devil do you bother me?" Kimball cried.

Reggie sat up suddenly. "Because this is something you must know." He rearranged his coat and slid down into the chair again, and drawled out what he had to say. "Some time the end of last year—point of fact—last December—bein' quite precise, from fifth to twenty-ninth—in one of the nursin'-homes in Queen Anne Street—speakin' strictly, No. 1003—there was a man bein' operated on by Sir Jenkin Totteridge for an affection of the middle ear. This chap was called Mason. You went to see him several times. Who was Mason?"

Kimball stared at him with singular intensity. Then he swung half round in his chair with one of his characteristic jerky movements, and pulled out his snuffbox. He took a pinch. "You've found a mare's nest," he said, with a laugh, and took another pinch.

As he spoke, Reggie sprang up with some vehemence, bumping into his arm. "Sorry—sorry. A mare's nest, you say? Now what exactly do you mean by that?"

Kimball stood up too. "I mean you're wasting my time," he said.

"That isn't what I should call an explanation," Reggie murmured. "For instance, do you mean you didn't go to see Mason?"

"Don't let's have any more of this damned trifling," Kimball cried. "Certainly I went to see Mason."

"Good! Who is he?"

"Jack Mason is a fellow I knew in my early days. I went up and he didn't. I've seen little of him this ten years. When he had that operation, poor chap, he wrote to me, and I went to see him for the sake of old times. And what the devil has it to do with Scotland Yard?"

"Mason is the man who was found at the Montmorency House flats with his face smashed in."

"God bless my soul! Mason! Poor chap, poor chap! But what are you talking about? The papers said that was a man called Rand."

"Mason, otherwise Rand. Rand, otherwise Mason. Who was Mason, and why did somebody kill him?"

Kimball made one of his jerky gestures. "Killed, was he? I thought he fell out of the window."

"He was murdered."

"Good God! Old Jack Mason! It's beyond me. I haven't a notice. You know this upsets me a good deal. I've seen little of him for a long time. I can hardly believe he's gone. But why the devil did he call himself Rand?"

"What was he?" said Reggie sharply.

"God bless me, I couldn't tell you," Kimball laughed. "He was always very close. An agent in a small way, when I knew him—colonial produce, and so forth. I fancy he went in for building land. Comfortably off always, but he never got on. Very reserved fellow. Loved to be mysterious. No. I suppose it isn't surprising he used two names."

"Why was he murdered?" said Reggie.

"I can't help you."

"That's all you can say?"

"Yes. Afraid so. Yes. Let me know as soon as you have anything more. Good morning, good morning." He bustled out.

"A bit hurried, as you might say," said Superintendent Bell.

Reggie picked up a paper-knife and fell on his knees. He rose with some fragments of white powder on the blade. "I suppose you saw me jog his arm," he said. "And that's cocaine." He tumbled Lomas's paper-clips out of their box and put the stuff in. "Do you remember the first time we had him here, he took snuff? I thought he was rather odd about it and after it, and I went over to the window where he stood to see if I could find any of the stuff he used. But he'd been careful. He is careful, is Kimball."

"He is damned careful," Lomas agreed, and began to write on a scribbling-pad, looking at each word critically.

There was a pause. "Beg your pardon, sir," said Superintendent Bell. "You talked about the murder being a madman's job. Do you mean Mr. Kimball, being a dope fiend, is not responsible for his actions?"

"O Lord, no. Kimball's not a dope fiend. He uses the stuff same like we use whisky. He's not a slave to it yet. Say he's a heavy drinker. It's just beginnin' to interfere with his efficiency. That's why he left the box behind in the bathroom; that's why he's a little jerky. But he's pretty adequate still."

"You talked about mad. You were emphatic, as you might say," Bell insisted. "What might you have in your mind, sir? Mr. Kimball's generally reckoned uncommon practical."

"He isn't ordinary mad," said Reggie. "He don't think he's Julius Caesar or a poached egg. He don't go out without his trousers. He don't see red and go it blind. But there is something queer in him. I doubt if they're physical, these perversions. Call it a disease of the soul."

"Ah, well, his soul," said Bell gravely. "I judge he's not a Christian man."

"I wish I did know his creed," said Reggie, with equal gravity. "It would be very instructive."

Lomas tapped his pencil impatiently. "We're not evangelists, we're policemen," he said. "And what do we do next?"

"Take out a warrant and arrest Kimball," said Reggie carelessly.

Bell and Lomas looked at each other and then at him. "I don't see my way," said Lomas.

"The corpse can be identified as Mason. I'll swear to the operation. Totteridge will swear it's the man he operated on as Mason. Kimball admits several visits to Mason. In the room from which the corpse was thrown was a gold snuff-box containing cocaine. Shortman's will swear that box is their make and exactly similar to a box sold to Kimball. And Kimball takes cocaine. It's a good prima facie case."

"Yes. Did you ever see a jury that would hang a man on it?"

"We do have to be so careful," Bell murmured.

Reggie laughed. "And Kimball's a Cabinet Minister."

"Damn it, Fortune, be fair!" Lomas cried. "If I had a sound case against a man, he would stand his trial whoever he was. I don't wink at a fellow who's got a pull. You know that. But there's reason in all things. I can't charge a Cabinet Minister with murder on evidence like this. What is it after all?" He picked up his scribbling-pad and read: "'Three circumstances—Kimball knew the murdered man; a snuff-box like Kimball's was found on the scene of the murder; that snuff-box held cocaine, and cocaine is what Kimball uses.' Circumstantial evidence at its weakest. Neither judge nor jury would look at it. There's no motive, there's no explanation of the method of the crime. My dear chap, suppose you were on the other side, you'd tear it to ribands in five minutes."

"On the other side?" Reggie repeated slowly. "I'm not an advocate, Lomas. I'm always on the same side. I'm for justice. I'm for the man who's been wronged."

Lomas stared at him. "Yes. Quite—quite. But we generally take all that for granted, don't we? My dear chap, you mustn't mind my saying so, but you do preach a good deal over this case."

"I had noticed the same thing myself," said Superintendent Bell, and they both looked curiously at Reggie.

"Why am I so moral? Because the thing's so damned immoral," said Reggie vehemently. "What's most crime? Human. Human greed, human lust, human hostility. But this is diabolical. Sheer evil for evil's sake. Lomas, I'll swear, when we have it all out, we'll find that it still looks unreasonable, futile, pure passion for wrong."

"Meaning Mr. Kimball mad. You do come back to that, sir," Bell said.

"Not legally mad. Probably not medically mad. I mean he has the devil in him."

"Really, my dear Fortune, you do surprise me," Lomas said. "I perceive that in all things you are too superstitious. The right honourable gentleman hath a devil! It isn't done, you know. This is the twentieth century. And you're a scientific man. Consider your reputation—and mine, if you don't mind. What the devil are we to do? Try exorcism?"

"You won't charge Kimball?" Lomas signified an impatient negative. "Very well. You say you don't let a man off because he's in the Government. Suppose you had a prime facie case like this against a nobody. Suppose I brought you as good grounds for arresting Sandford. Wouldn't you have him in the dock? On your conscience now!"

Again Bell and Lomas consulted each other's faces. "I wonder why you drag in Sandford?" said Lomas slowly.

"He's in it all right. I asked you a question."

"Well, if you insist. One might charge a man on a prima facie case, to hear his defence."

Reggie struck his hand on the table. "There it is! A man who is nobody—he can stand trial. Not a Cabinet Minister. Oh dear, no!"

"My dear fellow, the world is what it is. You know very well that if I wanted to charge Kimball on this evidence it would be turned down. I couldn't force the issue without a stronger case. Do have some sense of the practical."

Reggie smiled. "I'm not blaming you. I only want to rub it in."

"Thanks very much. We are to suspect Kimball, I suppose."

"Like the devil, and watch him."

"I see. Yes, I think we shall be quite justified in watching Mr. Kimball. But, my dear fellow, you are rather odd this morning. If you want Kimball watched, why the devil do you handle him so violently? You know, you almost accused him of the murder. Anything more likely to put him on his guard I can't imagine."

"Yes, yes. I think I made him jump," said Reggie, with satisfaction. "Quite intentional, Lomas, old thing. He's on his guard all right. But he don't know how little we know. I meant to put him in a funk. I want to see what a funk will make him do."

Lomas looked at him steadily. "For a very moral man," he said, "you have a good deal of the devil about you."

"I think I ought to say, Mr. Fortune," said Bell, "we've all been in a hurry to judge Mr. Kimball. I said things myself. And I do say he's not a Christian man—an unbeliever, I'm afraid. But I had ought to say too, he lives a very clean life. Always has. Temperate, very quiet style, a thorough good master, generous to his employees, and always ready to come down handsome for a good cause."

"Who is Kimball, Bell?" said Reggie quietly.

"Sir?" Bell stared. "He's always been known, sir. Started in Liverpool on the Cotton Exchange. Went into rubber. Came to London. That's his career. All quite open and straight."

"And we don't know a damned thing about him."

"Well, really, Fortune, you're rather exacting. You're after his soul, I suppose," said Lomas, with something like a sneer.

"Who is Kimball?" Reggie insisted. "There's two unknown quantities. Who is Kimball? Who is Sandford?"

"I'm afraid you want the Day of Judgment, my dear fellow," said Lomas. "'Unto whom all hearts are open, all desires known'—that sort of thing. Well, we can't ring up the Recording Angel from here. It's a trunk call."

"I know you're worldly. But you might know your world. Look about, Lomas, old thing. I've been looking about." He took out a newspaper cutting.

Lomas read: "'Sandford. Any one who can give any information about Mrs. Ellen Edith Sandford, resident Llanfairfechan from 1882–1900, formerly of Lancashire, is urgently begged to communicate with XYZ.'" He looked up. "Of Lancashire? That's a guess?"

Reggie nodded. "North Wales is mostly Lancashire people."

"Well, there's no harm in it. Do you want us to advertise for Kimball's wet nurse?"

"And his sisters and his cousins and his aunts. Yes. All in good time. But watch him first. Watch them both." He nodded, and sauntered out.

Lomas lit a cigarette and pushed the box to Bell. Both men smoked a minute in silence. Then Lomas said, "That's a damned clever fellow, Bell."

"Yes, sir."

"I've often thought he was too clever by half. But, damme, I don't remember thinking he was uncanny before."

"I have noticed it," said Bell diffidently, "in a manner of speaking. Of course he does know a lot, does Mr. Fortune, a rare lot of stuff. But that's natural, as it were. What upsets you is the sort of way he feels men. It's as if he had senses you haven't got. Very strange the way he knows men."

PHASE V: THE REPLY

Their admiration for Reggie Fortune received a shock the next day. It came by telephone. Just after his late and lazy breakfast, Reggie was rung up from Scotland Yard. Bell spoke. Mr. Lomas thought that Mr. Fortune would like to know that Sandford had gone down to Mr. Kimball's place. Reggie answered, "Oh, Peter!" In a quarter of an hour he was in Lomas's room asking for confirmation. There was no doubt. The detective watching Sandford's chambers had followed him to Victoria, and heard him take a ticket to Alwynstow, Kimball's place, and was gone with him.

"So that's the next move," said Lomas, "and if you can tell me what it means I shall be obliged to you."

Reggie dropped his hand on the table. "Not a guess," he said. "How can a man guess? We don't even know how much they know, or whether one knows what the other knows. I could fancy Sandford—what's the use?

"So runs my dream. But what am I?
An infant crying in the night,
An infant crying for the light,
And with no language but a cry.

"Same like you, Lomas."

"I notice you are not so much the moral sage this morning," Lomas said sourly.

"Lomas, dear, don't be unkind. I can't abear it. I wish to God I was down there!"

"Damn it, we've got two men down there now—one on Sandford, one on Kimball. They'll be knocking their heads together. What the devil do you think you could do?"

"Nothing. Lord, don't I know it? Nothing. That's what makes me peevish."

Lomas said severely that he had work to do, and Reggie left him, promising to come back and take him out to lunch, which he received as if it were a threat.

But when Reggie did come back, Superintendent Bell was in the room and Lomas listening to the telephone. Bell looked oddly at Reggie. Lomas raised a blank and pallid face from the receiver. "Sandford has murdered Kimball," he said.

"Oh, Peter! I wonder if he's brought it off," Reggie murmured. "Has he brought it off after all?" He bit his lip. Lomas was talking into the telephone. Asking for details, giving instructions. "Hold the line. Cut that out," said Reggie. "We'll go down, Lomas, please. Tell your chap to meet us at the house. My car's here."

Lomas gave the orders and rang off. "I'll have to go, I suppose," he agreed. "One doesn't kill Cabinet Ministers every day. More's the pity. Damn the case! There's nothing in it, though, Fortune. Sandford was walking up to the house. He met Kimball in the lane. They were crossing the ornamental water in the park when they had a quarrel. Kimball was thrown in. He called out, 'You scoundrel, you have murdered me.' When they got Kimball out he was dead. That's all. I'm afraid it washes your stuff about Kimball right out."

"Well, well," Reggie drawled, looking through his eyelashes. "Where is he that knows, Lomas? From the great deep to the great deep he goes, Lomas. We'll get on."

"What about lunch?"

"Damn lunch!" said Reggie, and went out.

The other two, who liked food far less than he but could not go without it, lingered to collect sandwiches, and found him chafing in the driver's seat.

They exchanged looks of horror. "I'm too old for Mr. Fortune's driving, and that's a fact," Bell mumbled.

"When I got out alive after that day at Woking I swore I'd never go again," said Lomas.

But they quailed before Reggie's virulent politeness when he asked them if they would please get in. . . . It is in the evidence of Lomas that they only slowed once, when an old lady dropped her handkerchief in the middle of Croydon. He is in conflict with the statement of Bell as to the most awful moment. For he selects the episode of the traction-engine with trucks at the Alwynstow crossroads, and Bell chooses the affair of the motor-bus and the caravan at Merstham. They agree that they arrived at Alwynstow Park in a cold sweat.

A detective came out on the steps to meet them, and watched reverently Bell and Lomas helping each other out. Reggie ran up to him. "Which are you?"

"Beg pardon, sir? Oh, I'm Hall. I had Mr. Kimball. It was Parker had Mr. Sandford." He turned to Lomas. "Good morning, sir. I tried to get you on the telephone, but they said you were on your way down."

"Oh, you've been on the telephone too?"

"When I heard what Parker's information was I rung up quick, sir. It's a very queer business, sir."

"Where is Parker? And where's Sandford? I suppose you've arrested him?"

"Well, no, sir. Not strictly speaking. We detained him pending instructions."

"Damme, you're very careful. Parker saw the murder committed, didn't he?"

"Well, sir, if I may say so, that's drawing conclusions. I don't understand Parker would go as far as that."

"Good Gad!" said Lomas. "Where the devil is Parker?"

"Keeping Mr. Sandford under observation, sir, according to instructions. Beg your pardon, sir. I've heard his story, and I quite agree it all happened like that. But you haven't heard mine."

Lomas looked round him. The house was too near. "We'll walk on the lawn," he announced. "Now then. Parker says the two men quarrelled on the bridge over the lake and Kimball was thrown in, and as he fell he called out, 'You scoundrel, you've murdered me!' And you say that isn't murder."

"Did Serjeant Parker say 'thrown in'?" said Hall, with surprise in his face and his voice.

"I believe he didn't," said Lomas slowly. "No. He said Kimball was thrown off, and as he fell in he called out."

"That's right, sir," said Hall heartily. "But I reckon there is more to it than that. When Mr. Kimball came out this morning I was waiting for him in the park. It was rather touch and go, because he had some men at work above the lake. He went down that way to the station. As he was crossing the bridge he tried the rails. It's very odd, sir, but a bit of the bar—it's a sort of rustic stuff—was that loose it came off in his hand. He put it back and went on. He met Mr. Sandford in the road and turned back with him. I had to get out of the way quick. I judged they were coming back to the house, so I did a run and dropped over the fence, and was away on the other side of the lake. Then I went into the rhododendrons and waited for them to pass. You see, sir, Parker had to keep well out of sight behind, and I was as near as makes no matter.

Well, if you'll believe me, it was Mr. Kimball made the quarrel, and all in a minute he made it. One minute they were walking quite friendly, the next he whips round on Mr. Sandford and he called him a bad name. I couldn't hear all, he was talking so quick, but there was ugly words in it. Then he made to strike Mr. Sandford, and Mr. Sandford closed and chucked him back, and into the water he went just where that same rail that he looked at was loose. But it's true enough as he fell he called out, 'You scoundrel, you've murdered me!' "

"Well, well. So he didn't bring it off after all," said Reggie. "We trumped his last card."

"Sir?" said the detective.

"You were the trump," said Reggie. "Oh, my aunt, I feel much better! I wonder if there's any lunch in these parts? What about it, Lomas, old thing?"

"I'm damned if I understand," said Lomas. "I want Sandford. Let's go up to the house."

They found Sandford sitting in an easy-chair in the dead man's library. He was reading; to Reggie's ineffable admiration he was reading a book by Mr. Sidney Webb on the history of trade unions. Serjeant Parker, the detective, made himself uncomfortable at the table and pored over his notebook.

"All right, all right, Parker. Quite understood." Lomas waved him away. "Good afternoon, Mr. Sandford. Sorry to detain you. Most unfortunate affair."

"Good afternoon. It is not necessary to apologize," said Sandford, completely himself. "I realize that the police must require my account of the affair. Yesterday afternoon Mr. Kimball rang me up at my rooms. I did not learn from where he was speaking. He said that my affair—that was his phrase—my affair had taken a new turn, and he wished me to come and see him here this morning. He named the train by which I was to travel. I thought it strange that he should bring me into the country, but I had no valid ground of objection. Accordingly I came this morning. I thought it strange that he sent no conveyance to meet me. I started to walk to the house. In the lane he met me walking. He talked of indifferent things in a rather broken manner, I thought, but that was common with him, and yet I was surprised he did not come to the point. He was, however, quite friendly until we reached the bridge over the lake. Then without any warning or reason he turned upon me and was violently abusive. His language was vulgar and even filthy. He attempted to strike me, and I defended myself. I was, in fact, a good deal alarmed, for he was, as you know, much bigger and heavier than I, and he was in a frenzy of rage. To my surprise, I may say my relief, I was able to resist him. I pushed him off—really, you know, it seemed quite easy—and the hand-rail behind him gave way and he fell into the water. As he fell he called out,

'You scoundrel, you have murdered me!' I can only suppose he was not responsible for his actions."

"Much obliged," said Lomas. "I'm afraid you've had a distressing time."

"It has been a remarkable experience," said Sandford. "May I ask if there is any reason why I should not return to town?"

"No, no." Lomas looked at him queerly. "You have an uncommon cool head. They'll want your evidence at the inquest, of course. But it's fair to say I quite accept your story."

"I am obliged to you," said Sandford, in a tone of surprise, as if he could not conceive that any one should not. "I am told there is a train at 3:35. Good afternoon."

"One moment. One moment," said Reggie. "Do you know of any reason in the world Kimball had to hate you?"

"Certainly not," said Sandford, in offended dignity. "Our relations were short and wholly official. I conceive that he had no reason to complain of my services."

"And yet he meant to murder you or have you hanged for his murder."

"If he did, I can only suppose that he was out of his mind."

"Was he out of his mind when he worked the Coal Ramp to ruin you?"

"Dear me," said Sandford, "do you really suggest, sir, that Mr. Kimball was responsible for that scandalous piece of finance?"

"Who else?"

"But really—you startle me. That is to say, as a Minister he betrayed the secrets of the department?"

"Well, he didn't stick at a trifle, did he?"

"The poor fellow must have been mad," said Sandford, with grave sympathy.

"Yes, yes. But why was he mad? Why did he hate you? My dear chap, do search your memory. Can you think of any sort of connection between Kimball and you?"

"I never heard of him till he became prominent in the House. I never saw him till he came into the office. Our relations were always perfectly correct. No, I can only suppose that he was insane. Is it any use to try to discover reasons for the antipathies of madness? I have not studied the subject, but it seems obvious that they must be irrational. I am sorry I cannot help your investigations. I believe I had better catch my train. Good afternoon."

"You know, I begin to like that fellow. He's so damned honest," said Reggie.

"Cold-blooded fish," said Lomas. "Begad, he don't know how near he was to dead. Did you ever hear anything less plausible than that yarn of his? If we didn't know it was true we wouldn't believe a word of it. Good God, suppose Hall hadn't been down here watching! We should have had the outside facts. Sandford, who had been accused and suspended by Kimball, suddenly comes down to Kimball's house, meets him, quarrels with him, and throws him into the lake."

"And the men working in the park a little way off just saw the struggle, just heard Kimball call out that he was murdered," said Reggie. "Don't forget the men. They're a most interesting touch. He always thought of everything, did Mr. Kimball. He had them there, just the right distance for the evidence he wanted. I don't know if you see the full significance of those men working in the park."

Lomas sat down. "I don't mind owning I thought they were accidental."

"My dear chap! Oh, my dear chap, there was very little accidental in the vicinity of the late Kimball. They were there to give evidence that would hang Sandford. And that proves Kimball didn't mean to throw Sandford into the lake. He wanted to be thrown in, he wanted to be killed, and get Sandford hanged for it."

"I suppose so," Lomas agreed. "It's a case that's happened before. And you couldn't always say the creatures that planned it were mad."

"Not legally mad. Not medically mad. I always said that. No, I don't know that it's even very strange. Quite a lot of people would be ready to die if they could get their enemies killed by their death. Only they don't see their way. But he was an able fellow, the late Kimball."

"Able! I should say so. If our men hadn't been here, Sandford would have been as good as hanged. Nobody could have believed his story. Why did he come here? There could be no evidence of Kimball's telephone call. What did Sandford come for? There's no reasonable reason. Kimball put him under a cloud, he was furious, he meant murder, and did it. The jury wouldn't leave the box."

"That's right, sir," said Superintendent Bell. "If it wasn't for Mr. Fortune he'd be down and out. What you might call a rarity in our work, that is, to save a man from a charge of murder before it comes along."

"How do you mean?" Reggie seemed to come back from other thoughts. "Oh, because I told you to have Kimball watched. Well, it was pretty clear he wasn't the kind to go about without a chaperon. We took that trick. I suppose Kimball's thinking, wherever he is, that we won the game. But I wouldn't say that—I wouldn't say that. Why did he hate Sandford?"

"My dear fellow, the man was mad."

"You mean he didn't like the way Sandford does his hair—or he thought Sandford was a German spy. No. He wasn't that kind of mad. There's something we don't know, Lomas, old thing. I dare say it's crazy enough. I'll bet you my favourite shirt it's something the ordinary sane man feels."

"If we are to go looking for something crazy which sane men feel!" said Lomas.

"Speakin' broadly, all the human emotions," said Reggie. "Didn't you ever hate a man because he married a girl who was pretty? Don't be so godlike."

"They weren't either of them married, sir," said Bell, in grave surprise.

"How do you know?" Reggie snapped. "No, I don't suppose they were. But we don't know. We don't know anything. That's why I say we haven't won the game. Well, well. For God's sake let's have some food! There was a modest pub in the village. I saw it when you let off your futile scream at the traction-engine. Let's go. I don't seem to want to eat Kimball's grub."

PHASE VI: JANE BROWN

Two or three days after Lomas received an invitation to lunch in Wimpole Street. I owe you one," Reggie wrote. "I owe myself one. I want to forget the high tea of Alwynstow. Do you remember the pickles? And the bacon? What had that pig been doing? A neurasthenic, I fear. A student of the Nematoda."

So naturally when Lomas came his first question was what may Nematoda be.

"Never mind," Reggie sighed. "It's a painful subject. A disgusting subject. Same like what we make our living by. They are among the criminals of animal life. Real bad eggs. A sad world, Lomas, old thing. Let's forget all about crime."

They did. For an hour and a half. At the end of which Lomas said dreamily, "You're a remarkable fellow, Fortune. I don't know how you can retain any brain. You do yourself so well. Yes, most seductive habit of life. I meant to say something when I came. What was it? I believe you have talked of everything else in creation. Ah yes, did you ever hear of the Kimball case? Well, I think we have combed it all out."

"Have you, though?" Reggie sat up.

"Yes. We've been dealing with a stockbroker or two. I'm really afraid there was a little bullying. We hinted that there might be developments about a certain murder case. And two of them began to talk. We've got Rand-Mason's past."

"Oh, that!" Reggie said, "Quite obvious, wasn't it? Kimball meant to use this coal scheme to ruin Sandford. He sent Mason, who had probably been his go-between in other financial things, to give the brokers the tip. It was also Rand-Mason who paid the money into Sandford's account. Remember the stout man in glasses. Then probably he struck for better pay or they had a row. Anyway, he threatened to give the show away. Kimball couldn't trust him any more. Daren't trust him. So he wiped Rand-Mason out. Is that right, sir?"

"I'm not omniscient myself. But certainly Rand-Mason was the man who put the brokers on to it. There is not much doubt he went to Sandford's bank. By the way, Kimball had several big sticks. His valet says he liked weight."

"I dare say. Had Kimball any papers?"

"Not a line that throws light on this. As you know everything, I'd like to hear why Kimball tried this murder plan last instead of first?"

"How can you be so unkind, Lomas? I keep telling you I don't know anything. I come and shout it in your ear. I don't know the thing that really matters. Who was Kimball? Who is Sandford? What is he that Kimball couldn't bear him? I said that at the beginning. I say it now in italics. Good Lord, you can hear Kimball laughing at us!"

"Don't be uncanny."

"Well, I'm not really sure he is laughing at us. Wait a while. But why did Kimball try murder last instead of first? Oh, that's easy. He was an epicure in hate! He didn't want mere blood. He wanted the beggar to suffer—to be ruined, not just dead. Hence he went to break Sandford. Then Rand-Mason complicated the affair. Kimball had a murder on his back and I scared him. He thought we had enough to convict him or that we'd get it. He said to himself, 'I'm for it, anyway. I'll have to die. Well, why shouldn't my death hang Sandford?' And he played that last card."

"I suppose so," Lomas agreed. "In a way it's all quite rational, isn't it?"

"I always said it would be. Grant that it was worth anything to ruin Sandford and Kimball's a most efficient fellow. But why was it worth anything to ruin Sandford?"

"Ah, God knows," said Lomas gravely.

"Yes. I wonder if Jane Brown does." He handed Lomas a letter.

Dear Sir,—Your advertisement for information about Mrs. Ellen Edith Sandford. I have some which is at your service if you can satisfy me why you want it.—Yours truly, JANE BROWN.

"I should say Jane is a character," said Lomas.

"Yes, she allured me. I told her who I was and she said she'd come to tea."

She kept her appointment. Reggie found himself facing a large young woman. In her construction nature had been very happy. She had decorated its work with admirable art. She was physically in the grand style, but she had a merry eye, and her clothes were not only charming but of a sophisticated elegance.

Reggie, there is no doubt, stared at her for a moment and a half. "Miss—Jane—Brown," he said slowly.

"I haven't brought my godfathers and godmothers, Mr. Fortune," she smiled. "But I am Jane Brown really. I always felt I couldn't live up to it. I see you know me."

"If seeing were knowing, I should know Miss Joan Amber very well. It's delightful to be able to thank her for the real Rosalind—all the Rosalind there is."

She made him a curtsey. "I'm lucky. I didn't think you'd be like this. I expected an old man with glasses and—"

"This," said Reggie maliciously—"this is the Chief of the Criminal Investigation Department—Mr. Lomas."

Lomas let his eyeglass fall. "I also am young enough to go to the theatre. I shall go on being young as long as Miss Amber is acting."

"May I sit down?" said she pathetically. "You're rather overwhelming. I thought it would be terrific and severe and suspicious. But you know you are bland— simply bland."

"This is your fault, Lomas," said Reggie severely. "I have often been called flippant and even futile, but never bland before—never bland."

"It is a tribute to your maturity, my dear Fortune."

Her golden eyes sent a glance at Reggie. "Mature!" she said. "I suppose you are real? Oh, let's be serious. I am Jane Brown, you know. Amber—of course I had to have another name for the stage—Amber because of my hair." She touched it.

"And your eyes," said Reggie.

"Never mind," said she, with another glance, but the gaiety had gone out of them. "My father was a doctor in Liverpool. He is worth twenty thousand of me, and he never made enough to live on. A poor middle-class practice, the work wore him out by the time he was fifty, and now he's an invalid in Devonshire. He can't walk upstairs even—heart, you know. And he simply pines to work. Oh, I know this doesn't matter to you, but I can't forget it. If only people were paid what they're worth! I beg your pardon. This isn't business-like. Well, he was the doctor the Kimball family went to. Old Mr. Kimball was a clerk, and the son, the man who was drowned the other day, began like that too. The old people died about the time young Mr. Kimball and his sister grew up. She kept house for her brother. He began as a broker and got on. In a way—my father always says that—in a way he was devoted to her. Nothing he could pay for was too good for her. He always wanted her with him. But he made awful demands on her. She mustn't have any interests of her own. She mustn't make any friends. Like some men are with their wives, you know. Horrible, isn't it?" She turned upon Reggie.

"Common form of selfishness. Passing into mania. Not only male, you know. Some mothers are like that."

"Yes, I know they are. But it's worst with men and their wives."

"The wife can't grow up. The children can," Reggie agreed.

"It is exactly that," said she eagerly. "You understand. Oh, well, this isn't business-like either. Ellen Kimball fell in love. He was just an ordinary sort of man, a clerk of some sort—Sandford was his name. Horace Kimball was furious. My father says Sandford was nothing in particular. There was no special reason why she should marry him or why she shouldn't. He was insignificant."

"Heredity." Reggie nodded to Lomas.

"I beg your pardon?"

"Your father understood men, Miss Amber."

"Indeed he does. Of course Horace Kimball did the absurd thing, said she mustn't marry, abused Sandford, and so on, and of course that made her marry. Unfortunately—this really seems to be the only thing against her—unfortunately she was married in a sly, secret sort of way. She didn't tell her brother she'd made up her mind, or when the marriage was to be or anything. She simply slunk out of his house and left him to find out. I suppose he had terrified her, poor thing, or his bullying made her sullen," said Miss Amber. "It was rather feeble of her. Only one hates to blame her. Her brother was furious. My father says that he never saw such a strange case of a man holding down a passionate rage. He thought at one time that Horace Kimball would have gone mad. The thing seemed like an obsession. Doesn't it seem paltry? A man wild with temper because he was jealous of his sister marrying!"

"Most jealousy is paltry." Lomas shrugged.

"Jealous of his sister marrying," Reggie repeated. "Yes, I dare say seven men in ten are. Common human emotion. Commonest in the form of mothers hating their sons' wives, Miss Amber. Still, men do their bit. Fathers proverbially object to daughters marrying. Brothers—well, there's quite a lot of folk-lore about brothers killing their sisters' lovers. Yes, common human emotion."

"I think jealousy is simply loathsome," said Miss Amber, with a quiver of her admirable nose. "Well, it's fair to say Horace Kimball seemed to get over the worst of his. He just lost himself in his business, my father says. He wouldn't see his sister again, not even when her child was born (it was a boy). He simply swept her out of his life. Even when Sandford got into trouble, he wouldn't hear of helping her. My father quarrelled with him over that. He said to my father, 'She's made her bed, and they can all die in it.' Oh, I know he's dead, and one oughtn't to say things. But I call that simply devilish."

"Yes, I believe in the devil too," said Reggie. "Devilish! You're exactly right, Miss Amber. Sandford got into trouble, did he? What was that?"

"It was some scandal about his business. A breach of trust in some way. His employers didn't prosecute, but they dismissed him in disgrace. My father doesn't remember the details. It was giving away some business secrets."

Reggie looked at Lomas. "That's very interesting," he said.

"Interesting! Poor people, it was misery for them. Sandford was ruined. My father says he never really tried to make a fresh start. He just died because he didn't want to go on living. And his wife broke her heart over it. She seemed like a woman frightened out of her senses, my father says. She got it into her head that it was all her brother's fault, that he had planned the whole thing. It was absurd, of course, but can you wonder?"

"I don't wonder," said Reggie.

"She was deadly afraid of her brother. She made up her mind that he would be the death of her baby too. So she ran away from Liverpool and hid in a little village in North Wales, Llanfairfechan, and nobody knew where she had gone. She had a little money of her own, and her husband had been well insured. She had just enough, and she lived quite alone in a cottage off the road to the mountains, and there she died. My father says her son did rather well. He got scholarships to Oxford, and my father fancies he went into the Civil Service, but he lost sight of him after the mother died."

"I'm infinitely obliged to you, Miss Amber," said Reggie, and rang for tea.

"Oh no, don't! I always thought that poor woman's story was too miserably sad. I don't know why you wanted it—no, no, I'm not asking—but if it could set anything right, or do anybody any good, it seems somehow to make it better. It wouldn't be so uselessly cruel."

"Over the past the gods themselves have no power," Reggie said. "We can't help her, poor soul. I dare say it's something to her to know that her son is safe and making good—in spite of all the devilry."

"Something to her—of course it is!" said Miss Amber, and looked divine.

"There's that," said Reggie, watching her.

"You won't mind my saying professionally that you have been very useful, Miss Amber," said Lomas. "You have cleared up what was a very tiresome mystery. I was being bothered. That's a serious disturbance of the machinery of Empire." He succeeded, as he desired, in setting the conversation to a lighter tune. He made Miss Amber's eyes again merry. He did not prevent Reggie from looking at her. "You must promise me another opportunity to thank you," he said, as she was going.

"Dear me, I thought you had been doing nothing else," said she demurely, and looked at the table and made a face. "Oh, Mr. Fortune, what, what a tea! I leave all my reputation behind me. Men hate to see women eat, don't they? But do men always make teas like this?"

"I've a simple mind. I live the simple life."

She looked at him fairly. "You said simple. Do you know how I feel? I feel as if I hadn't a secret left all my own," and she swept away. He was a long time gone letting her out.

"And that's that," Reggie said when he came back.

"Really?" Lomas was dim behind cigar smoke.

"All quite natural now, isn't it?"

"My dear fellow, you knew it all and you knew it right. You told me so. Kamerad, kamerad."

Reggie lit his pipe. "Jealousy, hate, mania. He broke the man the girl married. Curious that affair, wasn't it? Even the great criminal, he runs in a groove, he keeps to one kind of crime. The same dodge for the son that he used for the father. Then either he lost track of the mother or he preferred to hurt her through the son. He was an epicure in his little pleasures. The son came along. I dare say Kimball took that department because the son was in it. And then he was ready to smash everything for the sake of his hate—damage his own career, do a filthy murder, die himself, if he could torture his sister's child. Yes. The devil is with power, Lomas."

"I fancy you annoy him a little, my dear Fortune. But how can you believe in the devil? You have just seen—her."

Reggie smiled. "She is a woman, isn't she?"

"I think you might act on that theory. When is it to be?"

"Lomas, old thing, you're not only bland, you're obvious. Which is much worse."

THE BIG BOW MYSTERY

Israel Zangwill

I

On a memorable morning of early December, London opened its eyes on a frigid grey mist. There are mornings when King Fog masses his molecules of carbon in serried squadrons in the city, while he scatters them tenuously in the suburbs; so that your morning train may bear you from twilight to darkness. But to-day the enemy's manœuvring was more monotonous. From Bow even unto Hammersmith there draggled a dull, wretched vapour, like the wraith of an impecunious suicide come into a fortune immediately after the fatal deed. The barometers and thermometers had sympathetically shared its depression, and their spirits (when they had any) were low. The cold cut like a many-bladed knife.

Mrs. Drabdump, of 11 Glover Street, Bow, was one of the few persons in London whom fog did not depress. She went about her work quite as cheerlessly as usual. She had been among the earliest to be aware of the enemy's advent, picking out the strands of fog from the coils of darkness the moment she rolled up her bedroom blind and unveiled the sombre picture of the winter morning. She knew that the fog had come to stay for the day at least, and that the gas-bill for the quarter was going to beat the record in high-jumping. She also knew that this was because she had allowed her new gentleman lodger, Mr. Arthur Constant, to pay a fixed sum of a shilling a week for gas, instead of charging him a proportion of the actual account for the whole house. The meteorologists might have saved the credit of their science if they had reckoned with Mrs. Drabdump's next gas-bill when they predicted the weather and made "Snow" the favourite, and said that "Fog" would be nowhere. Fog was everywhere, yet Mrs. Drabdump took no credit to herself for her prescience. Mrs. Drabdump indeed took no credit for anything, paying her way along doggedly, and struggling through life like a wearied swimmer trying to touch the horizon. That things always went as badly as she had foreseen did not exhilarate her in the least.

Mrs. Drabdump was a widow. Widows are not born but made, else you might have fancied Mrs. Drabdump had always been a widow. Nature had given her that tall, spare form, and that pale, thin-lipped, elongated, hard-eyed visage, and that painfully precise hair, which are always associated with widowhood in low life. It is only in higher circles that women can lose their husbands and yet remain bewitching. The late Mr. Drabdump had scratched the base of his thumb with a rusty nail, and Mrs. Drabdump's foreboding that he would die of lockjaw had not prevented her wrestling day and night with the shadow of Death, as she had wrestled with it vainly twice before, when Katie died of diphtheria and little Johnny of scarlet fever. Perhaps it is from overwork among the poor that Death has been reduced to a shadow.

Mrs. Drabdump was lighting the kitchen fire. She did it very scientifically, as knowing the contrariety of coal and the anxiety of flaming sticks to end in smoke unless rigidly kept up to the mark. Science was a success as usual; and Mrs. Drabdump rose from her knees content, like a Parsee priestess who had duly paid her morning devotions to her deity. Then she started violently, and nearly lost her balance. Her eye had caught the hands of the clock on the mantel. They pointed to fifteen minutes to seven. Mrs. Drabdump's devotion to the kitchen fire invariably terminated at fifteen minutes past six. What was the matter with the clock?

Mrs. Drabdump had an immediate vision of Snoppet, the neighbouring horologist, keeping the clock in hand for weeks and then returning it only superficially repaired and secretly injured more vitally "for the good of the trade." The evil vision vanished as quickly as it came, exorcised by the deep boom of St. Dunstan's bells chiming the three-quarters. In its place a great horror surged. Instinct had failed; Mrs. Drabdump had risen at half-past six instead of six. Now she understood why she had been feeling so dazed and strange and sleepy. She had overslept herself.

Chagrined and puzzled, she hastily set the kettle over the crackling coal, discovering a second later that she had overslept herself because Mr. Constant wished to be woke three-quarters of an hour earlier than usual, and to have his breakfast at seven, having to speak at an early meeting of discontented tram-men. She ran at once, candle in hand, to his bedroom. It was upstairs. All "upstairs" was Arthur Constant's domain, for it consisted of but two mutually independent rooms. Mrs. Drabdump knocked viciously at the door of the one he used for a bedroom, crying, "Seven o'clock, sir. You'll be late, sir. You must get up at once." The usual slumbrous "All right" was not forthcoming; but, as she herself had varied her morning salute, her ear was less expectant of the echo. She went downstairs, with no foreboding save that the kettle would come off second best in the race between its boiling and her lodger's dressing.

For she knew there was no fear of Arthur Constant's lying deaf to the call of Duty—temporarily represented by Mrs. Drabdump. He was a light sleeper, and the tram-conductors' bells were probably ringing in his ears, summoning him to the meeting. Why Arthur Constant, B.A.—white-handed and white-shirted, and gentleman to the very purse of him—should concern himself with tram-men, when fortune had confined his necessary relations with drivers to cabmen at the least, Mrs. Drabdump could not quite make out. He probably aspired to represent Bow in Parliament; but then it would surely have been wiser to lodge with a landlady who possessed a vote by having a husband alive. Nor was there much practical wisdom in his wish to black his own boots (an occupation in which he shone but little), and to live in every way like a Bow working man. Bow working men were not so lavish in their patronage of water, whether existing in drinking-glasses, morning tubs, or laundress's establishments. Nor did they eat the delicacies with which Mrs. Drabdump supplied him, with the assurance that they were the artisan's appanage. She could not bear to see him eat things unbefitting his station. Arthur Constant opened his mouth and ate what his landlady gave him, not first deliberately shutting his eyes according to the formula, the rather pluming himself on keeping them very wide open. But it is difficult for saints to see through their own halos; and in practice an aureola about the head is often indistinguishable from a mist.

The tea to be scalded in Mr. Constant's pot, when that cantankerous kettle should boil, was not the coarse mixture of black and green sacred to herself and Mr. Mortlake, of whom the thoughts of breakfast now reminded her. Poor Mr. Mortlake, gone off without any to Devonport, somewhere about four in the fog-thickened darkness of a winter night! Well, she hoped his journey would be duly rewarded, that his perks would be heavy, and that he would make as good a thing out of the "travelling expenses" as rival labour leaders roundly accused him of to other people's faces. She did not grudge him his gains, nor was it her business if, as they alleged, in introducing Mr. Constant to her vacant rooms, his idea was not merely to benefit his landlady. He had done her an uncommon good turn, queer as was the lodger thus introduced. His own apostleship to the sons of toil gave Mrs. Drabdump no twinges of perplexity. Tom Mortlake had been a compositor; and apostleship was obviously a profession better paid and of a higher social status. Tom Mortlake—the hero of a hundred strikes—set up in print on a poster, was unmistakably superior to Tom Mortlake setting up other men's names at a case. Still, the work was not all beer and skittles, and Mrs. Drabdump felt that Tom's latest job was not enviable.

She shook his door as she passed it on her way back to the kitchen, but there was no response. The street door was only a few feet off down the passage, and a glance at it dispelled the last hope that Tom had abandoned the journey. The door was unbolted and unchained, and the only security was the latch-key lock. Mrs. Drabdump felt a whit uneasy, though, to give her her due, she never suffered as much as most good housewives do from criminals who never come. Not quite opposite, but still only a few doors off, on the other side of the street, lived the celebrated ex-detective Grodman, and, illogically enough, his presence in the street gave Mrs. Drabdump a curious sense of security, as of a believer living under the shadow of the fane. That any human being of ill odour should consciously come within a mile of the scent of so famous a sleuth-hound seemed to her highly improbable. Grodman had retired (with a competence) and was only a sleeping dog now; still, even criminals would have sense enough to let him lie.

So Mrs. Drabdump did not really feel that there had been any danger, especially as a second glance at the street door showed that Mortlake had been thoughtful enough to slip the loop that held back the bolt of the big lock. She allowed herself another throb of sympathy for the labour leader whirling on his dreary way towards Devonport Dockyard. Not that he had told her anything of his journey, beyond the town; but she knew Devonport had a Dockyard because Jessie Dymond—Tom's sweetheart—once mentioned that her aunt lived near there, and it lay on the surface that Tom had gone to help the dockers, who were imitating their London brethren. Mrs. Drabdump did not need to be told things to be aware of them. She went back to prepare Mr. Constant's superfine tea, vaguely wondering why people were so discontented nowadays. But when she brought up the tea and the toast and the eggs to Mr. Constant's sitting-room (which adjoined his bedroom, though without communicating with it), Mr. Constant was not sitting in it. She lit the gas, and laid the cloth; then she returned to the landing and beat at the bedroom door with an imperative palm. Silence alone answered her. She called him by name and told him the hour, but hers was the only voice she heard, and it sounded strangely to her in the shadows of the staircase. Then, mutter-ing, "Poor gentleman, he had the toothache last night; and p'r'aps he's only just got a wink o' sleep. Pity to disturb him for the sake of them grizzling conductors. I'll let him sleep his usual time," she bore the tea-pot downstairs with a mournful, almost poetic, consciousness that soft-boiled eggs (like love) must grow cold.

Half-past seven came—and she knocked again. But Constant slept on.

His letters, always a strange assortment, arrived at eight, and a telegram came soon after. Mrs. Drabdump rattled his door, shouted, and at last put the wire under it. Her heart was beating fast enough now, though there seemed to be a cold, clammy snake curling round it. She went downstairs again and turned the handle of Mortlake's room, and went in without knowing why. The coverlet of the bed showed that the occupant had only lain down in his clothes, as if fearing to miss the early train. She had not for a moment expected to find him in the room; yet somehow the consciousness that she was alone in the house with the sleeping Constant seemed to flash for the first time upon her, and the clammy snake tightened its folds round her heart.

She opened the street door, and her eye wandered nervously up and down. It was half-past eight. The little street stretched cold and still in the grey mist, blinking bleary eyes at either end, where the street lamps smouldered on. No one was visible for the moment, though smoke was rising from many of the chimneys to greet its sister mist. At the house of the detective across the way the blinds were still down and the shutters up. Yet the familiar, prosaic aspect of the street calmed her. The bleak air set her coughing; she slammed the door to, and returned to the kitchen to make fresh tea for Constant, who could only be in a deep sleep. But the canister trembled in her grasp. She did not know whether she dropped it or threw it down, but there was nothing in the hand that battered again a moment later at the bedroom door. No sound within answered the clamour without. She rained blow upon blow in a sort of spasm of frenzy, scarce remembering that her object was merely to wake her lodger, and almost staving in the lower panels with her kicks. Then she turned the handle and tried to open the door, but it was locked. The resistance recalled her to herself—she had a moment of shocked decency at the thought that she had been about to enter Constant's bedroom. Then the terror came over her afresh. She felt that she was alone in the house with a corpse. She sank to the floor, cowering; with difficulty stifling a desire to scream. Then she rose with a jerk and raced down the stairs without looking behind her, and threw open the door and ran out into the street, only pulling up with her hand violently agitating Grodman's door-knocker. In a moment the first-floor window was raised—the little house was of the same pattern as her own—and Grodman's full fleshy face loomed through the fog in sleepy irritation from under a nightcap. Despite its scowl the ex-detective's face dawned upon her like the sun upon an occupant of the haunted chamber.

"What in the devil's the matter?" he growled. Grodman was not an early bird, now that he had no worms to catch. He could afford to despise proverbs now, for the house in which he lived was his, and he lived in it because several other houses in the street were also his, and it is well for the landlord to be about his own estate in Bow, where poachers often shoot the moon. Perhaps the desire to enjoy his greatness among his early cronies counted for something, too, for he had been born and bred at Bow, receiving when a youth his first engagement from the local police quarters, whence he had drawn a few shillings a week as an amateur detective in his leisure hours.

Grodman was still a bachelor. In the celestial matrimonial bureau a partner might have been selected for him, but he had never been able to discover her. It was his one failure as a detective. He was a self-sufficing person, who preferred a gas stove to a domestic; but in deference to Glover Street opinion he admitted a female factotum between ten A.M. and ten P.M., and, equally in deference to Glover Street opinion, excluded her between ten P.M. and ten A.M.

"I want you to come across at once," Mrs. Drabdump gasped. "Something has happened to Mr. Constant."

"What! Not bludgeoned by the police at the meeting this morning, I hope?"

"No, no! He didn't go. He is dead."

"Dead?" Grodman's face grew very serious now.

"Yes. Murdered!"

"What?" almost shouted the ex-detective. "How? When? Where? Who?"

"I don't know. I can't get to him. I have beaten at his door. He does not answer."
Grodman's face lit up with relief.

"You silly woman! Is that all? I shall have a cold in my head. Bitter weather. He's
dog-tired after yesterday—processions, three speeches, kindergarten, lecture on 'the
moon,' article on coöperation. That's his style." It was also Grodman's style. He never
wasted words.

"No," Mrs. Drabdump breathed up at him solemnly, "he's dead."

"All right; go back. Don't alarm the neighbourhood unnecessarily. Wait for me.
Down in five minutes." Grodman did not take this Cassandra of the kitchen too seriously. Probably he knew his woman. His small, bead-like eyes glittered with an almost
amused smile as he withdrew them from Mrs. Drabdump's ken, and shut down the
sash with a bang. The poor woman ran back across the road and through her door,
which she would not close behind her. It seemed to shut her in with the dead. She
waited in the passage. After an age—seven minutes by any honest clock—Grodman
made his appearance, looking as dressed as usual, but with unkempt hair and with disconsolate side-whisker. He was not quite used to that side-whisker yet, for it had only
recently come within the margin of cultivation. In active service Grodman had been
clean-shaven, like all members of *the* profession—for surely your detective is the most
versatile of actors. Mrs. Drabdump closed the street door quietly, and pointed to the
stairs, fear operating like a polite desire to give him precedence. Grodman ascended,
amusement still glimmering in his eyes. Arrived on the landing he knocked peremptorily at the door, crying, "Nine o'clock, Mr. Constant; nine o'clock!" When he ceased
there was no other sound or movement. His face grew more serious. He waited, then
knocked, and cried louder. He turned the handle but the door was fast. He tried to
peer through the keyhole, but it was blocked. He shook the upper panels, but the door
seemed bolted as well as locked. He stood still, his face set and rigid, for he liked and
esteemed the man.

"Ay, knock your loudest," whispered the pale-faced woman. "You'll not wake
him now."

The grey mist had followed them through the street door, and hovered about the
staircase, charging the air with a moist sepulchral odour.

"Locked and bolted," muttered Grodman, shaking the door afresh.

"Burst it open," breathed the woman, trembling violently all over, and holding her hands before her as if to ward off the dreadful vision. Without another word, Grodman applied his shoulder to the door, and made a violent muscular effort. He had been an athlete in his time, and the sap was yet in him. The door creaked, little by little it began to give, the woodwork enclosing the bolt of the lock splintered, the panels bent inwards, the large upper bolt tore off its iron staple; the door flew back with a crash. Grodman rushed in.

"My God!" he cried. The woman shrieked. The sight was too terrible.

Within a few hours the jubilant newsboys were shrieking "Horrible Suicide in Bow," and The Moon poster added, for the satisfaction of those too poor to purchase, "A Philanthropist Cuts His Throat."

II

But the newspapers were premature. Scotland Yard refused to prejudice the case despite the penny-a-liners. Several arrests were made, so that the later editions were compelled to soften "Suicide" into "Mystery." The people arrested were a nondescript collection of tramps. Most of them had committed other offences for which the police had not arrested them. One bewildered-looking gentleman gave himself up (as if he were a riddle), but the police would have none of him, and restored him forthwith to his friends and keepers. The number of candidates for each new opening in Newgate is astonishing.

The full significance of this tragedy of a noble young life cut short had hardly time to filter into the public mind, when a fresh sensation absorbed it. Tom Mortlake had been arrested the same day at Liverpool on suspicion of being concerned in the death of his fellow-lodger. The news fell like a bombshell upon a land in which Tom Mortlake's name was a household word. That the gifted artisan orator, who had never shrunk upon occasion from launching red rhetoric at society, should actually have shed blood seemed too startling, especially as the blood shed was not blue, but the property of a lovable young middle-class idealist, who had now literally given his life to the Cause. But this supplementary sensation did not grow to a head, and everybody (save a few labour leaders) was relieved to hear that Tom had been released almost immediately, being merely subpœnaed to appear at the inquest. In an interview which he accorded to the representative of a Liverpool paper the same afternoon, he stated that he put his arrest down entirely to the enmity and rancour entertained towards him by the police throughout the country. He had come to Liverpool to trace the movements of a friend about whom he was very uneasy, and he was making anxious inquiries at the docks to discover at what times steamers left for America, when the detectives stationed there had, in accordance with instructions from headquarters, arrested him as a suspicious-looking character. "Though," said Tom, "they must very well have known my phiz, as I have been sketched and caricatured all over the shop. When I told them who I was they had the decency to let me go. They thought they'd scored off me enough, I reckon. Yes, it certainly *is* a strange coincidence that I might actually have had something to do with the poor fellow's death, which has cut me up as much as anybody; though if they had known I had just come from the 'scene of the crime,' and actually lived in the house, they would probably have—let me alone." He laughed sarcastically. "They are a queer lot of muddle-heads, are the police. Their motto is, 'First catch your man, then cook the evidence.' If you're on the spot you're guilty because you're there, and if you're elsewhere you're guilty because you have gone away. Oh, I know them! If they could have seen their way to clap me in quod, they'd ha' done it. Luckily I know the number of the cabman who took me to Euston before five this morning."

"If they clapped you in quod," the interviewer reported himself as facetiously observing, "the prisoners would be on strike in a week."

"Yes, but there would be so many blacklegs ready to take their places," Mortlake flashed back, "that I'm afraid it 'ould be no go. But do excuse me. I am so upset about my friend. I'm afraid he has left England, and I have to make inquiries; and now there's poor Constant gone—horrible! horrible! and I'm due in London at the inquest. I must really run away. Good-by. Tell your readers it's all a police grudge."

"One last word, Mr. Mortlake, if you please. Is it true that you were billed to preside at a great meeting of clerks at St. James's Hall between one and two to-day to protest against the German invasion?"

"Whew! so I was. But the beggars arrested me just before one, when I was going to wire, and then the news of poor Constant's end drove it out of my head. What a nuisance! Lord, how troubles do come together! Well, good-by, send me a copy of the paper."

Tom Mortlake's evidence at the inquest added little beyond this to the public knowledge of his movements on the morning of the Mystery. The cabman who drove him to Euston had written indignantly to the papers to say that he picked up his celebrated fare at Bow Railway Station at about half-past four A.M., and the arrest was a deliberate insult to democracy, and he offered to make an affidavit to that effect, leaving it dubious to which effect. But Scotland Yard betrayed no itch for the affidavit in question, and No. 2138 subsided again into the obscurity of his rank. Mortlake—whose face was very pale below the black mane brushed back from his fine forehead—gave his evidence in low, sympathetic tones. He had known the deceased for over a year, coming constantly across him in their common political and social work, and had found the furnished rooms for him in Glover Street at his own request, they just being to let when Constant resolved to leave his rooms at Oxford House in Bethnal Green, and to share the actual life of the people. The locality suited the deceased, as being near the People's Palace. He respected and admired the deceased, whose genuine goodness had won all hearts. The deceased was an untiring worker; never grumbled, was always in fair spirits, regarded his life and wealth as a sacred trust to be used for the benefit of humanity. He had last seen him at a quarter past nine P.M. on the day preceding his death. He (witness) had received a letter by the last post which made him uneasy about a friend. He went up to consult deceased about it. Deceased was evidently suffering from toothache, and was fixing a piece of cotton-wool in a hollow tooth, but he did not complain. Deceased seemed rather upset by the news he brought, and they both discussed it rather excitedly.

By a JURYMAN: Did the news concern him?

MORTLAKE: Only impersonally. He knew my friend, and was keenly sympathetic when one was in trouble.

CORONER: Could you show the jury the letter you received?

MORTLAKE: I have mislaid it, and cannot make out where it has got to. If you, sir, think it relevant or essential, I will state what the trouble was.

CORONER: Was the toothache very violent?

MORTLAKE: I cannot tell. I think not, though he told me it had disturbed his rest the night before.

CORONER: What time did you leave him?

MORTLAKE: About twenty to ten.

CORONER: And what did you do then?

MORTLAKE: I went out for an hour or so to make some inquiries. Then I returned, and told my landlady I should be leaving by an early train for—for the country.

CORONER: And that was the last you saw of the deceased?

MORTLAKE (with emotion): The last.

CORONER: How was he when you left him?

MORTLAKE: Mainly concerned about my trouble.

CORONER: Otherwise you saw nothing unusual about him?

MORTLAKE: Nothing.

CORONER: What time did you leave the house on Tuesday morning?

MORTLAKE: At about five-and-twenty minutes past four.

CORONER: Are you sure that you shut the street door?

MORTLAKE: Quite sure. Knowing my landlady was rather a timid person, I even slipped the bolt of the big lock, which was usually tied back. It was impossible for any one to get in, even with a latch-key.

Mrs. Drabdump's evidence (which, of course, preceded his) was more important, and occupied a considerable time, unduly eked out by Drabdumpian padding. Thus she not only deposed that Mr. Constant had the toothache, but that it was going to last about a week; in tragi-comic indifference to the radical cure that had been effected. Her account of the last hours of the deceased tallied with Mortlake's, only that she feared Mortlake was quarrelling with him over something in the letter that came by the nine o'clock post. Deceased had left the house a little after Mortlake, but had returned before him, and had gone straight to his bedroom. She had not actually seen him come in, having been in the kitchen, but she heard his latch-key, followed by his light step up the stairs.

A JURYMAN: How do you know it was not somebody else? (*Sensation, of which the juryman tries to look unconscious.*)

WITNESS: He called down to me over the banisters, and says in his sweetish voice, "Be hextra sure to wake me at a quarter to seven, Mrs. Drabdump, or else I shan't get to my tram meeting."

(*Juryman collapses.*)

CORONER: And did you wake him?

MRS. DRABDUMP (breaking down): Oh, my lud, how can you ask?

CORONER: There, there, compose yourself. I mean did you try to wake him?

MRS. DRABDUMP: I have taken in and done for lodgers this seventeen years, my lud, and have always gave satisfaction; and Mr. Mortlake, he wouldn't ha' recommended me otherwise, though I wish to Heaven the poor gentleman had never—

CORONER: Yes, yes, of course. You tried to rouse him?

But it was some time before Mrs. Drabdump was sufficiently calm to explain that, though she had overslept herself, and though it would have been all the same any-how, she *had* come up to time. Bit by bit the tragic story was forced from her lips—a tragedy that even her telling could not make tawdry. She told with superfluous detail how—when Mr. Grodman broke in the door—she saw her unhappy gentleman-lodger lying on his back in bed, stone dead, with a gaping red wound in his throat; how her stronger-minded companion calmed her a little by spreading a handkerchief over the distorted face; how they then looked vainly about and under the bed for any instrument by which the deed could have been done, the veteran detective carefully making a rapid inventory of the contents of the room, and taking notes of the precise position and condition of the body before anything was disturbed by the arrival of gapers or bunglers; how she had pointed out to him that both the windows were firmly bolted to keep out the cold night air; how, having noted this down with a puzzled, pity- ing shake of the head, he had opened the window to summon the police, and espied in the fog one Denzil Cantercot, whom he called, and told to run to the nearest police-station and ask them to send on an inspector and a surgeon; how they both remained in the room till the police arrived, Grodman pondering deeply the while and making notes every now and again, as fresh points occurred to him, and asking her questions about the poor, weak-headed young man. Pressed as to what she meant by calling the deceased "weak-headed," she replied that some of her neighbours wrote him begging letters, though, Heaven knew, they were better off than herself, who had to scrape her fingers to the bone for every penny she earned. Under further pressure from Mr. Talbot, who was watching the inquiry on behalf of Arthur Constant's family, Mrs. Drabdump admitted that the deceased had behaved like a human being, nor was there anything externally eccentric or queer in his conduct. He was always cheerful and pleasant spoken, though certainly soft—God rest his soul. No; he never shaved, but wore all the hair that Heaven had given him.

By a JURYMAN: She thought deceased was in the habit of locking his door when he went to bed. Of course, she couldn't say for certain. (Laughter.) There was no need to bolt the door as well. The bolt slid upwards, and was at the top of the door. When she first let lodgings, her reasons for which she seemed anxious to publish, there had only been a bolt, but a suspicious lodger, she would not call him a gentleman, had com- plained that he could not fasten his door behind him, and so she had been put to the expense of having a lock made. The complaining lodger went off soon after without paying his rent. (Laughter.) She had always known he would.

The CORONER: Was deceased at all nervous?

WITNESS: No, he was a very nice gentleman. (A laugh.)

CORONER: I mean did he seem afraid of being robbed?

WITNESS: No, he was always goin' to demonstrations. (Laughter.) I told him to be careful. I told him I lost a purse with 3s. 2d. myself on Jubilee Day.

Mrs. Drabdump resumed her seat, weeping vaguely.

The CORONER: Gentlemen, we shall have an opportunity of viewing the room shortly.

The story of the discovery of the body was retold, though more scientifically, by Mr. George Grodman, whose unexpected resurgence into the realm of his early exploits excited as keen a curiosity as the reappearance "for this occasion only" of a retired prima donna. His book, *Criminals I have Caught*, passed from the twenty-third to the twenty-fourth edition merely on the strength of it. Mr. Grodman stated that the body was still warm when he found it. He thought that death was quite recent. The door he had had to burst was bolted as well as locked. He confirmed Mrs. Drabdump's statement about the windows; the chimney was very narrow. The cut looked as if done by a razor. There was no instrument lying about the room. He had known the deceased about a month. He seemed a very earnest, simple-minded young fellow, who spoke a great deal about the brotherhood of man. (The hardened old man-hunter's voice was not free from a tremor as he spoke jerkily of the dead man's enthusiasms.) He should have thought the deceased the last man in the world to commit suicide.

Mr. DENZIL CANTERCOT was next called: He was a poet. (Laughter.) He was on his way to Mr. Grodman's house to tell him he had been unable to do some writing for him because he was suffering from writer's cramp, when Mr. Grodman called to him from the window of No. 11 and asked him to run for the police. No, he did not run; he was a philosopher. (Laughter.) He returned with them to the door, but did not go up. He had no stomach for crude sensations. (Laughter.) The grey fog was sufficiently unbeautiful for him for one morning. (Laughter.)

Inspector HOWLETT said: About 9:45 on the morning of Tuesday, 4th December, from information received, he went with Sergeant Runnymede and Dr. Robinson to 11 Glover Street, Bow, and there found the dead body of a young man, lying on his back with his throat cut. The door of the room had been smashed in, and the lock and the bolt evidently forced. The room was tidy. There were no marks of blood on the floor. A purse full of gold was on the dressing-table beside a big book. A hip-bath, with cold water, stood beside the bed, over which was a hanging bookcase. There was a large wardrobe against the wall next to the door. The chimney was very narrow. There were two windows, one bolted. It was about eighteen feet to the pavement. There was no way of climbing up. No one could possibly have got out of the room, and then bolted the doors and windows behind him; and he had searched all parts of the room in which any one might have been concealed. He had been unable to find any instrument in the room in spite of exhaustive search, there being not even a penknife in the pockets of the clothes of the deceased, which lay on a chair. The house and the back yard, and the adjacent pavement, had also been fruitlessly searched.

Sergeant RUNNYMEDE made an identical statement, saving only that *he* had gone with Dr. Robinson and Inspector Howlett.

Dr. ROBINSON, divisional surgeon, said: "The deceased was lying on his back, with his throat cut. The body was not yet cold, the abdominal region being quite warm. Rigor mortis had set in in the lower jaw, neck, and upper extremities. The muscles contracted when beaten. I inferred that life had been extinct some two or three hours, probably not longer, it might have been less. The bed-clothes would keep the lower part warm for some time. The wound, which was a deep one, was five and a half inches from right to left across the throat to a point under the left ear. The upper portion of the windpipe was severed, and likewise the jugular vein. The muscular coating of the carotid artery was divided. There was a slight cut, as if in continuation of the wound, on the thumb of the left hand. The hands were clasped underneath the head. There was no blood on the right hand. The wound could not have been self-inflicted. A sharp instrument had been used, such as a razor. The cut might have been made by a left-handed person. No doubt death was practically instantaneous. I saw no signs of a struggle about the body or the room. I noticed a purse on the dressing-table, lying next to Madame Blavatsky's big book on Theosophy. Sergeant Runnymede drew my attention to the fact that the door had evidently been locked and bolted from within."

By a JURYMAN: I do not say the cuts could not have been made by a right-handed person. I can offer no suggestion as to how the inflictor of the wound got in or out. Extremely improbable that the cut was self-inflicted. There was little trace of the outside fog in the room.

Police constable WILLIAMS said he was on duty in the early hours of the morning of the 4th inst. Glover Street lay within his beat. He saw or heard nothing suspicious. The fog was never very dense, though nasty to the throat. He had passed through Glover Street about half-past four. He had not seen Mr. Mortlake or anybody else leave the house.

The Court here adjourned, the coroner and the jury repairing in a body to 11 Glover Street, to view the house and the bedroom of the deceased. And the evening posters announced "The Bow Mystery Thickens."

III

Before the inquiry was resumed, all the poor wretches in custody had been released on suspicion that they were innocent; there was not a single case even for a magistrate. Clues, which at such seasons are gathered by the police like blackberries off the hedges, were scanty and unripe. Inferior specimens were offered them by bushels, but there was not a good one among the lot. The police could not even manufacture a clue.

Arthur Constant's death was already the theme of every hearth, railway-carriage, and public-house. The dead idealist had points of contact with so many spheres. The East-end and the West-end alike were moved and excited, the Democratic Leagues and the Churches, the Doss-houses and the Universities. The pity of it! And then the impenetrable mystery of it!

The evidence given in the concluding portion of the investigation was necessarily less sensational. There were no more witnesses to bring the scent of blood over the coroner's table; those who had yet to be heard were merely relatives and friends of the deceased, who spoke of him as he had been in life. His parents were dead, perhaps happily for them; his relatives had seen little of him, and had scarce heard as much about him as the outside world. No man is a prophet in his own country, and, even if he migrates, it is advisable for him to leave his family at home. His friends were a motley crew; friends of the same friend are not necessarily friends of one another. But their diversity only made the congruity of the tale they had to tell more striking. It was the tale of a man who had never made an enemy even by benefiting him, nor lost a friend even by refusing his favours; the tale of a man whose heart overflowed with peace and goodwill to all men all the year round; of a man to whom Christmas came not once, but three hundred and sixty-five times a year; it was the tale of a brilliant intellect, who gave up to mankind what was meant for himself, and worked as a labourer in the vineyard of humanity, never crying that the grapes were sour; of a man uniformly cheerful and of good courage, living in that forgetfulness of self which is the truest antidote to despair. And yet there was not quite wanting the note of pain to jar the harmony and make it human. Richard Elton, his chum from boyhood, and vicar of Somerton, in Midlandshire, handed to the coroner a letter received from the deceased about ten days before his death, containing some passages which the coroner read aloud:—"Do you know anything of Schopenhauer? I mean anything beyond the current misconceptions? I have been making his acquaintance lately. He is an agreeable rattle of a pessimist; his essay on 'The Misery of Mankind' is quite lively reading. At first his assimilation of Christianity and Pessimism (it occurs in his essay on 'Suicide') dazzled me as an audacious paradox. But there is truth in it. Verily the whole creation groaneth and travaileth, and man is a degraded monster, and sin is over all. Ah, my friend, I have shed many of my illusions since I came to this seething hive of misery and wrongdoing. What shall one man's life—a million men's lives—avail against the corruption, the vulgarity, and the squalor of civilisation? Sometimes I feel like a farthing rushlight in the Hall of Eblis. Selfishness is so long and life so short. And the worst of it is that everybody is so beastly contented. The poor no more desire comfort than the rich culture. The woman, to whom a penny school fee for her child represents an appreciable slice of her income, is satisfied that the rich we shall always have with us.

"The real old Tories are the paupers in the Workhouse. The radical working men are jealous of their own leaders, and the leaders are jealous of one another. Schopenhauer must have organized a Labour Party in his salad days. And yet one can't help feeling that he committed suicide as a philosopher by not committing it as a man. He claims kinship with Buddha, too; though Esoteric Buddhism at least seems spheres removed from the philosophy of 'the Will and the Idea.' What a wonderful woman Madame Blavatsky must be! I can't say I follow her, for she is up in the clouds nearly all the time, and I haven't as yet developed an astral body. Shall I send you on her book? It is fascinating. . . . I am becoming quite a fluent orator. One soon gets into the way of it. The horrible thing is that you catch yourself saying things to lead up to 'Cheers' instead of sticking to the plain realities of the business. Lucy is still doing the galleries in Italy. It used to pain me sometimes to think of my darling's happiness when I came across a flat-chested factory-girl. Now I feel her happiness is as important as a factory-girl's."

Lucy, the witness explained, was Lucy Brent, the betrothed of the deceased. The poor girl had been telegraphed for, and had started for England. The witness stated that the outburst of despondency in this letter was almost a solitary one, most of the letters in his possession being bright, buoyant, and hopeful. Even this letter ended with a humorous statement of the writer's manifold plans and projects for the New Year. The deceased was a good Churchman.

CORONER: Was there any private trouble in his own life to account for the temporary despondency?

WITNESS: Not so far as I am aware. His financial position was exceptionally favourable.

CORONER: There had been no quarrel with Miss Brent?

WITNESS: I have the best authority for saying that no shadow of difference had ever come between them.

CORONER: Was the deceased left-handed?

WITNESS: Certainly not. He was not even ambidexter.

A JURYMAN: Isn't Shoppinhour one of the infidel writers, published by the Freethought Publication Society?

WITNESS: I do not know who publishes his books.

The JURYMAN (a small grocer and big raw-boned Scotchman, rejoicing in the name of Sandy Sanderson and the dignities of deaconry and membership of the committee of the Bow Conservative Association): No equeevocation, sir. Is he not a secularist, who has lectured at the Hall of Science?

WITNESS: No, he is a foreign writer—(Mr. Sanderson was heard to thank heaven for this small mercy)—who believes that life is not worth living.

The JURYMAN: Were you not shocked to find the friend of a meenister reading such impure leeterature?

WITNESS: The deceased read everything. Schopenhauer is the author of a system of philosophy, and not what you seem to imagine. Perhaps you would like to inspect the book? (Laughter.)

The Juryman: I would na' touch it with a pitchfork. Such books should be burnt. And this Madame Blavatsky's book—what is that? Is that also pheelosophy?

Witness: No. It is Theosophy. (Laughter.)

Mr. Allan Smith, secretary of the Tram-men's Union, stated that he had had an interview with the deceased on the day before his death, when he (the deceased) spoke hopefully of the prospects of the movement, and wrote him out a check for ten guineas for his Union. Deceased promised to speak at a meeting called for a quarter past seven a.m. the next day.

Mr. Edward Wimp, of the Scotland Yard Detective Department, said that the letters and papers of the deceased threw no light upon the manner of his death, and they would be handed back to the family. His Department had not formed any theory on the subject.

The coroner proceeded to sum up the evidence. "We have to deal, gentlemen," he said, "with a most incomprehensible and mysterious case, the details of which are yet astonishingly simple. On the morning of Tuesday, the 4th inst., Mrs. Drabdump, a worthy hard-working widow, who lets lodgings at 11 Glover Street, Bow, was unable to arouse the deceased, who occupied the entire upper floor of the house. Becoming alarmed, she went across to fetch Mr. George Grodman, a gentleman known to us all by reputation, and to whose clear and scientific evidence we are much indebted, and got him to batter in the door. They found the deceased lying back in bed with a deep wound in his throat. Life had only recently become extinct. There was no trace of any instrument by which the cut could have been effected: there was no trace of any person who could have effected the cut. No person could apparently have got in or out. The medical evidence goes to show that the deceased could not have inflicted the wound himself. And yet, gentlemen, there are, in the nature of things, two—and only two—alternative explanations of his death. Either the wound was inflicted by his own hand, or it was inflicted by another's. I shall take each of these possibilities separately. First, did the deceased commit suicide? The medical evidence says deceased was lying with his hands clasped behind his head. Now the wound was made from right to left, and terminated by a cut on the left thumb. If the deceased had made it he would have had to do it with his right hand, while his left hand remained under his head—a most peculiar and unnatural position to assume. Moreover, in making a cut with the right hand, one would naturally move the hand from left to right. It is unlikely that the deceased would move his right hand so awkwardly and unnaturally, unless, of course, his object was to baffle suspicion. Another point is that on this hypothesis, the deceased would have had to replace his right hand beneath his head. But Dr. Robinson believes that death was instantaneous. If so, deceased could have had no time to pose so neatly. It is just possible the cut was made with the left hand, but then the deceased was right-handed. The absence of any signs of a possible weapon undoubtedly goes to corroborate the medical evidence. The police have made an exhaustive search in all places where the razor or other weapon or instrument might by any possibility have been concealed, including the bed-clothes, the mattress, the pillow, and the street into which it might have been dropped. But all theories involving the wilful conceal-ment of the fatal instrument have to reckon with the fact or probability that death was instantaneous, also with the fact that there was no blood about the floor. Finally, the instrument used was in all likelihood a razor, and the deceased did not shave, and was never known to be in possession of any such instrument. If, then, we were to confine ourselves to the medical and police evidence, there would, I think, be little hesitation in dismissing the idea of suicide. Nevertheless, it is well to forget the physical aspect of the case for a moment and to apply our minds to an unprejudiced inquiry into the mental aspect of it. Was there any reason why the deceased should wish to take his own life? He was young, wealthy, and popular, loving and loved; life stretched fair before him. He had no vices. Plain living, high thinking, and noble doing were the three guiding stars of his life. If he had had ambition, an illustrious public career was within his reach. He was an orator of no mean power, a brilliant and industrious man. His outlook was always on the future—he was always sketching out ways in which he could be useful to his fellow-men. His purse and his time were ever at the command of whosoever could show fair claim upon them. If such a man were likely to end his own life, the science of human nature would be at an end. Still, some of the shadows of the picture have been presented to us. The man had his moments of despondency—as which of us has not? But they seem to have been few and passing. Anyhow, he was cheerful enough on the day before his death. He was suffering, too, from toothache. But it does not seem to have been violent, nor did he complain. Possibly, of course, the pain became very acute in the night. Nor must we forget that he may have overworked himself, and got his nerves into a morbid state. He worked very hard, never rising later than half-past seven, and doing far more than the professional 'labour leader.' He taught, and wrote, as well as spoke and organised. But on the other hand all witnesses agreed that he was looking forward eagerly to the meeting of tram-men on the morn-ing of the 4th inst. His whole heart was in the movement. Is it likely that this was the night he would choose for quitting the scene of his usefulness? Is it likely that if he had chosen it, he would not have left letters and a statement behind, or made a last will and testament? Mr. Wimp has found no possible clue to such conduct in his papers. Or is it likely he would have concealed the instrument? The only positive sign of intention is the bolting of his door in addition to the usual locking of it, but one cannot lay much

stress on that. Regarding the mental aspects alone, the balance is largely against suicide; looking at the physical aspects, suicide is well-nigh impossible. Putting the two
together, the case against suicide is all but mathematically complete. The answer, then,
to our first question, Did the deceased commit suicide? is, that he did not."

The coroner paused, and everybody drew a long breath. The lucid exposition had
been followed with admiration. If the coroner had stopped now, the jury would have
unhesitatingly returned a verdict of "murder." But the coroner swallowed a mouthful
of water and went on:—

"We now come to the second alternative—was the deceased the victim of homi-
cide? In order to answer that question in the affirmative it is essential that we should
be able to form some conception of the *modus operandi*. It is all very well for Dr.
Robinson to say the cut was made by another hand; but in the absence of any theory
as to how the cut could possibly have been made by that other hand, we should be
driven back to the theory of self-infliction, however improbable it may seem to medical gentlemen. Now, what are the facts? When Mrs. Drabdump and Mr. Grodman
found the body it was yet warm, and Mr. Grodman, a witness fortunately qualified by
special experience, states that death had been quite recent. This tallies closely enough
with the view of Dr. Robinson, who, examining the body about an hour later, put
the time of death at two or three hours before, say seven o'clock. Mrs. Drabdump
had attempted to wake the deceased at a quarter to seven, which would put back the
act to a little earlier. As I understand from Dr. Robinson, that it is impossible to fix
the time very precisely, death may have very well taken place several hours before
Mrs. Drabdump's first attempt to wake deceased. Of course, it may have taken place
between the first and second calls, as he may merely have been sound asleep at first;
it may also not impossibly have taken place considerably earlier than the first call, for
all the physical data seem to prove. Nevertheless, on the whole, I think we shall be
least likely to err if we assume the time of death to be half-past six. Gentlemen, let us
picture to ourselves No. 11 Glover Street, at half-past six. We have seen the house; we
know exactly how it is constructed. On the ground floor a front room tenanted by Mr.
Mortlake, with two windows giving on the street, both securely bolted; a back room
occupied by the landlady; and a kitchen. Mrs. Drabdump did not leave her bedroom
till half-past six, so that we may be sure all the various doors and windows have not
yet been unfastened; while the season of the year is a guarantee that nothing had been
left open. The front door, through which Mr. Mortlake has gone out before half-past
four, is guarded by the latch-key lock and the big lock. On the upper floor are two
rooms—a front room used by deceased for a bedroom, and a back room which he
used as a sitting-room. The back room has been left open, with the key inside, but

the window is fastened. The door of the front room is not only locked but bolted. We have seen the splintered mortice and the staple of the upper bolt violently forced from the woodwork and resting on the pin. The windows are bolted, the fasteners being firmly fixed in the catches. The chimney is too narrow to admit of the passage of even a child. This room, in fact, is as firmly barred in as if besieged. It has no communication with any other part of the house. It is as absolutely self-centred and isolated as if it were a fort in the sea or a log-hut in the forest. Even if any strange person is in the house, nay, in the very sitting-room of the deceased, he cannot get into the bedroom, for the house is one built for the poor, with no communication between the different rooms, so that separate families, if need be, may inhabit each. Now, however, let us grant that some person has achieved the miracle of getting into the front room, first floor, 18 feet from the ground. At half-past six, or thereabouts, he cuts the throat of the sleeping occupant. How is he then to get out without attracting the attention of the now roused landlady? But let us concede him that miracle, too. How is he to go away and yet leave the doors and windows locked and bolted from within? This is a degree of miracle at which my credulity must draw the line. No, the room had been closed all night—there is scarce a trace of fog in it. No one could get in or out. Finally, murders do not take place without motive. Robbery and revenge are the only conceivable motives. The deceased had not an enemy in the world; his money and valuables were left untouched. Everything was in order. There were no signs of a struggle. The answer, then, to our second inquiry, Was the deceased killed by another person? is, that he was not.

"Gentlemen, I am aware that this sounds impossible and contradictory. But it is the facts that contradict themselves. It seems clear that the deceased did not commit suicide. It seems equally clear that the deceased was not murdered. There is nothing for it, therefore, gentlemen, but to return a verdict tantamount to an acknowledgment of our incompetence to come to any adequately grounded conviction whatever as to the means or the manner by which the deceased met his death. It is the most inexplicable mystery in all my experience." (Sensation.)

The FOREMAN (after a colloquy with Mr. Sandy Sanderson): We are not agreed, sir. One of the jurors insists on a verdict of "Death from visitation by the act of God."

IV

But Sandy Sanderson's burning solicitude to fix the crime flickered out in the face of opposition, and in the end he bowed his head to the inevitable "open verdict." Then the floodgates of inkland were opened, and the deluge pattered for nine days on the deaf coffin where the poor idealist mouldered. The tongues of the Press were loosened, and the leader-writers revelled in recapitulating the circumstances of "The Big Bow Mystery," though they could contribute nothing but adjectives to the solution. The papers teemed with letters—it was a kind of Indian summer of the silly season. But the editors could not keep them out, nor cared to. The mystery was the one topic of conversation everywhere—it was on the carpet and the bare boards alike, in the kitchen and the drawing-room. It was discussed with science or stupidity, with aspirates or without. It came up for breakfast with the rolls, and was swept off the supper-table with the last crumbs.

No. 11 Glover Street, Bow, remained for days a shrine of pilgrimage. The once sleepy little street buzzed from morning till night. From all parts of the town people came to stare up at the bedroom window and wonder with a foolish face of horror. The pavement was often blocked for hours together, and itinerant vendors of refreshment made it a new market centre, while vocalists hastened thither to sing the delectable ditty of the deed without having any voice in the matter. It was a pity the Government did not erect a toll-gate at either end of the street. But Chancellors of the Exchequer rarely avail themselves of the more obvious expedients for paying off the National Debt.

Finally, familiarity bred contempt, and the wits grew facetious at the expense of the Mystery. Jokes on the subject appeared even in the comic papers.

To the proverb, "You must not say Bo to a goose," one added, "or else she will explain you the Mystery." The name of the gentleman who asked whether the Bow Mystery was not 'arrowing shall not be divulged. There was more point in "Dagonet's" remark that, if he had been one of the unhappy jurymen, he should have been driven to "suicide." A professional paradox-monger pointed triumphantly to the somewhat similar situation in "the murder in the Rue Morgue," and said that Nature had been plagiarising again—like the monkey she was—and he recommended Poe's publishers to apply for an injunction. More seriously, Poe's solution was re-suggested by "Constant Reader" as an original idea. He thought that a small organ-grinder's monkey might have got down the chimney with its master's razor, and, after attempting to shave the occupant of the bed, have returned the way it came. This idea created considerable sensation, but a correspondent with a long train of letters draggling after his name pointed out that a monkey small enough to get down so narrow a flue would not be strong enough to inflict so deep a wound. This was disputed by a third writer, and the contest raged so keenly about the power of monkeys' muscles that it was almost taken for granted that a monkey was the guilty party. The bubble was pricked by the pen of "Common Sense," who laconically remarked that no traces of soot or blood had been discovered on the floor, or on the nightshirt, or the counterpane. The *Lancet*'s leader on the Mystery was awaited with interest. It said: "We cannot join in the praises that have been showered upon the coroner's summing up. It shows again the evils resulting from having coroners who are not medical men. He seems to have appreciated but inadequately the significance of the medical evidence. He should certainly have directed the jury to return a verdict of murder on that. What was it to do with him that he could see no way by which the wound could have been inflicted by an outside agency? It was for the police to find how that was done. Enough that it was impossible for the unhappy young man to have inflicted such a wound, and then to have strength and will power enough to hide the instrument and to remove perfectly every trace of his having left the bed for the purpose." It is impossible to enumerate all the theories propounded by the amateur detectives, while Scotland Yard religiously held its tongue. Ultimately the interest on the subject became confined to a few papers which had received the best letters. Those papers that couldn't get interesting letters stopped the correspondence and sneered at the "sensationalism" of those that could. Among the mass of fantasy there were not a few notable solutions, which failed brilliantly, like rockets posing as fixed stars. One was that in the obscurity of the fog the murderer had ascended to the window of the bedroom by means of a ladder from the pavement. He had then with a diamond cut one of the panes away, and effected an entry through the aperture. On leaving he fixed in the pane of glass again (or another which he had brought with him) and thus the room remained with its bolts and locks untouched. On its being pointed out that the panes were too small, a third correspondent showed that that didn't matter, as it was only necessary to insert the hand and undo the fastening, when the entire window could be opened, the process being reversed by the murderer on leaving. This pretty edifice of glass was smashed by a glazier, who wrote to say that a pane could hardly be fixed in from only one side of a window frame, that it would fall out when touched, and that in any case the wet putty could not have escaped detection. A door panel sliced out and replaced was also put forward, and as many trap-doors and secret passages were ascribed to No. 11 Glover Street, as if it were a mediæval castle. Another of these clever theories was that the murderer was in the room the whole time the police were there—hidden in the wardrobe. Or he had got behind the door when Grodman broke it open, so that he was not noticed in the excitement of the discovery, and escaped with his weapon at the moment when Grodman and Mrs. Drabdump were examining the window fastenings.

Scientific explanations also were to hand to explain how the assassin locked and bolted the door behind him. Powerful magnets outside the door had been used to turn the key and push the bolt within. Murderers armed with magnets loomed on the popular imagination like a new microbe. There was only one defect in this ingenious theory—the thing could not be done. A physiologist recalled the conjurers who swallow swords—by an anatomical peculiarity of the throat—and said that the deceased might have swallowed the weapon after cutting his own throat. This was too much for the public to swallow. As for the idea that the suicide had been effected with a penknife or its blade, or a bit of steel, which had then got buried in the wound, not even the quotation of Shelley's line:—

Makes such a wound, the knife is lost in it,

could secure it a moment's acceptance. The same reception was accorded to the idea that the cut had been made with a candle-stick (or other harmless necessary bedroom article) constructed like a sword stick. Theories of this sort caused a humorist to explain that the deceased had hidden the razor in his hollow tooth! Some kind friend of Messrs. Maskelyne and Cook suggested that they were the only persons who could have done the deed, as no one else could get out of a locked cabinet. But perhaps the most brilliant of these flashes of false fire was the facetious, yet probably half-seriously meant letter that appeared in the *Pell Mell Press* under the heading of

THE BIG BOW MYSTERY SOLVED

Sir,—You will remember that when the Whitechapel murders were agitating the universe, I suggested that the district coroner was the assassin. My suggestion has been disregarded. The coroner is still at large. So is the Whitechapel murderer. Perhaps this suggestive coincidence will incline the authorities to pay more attention to me this time. The problem seems to be this. The deceased could not have cut his own throat. The deceased could not have had his throat cut for him. As one of the two must have happened, this is obvious nonsense. As this is obvious nonsense I am justified in disbelieving it. As this obvious nonsense was primarily put in circulation by Mrs. Drabdump and Mr. Grodman, I am justified in disbelieving *them*. In short, sir, what guarantee have we that the whole tale is not a cock-and-bull story, invented by the two persons who first found the body? What proof is there that the deed was not done by these persons themselves, who then went to work to smash the door and break the locks and the bolts, and fasten up all the windows before they called the police in?—I enclose my card, and am, sir, yours truly,

ONE WHO LOOKS THROUGH HIS OWN SPECTACLES

[Our correspondent's theory is not so audaciously original as he seems to imagine. Has he not looked through the spectacles of the people who persistently suggested that the Whitechapel murderer was invariably the policeman who found the body? *Somebody* must find the body, if it is to be found at all.—Ed. *P.M.P.*]

The editor had reason to be pleased that he inserted this letter, for it drew the following interesting communication from the great detective himself:—

THE BIG BOW MYSTERY SOLVED

Sir,—I do not agree with you that your correspondent's theory lacks originality. On the contrary, I think it is delightfully original. In fact it has given me an idea. What that idea is I do not yet propose to say, but if 'One who looks through his own spectacles' will favour me with his name and address I shall be happy to inform him a little before the rest of the world whether his germ has borne any fruit. I feel he is a kindred spirit, and take this opportunity of saying publicly that I was extremely disappointed at the unsatisfactory verdict. The thing was a palpable assassination; an open verdict has a tendency to relax the exertions of Scotland Yard. I hope I shall not be accused of immodesty, or of making personal reflections, when I say that the Department has had several notorious failures of late. It is not what it used to be. Crime is becoming impertinent. It no longer knows its place, so to speak. It throws down the gauntlet where once it used to cower in its fastnesses. I repeat, I make these remarks solely in the interest of law and order. I do not for one moment believe that Arthur Constant killed himself, and if Scotland Yard satisfies itself with that explanation, and turns on its other side and goes to sleep again, then, sir, one of the foulest and most horrible crimes of the century will for ever go unpunished. My acquaintance with the unhappy victim was but recent; still, I saw and knew enough of the man to be certain (and I hope I have seen and known enough of other men to judge) that he was a man constitutionally incapable of committing an act of violence, whether against himself or anybody else. He would not hurt a fly, as the saying goes. And a man of that gentle stamp always lacks the active energy to lay hands on himself. He was a man to be esteemed in no common degree, and I feel proud to be able to say that he considered me a friend. I am hardly at the time of life at which a man cares to put on his harness again; but, sir, it is impossible that I should ever know a day's rest till the perpetrator of this foul deed is discovered. I have already put myself in communication with the family of the victim, who, I am pleased to say, have every confidence in me, and look to me to clear the name of their unhappy relative from the semi-imputation of suicide. I shall be pleased if any one who shares my distrust of the authorities, and who has any clue whatever to this terrible mystery or any plausible suggestion to offer, if, in brief, any 'One who looks through his own spectacles' will communicate with me. If I were asked to indicate the direction in which new clues might be most usefully sought, I should say, in the first instance, anything is valuable that helps us to piece together a complete picture of the manifold activities of the man in the East-end. He entered one way or another into the lives of a good many people; is it true that he nowhere made enemies? With the best intentions a man may wound or offend; his interference may be resented; he may even excite jealousy. A young man like the late Mr. Constant could not have had as much practical sagacity as he had goodness. Whose corns did he tread on? The more we know of the last few months of his life the more we shall know of the manner of his death. Thanking you by anticipation for the insertion of this letter in your valuable columns, I am, sir, yours truly,

GEORGE GRODMAN

46 Glover Street, Bow.

P. S.—Since writing the above lines, I have, by the kindness of Miss Brent, been placed in possession of a most valuable letter, probably the last letter written by the unhappy gentleman. It is dated Monday, 3 December, the very eve of the murder, and was addressed to her at Florence, and has now, after some delay, followed her back to London where the sad news unexpectedly brought her. It is a letter couched, on the whole, in the most hopeful spirit, and speaks in detail of his schemes. Of course there are things in it not meant for the ears of the public, but there can be no harm in transcribing an important passage:—

"You seem to have imbibed the idea that the East-end is a kind of Golgotha, and this despite that the books out of which you probably got it are carefully labelled 'Fiction.' Lamb says somewhere that we think of the 'Dark Ages' as literally without sunlight, and so I fancy people like you, dear, think of the 'East-end' as a mixture of mire, misery, and murder. How's that for alliteration? Why, within five minutes' walk of me there are the loveliest houses, with gardens back and front, inhabited by very fine people and furniture. Many of my university friends' mouths would water if they knew the income of some of the shopkeepers in the High Road.

"The rich people about here may not be so fashionable as those in Kensington and Bayswater, but they are every bit as stupid and materialistic. I don't deny, Lucy, I do have my black moments, and I do sometimes pine to get away from all this to the lands of sun and lotus-eating. But, on the whole, I am too busy even to dream of dreaming. My real black moments are when I doubt if I am really doing any good. But yet on the whole my conscience or my self-conceit tells me that I am. If one cannot do much with the mass, there is at least the consolation of doing good to the individual. And, after all, is it not enough to have been an influence for good over one or two human souls? There are quite fine characters hereabout—especially in the women— natures capable not only of self-sacrifice, but of delicacy of sentiment. To have learnt to know of such, to have been of service to one or two of such—is not this ample return? I could not get to St. James's Hall to hear your friend's symphony at the Henschel concert. I have been reading Mme. Blavatsky's latest book, and getting quite interested in occult philosophy. Unfortunately I have to do all my reading in bed, and I don't find the book as soothing a soporific as most new books. For keeping one awake I find Theosophy as bad as toothache. . . ."

THE BIG BOW MYSTERY SOLVED

Sir,—I wonder if any one besides myself has been struck by the incredible bad taste of Mr. Grodman's letter in your last issue. That he, a former servant of the Department, should publicly insult and run it down can only be charitably explained by the supposition that his judgment is failing him in his old age. In view of this letter, are the relatives of the deceased justified in entrusting him with any private documents? It is, no doubt, very good of him to undertake to avenge one whom he seems snobbishly anxious to claim as a friend; but, all things considered, should not his letter have been headed "The Big Bow Mystery Shelved"? I enclose my card, and am, sir,

Your obedient servant,
SCOTLAND YARD

George Grodman read this letter with annoyance, and crumpling up the paper, murmured scornfully, "Edward Wimp!"

V

"Yes, but what will become of the Beautiful?" said Denzil Cantercot.

"Hang the Beautiful!" said Peter Crowl, as if he were on the committee of the Academy. "Give me the True."

Denzil did nothing of the sort. He didn't happen to have it about him.

Denzil Cantercot stood smoking a cigarette in his landlord's shop, and imparting an air of distinction and an agreeable aroma to the close leathery atmosphere. Crowl cobbled away, talking to his tenant without raising his eyes. He was a small, big-headed, sallow, sad-eyed man, with a greasy apron. Denzil was wearing a heavy overcoat with a fur collar. He was never seen without it in public during the winter. In private he removed it and sat in his shirt sleeves. Crowl was a thinker, or thought he was—which seems to involve original thinking anyway. His hair was thinning rapidly at the top, as if his brain was struggling to get as near as possible to the realities of things. He prided himself on having no fads. Few men are without some foible or hobby; Crowl felt almost lonely at times in his superiority. He was a Vegetarian, a Secularist, a Blue Ribbonite, a Republican, and an Anti-tobacconist. Meat was a fad. Drink was a fad. Religion was a fad. Monarchy was a fad. Tobacco was a fad. "A plain man like me," Crowl used to say, "can live without fads." "A plain man" was Crowl's catchword. When of a Sunday morning he stood on Mile-end Waste, which was opposite his shop—and held forth to the crowd on the evils of kings, priests, and mutton chops, the "plain man" turned up at intervals like the "theme" of a symphonic movement. "I am only a plain man and I want to know." It was a phrase that sabred the spider-webs of logical refinement, and held them up scornfully on the point. When Crowl went for a little recreation in Victoria Park on Sunday afternoons, it was with this phrase that he invariably routed the supernaturalists. Crowl knew his Bible better than most ministers, and always carried a minutely printed copy in his pocket, dog's-eared to mark contradictions in the text. The second chapter of Jeremiah says one thing; the first chapter of Corinthians says another. Two contradictory statements *may* both be true, but "I am only a plain man, and I want to know." Crowl spent a large part of his time in setting "the word against the word." Cock-fighting affords its votaries no acuter pleasure than Crowl derived from setting two texts by the ears. Crowl had a metaphysical genius which sent his Sunday morning disciples frantic with admiration, and struck the enemy dumb with dismay. He had discovered, for instance, that the Deity could not move, owing to already filling all space. He was also the first to invent, for the confusion of the clerical, the crucial case of a saint dying at the Antipodes contemporaneously with another in London. Both went skyward to heaven, yet the two travelled in directly opposite directions. In all eternity they would never meet. Which, then, got to heaven? Or was there no such place? "I am only a plain man, and I want to know."

Preserve us our open spaces; they exist to testify to the incurable interest of humanity in the Unknown and the Misunderstood. Even 'Arry is capable of five minutes' attention to speculative theology, if 'Arriet isn't in a 'urry.

Peter Crowl was not sorry to have a lodger like Denzil Cantercot, who, though a man of parts and thus worth powder and shot, was so hopelessly wrong on all subjects under the sun. In only one point did Peter Crowl agree with Denzil Cantercot—he admired Denzil Cantercot secretly. When he asked him for the True—which was about twice a day on the average—he didn't really expect to get it from him. He knew that Denzil was a poet.

"The Beautiful," he went on, "is a thing that only appeals to men like you. The True is for all men. The majority have the first claim. Till then you poets must stand aside. The True and the Useful—that's what we want. The Good of Society is the only test of things. Everything stands or falls by the Good of Society."

"The Good of Society!" echoed Denzil, scornfully. "What's the good of Society? The Individual is before all. The mass must be sacrificed to the Great Man. Otherwise the Great Man will be sacrificed to the mass. Without great men there would be no art. Without art life would be a blank."

"Ah, but we should fill it up with bread and butter," said Peter Crowl.

"Yes, it is bread and butter that kills the Beautiful," said Denzil Cantercot, bitterly. "Many of us start by following the butterfly through the verdant meadows, but we turn aside—"

"To get the grub," chuckled Peter, cobbling away.

"Peter, if you make a jest of everything, I'll not waste my time on you."

Denzil's wild eyes flashed angrily. He shook his long hair. Life was very serious to him. He never wrote comic verse intentionally.

There are three reasons why men of genius have long hair. One is, that they forget it is growing. The second is, that they like it. The third is, that it comes cheaper; they wear it long for the same reason that they wear their hats long.

Owing to this peculiarity of genius, you may get quite a reputation for lack of twopence. The economic reason did not apply to Denzil, who could always get credit with the profession on the strength of his appearance. Therefore, when street arabs vocally commanded him to get his hair cut, they were doing no service to barbers. Why does all the world watch over barbers and conspire to promote their interests? Denzil would have told you it was not to serve the barbers, but to gratify the crowd's instinctive resentment of originality. In his palmy days Denzil had been an editor, but he no more thought of turning his scissors against himself than of swallowing his paste. The efficacy of hair has changed since the days of Samson, otherwise Denzil would have been a Hercules instead of a long, thin, nervous man, looking too brittle and delicate to be used even for a pipe-cleaner. The narrow oval of his face sloped to a pointed, untrimmed beard. His linen was reproachable, his dingy boots were down at heel, and his cocked hat was drab with dust. Such are the effects of a love for the Beautiful.

Peter Crowl was impressed with Denzil's condemnation of flippancy, and he hastened to turn off the joke.

"I'm quite serious," he said. "Butterflies are no good to nothing or nobody; caterpillars at least save the birds from starving."

"Just like your view of things, Peter," said Denzil. "Good morning, madam." This to Mrs. Crowl, to whom he removed his hat with elaborate courtesy.

Mrs. Crowl grunted and looked at her husband with a note of interrogation in each eye. For some seconds Crowl stuck to his last, endeavouring not to see the question. He shifted uneasily on his stool. His wife coughed grimly. He looked up, saw her towering over him, and helplessly shook his head in a horizontal direction. It was wonderful how Mrs. Crowl towered over Mr. Crowl, even when he stood up in his shoes. She measured half an inch less. It was quite an optical illusion.

"Mr. Crowl," said Mrs. Crowl, "then I'll tell him."

"No, no, my dear, not yet," faltered Peter, helplessly; "leave it to me."

"I've left it to you long enough. You'll never do nothing. If it was a question of provin' to a lot of chuckleheads that Jollygee and Genesis, or some other dead and gone Scripture folk that don't consarn no mortal soul, used to contradict each other, your tongue 'ud run thirteen to the dozen. But when it's a matter of takin' the bread out o' the mouths o' your own children, you ain't got no more to say for yourself than a lamp-post. Here's a man stayin' with you for weeks and weeks—eatin' and drinkin' the flesh off your bones—without payin' a far—"

"Hush, hush, mother; it's all right," said poor Crowl, red as fire.

Denzil looked at her dreamily. "Is it possible you are alluding to me, Mrs. Crowl?" he said.

"Who then should I be alludin' to, Mr. Cantercot? Here's seven weeks come and gone, and not a blessed 'aypenny have I—"

"My dear Mrs. Crowl," said Denzil, removing his cigarette from his mouth with a pained air, "why reproach *me for* your neglect?"

"*My* neglect! I like that!"

"I don't," said Denzil more sharply. "If you had sent me in the bill you would have had the money long ago. How do you expect me to think of these details?"

"We ain't so grand down here. People pays their way—they don't get no bills," said Mrs. Crowl, accentuating the word with infinite scorn.

Peter hammered away at a nail, as though to drown his spouse's voice.

"It's three pounds fourteen and eightpence, if you're so anxious to know," Mrs. Crowl resumed. "And there ain't a woman in the Mile End Road as 'ud a-done it cheaper, with bread at fourpence three-farden a quartern and landlords clamburin' for rent every Monday morning almost afore the sun's up and folks draggin' and slidderin' on till their shoes is only fit to throw after brides and Christmas comin' and sevenpence a week for schoolin'!"

Peter winced under the last item. He had felt it coming—like Christmas. His wife and he parted company on the question of Free Education. Peter felt that, having brought nine children into the world, it was only fair he should pay a penny a week for each of those old enough to bear educating. His better half argued that, having so many children, they ought in reason to be exempted. Only people who had few children could spare the penny. But the one point on which the cobbler-sceptic of the Mile End Road got his way was this of the fees. It was a question of conscience, and Mrs. Crowl had never made application for their remission, though she often slapped her children in vexation instead. They were used to slapping, and when nobody else slapped them they slapped one another. They were bright, ill-mannered brats, who pestered their parents and worried their teachers, and were as happy as the Road was long.

"Bother the school fees!" Peter retorted, vexed. "Mr. Cantercot's not responsible for your children."

"I should hope not, indeed, Mr. Crowl," Mrs. Crowl said sternly. "I'm ashamed of you." And with that she flounced out of the shop into the back parlour.

"It's all right," Peter called after her soothingly. "The money'll be all right, mother."

In lower circles it is customary to call your wife your mother; in somewhat superior circles it is the fashion to speak of her as "the wife," as you speak of "the Stock Exchange," or "the Thames," without claiming any peculiar property. Instinctively men are ashamed of being moral and domesticated.

Denzil puffed his cigarette, unembarrassed. Peter bent attentively over his work, making nervous stabs with his awl. There was a long silence. An organ-grinder played a waltz outside, unregarded; and, failing to annoy anybody, moved on. Denzil lit another cigarette. The dirty-faced clock on the wall chimed twelve.

"What do you think," said Crowl, "of Republics?"

"They are low," Denzil replied. "Without a Monarch there is no visible incarnation of Authority."

"What! do you call Queen Victoria visible?"

"Peter, do you want to drive me from the house? Leave frivolousness to women, whose minds are only large enough for domestic difficulties. Republics are low. Plato mercifully kept the poets out of his. Republics are not congenial soil for poetry."

"What nonsense! If England dropped its fad of Monarchy and became a Republic to-morrow, do you mean to say that——?"

"I mean to say there would be no Poet Laureate to begin with."

"Who's fribbling now, you or me, Cantercot? But I don't care a button-hook about poets, present company always excepted. I'm only a plain man, and I want to know where's the sense of givin' any one person authority over everybody else?"

"Ah, that's what Tom Mortlake used to say. Wait till you're in power, Peter, with trade-union money to control, and working men bursting to give you flying angels and to carry you aloft, like a banner, huzzahing."

"Ah, that's because he's head and shoulders above 'em already," said Crowl, with a flash in his sad grey eyes. "Still, it don't prove that I'd talk any different. And I think you're quite wrong about his being spoilt. Tom's a fine fellow—a man every inch of him, and that's a good many. I don't deny he has his weaknesses, and there was a time when he stood in this very shop and denounced that poor dead Constant. 'Crowl,' said he, 'that man'll do mischief. I don't like these kid-glove philanthropists mixing themselves up in practical labour disputes they don't understand.' "

Denzil whistled involuntarily. It was a piece of news.

"I dare say," continued Crowl, "he's a bit jealous of anybody's interference with his influence. But in this case the jealousy did wear off, you see, for the poor fellow and he got quite pals, as everybody knows. Tom's not the man to hug a prejudice. However, all that don't prove nothing against Republics. Look at the Czar and the Jews. I'm only a plain man, but I wouldn't live in Russia not for—not for all the leather in it! An Englishman, taxed as he is to keep up his Fad of Monarchy, is at least king in his own castle, whoever bosses it at Windsor. Excuse me a minute, the missus is callin'."

"Excuse *me* a minute. I'm going, and I want to say before I go—I feel it only right you should know at once—that after what has passed to-day I can never be on the same footing here as in the—shall I say pleasant?—days of yore."

"Oh, no, Cantercot. Don't say that; don't say that!" pleaded the little cobbler.

"Well, shall I say unpleasant, then?"

"No, no, Cantercot. Don't misunderstand me. Mother has been very much put to it lately to rub along. You see she has such a growing family. It grows—daily. But never mind her. You pay whenever you've got the money."

Denzil shook his head. "It cannot be. You know when I came here first I rented your top room and boarded myself. Then I learnt to know you. We talked together. Of the Beautiful. And the Useful. I found you had no soul. But you were honest, and I liked you. I went so far as to take my meals with your family. I made myself at home in your back parlour. But the vase has been shattered (I do not refer to that on the mantelpiece), and though the scent of the roses may cling to it still, it can be pieced together—nevermore." He shook his hair sadly and shambled out of the shop. Crowl would have gone after him, but Mrs. Crowl was still calling, and ladies must have the precedence in all polite societies.

Cantercot went straight—or as straight as his loose gait permitted—to 46 Glover Street, and knocked at the door. Grodman's factotum opened it. She was a pock-marked person, with a brickdust complexion and a coquettish manner.

"Oh! here we are again!" she said vivaciously.

"Don't talk like a clown," Cantercot snapped. "Is Mr. Grodman in?"

"No, you've put him out," growled the gentleman himself, suddenly appearing in his slippers. "Come in. What the devil have you been doing with yourself since the inquest? Drinking again?"

"I've sworn off. Haven't touched a drop since—"

"The murder?"

"Eh?" said Denzil Cantercot, startled. "What do you mean?"

"What I say. Since December 4. I reckon everything from that murder, now, as they reckon longitude from Greenwich."

"Oh," said Denzil Cantercot.

"Let me see. Nearly a fortnight. What a long time to keep away from Drink—and Me."

"I don't know which is worse," said Denzil, irritated. "You both steal away my brains."

"Indeed?" said Grodman, with an amused smile. "Well, it's only petty pilfering, after all. What's put salt on your wounds?"

"The twenty-fourth edition of my book."

"*Whose* book?"

"Well, *your* book. You must be making piles of money out of *Criminals I have Caught.*"

" 'Criminals *I* have Caught,' " corrected Grodman. "My dear Denzil, how often am I to point out that *I* went through the experiences that make the backbone of my book, not *you*? In each case *I* cooked the criminal's goose. Any journalist could have supplied the dressing."

"The contrary. The journeymen of journalism would have left the truth naked. You yourself could have done that—for there is no man to beat you at cold, lucid, scientific statement. But I idealised the bare facts and lifted them into the realm of poetry and literature. The twenty-fourth edition of the book attests my success."

"Rot! The twenty-fourth edition was all owing to the murder. Did you do that?"

"You take one up so sharply, Mr. Grodman," said Denzil, changing his tone.

"No—I've retired," laughed Grodman.

Denzil did not reprove the ex-detective's flippancy. He even laughed a little.

"Well, give me another fiver, and I'll cry 'quits.' I'm in debt."

"Not a penny. Why haven't you been to see me since the murder? I had to write that letter to the *Pell Mell Press* myself. You might have earned a crown."

"I've had writer's cramp, and couldn't do your last job. I was coming to tell you so on the morning of the—"

"Murder. So you said at the inquest."

"It's true."

"Of course. Weren't you on your oath? It was very zealous of you to get up so early to tell me. In which hand did you have this cramp?"

"Why, in the right of course."

"And you couldn't write with your left?"

"I don't think I could even hold a pen."

"Or any other instrument, mayhap. What had you been doing to bring it on?"

"Writing too much. That is the only possible cause."

"Oh! I didn't know. Writing what?"

Denzil hesitated. "An epic poem."

"No wonder you're in debt. Will a sovereign get you out of it?"

"No; it wouldn't be the least use to me."

"Here it is, then."

Denzil took the coin and his hat.

"Aren't you going to earn it, you beggar? Sit down and write something for me."

Denzil got pen and paper, and took his place.

"What do you want me to write?"

"Your Epic Poem."

Denzil started and flushed. But he set to work. Grodman leaned back in his armchair and laughed, studying the poet's grave face.

Denzil wrote three lines and paused.

"Can't remember any more? Well, read me the start."

Denzil read:—

> "Of man's first disobedience and the fruit
> Of that forbidden tree whose mortal taste
> Brought death into the world—"

"Hold on!" cried Grodman. "What morbid subjects you choose, to be sure!"

"Morbid! Why, Milton chose the same subject!"

"Blow Milton. Take yourself off—you and your Epics."

Denzil went. The pock-marked person opened the street door for him.

"When am I to have that new dress, dear?" she whispered coquettishly.

"I have no money, Jane," he said shortly.

"You have a sovereign."

Denzil gave her the sovereign, and slammed the door viciously. Grodman overheard their whispers, and laughed silently. His hearing was acute. Jane had first introduced Denzil to his acquaintance about two years ago, when he spoke of getting an amanuensis, and the poet had been doing odd jobs for him ever since. Grodman argued that Jane had her reasons. Without knowing them, he got a hold over both. There was no one, he felt, he could not get a hold over. All men—and women—have something to conceal, and you have only to pretend to know what it is. Thus Grodman, who was nothing if not scientific.

Denzil Cantercot shambled home thoughtfully, and abstractedly took his place at the Crowl dinner-table.

VI

Mrs. Crowl surveyed Denzil Cantercot so stonily and cut him his beef so savagely that he said grace when the dinner was over. Peter fed his metaphysical genius on tomatoes. He was tolerant enough to allow his family to follow their Fads; but no savoury smells ever tempted him to be false to his vegetable loves. Besides, meat might have reminded him too much of his work. There is nothing like leather, but Bow beefsteaks occasionally come very near it.

After dinner Denzil usually indulged in poetic reverie. But to-day he did not take his nap. He went out at once to "raise the wind." But there was a dead calm everywhere. In vain he asked for an advance at the office of the *Mile End Mirror*, to which he contributed scathing leaderettes about vestrymen. In vain he trudged to the City and offered to write the *Ham and Eggs Gazette* an essay on the modern methods of bacon-curing. Denzil knew a great deal about the breeding and slaughtering of pigs, smoke-lofts and drying processes, having for years dictated the policy of the *New Pork Herald* in these momentous matters. Denzil also knew a great deal about many other esoteric matters, including weaving machines, the manufacture of cabbage leaves and snuff, and the inner economy of drain-pipes. He had written for the trade papers since boyhood. But there is great competition on these papers. So many men of literary gifts know all about the intricate technicalities of manufactures and markets, and are eager to set the trade right. Grodman perhaps hardly allowed sufficiently for the step backwards that Denzil made when he devoted his whole time for months to *Criminals I have Caught*. It was as damaging as a debauch. For when your rivals are pushing forwards, to stand still is to go back.

In despair Denzil shambled toilsomely to Bethnal Green. He paused before the window of a little tobacconist's shop, wherein was displayed a placard announcing

PLOTS FOR SALE

The announcement went on to state that a large stock of plots was to be obtained on the premises—embracing sensational plots, humorous plots, love plots, religious plots, and poetic plots; also complete manuscripts, original novels, poems, and tales. Apply within.

It was a very dirty-looking shop, with begrimed bricks and blackened woodwork. The window contained some musty old books, an assortment of pipes and tobacco, and a large number of the vilest daubs unhung, painted in oil on Academy boards, and unframed. These were intended for landscapes, as you could tell from the titles. The most expensive was "Chingford Church," and it was marked 1s. 9d. The others ran from 6d. to 1s. 3d., and were mostly representations of Scottish scenery—a loch with mountains in the background, with solid reflections in the water and a tree in the foreground. Sometimes the tree would be in the background. Then the loch would be in the foreground. Sky and water were intensely blue in all. The name of the collection was "Original oil-paintings done by hand." Dust lay thick upon everything, as if carefully shovelled on; and the proprietor looked as if he slept in his shop-window at night without taking his clothes off. He was a gaunt man with a red nose, long but scanty black locks covered by a smoking-cap, and a luxuriant black moustache. He smoked a long clay pipe, and had the air of a broken-down operatic villain.

"Ah, good afternoon, Mr. Cantercot," he said, rubbing his hands, half from cold, half from usage; "what have you brought me?"

"Nothing," said Denzil, "but if you will lend me a sovereign I'll do you a stunner."

The operatic villain shook his locks, his eyes full of pawky cunning. "If you did it after that, it *would* be a stunner."

What the operatic villain did with these plots, and who bought them, Cantercot never knew nor cared to know. Brains are cheap to-day, and Denzil was glad enough to find a customer.

"Surely you've known me long enough to trust me," he cried.

"Trust is dead," said the operatic villain, puffing away.

"So is Queen Anne," cried the irritated poet. His eyes took a dangerous hunted look. Money he must have. But the operatic villain was inflexible. No plot, no supper.

Poor Denzil went out flaming. He knew not where to turn. Temporarily he turned on his heel again and stared despairingly at the shop-window. Again he read the legend

PLOTS FOR SALE

He stared so long at this that it lost its meaning. When the sense of the words suddenly flashed upon him again, they bore a new significance. He went in meekly, and borrowed fourpence of the operatic villain. Then he took the 'bus for Scotland Yard. There was a not ill-looking servant girl in the 'bus. The rhythm of the vehicle shaped itself into rhymes in his brain. He forgot all about his situation and his object. He had never really written an epic—except "Paradise Lost"—but he composed lyrics about wine and women and often wept to think how miserable he was. But nobody ever bought anything of him, except articles on bacon-curing or attacks on vestrymen. He was a strange, wild creature, and the wench felt quite pretty under his ardent gaze. It almost hypnotised her, though, and she looked down at her new French kid boots to escape it.

At Scotland Yard Denzil asked for Edward Wimp. Edward Wimp was not on view. Like kings and editors, detectives are difficult of approach—unless you are a criminal, when you cannot see anything of them at all. Denzil knew of Edward Wimp, principally because of Grodman's contempt for his successor. Wimp was a man of taste and culture. Grodman's interests were entirely concentrated on the problems of logic and evidence. Books about these formed his sole reading; for *belles lettres* he cared not a straw. Wimp, with his flexible intellect, had a great contempt for Grodman and his slow, laborious, ponderous, almost Teutonic methods. Worse, he almost threatened to eclipse the radiant tradition of Grodman by some wonderfully ingenious bits of workmanship. Wimp was at his greatest in collecting circumstantial evidence; in putting two and two together to make five. He would collect together a number of dark and disconnected data and flash across them the electric light of some unifying hypothesis in a way which would have done credit to a Darwin or a Faraday. An intellect which might have served to unveil the secret workings of nature was subverted to the protection of a capitalistic civilisation.

By the assistance of a friendly policeman, whom the poet magnetised into the belief that his business was a matter of life and death, Denzil obtained the great detective's private address. It was near King's Cross. By a miracle Wimp was at home in the afternoon. He was writing when Denzil was ushered up three pairs of stairs into his presence, but he got up and flashed the bull's-eye of his glance upon the visitor.

"Mr. Denzil Cantercot, I believe," said Wimp.

Denzil started. He had not sent up his name, merely describing himself as a gentleman.

"That is my name," he murmured.

"You were one of the witnesses at the inquest on the body of the late Arthur Constant. I have your evidence there." He pointed to a file. "Why have you come to give fresh evidence?"

Again Denzil started, flushing in addition this time. "I want money," he said, almost involuntarily.

"Sit down." Denzil sat. Wimp stood.

Wimp was young and fresh-coloured. He had a Roman nose, and was smartly dressed. He had beaten Grodman by discovering the wife Heaven meant for him. He had a bouncing boy, who stole jam out of the pantry without any one being the wiser. Wimp did what work he could do at home in a secluded study at the top of the house. Outside his chamber of horrors he was the ordinary husband of commerce. He adored his wife, who thought poorly of his intellect but highly of his heart. In domestic difficulties Wimp was helpless. He could not tell even whether the servant's "character" was forged or genuine. Probably he could not level himself to such petty problems. He was like the senior wrangler who has forgotten how to do quadratics, and has to solve equations of the second degree by the calculus.

"How much money do you want?" he asked.

"I do not make bargains," Denzil replied, his calm come back by this time. "I came here to tender you a suggestion. It struck me that you might offer me a fiver for my trouble. Should you do so, I shall not refuse it."

"You shall not refuse it—if you deserve it."

"Good. I will come to the point at once. My suggestion concerns—Tom Mortlake."

Denzil threw out the name as if it were a torpedo. Wimp did not move.

"Tom Mortlake," went on Denzil, looking disappointed, "had a sweetheart." He paused impressively.

Wimp said, "Yes?"

"Where is that sweetheart now?"

"Where, indeed?"

"You know about her disappearance?"

"You have just informed me of it."

"Yes, she is gone—without a trace. She went about a fortnight before Mr. Constant's murder."

"Murder? How do you know it was murder?"

"Mr. Grodman says so," said Denzil, startled again.

"H'm! Isn't that rather a proof that it was suicide? Well, go on."

"About a fortnight before the suicide, Jessie Dymond disappeared. So they tell me in Stepney Green, where she lodged and worked."

"What was she?"

"She was a dressmaker. She had a wonderful talent. Quite fashionable ladies got to know of it. One of her dresses was presented at Court. I think the lady forgot to pay for it; so Jessie's landlady said."

"Did she live alone?"

"She had no parents, but the house was respectable."

"Good-looking, I suppose?"

"As a poet's dream."

"As yours, for instance?"

"I am a poet; I dream."

"You dream you are a poet. Well, well! She was engaged to Mortlake?"

"Oh, yes! They made no secret of it. The engagement was an old one. When he was earning 36s. a week as a compositor, they were saving up to buy a home. He worked at Railton and Hockes who print the *New Pork Herald*. I used to take my 'copy' into the comps' room, and one day the Father of the Chapel told me all about 'Mortlake and his young woman.' Ye gods! How times are changed! Two years ago Mortlake had to struggle with my calligraphy—now he is in with all the nobs, and goes to the 'At Homes' of the aristocracy."

"Radical M.P.'s," murmured Wimp, smiling.

"While I am still barred from the dazzling drawing-rooms, where beauty and intellect foregather. A mere artisan! A manual labourer!" Denzil's eyes flashed angrily. He rose with excitement. "They say he always was a jabberer in the composing-room, and he has jabbered himself right out of it and into a pretty good thing. He didn't have much to say about the crimes of capital when he was set up to second the toast of 'Railton and Hockes' at the beanfeast."

"Toast and butter, toast and butter," said Wimp, genially. "I shouldn't blame a man for serving the two together, Mr. Cantercot."

Denzil forced a laugh. "Yes; but consistency's my motto. I like to see the royal soul immaculate, unchanging, immovable by fortune. Anyhow, when better times came for Mortlake the engagement still dragged on. He did not visit her so much. This last autumn he saw very little of her."

"How do you know?"

"I—I was often in Stepney Green. My business took me past the house of an evening. Sometimes there was no light in her room. That meant she was downstairs gossiping with the landlady."

"She might have been out with Tom?"

"No, sir; I knew Tom was on the platform somewhere or other. He was working up to all hours organising the eight hours' working movement."

"A very good reason for relaxing his sweethearting."

"It was. He never went to Stepney Green on a week night."

"But you always did."

"No—not every night."

"You didn't go in?"

"Never. She wouldn't permit my visits. She was a girl of strong character. She always reminded me of Flora Macdonald."

"Another lady of your acquaintance?"

"A lady I know better than the shadows who surround me, who is more real to me than the women who pester me for the price of apartments. Jessie Dymond, too, was of the race of heroines. Her eyes were clear blue, two wells with Truth at the bottom of each. When I looked into those eyes my own were dazzled. They were the only eyes I could never make dreamy." He waved his hand as if making a pass with it. "It was she who had the influence over me."

"You knew her, then?"

"Oh, yes. I knew Tom from the old *New Pork Herald* days, and when I first met him with Jessie hanging on his arm he was quite proud to introduce her to a poet. When he got on he tried to shake me off."

"You should have repaid him what you borrowed."

"It—it—was only a trifle," stammered Denzil.

"Yes, but the world turns on trifles," said the wise Wimp.

"The world is itself a trifle," said the pensive poet. "The Beautiful alone is deserving of our regard."

"And when the Beautiful was not gossiping with her landlady, did she gossip with you as you passed the door?"

"Alas, no! She sat in her room reading, and cast a shadow—"

"On your life?"

"No; on the blind."

"Always one shadow?"

"No, sir. Once or twice, two."

"Ah, you had been drinking."

"On my life, not. I have sworn off the treacherous wine-cup."

"That's right. Beer is bad for poets. It makes their feet shaky. Whose was the second shadow?"

"A man's."

"Naturally. Mortlake's, perhaps."

"Impossible. He was still striking eight hours."

"You found out whose shadow? You didn't leave a shadow of doubt?"

"No; I waited till the substance came out."

"It was Arthur Constant."

"You are a magician! You—you terrify me. Yes, it was he."

"Only once or twice, you say?"

"I didn't keep watch over them."

"No, no, of course not. You only passed casually. I understand you thoroughly."

Denzil did not feel comfortable at the assertion.

"What did he go there for?" Wimp went on.

"I don't know. I'd stake my soul on Jessie's honour."

"You might double your stake without risk."

"Yes, I might! I would! You see her with my eyes."

"For the moment they are the only ones available. When was the last time you saw the two together?"

"About the middle of November."

"Mortlake knew nothing of the meetings?"

"I don't know. Perhaps he did. Mr. Constant had probably enlisted her in his social mission work. I knew she was one of the attendants at the big children's tea in the Great Assembly Hall early in November. He treated her quite like a lady. She was the only attendant who worked with her hands."

"The others carried the cups on their feet, I suppose."

"No; how could that be? My meaning is that all the other attendants were real ladies, and Jessie was only an amateur, so to speak. There was no novelty for her in handing kids cups of tea. I dare say she had helped her landlady often enough at that—there's quite a bushel of brats below stairs. It's almost as bad as at friend Crowl's. Jessie was a real brick. But perhaps Tom didn't know her value. Perhaps he didn't like Constant to call on her, and it led to a quarrel. Anyhow, she's disappeared, like the snowfall on the river. There's not a trace. The landlady, who was such a friend of hers that Jessie used to make up her stuff into dresses for nothing, tells me that she's dreadfully annoyed at not having been left the slightest clue to her late tenant's whereabouts."

"You have been making inquiries on your own account apparently?"

"Only of the landlady. Jessie never even gave her the week's notice, but paid her in lieu of it, and left immediately. The landlady told me I could have knocked her down with a feather. Unfortunately, I wasn't there to do it, or I should certainly have knocked her down for not keeping her eyes open better. She says if she had only had the least suspicion beforehand that the minx (she dared to call Jessie a minx) was going, she'd have known where, or her name would have been somebody else's. And yet she admits that Jessie was looking ill and worried. Stupid old hag!"

"A woman of character," murmured the detective.

"Didn't I tell you so?" cried Denzil, eagerly. "Another girl would have let out that she was going. But no, not a word. She plumped down the money and walked out. The landlady ran upstairs. None of Jessie's things were there. She must have quietly sold them off, or transferred them to the new place. I never in my life met a girl who so thoroughly knew her own mind or had a mind so worth knowing. She always reminded me of the Maid of Saragossa."

"Indeed! And when did she leave?"

"On the 19th of November."

"Mortlake of course knows where she is?"

"I can't say. Last time I was at the house to inquire—it was at the end of November—he hadn't been seen there for six weeks. He wrote to her, of course, sometimes—the landlady knew his writing."

Wimp looked Denzil straight in the eyes, and said, "You mean, of course, to accuse Mortlake of the murder of Mr. Constant?"

"N-n-no, not at all," stammered Denzil, "only you know what Mr. Grodman wrote to the *Pell Mell*. The more we know about Mr. Constant's life the more we shall know about the manner of his death. I thought my information would be valuable to you, and I brought it."

"And why didn't you take it to Mr. Grodman?"

"Because I thought it wouldn't be valuable to me."

"You wrote *Criminals I have Caught*?"

"How—how do you know that?" Wimp was startling him to-day with a vengeance.

"Your style, my dear Mr. Cantercot. The unique, noble style."

"Yes, I was afraid it would betray me," said Denzil. "And since you know, I may tell you that Grodman's a mean curmudgeon. What does he want with all that money and those houses—a man with no sense of the Beautiful? He'd have taken my information, and given me more kicks than ha'pence for it, so to speak."

"Yes, he is a shrewd man after all. I don't see anything valuable in your evidence against Mortlake."

"No!" said Denzil in a disappointed tone, and fearing he was going to be robbed. "Not when Mortlake was already jealous of Mr. Constant, who was a sort of rival organiser, unpaid! A kind of blackleg doing the work cheaper—nay, for nothing."

"Did Mortlake tell you he was jealous?" said Wimp, a shade of sarcastic contempt piercing through his tones.

"Oh, yes! He said to me, 'That man will work mischief. I don't like your kid-glove philanthropists meddling in matters they don't understand.'"

"Those were his very words?"

"His *ipsissima verba*."

"Very well. I have your address in my files. Here is a sovereign for you."

"Only one sovereign! It's not the least use to me."

"Very well. It's of great use to me. I have a wife to keep."

"I haven't," said Denzil, with a sickly smile, "so perhaps I can manage on it after all." He took his hat and the sovereign.

Outside the door he met a rather pretty servant just bringing in some tea to her master. He nearly upset her tray at sight of her. She seemed more amused at the rencontre than he.

"Good afternoon, dear," she said coquettishly. "You might let me have that sovereign. I do so want a new Sunday bonnet."

Denzil gave her the sovereign, and slammed the hall-door viciously when he got to the bottom of the stairs. He seemed to be walking arm-in-arm with the long arm of coincidence. Wimp did not hear the duologue. He was already busy on his evening's report to headquarters. The next day Denzil had a body-guard wherever he went. It might have gratified his vanity had he known it. But to-night he was yet unattended, so no one noted that he went to 46 Glover Street, after the early Crowl supper. He could not help going. He wanted to get another sovereign. He also itched to taunt Grodman. Not succeeding in the former object, he felt the road open for the second.

"Do you still hope to discover the Bow murderer?" he asked the old bloodhound.

"I can lay my hand on him now," Grodman announced curtly.

Denzil hitched his chair back involuntarily. He found conversation with detectives as lively as playing at skittles with bombshells. They got on his nerves terribly, these undemonstrative gentlemen with no sense of the Beautiful.

"But why don't you give him up to justice?" he murmured.

"Ah—it has to be proved yet. But it is only a matter of time."

"Oh!" said Denzil, "and shall I write the story for you?"

"No. You will not live long enough."

Denzil turned white. "Nonsense! I am years younger than you," he gasped.

"Yes," said Grodman, "but you drink so much."

VII

When Wimp invited Grodman to eat his Christmas plum-pudding at King's Cross, Grodman was only a little surprised. The two men were always overwhelmingly cordial when they met, in order to disguise their mutual detestation. When people really like each other, they make no concealment of their mutual contempt. In his letter to Grodman, Wimp said that he thought it might be nicer for him to keep Christmas in company than in solitary state. There seems to be a general prejudice in favour of Christmas numbers, and Grodman yielded to it. Besides, he thought that a peep at the Wimp domestic interior would be as good as a pantomime. He quite enjoyed the fun that was coming, for he knew that Wimp had not invited him out of mere "peace and goodwill."

There was only one other guest at the festive board. This was Wimp's wife's mother's mother, a lady of sweet seventy. Only a minority of mankind can obtain a grandmother-in-law by marrying, but Wimp was not unduly conceited. The old lady suffered from delusions. One of them was that she was a centenarian. She dressed for the part. It is extraordinary what pains ladies will take to conceal their age. Another of Wimp's grandmother-in-law's delusions was that Wimp had married to get her into the family. Not to frustrate his design, she always gave him her company on high-days and holidays. Wilfred Wimp—the little boy who stole the jam—was in great form at the Christmas dinner. The only drawback to his enjoyment was that its sweets needed no stealing. His mother presided over the platters, and thought how much cleverer Grodman was than her husband. When the pretty servant who waited on them was momentarily out of the room, Grodman had remarked that she seemed very inquisitive. This coincided with Mrs. Wimp's own convictions, though Mr. Wimp could never be brought to see anything unsatisfactory or suspicious about the girl, not even though there were faults in spelling in the "character" with which her last mistress had supplied her.

It was true that the puss had pricked up her ears when Denzil Cantercot's name was mentioned. Grodman saw it, and watched her, and fooled Wimp to the top of his bent. It was, of course, Wimp who introduced the poet's name, and he did it so casually that Grodman perceived at once that he wished to pump him. The idea that the rival bloodhound should come to him for confirmation of suspicions against his own pet jackal was too funny. It was almost as funny to Grodman that evidence of some sort should be obviously lying to hand in the bosom of Wimp's hand-maiden; so obviously that Wimp could not see it. Grodman enjoyed his Christmas dinner, secure that he had not found a successor after all. Wimp, for his part, contemptuously wondered at the way Grodman's thought hovered about Denzil without grazing the truth. A man constantly about him, too!

"Denzil is a man of genius," said Grodman. "And as such comes under the heading of Suspicious Characters. He has written an Epic Poem and read it to me. It is morbid from start to finish. There is 'death' in the third line. I dare say you know he polished up my book?" Grodman's artlessness was perfect.

"No. You surprise me," Wimp replied. "I'm sure he couldn't have done much to it. Look at your letter in the *Pell Mell*. Who wants more polish and refinement than that showed?"

"Ah, I didn't know you did me the honour of reading that."

"Oh, yes; we both read it," put in Mrs. Wimp. "I told Mr. Wimp it was very clever and cogent. After that quotation from the letter to the poor fellow's *fiancée* there could be no more doubt but that it was murder. Mr. Wimp was convinced by it too, weren't you, Edward?"

Edward coughed uneasily. It was a true statement, and therefore an indiscreet. Grodman would plume himself terribly. At this moment Wimp felt that Grodman had been right in remaining a bachelor. Grodman perceived the humour of the situation, and wore a curious, sub-mocking smile.

"On the day I was born," said Wimp's grandmother-in-law, "over a hundred years ago, there was a babe murdered."—Wimp found himself wishing it had been she. He was anxious to get back to Cantercot. "Don't let us talk shop on Christmas Day," he said, smiling at Grodman. "Besides, murder isn't a very appropriate subject."

"No, it ain't," said Grodman. "How did we get on to it? Oh, yes—Denzil Cantercot. Ha! ha! ha! That's curious, for since Denzil revised *Criminals I have Caught*, his mind's running on nothing but murders. A poet's brain is easily turned."

Wimp's eye glittered with excitement and contempt for Grodman's blindness. In Grodman's eye there danced an amused scorn of Wimp; to the outsider his amusement appeared at the expense of the poet.

Having wrought his rival up to the highest pitch, Grodman slyly and suddenly unstrung him.

"How lucky for Denzil!" he said, still in the same naïve, facetious Christmasy tone, "that he can prove an alibi in this Constant affair."

"An alibi!" gasped Wimp. "Really?"

"Oh, yes. He was with his wife, you know. She's my woman of all work, Jane. She happened to mention his being with her."

Jane had done nothing of the kind. After the colloquy he had overheard, Grodman had set himself to find out the relation between his two employees. By casually referring to Denzil as "your husband," he so startled the poor woman that she did not attempt to deny the bond. Only once did he use the two words, but he was satisfied. As to the alibi, he had not yet troubled her; but to take its existence for granted would upset and discomfort Wimp. For the moment that was triumph enough for Wimp's guest.

"Par," said Wilfred Wimp, "what's a alleybi? A marble?"

"No, my lad," said Grodman, "it means being somewhere else when you're supposed to be somewhere."

"Ah, playing truant," said Wilfred, self-consciously; his schoolmaster had often proved an alibi against him. "Then Denzil will be hanged."

Was it a prophecy? Wimp accepted it as such; as an oracle from the gods bidding him mistrust Grodman. Out of the mouths of little children issueth wisdom; sometimes even when they are not saying their lessons.

"When I was in my cradle, a century ago," said Wimp's grandmother-in-law, "men were hanged for stealing horses."

They silenced her with snapdragon performances.

Wimp was busy thinking how to get at Grodman's factotum.

Grodman was busy thinking how to get at Wimp's domestic.

Neither received any of the usual messages from the Christmas Bells.

The next day was sloppy and uncertain. A thin rain drizzled languidly. One can stand that sort of thing on a summer Bank Holiday; one expects it. But to have a bad December Bank Holiday is too much of a bad thing. Some steps should surely be taken to confuse the weather clerk's chronology. Once let him know that Bank Holiday is coming, and he writes to the company for more water. To-day his stock seemed low, and he was dribbling it out; at times the wintry sun would shine in a feeble, diluted way, and though the holiday-makers would have preferred to take their sunshine neat, they swarmed forth in their myriads whenever there was a ray of hope. But it was only dodging the raindrops; up went the umbrellas again, and the streets became meadows of ambulating mushrooms.

Denzil Cantercot sat in his fur overcoat at the open window, looking at the landscape in watercolours. He smoked an after-dinner cigarette, and spoke of the Beautiful. Crowl was with him. They were in the first floor front, Crowl's bedroom, which, from its view of the Mile End Road, was livelier than the parlour with its outlook on the backyard. Mrs. Crowl was an anti-tobacconist as regards the best bedroom; but Peter did not like to put the poet or his cigarette out. He felt there was something in common between smoke and poetry, over and above their being both Fads. Besides, Mrs. Crowl was sulking in the kitchen. She had been arranging for an excursion with Peter and the children to Victoria Park. (She had dreamed of the Crystal Palace, but Santa Claus had put no gifts in the cobbler's shoes.) Now she could not risk spoiling the feather in her bonnet. The nine brats expressed their disappointment by slapping one another on the staircases. Peter felt that Mrs. Crowl connected him in some way with the rainfall, and was unhappy. Was it not enough that he had been deprived of the pleasure of pointing out to a superstitious majority the mutual contradictions of Leviticus and the Song of Solomon? It was not often that Crowl could count on such an audience.

"And you still call Nature Beautiful?" he said to Denzil, pointing to the ragged sky and the dripping eaves. "Ugly old scarecrow!"

"Ugly she seems to-day," admitted Denzil. "But what is Ugliness but a higher form of Beauty? You have to look deeper into it to see it; such vision is the priceless gift of the few. To me this wan desolation of sighing rain is lovely as the sea-washed ruins of cities."

"Ah, but you wouldn't like to go out into it," said Peter Crowl. As he spoke the drizzle suddenly thickened into a torrent.

"We do not always kiss the woman we love."

"Speak for yourself, Denzil. I'm only a plain man, and I want to know if Nature isn't a Fad. Hallo, there goes Mortlake! Lord, a minute of this will soak him to the skin."

The labour leader was walking along with bowed head. He did not seem to mind the shower. It was some seconds before he even heard Crowl's invitation to him to take shelter. When he did hear it he shook his head.

"I know I can't offer you a drawing-room with duchesses stuck about it," said Peter, vexed.

Tom turned the handle of the shop door and went in. There was nothing in the world which now galled him more than the suspicion that he was stuck-up and wished to cut old friends. He picked his way through the nine brats who clung affectionately to his wet knees, dispersing them finally by a jet of coppers to scramble for. Peter met him on the stairs and shook his hand lovingly and admiringly, and took him into Mrs. Crowl's bedroom.

"Don't mind what I say, Tom. I'm only a plain man, and my tongue will say what comes uppermost! But it ain't from the soul, Tom, it ain't from the soul," said Peter, punning feebly, and letting a mirthless smile play over his sallow features. "You know Mr. Cantercot, I suppose? The Poet."

"Oh, yes; how do you do, Tom?" cried the Poet. "Seen the New Pork Herald lately? Not bad, those old times, eh?"

"No," said Tom, "I wish I was back in them."

"Nonsense, nonsense," said Peter, in much concern. "Look at the good you are doing to the working man. Look how you are sweeping away the Fads. Ah, it's a grand thing to be gifted, Tom. The idea of your chuckin' yourself away on a composin'-room! Manual labour is all very well for plain men like me, with no gift but just enough brains to see into the realities of things—to understand that we've got no soul and no immortality, and all that—and too selfish to look after anybody's comfort but my own and mother's and the kids'. But men like you and Cantercot—it ain't right that you should be peggin' away at low material things. Not that I think Cantercot's gospel any value to the masses. The Beautiful is all very well for folks who've got nothing else to think of, but give me the True. You're the man for my money, Mortlake. No reference to the funds, Tom, to which I contribute little enough, Heaven knows; though how a place can know anything, Heaven alone knows. You give us the Useful, Tom; that's what the world wants more than the Beautiful."

"Socrates said that the Useful is the Beautiful," said Denzil.

"That may be," said Peter, "but the Beautiful ain't the Useful."

"Nonsense!" said Denzil. "What about Jessie—I mean Miss Dymond? There's a combination for you. She always reminds me of Grace Darling. How is she, Tom?"

"She's dead!" snapped Tom.

"What?" Denzil turned as white as a Christmas ghost.

"It was in the papers," said Tom; "all about her and the lifeboat."

"Oh, you mean Grace Darling," said Denzil, visibly relieved. "I meant Miss Dymond."

"You needn't be so interested in her," said Tom surlily. "She don't appreciate it. Ah, the shower is over. I must be going."

"No, stay a little longer, Tom," pleaded Peter. "I see a lot about you in the papers, but very little of your dear old phiz now. I can't spare the time to go and hear you. But I really must give myself a treat. When's your next show?"

"Oh, I am always giving shows," said Tom, smiling a little. "But my next big performance is on the twenty-first of January, when that picture of poor Mr. Constant is to be unveiled at the Bow Break o' Day Club. They have written to Gladstone and other big pots to come down. I do hope the old man accepts. A non-political gathering like this is the only occasion we could both speak at, and I have never been on the same platform with Gladstone."

He forgot his depression and ill-temper in the prospect, and spoke with more animation.

"No, I should hope not, Tom," said Peter. "What with his Fads about the Bible being a Rock, and Monarchy being the right thing, he is a most dangerous man to lead the Radicals. He never lays his axe to the root of anything—except oak trees."

"Mr. Cantycot!" It was Mrs. Crowl's voice that broke in upon the tirade. "There's a gentleman to see you." The astonishment Mrs. Crowl put into the "gentleman" was delightful. It was almost as good as a week's rent to her to give vent to her feelings. The controversial couple had moved away from the window when Tom entered, and had not noticed the immediate advent of another visitor who had spent his time profitably in listening to Mrs. Crowl before asking to see the presumable object of his visit.

"Ask him up if it's a friend of yours, Cantercot," said Peter. It was Wimp. Denzil was rather dubious as to the friendship, but he preferred to take Wimp diluted. "Mortlake's upstairs," he said; "will you come up and see him?"

Wimp had intended a duologue, but he made no objection, so he, too, stumbled through the nine brats to Mrs. Crowl's bedroom. It was a queer quartette. Wimp had hardly expected to find anybody at the house on Boxing Day, but he did not care to waste a day. Was not Grodman, too, on the track? How lucky it was that Denzil had made the first overtures, so that he could approach him without exciting suspicion.

Mortlake scowled when he saw the detective. He objected to the police—on principle. But Crowl had no idea who the visitor was, even when told his name. He was rather pleased to meet one of Denzil's high-class friends, and welcomed him warmly. Probably he was some famous editor, which would account for his name stirring vague recollections. He summoned the eldest brat and sent him for beer (people would have their Fads), and not without trepidation called down to "Mother" for glasses. "Mother" observed at night (in the same apartment) that the beer money might have paid the week's school fees for half the family.

"We were just talking of poor Mr. Constant's portrait, Mr. Wimp," said the unconscious Crowl; "they're going to unveil it, Mortlake tells me, on the twenty-first of next month at the Bow Break o' Day Club."

"Ah," said Wimp, elate at being spared the trouble of manoeuvring the conversation; "mysterious affair that, Mr. Crowl."

"No; it's the right thing," said Peter. "There ought to be some memorial of the man in the district where he worked and where he died, poor chap." The cobbler brushed away a tear.

"Yes, it's only right," echoed Mortlake, a whit eagerly. "He was a noble fellow, a true philanthropist—the only thoroughly unselfish worker I've ever met."

"He was that," said Peter; "and it's a rare pattern is unselfishness. Poor fellow, poor fellow. He preached the Useful, too. I've never met his like. Ah, I wish there was a heaven for him to go to!" He blew his nose violently with a red pocket-handkerchief.

"Well, he's there, if there is," said Tom.

"I hope he is," added Wimp, fervently; "but I shouldn't like to go there the way he did."

"You were the last person to see him, Tom, weren't you?" said Denzil.

"Oh, no," answered Tom, quickly. "You remember he went out after me; at least, so Mrs. Drabdump said at the inquest."

"That last conversation he had with you, Tom," said Denzil. "He didn't say anything to you that would lead you to suppose—"

"No, of course not!" interrupted Mortlake, impatiently.

"Do you really think he was murdered, Tom?" said Denzil.

"Mr. Wimp's opinion on that point is more valuable than mine," replied Tom, testily. "It may have been suicide. Men often get sick of life—especially if they are bored," he added meaningly.

"Ah, but you were the last person known to be with him," said Denzil.

Crowl laughed. "Had you there, Tom."

But they did not have Tom there much longer, for he departed, looking even worse-tempered than when he came. Wimp went soon after, and Crowl and Denzil were left to their interminable argumentation concerning the Useful and the Beautiful.

Wimp went West. He had several strings (or cords) to his bow, and he ultimately found himself at Kensal Green Cemetery. Being there, he went down the avenues of the dead to a grave to note down the exact date of a death. It was a day on which the dead seemed enviable. The dull, sodden sky, the dripping, leafless trees, the wet, spongy soil, the reeking grass—everything combined to make one long to be in a warm, comfortable grave away from the leaden ennuis of life. Suddenly the detective's keen eye caught sight of a figure that made his heart throb with sudden excitement. It was that of a woman in a grey shawl and a brown bonnet, standing before a railed-in grave. She had no umbrella. The rain plashed mournfully upon her, but left no trace on her soaking garments. Wimp crept up behind her, but she paid no heed to him. Her eyes were lowered to the grave, which seemed to be drawing them towards it by some strange morbid fascination. His eyes followed hers. The simple headstone bore the name, "Arthur Constant."

Wimp tapped her suddenly on the shoulder.

"How do you do, Mrs. Drabdump?"

Mrs. Drabdump went deadly white. She turned round, staring at Wimp without any recognition.

"You remember me, surely," he said; "I've been down once or twice to your place about that poor gentleman's papers." His eye indicated the grave.

"Lor! I remember you now," said Mrs. Drabdump.

"Won't you come under my umbrella? You must be drenched to the skin."

"It don't matter, sir. I can't take no hurt. I've had the rheumatics this twenty year."

Mrs. Drabdump shrank from accepting Wimp's attentions, not so much perhaps because he was a man as because he was a gentleman. Mrs. Drabdump liked to see the fine folks keep their place, and not contaminate their skirts by contact with the lower castes. "It's set wet, it'll rain right into the new year," she announced. "And they say a bad beginnin' makes a worse endin'." Mrs. Drabdump was one of those persons who give you the idea that they just missed being born barometers.

"But what are you doing in this miserable spot, so far from home?" queried the detective.

"It's Bank Holiday," Mrs. Drabdump reminded him in tones of acute surprise. "I always make a hexcursion on Bank Holiday."

VIII

The New Year drew Mrs. Drabdump a new lodger. He was an old gentleman with a long grey beard. He rented the rooms of the late Mr. Constant, and lived a very retired life. Haunted rooms—or rooms that ought to be haunted if the ghosts of those murdered in them had any self-respect—are supposed to fetch a lower rent in the market. The whole Irish problem might be solved if the spirits of "Mr. Balfour's victims" would only depreciate the value of property to a point consistent with the support of an agricultural population. But Mrs. Drabdump's new lodger paid so much for his rooms that he laid himself open to a suspicion of a special interest in ghosts. Perhaps he was a member of the Psychical Society. The neighbourhood imagined him another mad philanthropist, but as he did not appear to be doing any good to anybody it relented and conceded his sanity. Mortlake, who occasionally stumbled across him in the passage, did not trouble himself to think about him at all. He was too full of other troubles and cares. Though he worked harder than ever, the spirit seemed to have gone out of him. Sometimes he forgot himself in a fine rapture of eloquence—lashing himself up into a divine resentment of injustice or a passion of sympathy with the sufferings of his brethren—but mostly he plodded on in dull, mechanical fashion. He still made brief provincial tours, starring a day here and a day there, and everywhere his admirers remarked how jaded and overworked he looked. There was talk of starting a subscription to give him a holiday on the Continent—a luxury obviously unobtainable on the few pounds allowed him per week. The new lodger would doubtless have been pleased to subscribe, for he seemed quite to like occupying Mortlake's chamber the nights he was absent, though he was thoughtful enough not to disturb the hard-worked landlady in the adjoining room by unseemly noise. Wimp was always a quiet man.

Meantime the twenty-first of the month approached, and the East-end was in excitement. Mr. Gladstone had consented to be present at the ceremony of unveiling the portrait of Arthur Constant, presented by an unknown donor to the Bow Break o' Day Club, and it was to be a great function. The whole affair was outside the lines of party politics, so that even Conservatives and Socialists considered themselves justified in pestering the committee for tickets. To say nothing of ladies! As the committee desired to be present themselves, nine-tenths of the applications for admission had to be refused, as is usual on these occasions. The committee agreed among themselves to exclude the fair sex altogether as the only way of disposing of their womankind, who were making speeches as long as Mr. Gladstone's. Each committeeman told his sisters, female cousins, and aunts, that the other committeemen had insisted on divesting the function of all grace; and what could a man do when he was in a minority of one?

Crowl, who was not a member of the Break o' Day Club, was particularly anxious to hear the great orator whom he despised; fortunately Mortlake remembered the cobbler's anxiety to hear himself, and on the eve of the ceremony sent him a ticket. Crowl was in the first flush of possession when Denzil Cantercot returned, after a sudden and unannounced absence of three days. His clothes were muddy and tattered, his cocked hat was deformed, his cavalier beard was matted, and his eyes were bloodshot. The cobbler nearly dropped the ticket at the sight of him. "Hallo, Cantercot!" he gasped. "Why, where have you been all these days?"

"Terribly busy!" said Denzil. "Here, give me a glass of water. I'm dry as the Sahara."

Crowl ran inside and got the water, trying hard not to inform Mrs. Crowl of their lodger's return. "Mother" had expressed herself freely on the subject of the poet during his absence, and not in terms which would have commended themselves to the poet's fastidious literary sense. Indeed, she did not hesitate to call him a sponger and a low swindler, who had run away to avoid paying the piper. Her fool of a husband might be quite sure he would never set eyes on the scoundrel again. However, Mrs. Crowl was wrong. Here was Denzil back again. And yet Mr. Crowl felt no sense of victory. He had no desire to crow over his partner and to utter that "See! didn't I tell you so?" which is a greater consolation than religion in most of the misfortunes of life. Unfortunately, to get the water, Crowl had to go to the kitchen; and as he was usually such a temperate man, this desire for drink in the middle of the day attracted the attention of the lady in possession. Crowl had to explain the situation. Mrs. Crowl ran into the shop to improve it. Mr. Crowl followed in dismay, leaving a trail of spilt water in his wake.

"You good-for-nothing, disreputable scare-crow, where have—"

"Hush, mother. Let him drink. Mr. Cantercot is thirsty."

"Does he care if my children are hungry?"

Denzil tossed the water greedily down his throat almost at a gulp, as if it were brandy.

"Madam," he said, smacking his lips, "I do care. I care intensely. Few things in life would grieve me more deeply than to hear that a child, a dear little child—the Beautiful in a nutshell—had suffered hunger. You wrong me." His voice was tremulous with the sense of injury. Tears stood in his eyes.

"Wrong you? I've no wish to *wrong* you," said Mrs. Crowl. "I should like to hang you."

"Don't talk of such ugly things," said Denzil, touching his throat nervously.

"Well, what have you been doin' all this time?"

"Why, what should I be doing?"

"How should I know what became of you? I thought it was another murder."

"What!" Denzil's glass dashed to fragments on the floor. "What do you mean?"

But Mrs. Crowl was glaring too viciously at Mr. Crowl to reply. He understood the message as if it were printed. It ran: "You have broken one of my best glasses. You have annihilated threepence, or a week's school fees for half the family." Peter wished she would turn the lightning upon Denzil, a conductor down whom it would run innocuously. He stooped down and picked up the pieces as carefully as if they were cuttings from the Koh-i-noor. Thus the lightning passed harmlessly over his head and flew towards Cantercot.

"What do I mean?" Mrs. Crowl echoed, as if there had been no interval. "I mean that it would be a good thing if you had been murdered."

"What unbeautiful ideas you have to be sure!" murmured Denzil.

"Yes; but they'd be useful," said Mrs. Crowl, who had not lived with Peter all these years for nothing. "And if you haven't been murdered, what have you been doing?"

"My dear, my dear," put in Crowl, deprecatingly, looking up from his quadrupedal position like a sad dog, "you are not Cantercot's keeper."

"Oh, ain't I?" flashed his spouse. "Who else keeps him, I should like to know?"

Peter went on picking up the pieces of the Koh-i-noor.

"I have no secrets from Mrs. Crowl," Denzil explained courteously. "I have been working day and night bringing out a new paper. Haven't had a wink of sleep for three nights."

Peter looked up at his bloodshot eyes with respectful interest.

"The capitalist met me in the street—an old friend of mine—I was overjoyed at the *rencontre* and told him the idea I'd been brooding over for months, and he promised to stand all the racket."

"What sort of a paper?" said Peter.

"Can you ask? To what do you think I've been devoting my days and nights but to the cultivation of the Beautiful?"

"Is that what the paper will be devoted to?"

"Yes. To the Beautiful."

"I know," snorted Mrs. Crowl, "with portraits of actresses."

"Portraits? Oh, no!" said Denzil. "That would be the True, not the Beautiful."

"And what's the name of the paper?" asked Crowl.

"Ah, that's a secret, Peter. Like Scott, I prefer to remain anonymous."

"Just like your Fads. I'm only a plain man, and I want to know where the fun of anonymity comes in. If I had any gifts, I should like to get the credit. It's a right and natural feeling to my thinking."

"Unnatural, Peter; unnatural. We're all born anonymous, and I'm for sticking close to Nature. Enough for me that I disseminate the Beautiful. Any letters come during my absence, Mrs. Crowl?"

"No," she snapped. "But a gent named Grodman called. He said you hadn't been to see him for some time, and looked annoyed to hear you'd disappeared. How much have you let *him* in for?"

"The man's in *my* debt," said Denzil, annoyed. "I wrote a book for him and he's taken all the credit for it, the rogue! My name doesn't appear even in the Preface. What's that ticket you're looking so lovingly at, Peter?"

"That's for to-night—the unveiling of Constant's portrait. Gladstone speaks. Awful demand for places."

"Gladstone!" sneered Denzil. "Who wants to hear Gladstone? A man who's devoted his life to pulling down the pillars of Church and State."

"A man who's devoted his whole life to propping up the crumbling Fads of Religion and Monarchy. But, for all that, the man has his gifts, and I'm burnin' to hear him."

"I wouldn't go out of my way an inch to hear him," said Denzil; and went up to his room, and when Mrs. Crowl sent him up a cup of nice strong tea at tea-time, the brat who bore it found him lying dressed on the bed, snoring unbeautifully.

The evening wore on. It was fine frosty weather. The Whitechapel Road swarmed with noisy life, as though it were a Saturday night. The stars flared in the sky like the lights of celestial costermongers. Everybody was on the alert for the advent of Mr. Gladstone. He must surely come through the Road on his journey from the West Bow-wards. But nobody saw him or his carriage, except those about the Hall. Probably he went by tram most of the way. He would have caught cold in an open carriage, or bobbing his head out of the window of a closed.

"If he had only been a German prince, or a cannibal king," said Crowl, bitterly, as he plodded towards the Club, "we should have disguised Mile End in bunting and blue fire. But perhaps it's a compliment. He knows his London, and it's no use trying to hide the facts from him. They must have queer notions of cities, those monarchs. They must fancy everybody lives in a flutter of flags and walks about under triumphal arches, like as if I were to stitch shoes in my Sunday clothes." By a defiance of chronology Crowl had them on to-day, and they seemed to accentuate the simile.

"And why shouldn't life be fuller of the Beautiful?" said Denzil. The poet had brushed the reluctant mud off his garments to the extent it was willing to go, and had washed his face, but his eyes were still bloodshot from the cultivation of the Beautiful. Denzil was accompanying Crowl to the door of the Club out of good fellowship. Denzil was himself accompanied by Grodman, though less obtrusively. Least obtrusively was he accompanied by his usual Scotland Yard shadows, Wimp's agents. There was a surging nondescript crowd about the Club, so that the police, and the doorkeeper, and the stewards could with difficulty keep out the tide of the ticketless, through which the current of the privileged had equal difficulty in permeating. The streets all around were thronged with people longing for a glimpse of Gladstone. Mortlake drove up in a hansom (his head a self-conscious pendulum of popularity, swaying and bowing to right and left) and received all the pent-up enthusiasm.

"Well, good-by, Cantercot," said Crowl.

"No, I'll see you to the door, Peter."

They fought their way shoulder to shoulder.

Now that Grodman had found Denzil he was not going to lose him again. He had only found him by accident, for he was himself bound to the unveiling ceremony, to which he had been invited in view of his known devotion to the task of unveiling the Mystery. He spoke to one of the policemen about, who said, "Ay, ay, sir," and he was prepared to follow Denzil, if necessary, and to give up the pleasure of hearing Gladstone for an acuter thrill. The arrest must be delayed no longer.

But Denzil seemed as if he were going in on the heels of Crowl. This would suit Grodman better. He could then have the two pleasures. But Denzil was stopped half-way through the door.

"Ticket, sir!"

Denzil drew himself up to his full height.

"Press," he said majestically. All the glories and grandeurs of the Fourth Estate were concentrated in that haughty monosyllable. Heaven itself is full of journalists who have overawed St. Peter. But the doorkeeper was a veritable dragon.

"What paper, sir?"

"*New Pork Herald*," said Denzil, sharply. He did not relish his word being distrusted.

"*New Pork Herald*," said one of the bystanding stewards, scarce catching the sounds. "Pass him in."

And in the twinkling of an eye Denzil had eagerly slipped inside.

But during the brief altercation Wimp had come up. Even he could not make his face quite impassive, and there was a suppressed intensity in the eyes and a quiver about the mouth. He went in on Denzil's heels, blocking up the doorway with Grodman. The two men were so full of their coming coups that they struggled for some seconds, side by side, before they recognised each other. Then they shook hands heartily.

"That was Cantercot just went in, wasn't it, Grodman?" said Wimp.

"I didn't notice," said Grodman, in tones of utter indifference.

At bottom Wimp was terribly excited. He felt that his coup was going to be executed under very sensational circumstances. Everything would combine to turn the eyes of the country upon him—nay, of the world, for had not the Big Bow Mystery been discussed in every language under the sun? In these electric times the criminal receives a cosmopolitan reputation. It is a privilege he shares with few other artists. This time Wimp would be one of them. And he felt deservedly so. If the criminal had been cunning to the point of genius in planning the murder, he had been acute to the point of divination in detecting it. Never before had he pieced together so broken a chain. He could not resist the unique opportunity of setting a sensational scheme in a sensational framework. The dramatic instinct was strong in him; he felt like a playwright who has constructed a strong melodramatic plot, and has the Drury Lane stage suddenly offered him to present it on. It would be folly to deny himself the luxury, though the presence of Mr. Gladstone and the nature of the ceremony should perhaps have given him pause. Yet, on the other hand, these were the very factors of the temptation. Wimp went in and took a seat behind Denzil. All the seats were numbered, so that everybody might have the satisfaction of occupying somebody else's. Denzil was in the special reserved places in the front row just by the central gangway; Crowl was squeezed into a corner behind a pillar near the back of the hall. Grodman had been honoured with a seat on the platform, which was accessible by steps on the right and left, but he kept his eye on Denzil. The picture of the poor idealist hung on the wall behind Grodman's head, covered by its curtain of brown holland. There was a subdued buzz of excitement about the hall, which swelled into cheers every now and again as some gentleman known to fame or Bow took his place upon the platform. It was occupied by several local M.P.'s of varying politics, a number of other Parliamentary satellites of the great man, three or four labour leaders, a peer or two of philanthropic pretensions, a sprinkling of Toynbee and Oxford Hall men, the president and other honorary officials, some of the family and friends of the deceased, together with the inevitable percentage of persons who had no claim to be there save cheek. Gladstone was late—later than Mortlake, who was cheered to the echo when he arrived, some one starting "For He's a Jolly Good Fellow," as if it were a political meeting. Gladstone came in just in time to acknowledge the compliment. The noise of the song, trolled out from iron lungs, had drowned the huzzahs heralding the old man's advent. The convivial chorus went to Mortlake's head, as if champagne had really preceded it. His eyes grew moist and dim. He saw himself swimming to the Millennium on waves of enthusiasm. Ah, how his brother toilers should be rewarded for their trust in him!

With his usual courtesy and consideration, Mr. Gladstone had refused to perform the actual unveiling of Arthur Constant's portrait. "That," he said in his postcard, "will fall most appropriately to Mr. Mortlake, a gentleman who has, I am given to understand, enjoyed the personal friendship of the late Mr. Constant, and has coöperated with him in various schemes for the organisation of skilled and unskilled classes of labour, as well as for the diffusion of better ideals—ideals of self-culture and self-restraint—among the working men of Bow, who have been fortunate, so far as I can perceive, in the possession (if in one case unhappily only temporary possession) of two such men of undoubted ability and honesty to direct their divided counsels and to lead them along a road, which, though I cannot pledge myself to approve of it in all its turnings and windings, is yet not unfitted to bring them somewhat nearer to goals to which there are few of us but would extend some measure of hope that the working classes of this great Empire may in due course, yet with no unnecessary delay, be enabled to arrive."

Mr. Gladstone's speech was an expansion of his postcard, punctuated by cheers. The only new thing in it was the graceful and touching way in which he revealed what had been a secret up till then—that the portrait had been painted and presented to the Bow Break o' Day Club, by Lucy Brent, who in the fulness of time would have been Arthur Constant's wife. It was a painting for which he had sat to her while alive, and she had stifled yet pampered her grief by working hard at it since his death. The fact added the last touch of pathos to the occasion. Crowl's face was hidden behind his red handkerchief; even the fire of excitement in Wimp's eye was quenched for a moment by a teardrop, as he thought of Mrs. Wimp and Wilfred. As for Grodman, there was almost a lump in his throat. Denzil Cantercot was the only unmoved man in the room. He thought the episode quite too Beautiful, and was already weaving it into rhyme.

At the conclusion of his speech Mr. Gladstone called upon Tom Mortlake to unveil the portrait. Tom rose, pale and excited. He faltered as he touched the cord. He seemed overcome with emotion. Was it the mention of Lucy Brent that had moved him to his depths?

The brown holland fell away—the dead stood revealed as he had been in life. Every feature, painted by the hand of Love, was instinct with vitality: the fine, earnest face, the sad kindly eyes, the noble brow, seeming still a-throb with the thought of Humanity. A thrill ran through the room—there was a low, undefinable murmur. Oh, the pathos and the tragedy of it! Every eye was fixed, misty with emotion, upon the dead man in the picture, and the living man who stood, pale and agitated, and visibly unable to commence his speech, at the side of the canvas. Suddenly a hand was laid upon the labour leader's shoulder, and there rang through the hall in Wimp's clear, decisive tones the words—"Tom Mortlake, I arrest you for the murder of Arthur Constant!"

IX

For a moment there was an acute, terrible silence. Mortlake's face was that of a corpse; the face of the dead man at his side was flushed with the hues of life. To the overstrung nerves of the onlookers, the brooding eyes of the picture seemed sad and stern with menace, and charged with the lightnings of doom.

It was a horrible contrast. For Wimp, alone, the painted face had fuller, more tragical meanings. The audience seemed turned to stone. They sat or stood—in every variety of attitude—frozen, rigid. Arthur Constant's picture dominated the scene, the only living thing in a hall of the dead.

But only for a moment. Mortlake shook off the detective's hand.

"Boys!" he cried, in accents of infinite indignation, "this is a police conspiracy."

His words relaxed the tension. The stony figures were agitated. A dull excited hubbub answered him. The little cobbler darted from behind his pillar, and leapt upon a bench. The cords of his brow were swollen with excitement. He seemed a giant overshadowing the hall.

"Boys!" he roared, in his best Victoria Park voice, "listen to me. This charge is a foul and damnable lie."

"Bravo!" "Hear, hear!" "Hooray!" "It is!" was roared back at him from all parts of the room. Everybody rose and stood in tentative attitudes, excited to the last degree.

"Boys!" Peter roared on, "you all know me. I'm a plain man, and I want to know if it's likely a man would murder his best friend."

"No!" in a mighty volume of sound.

Wimp had scarcely calculated upon Mortlake's popularity. He stood on the platform, pale and anxious as his prisoner.

"And if he did, why didn't they prove it the first time?"

"HEAR, HEAR!"

"And if they want to arrest him, why couldn't they leave it till the ceremony was over? Tom Mortlake's not the man to run away."

"Tom Mortlake! Tom Mortlake! Three cheers for Tom Mortlake!" "Hip, hip, hip, hooray!"

"Three groans for the police!" "Hoo! Oo! Oo!"

Wimp's melodrama was not going well. He felt like the author to whose ears is borne the ominous sibilance of the pit. He almost wished he had not followed the curtain-raiser with his own stronger drama. Unconsciously the police, scattered about the hall, drew together. The people on the platform knew not what to do. They had all risen and stood in a densely packed mass. Even Mr. Gladstone's speech failed him in circumstances so novel. The groans died away; the cheers for Mortlake rose and swelled and fell and rose again. Sticks and umbrellas were banged and rattled, handkerchiefs were waved, the thunder deepened. The motley crowd still surging about the hall took up the cheers, and for hundreds of yards around people were going black in the face out of mere irresponsible enthusiasm. At last Tom waved his hand—the thunder dwindled, died. The prisoner was master of the situation.

Grodman stood on the platform, grasping the back of his chair, a curious mocking Mephistophelian glitter about his eyes, his lips wreathed into a half smile. There was no hurry for him to get Denzil Cantercot arrested now. Wimp had made an egregious, a colossal blunder. In Grodman's heart there was a great, glad calm as of a man who has strained his sinews to win in a famous match, and has heard the judge's word. He felt almost kindly to Denzil now.

Tom Mortlake spoke. His face was set and stony. His tall figure was drawn up haughtily to its full height. He pushed the black mane back from his forehead with a characteristic gesture. The fevered audience hung upon his lips—the men at the back leaned eagerly forward—the reporters were breathless with fear lest they should miss a word. What would the great labour leader have to say at this supreme moment?

"Mr. Chairman and gentlemen. It is to me a melancholy pleasure to have been honoured with the task of unveiling to-night this portrait of a great benefactor to Bow and a true friend to the labouring classes. Except that he honoured me with his friendship while living, and that the aspirations of my life have, in my small and restricted way, been identical with his, there is little reason why this honourable duty should have fallen upon me. Gentlemen, I trust that we shall all find an inspiring influence in the daily vision of the dead, who yet liveth in our hearts and in this noble work of art—wrought, as Mr. Gladstone has told us, by the hand of one who loved him." The speaker paused a moment, his low vibrant tones faltering into silence. "If we humble working men of Bow can never hope to exert individually a tithe of the beneficial influence wielded by Arthur Constant, it is yet possible for each of us to walk in the light he has kindled in our midst—a perpetual lamp of self-sacrifice and brotherhood."

That was all. The room rang with cheers. Tom Mortlake resumed his seat. To Wimp the man's audacity verged on the Sublime; to Denzil on the Beautiful. Again there was a breathless hush. Mr. Gladstone's mobile face was working with excitement. No such extraordinary scene had occurred in the whole of his extraordinary experience. He seemed about to rise. The cheering subsided to a painful stillness. Wimp cut the situation by laying his hand again upon Tom's shoulder.

"Come quietly with me," he said. The words were almost a whisper, but in the supreme silence they travelled to the ends of the hall.

"Don't you go, Tom!" The trumpet tones were Peter's. The call thrilled an answering chord of defiance in every breast, and a low ominous murmur swept through the hall.

Tom rose, and there was silence again. "Boys," he said, "let me go. Don't make any noise about it. I shall be with you again to-morrow."

But the blood of the Break o' Day boys was at fever heat. A hurtling mass of men struggled confusedly from their seats. In a moment all was chaos. Tom did not move. Half-a-dozen men headed by Peter scaled the platform. Wimp was thrown to one side, and the invaders formed a ring round Tom's chair. The platform people scampered like mice from the centre. Some huddled together in the corners, others slipped out at the rear. The committee congratulated themselves on having had the self-denial to exclude ladies. Mr. Gladstone's satellites hurried the old man off and into his carriage, though the fight promised to become Homeric. Grodman stood at the side of the platform secretly more amused than ever, concerning himself no more with Denzil Cantercot, who was already strengthening his nerves at the bar upstairs. The police about the hall blew their whistles, and policemen came rushing in from outside and the neighbourhood. An Irish M.P. on the platform was waving his gingham like a shillelagh in sheer excitement, forgetting his new-found respectability and dreaming himself back at Donnybrook Fair. Him a conscientious constable floored with a truncheon. But a shower of fists fell on the zealot's face, and he tottered back bleeding. Then the storm broke in all its fury. The upper air was black with staves, sticks, and umbrellas, mingled with the pallid hailstones of knobby fists. Yells, and groans, and hoots, and battle-cries blent in grotesque chorus, like one of Dvořák's weird diabolical movements. Mortlake stood impassive, with arms folded, making no further effort, and the battle raged round him as the water swirls round some steadfast rock. A posse of police from the back fought their way steadily towards him, and charged up the heights of the platform steps, only to be sent tumbling backwards, as their leader was hurled at them like a battering-ram. Upon the top of the heap he fell, surmounting the strata of policemen. But others clambered upon them, escalading the platform. A moment more and Mortlake would have been taken. Then the miracle happened.

As when of old a reputable goddess *ex machinâ* saw her favourite hero in dire peril, straightway she drew down a cloud from the celestial stores of Jupiter and enveloped her fondling in kindly night, so that his adversary strove with the darkness, so did Crowl, the cunning cobbler, the much-daring, essay to ensure his friend's safety. He turned off the gas at the meter.

An Arctic night—unpreceded by twilight—fell, and there dawned the sabbath of the witches. The darkness could be felt—and it left blood and bruises behind it. When the lights were turned on again, Mortlake was gone. But several of the rioters were arrested, triumphantly.

And through all, and over all, the face of the dead man, who had sought to bring peace on earth, brooded.

Crowl sat meekly eating his supper of bread and cheese, with his head bandaged, while Denzil Cantercot told him the story of how he had rescued Tom Mortlake. He had been among the first to scale the height, and had never budged from Tom's side or from the forefront of the battle till he had seen him safely outside and into a by-street.

"I am so glad you saw that he got away safely," said Crowl, "I wasn't quite sure he would."

"Yes; but I wish some cowardly fool hadn't turned off the gas. I like men to see that they are beaten."

"But it seemed—easier," faltered Crowl.

"Easier!" echoed Denzil, taking a deep draught of bitter. "Really, Peter, I'm sorry to find you always will take such low views. It may be easier, but it's shabby. It shocks one's sense of the Beautiful."

Crowl ate his bread and cheese shamefacedly.

"But what was the use of breaking your head to save him?" said Mrs. Crowl, with an unconscious pun. "He must be caught."

"Ah, I don't see how the Useful does come in, now," said Peter, thoughtfully. "But I didn't think of that at the time."

He swallowed his water quickly, and it went the wrong way and added to his confusion. It also began to dawn upon him that he might be called to account. Let it be said at once that he wasn't. He had taken too prominent a part.

Meantime, Mrs. Wimp was bathing Mr. Wimp's eye, and rubbing him generally with arnica. Wimp's melodrama had been, indeed, a sight for the gods. Only virtue was vanquished and vice triumphant. The villain had escaped, and without striking a blow.

X

There was matter and to spare for the papers the next day. The striking ceremony—Mr. Gladstone's speech—the sensational arrest—these would of themselves have made excellent themes for reports and leaders. But the personality of the man arrested, and the Big Bow Mystery Battle—as it came to be called—gave additional piquancy to the paragraphs and the posters. The behaviour of Mortlake put the last touch to the picturesqueness of the position. He left the hall when the lights went out, and walked unnoticed and unmolested through pleiads of policemen to the nearest police station, where the superintendent was almost too excited to take any notice of his demand to be arrested. But to do him justice, the official yielded as soon as he understood the situation. It seems inconceivable that he did not violate some red-tape regulation in so doing. To some this self-surrender was limpid proof of innocence; to others it was the damning token of despairing guilt.

The morning papers were pleasant reading for Grodman, who chuckled as continuously over his morning egg, as if he had laid it. Jane was alarmed for the sanity of her saturnine master. As her husband would have said, Grodman's grins were not

Beautiful. But he made no effort to suppress them. Not only had Wimp perpetrated a grotesque blunder, but the journalists to a man were down on his great sensation tableau, though their denunciations did not appear in the dramatic columns. The Liberal papers said that he had endangered Mr. Gladstone's life; the Conservative that he had unloosed the raging elements of Bow blackguardism, and set in motion forces which might have easily swelled to a riot, involving severe destruction of property. But "Tom Mortlake" was, after all, the thought swamping every other. It was, in a sense, a triumph for the man.

But Wimp's turn came when Mortlake, who reserved his defence, was brought up before a magistrate, and by force of the new evidence, fully committed for trial on the charge of murdering Arthur Constant. Then men's thoughts centred again on the Mystery, and the solution of the inexplicable problem agitated mankind from China to Peru.

In the middle of February, the great trial befell. It was another of the opportunities which the Chancellor of the Exchequer neglects. So stirring a drama might have easily cleared its expenses—despite the length of the cast, the salaries of the stars, and the rent of the house—in mere advance booking. For it was a drama which (by the rights of Magna Charta) could never be repeated; a drama which ladies of fashion would have given their earrings to witness, even with the central figure not a woman. And there *was* a woman in it anyhow, to judge by the little that had transpired at the magisterial examination, and the fact that the country was placarded with bills offering a reward for information concerning a Miss Jessie Dymond. Mortlake was defended by Sir Charles Brown-Harland, Q.C., retained at the expense of the Mortlake Defence Fund (subscriptions to which came also from Australia and the Continent), and set on his mettle by the fact that he was the accepted labour candidate for an East-end constituency. Their Majesties, Victoria and the Law, were represented by Mr. Robert Spigot, Q.C.

Mr. SPIGOT, Q.C, in presenting his case, said: "I propose to show that the prisoner murdered his friend and fellow-lodger, Mr. Arthur Constant, in cold blood, and with the most careful premeditation; premeditation so studied, as to leave the circumstances of the death an impenetrable mystery for weeks to all the world, though, fortunately, without altogether baffling the almost superhuman ingenuity of Mr. Edward Wimp, of the Scotland Yard Detective Department. I propose to show that the motives of the prisoner were jealousy and revenge; jealousy, not only of his friend's superior influence over the working men he himself aspired to lead, but the more commonplace animosity engendered by the disturbing element of a woman having relations to both. If, before my case is complete, it will be my painful duty to show that the murdered man was not the saint the world has agreed to paint him, I shall not shrink from unveiling the truer picture, in the interests of justice, which cannot say *nil nisi bonum* even of the dead. I propose to show that the murder was committed by the prisoner shortly before half-past six on the morning of December 4th, and that the prisoner having, with the remarkable ingenuity which he has shown throughout, attempted to prepare an alibi by feigning to leave London by the *first* train to Liverpool, returned home, got in with his latch-key through the street door, which he had left on the latch, unlocked his victim's bedroom with a key which he possessed, cut the sleeping man's throat, pocketed his razor, locked the door again, and gave it the appearance of being bolted, went downstairs, unslipped the bolt of the big lock, closed the door behind him, and got to Euston in time for the *second* train to Liverpool. The fog helped his proceedings throughout." Such was in sum the theory of the prosecution. The pale, defiant figure in the dock winced perceptibly under parts of it.

Mrs. Drabdump was the first witness called for the prosecution. She was quite used to legal inquisitiveness by this time, but did not appear in good spirits.

"On the night of December 3rd, you gave the prisoner a letter?"

"Yes, your ludship."

"How did he behave when he read it?"

"He turned very pale and excited. He went up to the poor gentleman's room, and I'm afraid he quarrelled with him. He might have left his last hours peaceful." (Amusement.)

"What happened then?"

"Mr. Mortlake went out in a passion, and came in again in about an hour."

"He told you he was going away to Liverpool very early the next morning?"

"No, your ludship, he said he was going to Devonport." (Sensation.)

"What time did you get up the next morning?"

"Half-past six."

"That is not your usual time?"

"No, I always get up at six."

"How do you account for the extra sleepiness?"

"Misfortunes will happen."

"It wasn't the dull, foggy weather?"

"No, my lud, else I should never get up early." (Laughter.)

"You drink something before going to bed?"

"I like my cup o' tea. I take it strong, without sugar. It always steadies my nerves."

"Quite so. Where were you when the prisoner told you he was going to Devonport?"

"Drinkin' my tea in the kitchen."

"What should you say if prisoner dropped something in it to make you sleep late?"

WITNESS (startled): "He ought to be shot."

"He might have done it without your noticing it, I suppose?"

"If he was clever enough to murder the poor gentleman, he was clever enough to try and poison me."

The JUDGE: "The witness in her replies must confine herself to the evidence."

Mr. SPIGOT, Q.C.: "I must submit to your lordship that it is a very logical answer, and exactly illustrates the interdependence of the probabilities. Now, Mrs. Drabdump, let us know what happened when you awoke at half-past six the next morning." Thereupon Mrs. Drabdump recapitulated the evidence (with new redundancies, but slight variations) given by her at the inquest. How she became alarmed—how she found the street door locked by the big lock—how she roused Grodman, and got him to burst open the door—how they found the body—all this with which the public was already familiar *ad nauseam* was extorted from her afresh.

"Look at this key (key passed to witness). Do you recognise it?"

"Yes; how did you get it? It's the key of my first-floor front. I am sure I left it sticking in the door."

"Did you know a Miss Dymond?"

"Yes, Mr. Mortlake's sweetheart. But I knew he would never marry her, poor thing." (Sensation.)

"Why not?"

"He was getting too grand for her." (Amusement.)

"You don't mean anything more than that?"

"I don't know; she only came to my place once or twice. The last time I set eyes on her must have been in October."

"How did she appear?"

"She was very miserable, but she wouldn't let you see it." (Laughter.)

"How has the prisoner behaved since the murder?"

"He always seemed very glum and sorry for it."

Cross-examined: "Did not the prisoner once occupy the bedroom of Mr. Constant, and give it up to him, so that Mr. Constant might have the two rooms on the same floor?"

"Yes, but he didn't pay as much."

"And, while occupying this front bedroom, did not the prisoner once lose his key and have another made?"

"He did; he was very careless."

"Do you know what the prisoner and Mr. Constant spoke about on the night of December 3rd?"

"No; I couldn't hear."

"Then how did you know they were quarrelling?"

"They were talkin' so loud."

Sir CHARLES BROWN-HARLAND, Q.C. (sharply): "But I'm talking loudly to you now. Should you say I was quarrelling?"

"It takes two to make a quarrel." (Laughter.)

"Was prisoner the sort of man who, in your opinion, would commit a murder?"

"No, I never should ha' guessed it was him."

"He always struck you as a thorough gentleman?"

"No, my lud. I knew he was only a comp."

"You say the prisoner has seemed depressed since the murder. Might not that have been due to the disappearance of his sweetheart?"

"No, he'd more likely be glad to get rid of her."

"Then he wouldn't be jealous if Mr. Constant took her off his hands?" (Sensation.)

"Men are dog-in-the-mangers."

"Never mind about men, Mrs. Drabdump. Had the prisoner ceased to care for Miss Dymond?"

"He didn't seem to think of her, my lud. When he got a letter in her handwriting among his heap he used to throw it aside till he'd torn open the others."

BROWN-HARLAND, Q.C. (with a triumphant ring in his voice): "Thank you, Mrs. Drabdump. You may sit down."

SPIGOT, Q.C.: "One moment, Mrs. Drabdump. You say the prisoner had ceased to care for Miss Dymond. Might not this have been in consequence of his suspecting for some time that she had relations with Mr. Constant?"

The JUDGE: "That is not a fair question."

SPIGOT, Q.C.: "That will do, thank you, Mrs. Drabdump."

BROWN-HARLAND, Q.C.: "No; one question more, Mrs. Drabdump. Did you ever see anything—say, when Miss Dymond came to your house—to make you suspect anything between Mr. Constant and the prisoner's sweetheart?"

"She did meet him once when Mr. Mortlake was out." (Sensation.)

"Where did she meet him?"

"In the passage. He was going out when she knocked and he opened the door." (Amusement.)

"You didn't hear what they said?"

"I ain't a eavesdropper. They spoke friendly and went away together."

Mr. GEORGE GRODMAN was called, and repeated his evidence at the inquest. Cross-examined, he testified to the warm friendship between Mr. Constant and the prisoner. He knew very little about Miss Dymond, having scarcely seen her. Prisoner had never spoken to him much about her. He should not think she was much in prisoner's thoughts. Naturally the prisoner had been depressed by the death of his friend. Besides, he was overworked. Witness thought highly of Mortlake's character. It was incredible that Constant had had improper relations of any kind with his friend's promised wife. Grodman's evidence made a very favourable impression on the jury; the prisoner looked his gratitude; and the prosecution felt sorry it had been necessary to call this witness.

Inspector HOWLETT and Sergeant RUNNYMEDE had also to repeat their evidence. Dr. ROBINSON, police surgeon, likewise retendered his evidence as to the nature of the wound, and the approximate hour of death. But this time he was much more severely examined. He would not bind himself down to state the time within an hour or two. He thought life had been extinct two or three hours when he arrived, so that the deed had been committed between seven and eight. Under gentle pressure from the prosecuting counsel, he admitted that it might possibly have been between six and seven. Cross-examined, he reiterated his impression in favour of the later hour.

Supplementary evidence from medical experts proved as dubious and uncertain as if the court had confined itself to the original witness. It seemed to be generally agreed that the data for determining the time of death of any body were too complex and variable to admit of very precise inference; rigor mortis and other symptoms setting in within very wide limits and differing largely in different persons. All agreed that death from such a cut must have been practically instantaneous, and the theory of suicide was rejected by all. As a whole the medical evidence tended to fix the time of death, with a high degree of probability, between the hours of six and half-past eight. The efforts of the prosecution were bent upon throwing back the time of death to as early as possible after about half-past five. The defence spent all its strength upon pinning the experts to the conclusion that death could not have been earlier than seven. Evidently the prosecution was going to fight hard for the hypothesis that Mortlake had committed the crime in the interval between the first and second trains for Liverpool; while the defence was concentrating itself on an alibi, showing that the prisoner had travelled by the second train which left Euston Station at a quarter-past seven, so that there could have been no possible time for the passage between Bow and Euston. It was an exciting struggle. As yet the contending forces seemed equally matched. The evidence had gone as much for as against the prisoner. But everybody knew that worse lay behind.

"Call Edward Wimp."

The story EDWARD WIMP had to tell began tamely enough with thrice-threshed-out facts. But at last the new facts came.

"In consequence of suspicions that had formed in your mind you took up your quarters, disguised, in the late Mr. Constant's rooms?"

"I did; at the commencement of the year. My suspicions had gradually gathered against the occupants of No. 11 Glover Street, and I resolved to quash or confirm these suspicions once for all."

"Will you tell the jury what followed?"

"Whenever the prisoner was away for the night I searched his room. I found the key of Mr. Constant's bedroom buried deeply in the side of prisoner's leather sofa. I found what I imagine to be the letter he received on December 3rd, in the pages of a 'Bradshaw' lying under the same sofa. There were two razors about."

Mr. SPIGOT, Q.C., said: "The key has already been identified by Mrs. Drabdump. The letter I now propose to read."

It was undated, and ran as follows:—

Dear Tom,—This is to bid you farewell. It is best for us all. I am going a long way, dearest. Do not seek to find me, for it will be useless. Think of me as one swallowed up by the waters, and be assured that it is only to spare you shame and humiliation in the future that I tear myself from you and all the sweetness of life. Darling, there is no other way. I feel you could never marry me now. I have felt it for months. Dear Tom, you will understand what I mean. We must look facts in the face. I hope you will always be friends with Mr. Constant. Good-by, dear. God bless you! May you always be happy, and find a worthier wife than I. Perhaps when you are great, and rich, and famous, as you deserve, you will sometimes think not unkindly of one who, however faulty and unworthy of you, will at least love you till the end.—Yours, till death,

JESSIE

By the time this letter was finished numerous old gentlemen, with wigs or without, were observed to be polishing their glasses. Mr. Wimp's examination was resumed.

"After making these discoveries what did you do?"

"I made inquiries about Miss Dymond, and found Mr. Constant had visited her once or twice in the evening. I imagined there would be some traces of a pecuniary connection. I was allowed by the family to inspect Mr. Constant's cheque-book, and found a paid cheque made out for £25 in the name of Miss Dymond. By inquiry at the

Bank, I found it had been cashed on November 12th of last year. I then applied for a warrant against the prisoner."

Cross-examined: "Do you suggest that the prisoner opened Mr. Constant's bed-room with the key you found?"

"Certainly."

BROWN-HARLAND, Q.C. (sarcastically): "And locked the door from within with it on leaving?"

"Certainly."

"Will you have the goodness to explain how the trick was done?"

"It wasn't done. (Laughter.) The prisoner probably locked the door from the out-side. Those who broke it open naturally imagined it had been locked from the inside when they found the key inside. The key would, on this theory, be on the floor as the outside locking could not have been effected if it had been in the lock. The first persons to enter the room would naturally believe it had been thrown down in the bursting of the door. Or it might have been left sticking very loosely inside the lock so as not to interfere with the turning of the outside key, in which case it would also probably have been thrown to the ground."

"Indeed. Very ingenious. And can you also explain how the prisoner could have bolted the door within from the outside?"

"I can. (Renewed sensation.) There is only one way in which it was possible—and that was, of course, a mere conjurer's illusion. To cause a locked door to appear bolted in addition, it would only be necessary for the person on the inside of the door to wrest the staple containing the bolt from the woodwork. The bolt in Mr. Constant's bed-room worked perpendicularly. When the staple was torn off, it would simply remain at rest on the pin of the bolt instead of supporting it or keeping it fixed. A person bursting open the door and finding the staple resting on the pin and torn away from the lintel of the door, would, of course, imagine he had torn it away, never dreaming the wresting off had been done beforehand." (Applause in court, which was instantly checked by the ushers.) The counsel for the defence felt he had been entrapped in attempting to be sarcastic with the redoubtable detective. Grodman seemed green with envy. It was the one thing he had not thought of.

Mrs. Drabdump, Grodman, Inspector Howlett, and Sergeant Runnymede were recalled and reëxammed by the embarrassed Sir Charles Brown-Harland as to the exact condition of the lock and the bolt and the position of the key. It turned out as Wimp had suggested; so prepossessed were the witnesses with the conviction that the door was locked and bolted from the inside when it was burst open that they were a little hazy about the exact details. The damage had been repaired, so that it was all a question of precise past observation. The inspector and the sergeant testified that the key was in the lock when they saw it, though both the mortice and the bolt were broken. They were not prepared to say that Wimp's theory was impossible; they would even admit it was quite possible that the staple of the bolt had been torn off beforehand. Mrs. Drabdump could give no clear account of such petty facts in view of her immediate engrossing interest in the horrible sight of the corpse. Grodman alone was positive that the key was in the door when he burst it open. No, he did not remember picking it up from the floor and putting it in. And he was certain that the staple of the bolt was *not* broken, from the resistance he experienced in trying to shake the upper panels of the door.

By the Prosecution: "Don't you think, from the comparative ease with which the door yielded to your onslaught, that it is highly probable that the pin of the bolt was not in a firmly fixed staple, but in one already detached from the woodwork of the lintel?"

"The door did not yield so easily."

"But you must be a Hercules."

"Not quite; the bolt was old, and the woodwork crumbling; the lock was new and shoddy. But I have always been a strong man."

"Very well, Mr. Grodman. I hope you will never appear at the music-halls." (Laughter.)

Jessie Dymond's landlady was the next witness for the prosecution. She corroborated Wimp's statements as to Constant's occasional visits, and narrated how the girl had been enlisted by the dead philanthropist as a collaborator in some of his enterprises. But the most telling portion of her evidence was the story of how, late at night, on December 3rd, the prisoner called upon her and inquired wildly about the whereabouts of his sweetheart. He said he had just received a mysterious letter from Miss Dymond saying she was gone. She (the landlady) replied that she could have told him that weeks ago, as her ungrateful lodger was gone now some three weeks without leaving a hint behind her. In answer to his most ungentlemanly raging and raving, she told him it served him right, as he should have looked after her better, and not kept away for so long. She reminded him that there were as good fish in the sea as ever came out, and a girl of Jessie's attractions need not pine away (as she had seemed to be pining away) for lack of appreciation. He then called her a liar and left her, and she hoped never to see his face again, though she was not surprised to see it in the dock.

Mr. FITZJAMES MONTGOMERY, a bank clerk, remembered cashing the cheque produced. He particularly remembered it, because he paid the money to a very pretty girl. She took the entire amount in gold. At this point the case was adjourned.

DENZIL CANTERCOT was the first witness called for the prosecution on the resumption of the trial. Pressed as to whether he had not told Mr. Wimp that he had overheard the prisoner denouncing Mr. Constant, he could not say. He had not actually heard the prisoner's denunciations; he might have given Mr. Wimp a false impression, but then Mr. Wimp was so prosaically literal. (Laughter.) Mr. Crowl had told him something of the kind. Cross-examined, he said Jessie Dymond was a rare spirit and she always reminded him of Joan of Arc.

Mr. CROWL, being called, was extremely agitated. He refused to take the oath, and informed the court that the Bible was a Fad. He could not swear by anything so self-contradictory. He would affirm. He could not deny—though he looked like wishing to—that the prisoner had at first been rather mistrustful of Mr. Constant, but he was certain that the feeling had quickly worn off. Yes, he was a great friend of the prisoner, but he didn't see why that should invalidate his testimony, especially as he had not taken an oath. Certainly the prisoner seemed rather depressed when he saw him on Bank Holiday, but it was overwork on behalf of the people and for the demolition of the Fads.

Several other familiars of the prisoner gave more or less reluctant testimony as to his sometime prejudice against the amateur rival labour leader. His expressions of dislike had been strong and bitter. The prosecution also produced a poster announcing that the prisoner would preside at a great meeting of clerks on December 4th. He had not turned up at this meeting nor sent any explanation. Finally, there was the evidence of the detectives who originally arrested him at Liverpool Docks in view of his suspicious demeanour. This completed the case for the prosecution.

Sir CHARLES BROWN-HARLAND, Q.C., rose with a swagger and a rustle of his silk gown, and proceeded to set forth the theory of the defence. He said he did not purpose to call many witnesses. The hypothesis of the prosecution was so inherently childish and inconsequential, and so dependent upon a bundle of interdependent probabilities that it crumbled away at the merest touch. The prisoner's character was of unblemished integrity, his last public appearance had been made on the same platform with Mr. Gladstone, and his honesty and highmindedness had been vouched for by statesmen of the highest standing. His movements could be accounted for from hour to hour—and those with which the prosecution credited him rested on no tangible evidence whatever. He was also credited with superhuman ingenuity and diabolical cunning of which he had shown no previous symptom. Hypothesis was piled on hypothesis, as in the old Oriental legend, where the world rested on the elephant and the elephant on the tortoise. It might be worth while, however, to point out that it was at least quite likely that the death of Mr. Constant had not taken place before seven, and as the prisoner left Euston Station at 7:15 A.M. for Liverpool, he could certainly not have got there from Bow in the time; also that it was hardly possible for the prisoner, who could prove being at Euston Station at 5:25 A.M., to travel backwards and forwards to Glover Street and commit the crime all within less than two hours. "The real facts," said Sir Charles, impressively, "are most simple. The prisoner, partly from pressure of work, partly (he had no wish to conceal) from worldly ambition, had begun to neglect Miss Dymond, to whom he was engaged to be married. The man was but human, and his head was a little turned by his growing importance. Nevertheless, at heart he was still deeply attached to Miss Dymond. She, however, appears to have jumped to the conclusion that he had ceased to love her, that she was unworthy of him, unfitted by education to take her place side by side with him in the new spheres to which he was mounting—that, in short, she was a drag on his career. Being, by all accounts, a girl of remarkable force of character, she resolved to cut the Gordian knot by leaving London, and, fearing lest her affianced husband's conscientiousness should induce him to sacrifice himself to her; dreading also, perhaps, her own weakness, she made the parting absolute, and the place of her refuge a mystery. A theory has been suggested which drags an honoured name in the mire—a theory so superfluous that I shall only allude to it. That Arthur Constant could have seduced, or had any improper relations with his friend's betrothed is a hypothesis to which the lives of both give the lie. Before leaving London—or England—Miss Dymond wrote to her aunt in Devonport—her only living relative in this country—asking her as a great favour to forward an addressed letter to the prisoner, a fortnight after receipt. The aunt obeyed implicitly. This was the letter which fell like a thunderbolt on the prisoner on the night of December 3rd. All his old love returned—he was full of self-reproach and pity for the poor girl. The letter read ominously. Perhaps she was going to put an end to herself. His first thought was to rush up to his friend, Constant, to seek his advice. Perhaps Constant knew something of the affair. The prisoner knew the two were in not infrequent communication. It is possible—my lord and gentlemen of the jury, I do not wish to follow the methods of the prosecution and confuse theory with fact, so I say it is possible—that Mr. Constant had supplied her with the £25 to leave the country. He was like a brother to her, perhaps even acted imprudently in calling upon her, though neither dreamed of evil. It is possible that he may have encouraged her in her abnegation and in her altruistic aspirations, perhaps even without knowing their exact drift, for does he not speak in his very last letter of the fine female characters he was meeting, and the influence for good he had over individual human souls? Still, this we can now never know, unless the dead speak or the absent return. It is also not impossible that Miss Dymond was entrusted with the £25 for charitable purposes.

But to come back to certainties. The prisoner consulted Mr. Constant about the letter. He then ran to Miss Dymond's lodgings in Stepney Green, knowing beforehand his trouble would be futile. The letter bore the postmark of Devonport. He knew the girl had an aunt there; possibly she might have gone to her. He could not telegraph, for he was ignorant of the address. He consulted his 'Bradshaw,' and resolved to leave by the 5:30 A.M. from Paddington, and told his landlady so. He left the letter in the 'Bradshaw,' which ultimately got thrust among a pile of papers under the sofa, so that he had to get another. He was careless and disorderly, and the key found by Mr. Wimp in his sofa, which he was absurdly supposed to have hidden there after the murder, must have lain there for some years, having been lost there in the days when he occupied the bedroom afterwards rented by Mr. Constant. For it was his own sofa, removed from that room, and the suction of sofas was well known. Afraid to miss his train, he did not undress on that distressful night. Meantime the thought occurred to him that Jessie was too clever a girl to leave so easy a trail, and he jumped to the conclusion that she would be going to her married brother in America, and had gone to Devonport merely to bid her aunt farewell. He determined therefore to get to Liverpool, without wasting time at Devonport, to institute inquiries. Not suspecting the delay in the transit of the letter, he thought he might yet stop her, even at the landing-stage or on the tender. Unfortunately his cab went slowly in the fog, he missed the first train, and wandered about brooding disconsolately in the mist till the second. At Liverpool his suspicious, excited demeanour procured his momentary arrest. Since then the thought of the lost girl has haunted and broken him. That is the whole, the plain, and the sufficing story."

The effective witnesses for the defence were, indeed, few. It is so hard to prove a negative. There was Jessie's aunt, who bore out the statement of the counsel for the defence. There were the porters who saw him leave Euston by the 7:15 train for Liverpool, and arrive just too late for the 5:15; there was the cabman (2138), who drove him to Euston just in time, he (witness) thought, to catch the 5:15 A.M. Under cross-examination, the cabman got a little confused; he was asked whether, if he really picked up the prisoner at Bow Railway Station at about 4.30, he ought not to have caught the first train at Euston. He said the fog made him drive rather slowly, but admitted the mist was transparent enough to warrant full speed. He also admitted being a strong trade unionist, SPIGOT, Q.C., artfully extorting the admission as if it were of the utmost significance. Finally, there were numerous witnesses—of all sorts and conditions—to the prisoner's high character, as well as to Arthur Constant's blameless and moral life.

In his closing speech on the third day of the trial, Sir CHARLES pointed out with great exhaustiveness and cogency the flimsiness of the case for the prosecution, the number of hypotheses it involved, and their mutual interdependence. Mrs. Drabdump was a witness whose evidence must be accepted with extreme caution. The jury must remember that she was unable to dissociate her observations from her inferences, and thought that the prisoner and Mr. Constant were quarrelling merely because they were agitated. He dissected her evidence, and showed that it entirely bore out the story of the defence. He asked the jury to bear in mind that no positive evidence (whether of cabmen or others) had been given of the various and complicated movements attributed to the prisoner on the morning of December 4th, between the hours of 5:25 and 7:15 A.M., and that the most important witness on the theory of the prosecution—he meant, of course, Miss Dymond—had not been produced. Even if she were dead, and her body were found, no countenance would be given to the theory of the prosecution, for the mere conviction that her lover had deserted her would be a sufficient explanation of her suicide. Beyond the ambiguous letter, no tittle of evidence of her dishonour—on which the bulk of the case against the prisoner rested—had been adduced. As for the motive of political jealousy that had been a mere passing cloud. The two men had become fast friends. As to the circumstances of the alleged crime, the medical evidence was on the whole in favour of the time of death being late; and the prisoner had left London at a quarter-past seven. The drugging theory was absurd, and as for the too clever bolt and lock theories, Mr. Grodman, a trained scientific observer, had pooh-poohed them. He would solemnly exhort the jury to remember that if they condemned the prisoner they would not only send an innocent man to an ignominious death on the flimsiest circumstantial evidence, but they would deprive the working men of this country of one of their truest friends and their ablest leader.

The conclusion of Sir Charles's vigorous speech was greeted with irrepressible applause.

Mr. Spigot, Q.C., in closing the case for the prosecution, asked the jury to return a verdict against the prisoner for as malicious and premeditated a crime as ever disgraced the annals of any civilised country. His cleverness and education had only been utilised for the devil's ends, while his reputation had been used as a cloak. Everything pointed strongly to the prisoner's guilt. On receiving Miss Dymond's letter announcing her shame, and (probably) her intention to commit suicide, he had hastened upstairs to denounce Constant. He had then rushed to the girl's lodgings, and, finding his worst fears confirmed, planned at once his diabolically ingenious scheme of revenge. He told his landlady he was going to Devonport, so that if he bungled, the police would be put temporarily off his track. His real destination was Liverpool, for he intended to leave the country. Lest, however, his plan should break down here, too, he arranged an ingenious alibi by being driven to Euston for the 5:15 train to Liverpool. The cabman would not know he did not intend to go by it, but meant to return to 11 Glover Street, there to perpetrate this foul crime, interruption to which he had possibly barred by drugging his landlady. His presence at Liverpool (whither he really went by the second train) would corroborate the cabman's story. That night he had not undressed nor gone to bed; he had plotted out his devilish scheme till it was perfect; the fog came as an unexpected ally to cover his movements. Jealousy, outraged affection, the desire for revenge, the lust for political power—these were human. They might pity the criminal, they could not find him innocent of the crime.

Mr. Justice CROGIE, summing up, began dead against the prisoner. Reviewing the evidence, he pointed out that plausible hypotheses neatly dove-tailed did not necessarily weaken one another, the fitting so well together of the whole rather making for the truth of the parts. Besides, the case for the prosecution was as far from being all hypothesis as the case for the defence was from excluding hypotheses. The key, the letter, the reluctance to produce the letter, the heated interview with Constant, the misstatement about the prisoner's destination, the flight to Liverpool, the false tale about searching for a "him," the denunciations of Constant, all these were facts. On the other hand, there were various lacunæ and hypotheses in the case for the defence. Even conceding the somewhat dubious alibi afforded by the prisoner's presence at Euston at 5:25 A.M., there was no attempt to account for his movements between that and 7:15 A.M. It was as possible that he returned to Bow as that he lingered about Euston. There was nothing in the medical evidence to make his guilt impossible. Nor was there anything inherently impossible in Constant's yielding to the sudden temptation of a beautiful girl, nor in a working girl deeming herself deserted, temporarily succumbing to the fascinations of a gentleman and regretting it bitterly afterwards. What had become of the girl was a mystery. Hers might have been one of those nameless corpses which the tide swirls up on slimy river banks. The jury must remember, too, that the relation might not have actually passed into dishonour, it might have been just grave enough to smite the girl's conscience, and to induce her to behave as she had done. It was enough that her letter should have excited the jealousy of the prisoner. There was one other point which he would like to impress on the jury, and which the counsel for the prosecution had not sufficiently insisted upon. This was that the prisoner's guiltiness was the only plausible solution that had ever been advanced of the Bow Mystery. The medical evidence agreed that Mr. Constant did not die by his own hand. Some one must therefore have murdered him. The number of people who could have had any possible reason or opportunity to murder him was extremely small. The prisoner had both reason and opportunity. By what logicians called the method of exclusion, suspicion would attach to him on even slight evidence. The actual evidence was strong and plausible, and now that Mr. Wimp's ingenious theory had enabled them to understand how the door could have been apparently locked and bolted from within, the last difficulty and the last argument for suicide had been removed. The prisoner's guilt was as clear as circumstantial evidence could make it. If they let him go free, the Bow Mystery might henceforward be placed among the archives of unavenged assassinations. Having thus well-nigh hung the prisoner, the judge wound up by insisting on the high probability of the story for the defence, though that, too, was dependent in important details upon the prisoner's mere private statements to his counsel. The jury, being by this time sufficiently muddled by his impartiality, were dismissed, with the exhortation to allow due weight to every fact and probability in determining their righteous verdict.

The minutes ran into hours, but the jury did not return. The shadows of night fell across the reeking, fevered court before they announced their verdict—

"Guilty!"

The judge put on his black cap.

The great reception arranged outside was a fiasco; the evening banquet was indefinitely postponed. Wimp had won; Grodman felt like a whipped cur.

XI

"So you were right," Denzil could not help saying as he greeted Grodman a week afterwards. "I shall not live to tell the story of how you discovered the Bow murderer."

"Sit down," growled Grodman; "perhaps you will after all." There was a dangerous gleam in his eyes. Denzil was sorry he had spoken.

"I sent for you," Grodman said, "to tell you that on the night Wimp arrested Mortlake I had made preparations for your arrest."

Denzil gasped, "What for?"

"My dear Denzil, there is a little law in this country invented for the confusion of the poetic. The greatest exponent of the Beautiful is only allowed the same number of wives as the greengrocer. I do not blame you for not being satisfied with Jane—she is a good servant but a bad mistress—but it was cruel to Kitty not to inform her that Jane had a prior right in you, and unjust to Jane not to let her know of the contract with Kitty."

"They both know it now well enough, curse 'em," said the poet.

"Yes; your secrets are like your situations—you can't keep 'em long. My poor poet, I pity you—betwixt the devil and the deep sea."

"They're a pair of harpies, each holding over me the Damocles sword of an arrest for bigamy. Neither loves me."

"I should think they would come in very useful to you. You plant one in my house to tell my secrets to Wimp, and you plant one in Wimp's house to tell Wimp's secrets to me, I suppose. Out with some, then."

"Upon my honour, you wrong me. Jane brought *me* here, not I Jane. As for Kitty, I never had such a shock in my life as at finding her installed in Wimp's house."

"She thought it safer to have the law handy for your arrest. Besides, she probably desired to occupy a parallel position to Jane's. She must do something for a living; you wouldn't do anything for hers. And so you couldn't go anywhere without meeting a wife! Ha! ha! ha! Serve you right, my polygamous poet."

"But why should you arrest me?"

"Revenge, Denzil. I have been the best friend you ever had in this cold, pro-saic world. You have eaten my bread, drunk my claret, written my book, smoked my cigars, and pocketed my money. And yet, when you have an important piece of infor-mation bearing on a mystery about which I am thinking day and night, you calmly go and sell it to Wimp."

"I did-didn't," stammered Denzil.

"Liar! Do you think Kitty has any secrets from me? As soon as I discovered your two marriages I determined to have you arrested for—your treachery. But when I found you had, as I thought, put Wimp on the wrong scent, when I felt sure that by arresting Mortlake he was going to make a greater ass of himself than even nature had been able to do, then I forgave you. I let you walk about the earth—and drink—freely. Now it is Wimp who crows—everybody pats him on the back—they call him the mystery man of the Scotland Yard tribe. Poor Tom Mortlake will be hanged, and all through your telling Wimp about Jessie Dymond!"

"It was you yourself," said Denzil, sullenly. "Everybody was giving it up. But you said 'Let us find out all that Arthur Constant did in the last few months of his life.' Wimp couldn't miss stumbling on Jessie sooner or later. I'd have throttled Constant, if I had known he'd touched her," he wound up with irrelevant indignation.

Grodman winced at the idea that he himself had worked *ad majorem gloriam* of Wimp. And yet, had not Mrs. Wimp let out as much at the Christmas dinner?

"What's past is past," he said gruffly. "But if Tom Mortlake hangs, you go to Portland."

"How can I help Tom hanging?"

"Help the agitation as much as you can. Write letters under all sorts of names to all the papers. Get everybody you know to sign the great petition. Find out where Jessie Dymond is—the girl who holds the proof of Mortlake's innocence."

"You really believe him innocent?"

"Don't be satirical, Denzil. Haven't I taken the chair at all the meetings? Am I not the most copious correspondent of the Press?"

"I thought it was only to spite Wimp."

"Rubbish. It's to save poor Tom. He no more murdered Arthur Constant than— you did!" He laughed an unpleasant laugh.

Denzil bade him farewell, frigid with fear.

Grodman was up to his ears in letters and telegrams. Somehow he had become the leader of the rescue party—suggestions, subscriptions came from all sides. The suggestions were burnt, the subscriptions acknowledged in the papers and used for hunting up the missing girl. Lucy Brent headed the list with a hundred pounds. It was a fine testimony to her faith in her dead lover's honour.

The release of the Jury had unloosed "The Greater Jury," which always now sits upon the smaller. Every means was taken to nullify the value of the "palladium of British liberty." The foreman and the jurors were interviewed, the judge was judged, and by those who were no judges. The Home Secretary (who had done nothing beyond accepting office under the Crown) was vituperated, and sundry provincial persons wrote confidentially to the Queen. Arthur Constant's backsliding cheered many by convincing them that others were as bad as themselves; and well-to-do tradesmen saw in Mortlake's wickedness the pernicious effects of Socialism. A dozen new theories were afloat. Constant had committed suicide by Esoteric Buddhism, as witness his devotion to Mme. Blavatsky, or he had been murdered by his Mahatma or victimised by Hypnotism, Mesmerism, Somnambulism, and other weird abstractions. Grodman's great point was—Jessie Dymond must be produced, dead or alive. The electric current scoured the civilised world in search of her. What wonder if the shrewder sort divined that the indomitable detective had fixed his last hope on the girl's guilt? If Jessie had wrongs why should she not have avenged them herself? Did she not always remind the poet of Joan of Arc?

Another week passed; the shadow of the gallows crept over the days; on, on, remorselessly drawing nearer, as the last ray of hope sank below the horizon. The Home Secretary remained inflexible; the great petitions discharged their signatures at him in vain. He was a Conservative, sternly conscientious; and the mere insinuation that his obstinacy was due to the politics of the condemned only hardened him against the temptation of a cheap reputation for magnanimity. He would not even grant a respite, to increase the chances of the discovery of Jessie Dymond. In the last of the three weeks there was a final monster meeting of protest. Grodman again took the chair, and several distinguished faddists were present, as well as numerous respectable members of society. The Home Secretary acknowledged the receipt of their resolutions. The Trade Unions were divided in their allegiance; some whispered of faith and hope, others of financial defalcations. The former essayed to organise a procession and an indignation meeting on the Sunday preceding the Tuesday fixed for the execution, but it fell through on a rumour of confession. The Monday papers contained a last masterly letter from Grodman exposing the weakness of the evidence, but they knew nothing of a confession. The prisoner was mute and disdainful, professing little regard for a life empty of love and burdened with self-reproach. He refused to see clergymen. He was accorded an interview with Miss Brent in the presence of a gaoler, and solemnly asseverated his respect for her dead lover's memory. Monday buzzed with rumours; the evening papers chronicled them hour by hour. A poignant anxiety was abroad. The girl would be found. Some miracle would happen. A reprieve would arrive. The sentence would be commuted. But the short day darkened into night even as Mortlake's short day was darkening. And the shadow of the gallows crept on and on, and seemed to mingle with the twilight.

Crowl stood at the door of his shop, unable to work. His big grey eyes were heavy with unshed tears. The dingy wintry road seemed one vast cemetery; the street lamps twinkled like corpse-lights. The confused sounds of the street life reached his ear as from another world. He did not see the people who flitted to and fro amid the gathering shadows of the cold, dreary night. One ghastly vision flashed and faded and flashed upon the background of the duskiness.

Denzil stood beside him, smoking in silence. A cold fear was at his heart. That terrible Grodman! As the hangman's cord was tightening round Mortlake, he felt the convict's chains tightening round himself. And yet there was one gleam of hope, feeble as the yellow flicker of the gas-lamp across the way. Grodman had obtained an interview with the condemned late that afternoon, and the parting had been painful, but the evening paper, that in its turn had obtained an interview with the ex-detective, announced on its placard

GRODMAN STILL CONFIDENT

and the thousands who yet pinned their faith on this extraordinary man refused to extinguish the last sparks of hope. Denzil had bought the paper and scanned it eagerly, but there was nothing save the vague assurance that the indefatigable Grodman was still almost pathetically expectant of the miracle. Denzil did not share the expectation; he meditated flight.

"Peter," he said at last, "I'm afraid it's all over."

Crowl nodded, heart-broken. "All over!" he repeated, "and to think that he dies—and it is—all over!"

He looked despairingly at the blank winter sky, where leaden clouds shut out the stars. "Poor, poor young fellow! To-night alive and thinking. To-morrow night a clod, with no more sense or motion than a bit of leather! No compensation nowhere for being cut off innocent in the pride of youth and strength! A man who has always preached the Useful day and night, and toiled and suffered for his fellows. Where's the justice of it, where's the justice of it?" he demanded fiercely. Again his wet eyes wandered upwards towards heaven, that heaven away from which the soul of a dead saint at the Antipodes was speeding into infinite space.

"Well, where was the justice for Arthur Constant if he, too, was innocent?" said Denzil. "Really, Peter, I don't see why you should take it for granted that Tom is so dreadfully injured. Your horny-handed labour leaders are, after all, men of no aesthetic refinement, with no sense of the Beautiful; you cannot expect them to be exempt from the coarser forms of crime. Humanity must look to far other leaders—to the seers and the poets!"

"Cantercot, if you say Tom's guilty I'll knock you down." The little cobbler turned upon his tall friend like a roused lion. Then he added, "I beg your pardon, Cantercot, I don't mean that. After all, I've no grounds. The judge is an honest man, and with gifts I can't lay claim to. But I believe in Tom with all my heart. And if Tom is guilty I believe in the Cause of the People with all my heart all the same. The Fads are doomed to death, they may be reprieved, but they must die at last."

He drew a deep sigh, and looked along the dreary Road. It was quite dark now, but by the light of the lamps and the gas in the shop windows the dull, monotonous Road lay revealed in all its sordid, familiar outlines; with its long stretches of chill pavement, its unlovely architecture, and its endless stream of prosaic pedestrians.

A sudden consciousness of the futility of his existence pierced the little cobbler like an icy wind. He saw his own life, and a hundred million lives like his, swelling and breaking like bubbles on a dark ocean, unheeded, uncared for.

A newsboy passed along, clamouring "The Bow murderer, preparaitions for the hexecution!"

A terrible shudder shook the cobbler's frame. His eyes ranged sightlessly after the boy; the merciful tears filled them at last.

"The Cause of the People," he murmured brokenly, "I believe in the Cause of the People. There is nothing else."

"Peter, come in to tea, you'll catch cold," said Mrs. Crowl.

Denzil went in to tea and Peter followed.

• • •

Meantime, round the house of the Home Secretary, who was in town, an ever-augmenting crowd was gathered, eager to catch the first whisper of a reprieve.

The house was guarded by a cordon of police, for there was no inconsiderable danger of a popular riot. At times a section of the crowd groaned and hooted. Once a volley of stones was discharged at the windows. The newsboys were busy vending their special editions, and the reporters struggled through the crowd, clutching descriptive pencils, and ready to rush off to telegraph offices should anything "extra special" occur. Telegraph boys were coming up every now and again with threats, messages, petitions, and exhortations from all parts of the country to the unfortunate Home Secretary, who was striving to keep his aching head cool as he went through the voluminous evidence for the last time and pondered over the more important letters which "The Greater Jury" had contributed to the obscuration of the problem. Grodman's letter in that morning's paper shook him most; under his scientific analysis the circumstantial chain seemed forged of painted cardboard. Then the poor man read the judge's summing up, and the chain became tempered steel. The noise of the crowd outside broke upon his ear in his study like the roar of a distant ocean. The more the rabble hooted him, the more he essayed to hold scrupulously the scales of life and death. And the crowd grew and grew, as men came away from their work. There were many that loved the man who lay in the jaws of death, and a spirit of mad revolt surged in their breasts. And the sky was grey, and the bleak night deepened, and the shadow of the gallows crept on.

Suddenly a strange inarticulate murmur spread through the crowd, a vague whisper of no one knew what. Something had happened. Somebody was coming. A second later and one of the outskirts of the throng was agitated, and a convulsive cheer went up from it, and was taken up infectiously all along the street. The crowd parted—a hansom dashed through the centre. "Grodman! Grodman!" shouted those who recognised the occupant. "Grodman! Hurrah!" Grodman was outwardly calm and pale, but his eyes glittered; he waved his hand encouragingly as the hansom dashed up to the door, cleaving the turbulent crowd as a canoe cleaves the waters. Grodman sprang out, the constables at the portal made way for him respectfully. He knocked imperatively, the door was opened cautiously; a boy rushed up and delivered a telegram; Grodman forced his way in, gave his name, and insisted on seeing the Home Secretary on a matter of life and death. Those near the door heard his words and cheered, and the crowd divined the good omen, and the air throbbed with cannonades of joyous sound. The cheers rang in Grodman's ears as the door slammed behind him. The reporters struggled to the front. An excited knot of working men pressed round the arrested hansom; they took the horse out. A dozen enthusiasts struggled for the honour of placing themselves between the shafts. And the crowd awaited Grodman.

XII

Grodman was ushered into the conscientious Minister's study. The doughty chief of the agitation was, perhaps, the one man who could not be denied. As he entered, the Home Secretary's face seemed lit up with relief. At a sign from his master, the amanuensis who had brought in the last telegram took it back with him into the outer room where he worked. Needless to say not a tithe of the Minister's correspondence ever came under his own eyes.

"You have a valid reason for troubling me, I suppose, Mr. Grodman?" said the Home Secretary, almost cheerfully. "Of course it is about Mortlake?"

"It is; and I have the best of all reasons."

"Take a seat. Proceed."

"Pray do not consider me impertinent, but have you ever given any attention to the science of evidence?"

"How do you mean?" asked the Home Secretary, rather puzzled, adding, with a melancholy smile, "I have had to lately. Of course, I've never been a criminal lawyer, like some of my predecessors. But I should hardly speak of it as a science; I look upon it as a question of common-sense."

"Pardon me, sir. It is the most subtle and difficult of all the sciences. It is, indeed, rather the science of the sciences. What is the whole of Inductive Logic, as laid down, say, by Bacon and Mill, but an attempt to appraise the value of evidence, the said evidence being the trails left by the Creator, so to speak? The Creator has—I say it in all reverence—drawn a myriad red herrings across the track, but the true scientist refuses to be baffled by superficial appearances in detecting the secrets of Nature. The vulgar herd catches at the gross apparent fact, but the man of insight knows that what lies on the surface does lie."

"Very interesting, Mr. Grodman, but really—"

"Bear with me, sir. The science of evidence being thus so extremely subtle, and demanding the most acute and trained observation of facts, the most comprehensive understanding of human psychology, is naturally given over to professors who have not the remotest idea that 'things are not what they seem,' and that everything is other than it appears; to professors, most of whom by their year-long devotion to the shop-counter or the desk, have acquired an intimate acquaintance with all the infinite shades and complexities of things and human nature. When twelve of these professors are put in a box, it is called a jury. When one of these professors is put in a box by himself, he is called a witness. The retailing of evidence—the observation of the facts—is given over to people who go through their lives without eyes; the appreciation of evidence—the judging of these facts—is surrendered to people who may possibly be adepts in weighing out pounds of sugar. Apart from their sheer inability to fulfil either function—to observe, or to judge—their observation and their judgment alike are vitiated by all sorts of irrelevant prejudices."

"You are attacking trial by jury."

"Not necessarily. I am prepared to accept that scientifically, on the ground that, as there are, as a rule, only two alternatives, the balance of probability is slightly in favour of the true decision being come to. Then, in cases where experts like myself have got up the evidence, the jury can be made to see through trained eyes."

The Home Secretary tapped impatiently with his foot.

"I can't listen to abstract theorising," he said. "Have you any fresh concrete evidence?"

"Sir, everything depends on our getting down to the root of the matter. What percentage of average evidence should you think is thorough, plain, simple, unvarnished fact, 'the truth, the whole truth, and nothing but the truth'?"

"Fifty?" said the Minister, humouring him a little.

"Not five. I say nothing of lapses of memory, of inborn defects of observational power—though the suspiciously precise recollection of dates and events possessed by ordinary witnesses in important trials taking place years after the occurrences involved, is one of the most amazing things in the curiosities of modern jurisprudence. I defy you, sir, to tell me what you had for dinner last Monday, or what exactly you were saying and doing at five o'clock last Tuesday afternoon. Nobody whose life does not run in mechanical grooves can do anything of the sort; unless, of course, the facts have been very impressive. But this by the way. The great obstacle to veracious observation is the element of prepossession in all vision. Has it ever struck you, sir, that we never *see* any one more than once, if that? The first time we meet a man we may possibly see him as he is; the second time our vision is coloured and modified by the memory of the first. Do our friends appear to us as they appear to strangers? Do our rooms, our furniture, our pipes strike our eye as they would strike the eye of an outsider, looking on them for the first time? Can a mother see her babe's ugliness, or a lover his mistress's shortcomings, though they stare everybody else in the face? Can we see ourselves as others see us? No; habit, prepossession changes all. The mind is a large factor of every so-called external fact. The eye sees, sometimes, what it wishes to see, more often what it expects to see. You follow me, sir?"

The Home Secretary nodded his head less impatiently. He was beginning to be interested. The hubbub from without broke faintly upon their ears.

"To give you a definite example. Mr. Wimp says that when I burst open the door of Mr. Constant's room on the morning of December 4th, and saw that the staple of the bolt had been wrested by the pin from the lintel, I jumped at once to the conclusion that I had broken the bolt. Now I admit that this was so, only in things like this you do not seem to conclude, you jump so fast that you see, or seem to. On the other hand, when you see a standing ring of fire produced by whirling a burning stick, you do not believe in its continuous existence. It is the same when witnessing a legerdemain performance. Seeing is not always believing, despite the proverb; but believing is often seeing. It is not to the point that in that little matter of the door Wimp was as hopelessly and incurably wrong as he has been in everything all along. The door was securely bolted. Still I confess that I should have seen that I had broken the bolt in forcing the door, even if it had been broken beforehand. Never once since December 4th did this possibility occur to me, till Wimp with perverted ingenuity suggested it. If this is the case with a trained observer, one moreover fully conscious of this ineradicable tendency of the human mind, how must it be with an untrained observer?"

"Come to the point, come to the point," said the Home Secretary, putting out his hand as if it itched to touch the bell on the writing-table.

"Such as," went on Grodman, imperturbably, "such as—Mrs. Drabdump. That worthy person is unable, by repeated violent knocking, to arouse her lodger who yet desires to be aroused; she becomes alarmed, she rushes across to get my assistance; I burst open the door—what do you think the good lady expected to see?"

"Mr. Constant murdered, I suppose," murmured the Home Secretary, wonderingly.

"Exactly. And so she saw it. And what should you think was the condition of Arthur Constant when the door yielded to my violent exertions and flew open?"

"Why, was he not dead?" gasped the Home Secretary, his heart fluttering violently.

"Dead? A young, healthy fellow like that! When the door flew open, Arthur Constant was sleeping the sleep of the just. It was a deep, a very deep sleep, of course, else the blows at his door would long since have awakened him. But all the while Mrs. Drabdump's fancy was picturing her lodger cold and stark, the poor young fellow was lying in bed in a nice warm sleep."

"You mean to say you found Arthur Constant alive?"

"As you were last night."

The Minister was silent, striving confusedly to take in the situation. Outside the crowd was cheering again. It was probably to pass the time.

"Then, when was he murdered?"

"Immediately afterwards."

"By whom?"

"Well, that is, if you will pardon me, not a very intelligent question. Science and common-sense are in accord for once. Try the method of exhaustion. It must have been either by Mrs. Drabdump or myself."

"You mean to say that Mrs. Drabdump——!"

"Poor dear Mrs. Drabdump, you don't deserve this of your Home Secretary! The idea of that good lady!"

"It was you!!"

"Calm yourself, my dear Home Secretary. There is nothing to be alarmed at. It was a solitary experiment, and I intend it to remain so." The noise without grew louder. "Three cheers for Grodman! Hip, hip, hip, hooray," fell faintly on their ears.

But the Minister, pallid and deeply moved, touched the bell. The Home Secretary's home secretary appeared. He looked at the great man's agitated face with suppressed surprise.

"Thank you for calling in your amanuensis," said Grodman. "I intended to ask you to lend me his services. I suppose he can write shorthand."

The Minister nodded, speechless.

"That is well. I intend this statement to form the basis of an appendix to the twenty-fifth edition—sort of silver wedding—of my book, Criminals I have Caught. Mr. Denzil Cantercot, who, by the will I have made to-day, is appointed my literary executor, will have the task of working it up with literary and dramatic touches after the model of the other chapters of my book. I have every confidence he will be able to do me as much justice, from a literary point of view, as you, sir, no doubt will from a legal. I feel certain he will succeed in catching the style of the other chapters to perfection."

"Templeton," whispered the Home Secretary, "this man may be a lunatic. The effort to solve the Big Bow Mystery may have addled his brain. Still," he added aloud, "it will be as well for you to take down his statement in shorthand."

"Thank you, sir," said Grodman, heartily. "Ready, Mr. Templeton? Here goes. My career till I left the Scotland Yard Detective Department is known to all the world. Is that too fast for you, Mr. Templeton? A little? Well, I'll go slower; but pull me up if I forget to keep the brake on. When I retired, I discovered that I was a bachelor. But it was too late to marry. Time hung heavy on my hands. The preparation of my book, Criminals I have Caught, kept me occupied for some months. When it was published, I had nothing more to do but think. I had plenty of money, and it was safely invested; there was no call for speculation. The future was meaningless to me; I regretted I had not elected to die in harness. As idle old men must, I lived in the past. I went over and over again my ancient exploits; I re-read my book. And as I thought and thought, away from the excitement of the actual hunt, and seeing the facts in a truer perspective, so it grew daily clearer to me that criminals were more fools than rogues. Every crime I had traced, however cleverly perpetrated, was from the point of view of penetrability a weak failure. Traces and trails were left on all sides—ragged edges, rough-hewn corners; in short, the job was botched, artistic completeness unattained. To the vulgar, my feats might seem marvellous—the average man is mystified to grasp how you detect the letter 'e' in a simple cryptogram—to myself they were as commonplace as the crimes they unveiled. To me now, with my lifelong study of the science of evidence, it seemed possible to commit not merely one but a thousand crimes that should be absolutely undiscoverable. And yet criminals would go on sinning, and giving themselves away, in the same old grooves—no originality, no dash, no individual insight, no fresh conception! One would imagine there were an Academy of crime with forty thousand armchairs. And gradually, as I pondered and brooded over the thought, there came upon me the desire to commit a crime that should baffle detection. I could invent hundreds of such crimes, and please myself by imagining them done; but would they really work out in practice? Evidently the sole performer of my experiment must be myself; the subject—whom or what? Accident should determine. I itched to commence with murder—to tackle the stiffest problems first, and I burned to startle and baffle the world—especially the world of which I had ceased to be. Outwardly I was calm, and spoke to the people about me as usual. Inwardly I was on fire with a consuming scientific passion. I sported with my pet theories, and fitted them mentally on every one I met. Every friend or acquaintance I sat and gossiped with, I was plotting how to murder without leaving a clue. There is not one of my friends or acquaintances I have not done away with in thought. There is no public man—have no fear, my dear Home Secretary—I have not planned to assassinate secretly, mysteriously, unintelligibly, undiscoverably. Ah, how I could give the stock criminals points—with their second-hand motives, their conventional conceptions, their commonplace details, their lack of artistic feeling and restraint."

The crowd had again started cheering. Impatient as the watchers were, they felt that no news was good news. The longer the interview accorded by the Home Secretary to the chairman of the Defence Committee, the greater the hope his obduracy was melting. The idol of the people would be saved, and "Grodman" and "Tom Mortlake" were mingled in the exultant plaudits.

"The late Arthur Constant," continued the great criminologist, "came to live nearly opposite me. I cultivated his acquaintance—he was a lovable young fellow, an excellent subject for experiment. I do not know when I have ever taken to a man more. From the moment I first set eyes on him, there was a peculiar sympathy between us. We were drawn to each other. I felt instinctively he would be the man. I loved to hear him speak enthusiastically of the Brotherhood of Man—I, who knew the brotherhood of man was to the ape, the serpent, and the tiger—and he seemed to find a pleasure in stealing a moment's chat with me from his engrossing self-appointed duties. It is a pity humanity should have been robbed of so valuable a life. But it had to be. At a quarter to ten on the night of December 3rd he came to me. Naturally I said nothing about this visit at the inquest or the trial. His object was to consult me mysteriously about some girl. He said he had privately lent her money—which she was to repay at her convenience. What the money was for he did not know, except that it was somehow connected with an act of abnegation in which he had vaguely encouraged her. The girl had since disappeared, and he was in distress about her. He would not tell me who it was—of course now, sir, you know as well as I it was Jessie Dymond—but asked for advice as to how to set about finding her. He mentioned that Mortlake was leaving for Devonport by the first train on the next day. Of old I should have connected these two facts and sought the thread; now, as he spoke, all my thoughts were dyed red. He was suffering perceptibly from toothache, and in answer to my sympathetic inquiries told me it had been allowing him very little sleep. Everything combined to invite the trial of one of my favourite theories. I spoke to him in a fatherly way, and when I had tendered some vague advice about the girl, I made him promise to secure a night's rest (before he faced the arduous tram-men's meeting in the morning) by taking a sleeping draught. I gave him a quantity of sulfonal in a phial. It is a new drug, which produces protracted sleep without disturbing digestion, and which I use myself. He promised faithfully to take the draught; and I also exhorted him earnestly to bolt and bar and lock himself in so as to stop up every chink or aperture by which the cold air of the winter's night might creep into the room. I remonstrated with him on the careless manner he treated his body, and he laughed in his good-humoured, gentle way, and promised to obey me in all things. And he did. That Mrs. Drabdump, failing to rouse him, would cry 'Murder!' I took for certain. She is built that way. As even Sir Charles Brown-Harland remarked, she habitually takes her prepossessions for facts, her inferences for observations. She forecasts the future in grey. Most women of Mrs. Drabdump's class would have behaved as she did. She happened to be a peculiarly favourable specimen for working on by 'suggestion,' but I would have undertaken to produce the same effect on almost any woman. The key to the Big Bow Mystery is feminine psychology. The only uncertain link in the chain was, Would Mrs. Drabdump rush across to get me to break open the door?

Women always rush for a man. I was well-nigh the nearest, and certainly the most authoritative man in the street, and I took it for granted she would."

"But suppose she hadn't?" the Home Secretary could not help asking.

"Then the murder wouldn't have happened, that's all. In due course Arthur Constant would have awoke, or somebody else breaking open the door would have found him sleeping; no harm done, nobody any the wiser. I could hardly sleep myself that night. The thought of the extraordinary crime I was about to commit—a burning curiosity to know whether Wimp would detect the modus operandi—the prospect of sharing the feelings of murderers with whom I had been in contact all my life without being in touch with the terrible joys of their inner life—the fear lest I should be too fast asleep to hear Mrs. Drabdump's knock—these things agitated me and disturbed my rest. I lay tossing on my bed, planning every detail of poor Constant's end. The hours dragged slowly and wretchedly on towards the misty dawn. I was racked with suspense. Was I to be disappointed after all? At last the welcome sound came—the rat-tat-tat of murder. The echoes of that knock are yet in my ear. 'Come over and kill him!' I put my night-capped head out of the window and told her to wait for me. I dressed hurriedly, took my razor, and went across to 11 Glover Street. As I broke open the door of the bedroom in which Arthur Constant lay sleeping, his head resting on his hands, I cried, 'My God!' as if I saw some awful vision. A mist as of blood swam before Mrs. Drabdump's eyes. She cowered back, for an instant (I divined rather than saw the action) she shut off the dreaded sight with her hands. In that instant I had made my cut—precisely, scientifically—made so deep a cut and drawn out the weapon so sharply that there was scarce a drop of blood on it; then there came from the throat a jet of blood which Mrs. Drabdump, conscious only of the horrid gash, saw but vaguely. I covered up the face quickly with a handkerchief to hide any convulsive distortion. But as the medical evidence (in this detail accurate) testified, death was instantaneous. I pocketed the razor and the empty sulfonal phial. With a woman like Mrs. Drabdump to watch me, I could do anything I pleased. I got her to draw my attention to the fact that both the windows were fastened. Some fool, by the by, thought there was a discrepancy in the evidence because the police found only one window fastened, forgetting that, in my innocence I took care not to refasten the window I had opened to call for aid. Naturally I did not call for aid before a considerable time had elapsed. There was Mrs. Drabdump to quiet, and the excuse of making notes—as an old hand. My object was to gain time. I wanted the body to be fairly cold and stiff before being discovered, though there was not much danger here; for, as you saw by the medical evidence, there is no telling the time of death to an hour or two. The frank way in which I said the death was very recent disarmed all suspicion, and even Dr. Robinson was unconsciously worked upon, in adjudging the time of death, by the knowledge (query here, Mr. Templeton) that it had preceded my advent on the scene.

"Before leaving Mrs. Drabdump, there is just one point I should like to say a word about. You have listened so patiently, sir, to my lectures on the science of sciences that you will not refuse to hear the last. A good deal of importance has been attached to Mrs. Drabdump's oversleeping herself by half an hour. It happens that this (like the innocent fog which has also been made responsible for much) is a purely accidental and irrelevant circumstance. In all works on inductive logic it is thoroughly recognised that only some of the circumstances of a phenomenon are of its essence and casually interconnected; there is always a certain proportion of heterogeneous accompaniments which have no intimate relation whatever with the phenomenon. Yet, so crude is as yet the comprehension of the science of evidence, that every feature of the phenomenon under investigation is made equally important, and sought to be linked with the chain of evidence. To attempt to explain everything is always the mark of the tyro. The fog and Mrs. Drabdump's oversleeping herself were mere accidents. There are always these irrelevant accompaniments, and the true scientist allows for this element of (so to speak) chemically unrelated detail. Even I never counted on the unfortunate series of accidental phenomena which have led to Mortlake's implication in a network of suspicion. On the other hand, the fact that my servant, Jane, who usually goes about ten, left a few minutes earlier on the night of December 3rd, so that she didn't know of Constant's visit, was a relevant accident. In fact, just as the art of the artist or the editor consists largely in knowing what to leave out, so does the art of the scientific detector of crime consist in knowing what details to ignore. In short, to explain everything is to explain too much. And too much is worse than too little.

"To return to my experiment. My success exceeded my wildest dreams. None had an inkling of the truth. The insolubility of the Big Bow Mystery teased the acutest minds in Europe and the civilised world. That a man could have been murdered in a thoroughly inaccessible room savoured of the ages of magic. The redoubtable Wimp, who had been blazoned as my successor, fell back on the theory of suicide. The mystery would have slept till my death, but—I fear—for my own ingenuity. I tried to stand outside myself, and to look at the crime with the eyes of another, or of my old self. I found the work of art so perfect as to leave only one sublimely simple solution. The very terms of the problem were so inconceivable that, had I not been the murderer, I should have suspected myself, in conjunction, of course, with Mrs. Drabdump. The first persons to enter the room would have seemed to me guilty. I wrote at once (in a disguised hand and over the signature of 'One who looks through his own spectacles') to the Pell Mell Press to suggest this. By associating myself thus with Mrs. Drabdump I made it difficult for people to dissociate the two who entered the room together. To dash a half-truth in the world's eyes is the surest way of blinding it altogether. This pseudonymous letter of mine I contradicted (in my own name) the next day, and in the course of the long letter which I was tempted to write, I adduced fresh evidence against the theory of suicide. I was disgusted with the open verdict, and wanted men to be up and doing and trying to find me out. I enjoyed the hunt more.

"Unfortunately, Wimp, set on the chase again by my own letter, by dint of persistent blundering, blundered into a track which—by a devilish tissue of coincidences I had neither foreseen nor dreamt of—seemed to the world the true. Mortlake was arrested and condemned. Wimp had apparently crowned his reputation. This was too much. I had taken all this trouble merely to put a feather in Wimp's cap, whereas I had expected to shake his reputation by it. It was bad enough that an innocent man should suffer; but that Wimp should achieve a reputation he did not deserve, and overshadow all his predecessors by dint of a colossal mistake, this seemed to me intolerable. I have moved heaven and earth to get the verdict set aside, and to save the prisoner; I have exposed the weakness of the evidence; I have had the world searched for the missing girl; I have petitioned and agitated. In vain. I have failed. Now I play my last card. As the overweening Wimp could not be allowed to go down to posterity as the solver of this terrible mystery, I decided that the condemned man might just as well profit by his exposure. That is the reason I make the exposure to-night, before it is too late to save Mortlake."

"So that is the reason?" said the Home Secretary, with a suspicion of mockery in his tones.

"The sole reason."

Even as he spoke, a deeper roar than ever penetrated the study.

"A Reprieve! Hooray! Hooray!" The whole street seemed to rock with earthquake and the names of Grodman and Mortlake to be thrown up in a fiery jet. "A Reprieve! A Reprieve!" And then the very windows rattled with cheers for the Minister. And even above that roar rose the shrill voices of the newsboys, "Reprieve of Mortlake! Mortlake Reprieved!" Grodman looked wonderingly towards the street. "How do they know?" he murmured.

"Those evening papers are amazing," said the Minister, drily. "But I suppose they had everything ready in type for the contingency." He turned to his secretary.

"Templeton, have you got down every word of Mr. Grodman's confession?"

"Every word, sir."

"Then bring in the cable you received just as Mr. Grodman entered the house."

Templeton went back into the outer room and brought back the cablegram that had been lying on the Minister's writing-table when Grodman came in. The Home Secretary silently handed it to his visitor. It was from the Chief of Police of Melbourne, announcing that Jessie Dymond had just arrived in that city in a sailing vessel, ignorant of all that had occurred, and had been immediately despatched back to England, having made a statement entirely corroborating the theory of the defence.

"Pending further inquiries into this," said the Home Secretary, not without appreciation of the grim humour of the situation as he glanced at Grodman's ashen cheeks, "I have reprieved the prisoner. Mr. Templeton was about to despatch the messenger to the governor of Newgate as you entered this room. Mr. Wimp's card-castle would have tumbled to pieces without your assistance. Your still undiscoverable crime would have shaken his reputation as you intended."

A sudden explosion shook the room and blent with the cheers of the populace. Grodman had shot himself—very scientifically—in the heart. He fell at the Home Secretary's feet, stone dead.

Some of the working men who had been standing waiting by the shafts of the hansom helped to bear the stretcher.

ROOM NUMBER 3

Anna Katharine Green

I

Wmodels-hat door is that? You've opened all the others; why do you pass that one by?"

"Oh, that! That's only Number 3. A mere closet, gentlemen," responded the landlord in a pleasant voice. "To be sure, we sometimes use it as a sleeping-room when we are hard pushed. Jake, the clerk you saw below, used it last night. But it's not on our regular list. Do you want a peep at it?"

"Most assuredly. As you know, it's our duty to see every room in this house, whether it is on your regular list or not."

"All right. I haven't the key of this one with me. But—yes, I have. There, gentlemen!" he cried, unlocking the door and holding it open for them to look inside. "You see it no more answers the young lady's description than the others do. And I haven't another to show you. You have seen all those in front, and this is the last one in the rear. You'll have to believe our story. The old lady never put foot in this tavern."

The two men he addressed peered into the shadowy recesses before them, and one of them, a tall and uncommonly good-looking young man of stalwart build and unusually earnest manner, stepped softly inside. He was a gentleman farmer living near, recently appointed deputy sheriff on account of a recent outbreak of horse-stealing in the neighbourhood.

"I observe," he remarked, after a hurried glance about him, "that the paper on these walls is not at all like that she describes. She was very particular about the paper; said that it was of a muddy pink colour and had big scrolls on it which seemed to move and crawl about in whirls as you looked at it. This paper is blue and striped. Otherwise—"

"Let's go below," suggested his companion, who, from the deference with which his most casual word was received, was evidently a man of some authority. "It's cold here, and there are several new questions I should like to put to the young lady. Mr. Quimby,"—this to the landlord, "I've no doubt you are right, but we'll give this poor girl another chance. I believe in giving every one the utmost chance possible."

"My reputation is in your hands, Coroner Golden," was the quiet reply. Then, as they both turned, "my reputation against the word of an obviously demented girl."

The words made their own echo. As the third man moved to follow the other two into the hall, he seemed to catch this echo, for he involuntarily cast another look behind him as if expectant of some contradiction reaching him from the bare and melancholy walls he was leaving. But no such contradiction came. Instead, he appeared to read confirmation there of the landlord's plain and unembittered statement. The dull blue paper with its old-fashioned and uninteresting stripes seemed to have disfigured the walls for years. It was not only grimy with age, but showed here and there huge discoloured spots, especially around the stovepipe-hole high up on the left-hand side. Certainly he was a dreamer to doubt such plain evidences as these. Yet—

Here his eye encountered Quimby's, and pulling himself up short, he hastily fell into the wake of his comrade now hastening down the narrow passage to the wider hall in front. Had it occurred to him to turn again before rounding the corner—but no, I doubt if he would have learned anything even then. The closing of a door by a careful hand—the slipping up behind him of an eager and noiseless step—what is there in these to re-awaken curiosity and fix suspicion? Nothing, when the man concerned is Jacob Quimby; nothing. Better that he failed to look back; it left his judgment freer for the question confronting him in the room below.

Three Forks Tavern has been long forgotten, but at the time of which I write it was a well-known but little-frequented house, situated just back of the highway on the verge of the forest lying between the two towns of Chester and Danton in southern Ohio. It was of ancient build, and had all the picturesquesness of age and the English traditions of its original builder. Though so near two thriving towns, it retained its own quality of apparent remoteness from city life and city ways. This in a measure was made possible by the nearness of the woods which almost enveloped it; but the character of the man who ran it had still more to do with it, his sympathies being entirely with the old, and not at all with the new, as witness the old-style glazing still retained in its ancient doorway. This, while it appealed to a certain class of summer boarders, did not so much meet the wants of the casual traveller, so that while the house might from some reason or other be overfilled one night, it was just as likely to be almost empty the next, save for the faithful few who loved the woods and the ancient ways of the easy-mannered host and his attentive, soft-stepping help. The building itself was of wooden construction, high in front and low in the rear, with gables toward the highway, projecting here and there above a strip of rude old-fashioned carving. These gables were new, that is, they were only a century old; the portion now called the extension, in the passages of which we first found the men we have introduced to you, was the original house. Then it may have enjoyed the sunshine and air of the valley it overlooked, but now it was so hemmed in by yards and outbuildings as to be considered the most undesirable part of the house, and Number 3 the most undesirable of its rooms; which certainly does not speak well for it.

But we are getting away from our new friends and their mysterious errand. As I have already intimated, this tavern with the curious name (a name totally unsuggestive, by the way, of its location on a perfectly straight road) had for its southern aspect the road and a broad expanse beyond of varied landscape which made the front rooms cheerful even on a cloudy day; but it was otherwise with those in the rear and on the north end. They were never cheerful, and especially toward night were frequently so dark that artificial light was resorted to as early as three o'clock in the afternoon. It was so to-day in the remote parlour which these three now entered. A lamp had been lit, though the daylight still struggled feebly in, and it was in this conflicting light that there rose up before them the vision of a woman, who seen at any time and in any place would have drawn, if not held, the eye, but seen in her present attitude and at such a moment of question and suspense, struck the imagination with a force likely to fix her image forever in the mind, if not in the heart, of a sympathetic observer.

I should like to picture her as she stood there, because the impression she made at this instant determined the future action of the man I have introduced to you as not quite satisfied with the appearances he had observed above. Young, slender but vigorous, with a face whose details you missed in the fire of her eye and the wonderful red of her young, fresh but determined mouth, she stood, on guard as it were, before a shrouded form on a couch at the far end of the room. An imperative *Keep back!* spoke in her look, her attitude, and the silent gesture of one outspread hand, but it was the *Keep back!* of love, not of fear, the command of an outraged soul, conscious of its rights and instinctively alert to maintain them.

The landlord at sight of the rebuke thus given to their intrusion, stepped forward with a conciliatory bow.

"I beg pardon," said he, "but these gentlemen, Doctor Golden, the coroner from Chester, and Mr. Hammersmith, wish to ask you a few more questions about your mother's death. You will answer them, I am sure."

Slowly her eyes moved till they met those of the speaker.

"I am anxious to do so," said she, in a voice rich with many emotions. But seeing the open compassion in the landlord's face, the colour left her cheeks, almost her lips, and drawing back the hand which she had continued to hold outstretched, she threw a glance of helpless inquiry about her which touched the younger man's heart and induced him to say:

"The truth should not be hard to find in a case like this. I'm sure the young lady can explain. Doctor Golden, are you ready for her story?"

The coroner, who had been silent up till now, probably from sheer surprise at the beauty and simple, natural elegance of the woman caught, as he believed, in a net of dreadful tragedy, roused himself at this direct question, and bowing with an assumption of dignity far from encouraging to the man and woman anxiously watching him, replied:

"We will hear what she has to say, of course, but the facts are well known. The woman she calls mother was found early this morning lying on her face in the adjoining woods quite dead. She had fallen over a half-concealed root, and with such force that she never moved again. If her daughter was with her at the time, then that daughter fled without attempting to raise her. The condition and position of the wound on the dead woman's forehead, together with such corroborative facts as have since come to light, preclude all argument on this point. But we'll listen to the young woman, notwithstanding; she has a right to speak, and she shall speak. Did not your mother die in the woods? No hocus-pocus, miss, but the plain unvarnished truth."

"Sirs,"—the term was general, but her appeal appeared to be directed solely to the one sympathetic figure before her, "if my mother died in the wood—and, for all I can say, she may have done so—it was not till after she had been in this house. She arrived in my company, and was given a room. I saw the room and I saw her in it. I cannot be deceived in this. If I am, then my mind has suddenly failed me;—something which I find it hard to believe."

"Mr. Quimby, did Mrs. Demarest come to the house with Miss Demarest?" inquired Mr. Hammersmith of the silent landlord.

"She says so," was the reply, accompanied by a compassionate shrug which spoke volumes. "And I am quite sure she means it," he added, with kindly emphasis. "But ask Jake, who was in the office all the evening. Ask my wife, who saw the young lady to her room. Ask anybody and everybody who was around the tavern last night. I'm not the only one to say that Miss Demarest came in alone. All will tell you that she arrived here without escort of any kind; declined supper, but wanted a room, and when I hesitated to give it to her, said by way of explanation of her lack of a companion that she had had trouble in Chester and had left town very hurriedly for her home. That her mother was coming to meet her and would probably arrive here very soon. That when this occurred I was to notify her; but if a gentleman called instead, I was to be very careful not to admit that any such person as herself was in the house. Indeed, to avoid any such possibility she prayed that her name might be left off the register—a favour which I was slow in granting her, but which I finally did, as you can see for yourselves."

"Oh!" came in indignant exclamation from the young woman before them. "I understand my position now. This man has a bad conscience. He has something to hide, or he would not take to lying about little things like that. I never asked him to allow me to leave my name off the register. On the contrary I wrote my name in it and my mother's name, too. Let him bring the book here and you will see."

"We have seen," responded the coroner. "We looked in the register ourselves. Your names are not there."

The flush of indignation which had crimsoned her cheeks faded till she looked as startling and individual in her pallor as she had the moment before in her passionate bloom.

"Not there?" fell from her lips in a frozen monotone as her eyes grew fixed upon the faces before her and her hand went groping around for some support.

Mr. Hammersmith approached with a chair.

"Sit," he whispered. Then, as she sank slowly into an attitude of repose, he added gently, "You shall have every consideration. Only tell the truth, the exact truth without any heightening from your imagination, and, above all, don't be frightened."

She may have heard his words, but she gave no sign of comprehending them. She was following the movements of the landlord, who had slipped out to procure the register, and now stood holding it out toward the coroner.

"Let her see for herself," he suggested, with a bland, almost fatherly, air.

Doctor Golden took the book and approached Miss Demarest.

"Here is a name very unlike yours," he pointed out, as her eye fell on the page he had opened to. "Annette Colvin, Lansing, Michigan."

"That is not my name or writing," said she.

"There is room below it for your name and that of your mother, but the space is blank, do you see?"

"Yes, yes, I see," she admitted, "Yet I wrote my name in the book! Or is it all a monstrous dream!"

The coroner returned the book to the landlord.

"Is this your only book?" he asked.

"The only book."

Miss Demarest's eyes flashed. Hammersmith, who had watched this scene with intense interest, saw, or believed that he saw, in this flash the natural indignation of a candid mind face to face with arrant knavery. But when he forced himself to consider the complacent Quimby he did not know what to think. His aspect of self-confidence equalled hers. Indeed, he showed the greater poise. Yet her tones rang true as she cried:

"You made up one plausible story, and you may well make up another. I demand the privilege of relating the whole occurrence as I remember it," she continued with an appealing look in the one sympathetic direction. "Then you can listen to him."

"We desire nothing better," returned the coroner.

"I shall have to mention a circumstance very mortifying to myself," she proceeded, with a sudden effort at self-control, which commanded the admiration even of the coroner. "My one adviser is dead," here her eyes flashed for a moment toward the silent form behind her. "If I make mistakes, if I seem unwomanly—but you have asked for the truth and you shall have it, all of it. I have no father. Since early this morning I have had no mother. But when I had, I found it my duty to work for her as well as for myself, that she might have the comforts she had been used to and could no longer afford. For this purpose I sought a situation in Chester, and found one in a family I had rather not name." A momentary tremor, quickly suppressed, betrayed the agitation which this allusion cost her. "My mother lived in Danton (the next town to the left). Anybody there will tell you what a good woman she was. I had wished her to live in Chester (that is, at first; later, I—I was glad she didn't), but she had been born in Danton, and could not accustom herself to strange surroundings. Once a week I went home, and once a week, usually on a Wednesday, she would come and meet me on the highroad, for a little visit. Once we met here, but this is a circumstance no one seems to remember. I was very fond of my mother and she of me. Had I loved no one else, I should have been happy still, and not been obliged to face strangers over her body and bare the secrets of my heart to preserve my good name. There is a man, he seems a thousand miles away from me now, so much have I lived since yesterday. He—he lived in the house where I did—was one of the family—always at table—always before my eyes. He fancied me. I—I might have fancied him had he been a better man. But he was far from being of the sort my mother approved, and when he urged his suit too far, I grew frightened and finally ran away. It was not so much that I could not trust him," she bravely added after a moment of silent confusion, "but that I could not trust myself. He had an unfortunate influence over me, which I hated while I half yielded to it."

"You ran away. When was this?"

"Yesterday afternoon at about six. He had vowed that he would see me again before the evening was over, and I took that way to prevent a meeting. There was no other so simple,—or such was my thought at the time. I did not dream that sorrows awaited me in this quiet tavern, and perplexities so much greater than any which could have followed a meeting with him that I feel my reason fail when I contemplate them."

"Go on," urged the coroner, after a moment of uneasy silence. "Let us hear what happened after you left your home in Chester."

"I went straight to the nearest telegraph office, and sent a message to my mother. I told her I was coming home, and for her to meet me on the road near this tavern. Then

I went to Hudson's and had supper, for I had not eaten before leaving my employer's. The sun had set when I finally started, and I walked fast so as to reach Three Forks before dark. If my mother had got the telegram at once, which I calculated on her doing, as she lived next door to the telegraph office in Danton, she would be very near this place on my arrival here. So I began to look for her as soon as I entered the woods. But I did not see her. I came as far as the tavern door, and still I did not see her. But farther on, just where the road turns to cross the railroad-track, I spied her coming, and ran to meet her. She was glad to see me, but asked a good many questions which I had some difficulty in answering. She saw this, and held me to the matter till I had satisfied her. When this was done it was late and cold, and we decided to come to the tavern for the night. *And we came!* Nothing shall ever make me deny so positive a fact. We came, and this man received us."

With her final repetition of this assertion, she rose and now stood upright, with her finger pointing straight at Quimby. Had he cringed or let his eyes waver from hers by so much as a hair's breadth, her accusation would have stood and her cause been won. But not a flicker disturbed the steady patience of his look, and Hammersmith, who had made no effort to hide his anxiety to believe her story, showed his disappointment with equal frankness as he asked:

"Who else was in the office? Surely Mr. Quimby was not there alone?"

She reseated herself before answering. Hammersmith could see the effort she made to recall that simple scene. He found himself trying to recall it, too—the old-fashioned, smoke-begrimed office, with its one long window toward the road and the glass-paned door leading into the hall of entrance. They had come in by that door and crossed to the bar, which was also the desk in this curious old hostelry. He could see them standing there in the light of possibly a solitary lamp, the rest of the room in shadow unless a game of checkers were on, which evidently was not so on this night. Had she turned her head to peer into those shadows? It was not likely. She was supported by her mother's presence, and this she was going to say. By some strange telepathy that he would have laughed at a few hours before, he feels confident of her words before she speaks. Yet he listens intently as she finally looks up and answers:

"There was a man, I am sure there was a man somewhere at the other end of the office. But I paid no attention to him. I was bargaining for two rooms and registering my name and that of my mother."

"Two rooms; why two? You are not a fashionable young lady to require a room alone."

"Gentlemen, I was tired. I had been through a wearing half-hour. I knew that if we occupied the same room or even adjoining ones that nothing could keep us from a night of useless and depressing conversation. I did not feel equal to it, so I asked for two rooms a short distance apart."

An explanation which could at least be accepted. Mr. Hammersmith felt an increase of courage and scarcely winced as his colder-blooded companion continued this unofficial examination by asking:

"Where were you standing when making these arrangements with Mr. Quimby?"

"Right before the desk."

"And your mother?"

"She was at my left and a little behind me. She was a shy woman. I usually took the lead when we were together."

"Was she veiled?" the coroner continued quietly.

"I think so. She had been crying—" The bereaved daughter paused.

"But don't you know?"

"My impression is that her veil was down when we came into the room. She may have lifted it as she stood there. I know that it was lifted as we went upstairs. I remember feeling glad that the lamps gave so poor a light, she looked so distressed."

"Physically, do you mean, or mentally?"

Mr. Hammersmith asked this question. It seemed to rouse some new train of thought in the girl's mind. For a minute she looked intently at the speaker, then she replied in a disturbed tone:

"Both. I wonder—" Here her thought wavered and she ceased.

"Go on," ordered the coroner impatiently. "Tell your story. It contradicts that of the landlord in almost every point, but we've promised to hear it out, and we will."

Rousing, she hastened to obey him.

"Mr. Quimby told the truth when he said that he asked me if I would have supper, also when he repeated what I said about a gentleman, but not when he declared that I wished to be told if my mother should come and ask for me. My mother was at my side all the time we stood there talking, and I did not need to make any requests concerning her. When we went to our rooms a woman accompanied us. He says she is his wife. I should like to see that woman."

"I am here, miss," spoke up a voice from a murky corner no one had thought of looking in till now.

Miss Demarest at once rose, waiting for the woman to come forward. This she did with a quick, natural step which insensibly prepared the mind for the brisk, assertive woman who now presented herself. Mr. Hammersmith, at sight of her open, not unpleasing face, understood for the first time the decided attitude of the coroner. If this woman corroborated her husband's account, the poor young girl, with her incongruous beauty and emotional temperament, would not have much show. He looked to see her quailing now. But instead of that she stood firm, determined, and feverishly beautiful.

"Let her tell you what took place upstairs," she cried. "She showed us the rooms and carried water afterward to the one my mother occupied."

"I am sorry to contradict the young lady," came in even tones from the unembarrassed, motherly looking woman thus appealed to. "She thinks that her mother was with her and that I conducted this mother to another room after showing her to her own. I don't doubt in the least that she has worked herself up to the point of absolutely believing this. But the facts are these: She came alone and went to her room unattended by any one but myself. And what is more, she seemed entirely composed at the time, and I never thought of suspecting the least thing wrong. Yet her mother lay all that time in the wood—"

"Silence!"

This word was shot at her by Miss Demarest, who had risen to her full height and now fairly flamed upon them all in her passionate indignation. "I will not listen to such words till I have finished all I have to say and put these liars to the blush. My mother was with me, and this woman witnessed our good-night embrace, and then showed my mother to her own room. I watched them going. They went down the hall to the left and around a certain corner. I stood looking after them till they turned this corner, then I closed my door and began to take off my hat. But I wasn't quite satisfied with the good-night which had passed between my poor mother and myself, and presently I opened my door and ran down the hall and around the corner on a chance of finding her room. I don't remember very well how that hall looked. I passed several doors seemingly shut for the night, and should have turned back, confused, if at that moment I had not spied the landlady's figure, your figure, madam, coming out of one room on your way to another. You were carrying a pitcher, and I made haste and ran after you and reached the door just before you turned to shut it. Can you deny that, or that you stepped aside while I ran in and gave my mother another hug? If you can and do, then you are a dangerous and lying woman, or I— But I won't admit that I'm not all right. It is you, base and untruthful woman, who for some end I cannot fathom persist in denying facts on which my honour, if not my life, depends. Why, gentlemen, you, one of you at least, have heard me describe the very room in which I saw my mother. It is imprinted on my mind. I didn't know at the time that I took especial notice of it, but hardly a detail escaped me. The paper on the wall—"

"We have been looking through the rooms," interpolated the coroner. "We do not find any papered with the muddy pink you talk about."

She stared, drew back from them all, and finally sank into a chair. "You do not find— But you have not been shown them all."

"I think so."

"You have not. There *is* such a room. I could not have dreamed it."

Silence met this suggestion.

Throwing up her hands like one who realises for the first time that the battle is for life, she let an expression of her despair and desolation rush in frenzy from her lips:

"It's a conspiracy. The whole thing is a conspiracy. If my mother had had money on her or had worn valuable jewelry, I should believe her to have been a victim of this lying man and woman. As it is, I don't trust them. They say that my poor mother was found lying ready dressed and quite dead in the wood. That may be true, for I saw men bringing her in. But if so, what warrant have we that she was not lured there, slaughtered, and made to seem the victim of accident by this unscrupulous man and woman? Such things have been done; but for a daughter to fabricate such a plot as they impute to me is past belief, out of Nature and impossible. With all their wiles, they cannot prove it. I dare them to do so; I dare any one to do so."

Then she begged to be allowed to search the house for the room she so well remembered. "When I show you that," she cried, with ringing assurance, "you will believe the rest of my story."

"Shall I take the young lady up myself?" asked Mr. Quimby. "Or will it be enough if my wife accompanies her?"

"We will all accompany her," said the coroner.

"Very good," came in hearty acquiescence.

"It's the only way to quiet her," he whispered in Mr. Hammersmith's ear.

The latter turned on him suddenly.

"None of your insinuations," he cried. "She's as far from insane as I am myself. We shall find the room."

"You, too," fell softly from the other's lips as he stepped back into the coroner's wake. Mr. Hammersmith gave his arm to Miss Demarest, and the landlady brought up the rear.

"Upstairs," ordered the trembling girl. "We will go first to the room I occupied."

As they reached the door, she motioned them all back, and started away from them down the hall. Quickly they followed. "It was around a corner," she muttered broodingly, halting at the first turning. "That is all I remember. But we'll visit every room."

"We have already," objected the coroner, but meeting Mr. Hammersmith's warning look, he desisted from further interference.

"I remember its appearance perfectly. I remember it as if it were my own," she persisted, as door after door was thrown back and as quickly shut again at a shake of her head. "Isn't there another hall? Might I not have turned some other corner?"

"Yes, there is another hall," acquiesced the landlord, leading the way into the passage communicating with the extension.

"Oh!" she murmured, as she noted the increased interest in both the coroner and his companion; "we shall find it here."

"Do you recognise the hall?" asked the coroner as they stepped through a narrow opening into the old part.

"No, but I shall recognise the room."

"Wait!" It was Hammersmith who called her back as she was starting forward. "I should like you to repeat just how much furniture this room contained and where it stood."

She stopped, startled, and then said:

"It was awfully bare; a bed was on the left—"

"On the left?"

"She said the left," quoth the landlord, "though I don't see that it matters; it's all fancy with her."

"Go on," kindly urged Hammersmith.

"There was a window. I saw the dismal panes and my mother standing between them and me. I can't describe the little things."

"Possibly because there were none to describe," whispered Hammersmith in his superior's ear.

Meanwhile the landlord and his wife awaited their advance with studied patience. As Miss Demarest joined him, he handed her a bunch of keys, with the remark:

"None of these rooms are occupied to-day, so you can open them without hesitation."

She stared at him and ran quickly forward. Mr. Hammersmith followed speedily after. Suddenly both paused. She had lost the thread of her intention before opening a single door.

"I thought I could go straight to it," she declared. "I shall have to open all the doors, as we did in the other hall."

"Let me help you," proffered Mr. Hammersmith. She accepted his aid, and the search recommenced with the same results as before. Hope sank to disappointment as each door was passed. The vigour of her step was gone, and as she paused heartsick before the last and only remaining door, it was with an ashy face she watched Mr. Hammersmith stoop to insert the key.

He, on his part, as the door fell back, watched her for some token of awakened interest. But he watched in vain. The smallness of the room, its bareness, its one window, the absence of all furniture save the solitary cot drawn up on the right (not on the left, as she had said), seemed to make little or no impression on her.

"The last! the last! and I have not found it. Oh, sir," she moaned, catching at Mr. Hammersmith's arm, "am I then mad? Was it a dream? Or is this a dream? I feel that I no longer know." Then, as the landlady officiously stepped up, she clung with increased frenzy to Mr. Hammersmith, crying, with positive wildness, "*This* is the dream! The room I remember is a real one and my story is real. Prove it, or my reason will leave me. I feel it going—going—"

"Hush!" It was Hammersmith who sought thus to calm her. "Your story *is* real and I will prove it so. Meanwhile trust your reason. It will not fail you."

He had observed the corners of the landlord's hitherto restrained lips settle into a slightly sarcastic curl as the door of this room closed for the second time.

II

The girl's beauty has imposed on you."

"I don't think so. I should be sorry to think myself so weak. I simply credit her story more than I do that of Quimby."

"But his is supported by several witnesses. Hers has no support at all."

"That is what strikes me as so significant. This man Quimby understands himself. Who are his witnesses? His wife and his head man. There is nobody else. In the half-hour which has just passed I have searched diligently for some disinterested testimony supporting his assertion, but I have found none. No one knows anything. Of the three persons occupying rooms in the extension last night, two were asleep and the third overcome with drink. The maids won't talk. They seem uneasy, and I detected a sly look pass from the one to the other at some question I asked, but they won't talk. There's a conspiracy somewhere. I'm as sure of it as that I am standing here."

"Nonsense! What should there be a conspiracy about? You would make this old woman an important character. Now we know that she wasn't. Look at the matter as it presents itself to an unprejudiced mind. A young and susceptible girl falls in love with a man, who is at once a gentleman and a scamp. She may have tried to resist her feelings, and she may not have. Your judgment and mine would probably differ on this point. What she does *not* do is to let her mother into her confidence. She sees the man—runs upon him, if you will, in places or under circumstances she cannot avoid—till her judgment leaves her and the point of catastrophe is reached. Then, possibly, she awakens, or what is more probable, seeks to protect herself from the penetration and opposition of his friends by meetings less open than those in which they had lately indulged. She says that she left the house to escape seeing him again last night. But this is not true. On the contrary, she must have given him to understand where she was going, for she had an interview with him in the woods before she came upon her mother. He acknowledges to the interview. I have just had a talk with him over the telephone."

"Then you know his name?"

"Yes, of course, she had to tell me. It's young Maxwell. I suspected it from the first."

"Maxwell!" Mr. Hammersmith's cheek showed an indignant colour. Or was it a reflection from the setting sun? "You called him a scamp a few minutes ago. A scamp's word isn't worth much."

"No, but it's evidence when on oath, and I fancy he will swear to the interview."

"Well, well, say there was an interview."

"It changes things, Mr. Hammersmith. It changes things. It makes possible a certain theory of mine which accounts for all the facts."

"It does!"

"Yes. I don't think this girl is really responsible. I don't believe she struck her mother or is deliberately telling a tissue of lies to cover up some dreadful crime. I consider her the victim of a mental hallucination, the result of some great shock. Now what was the shock? I'll tell you. This is how I see it, how Mr. Quimby sees it, and such others in the house as have ventured an opinion. She was having this conversation with her lover in the woods below here when her mother came in sight. Surprised, for she had evidently not expected her mother to be so prompt, she hustled her lover off and hastened to meet the approaching figure. But it was too late. The mother had seen the man, and in the excitement of the discovery and the altercation which undoubtedly followed, made such a sudden move, possibly of indignant departure, that her foot was caught by one of the roots protruding at this point and she fell her whole length and with such violence as to cause immediate death. Now, Mr. Hammersmith, stop a minute and grasp the situation. If, as I believe at this point in the inquiry, Miss Demarest had encountered a passionate opposition to her desires from this upright and thoughtful mother, the spectacle of this mother lying dead before her, with all opposition gone and the way cleared in an instant to her wishes, but cleared in a manner which must haunt her to her own dying day, was enough to turn a brain already heated with contending emotions. Fancies took the place of facts, and by the time she reached this house had so woven themselves into a concrete form that no word she now utters can be relied on. This is how I see it, Mr. Hammersmith, and it is on this basis I shall act."

Hammersmith made an effort and, nodding slightly, said in a restrained tone:

"Perhaps you are justified. I have no wish to force my own ideas upon you; they are much too vague at present. I will only suggest that this is not the first time the attention of the police has been drawn to this house by some mysterious occurrence. You remember the Stevens case? There must have been notes to the amount of seven thousand dollars in the pile he declared had been taken from him some time during the day and night he lodged here."

"Stevens! I remember something about it. But they couldn't locate the theft here. The fellow had been to the fair in Chester all day and couldn't swear that he had seen his notes after leaving the grounds."

"I know. But he always looked on Quimby as the man. Then there is the adventure of little Miss Thistlewaite."

"I don't remember that."

"It didn't get into the papers; but it was talked about in the neighbourhood. She is a quaint one, full of her crotchets, but clear—clear as a bell where her interests are involved. She took a notion to spend a summer here—in this house, I mean. She had a room in one of the corners overlooking the woods, and professing to prefer Nature to everything else, was happy enough till she began to miss things—rings, pins, a bracelet and, finally, a really valuable chain. She didn't complain at first—the objects were trivial, and she herself somewhat to blame for leaving them lying around in her room, often without locking the door. But when the chain went, the matter became serious, and she called Mr. Quimby's attention to her losses. He advised her to lock her door, which she was careful to do after that, but not with the expected result. She continued to miss things, mostly jewelry of which she had a ridiculous store. Various domestics were dismissed, and finally one of the permanent boarders was requested to leave, but still the thefts went on till, her patience being exhausted, she notified the police and a detective was sent: I have always wished I had been that detective. The case ended in what was always considered a joke. Another object disappeared while he was there, and it having been conclusively proved to him that it could not have been taken by way of the door, he turned his attention to the window which it was one of her freaks always to keep wide open. The result was curious. One day he spied from a hiding-place he had made in the bushes a bird flying out from that window, and following the creature till she alighted in her nest he climbed the tree and searched that nest. It was encrusted with jewels. The bird was a magpie and had followed its usual habits, but—the chain was not there, nor one or two other articles of decided value. Nor were they ever found. The bird bore the blame; the objects missing were all heavy and might have been dropped in its flight, but I have always thought that the bird had an accomplice, a knowing fellow who understood what's what and how to pick out his share."

The coroner smiled. There was little conviction and much sarcasm in that smile. Hammersmith turned away. "Have you any instructions for me?" he said.

"Yes, you had better stay here. I will return in the morning with my jury. It won't take long after that to see this thing through."

The look he received in reply was happily hidden from him.

III

Yes, I'm going to stay here to-night. As it's a mere formality, I shall want a room to sit in, and if you have no objection I'll take Number 3 on the rear corridor."

"I'm sorry, but Number 3 is totally unfit for use, as you've already seen."

"Oh, I'm not particular. Put a table in and a good light, and I'll get along with the rest. I have something to do. Number 3 will answer."

The landlord shifted his feet, cast a quick scrutinising look at the other's composed face, and threw back his head with a quick laugh.

"As you will. I can't make you comfortable on such short notice, but that's your lookout. I've several other rooms vacant."

"I fancy that room," was all the reply he got.

Mr. Quimby at once gave his orders. They were received by Jake with surprise.

Fifteen minutes later Hammersmith prepared to install himself in these desolate quarters. But before doing so he walked straight to the small parlour where he had last seen Miss Demarest and, knocking, asked for the privilege of a word with her. It was not her figure, however, which appeared in the doorway, but that of the landlady.

"Miss Demarest is not here," announced that buxom and smooth-tongued woman. "She was like to faint after you gentlemen left the room, and I just took her upstairs to a quiet place by herself."

"On the rear corridor?"

"Oh, no, sir; a nice front room; we don't consider money in a case like this."

"Will you give me its number?"

Her suave and steady look changed to one of indignation.

"You're asking a good deal, aren't you? I doubt if the young lady—"

"The number, if you please," he quietly put in.

"Thirty-two," she snapped out. "She will have every care," she hastened to assure him as he turned away.

"I've no doubt. I do not intend to sleep to-night; if the young lady is worse, you will communicate the fact to me. You will find *me* in Number 3."

He had turned back to make this reply, and was looking straight at her as the number dropped from his lips. It did not disturb her set smile, but in some inscrutable way all meaning seemed to leave that smile, and she forgot to drop her hand which had been stretched out in an attempted gesture.

"Number 3," he repeated. "Don't forget, madam."

The injunction seemed superfluous. She had not dropped her hand when he wheeled around once more in taking the turn at the foot of the staircase.

Jake and a very sleepy maid were on the floor above when he reached it. He paid no attention to Jake, but he eyed the girl somewhat curiously. She was comparatively a new domestic in the tavern, having been an inmate there for only three weeks. He had held a few minutes' conversation with her during the half-hour of secret inquiry in which he had previously indulged and he remembered some of her careful answers, also the air of fascination with which she had watched him all the time they were together. He had made nothing of her then, but the impression had remained that she was the one hopeful source of knowledge in the house. Now she looked dull and moved about in Jake's wake like an automaton. Yet Hammersmith made up his mind to speak to her as soon as the least opportunity offered.

"Where is 32?" he asked as he moved away from them in the opposite direction from the course they were taking.

"I thought you were to have room Number 3," blurted out Jake.

"I am. But where is 32?"

"Round there," said she. "A lady's in there now. The one—"

"Come on," urged Jake. "Huldah, you may go now. I'll show the gentleman his room."

Huldah dropped her head, and began to move off, but not before Hammersmith had caught her eye.

"Thirty-two," he formed with his lips, showing her a scrap of paper which he held in his hand.

He thought she nodded, but he could not be sure. Nevertheless, he ventured to lay the scrap down on a small table he was passing, and when he again looked back, saw that it was gone and Huldah with it. But whither, he could not be quite sure. There was always a risk in these attempts, and he only half trusted the girl. She might carry it to 32, and she might carry it to Quimby. In the first case, Miss Demarest would know that she had an active and watchful friend in the house; in the other, the dubious landlord would but receive an open instead of veiled intimation that the young deputy had his eye on him and was not to be fooled by appearances and the lack of evidence to support his honest convictions.

They had done little more than he had suggested to make Number 3 habitable. As the door swung open under Jake's impatient hand, the half-lighted hollow of the almost empty room gaped uninvitingly before them, with just a wooden-bottomed chair and a rickety table added to the small cot-bed which had been almost its sole furnishing when he saw it last. The walls, bare as his hand, stretched without relief from base-board to ceiling, and the floor from door to window showed an unbroken expanse of unpainted boards, save for the narrow space between chair and table, where a small rug had been laid. A cheerless outlook for a tired man, but it seemed to please Hammersmith. There was paper and ink on the table, and the lamp which he took care to examine held oil enough to last till morning. With a tray of eatables, this ought to suffice, or so his manner conveyed, and Jake, who had already supplied the eatables, was backing slowly out when his eye, which seemingly against his will had been travelling curiously up and down the walls, was caught by that of Hammersmith, and he plunged from the room, with a flush visible even in that half light.

It was a trivial circumstance, but it fitted in with Hammersmith's trend of thought at the moment, and when the man was gone he stood for several minutes with his own eye travelling up and down those dusky walls in an inquiry which this distant inspection did not seem thoroughly to satisfy, for in another instant he had lifted a glass of water from the tray and, going to the nearest wall, began to moisten the paper at one of the edges. When it was quite wet, he took out his penknife, but before using it, he looked behind him, first at the door, and then at the window. The door was shut; the window seemingly guarded by an outside blind; but the former was not locked, and the latter showed, upon closer inspection, a space between the slats which he did not like. Crossing to the door, he carefully turned the key, then proceeding to the window, he endeavoured to throw up the sash in order to close the blinds more effectually. But he found himself balked in the attempt. The cord had been cut and the sash refused to move under his hand.

Casting a glance of mingled threat and sarcasm out into the night, he walked back to the wall and, dashing more water over the spot he had already moistened, began to pick at the loosened edges of the paper which were slowly falling away. The result was a disappointment; how great a disappointment he presently realised, as his knife-point encountered only plaster under the peeling edges of the paper. He had hoped to find other paper under the blue—the paper which Miss Demarest remembered—and not finding it, was conscious of a sinking of the heart which had never attended any of his miscalculations before. Were his own feelings involved in this matter? It would certainly seem so.

Astonished at his own sensations, he crossed back to the table, and sinking into the chair beside it, endeavoured to call up his common sense, or at least shake himself free from the glamour which had seized him. But this especial sort of glamour is not so easily shaken off. Minutes passed—an hour, and little else filled his thoughts than the position of this bewitching girl and the claims she had on his sense of justice. If he listened, it was to hear her voice raised in appeal at his door. If he closed his eyes, it was to see her image more plainly on the background of his consciousness. The stillness into which the house had sunk aided this absorption and made his battle a losing one. There was naught to distract his mind, and when he dozed, as he did for a while after midnight, it was to fall under the conjuring effect of dreams in which her form dominated with all the force of an unfettered fancy. The pictures which his imagination thus brought before him were startling and never to be forgotten. The first was that of an angry sea in the blue light of an arctic winter. Stars flecked the zenith and shed a pale lustre on the moving ice-floes hurrying toward a horizon of skurrying clouds and rising waves. On one of those floes stood a woman alone, with face set toward her death.

The scene changed. A desert stretched out before him. Limitless, with the blazing colours of the arid sand topped by a cloudless sky, it revealed but one suggestion of life in its herbless, waterless, shadowless solitude. She stood in the midst of this desert, and as he had seen her sway on the ice-floe, so he saw her now stretching unavailing arms to the brazen heavens and sink— No! it was not a desert, it was not a sea, ice-bound or torrid, it was a toppling city, massed against impenetrable night one moment, then shown to its awful full the next by the sudden tearing through of lightning-flashes. He saw it all—houses, churches, towers, erect and with steadfast line, a silhouette of quiet rest awaiting dawn; then at a flash, the doom, the quake, the breaking down of outline, the caving in of walls, followed by the sickening collapse in which life, wealth, and innumerable beating human hearts went down into the unseen and unknowable. He saw and he heard, but his eyes clung to but one point, his ears listened for but one cry. There at the extremity of a cornice, clinging to a bending beam, was the figure again—the woman of the ice-floe and the desert. She seemed nearer now. He could see the straining muscles of her arm, the white despair of her set features. He wished to call aloud to her not to look down—then, as the sudden darkness yielded to another illuminating gleam, his mind changed and he would fain have begged her to look, slip, and end all, for subtly, quietly, ominously somewhere below her feet, he had caught the glimpsing of a feathery line of smoke curling up from the lower debris. Flame was there; a creeping devil which soon—

Horror! it was no dream! He was awake, he, Hammersmith, in this small solitary hotel in Ohio, and there was fire, real fire in the air, and in his ears the echo of a shriek such as a man hears but few times in his life, even if his lot casts him continually among the reckless and the suffering. Was it *hers*? Had these dreams been forerunners of some menacing danger? He was on his feet, his eyes staring at the floor beneath him, through the cracks of which wisps of smoke were forcing their way up. The tavern was not only on fire, *but on fire directly under him*. This discovery woke him effectually. He bounded to the door; it would not open. He wrenched at the key; but it would not turn, it was hampered in the lock. Drawing back, he threw his whole weight against the panels, uttering loud cries for help. The effort was useless. No yielding in the door, no rush to his assistance from without. Aroused now to his danger—reading the signs of the broken cord and hampered lock only too well—he desisted from his vain attempts and turned desperately toward the window. Though it might be impossible to hold up the sash and crawl under it at the same time, his only hope of exit lay there, as well as his only means of surviving the inroad of smoke which was fast becoming unendurable. He would break the sash and seek escape that way. They had doomed him to death, but he could climb roofs like a cat and feared nothing when once relieved from this smoke. Catching up the chair, he advanced toward the window.

But before reaching it he paused. It was not only he they sought to destroy, but the room. There was evidence of crime in the room. In that moment of keenly aroused intelligence he felt sure of it. What was to be done? How could he save the room, and, by these means, save himself and her? A single glance about assured him that he could not save it. The boards under his feet were hot. Glints of yellow light streaking through the shutters showed that the lower storey had already burst into flame. The room must go and with it every clue to the problem which was agitating him. Meanwhile, his eyeballs were smarting, his head growing dizzy. No longer sure of his feet, he staggered over to the wall and was about to make use of its support in his effort to reach the window, when his eyes fell on the spot from which he had peeled the paper, and he came to a sudden standstill. A bit of pink was showing under one edge of the blue.

Dropping the chair which he still held, he fumbled for his knife, found it, made a dash at that wall, and for a few frenzied moments worked at the plaster till he had hacked off a piece which he thrust into his pocket. Then seizing the chair again, he made for the window and threw it with all his force against the panes. They crashed and the air came rushing in, reviving him enough for the second attempt. This not only smashed the pane, but loosened the shutters, and in one instant two sights burst upon his view—the face of a man in an upper window of the adjoining barn and the sudden swooping up from below of a column of deadly smoke which seemed to cut off all hope of his saving himself by the means he had calculated on. Yet no other way offered. It would be folly to try the door again. This was the only road, threatening as it looked, to possible safety for himself and her. He would take it, and if he succumbed in the effort, it should be with a final thought of her who was fast becoming an integral part of his own being.

Meanwhile he had mounted to the sill and taken another outward look. This room, as I have already intimated, was in the rear of an extension running back from the centre of the main building. It consisted of only two stories, surmounted by a long, slightly-peaked roof. As the ceilings were low in this portion of the house, the gutter of this roof was very near the top of the window. To reach it was not a difficult feat for one of his strength and agility, and if only the smoke would blow aside—Ah, it is doing so! A sudden change of wind had come to his rescue, and for the moment the way is clear for him to work himself out and up on to the ledge above. But once there, horror makes him weak again. A window, high up in the main building overlooking the extension, had come in sight, and in it sways a frantic woman ready to throw herself out. She screamed as he measured with his eye the height of that window from the sloping roof and thence to the ground, and he recognised the voice. It was the same he had heard before, but it was not hers. She would not be up so high, besides the shape and attitude, shown fitfully by the light of the now leaping flames, were those of a heavier, and less-refined woman. It was one of the maids—it was *the* maid Huldah, the one from whom he had hoped to win some light on this affair. Was she locked in, too? Her frenzy and mad looking behind and below her seemed to argue that she was. What deviltry! and, ah! what a confession of guilt on the part of the vile man who had planned this abominable end for the two persons whose evidence he dreaded. Helpless with horror, he became a man again in his indignation. Such villainy should not succeed. He would fight not only for his own life, but for this woman's. Miss Demarest was doubtless safe. Yet he wished he were sure of it; he could work with so much better heart. Her window was not visible from where he crouched. It was on the other side of the house. If she screamed, he would not be able to hear her. He must trust her to Providence. But his dream! his dream! The power of it was still upon him; a forerunner of fate, a picture possibly of her doom. The hesitation which this awful thought caused him warned him that not in this way could he make himself effective. The woman he saw stood in need of his help, and to her he must make his way. The bustle which now took place in the yards beneath, the sudden shouts and the hurried throwing up of windows all over the house showed that the alarm had now become general. Another moment, and the appalling cry—the most appalling which leaves human lips—of fire! fire! rang from end to end of the threatened building. It was followed by women's shrieks and men's curses and then—by flames.

"She will hear, she will wake now," he thought, with his whole heart pulling him her way. But he did not desist from his intention to drop his eyes from the distraught figure entrapped between a locked door and a fall of thirty feet. He could reach her if he kept his nerve. A slow but steady hitch along the gutter was bringing him nearer every instant. Would she see him and take courage? No! her eyes were on the flames which were so bright now that he could actually see them glassed in her eyeballs. Would a shout attract her? The air was full of cries as the yards filled with escaping figures, but he would attempt it at the first lull—now—while her head was turned his way. Did she hear him? Yes. She is looking at him.

"Don't jump," he cried. "Tie your sheet to the bed-post. Tie it strong and fasten the other one to it and throw down the end. I will be here to catch it. Then you must come down hand over hand."

She threw up her arms, staring down at him in mortal terror; then, as the whole air grew lurid, nodded and tottered back. With incredible anxiety he watched for her reappearance. His post was becoming perilous. The fire had not yet reached the roof, but it was rapidly undermining its supports, and the heat was unendurable. Would he have to jump to the ground in his own despite? Was it his duty to wait for this girl, possibly already overcome by her fears and lying insensible? Yes; so long as he could hold out against the heat, it was his duty, but—Ah! what was that? Some one was shouting to him. He had been seen at last, and men, half-clad but eager, were rushing up the yard with a ladder. He could see their faces. How they glared in the red light. Help and determination were there, and perhaps when she saw the promise of this support, it would give nerve to her fingers and—

But it was not to be. As he watched their eager approach, he saw them stop, look back, swerve and rush around the corner of the house. Some one had directed them elsewhere. He could see the pointing hand, the baleful face. Quimby had realised his own danger in this prospect of Hammersmith's escape, and had intervened to prevent it. It was a murderer's natural impulse, and did not surprise him, but it added another element of danger to his position, and if this woman delayed much longer—but she is coming; a blanket is thrown out, then a dangling end of cloth appears above the sill. It descends. Another moment he has crawled up the roof to the ridge and grasped it.

"Slowly now!" he shouts. "Take time and hold on tight. I will guide you." He feels the frail support stiffen. She has drawn it into her hands; now she is on the sill, and is working herself off. He clutched his end firmly, steadying himself as best he might by bestriding the ridge of the roof. The strain becomes greater, he feels her weight, she is slipping down, down. Her hands strike a knot; the jerk almost throws him off his balance. He utters a word of caution, lost in the growing roar of the flames whose hungry tongues have begun to leap above the gutter. She looks down, sees the approaching peril, and hastens her descent. He is all astrain, with heart and hand nerved for the awful possibilities of the coming moments when—ping! Something goes whistling by his ear, which for the instant sets his hair bristling on his head, and almost paralyses every muscle. A bullet! The flame is not threatening enough! Some one is shooting at him from the dark.

IV

Well! death which comes one way cannot come another, and a bullet is more merciful than flame. The thought steadies Hammersmith; besides he has nothing to do with what is taking place behind his back. His duty is here, to guide and support this rapidly-descending figure now almost within his reach. And he fulfils this duty, though that deadly "ping" is followed by another, and his starting eyes behold the hole made by the missile in the clap-board just before him.

She is down. They stand toppling together on the slippery ridge with no support but the rapidly heating wall down which she had come. He looks one way, then another. Ten feet either way to the gutter! On one side leap the flames; beneath the other crouches their secret enemy. They cannot meet the first and live; needs must they face the latter. Bullets do not always strike the mark, as witness the two they had escaped. Besides, there are friends as well as enemies in the yard on this side. He can hear their encouraging cries. He will toss down the blanket; perhaps there will be hands to hold it and so break her fall, if not his.

With a courage which drew strength from her weakness, he carried out this plan and saw her land in safety amid half a dozen upstretched arms. Then he prepared to follow her, but felt his courage fail and his strength ooze without knowing the cause. Had a bullet struck him? He did not feel it. He was conscious of the heat, but of no other suffering; yet his limbs lacked life, and it no longer seemed possible for him to twist himself about so as to fall easily from the gutter.

"Come on! Come on!" rose in yells from below, but there was no movement in him.

"We can't wait. The wall will fall," rose affrightedly from below. But he simply clung and the doom of flame and collapsing timbers was rushing mercilessly upon him when, in the glare which lit up the whole dreadful scenery, there rose before his fainting eyes the sight of Miss Demarest's face turned his way from the crowd below, with all the terror of a woman's bleeding heart behind it. The joy which this recognition brought cleared his brain and gave him strength to struggle with his lethargy. Raising himself on one elbow, he slid his feet over the gutter, and with a frantic catch at its frail support, hung for one instant suspended, then dropped softly into the blanket which a dozen eager hands held out for him.

As he did so, a single gasping cry went up from the hushed throng. He knew the voice. His rescue had relieved one heart. His own beat tumultuously and the blood throbbed in his veins as he realised this.

The next thing he remembered was standing far from the collapsing building, with a dozen men and boys grouped about him. A woman at his feet was clasping his knees in thankfulness, another sinking in a faint at the edge of the shadow, but he saw neither, for the blood was streaming over his eyes from a wound not yet accounted for, and as he felt the burning flow, he realised a fresh duty.

"Where is Quimby?" he demanded loudly. "He made this hole in my forehead. He's a murderer and a thief, and I order you all in the name of the law to assist me in arresting him."

With the confused cry of many voices, the circle widened. Brushing the blood from his brow, he caught at the nearest man, and with one glance toward the tottering building, pointed to the wall where he and the girl Huldah had clung.

"Look!" he shouted, "do you see that black spot? Wait till the smoke blows aside. There! now! the spot just below the dangling sheet. It's a bullet-hole. It was made while I crouched there. Quimby held the gun. He had his reasons for hindering our escape. The girl can tell you—"

"Yes, yes," rose up from the ground at his feet. "Quimby is a wicked man. He knew that I knew it and he locked my door when he saw the flames coming. I'm willing to tell now. I was afraid before."

They stared at her with all the wonder of uncomprehending minds as she rose with a resolute air to confront them; but as the full meaning of her words penetrated their benumbed brains, slowly, man by man, they crept away to peer about in the barns, and among the clustering shadows for the man who had been thus denounced. Hammersmith followed them, and for a few minutes nothing but chase was in any man's mind. That part of the building in which lay hidden the room of shadows shook, tottered, and fell, loading the heavens with sparks and lighting up the pursuit now become as wild and reckless as the scene itself. To Miss Demarest's eyes, just struggling back to sight and hearing from the nethermost depths of unconsciousness, it looked like the swirling flight of spirits lost in the vortex of hell. For one wild moment she thought that she herself had passed the gates of life and was one of those unhappy souls whirling over a gulf of flame. The next moment she realised her mistake. A kindly voice was in her ear, a kindly hand was pressing a half-burned blanket about her.

"Don't stare so," the voice said. "It is only people routing out Quimby. They say he set fire to the tavern himself, to hide his crime and do away with the one man who knew about it. I know that he locked me in because I—Oh, see! they've got him! they've got him! and with a gun in his hand!"

The friendly hand fell; both women started upright panting with terror and excitement. Then one of them drew back, crying in a tone of sudden anguish, "Why, no! It's Jake, Jake!"

Daybreak! and with it Doctor Golden, who at the first alarm had ridden out post-haste without waiting to collect his jury. As he stepped to the ground before the hollow shell and smoking pile which were all that remained to mark the scene of yesterday's events, he looked about among the half-clad, shivering men and women peering from the barns and stables where they had taken refuge, till his eyes rested on Hammersmith standing like a sentinel before one of the doors.

"What's this? what's this?" he cried, as the other quickly approached. "Fire, with a man like you in the house?"

"Fire because I was in the house. They evidently felt obliged to get rid of me somehow. It's been a night of great experiences for me. When they found I was not likely to perish in the flames they resorted to shooting. I believe that my forehead shows where one bullet passed. Jake's aim might be improved. Not that I am anxious for it."

"Jake? Do you mean the clerk? Did he fire at you?"

"Yes, while I was on the roof engaged in rescuing one of the women."

"The miserable cur! You arrested him, of course, as soon as you could lay your hands on him?"

"Yes. He's back of me in this outhouse."

"And Quimby? What about Quimby?"

"He's missing."

"And Mrs. Quimby?"

"Missing, too. They are the only persons unaccounted for."

"Lost in the fire?"

"We don't think so. He was the incendiary and she, undoubtedly, his accomplice. They would certainly look out for themselves. Doctor Golden, it was not for insurance money they fired the place; it was to cover up a crime."

The coroner, more or less prepared for this statement by what Hammersmith had already told him, showed but little additional excitement as he dubiously remarked:

"So you still hold to that idea."

Hammersmith glanced about him and, catching more than one curious eye turned their way from the crowd now rapidly collecting in all directions, drew the coroner aside and in a few graphic words related the night's occurrences and the conclusions these had forced upon him. Doctor Golden listened and seemed impressed at last, especially by one point.

"You saw Quimby," he repeated; "saw his face distinctly looking toward your room from one of the stable windows?"

"I can swear to it. I even caught his expression. It was malignant in the extreme, quite unlike that he usually turns upon his guests."

"Which window was it?"

Hammersmith pointed it out.

"You have been there? Searched the room and the stable?"

"Thoroughly, just as soon as it was light enough to see."

"And found——"

"Nothing; not even a clue."

"The man is lying dead in that heap. She, too, perhaps. We'll have to put the screws on Jake. A conspiracy like this must be unearthed. Show me the rascal."

"He's in a most careless mood. *He* doesn't think his master and mistress perished in the fire."

"Careless, eh? Well, we'll see. I know that sort."

But when a few minutes later he came to confront the clerk he saw that his task was not likely to prove quite so easy as his former experience had led him to expect. Save for a slight nervous trembling of limb and shoulder—surely not unnatural after such a night—Jake bore himself with very much the same indifferent ease he had shown the day before.

Doctor Golden surveyed him with becoming sternness.

"At what time did this fire start?" he asked.

Jake had a harsh voice, but he mellowed it wonderfully as he replied:

"Somewhere about one. I don't carry a watch, so I don't know the exact time."

"The exact time isn't necessary. Near one answers well enough. How came you to be completely dressed at near one in a country tavern like this?"

"I was on watch. There was death in the house."

"Then you were in the house?"

"Yes." His tongue faltered, but not his gaze; that was as direct as ever. "I was in the house, but not at the moment the fire started. I had gone to the stable to get a newspaper. My room is in the stable, the little one high in the cock-loft. I did not find the paper at once and when I did I stopped to read a few lines. I'm a slow reader, and by the time I was ready to cross back to the house, smoke was pouring out of the rear windows, and I stopped short, horrified! I'm mortally afraid of fire."

"You have shown it. I have not heard that you raised the least alarm."

"I'm afraid you're right. I lost my head like a fool. You see, I've never lived any-where else for the last ten years, and to see my home on fire was more than I could stand. You wouldn't think me so weak to look at these muscles."

Baring his arm, he stared down at it with a forlorn shake of his head. The coro-ner glanced at Hammersmith. What sort of fellow was this! A giant with the air of a child, a rascal with the smile of a humourist. Delicate business, this; or were they both deceived and the man just a good-humoured silly?

Hammersmith answered the appeal by a nod toward an inner door. The coroner understood and turned back to Jake with the seemingly irrelevant inquiry:

"Where did you leave Mr. Quimby when you went to the cock-loft?"

"In the house?"

"Asleep?"

"No, he was making up his accounts."

"In the office?"

"Yes."

"And that was where you left him?"

"Yes, it was."

"Then, how came he to be looking out of your window just before the fire broke out?"

"He?" Jake's jaw fell and his enormous shoulders drooped; but only for a moment. With something between a hitch and a shrug, he drew himself upright and with some slight display of temper cried out, "Who says he was there?"

The coroner answered him. "The man behind you. He saw him."

Jake's hand closed in a nervous grip. Had the trigger been against his finger at that moment it would doubtless have been snapped with some satisfaction, so the barrel had been pointing at Hammersmith.

"Saw him distinctly," the coroner repeated. "Mr. Quimby's face is not to be mistaken."

"If he saw him," retorted Jake, with unexpected cunning, "then the flames had got a start. One don't see in the dark. They hadn't got much of a start when I left. So he must have gone up to my room after I came down."

"It was before the alarm was given; before Mr. Hammersmith here had crawled out of his room window."

"I can't help that, sir. It was after I left the stable. You can't mix me up with Quimby's doings."

"Can't we? Jake, you're no lawyer and you don't know how to manage a lie. Make a clean breast of it. It may help you and it won't hurt Quimby. Begin with the old lady's coming. What turned Quimby against her? What's the plot?"

"I don't know of any plot. What Quimby told you is true. You needn't expect me to contradict it!"

A leaden doggedness had taken the place of his whilom good nature. Nothing is more difficult to contend with. Nothing is more dreaded by the inquisitor. Hammersmith realised the difficulties of the situation and repeated the gesture he had previously made toward the door leading into an adjoining compartment. The coroner nodded as before and changed the tone of his inquiry.

"Jake," he declared, "you are in a more serious position than you realise. You may be devoted to Quimby, but there are others who are not. A night such as you have been through quickens the conscience of women if it does not that of men. One has been near death. The story of such a woman is apt to be truthful. Do you want to hear it? I have no objections to your doing so."

"What story? I don't know of any story. Women have easy tongues; they talk even when they have nothing to say."

"This woman has something to say, or why should she have asked to be confronted with you? Have her in, Mr. Hammersmith. I imagine that a sight of this man will make her voluble."

A sneer from Jake; but when Hammersmith, crossing to the door I've just mentioned, opened it and let in Huldah, this token of bravado gave way to a very different expression and he exclaimed half ironically, half caressingly:

"Why, she's my sweetheart! What can she have to say except that she was mighty fortunate not to have been burned up in the fire last night?"

Doctor Golden and the detective crossed looks in some anxiety. They had not been told of this relation between the two, either by the girl herself or by the others. Gifted with a mighty close mouth, she had nevertheless confided to Hammersmith that she could tell things and would, if he brought her face to face with the man who tried to shoot him while he was helping her down from the roof. Would her indignation hold out under the insinuating smile with which the artful rascal awaited her words? It gave every evidence of doing so, for her eye flashed threateningly and her whole body showed the tension of extreme feeling as she came hastily forward, and pausing just beyond the reach of his arm, cried out:

"You had a hand in locking me in. You're tired of me. If you're not, why did you fire those bullets my way? I was escaping and—"

Jake thrust in a quick word. "That was Quimby's move—locking your door. He had some game up. I don't know what it was. I had nothing to do with it."

This denial seemed to influence her. She looked at him and her breast heaved. He was good to look at; he must have been more than that to one of her restricted experience. Hammersmith trembled for the success of their venture. Would this blond young giant's sturdy figure and provoking smile prevail against the good sense which must tell her that he was criminal to the core, and that neither his principle nor his love were to be depended on? No, not yet. With a deepening flush, she flashed out:

"You hadn't? You didn't want me dead? Why, then, those bullets? You might have killed me as well as Mr. Hammersmith when you fired!"

"Huldah!" Astonishment and reproach in the tone and something more than either in the look which accompanied it. Both were very artful and betrayed resources not to be expected from one of his ordinarily careless and good-humoured aspect. "You haven't heard what I've said about that?"

"What could you say?"

"Why, the truth, Huldah. I saw you on the roof. The fire was near. I thought that neither you nor the man helping you could escape. A death of that kind is horrible. I loved you too well to see you suffer. My gun was behind the barn door. I got it and fired out of mercy."

She gasped. So, in a way, did the two officials. The plea was so specious, and its likely effect upon her so evident.

"Jake, can I believe you?" she murmured.

For answer, he fumbled in his pocket and drew out a small object which he held up before her between his fat forefinger and thumb. It was a ring, a thin, plain hoop of gold worth possibly a couple of dollars, but which in her eyes seemed to possess an incalculable value, for she had no sooner seen it than her whole face flushed and a look of positive delight supplanted the passionately aggrieved one with which she had hitherto faced him.

"You had bought *that*?"

He smiled and returned it to his pocket.

"For you," he simply said.

The joy and pride with which she regarded him, despite the protesting murmur of the discomfited Hammersmith, proved that the wily Jake had been too much for them.

"You see!" This to Hammersmith. "Jake didn't mean any harm, only kindness to us both. If you will let him go, I'll be more thankful than when you helped me down off the roof. We're wanting to be married. Didn't you see him show me the ring?"

It was for the coroner to answer.

"We'll let him go when we're assured that he means all that he says. I haven't as good an opinion of him as you have. I think he's deceiving you and that you are a very foolish girl to trust him. Men don't fire on the women they love, for any reason. You'd better tell me what you have against him."

"I haven't anything against him *now*."

"But you were going to tell us something—"

"I guess I was fooling."

"People are not apt to fool who have just been in terror of their lives."

Her eyes sought the ground. "I'm just a hardworking girl," she muttered almost sullenly. "What should I know about that man Quimby's dreadful doings?"

"Dreadful? You call them dreadful?" It was Doctor Golden who spoke.

"He locked me in my room," she violently declared. "That wasn't done for fun."

"And is that all you can tell us? Don't look at Jake. Look at me."

"But I don't know what to say. I don't even know what you want."

"I'll tell you. Your work in the house has been upstairs work, hasn't it?"

"Yes, sir. I did up the rooms—some of them," she added cautiously.

"What rooms? Front rooms, rear rooms, or both?"

"Rooms in front; those on the third floor."

"But you sometimes went into the extension?"

"I've been down the hall."

"Haven't you been in any of the rooms there,—Number 3, for instance?"

"No, sir; my work didn't take me there."

"But you've heard of the room?"

"Yes, sir. The girls sometimes spoke of it. It had a bad name, and wasn't often used. No girl liked to go there. A man was found dead in it once. They said he killed his own self."

"Have you ever heard any one describe this room?"

"No, sir."

"Tell what paper was on the wall?"

"No, sir."

"Perhaps Jake here can help us. He's been in the room often."

"The paper was blue; you know that; you saw it yourselves yesterday," blurted forth the man thus appealed to.

"Always blue? Never any other colour that you remember?"

"No; but I've been in the house only ten years."

"Oh, is that all! And do you mean to say that this room has not been redecorated in ten years?"

"How can I tell? I can't remember every time a room is repapered."

"You ought to remember this one."

"Why?"

"Because of a very curious circumstance connected with it."

"I don't know of any circumstance."

"You heard what Miss Demarest had to say about a room whose walls were covered with muddy pink scrolls."

"Oh, she!" His shrug was very expressive. Huldah continued to look down.

"Miss Demarest seemed to know what she was talking about," pursued the coroner in direct contradiction of the tone he had taken the day before. "Her description was quite vivid. It would be strange now if those walls had once been covered with just such paper as she described."

An ironic stare, followed by an incredulous smile from Jake; dead silence and immobility on the part of Huldah.

"Was it?" shot from Doctor Golden's lips with all the vehemence of conscious authority.

There was an instant's pause, during which Huldah's breast ceased its regular rise and fall; then the clerk laughed sharply and cried with the apparent lightness of a happy-go-lucky temperament:

"I should like to know if it was. I'd think it a very curious quin—quin— What's the word? quincedence, or something like that."

"The deepest fellow I know," grumbled the baffled coroner into Hammersmith's ear, as the latter stepped his way, "or just the most simple." Then added aloud: "Lift up my coat there, please."

Hammersmith did so. The garment mentioned lay across a small table which formed the sole furnishing of the place, and when Hammersmith raised it, there appeared lying underneath several small pieces of plaster which Doctor Golden immediately pointed out to Jake.

"Do you see these bits from a papered wall?" he asked. "They were torn from that of Number 3, between the breaking out of the fire and Mr. Hammersmith's escape from the room. Come closer; you may look at them, but keep your fingers off. You see that the coincidence you mentioned holds."

Jake laughed again loudly, in a way he probably meant to express derision; then he stood silent, gazing curiously down at the pieces before him. The blue paper peeling away from the pink made it impossible for him to deny that just such paper as Miss Demarest described had been on the wall prior to the one they had all seen and remembered.*

"Well, I vum!" Jake finally broke out, turning and looking from one face to another with a very obvious attempt to carry off the matter jovially. "She must have a great eye; a—a—(another hard word! What is it now?) Well! no matter. One of the kind what sees through the outside of things to what's underneath. I always thought her queer, but not so queer as that. I'd like to have that sort of power myself. Wouldn't you, Huldah?"

The girl, whose eye, as Hammersmith was careful to note, had hardly dwelt for an instant on these bits, not so long by any means as a woman's natural curiosity would seem to prompt, started as attention was thus drawn to herself and attempted a sickly smile.

But the coroner had small appreciation for this attempted display of humour, and motioning to Hammersmith to take her away, he subjected the clerk to a second examination which, though much more searching and rigorous than the first, resulted in the single discovery that for all his specious love-making he cared no more for the girl than for one of his old hats. This the coroner confided to Hammersmith when he came in looking disconsolate at his own failure to elicit anything further from the resolute Huldah.

"But you can't make her believe that now," whispered Hammersmith.

"Then we must trick him into showing her his real feelings."

"How would you set to work? He's warned, she's warned, and life if not love is at stake."

"It don't look very promising," muttered Doctor Golden, "but—"

He was interrupted by a sudden sound of hubbub without.

"It's Quimby, Quimby!" declared Hammersmith in his sudden excitement.

But again he was mistaken. It was not the landlord, but his wife, wild-eyed, dishevelled, with bits of straw in her hair from some sheltering hayrick and in her hand a heavy gold chain which, as the morning sun shone across it, showed sparkles of liquid clearness at short intervals along its whole length.

Diamonds! Miss Thistlewaite's diamonds, and the woman who held them was gibbering like an idiot!

The effect on Jake was remarkable. Uttering a piteous cry, he bounded from their hands and fell at the woman's feet.

---

*Hammersmith's first attempt to settle this fact must have failed from his having chosen a spot for his experiment where the old paper had been stripped away before the new was put on.

"Mother Quimby!" he moaned. "Mother Quimby!" and sought to kiss her hand and wake some intelligence in her eye.

Meanwhile the coroner and Hammersmith looked on, astonished at these evidences of real feeling. Then their eyes stole behind them, and simultaneously both started back for the outhouse they had just left. Huldah was standing in the doorway, surveying the group before her with trembling, half-parted lips.

"Jealous!" muttered Hammersmith. "Providence has done our little trick for us. She will talk now. Look! She's beckoning to us."

V

Speak quickly. You'll never regret it, Huldah. He's no mate for you, and you ought to know it. You have seen this paper covered with the pink scrolls before?"

The coroner had again drawn aside his coat from the bits of plaster.

"Yes," she gasped, with quick glances at her lover through the open doorway. "He never shed tears for me!" she exclaimed bitterly. "I didn't know he could for anybody. Oh, I'll tell what I've kept quiet here," and she struck her breast violently. "I wouldn't keep the truth back now if the minister was waiting to marry us. He loves that old woman and he doesn't love me. Hear him call her 'mother.' Are mothers dearer than sweethearts? Oh, I'll tell! I don't know anything about the old lady, but I do know that room 3 was repapered the night before last, and secretly, by him. I didn't see him do it, nobody did, but this is how I know: Some weeks ago I was hunting for something in the attic, when I stumbled upon some rolls of old wall-paper lying in a little cubby-hole under the eaves. The end of one of the rolls was torn and lay across the floor. I couldn't help seeing it or remembering its colour. It was like this, blue and striped. Exactly like it," she repeated, "just as shabby and old-looking. The rain had poured in on it, and it was all mouldy and stained. It smelt musty. I didn't give two thoughts to it then, but when after the old lady's death I heard one of the girls say something in the kitchen about a room being blue now which only a little while ago was pink, I stole up into the attic to see if those rolls were still there and found them every one gone. Oh, what is happening now?"

"One of the men is trying to take the diamonds from the woman and she won't let him. Her wits are evidently gone—frightened away by the horrors of the night—or she wouldn't try to cling to what has branded her at once as a thief."

The word seemed to pierce the girl. She stared out at her former mistress, who was again being soothed by the clerk, and murmured hoarsely:

"A thief! and he don't seem to mind, but is just as good to her! Oh, oh, I once served a term myself for—for a smaller thing than that and I thought that was why—

Oh, sir, oh, sir, there's no mistake about the paper. For I went looking about in the barrels and where they throw the refuse, for bits to prove that this papering had been done in the night. It seemed so wonderful to me that any one, even Jake, who is the smartest man you ever saw, could do such a job as that and no one know. And though I found nothing in the barrels, I did in the laundry stove. It was full of burned paper, and some of it showed colour, and it was just that musty old blue I had seen in the attic."

She paused with a terrified gasp; Jake was looking at her from the open door.

"Oh, Jake!" she wailed out, "why weren't you true to me? Why did you pretend to love me when you didn't?"

He gave her a look, then turned on his heel. He was very much subdued in aspect and did not think to brush away the tear still glistening on his cheek.

"I've said my last word to *you*," he quietly declared, then stood silent a moment, with slowly labouring chest and an air of deepest gloom. But, as his eye stole outside again, they saw the spirit melt within him and simple human grief take the place of icy resolution. "She was like a mother to me," he murmured. "And now they say she'll never be herself again as long as she lives." Suddenly his head rose and he faced the coroner.

"You're right," said he. "It's all up with me. No home, no sweetheart, no missus. *She* [there was no doubt as to whom he meant by that tremulous *she*] was the only one I've ever cared for and she's just shown herself a thief. I'm no better. This is our story."

I will not give it in his words, but in my own. It will be shorter and possibly more intelligible.

The gang, if you may call it so, consisted of Quimby and these two, with a servant or so in addition. Robbery was its aim; a discreet and none too frequent spoliation of such of their patrons as lent themselves to their schemes. Quimby was the head, his wife the soul of this business, and Jake their devoted tool. The undermining of the latter's character had been begun early; a very dangerous undermining, because it had for one of its elements good humour and affectionate suggestion. At fourteen he was ready for any crime, but he was mercifully kept out of the worst till he was a full-grown man. Then he did his part. The affair of the old woman was an unpremeditated one. It happened in this wise: Miss Demarest's story had been true in every particular. Her mother was with her when she came to the house, and he, Jake, was the person sitting far back in the shadows at the time the young lady registered. There was nothing peculiar in the occurrence or in their behaviour except the decided demand which Miss Demarest made for separate rooms. This attracted his attention, for the house was pretty full and only one room was available in the portion reserved for transients. What would Quimby do? He couldn't send two women away, and he was entirely too conciliatory and smooth to refuse a request made so peremptorily. Quimby did nothing. He hemmed, hawed, and looked about for his wife. She was in the inner office back of him, and, attracted by his uneasy movements, showed herself. A whispered consultation followed, during which she cast a glance Jake's way. He understood her instantly and lounged carelessly forward. "Let them have Number 3," he said. "It's all fixed for the night. I can sleep anywhere, on the settle here or even on the floor of the inner office."

He had whispered these words, for the offer meant more than appeared. Number 3 was never given to guests. It was little more than a closet and was not even furnished. A cot had been put in that very afternoon, but only to meet a special emergency. A long-impending conference was going to be held between him and his employers subsequent to closing up time, and he had planned this impromptu refuge to save himself a late walk to the stable. At his offer to pass the same over to the Demarests, the difficulty of the moment vanished. Miss Demarest was shown to the one empty room in front, and the mother—as being the one less likely to be governed by superstitious fears if it so happened that some rumour of the undesirability of the haunted Number 3 should have reached them—to the small closet so hastily prepared for the clerk. Mrs. Quimby accompanied her, and afterward visited her again for the purpose of carrying her a bowl and some water. It was then she encountered Miss Demarest, who, anxious for a second and more affectionate good-night from her mother, had been wandering the halls in a search for her room. There was nothing to note in this simple occurrence, and Mrs. Quimby might have forgotten all about it if Miss Demarest had not made a certain remark on leaving the room. The bareness and inhospitable aspect of the place may have struck her, for she stopped in the doorway and, looking back, exclaimed: "What ugly paper! Magenta, too, the one colour my mother hates." This Mrs. Quimby remembered, for she also hated magenta, and never went into this room if she could help it.

The business which kept them all up that night was one totally disconnected with the Demarests or any one else in the house. A large outstanding obligation was coming due which Quimby lacked the money to meet. Something must be done with the stolen notes and jewelry which they had accumulated in times past and had never found the will or courage to dispose of. A choice must be made of what was salable. But what choice? It was a question that opened the door to endless controversy and possibly to a great difference of opinion; for in his way Quimby was a miser of the worst type and cared less for what money would do than for the sight and feeling of the money itself, while Mrs. Quimby was even more tenacious in her passion for the trinkets and gems which she looked upon as her part of the booty. Jake, on the contrary, cared little for anything but the good of the couple to whom he had attached himself. He wished Quimby to be satisfied, but not at Mrs. Quimby's expense. He was really fond of the woman and he was resolved that she should have no cause to grieve, even if he had to break with the old man. Little did any of them foresee what the night really held for them, or on what a jagged and unsuspected rock their frail bark was about to split.

Shutting-up time came, and with it the usual midnight quiet. All the doors had been locked and the curtains drawn over the windows and across the glass doors of the office. They were determined to do what they had never done before, lay out the loot and make a division. Quimby was resolved to see the diamonds which his wife had kept hidden for so long, and she, the securities, concerning the value of which he had contradicted himself so often. Jake's presence would keep the peace; they had no reason to fear any undue urging of his claims. All this he knew, and he was not therefore surprised, only greatly excited, when, after a last quiet look and some listening at the foot of the stairs, Mr. Quimby beckoned him into the office and, telling him to lock the door behind him, stepped around the bar to summon his wife. Jake never knew how it happened. He flung the door to and locked it, as he thought, but he must have turned the key too quickly, for the bolt of the lock did not enter the jamb, as they afterward found. Meanwhile they felt perfectly secure. The jewels were brought out of Mrs. Quimby's bedroom and laid on the desk. The securities were soon laid beside them. They had been concealed behind a movable brick at the side of the fireplace. Then the discussion began, involving more or less heat and excitement.

How long this lasted no one ever knew. At half-past eleven no change of attitude had taken place either in Quimby or his wife. At twelve the only difference marked by Jake was the removal of the securities to Quimby's breast pocket, and of the diamond-studded chain to Mrs. Quimby's neck. The former were too large for the pocket, the latter too brilliant for the dark calico background they blazed against. Jake, who was no fool, noted both facts, but had no words for the situation. He was absorbed, and he saw that Quimby was absorbed, in watching her broad hand creeping over those diamonds and huddling them up in a burning heap against her heart. There was fear in the action, fierce and overmastering fear, and so there was in her eyes which, fixed and glassy, stared over their shoulders at the wall behind, as though something had reached out from that wall and struck at the very root of her being. What did it mean? There was nothing in the room to affright her. Had she gone daft? Or—

Suddenly they both felt the blood congeal in their own veins; each turned to each a horrified face, then slowly and as if drawn by a power supernatural and quite outside of their own will, their two heads turned in the direction she was looking, and they beheld standing in their midst a spectre—no, it was the figure of a living, breathing woman, with eyes fastened on those jewels,—those well-known, much-advertised jewels! So much they saw in that instant flash, then nothing! For Quimby, in a frenzy of unreasoning fear, had taken the chair from under him and had swung it at the figure. A lamp had stood on the bar top. It was caught by the backward swing of the chair, overturned and quenched. The splintering of glass mingled its small sound with an ominous thud in the thick darkness. It was the end of all things; the falling of an impenetrable curtain over a horror half sensed, yet all the greater for its mystery.

The silence—the terror—the unspeakable sense of doom which gripped them all was not broken by a heart-beat. All listened for a stir, a movement where they could see nothing. But the stillness remained unbroken. The silence was absolute. The figure which they had believed themselves to have seen had been a dream, an imagination of their overwrought minds. It could not be otherwise. The door had been locked, entrance was impossible; yet doubt held them powerless. The moments were making years of themselves. To each came in a flash a review of every earthly incident they had experienced, every wicked deed, every unholy aspiration. Quimby gritted his teeth. It was the first sound which had followed that thud and, slight as it was, it released them somewhat from their awful tension. Jake felt that he could move now, and was about to let forth his imprisoned breath when he felt the touch of icy fingers trailing over his cheek, and started back with a curse. It was Mrs. Quimby feeling about for him in the impenetrable darkness, and in another moment he could hear her smothered whisper:

"Are you there, Jake?"

"Yes; where are you?"

"Here," said the woman, with an effort to keep her teeth from striking together.

"For God's sake, a light!" came from the hollow darkness beyond.

It was Quimby's voice at last. Jake answered:

"No light for me. I'll stay where I am till daybreak."

"Get a light, you fool!" commanded Quimby, but not without a tremble in his usually mild tone.

Hard breathing from Jake, but no other response. Quimby seemed to take a step nearer, for his voice was almost at their ears now.

"Jake, you can have anything I've got so as you get a light now."

"There ain't nothing to light here. You broke the lamp."

Quiet for a moment, then Quimby muttered hoarsely:

"If you ain't scared out of your seven senses, you can go down cellar and bring up that bit of candle 'longside the ale-barrels."

Into the cellar! Not Jake. The moving of the rickety table which his fat hand had found and rested on spoke for him.

Another curse from Quimby. Then the woman, though with some hesitation, said with more self-control than could be expected:

"I'll get it," and they heard her move away from *it* toward the trap-door behind the bar.

The two men made no objection. To her that cold, black cellar might seem a refuge from the unseen horror centred here. It had not struck them so. It had its own possibilities, and Jake wondered at her courage, as he caught the sound of her groping advance and the sudden clatter and clink of bottles as the door came up and struck the edge of the bar. There was life and a suggestion of home in that clatter and clink, and all breathed easier for a moment, but only for a moment. The something lying there behind them, or was it almost under their feet, soon got its hold again upon their fears, and Jake found himself standing stock-still, listening both ways for that dreaded, or would it be welcome, movement on the floor behind, and to the dragging sound of Mrs. Quimby's skirt and petticoat as she made her first step down those cellar-stairs. What an endless time it took! He could rush down there in a minute, but she—she could not have reached the third step yet, for that always creaked. Now it did creak. Then there was no sound for some time, unless it was the panting of Quimby's breath somewhere over by the bar. Then the stair creaked again. She must be nearly up.

"Here's matches and the candle," came in a hollow voice from the trap-stairs.

A faint streak appeared for an instant against the dark, then disappeared. Another; but no lasting light. The matches were too damp to burn.

"Jake, ain't you got a match?" appealed the voice of Quimby in half-choked accents.

After a bit of fumbling a small blaze shot up from where Jake stood. Its sulphurous smell may have suggested to all, as it did to one, the immeasurable distance of heaven at that moment, and the awful nearness of hell. They could see now, but not one of them looked in the direction where all their thoughts lay. Instead of that, they rolled their eyes on each other, while the match burned slowly out: Mrs. Quimby from the trap, her husband from the bar, and Jake. Suddenly he found words, and his cry rang through the room:

"The candle! the candle! this is my only match. Where is the candle?"

Quimby leaped forward and with shaking hand held the worn bit of candle to the flame. It failed to ignite. The horrible, dreaded darkness was about to close upon them again before—before— But another hand had seized the candle. Mrs. Quimby has come forward, and as the match sends up its last flicker, thrusts the wick against the flame and the candle flares up. It is lighted.

Over it they give each other one final appealing stare. There's no help for it now; they must look. Jake's head turned first, then Mrs. Quimby, and then that of the real aggressor.

A simultaneous gasp from them all betrays the worst. It had been no phantom called into being by their overtaxed nerves. A woman lay before them, face downward on the hard floor. A woman dressed in black, with hat on head and a little satchel clutched in one stiff, outstretched hand. Miss Demarest's mother! The little old lady who had come into the place four hours before!

With a muttered execration, Jake stepped over to her side and endeavoured to raise her; but he instantly desisted, and looking up at Quimby and his wife, moved his lips with the one fatal word which ends all hope:

"Dead!"

They listened appalled. "Dead?" echoed the now terrified Quimby.

"Dead?" repeated his no less agitated wife.

Jake was the least overcome of the three. With another glance at the motionless figure, he rose, and walking around the body, crossed to the door and seeing what he had done to make entrance possible, cursed himself and locked it properly. Meanwhile, Mrs. Quimby, with her eyes on her husband, had backed slowly away till she had reached the desk, against which she now stood with fierce and furious eyes, still clutching at her chain.

Quimby watched her fascinated. He had never seen her look like this before. What did it portend? They were soon to know.

"Coward!" fell from her lips, as she stared with unrelenting hate at her husband. "An old woman who was not even conscious of what she saw! I'll not stand for this killing, Jacob. You may count me out of this and the chain, too. If you don't—" a threatening gesture finished the sentence and the two men looking at her knew that they had come up against a wall.

"Susan!" Was that Quimby speaking? "Susan, are you going back on me now?"

She pointed at the motionless figure lying in its shrouding black like an ineffaceable blot on the office floor, then at the securities showing above the edge of his pocket.

"Were we not close enough to discovery, without drawing the attention of the police by such an unnecessary murder? She was walking in her sleep. I remember her eyes as she advanced toward me; there was no sight in them."

"You lie!" It was the only word which Quimby found to ease the shock which this simple statement caused him. But Jake saw from the nature of the glance he shot at his poor old victim that her words had struck home. His wife saw it, too, but it did not disturb the set line of her determined mouth.

"You'll let me keep the chain," she said, "and you'll use your wits, now that you have used your hand, to save yourself and myself from the charge of murder."

Quimby, who was a man of great intelligence when his faculties were undisturbed by anger or shock, knelt and turned his victim carefully over so that her face was uppermost.

"It was not murder," he uttered in an indescribable tone after a few minutes of cautious scrutiny. "The old lady fell and struck her forehead. See! the bruise is scarcely perceptible. Had she been younger—"

"A sudden death from any cause in this house at just this time is full of danger for us," coldly broke in his wife.

The landlord rose to his feet, walked away to the window, dropped his head, thought for a minute, and then slowly came back, glanced at the woman again, at her dress, her gloved hands, and her little satchel.

"She didn't die in this house," fell from his lips in his most oily accents. "She fell in the woods; the path is full of bared roots, and there she must be found to-morrow morning. Jake, are you up to the little game?"

Jake, who was drawing his first full breath, answered with a calm enough nod, whereupon Quimby bade his wife to take a look outside and see if the way was clear for them to carry the body out.

She did not move. He fell into a rage; an unusual thing for him.

"Bestir yourself! do as I bid you," he muttered.

Her eyes held his; her face took on the look he had learned to dread. Finally she spoke:

"And the daughter! What about the daughter?"

Quimby stood silent; then with a sidelong leer, and in a tone smooth as oil, but freighted with purpose, "The mother first; we'll look after the daughter later."

Mrs. Quimby shivered; then as her hand spread itself over the precious chain sparkling with the sinister gleam of serpent's eyes on her broad bosom, she grimly muttered:

"How? I'm for no more risks, I tell you."

Jake took a step forward. He thought his master was about to rush upon her. But he was only gathering up his faculties to meet the new problem she had flung at him.

"The girl's a mere child; we shall have no difficulty with her," he muttered broodingly. "Who saw these two come in?"

Then it came out that no one but themselves had been present at their arrival. Further consultation developed that the use to which Number 3 had been put was known to but one of the maids, who could easily be silenced. Whereupon Quimby told his scheme. Mrs. Quimby was satisfied, and he and Jake prepared to carry it out.

The sensations of the next half-hour, as told by Jake, would make your flesh creep. They did not dare to carry a lamp to light the gruesome task, and well as they knew the way, the possibilities of a stumble or a fall against some one of the many trees they had to pass filled them with constant terror. They did stumble once, and the low cry Jake uttered caused them new fears. Was that a window they heard flying up? No; but something moved in the bushes. They were sure of this and guiltily shook in their shoes; but nothing advanced out of the shadows, and they went on.

But the worst was when they had to turn their backs upon the body left lying face downward in the cold, damp woods. Men of no compassion, unreached by ordinary sympathies, they felt the furtive skulking back, step by step, along ways commonplace enough in the daytime, but begirt with terrors now and full of demoniac suggestion.

The sight of a single thread of light marking the door left ajar for them by Mrs. Quimby was a beacon of hope which was not even disturbed by the sight of her wild figure walking in a circle round and round the office, the stump of candle dripping unheeded over her fingers, and her eyes almost as sightless as those of the form left in the woods.

"Susan!" exclaimed her husband, laying hand on her.

She paused at once. The presence of the two men had restored her self-possession.

But all was not well yet. Jake drew Quimby's attention to the register where the two names of mother and daughter could be seen in plain black and white.

"Oh, that's nothing!" exclaimed the landlord, and, taking out his knife, he ripped the leaf out, together with the corresponding one in the back. "The devil's on our side all right, or why did she pass over the space at the bottom of the page and write their two names at the top of the next one?"

He started, for his wife had clutched his arm.

"Yes, the devil's on our side thus far," said she, "but here he stops. I have just remembered something that will upset our whole plan and possibly hang us. Miss Demarest visited her mother in Number 3 and noticed the room well, and particularly the paper. Now if she is able to describe that paper, it might not be so easy for us to have our story believed."

For a minute all stood aghast, then Jake quietly remarked: "It is now one by the clock. If you can find me some of that old blue paper I once chucked under the eaves in the front attic, I will engage to have it on those four walls before daylight. Bring the raggedest rolls you can find. If it shouldn't be dry to the touch when they come to see it to-morrow, it must look so stained and old that no one will think of laying hand on it. I'll go make the paste."

As Jake was one of the quickest and most precise of workers at anything he understood, this astonishing offer struck the other two as quite feasible. The paper was procured, the furniture moved back, and a transformation made in the room in question which astonished even those concerned in it. Dawn rose upon the completed work and, the self-possession of all three having been restored with the burning up of such scraps as remained after the four walls were covered, they each went to their several beds for a half-hour of possible rest. Jake's was in Number 3. He has never said what that half-hour was to him!

The rest we know. The scheme did not fully succeed, owing to the interest awakened in one man's mind by the beauty and seeming truth of Miss Demarest. Investigation followed which roused the landlord to the danger threatening them from the curiosity of Hammersmith, and it being neck or nothing with him, he planned the deeper crime of burning up room and occupant before further discoveries could be made. What became of him in the turmoil which followed, no one could tell, not even Jake. They had been together in Jake's room before the latter ran out with his gun, but beyond that the clerk knew nothing. Of Mrs. Quimby he could tell more. She had not been taken into their confidence regarding the fire, some small grains of humanity remaining in her which they feared might upset their scheme. She had only been given some pretext for locking Huldah in her room, and it was undoubtedly her horror at her own deed when she saw to what it had committed her which unsettled her brain and made her a gibbering idiot for life.

Or was it some secret knowledge of her husband's fate, unknown to others? We cannot tell, for no sign nor word of Jacob Quimby ever came to dispel the mystery of his disappearance.

And this is the story of Three Forks Tavern and the room numbered 3.

THE DOOMDORF MYSTERY

Melville Davisson Post

THE PIONEER WAS NOT THE ONLY MAN IN THE GREAT MOUNTAINS BEHIND Virginia. Strange aliens drifted in after the Colonial wars. All foreign armies are sprinkled with a cockle of adventurers that take root and remain. They were with Braddock and La Salle, and they rode north out of Mexico after her many empires went to pieces.

I think Doomdorf crossed the seas with Iturbide when that ill-starred adventurer returned to be shot against a wall; but there was no Southern blood in him. He came from some European race remote and barbaric. The evidences were all about him. He was a huge figure of a man, with a black spade beard, broad, thick hands, and square, flat fingers.

He had found a wedge of land between the Crown's grant to Daniel Davisson and a Washington survey. It was an uncovered triangle not worth the running of the lines; and so, no doubt, was left out, a sheer rock standing up out of the river for a base, and a peak of the mountain rising northward behind it for an apex.

Doomdorf squatted on the rock. He must have brought a belt of gold pieces when he took to his horse, for he hired old Robert Steuart's slaves and built a stone house on the rock, and he brought the furnishings overland from a frigate in the Chesapeake; and then in the handfuls of earth, wherever a root would hold, he planted the mountain behind his house with peach trees. The gold gave out; but the devil is fertile in resources. Doomdorf built a log still and turned the first fruits of the garden into a hell-brew. The idle and the vicious came with their stone jugs, and violence and riot flowed out.

The government of Virginia was remote and its arm short and feeble; but the men who held the lands west of the mountains against the savages under grants from George, and after that held them against George himself, were efficient and expeditious. They had long patience, but when that failed they went up from their fields and drove the thing before them out of the land, like a scourge of God.

There came a day, then, when my Uncle Abner and Squire Randolph rode through the gap of the mountains to have the thing out with Doomdorf. The work of this brew, which had the odors of Eden and the impulses of the devil in it, could be borne no longer. The drunken negroes had shot old Duncan's cattle and burned his haystacks, and the land was on its feet.

They rode alone, but they were worth an army of little men. Randolph was vain and pompous and given over to extravagance of words, but he was a gentleman beneath it, and fear was an alien and a stranger to him. And Abner was the right hand of the land.

It was a day in early summer and the sun lay hot. They crossed through the broken spine of the mountains and trailed along the river in the shade of the great chestnut trees. The road was only a path and the horses went one before the other. It left the river when the rock began to rise and, making a detour through the grove of peach trees, reached the house on the mountain side. Randolph and Abner got down, unsaddled their horses and turned them out to graze, for their business with Doomdorf would not be over in an hour. Then they took a steep path that brought them out on the mountain side of the house.

A man sat on a big red-roan horse in the paved court before the door. He was a gaunt old man. He sat bare-headed, the palms of his hands resting on the pommel of his saddle, his chin sunk in his black stock, his face in retrospection, the wind moving gently his great shock of voluminous white hair. Under him the huge red horse stood with his legs spread out like a horse of stone.

There was no sound. The door to the house was closed; insects moved in the sun; a shadow crept out from the motionless figure, and swarms of yellow butterflies maneuvered like an army.

Abner and Randolph stopped. They knew the tragic figure—a circuit rider of the hills who preached the invective of Isaiah as though he were the mouthpiece of a militant and avenging overlord; as though the government of Virginia were the awful theocracy of the Book of Kings. The horse was dripping with sweat and the man bore the dust and the evidences of a journey on him.

"Bronson," said Abner, "where is Doomdorf?"

The old man lifted his head and looked down at Abner over the pommel of the saddle.

" 'Surely,' he said, 'he covereth his feet in his summer chamber.' "

Abner went over and knocked on the closed door, and presently the white, frightened face of a woman looked out at him. She was a little, faded woman, with fair hair, a broad foreign face, but with the delicate evidences of gentle blood.

Abner repeated his question.

"Where is Doomdorf?"

"Oh, sir," she answered with a queer lisping accent, "he went to lie down in his south room after his midday meal, as his custom is; and I went to the orchard to gather any fruit that might be ripened." She hesitated and her voice lisped into a whisper: "He is not come out and I cannot wake him."

The two men followed her through the hall and up the stairway to the door.

"It is always bolted," she said, "when he goes to lie down." And she knocked feebly with the tips of her fingers.

There was no answer and Randolph rattled the doorknob.

"Come out, Doomdorf!" he called in his big, bellowing voice.

There was only silence and the echoes of the words among the rafters. Then Randolph set his shoulder to the door and burst it open.

They went in. The room was flooded with sun from the tall south windows. Doomdorf lay on a couch in a little offset of the room, a great scarlet patch on his bosom and a pool of scarlet on the floor.

The woman stood for a moment staring; then she cried out:

"At last I have killed him!" And she ran like a frightened hare.

The two men closed the door and went over to the couch. Doomdorf had been shot to death. There was a great ragged hole in his waistcoat. They began to look about for the weapon with which the deed had been accomplished, and in a moment found it—a fowling piece lying in two dogwood forks against the wall. The gun had just been fired; there was a freshly exploded paper cap under the hammer.

There was little else in the room—a loom-woven rag carpet on the floor; wooden shutters flung back from the windows; a great oak table, and on it a big, round, glass water bottle, filled to its glass stopper with raw liquor from the still. The stuff was limpid and clear as spring water; and, but for its pungent odor, one would have taken it for God's brew instead of Doomdorf's. The sun lay on it and against the wall where hung the weapon that had ejected the dead man out of life.

"Abner," said Randolf, "this is murder! The woman took that gun down from the wall and shot Doomdorf while he slept."

Abner was standing by the table, his fingers round his chin.

"Randolph," he replied, "what brought Bronson here?"

"The same outrages that brought us," said Randolph. "The mad old circuit rider has been preaching a crusade against Doomdorf far and wide in the hills."

Abner answered, without taking his fingers from about his chin:

"You think this woman killed Doomdorf? Well, let us go and ask Bronson who killed him."

They closed the door, leaving the dead man on his couch, and went down into the court.

The old circuit rider had put away his horse and got an ax. He had taken off his coat and pushed his shirtsleeves up over his long elbows. He was on his way to the still to destroy the barrels of liquor. He stopped when the two men came out, and Abner called to him.

"Bronson," he said, "who killed Doomdorf?"

"I killed him," replied the old man, and went on toward the still.

Randolph swore under his breath. "By the Almighty," he said, "everybody couldn't kill him!"

"Who can tell how many had a hand in it?" replied Abner.

"Two have confessed!" cried Randolph. "Was there perhaps a third? Did you kill him, Abner? And I too? Man, the thing is impossible!"

"The impossible," replied Abner, "looks here like the truth. Come with me, Randolph, and I will show you a thing more impossible than this."

They returned through the house and up the stairs to the room. Abner closed the door behind them.

"Look at this bolt," he said; "it is on the inside and not connected with the lock. How did the one who killed Doomdorf get into this room, since the door was bolted?"

"Through the windows," replied Randolph.

There were but two windows, facing the south, through which the sun entered. Abner led Randolph to them.

"Look!" he said. "The wall of the house is plumb with the sheer face of the rock. It is a hundred feet to the river and the rock is as smooth as a sheet of glass. But that is not all. Look at these window frames; they are cemented into their casement with dust and they are bound along their edges with cobwebs. These windows have not been opened. How did the assassin enter?"

"The answer is evident," said Randolph: "The one who killed Doomdorf hid in the room until he was asleep; then he shot him and went out."

"The explanation is excellent but for one thing," replied Abner: "How did the assassin bolt the door behind him on the inside of this room after he had gone out?"

Randolph flung out his arms with a hopeless gesture.

"Who knows?" he cried. "Maybe Doomdorf killed himself."

Abner laughed.

"And after firing a handful of shot into his heart he got up and put the gun back carefully into the forks against the wall!"

"Well," cried Randolph, "there is one open road out of this mystery. Bronson and this woman say they killed Doomdorf, and if they killed him they surely know how they did it. Let us go down and ask them."

"In the law court," replied Abner, "that procedure would be considered sound sense; but we are in God's court and things are managed there in a somewhat stranger way. Before we go let us find out, if we can, at what hour it was that Doomdorf died."

He went over and took a big silver watch out of the dead man's pocket. It was broken by a shot and the hands lay at one hour after noon. He stood for a moment fingering his chin.

"At one o'clock," he said. "Bronson, I think, was on the road to this place, and the woman was on the mountain among the peach trees."

Randolph threw back his shoulders.

"Why waste time in a speculation about it, Abner?" he said. "We know who did this thing. Let us go and get the story of it out of their own mouths. Doomdorf died by the hands of either Bronson or this woman."

"I could better believe it," replied Abner, "but for the running of a certain awful law."

"What law?" said Randolph. "Is it a statute of Virginia?"

"It is a statute," replied Abner, "of an authority somewhat higher. Mark the language of it: 'He that killeth with the sword must be killed with the sword.' "

He came over and took Randolph by the arm.

"Must! Randolph, did you mark particularly the word 'must'? It is a mandatory law. There is no room in it for the vicissitudes of chance or fortune. There is no way round that word. Thus, we reap what we sow and nothing else; thus, we receive what we give and nothing else. It is the weapon in our own hands that finally destroys us. You are looking at it now." And he turned him about so that the table and the weapon and the dead man were before him. " 'He that killeth with the sword must be killed with the sword.' And now," he said, "let us go and try the method of the law courts. Your faith is in the wisdom of their ways."

They found the old circuit rider at work in the still, staving in Doomdorf's liquor casks, splitting the oak heads with his ax.

"Bronson," said Randolph, "how did you kill Doomdorf?"

The old man stopped and stood leaning on his ax.

"I killed him," replied the old man, "as Elijah killed the captains of Ahaziah and their fifties. But not by the hand of any man did I pray the Lord God to destroy Doomdorf, but with fire from heaven to destroy him."

He stood up and extended his arms.

"His hands were full of blood," he said. "With his abomination from these groves of Baal he stirred up the people to contention, to strife and murder. The widow and the orphan cried to heaven against him. 'I will surely hear their cry,' is the promise written in the Book. The land was weary of him; and I prayed the Lord God to destroy him with fire from heaven, as he destroyed the Princes of Gomorrah in their palaces!"

Randolph made a gesture as of one who dismisses the impossible, but Abner's face took on a deep, strange look.

"With fire from heaven!" he repeated slowly to himself. Then he asked a question. "A little while ago," he said, "when we came, I asked you where Doomdorf was, and you answered me in the language of the third chapter of the Book of Judges. Why did you answer me like that, Bronson?—'Surely he covereth his feet in his summer chamber.' "

"The woman told me that he had not come down from the room where he had gone up to sleep," replied the old man, "and that the door was locked. And then I knew that he was dead in his summer chamber like Eglon, King of Moab."

He extended his arm toward the south.

"I came here from the Great Valley," he said, "to cut down these groves of Baal and to empty out this abomination; but I did not know that the Lord had heard my prayer and visited His wrath on Doomdorf until I was come up into these mountains to his door. When the woman spoke I knew it." And he went away to his horse, leaving the ax among the ruined barrels.

Randolph interrupted.

"Come, Abner," he said; "this is wasted time. Bronson did not kill Doomdorf."

Abner answered slowly in his deep, level voice: "Do you realize, Randolph, how Doomdorf died?"

"Not by fire from heaven, at any rate," said Randolph.

"Randolph," replied Abner, "are you sure?"

"Abner," cried Randolph, "you are pleased to jest, but I am in deadly earnest. A crime has been done here against the state. I am an officer of justice and I propose to discover the assassin if I can."

He walked away toward the house and Abner followed, his hands behind him and his great shoulders thrown loosely forward, with a grim smile about his mouth.

"It is no use to talk with the mad old preacher," Randolph went on. "Let him empty out the liquor and ride away. I won't issue a warrant against him. Prayer may be a handy implement to do a murder with, Abner, but it is not a deadly weapon under the statutes of Virginia. Doomdorf was dead when old Bronson got here with his Scriptural jargon. This woman killed Doomdorf. I shall put her to an inquisition."

"As you like," replied Abner. "Your faith remains in the methods of the law courts."

"Do you know of any better methods?" said Randolph.

"Perhaps," replied Abner, "when you have finished."

Night had entered the valley. The two men went into the house and set about preparing the corpse for burial. They got candles, and made a coffin, and put Doomdorf in it, and straightened out his limbs, and folded his arms across his shot-out heart. Then they set the coffin on benches in the hall.

They kindled a fire in the dining room and sat down before it, with the door open and the red firelight shining through on the dead man's narrow, everlasting house. The woman had put some cold meat, a golden cheese and a loaf on the table. They did not see her, but they heard her moving about the house; and finally, on the gravel court outside, her step and the whinny of a horse. Then she came in, dressed as for a journey. Randolph sprang up.

"Where are you going?" he said.

"To the sea and a ship," replied the woman. Then she indicated the hall with a gesture. "He is dead and I am free."

There was a sudden illumination in her face. Randolph took a step toward her. His voice was big and harsh.

"Who killed Doomdorf?" he cried.

"I killed him," replied the woman. "It was fair!"

"Fair!" echoed the justice. "What do you mean by that?"

The woman shrugged her shoulders and put out her hands with a foreign gesture.

"I remember an old, old man sitting against a sunny wall, and a little girl, and one who came and talked a long time with the old man, while the little girl plucked yellow flowers out of the grass and put them into her hair. Then finally the stranger gave the old man a gold chain and took the little girl away." She flung out her hands. "Oh, it was fair to kill him!" She looked up with a queer, pathetic smile.

"The old man will be gone by now," she said; "but I shall perhaps find the wall there, with the sun on it, and the yellow flowers in the grass. And now, may I go?"

It is a law of the story-teller's art that he does not tell a story. It is the listener who tells it. The story-teller does but provide him with the stimuli.

Randolph got up and walked about the floor. He was a justice of the peace in a day when that office was filled only by the landed gentry, after the English fashion; and the obligations of the law were strong on him. If he should take liberties with the letter of it, how could the weak and the evil be made to hold it in respect? Here was this woman before him a confessed assassin. Could he let her go?

Abner sat unmoving by the hearth, his elbow on the arm of his chair, his palm propping up his jaw, his face clouded in deep lines. Randolph was consumed with vanity and the weakness of ostentation, but he shouldered his duties for himself. Presently he stopped and looked at the woman, wan, faded like some prisoner of legend escaped out of fabled dungeons into the sun.

The firelight flickered past her to the box on the benches in the hall, and the vast, inscrutable justice of heaven entered and overcame him.

"Yes," he said. "Go! There is no jury in Virginia that would hold a woman for shooting a beast like that." And he thrust out his arm, with the fingers extended toward the dead man.

The woman made a little awkward curtsy.

"I thank you, sir." Then she hesitated and lisped, "But I have not shoot him."

"Not shoot him!" cried Randolph. "Why, the man's heart is riddled!"

"Yes, sir," she said simply, like a child. "I kill him, but have not shoot him."

Randolph took two long strides toward the woman.

"Not shoot him!" he repeated. "How then, in the name of heaven, did you kill Doomdorf?" And his big voice filled the empty places of the room.

"I will show you, sir," she said.

She turned and went away into the house. Presently she returned with something folded up in a linen towel. She put it on the table between the loaf of bread and the yellow cheese.

Randolph stood over the table, and the woman's deft fingers undid the towel from round its deadly contents; and presently the thing lay there uncovered.

It was a little crude model of a human figure done in wax with a needle thrust through the bosom.

Randolph stood up with a great intake of the breath.

"Magic! By the eternal!"

"Yes, sir," the woman explained, in her voice and manner of a child. "I have try to kill him many times—oh, very many times!—with witch words which I have remember; but always they fail. Then, at last, I make him in wax, and I put a needle through his heart; and I kill him very quickly."

It was as clear as daylight, even to Randolph, that the woman was innocent. Her little harmless magic was the pathetic effort of a child to kill a dragon. He hesitated a moment before he spoke, and then he decided like the gentleman he was. If it helped the child to believe that her enchanted straw had slain the monster—well, he would let her believe it.

"And now, sir, may I go?"

Randolph looked at the woman in a sort of wonder.

"Are you not afraid," he said, "of the night and the mountains, and the long road?"

"Oh no, sir," she replied simply. "The good God will be everywhere now."

It was an awful commentary on the dead man—that this strange half-child believed that all the evil in the world had gone out with him; that now that he was dead, the sunlight of heaven would fill every nook and corner.

It was not a faith that either of the two men wished to shatter, and they let her go. It would be daylight presently and the road through the mountains to the Chesapeake was open.

Randolph came back to the fireside after he had helped her into the saddle, and sat down. He tapped on the hearth for some time idly with the iron poker; and then finally he spoke.

"This is the strangest thing that ever happened," he said. "Here's a mad old preacher who thinks that he killed Doomdorf with fire from Heaven, like Elijah the Tishbite; and here is a simple child of a woman who thinks she killed him with a piece of magic of the Middle Ages—each as innocent of his death as I am. And yet, by the eternal, the beast is dead!"

He drummed on the hearth with the poker, lifting it up and letting it drop through the hollow of his fingers.

"Somebody shot Doomdorf. But who? And how did he get into and out of that shut-up room? The assassin that killed Doomdorf must have gotten into the room to kill him. Now, how did he get in?" He spoke as to himself; but my uncle sitting across the hearth replied:

"Through the window."

"Through the window!" echoed Randolph. "Why, man, you yourself showed me that the window had not been opened, and the precipice below it a fly could hardly climb. Do you tell me now that the window was opened?"

"No," said Abner, "it was never opened."

Randolph got on his feet.

"Abner," he cried, "are you saying that the one who killed Doomdorf climbed the sheer wall and got in through a closed window, without disturbing the dust or the cobwebs on the window frame?"

My uncle looked Randolph in the face.

"The murderer of Doomdorf did even more," he said. "That assassin not only climbed the face of that precipice and got in through the closed window, but he shot

Doomdorf to death and got out again through the closed window without leaving a single track or trace behind, and without disturbing a grain of dust or a thread of a cobweb."

Randolph swore a great oath.

"The thing is impossible!" he cried. "Men are not killed today in Virginia by black art or a curse of God."

"By black art, no," replied Abner; "but by the curse of God, yes. I think they are." Randolph drove his clenched right hand into the palm of his left.

"By the eternal!" he cried. "I would like to see the assassin who could do a murder like this, whether he be an imp from the pit or an angel out of Heaven."

"Very well," replied Abner, undisturbed. "When he comes back tomorrow I will show you the assassin who killed Doomdorf."

When day broke they dug a grave and buried the dead man against the mountain among his peach trees. It was noon when that work was ended. Abner threw down his spade and looked up at the sun.

"Randolph," he said, "let us go and lay an ambush for this assassin. He is on the way here."

And it was a strange ambush that he laid. When they were come again into the chamber where Doomdorf died he bolted the door; then he loaded the fowling piece and put it carefully back on its rack against the wall. After that he did another curious thing: He took the blood-stained coat, which they had stripped off the dead man when they had prepared his body for the earth, put a pillow in it and laid it on the couch precisely where Doomdorf had slept. And while he did these things Randolph stood in wonder and Abner talked:

"Look you, Randolph. . . . We will trick the murderer. . . . We will catch him in the act."

Then he went over and took the puzzled justice by the arm.

"Watch!" he said. "The assassin is coming along the wall!"

But Randolph heard nothing, saw nothing. Only the sun entered. Abner's hand tightened on his arm.

"It is here! Look!" And he pointed to the wall.

Randolph, following the extended finger, saw a tiny brilliant disk of light moving slowly up the wall toward the lock of the fowling piece. Abner's hand became a vise and his voice rang as over metal.

" 'He that killeth with the sword must be killed with the sword.' It is the water bottle, full of Doomdorf's liquor, focusing the sun. . . . And look, Randolph, how Bronson's prayer was answered!"

The tiny disk of light traveled on the plate of the lock.

"It is fire from heaven!"

The words rang above the roar of the fowling piece, and Randolph saw the dead man's coat leap up on the couch, riddled by the shot. The gun, in its natural position on the rack, pointed to the couch standing at the end of the chamber, beyond the offset of the wall, and the focused sun had exploded the percussion cap.

Randolph made a great gesture, with his arm extended.

"It is a world," he said, "filled with the mysterious joinder of accident!"

"It is a world," replied Abner, "filled with the mysterious justice of God!"

THE POISONED PEN

Arthur B. Reeve

KENNEDY'S SUIT-CASE WAS LYING OPEN ON THE BED, AND HE WAS LITERALLY throwing things into it from his chiffonier, as I entered after a hurried trip up-town from the *Star* office in response to an urgent message from him.

"Come, Walter," he cried, hastily stuffing in a package of clean laundry without taking off the wrapping-paper, "I've got your suit-case out. Pack up whatever you can in five minutes. We must take the six o'clock train for Danbridge."

I did not wait to hear any more. The mere mention of the name of the quaint and quiet little Connecticut town was sufficient. For Danbridge was on everybody's lips at that time. It was the scene of the now famous Danbridge poisoning case—a brutal case in which the pretty little actress, Vera Lytton, had been the victim.

"I've been retained by Senator Adrian Willard," he called from his room, as I was busy packing in mine. "The Willard family believe that that young Dr. Dixon is the victim of a conspiracy—or at least Alma Willard does, which comes to the same thing, and—well, the senator called me up on long-distance and offered me anything I would name in reason to take the case. Are you ready? Come on, then. We've simply got to make that train."

As we settled ourselves in the smoking-compartment of the Pullman, which for some reason or other we had to ourselves, Kennedy spoke again for the first time since our frantic dash across the city to catch the train.

"Now let us see, Walter," he began. "We've both read a good deal about this case in the papers. Let's try to get our knowledge in an orderly shape before we tackle the actual case itself."

"Ever been in Danbridge?" I asked.

"Never," he replied. "What sort of place is it?"

"Mighty interesting," I answered; "a combination of old New England and new, of ancestors and factories, of wealth and poverty, and above all it is interesting for its colony of New-Yorkers—what shall I call it?—a literary-artistic-musical combination, I guess."

"Yes," he resumed, "I thought as much. Vera Lytton belonged to the colony. A very talented girl, too—you remember her in 'The Taming of the New Woman' last season? Well, to get back to the facts as we know them at present.

"Here is a girl with a brilliant future on the stage discovered by her friend, Mrs. Boncour, in convulsions—practically insensible—with a bottle of headache-powder and a jar of ammonia on her dressing-table. Mrs. Boncour sends the maid for the nearest doctor, who happens to be a Dr. Waterworth. Meanwhile she tries to restore Miss Lytton, but with no result. She smells the ammonia and then just tastes the head-ache-powder, a very foolish thing to do, for by the time Dr. Waterworth arrives he has two patients."

"No," I corrected, "only one, for Miss Lytton was dead when he arrived, accord-ing to his latest statement."

"Very well, then—one. He arrives, Mrs. Boncour is ill, the maid knows nothing at all about it, and Vera Lytton is dead. He, too, smells the ammonia, tastes the headache-powder—just the merest trace—and then he has two patients, one of them himself. We must see him, for his experience must have been appalling. How he ever did it I can't imagine, but he saved both himself and Mrs. Boncour from poisoning—cyanide, the papers say, but of course we can't accept that until we see. It seems to me, Walter, that lately the papers have made the rule in murder cases: When in doubt, call it cyanide."

Not relishing Kennedy in the humor of expressing his real opinion of the news-papers, I hastily turned the conversation back again by asking, "How about the note from Dr. Dixon?"

"Ah, there is the crux of the whole case—that note from Dixon. Let us see. Dr. Dixon is, if I am informed correctly, of a fine and aristocratic family, though not wealthy. I believe it has been established that while he was an interne in a city hospital he became acquainted with Vera Lytton, after her divorce from that artist Thurston. Then comes his removal to Danbridge and his meeting and later his engagement with Miss Willard. On the whole, Walter, judging from the newspaper pictures, Alma Willard is quite the equal of Vera Lytton for looks, only of a different style of beauty. Oh, well, we shall see. Vera decided to spend the spring and summer at Danbridge in the bungalow of her friend, Mrs. Boncour, the novelist. That's when things began to happen."

"Yes," I put in, "when you come to know Danbridge as I did after that summer when you were abroad, you'll understand, too. Everybody knows everybody else's business. It is the main occupation of a certain set, and the per-capita output of gossip is a record that would stagger the census bureau. Still, you can't get away from the note, Craig. There it is, in Dixon's own handwriting, even if he does deny it: 'This will cure your headache. Dr. Dixon.' That's a damning piece of evidence."

"Quite right," he agreed hastily; "the note was queer, though, wasn't it? They found it crumpled up in the jar of ammonia. Oh, there are lots of problems the news-papers have failed to see the significance of, let alone trying to follow up."

Our first visit in Danbridge was to the prosecuting attorney, whose office was not far from the station on the main street. Craig had wired him, and he had kindly waited to see us, for it was evident that Danbridge respected Senator Willard and everyone connected with him.

"Would it be too much to ask just to see that note that was found in the Boncour bungalow?" asked Craig.

The prosecutor, an energetic young man, pulled out of a document-case a crumpled note which had been pressed flat again. On it in clear, deep black letters were the words, just as reported:

This will cure your headache.
Dr. Dixon

"How about the handwriting?" asked Kennedy.

The lawyer pulled out a number of letters. "I'm afraid they will have to admit it," he said with reluctance, as if down in his heart he hated to prosecute Dixon. "We have lots of these, and no handwriting expert could successfully deny the identity of the writing."

He stowed away the letters without letting Kennedy get a hint as to their contents. Kennedy was examining the note carefully.

"May I count on having this note for further examination, of course always at such times and under such conditions as you agree to?"

The attorney nodded. "I am perfectly willing to do anything not illegal to accommodate the senator," he said. "But, on the other hand, I am here to do my duty for the state, cost whom it may."

The Willard house was in a virtual state of siege. Newspaper reporters from Boston and New York were actually encamped at every gate, terrible as an army, with cameras. It was with some difficulty that we got in, even though we were expected, for some of the more enterprising had already fooled the family by posing as officers of the law and messengers from Dr. Dixon.

The house was a real, old colonial mansion with tall white pillars, a door with a glittering brass knocker, which gleamed out severely at you as you approached through a hedge of faultlessly trimmed boxwoods.

Senator, or rather former Senator Willard met us in the library, and a moment later his daughter Alma joined him. She was tall, like her father, a girl of poise and self-control. Yet even the schooling of twenty-two years in rigorous New England self-restraint could not hide the very human pallor of her face after the sleepless nights and nervous days since this trouble had broken on her placid existence. Yet there was a mark of strength and determination on her face that was fascinating. The man who would trifle with this girl, I felt, was playing fast and loose with her very life. I thought then, and I said to Kennedy afterward: "If this Dr. Dixon is guilty, you have no right to hide it from that girl. Anything less than the truth will only blacken the hideousness of the crime that has already been committed."

The senator greeted us gravely, and I could not but take it as a good omen when, in his pride of wealth and family and tradition, he laid bare everything to us, for the sake of Alma Willard. It was clear that in this family there was one word that stood above all others, "Duty."

As we were about to leave after an interview barren of new facts, a young man was announced, Mr. Halsey Post. He bowed politely to us, but it was evident why he had called, as his eye followed Alma about the room.

"The son of the late Halsey Post, of Post & Vance, silversmiths, who have the large factory in town, which you perhaps noticed," 'explained the senator. "My daughter has known him all her life. A very fine young man."

Later, we learned that the senator had bent every effort toward securing Halsey Post as a son-in-law, but his daughter had had views of her own on the subject.

Post waited until Alma had withdrawn before he disclosed the real object of his visit. In almost a whisper, lest she should still be listening, he said, "There is a story about town that Vera Lytton's former husband—an artist named Thurston—was here just before her death."

Senator Willard leaned forward as if expecting to hear Dixon immediately acquitted. None of us was prepared for the next remark.

"And the story goes on to say that he threatened to make a scene over a wrong he says he has suffered from Dixon. I don't know anything more about it, and I tell you only because I think you ought to know what Danbridge is saying under its breath."

We shook off the last of the reporters who affixed themselves to us, and for a moment Kennedy dropped in at the little bungalow to see Mrs. Boncour. She was much better, though she had suffered much. She had taken only a pinhead of the poison, but it had proved very nearly fatal.

"Had Miss Lytton any enemies whom you think of, people who were jealous of her professionally or personally?" asked Craig.

"I should not even have said Dr. Dixon was an enemy," she replied evasively.

"But this Mr. Thurston," put in Kennedy quickly. "One is not usually visited in perfect friendship by a husband who has been divorced."

She regarded him keenly for a moment. "Halsey Post told you that," she said. "No one else knew he was here. But Halsey Post was an old friend of both Vera and Mr. Thurston before they separated. By chance he happened to drop in the day Mr. Thurston was here, and later in the day I gave him a letter to forward to Mr. Thurston, which had come after the artist left. I'm sure no one else knew the artist. He was here the morning of the day she died, and—and—that's every bit I'm going to tell you about him, so there. I don't know why he came or where he went."

"That's a thing we must follow up later," remarked Kennedy as we made our adieus. "Just now I want to get the facts in hand. The next thing on my program is to see this Dr. Waterworth."

We found the doctor still in bed; in fact, a wreck as the result of his adventure. He had little to correct in the facts of the story which had been published so far. But there were many other details of the poisoning he was quite willing to discuss frankly.

"It was true about the jar of ammonia?" asked Kennedy.

"Yes," he answered. "It was standing on her dressing-table with the note crumpled up in it, just as the papers said."

"And you have no idea why it was there?"

"I didn't say that. I can guess. Fumes of ammonia are one of the antidotes for poisoning of this kind."

"But Vera Lytton could hardly have known that," objected Kennedy.

"No, of course not. But she probably did know that ammonia is good for just that sort of faintness which she must have experienced after taking the powder. Perhaps she thought of sal volatile, I don't know. But most people know that ammonia in some form is good for faintness of this sort, even if they don't know anything about cyanides and—"

"Then it *was* cyanide?" interrupted Craig.

"Yes," he replied slowly. It was evident that he was suffering great physical and nervous anguish as the result of his too intimate acquaintance with the poisons in question. "I will tell you precisely how it was, Professor Kennedy. When I was called in to see Miss Lytton I found her on the bed. I pried open her jaws and smelled the sweetish odor of the cyanogen gas. I knew then what she had taken, and at the moment she was dead. In the next room I heard some one moaning. The maid said that it was Mrs. Boncour, and that she was deathly sick. I ran into her room, and though she was beside herself with pain I managed to control her, though she struggled desperately against me. I was rushing her to the bathroom, passing through Miss Lytton's room. 'What's wrong?' I asked as I carried her along. 'I took some of that,' she replied, pointing to the bottle on the dressing-table.

"I put a small quantity of its crystal contents on my tongue. Then I realized the most tragic truth of my life. I had taken one of the deadliest poisons in the world. The odor of the released gas of cyanogen was strong. But more than that, the metallic taste and the horrible burning sensation told of the presence of some form of mercury, too. In that terrible moment my brain worked with the incredible swiftness of light. In a flash I knew that if I added malic acid to the mercury—perchloride of mercury or corrosive sublimate—I would have calomel or subchloride of mercury, the only thing that would switch the poison out of my system and Mrs. Boncour's.

"Seizing her about the waist, I hurried into the dining-room. On a sideboard was a dish of fruit. I took two apples. I made her eat one, core and all. I ate the other. The fruit contained the malic acid I needed to manufacture the calomel, and I made it right there in nature's own laboratory. But there was no time to stop. I had to act just as quickly to neutralize that cyanide, too. Remembering the ammonia, I rushed back with Mrs. Boncour, and we inhaled the fumes. Then I found a bottle of peroxide of hydrogen. I washed out her stomach with it, and then my own. Then I injected some of the peroxide into various parts of her body. The peroxide of hydrogen and hydrocyanic acid, you know, make oxamide, which is a harmless compound.

"The maid put Mrs. Boncour to bed, saved. I went to my house, a wreck. Since then I have not left this bed. With my legs paralyzed I lie here, expecting each hour to be my last."

"Would you taste an unknown drug again to discover the nature of a probable poison?" asked Craig.

"I don't know," he answered slowly, "but I suppose I would. In such a case a conscientious doctor has no thought of self. He is there to do things, and he does them, according to the best that is in him. In spite of the fact that I haven't had one hour of unbroken sleep since that fatal day, I suppose I would do it again."

When we were leaving, I remarked: "That is a martyr to science. Could anything be more dramatic than his willing penalty for his devotion to medicine?"

We walked along in silence. "Walter, did you notice he said not a word of condemnation of Dixon, though the note was before his eyes? Surely Dixon has some strong supporters in Danbridge, as well as enemies."

The next morning we continued our investigation. We found Dixon's lawyer, Leland, in consultation with his client in the bare cell of the county jail. Dixon proved to be a clear-eyed, clean-cut young man. The thing that impressed me most about him, aside from the prepossession in his favor due to the faith of Alma Willard, was the nerve he displayed, whether guilty or innocent. Even an innocent man might well have been staggered by the circumstantial evidence against him and the high tide of public feeling, in spite of the support that he was receiving. Leland, we learned, had been very active. By prompt work at the time of the young doctor's arrest he had managed to secure the greater part of Dr. Dixon's personal letters, though the prosecutor secured some, the contents of which had not been disclosed.

Kennedy spent most of the day in tracing out the movements of Thurston. Nothing that proved important was turned up, and even visits to near-by towns failed to show any sales of cyanide or sublimate to any one not entitled to buy them. Meanwhile, in turning over the gossip of the town, one of the newspapermen ran across the fact that the Boncour bungalow was owned by the Posts, and that Halsey Post, as the executor of the estate, was a more frequent visitor than the mere collection of the rent would warrant. Mrs. Boncour maintained a stolid silence that covered a seething internal fury when the newspaperman in question hinted that the landlord and tenant were on exceptionally good terms.

It was after a fruitless day of such search that we were sitting in the reading-room of the Fairfield Hotel. Leland entered. His face was positively white. Without a word he took us by the arm and led us across Main Street and up a flight of stairs to his office. Then he locked the door.

"What's the matter?" asked Kennedy.

"When I took this case," he said, "I believed down in my heart that Dixon was innocent. I still believe it, but my faith has been rudely shaken. I feel that you should know about what I have just found. As I told you, we secured nearly all of Dr. Dixon's letters. I had not read them all then. But I have been going through them to-night. Here is a letter from Vera Lytton herself. You will notice it is dated the day of her death."

He laid the letter before us. It was written in a curious greyish-black ink in a woman's hand, and read:

Dear Harris:

Since we agreed to disagree we have at least been good friends, if no longer lovers. I am not writing in anger to reproach you with your new love, so soon after the old. I suppose Alma Willard is far better suited to be your wife than is a poor little actress—rather looked down on in this Puritan society here. But there is something I wish to warn you about, for it concerns us all intimately.

We are in danger of an awful mix-up if we don't look out. Mr. Thurston—I had almost said my husband, though I don't know whether that is the truth or not—who has just come over from New York, tells me that there is some doubt about the validity of our divorce. You recall he was in the

South at the time I sued him, and the papers were served on him in Georgia. He now says the proof of service was fraudulent and that he can set aside the divorce. In that case you might figure in a suit for alienating my affections.

I do not write this with ill will, but simply to let you know how things stand. If we had married, I suppose I would be guilty of bigamy. At any rate, if he were disposed he could make a terrible scandal.

Oh, Harris, can't you settle with him if he asks anything? Don't forget so soon that we once thought we were going to be the happiest of mortals—at least I did. Don't desert me, or the very earth will cry out against you. I am frantic and hardly know what I am writing. My head aches, but it is my heart that is breaking. Harris, I am yours still, down in my heart, but not to be cast off like an old suit for a new one. You know the old saying about a woman scorned. I beg you not to go back on

Your poor little deserted

VERA

As we finished reading, Leland exclaimed, "That never must come before the jury."

Kennedy was examining the letter carefully. "Strange," he muttered. "See how it was folded. It was written on the wrong side of the sheet, or rather folded up with the writing outside. Where have these letters been?"

"Part of the time in my safe, part of the time this afternoon on my desk by the window."

"The office was locked, I suppose?" asked Kennedy. "There was no way to slip this letter in among the others since you obtained them?"

"None. The office has been locked, and there is no evidence of any one having entered or disturbed a thing."

He was hastily running over the pile of letters as if looking to see whether they were all there. Suddenly he stopped.

"Yes," he exclaimed excitedly, "one of them *is* gone." Nervously he fumbled through them again. "One is gone," he repeated, looking at us, startled.

"What was it about?" asked Craig.

"It was a note from an artist, Thurston, who gave the address of Mrs. Boncour's bungalow—ah, I see you have heard of him. He asked Dixon's recommendation of a certain patent headache medicine. I thought it possibly evidential, and I asked Dixon about it. He explained it by saying that he did not have a copy of his reply, but as near as he could recall, he wrote that the compound would not cure a headache except at the expense of reducing heart action dangerously. He says he sent no prescription. Indeed, he thought it a scheme to extract advice without incurring the charge for an office call and answered it only because he thought Vera had become reconciled to Thurston again. I can't find that letter of Thurston's. It is gone."

We looked at each other in amazement.

"Why, if Dixon contemplated anything against Miss Lytton, should he preserve this letter from her?" mused Kennedy. "Why didn't he destroy it?"

"That's what puzzles me," remarked Leland. "Do you suppose some one has broken in and substituted this Lytton letter for the Thurston letter?"

Kennedy was scrutinizing the letter, saying nothing. "I may keep it?" he asked at length. Leland was quite willing and even undertook to obtain some specimens of the writing of Vera Lytton. With these and the letter Kennedy was working far into the night and long after I had passed into a land troubled with many wild dreams of deadly poisons and secret intrigues of artists.

The next morning a message from our old friend First Deputy O'Connor in New York told briefly of locating the rooms of an artist named Thurston in one of the co-operative studio apartments. Thurston himself had not been there for several days and was reported to have gone to Maine to sketch. He had had a number of debts, but before he left they had all been paid—strange to say, by a notorious firm of shyster lawyers, Kerr & Kimmel. Kennedy wired back to find out the facts from Kerr & Kimmel and to locate Thurston at any cost.

Even the discovery of the new letter did not shake the wonderful self-possession of Dr. Dixon, He denied ever having received it and repeated his story of a letter from Thurston to which he had replied by sending an answer, care of Mrs. Boncour, as requested. He insisted that the engagement between Miss Lytton and himself had been broken before the announcement of his engagement with Miss Willard. As for Thurston, he said the man was little more than a name to him. He had known perfectly all the circumstances of the divorce, but had had no dealings with Thurston and no fear of him. Again and again he denied ever receiving the letter from Vera Lytton.

Kennedy did not tell the Willards of the new letter. The strain had begun to tell on Alma, and her father had had her quietly taken to a farm of his up in the country. To escape the curious eyes of reporters, Halsey Post had driven up one night in his closed car. She had entered it quickly with her father, and the journey had been made in the car, while Halsey Post had quietly dropped off on the outskirts of the town, where another car was waiting to take him back. It was evident that the Willard family relied implicitly on Halsey, and his assistance to them was most considerate. While he never forced himself forward, he kept in close touch with the progress of the case, and now that Alma was away his watchfulness increased proportionately, and twice a day he wrote a long report which was sent to her.

Kennedy was now bending every effort to locate the missing artist. When he left Danbridge, he teemed to have dropped out of sight completely. However, with O'Connor's aid, the police of all New England were on the lookout.

The Thurstons had been friends of Halsey's before Vera Lytton had ever met Dr. Dixon, we discovered from the Danbridge gossips, and I, at least, jumped to the conclusion that Halsey was shielding the artist, perhaps through a sense of friendship when he found that Kennedy was interested in Thurston's movements. I must say I rather liked Halsey, for he seemed very thoughtful of the Willards, and was never too busy to give an hour or so to any commission they wished carried out without publicity.

Two days passed with not a word from Thurston. Kennedy was obviously getting impatient. One day a rumor was received that he was in Bar Harbor; the next it was a report from Nova Scotia. At last, however, came the welcome news that he had been located in New Hampshire, arrested, and might be expected the next day.

At once Kennedy became all energy. He arranged for a secret conference in Senator Willard's house, the moment the artist was to arrive. The senator and his daughter made a flying trip back to town. Nothing was said to anyone about Thurston, but Kennedy quietly arranged with the district attorney to be present with the note and the jar of ammonia properly safeguarded. Leland of course came, although his client could not. Halsey Post seemed only too glad to be with Miss Willard, though he seemed to have lost interest in the case as soon as the Willards returned to look after it themselves. Mrs. Boncour was well enough to attend, and even Dr. Waterworth insisted on coming in a private ambulance which drove over from a near-by city especially for him. The time was fixed just before the arrival of the train that was to bring Thurston.

It was an anxious gathering of friends and foes of Dr. Dixon who sat impatiently waiting for Kennedy to begin this momentous exposition that was to establish the guilt or innocence of the calm young physician who sat impassively in the jail not half a mile from the room where his life and death were being debated.

"In many respects this is the most remarkable case that it has ever been my lot to handle," began Kennedy. "Never before have I felt so keenly my sense of responsibility. Therefore, though this is a somewhat irregular proceeding, let me begin by setting forth the facts as I see them.

"First, let us consider the dead woman. The question that arises here is, Was she murdered or did she commit suicide? I think you will discover the answer as I proceed. Miss Lytton, as you know, was two years ago, Mrs. Burgess Thurston. The Thurstons had temperament, and temperament is quite often the highway to the divorce court. It was so in this case. Mrs. Thurston discovered that her husband was paying much attention to other women. She sued for divorce in New York, and he accepted service in the South, where he happened to be. At least it was so testified by Mrs. Thurston's lawyer.

"Now here comes the remarkable feature of the case. The law firm of Kerr & Kimmel, I find, not long ago began to investigate the legality of this divorce. Before a notary Thurston made an affidavit that he had never been served by the lawyer for Miss Lytton, as she was now known. Her lawyer is dead, but his representative in the South who served the papers is alive. He was brought to New York and asserted squarely that he had served the papers properly.

"Here is where the shrewdness of Mose Kimmel, the shyster lawyer, came in. He arranged to have the Southern attorney identify the man he had served the papers on. For this purpose he was engaged in conversation with one of his own clerks when the lawyer was due to appear. Kimmel appeared to act confused, as if he had been caught napping. The Southern lawyer, who had seen Thurston only once, fell squarely into the trap and identified the clerk as Thurston. There were plenty of witnesses to it, and it was point number two for the great Mose Kimmel. Papers were drawn up to set aside the divorce decree.

"In the meantime, Miss Lytton, or Mrs. Thurston, had become acquainted with a young doctor in a New York hospital, and had become engaged to him. It matters not that the engagement was later broken. The fact remains that if the divorce were set aside an action would lie against Dr. Dixon for alienating Mrs. Thurston's affections, and a grave scandal would result. I need not add that in this quiet little town of Danbridge the most could be made of such a suit."

Kennedy was unfolding a piece of paper. As he laid it down, Leland, who was sitting next to me, exclaimed under his breath:

"My God, he's going to let the prosecutor know about that letter. Can't you stop him?"

It was too late. Kennedy had already begun to read Vera's letter. It was damning to Dixon, added to the other note found in the ammonia-jar.

When he had finished reading, you could almost hear the hearts throbbing in the room. A scowl overspread Senator Willard's features. Alma Willard was pale and staring wildly at Kennedy. Halsey Post, ever solicitous for her, handed her a glass of water from the table. Dr. Waterworth had forgotten his pain in his intense attention, and Mrs. Boncour seemed stunned with astonishment. The prosecuting attorney was eagerly taking notes.

"In some way," pursued Kennedy in an even voice, "this letter was either overlooked in the original correspondence of Dr. Dixon or it was added to it later. I shall come back to that presently. My next point is that Dr. Dixon says he received a letter from Thurston on the day the artist visited the Boncour bungalow. It asked about a certain headache compound, and his reply was brief and, as nearly as I can find out, read, 'This compound will not cure your headache except at the expense of reducing heart action dangerously.'

"Next comes the tragedy. On the evening of the day that Thurston left, after presumably telling Miss Lytton about what Kerr & Kimmel had discovered, Miss Lytton is found dying with a bottle containing cyanide and sublimate beside her. You are all familiar with the circumstances and with the note discovered in the jar of ammonia. Now, if the prosecutor will be so kind as to let me see that note—thank you, sir. This is the identical note. You have all heard the various theories of the jar and have read the note. Here it is in plain, cold black and white—in Dr. Dixon's own handwriting: 'This will cure your headache. Dr. Dixon.'"

Alma Willard seemed as one paralyzed. Was Kennedy, who had been engaged by her father to defend her fiancé, about to convict him?

"Before we draw the final conclusion," continued Kennedy gravely, "there are one or two points I wish to elaborate. Walter, will you open that door into the main hall?"

I did so, and two policemen stepped in with a prisoner. It was Thurston, but changed almost beyond recognition. His clothes were worn, his beard shaved off, and he had a generally hunted appearance.

Thurston was visibly nervous. Apparently he had heard all that Kennedy had said and intended he should hear, for as he entered he almost broke away from the police officers in his eagerness to speak.

"Before God," he cried dramatically, "I am as innocent as you are of this crime, Professor Kennedy."

"Are you prepared to swear before *me*," almost shouted Kennedy, his eyes blazing, "that you were never served properly by your wife's lawyers in that suit?"

The man cringed back as if a stinging blow had been delivered between his eyes. As he met Craig's fixed glare he knew there was no hope. Slowly, as if the words were being wrung from him syllable by syllable, he said in a muffled voice:

"No, I perjured myself. I was served in that suit. But—"

"And you swore falsely before Kimmel that you were not?" persisted Kennedy.

"Yes," he murmured. "But—"

"And you are prepared now to make another affidavit to that effect?"

"Yes," he replied. "If—"

"No buts or ifs, Thurston," cried Kennedy, sarcastically. "What did you make that affidavit for? What is *your* story?"

"Kimmel sent for me. I did not go to him. He offered to pay my debts if I would swear to such a statement. I did not ask why or for whom. I swore to it and gave him a list of my creditors. I waited until they were paid. Then my conscience"—I could not help revolting at the thought of conscience in such a wretch, and the word itself seemed to stick in his throat as he went on and saw how feeble an impression he was making on us—"my conscience began to trouble me. I determined to see Vera, tell her all, and find out whether it was she who wanted this statement. I saw her. When at last I told her, she scorned me. I can confirm that, for as I left a man entered. I now knew how grossly I had sinned, in listening to Mose Kimmel. I fled. I disappeared in Maine. I travelled. Every day my money grew less. At last I was overtaken, captured, and brought back here."

He stopped and sank wretchedly down in a chair and covered his face with his hands.

"A likely story," muttered Leland in my ear.

Kennedy was working quickly. Motioning the officers to be seated by Thurston, he uncovered a jar which he had placed on the table. The color had now appeared in Alma's cheeks, as if hope had again sprung in her heart, and I fancied that Halsey Post saw his claim on her favor declining correspondingly.

"I want you to examine the letters in this case with me," continued Kennedy. "Take the letter which I read from Miss Lytton, which was found following the strange disappearance of the note from Thurston."

He dipped a pen into a little bottle, and wrote on a piece of paper:

What is your opinion about Cross's Headache Cure? Would you recommend it for a nervous headache?

BURGESS THURSTON,
c/o Mrs. S. Boncour

Craig held up the writing so that we could all see that he had written what Dixon declared Thurston wrote in the note that had disappeared. Then he dipped another pen into a second bottle, and for some time he scrawled on another sheet of paper. He held it up, but it was still perfectly blank.

"Now," he added, "I am going to give a little demonstration which I expect to be successful only in a measure. Here in the open sunshine by this window I am going to place these two sheets of paper side by side. It will take longer than I care to wait to make my demonstration complete, but I can do enough to convince you."

For a quarter of an hour we sat in silence, wondering what he would do next. At last he beckoned us over to the window. As we approached he said, "On sheet number one I have written with quinoline; on sheet number two I wrote with a solution of nitrate of silver."

We bent over. The writing signed "Thurston" on sheet number one was faint, almost imperceptible, but on paper number two, in black letters, appeared what Kennedy had written: "Dear Harris: Since we agreed to disagree we have at least been good friends."

"It is like the start of the substituted letter, and the other is like the missing note," gasped Leland in a daze.

"Yes," said Kennedy quickly. "Leland, no one entered your office. No one stole the Thurston note. No one substituted the Lytton letter. According to your own story, you took them out of the safe and left them in the sunlight all day. The process that had been started earlier in ordinary light, slowly, was now quickly completed. In other words, there was writing which would soon fade away on one side of the paper and writing which was invisible but would soon appear on the other.

"For instance, quinoline rapidly disappears in sunlight. Starch with a slight trace of iodine writes a light blue, which disappears in air. It was something like that used in the Thurston letter. Then, too, silver nitrate dissolved in ammonia gradually turns black as it is acted on by light and air. Or magenta treated with a bleaching-agent in just sufficient quantity to decolorize it is invisible when used for writing. But the original color reappears as the oxygen of the air acts upon the pigment. I haven't a doubt but that my analyses of the inks are correct and on one side quinoline was used and on the other nitrate of silver. This explains the inexplicable disappearance of evidence incriminating one person, Thurston, and the sudden appearance of evidence incriminating another, Dr. Dixon. Sympathetic ink also accounts for the curious circumstance that the Lytton letter was folded up with the writing apparently outside. It was outside and unseen until the sunlight brought it out and destroyed the other, inside, writing— a change, I suspect, that was intended for the police to see after it was completed, not for the defense to witness as it was taking place."

We looked at each other aghast. Thurston was nervously opening and shutting his lips and moistening them as if he wanted to say something but could not find the words.

"Lastly," went on Craig, utterly regardless of Thurston's frantic efforts to speak, "we come to the note that was discovered so queerly crumpled up in the jar of ammonia on Vera Lytton's dressing-table. I have here a cylindrical glass jar in which I place some sal-ammoniac and quicklime. I will wet it and heat it a little. That produces the pungent gas of ammonia.

"On one side of this third piece of paper I myself write with this mercurous nitrate solution. You see, I leave no mark on the paper as I write. I fold it up and drop it into the jar—and in a few seconds withdraw it. Here is a very quick way of producing something like the slow result of sunlight with silver nitrate. The fumes of ammonia have formed the precipitate of black mercurous nitrate, a very distinct black writing which is almost indelible. That is what is technically called invisible rather than sympathetic ink."

We leaned over to read what he had written. It was the same as the note incriminating Dixon:

This will cure your headache.

Dr. Dixon

A servant entered with a telegram from New York. Scarcely stopping in his exposure, Kennedy tore it open, read it hastily, stuffed it into his pocket, and went on.

"Here in this fourth bottle I have an acid solution of iron chloride, diluted until the writing is invisible when dry," he hurried on. "I will just make a few scratches on this fourth sheet of paper—so. It leaves no mark. But it has the remarkable property of becoming red in vapor of sulpho-cyanide. Here is a long-necked flask of the gas, made by sulphuric acid acting on potassium sulpho-cyanide. Keep back, Dr. Waterworth, for it would be very dangerous for you to get even a whiff of this in your condition. Ah! See—the scratches I made on the paper are red."

Then hardly giving us more than a moment to let the fact impress itself on our minds, he seized the piece of paper and dashed it into the jar of ammonia. When he withdrew it, it was just a plain sheet of white paper again. The red marks which the gas in the flask had brought out of nothingness had been effaced by the ammonia. They had gone and left no trace.

"In this way I can alternately make the marks appear and disappear by using the sulpho-cyanide and the ammonia. Whoever wrote this note with Dr. Dixon's name on it must have had the doctor's reply to the Thurston letter containing the words, 'This will not cure your headache.' He carefully traced the words, holding the genuine note up to the light with a piece of paper over it, leaving out the word 'not' and using only such words as he needed. This note was then destroyed.

"But he forgot that after he had brought out the red writing by the use of the sulpho-cyanide, and though he could count on Vera Lytton's placing the note in the jar of ammonia and hence obliterating the writing, while at the same time the invisible writing in the mercurous nitrate involving Dr. Dixon's name would be brought out by the ammonia indelibly on the other side of the note—he forgot"—Kennedy was now speaking eagerly and loudly—"that the sulpho-cyanide vapors could always be made to bring back to accuse him the words that the ammonia had blotted out."

Before the prosecutor could interfere, Kennedy had picked up the note found in the ammonia-jar beside the dying girl and had jammed the state's evidence into the long-necked flask of sulpho-cyanide vapor.

"Don't fear," he said, trying to pacify the now furious prosecutor, "it will do nothing to the Dixon writing. That is permanent now, even if it is only a tracing."

When he withdrew the note, there was writing on both sides, the black of the original note and something in red on the other side.

We crowded around, and Craig read it with as much interest as any of us:

"Before taking the headache-powder, be sure to place the contents of this paper in a jar with a little warm water."

"Hum," commented Craig, "this was apparently written on the outside wrapper of a paper folded about some sal-ammoniac and quicklime. It goes on:

"'Just drop the whole thing in, *paper and all*. Then if you feel a faintness from the medicine the ammonia will quickly restore you. One spoonful of the headache-powder swallowed quickly is enough.'"

No name was signed to the directions, but they were plainly written, and "*paper and all*" was underscored heavily.

Craig pulled out some letters. "I have here specimens of writing of many persons connected with this case, but I can see at a glance which one corresponds to the writing on this red death-warrant by an almost inhuman fiend. I shall, however, leave that part of it to the handwriting experts to determine at the trial. Thurston, who was the man whom you saw enter the Boncour bungalow as you left—the constant visitor?"

Thurston had not yet regained his self-control, but with trembling forefinger he turned and pointed to Halsey Post.

"Yes, ladies and gentlemen," cried Kennedy as he slapped the telegram that had just come from New York down on the table decisively, "yes, the real client of Kerr & Kimmel, who bent Thurston to his purposes, was Halsey Post, once secret lover of Vera Lytton till threatened by scandal in Danbridge, Halsey Post, graduate in technology, student of sympathetic inks, forger of the Vera Lytton letter and the other notes, and dealer in cyanides in the silversmithing business, fortune-hunter for the Willard millions with which to recoup the Post & Vance losses, and hence rival of Dr. Dixon for the love of Alma Willard. That is the man who wielded the poisoned pen. "Dr. Dixon is innocent."

JUSTICE ENDS AT HOME

Rex Stout

I. THE PLEA

The courtroom of New York County General Sessions, Part VI, was unusually busy that April morning. The calling of the calendar occupied all of an hour, delayed as it was by arguments on postponements and various motions, with now and then a sound of raised voices as opposing attorneys entered into a wrangle that colored their logic with emotion.

Judge Fraser Manton cut off most of these disputes in the middle with a terse, final ruling on the point at issue. He seemed to have been made for the bench of justice. Rather young-looking for a judge of New York General Sessions, with bright, dark eyes and clear skin, he possessed nevertheless that air of natural authority and wisdom that sits so gracefully on some fortunate men.

Perched high above the others in the great leather chair on the daïs, black-gowned and black-collared, his was easily the most handsome face in the room. He was liked and admired by lawyers for his cool, swift decisions and imperturbable impartiality; and he was even more popular off the bench than on, for he was a wealthy bachelor and somewhat of a good fellow. He was a prominent clubman, and came from a family of high social position.

The first business after the calling of the calendar was a batch of indictments sent over from the Grand Jury.

Three gunmen, accused of holding up a jewelry store on Sixth Avenue, entered a plea of not guilty; they were represented by a large, jovial individual who was known to be high in the councils of Tammany. Then the attorney of a little black-haired Italian who was alleged—as the newspapers say—to have planted a bomb in his neighbor's hallway, asked permission to withhold his plea for twenty-four hours, which was granted. Two others followed—a druggist charged with illegal sales of heroin, and a weak-faced youth, whose employer had missed a thousand dollars from his safe. The clerk called out the next case, and a seedy-looking man was led to the bar by a sheriff's deputy, while Arthur Thornton, assistant district attorney, arose from his seat at a nearby table.

The prisoner—the seedy-looking man—was about forty years of age, and his clothing seemed nearly as old, so worn and dirty was it. His face, shaven that morning in the Tombs, had the hollow and haggard appearance that is the result of continued misery and misfortune, and his gray eyes were filled with the heroic indifference of a man who knows he is doomed and cares very little about the matter.

He gave his pedigree to the clerk in a low, even voice: William Mount, no address, age thirty-eight, American born, occupation bookkeeper.

Judge Fraser Manton, who had been gazing with keen interest at the prisoner during the questioning, now cleared his throat.

"William Mount," he said, "you have been charged before the grand jury with the murder of your wife, Mrs. Elaine Mount, known as Alice Reeves. Do you wish the indictment read?"

The prisoner looked up at the judge and the eyes of the two men met.

"No, sir; I don't want to hear the indictment," Mount replied.

"Very well. You are brought before me to enter a plea. You understand, this is not a trial, and you are not expected to say anything except a plea to the indictment. Are you guilty of the crime charged?"

A little light appeared in the prisoner's eyes, but speedily died out as he replied simply:

"I didn't do it, sir."

"Then you plead not guilty?"

"Yes, sir."

The judge turned to the clerk to instruct him to enter the plea, then his eyes went back to the prisoner.

"Are you represented by counsel? Have you a lawyer?"

The shadow of a scornful and bitter smile swept across Mount's lips.

"No, sir," he replied.

"Do you want one?"

"What if I did? I couldn't pay a lawyer. I haven't any money."

"I suppose not. Just so." The judge appeared to be examining the prisoner with attentive curiosity. "It's my duty, Mount, in the case that a man is charged with a capital crime is unable retain counsel, to assign an attorney to his defense. The attorney will be paid by the State, also all legitimate and necessary expenses incurred by him up to a certain amount. The State takes this precaution to safeguard the lives and liberties of its children. I will assign counsel to your case this afternoon, and he will probably see you tomorrow."

"Yes, sir," replied the prisoner without a show of interest. It was evident that he expected little assistance from any lawyer.

Judge Manton beckoned to the clerk, who handed him a file to which two or three sheets of paper were attached. The judge looked over them thoughtfully, then turned to the assistant district attorney.

I'll set the case for May eighteenth, Mr. Thornton. Will that be all right?"

"Perfectly, your honor," replied the prosecutor.

"Well, Mount, you will be tried on Tuesday, the eighteenth day of May. Your counsel will be notified to that effect. That's all."

As the prisoner was led from the courtroom his face wore exactly the same expression of resigned hopelessness that it had shown when he entered twenty minutes before.

Late that afternoon, in his chambers adjoining the courtroom, Judge Fraser Manton was enjoying a cigar and a chat with his friends, Hamilton Rogers, proprietor and editor of the *Bulletin*, and Richard Hammel, police commissioner, when his clerk approached with some letters and other documents to be signed.

"By the way," observed the clerk as he blotted the signatures, "there will be another, sir. Who are you going to give the Mount case to? He must be notified."

"Oh, yes," replied the judge. "Why, I don't know; let me see. I looked the list over this afternoon, and I thought of assigning it to Simon Leg." He hesitated. "Yes, give it to Leg. L, E, G, Leg; you'll find his address in the book."

"What!" exclaimed Police Commissioner Hammel; "old Simmie Leg?"

The clerk stopped short on his way out of the room, while an expression of surprise and amusement filled his eyes.

"Yes, sir," he said finally as he turned to go. A minute later the click of his typewriter was heard through the open door.

II. The Attorney for the Defense

In a nicely furnished office, consisting of two rooms, on the eighteenth floor of one of New York's highest buildings, situated on Broadway not far south of City Hall, a stenographer was talking to an office boy at nine o'clock in the morning. (Heavens! How many stenographers are there talking to office boys at nine o'clock in the morning?) This particular stenographer was, perhaps, a little prettier than the average, but otherwise she held strictly to type; whereas the office boy appeared to be really individual.

There was a light in his eyes and a form to his brow that spoke of intelligence, and he was genuinely, not superficially, neat in appearance. He was about twenty years of age, and his name was Dan Culp. As soon as the morning conversation with his coworker was finished, he took a heavy law volume down from a shelf and began reading in it.

The door opened and a man entered the office.

The office boy and the stenographer spoke together:

"Good morning, sir."

"Good morning, Mr. Leg."

The newcomer returned their greetings and hung his hat and spring overcoat in a closet. He was a middle-aged man of heavy build, with an elongated, sober-looking countenance, which formed an odd contrast with his pleasant, twinkling eyes.

"Any mail, Miss Venner?" he asked, turning.

"Yes, sir."

He took the two letters which the stenographer handed to him and passed into the other room, The office boy returned to his law volume. Miss Venner took a piece of embroidery from a drawer desk and started to work on it. From within came various small sounds as their employer opened his desk, pulled his chair back, and tore open his mail. Silence followed.

Presently his voice came:

"Dan!"

The office boy stuck a blotter in his book and went to the door of the other room.

"Yes, sir."

"Come here." Mr. Leg had wheeled himself about in his swivel chair and was gazing with an expression of puzzled astonishment at a typewritten letter in his hand. "Just come here, Dan, and look at this! Of all the—but just look at it!"

The youth's face took on a sudden expression of eager interest as he read the letter through to the end.

"It's a murder case, sir," he said with animation.

"So I see. But why, in Heaven's name, has it been assigned to me? Why should any case be assigned to me?"

The youth smiled. "It is surprising, sir."

"Surprising! It's outrageous! There's no reason for it! A murderer! Why, I wouldn't know how to talk to the fellow. They know very well I haven't had a case for ten years. Dan, it's an outrage!"

"Yes, sir."

"I won't take it."

"No, sir."

Mr. Leg got up from his chair with a gesture of indignation and walked to the window. Dan stood regarding him hesitatingly, with eagerness in his eyes, and finally inquired diffidently:

"Would that be ethical, Mr. Leg?"

The lawyer wheeled with a sharp: "What?"

"To refuse the case, sir."

"I don't know. No, it wouldn't. Hang it all, I suppose I'm in for it. But where's the sense in it? I don't know the first thing about murder. What if he's innocent? How could I prove it? Whoever this Mount is, God help him. I suppose I'll have to go and see him."

"Yes, sir."

Though Mr. Leg talked for another half-hour, while Dan listened respectfully, he could arrive at no other conclusion. There was no way out of it—he must go see the man, Mount. Heavens, what a frightful, unexpected thing, to have a murderer thrown on one's hands! Really, there ought to be a public defender.

At ten o'clock he put on his hat and coat and started for the Tombs.

Let us talk about him while he is on his way. Mr. Simon Leg was known among the members of his profession as well as any lawyer in the city, but not as a lawyer. In fact, he wasn't a lawyer at all, except in name. He hadn't had a case in ten years.

He had inherited a large fortune, and thus seeing no necessity for work of any kind, he refused to do any.

It was apparently to maintain his self-respect that he kept an office and spent his days in it, for all he ever did was sit in the swivel chair and consume novels and tales of adventure at the rate of five or six a week, with now and then a game of chess with Dan, who gave him odds of a rook and beat him. At first sight it would appear that Dan and Miss Venner had absolutely nothing to do, but they were in fact kept pretty busy picking up the novels and tales from the floor as their employer finished them, sending them to the Salvation Army.

As for Mr. Leg's wide popularity, among the members of his profession, that was accounted for by the fact that he was a member of the best clubs, a good fellow, and a liberal friend.

He is now at the Tombs. Entering the grim portals with an inward shudder, he explained his mission to the doorkeeper, and was at one ushered into the office of the warden, to whom he exhibited the letter from Judge Manton by way of credentials. The warden summoned the attendant, who conducted the lawyer to a small, bare room at the end of a dark corridor, and left him there. Five minutes later he door opened again and a uniformed turnkey appeared; ahead of him was a man with a white face and sunken eyes, wearing a seedy black suit.

The turnkey pointed to a button on the wall.

"Ring when you're through," he directed, and went out, closing the door behind him.

The lawyer rose and approached the other man, who stood near the door regarding him stolidly.

"Mr. Mount," said the attorney in an embarrassed tone of voice, holding out his hand. "I'm Mr. Leg, Simon Leg, your—that is; your counsel."

The other hesitated a moment, then took the proffered hand.

"Glad to meet you, Mr. Leg," he said. He appeared to be also ill at ease. It is a curious thing how lighter emotions, such as ordinary social embarrassment, continue to operate even when a man is in the shadow of death.

"Well—" began the lawyer, and stopped.

The other came to his rescue.

"I suppose," said Mount, "you've come to hear my side of it?"

"Exactly," Mr. Leg agreed. "But here, we may as well sit down."

They seated themselves, one on either side of the wooden table in the center of the room.

"You see, Mr. Mount," began the lawyer, "I don't know the first thing about this case. I was assigned to it by Judge Manton. And before you give me any confidences, I want to tell you that I have no criminal practice whatever. To tell the truth, I'm not much of a lawyer. I say this so you can ask the court to give you other counsel, and I think you better do it."

"It doesn't matter," returned Mount quietly. "There's no use putting in a defense, anyway."

Mr. Leg glanced at him quickly. "Oh," he observed. "What—do you mean you're guilty?"

The lawyer shrank back from the quick, burning light that leaped from the other's eyes.

"No!" Mount shouted fiercely. Then suddenly he was quiet again. "No," he continued calmly, "I'm not guilty, Mr. Leg. My God, do you think I could have killed her? But there's no use. I was caught—they found me there—"

"Wait," the lawyer interrupted. "I really think, Mr. Mount, that you'd better ask for other counsel."

"Well, I won't."

"But I'm incompetent."

"It doesn't matter. Nothing matters. She's dead, and that's all there is to it. What do I care? I tell you that I haven't any defense except that I didn't do it. No, I won't ask the judge for anything. Let it go."

Mr. Leg sighed.

"Then I'll do the best I can," he said hopelessly. "Now, Mr. Mount, tell me all you know about it. Tell me everything. And remember that my only chance to help you is if you tell me the whole truth."

"There's no use in it, sir," said the other in a dull tone of misery.

"Go on," returned the lawyer sternly.

And William Mount told his story.

III. The Amateur Detective

It was well past two o'clock when Mr. Leg returned to his office, having stopped at a restaurant for lunch on the way. As he entered, Miss Venner and Dan looked up with faces of expectant eagerness, and a faint smile of amusement curled the stenographer's pretty lips. Dan sprang to his feet to hang up his employer's coat, and a shadow of disappointment fell across his face as the lawyer nodded his greetings and thanks and passed without a word into the other room. But it was not long before his voice came:

"Dan!"

The youth hastened to the door.

"Yes, sir."

"Come here." Mr. Leg was seated at his desk with his feet upon its edge and his chin buried in his collar—his favorite reading attitude. "Dan," he said as the other stood before him, "this Mount case is a very sad affair. I'm sorrier than ever that I'm mixed up in it. As sure as Heaven, they're going to convict an innocent man."

"Yes, sir."

"He's innocent, beyond any doubt; but I don't know what to do. Sit down there and let me tell you about it. You're a bright boy; you play a good game of chess; maybe you'll think of something."

"Yes, sir," returned the youth eagerly, bringing forth a chair.

"You know," the lawyer began, "Mount is accused of murdering his wife. Well, she was his wife only in name. He hadn't been living with her for four years. He hadn't even seen her in that time. He married her seven years ago when he was thirty-two and she was twenty-one. He was head clerk in an insurance office, getting a good salary, and she had been a stenographer in a law office. For two years they lived together happily. Mount worshiped her. Then she seemed to become discontented, and one day, a year later, she suddenly disappeared, leaving a letter for him which indicated that she had found another man, but not saying so in so many words. He searched——"

"Has he got that letter?" interrupted Dan, who was listening intently.

"What letter?"

"The one his wife left."

"Oh, I don't know. I didn't ask him."

"All right, sir. Excuse me."

"He searched for her everywhere," the lawyer continued, "but found no trace whatever. He went to the police, but they had no better luck. By that time, he had lost his position, having continually absented himself from the office for two months. His heart was broken, and with his wife gone, he didn't care whether he lived or not. He went from bad to worse, and became practically a vagabond. Half mad from misery and grief, he tramped around looking vaguely for his lost wife. More than three years passed, and the edge of his sorrow dulled a little. He obtained a position as bookkeeper in a coal office, and held it faithfully for four months.

"One evening—this was April 2, a week ago last Friday—he was walking across One Hundred and Fourth Street on his way home from work, when a woman, coming in the opposite direction, stopped suddenly in front of him with a cry of surprise. It was his wife.

"Mount, of course, was staggered.

"He remembered afterward that she was very well dressed, even expensively, it seemed to him. She told him she had been searching for him the past six months; she had discovered that she really loved him and no one else, and she wanted to come back to him. Mount called attention to his pitiable condition, physical and sartorial, but she said that she had a great deal of money, enough to last them a very long time, many years. Poor Mount didn't even dare ask her where the money came from. He said he would take her back.

"She arranged to meet him the following night at nine o'clock at a drugstore on the corner of One Hundred and Sixteenth and Eighth Avenue. He begged her to go with him then, at once; but that she said she couldn't do. Finally, they separated. But Mount couldn't bear to let her get out of his sight, and he followed her.

"She took the subway at One Hundred and Third Street, and he managed to get on the same train without being discovered. At One Hundred and Fifty-seventh Street she got off, and he followed her to an apartment house near Broadway. Soon after she entered he saw a light appear in the east flat on the third floor, so he supposed she lived there. He stayed around until after eleven, but she didn't come out again.

"The next night Mount was at the drugstore ahead of time. She wasn't there, nor did she arrive at nine o'clock. He waited nearly two hours. At twenty minutes to eleven he went uptown to One Hundred and Fifty-seventh Street. From the pavement he saw a light in her windows.

"He entered her building; the outer door was open.

"A man was standing in the lower hall. Mount barely glanced at him as he passed to the stairs; he doesn't remember what the man looked like, only he has an indistinct recollection that he had a suitcase in his hand. Mount went upstairs to the third floor and rang the bell at the flat to the east. There was no answer, though he rang several times, and finally, finding the door unlocked, he pushed it open and entered.

"On the floor, with the electric lights glaring above her, was the dead body of his wife with the hilt of a knife protruding from her breast and blood everywhere. Mount screamed, leaped forward, and pulled out the knife; blood spurted on his hands and sleeves. His scream brought adjoining tenants to the scene. In ten minutes the police were there, and when they left, they took Mount with them."

Mr. Leg took one foot down from the desk, reached in his pocket for a packet of cigarettes, and lit one.

"That's Mount's story," said he, blowing a column of smoke into the air, "and I'm certain it's a true one. The man has an appearance of honesty."

A slight smile appeared on Dan's lips.

"You know, sir, you believe everything people tell you," he suggested diffidently.

"True," Mr. Leg frowned. "Yes, I suppose it's a fault not to be suspicious sometimes. But that's what the man told me, and I'm his counsel. I don't mind confessing to you, Dan, that I'm absolutely helpless. I haven't the slightest idea what to do. I thought of several things, but they all seemed absurd on analysis. I had it in mind during luncheon. I've put a lot of thought on it."

"Yes, sir."

"But I arrived nowhere. As I said before, Dan, you're a bright boy. Maybe you might suggest something—"

The youth's eyes were alive with eager intelligence. "I could think it over, sir. It's a mighty interesting case. There's one curious thing about it—very curious—"

"What is it?"

"I wouldn't like to mention it, sir, until I've examined it more. Maybe I can suggest something then."

"All right, Dan. If you're as good at detective work as you are at playing chess, Mount might do worse after all. Exercise your ingenuity, my boy. We'll talk it over again tomorrow."

"Yes, sir."

After Dan returned to the other room Mr. Leg sat for sometime thoughtfully regarding his inkwell. Presently he shook himself, heaved a sigh, and reached across the desk for a book bound in red cloth with a gilt title, *The Fight on the Amazon*.

He opened it at the first page and began to read. An expression of pure content appeared upon his face. The minutes passed unheeded. His chin sank deeper in his collar and his hands griped the book tightly as he came to the fourth chapter, "The Night Attack." At the end of an hour he had reached the most thrilling point of the fight and his eyes were glowing with unrestrained joy.

"Mr. Leg."

The lawyer looked up to find Dan standing before him.

"Well?"

"Why, this Mount case sir."

"What about it?"

"I've been thinking it over, sir, but before we can get anywhere we must obtain more information. Somebody ought to go up and examine the scene of the murder. I'd be only too glad to do it."

"All right, that's a good idea," agreed Mr. Leg, whose fingers were twitching impatiently as they held the place in his book.

"And there are other things we must do, too, sir. Things absolutely essential. I've made a little list of questions, if you'd like to look it over."

With a gesture of impatience the lawyer took the sheet of paper which Dan handed him. Evidently he had been making use of the stenographer's machine, for it was covered with typewriting:

First, to verify Mount's story:

1. Has he kept the letter his wife left when she ran away? If so, get it from him.
2. Where was he employed as bookkeeper during the four months previous to the crime? Verify.
3. Did he wait inside the drugstore at the corner of One Hundred and Sixteenth Street and Eighth Avenue on the night of April 3, or merely in its neighborhood? Find out if there is any one in the store or near it who remembers seeing him.
4. Does he drink to excess?
5. Does he appear nervous and excitable, or stolid and calm?

Second, from the police:

1. With what kind of knife was the crime committed? Were there finger-prints on it other than Mount's?

2. Exactly at what hour were the police summoned to the scene, and how long had the victim been dead, according to the doctor's report, when they arrived?

3. Did they take any papers or articles of any kind from the flat? If so, examine them, if possible.

4. Has either Mount or his wife any criminal record?

5. Get a photograph of Mount.

6. Did the body show any marks of violence besides the wound in the breast?

Having reached this point, halfway down the sheet, the lawyer stopped to look up at his office boy with an expression of admiration.

"All this is very sensible, Dan," he observed. "Remarkably sensible. These are serviceable ideas."

"Yes, sir." The youth smiled a little. "Of course, Mr. Leg, you won't be able to see Mount again till tomorrow morning, but you can get the information from the police this afternoon. I suppose headquarters—"

"You mean for *me* to go to the police?" interrupted Mr. Leg in dismay.

"Certainly, sir. They wouldn't pay much attention to me, and besides, I'm going uptown to the flat."

"Well, but—" Mr. Leg appeared to be dumbfounded to discover that there would actually be work for him to do. "All right," he said finally, "I suppose I'll have to. I'll go first thing in the morning."

"To see Mount, yes, sir. But you must go the police this afternoon, at once."

"This afternoon!" The lawyer glanced in helpless consternation at the book in his hand. "Now, Dan, there's no use rushing things. I'll go tomorrow. Anyway, what right has this Mount to upset my whole office like this?"

"He's your client, sir. This is April sixteenth, and the trial is set for the eighteenth of May. There's no time to be lost."

"Yes, hang it all, he's my client," the lawyer agreed. "So much the worse for him, but I suppose I ought to do the best I can. All right, I'll go this afternoon."

"Right away, sir."

"Yes. You want answers to all these questions, do you?"

"Yes, sir. And tomorrow, besides seeing Mount, you must go to the office where he says he worked, and other places. I'll see about the drugstore myself. There'll be a lot to do."

"There sure will, if we follow your orders." Mr. Leg was beginning to recover his good humor.

"Yes, sir. I'm going up to the flat now, and I—" the youth hesitated—"I may need some money for janitors and people like that. They talk better when you give them something."

"Dan, you're a cynic," Mr. Leg pulled out his wallet. "How much?"

"I think fifty dollars, sir."

"Here's a hundred."

"Thank you, sir."

Fifteen minutes later, having waited to see his employer safely started for police headquarters, Dan took his hat from the closet. On his way to the door he stopped beside the stenographer's desk, where that proud damsel was seated at work on her dainty embroidery.

"Maybe pretty soon you'll think I'm not just a boy anymore, Miss Venner."

The lady looked up.

"Oh! I suppose you think you're going to do something great."

"You bet I am." Enthusiasm and confidence shone from Dan's eyes. "You'll see. And then, when I want to tell you—er—tell you—"

"Well, tell me what?" Miss Venner s.miled with sweet maliciousness.

But Dan appeared to have no finish for his sentence. Suddenly he bent over and imprinted a loud kiss on the dainty piece of embroidery, and then, his face burning red, he made for the door.

IV. A Slip of Paper

It was nearly four o'clock when Dan arrived at the apartment house on One Hundred and Fifty-seventh Street, the address of which he obtained from Mr. Leg. He stood across the street and ran his eyes over the exterior. It was a five-story stone building, the oldest and smallest in the block, with fire escapes in front. Dan picked out the three east windows on the third floor as those of the flat in which Elaine Mount had met her death.

He crossed the street and rang the janitor's bell. After a minute's delay there appeared in the areaway below a hard-looking customer with a black mustache.

"What do you want?" he demanded gruffly, looking up at the boy on the stoop.

Dan smiled down at him.

"Are you the janitor?"

"Yes."

Dan descended to the areaway.

"I'm from Mr. Leg's office, the lawyer for the man held for the murder committed here. I want to look through the flat. Is there a policeman in charge?"

"In charge of what?"

"The flat."

"No."

"Is it sealed up?"

"No. They took the seal off day before yesterday. But I don't know who *you* are, young fellow."

"That's all right. I have a letter from Mr. Leg. See." As Dan pulled the letter from his pocket a five-dollar bill came with it. The letter was soon returned, but the bill found its way to the janitor's grimy palm.

"I'd like to go through the flat, if you don't mind," Dan repeated.

"All right," the other agreed more amiably. "There's no reason why you shouldn't, seeing as it's for rent."

He turned and led the way through the dark hall and up the stairs. Dan observed as they passed that the corridor on the ground floor was quite narrow and deserted, there being neither telephone switchboard nor elevator. This was evidently one of the old houses erected on the Heights between 1890 and 1900, with its entire lack of twentieth-century middle-class show.

"Here you are," said the janitor, stopping at the door on the right two flights up. He selected a key from a bunch, unlocked the door and passed within, with Dan at his heels.

With one foot across the threshold, Dan stopped short in amazed consternation. What he saw was a flat bare of furniture, with discolored wall paper and dirty floors; in short, that dreariest and dismalest of sights on earth, a vacant and empty apartment.

"But—but—" the youth stammered in dismay. "But there's nothing here."

"Nope. All empty," returned the janitor placidly.

"But how—do the police know of this?"

"Sure. I told you they was here day before yesterday and took the seal off. They said we could take the stuff out. One of the cops told me they had the man that did it, so there wasn't any use keeping it locked up any longer."

"Where's the furniture and things?"

"In storage. Hauled away yesterday."

For a minute Dan gazed at the dismantled flat in dismayed silence. If there had been anything here which would have been of value to his untrained eye it was now too late.

"Spilt milk," he finally observed aloud. "No use crying." He turned again to the janitor.

"Who got the stuff ready?"

"I did."

"Did you take away anything, did you leave papers and everything in the desks and drawers, if there were any?"

"Sure I did." The janitor appeared to be a little nettled at this slight aspersion to his integrity. "I didn't take nothing. Of course there was a lot of papers and trash and stuff I cleaned out."

"Did you throw it away?"

"Yes. I ain't gone yet, though; it's still down in the basement."

"Do you mind if I take a look at it?"

So they returned downstairs, and there, in a dark corner of the basement the janitor pointed out a dirty old bag filled with papers and all sorts of trash. With a feeling that he was making a silly fool of himself, Dan dragged the bag out into the light and dumped its contents on the cement floor. Then he began to pick the articles up one by one, examine them, and replace them in the bag.

There was a little bit of everything: magazines and newspapers, a broken inkwell, stubs of lead pencils, writing paper, banana skins, combings of hair, bills from butchers and delicatessen shops.

There was a lot of it, and he pawed through the stuff for an hour before he came across anything that appeared to him worthy of attention. This was a small piece of white paper, rectangular in shape. In one corner was an imprint of the seal of the County of New York, and across the middle of the sheet was written in ink:

Bonneau et Mouet—Sec.

Dan carried the paper to the window and examined it attentively, and ended by sticking it in his pocket.

"I'm crazy, I suppose," he murmured to himself. "It's all right to have an idea, but there is no sense in expecting— However, we'll see."

In another thirty minutes he had finished with the heap of trash, having found nothing else of interest. He found the janitor in the front room of the basement, smoking a pipe and reading a newspaper. On a table before him was a bucket of beer. Already Mr. Leg's five-dollar bill was cheering humanity.

"Through?" asked the janitor, glancing up with a grin that was supposed to be amiable. "Find anything?"

Dan shook his head. "No. And now, mister—I didn't get your name—"

"Yoakum, Bill Yoakum."

"I'd like to ask you a question or two, Mr. Yoakum, if you don't mind. Were you at home on the night of Saturday, April third, the night of the murder?"

"Yep. All evening."

"Did you hear or see anything unusual?"

Mr. Yoakum grinned, as though at some secret joke. "I sure didn't," he replied.

"Nothing whatever?"

"Absolutely nothin'."

"When did you first know of the murder? What time, I mean."

"Lets see, Monday morning," replied the janitor, still grinning.

"Monday morning!" exclaimed Dan in amazement. "Do you mean you didn't hear of it till thirty-six hours afterward?"

"I sure didn't."

"How was that?"

"Well, you see," replied Mr. Yoakum slowly, as though it was regretful that his joke must end, "I didn't get here until Monday morning."

"But you said you were at home—"

"Sure, I was home, so I wasn't here. I was janitor down on Ninety-eighth Street then. You see, I've only been here about ten days. I came after the murder was all over, though I had to clean up after it."

Mr. Yoakum cackled. Dan interrupted him:

"So you weren't here a week ago Saturday?"

"I sure wasn't."

"Do you know who was janitor here before you?"

"Nope. Don't know a thing about him, only he sure put the hot-water boiler on the bum. He was ignorant, that's all I know."

So there was nothing to be learned from Mr. Yoakum, except the name and address of the agent of the apartment house. Dan wrote this down in a memorandum book, refused Mr. Yoakum's offer of a glass of beer, and left to go above to the ground floor, when he rang the bell of the tenant on the right. By then it was nearly seven o'clock and quite dark outdoors, but the amateur detective had no thought of halting his investigations for anything so trivial as dinner.

His ring was answered by a woman in a dirty blue kimono, who informed that she had lived in the house only two months; that she had never seen a murdered woman, and that she didn't want to talk about so disgusting a subject as murder anyhow. The other flat on the ground floor was vacant.

Dan mounted a flight of stairs and tried again.

Here he had better luck. He was told by a pale young woman in a kitchen apron that she had spoken many times to the murdered woman, who had lived there under the name of Miss Alice Reeves. Miss Reeves had been an old tenant; she had been there when the pale young woman came, and that was over two years ago.

She had been very pretty, with dark eyes and hair, and a beautiful complexion; she was always quiet and reserved, not mixing with anyone; she had sometimes had callers, especially one gentleman, who came quite often. The pale young woman had never got a good look at him, having seen him only on the dark stairs; besides, he had always worn a sort of muffler over the lower part of his face, so she couldn't describe him except to say that he was rather tall and very well dressed and distinguished-looking. She wouldn't recognize him if she saw him.

Yes, said the pale young woman, they had a new janitor. She didn't know what had become of the old one, who had been a little gray-haired Irishman named Cummings. He had been there Saturday evening to take off the garbage, but at midnight, the time of the murder, he could not be found, nor did he return on Sunday; they had been compelled to go without hot water all day. Monday morning the new man was sent up by the agent. He wasn't as good as Cummings, who had been very capable and obliging.

It took an hour for the pale young woman to tell Dan all she knew.

At the other flat on that floor he found a new tenant, who could tell him nothing. Another flight up and he was on the floor on which Mrs. Mount, or Alice Reeves, had lived. Here, in the flat across the hall from hers, he met a Tartar in the person of an old music teacher who said that he lived there alone with his wife; that he never poked his nose into other people's business, and that he expected them to do the same.

Dan retreated in good order.

On the two top floors he had no better luck; he found no one who had known Miss Reeves, though some had seen her often; nor could he get any description of the mysterious caller who, according to the pale young woman, had always worn a muffler across the lower part of his face. He did find the persons who had arrived first at the scene of the murder, a young husband and wife on the floor above.

Their story tallied with Mount's; they had been attracted by his scream, which they described as piercing and terrible, and, running down to Miss Reeves's flat, they found her lying on the floor in a pool of blood, with Mount, the dripping knife in his hand, standing above her. It was the young husband who had summoned the police.

According to him, Mount had appeared absolutely dazed—half mad, in fact. He had made no attempt whatever to get away, but had remained kneeling over the dead body of his wife until the arrival of the police.

But Dan's great disappointment was that he was unable to find among the tenants any trace of the man who, according to Mount's story, was standing in the lower hall with a suitcase in his hand when Mount entered. No one had seen him or knew anything about him.

It was a quarter to nine when Dan found himself again on the street.

A block or two down Broadway he entered a dairy lunchroom for a sandwich and a glass of milk, after which he sought the subway on the downtown side. The train was well filled, though it was too late for the theater crowd, for everybody is always going somewhere in New York. At the Ninety-sixth Street station Dan got out, walked two blocks north on Broadway, and over to West End Avenue, and entered the marble reception hall of an ornate apartment house.

"I want to Mr. Leg," he said to the West Indian at the switchboard. "Tell him it's Dan Culp."

The Negro threw in a plug and presently spoke into the transmitter:

"Thirty-four? Dan Koolp to see Mr. Leg. All right, sir."

He disposed of Dan with a lordly gesture toward the elevator.

Mr. Leg appeared to be surprised, even alarmed, at the unexpected visit from his office boy. Dan, ushered in by the manservant, found his employer entertaining four or five friends in a session of the national game—not baseball.

"What is it, Dan? Something happened?" queried the lawyer, advancing to meet the youth at the door with a pair of kings in his hand.

"No, sir. That is, nothing important. I just wanted to find out if you got a photograph of Mount."

"Yes, the police let me have a copy of the one taken for the gallery."

"May I have it, sir? I'm going up to the drugstore to see if they remember seeing him there."

"By Jove, you certainly are on the job," smiled the lawyer. "Yes, of course you can have it." He went to a desk at the other end of the room and returned with a small unmounted photograph. "Here you are. But what's the hurry? Couldn't you have gone tomorrow just as well?"

"No, sir. You see, he was there at night, just about this time, so I'm more apt to find somebody who saw him. I didn't want to wait until tomorrow night." The youth appeared to hesitate, then continued, "there was something else, sir. May I have your night pass to the office building? I want to go down and look at something."

The lawyer's smile became a little impatient. "Well, really now, Dan, isn't that a little bit unnecessary? It isn't long till tomorrow morning."

"All right, sir, if you don't want—"

"Oh, I don't care. Wait a minute. I don't know where the blamed thing is."

This time Mr. Leg had to search for what he wanted, and it was finally found hidden under some papers in the bottom drawer of his desk.

Back uptown went Dan, to One Hundred and Sixteenth Street and Eighth Avenue, one of the busiest spots in Harlem, where he found a drugstore on the southwest corner. He failed to get any satisfactory information. The two clerks and the boy at the soda fountain declared that they had been on duty all evening on Saturday, April 3, but they had no recollection of seeing anyone who resembled the photograph of William Mount. The man at the newsstand outside said that he had an indistinct memory of such a man, but that he couldn't tell just when he had seen him.

"It's been two weeks, so I suppose I shouldn't expect anything," thought Dan as he turned away.

As he boarded a downtown train he was telling himself that Mr. Leg had stated the case mildly when he said that it was a little bit unnecessary to make a trip down to the office so late at night. It was worse than that, it was absurd.

Not for worlds would Dan have disclosed to anyone the extent of its absurdity by confessing the nature of his errand; he was himself trying to scoff at the wild idea that had entered his head that morning, and he felt that he was doubly a fool to entertain it as a possibility. Nevertheless, he was so completely possessed by it that he felt he couldn't sleep till he had sought the slight corroboration chance had offered him.

"But even if it's the same it won't really prove anything," he muttered, gazing out of the window down at the never-ending row of lighted shops as the elevated train rumbled along through the night.

At the office building he was admitted and passed into the night elevator by the watchman on showing Mr. Leg's card. He carried a key to the office, since he was always the first to arrive in the morning. A queer sense of strangeness and loneliness came over him as he switched on the electricity and saw his desk and Miss Venner's, all the familiar objects, revealed by its cold rays.

What a difference artificial light, with the night outside, makes in a room which we have previously seen illumined only by the soft, natural light of day!

Dan passed into the inner room, went straight to Mr. Leg's desk, turned on the electric reading globe, and cast his eye over the accumulation of books and papers. There were publishers' announcements, social invitations, personal letters, and other things. Almost at once, with an exclamation of satisfaction, he pounced on a typewritten sheet of paper with a name written at the bottom.

He spread this out on the desk, pulled from his pocket the slip he had found in Mr. Yoakum's bag of trash bearing the words "Bonneau et Mouet—Sec." and, sitting down in Mr. Leg's chair, began to examine with minute attention first the name on the letter, then the words on the slip. He did this for a full half-hour, with his brows wrinkled in concentration and the glow of discovery in his eyes."

"Of course," he muttered finally aloud, as he put the typewritten sheet back where he had found it, "I may not be a handwriting expert, but those were written by the same man as sure as my name's Dan Culp. He's mixed up in it somehow."

He placed the slip back in his pocket, and going to a case devoted to law volumes and similar works at one side of the room, took out a large blue book and carried it to the desk. He opened it at the front, ran his finger down the list of illustrations, stopped about the middle, and turned over the pages till he came to the one he wanted. It showed a full-page reproduction of a photograph of a man. He looked at it a moment, then carefully tore it out of the book, folded it, and placed it in his pocket.

There was a scared look on the youth's face as he turned out the lights and turned to leave the office. As the lock of the door clicked behind him there came faintly the sound of Trinity's midnight chimes.

V. The Police Commissioner

Despite the fact that he didn't get to bed till nearly two o'clock, having consumed half an hour explaining his late arrival to his mother and accepting her good-natured banter on his coming career as a great detective, Dan arrived at the office at half-past eight the following morning. He sat at his desk reading till nine, when Miss Venner appeared.

"Well, did you find the murderer?" she inquired sweetly, as he drew out her chair for her.

"Maybe," Dan replied in a tone so professionally cryptic that she burst into a peal of laughter.

"All right," continued Dan calmly, "wait and see."

"I'll tell you what I'll do," remarked Miss Venner as she sat down and took her embroidery from the drawer. "If you win Mr. Leg's case for him—for, of course, he can't do it—I'll give you the scarf I'm working on."

The splendid vanity of this proposal appeared not to occur to Dan. "No; do you mean it?" he exclaimed.

Miss Venner's reply was lost in the sound of the door opening to admit Mr. Leg. Greetings were exchanged. Dan sought his own desk.

A few minutes later, called into the other room by his employer, he proceeded to give him an account of his activities of the day before. He told him all that he had learned at the apartment house, from the janitor and tenants, and of his failure to find anyone at the drugstore who remembered seeing Mount. But there was one thing he did not mention: the slip of paper he had in his pocket; nor did he inform the lawyer that one of his books had been disfigured by having a photograph torn from it.

"And now I suppose you're ready for my report," observed Mr. Leg with an amused smile when Dan finished.

"If you please, sir."

"Well, to begin with, I had a hard time finding out anything." The lawyer took a sheet of paper covered with writing from his pocket. "First, I went to the office of Police Commissioner Hammel, who is a personal friend of mine, to get his authority, but he was out of town and wasn't expected back until this afternoon.

"I was afraid you'd call me down if I put it off, so I went to Inspector Brown, and he referred me to another inspector, Lobert, who is in charge of the case. Naturally, I suppose, they regard it as their business to convict Mount, but Lobert certainly didn't want me to tell anything. I got most of my information from a record of the testimony at the coroner's inquest and before the Grand Jury, of which I secured a copy.

"The police arrived at the scene of the murder at twenty-five minutes to twelve. The story of what happened after they got there is the same as Mount's. They say that the body of the victim was still quite warm; it wasn't examined by a doctor until the next morning at nine o'clock, and all they could say was that she had died between eight o'clock and midnight.

"They took nothing from the flat except the knife, and nothing from Mount's person of any significance. The knife was an ordinary steel paper knife with an ivory hilt, presumably the property of Mrs. Mount, or Alice Reeves, under which name the murdered woman was living there. The police didn't examine the hilt for fingerprints, as it was found in Mount's hand. Besides the wound in the breast, the body showed no marks of violence. Neither Mount nor his wife has any criminal record."

The lawyer handed the sheet of paper to Dan as he finished.

"So," observed the youth, "the knife doesn't tell us anything. I was hoping—"

"Well?" the other prodded him as he stopped.

"Nothing, sir. That is, nothing that is worth telling. But that doesn't matter; we've only begun. Of course, we can't expect any real help from the police; all they want is to convict somebody. Are you going to see Mount this morning, sir?"

"I suppose so." Mr. Leg frowned. "The Tombs is an extremely unpleasant place to visit, Dan. Extremely. But, of course, if it's necessary——"

Mr. Leg suddenly smiled, arose to his feet, drew himself up, and performed a clumsy imitation of a military salute.

"At your orders, Captain Culp."

When, a little later, the lawyer departed on his way to the Tombs, Dan remained behind to go over the testimony at the inquest. But he found nothing in it of importance except what Mr. Leg had already told him, and, having finished it, he left the office in care of Miss Venner and descended to the street.

A Broadway streetcar took him to a certain address near Union Square which he had got the day before from Mr. Yoakum. He entered a door marked in gilt lettering, "Levis & Levis, Real Estate," and, after explaining his errand to a clerk, was admitted to the private room of a junior member of the firm.

"Yes," replied the agent, in answer to his question; "we had a man named Cummings working for us. Patrick Cummings. Yes, he was janitor of the house where the murder took place. But we don't know where he is now."

"Isn't he with you any longer?"

"No. It was mighty curious. He disappeared suddenly, and the funny part of it is we still owe him fifteen dollars wages, which makes it really mysterious. All we know is that when one of our men went up there Sunday, on account of the murder, Cummings was nowhere to be found, although the tenants said he had been there Saturday evening. We haven't heard anything of him."

"I should think," observed Dan, "that you might have suspected his disappearance was connected with the murder."

The real estate agent smiled condescendingly. "You're a great little thinker, my lad. We did suspect it, and we communicated the fact to the police. I myself told Inspector Lobert about it. He said he'd let me know if they found him, but I haven't heard."

"Would you mind describing him to me, sir?"

"He was a little gray-haired man, about fifty, I should say, with light-colored eyes—I don't know if they were blue or gray—and a scraggly mustache. He was about five feet seven and weighed about one hundred and thirty-five pounds."

"Had he been working for you long?"

"About three years."

"Thank you, sir. One other thing; I'd like to get permission to go through Mrs. Mount's furniture and things—Miss Reeves, you know. The janitor says it is in storage. A letter from you, sir——"

"Nothing doing," returned the agent. "It's under jurisdiction of the probate court, and I couldn't give you permission if I wanted to. You'll have to get a court order."

So Dan went back down to Chambers Street, where, after interminable delays and examinations of his credentials from Mr. Leg, he obtained the sought-for permission. Then he had to wait another hour until a court officer was ready to accompany him to the storage warehouse; and in the end he had all his trouble for nothing. Among the hundreds of papers and books and other articles which he examined till late in the afternoon, he found absolutely nothing of significance.

"It's mighty curious," he muttered disgustedly, "that I shouldn't find one letter, or one book with his writing in it, or anything."

It was after four o'clock when he handed the court officer a two-dollar bill out of Mr. Leg's diminishing hundred and left him to go farther uptown. His destination was the house on One Hundred and Fifty-seventh Street, and when he arrived there he once more made a round of the tenants, from the top floor to the bottom.

To each of them he showed the photograph which he had torn out of the book in his employer's office, but no one remembered having seen the man; and when he asked the pale young woman on the second floor if the photograph resembled the man of whom she had spoken as a frequent caller at Miss Reeves's apartment, she replied that she really couldn't say, as she never had a good look at him.

But most of Dan's questions on this occasion concerned Patrick Cummings, the missing janitor. He learned little from the tenants; and then, realizing his mistake, he left the house and sought the basement next door.

The janitor here was a broken-down Scotchman with watery eyes. Yes, he replied, he had known Paddy Cummings well: and, urged on by another appropriation from Mr. Leg's hundred, he furnished a great deal of miscellaneous information concerning the character and habits of his missing confrère.

He said he had been a happy-go-lucky individual, much given, however, to unexpected fits of sullenness.

He had been unmarried, with no apparent relatives or friends whatever. Despite the fact that there was always money in his pocket, he had invariably cheated at pinocle. He had possessed the tastes of a gentleman, preferring whisky to beer. During the past year, however, he had contracted a disgusting fondness for motion pictures, having attended at least three times a week at the nickelodeon around the corner.

The Scotchman knew nothing of where he had gone; he missed him unspeakably, all the more on account of the insufferable Yoakum, who had taken his place.

Dan went back next door to see the insufferable Yoakum, from whom he learned that the former janitor had evidently departed unexpectedly and in a great hurry, as he had left his household goods behind him. Yoakum had found cooking utensils, a bed, two tables, some chairs, et cetera, in their places in the basement when he arrived; presumably they were the property of Cummings. Dan went through the place half a dozen times, but found nothing that gave any trace of the missing man's reasons for departure.

By the time he emerged again into the street the day was gone; a clock in the window at the Broadway corner said ten minutes past six. He entered and sought a telephone booth to call up the office, thinking it barely possible that Mr. Leg would be awaiting his return, but he got no answer.

He went home to sleep over the developments of the day.

At the office the next morning Mr. Leg submitted his report of the previous day's activities immediately upon his arrival. He had written down the answers to Dan's questions in their order:

1. Mount hasn't got the letter his wife left when she ran away. It was destroyed two years ago.
2. He was employed as bookkeeper at the office of Rafter & Co., coal dealers, foot of One Hundred and Twelfth Street, for the four months previous to the murder.
3. He was inside the drugstore only a few minutes. The rest of the time he waited outside on the corner. He bought a paper from the man at the news-stand and talked with him a little. He says this man might remember him.
4. He drank a great deal for the two years following his wife's disappearance, but not since then. He swears he didn't touch a drop that night.
5. He appears stolid and calm, with a lifeless indifference that is extraordinary, except when speaking of his wife, when he nearly breaks down with grief.

"There," said Mr. Leg, "that's what you wanted to know. I went to Rafter & Co., and they corroborated Mount, saying that he had worked for them a little over four months, and that he had been very satisfactory. He never drank any as far as they knew."

"I'm glad to hear that, sir," replied Dan. "That settles it as far as Mount's concerned. He's out of it, anyway; only I thought he might have done it in a fit of drunkenness. You see, sir, he couldn't have had any possible to kill his wife. The police supposition is that he found that she had been receiving another man in that flat, and killed her for revenge and jealousy.

"But, according to his story, he had agreed to take her back only the night before, knowing that in all probability she had done wrong. The reason I believe him is because of what he said about the money. He was even willing to make use of the money she was going to bring with her. No man would make up a thing like that about himself, even to save his own neck."

"Humph!" the lawyer grunted. "So you're a student of human nature, are you, Dan?"

"Yes, sir. I'm just beginning. I've had very little experience, but there's something else just as good. The people who say experience is the best school don't know what they're talking about. Most people could learn more about human nature in one week by studying Montaigne's *Essays* than in a lifetime of observation, because hardly anyone knows how to observe. Not that I don't need experience; I'm just beginning to get it. I always keep my eyes and ears open. You remember, sir, it was you who told me to read Montaigne."

"Yes, I believe I did," returned the lawyer. "I never got much out of him myself."

"No, sir; I suppose not. But to go back to Mount. I am certain now that he's innocent."

Mr. Leg frowned. "But that doesn't get us anywhere."

"No, sir. But I'm also pretty certain that I know who is responsible for the murder."

"What?" shouted Mr. Leg, nearly falling out of his chair in surprise.

"Yes, sir."

"You know who the murderer is!"

"No, sir, I didn't say that. I only know who is responsible for it, though it may be that he actually did it himself. I wouldn't think it possible, only I remember that Montaigne says, 'The passions smothered by modern civilization are doubly ferocious when awakened,' and that was nearly four hundred years ago."

"But, good Heavens, Dan, how did you—who is it?"

But that the boy wouldn't tell, saying that he might be wrong, and that he had no real evidence to support his suspicion. Mr. Leg insisted, but finally gave it up, and listened attentively while Dan recounted the story of the missing janitor, with all the details.

"There's just one thing we've got to do," finished the boy, "and that is find Patrick Cummings. It won't be easy, because it's certain that he's in hiding, if something worse hasn't happened to him. I looked around for a photograph of him, but couldn't find any."

"The thing to do is get the police after him," suggested Mr. Leg.

"Yes, sir," agreed Dan, but there was a curious expression in his eyes. "That's what I wanted to ask, will you go to Commissioner Hammel himself, since you know him?"

"Yes, I will," said the lawyer, "and I'll go right now."

And ten minutes later he was off, with a detailed description of Patrick Cummings, typewritten by Dan, in his pocket. A taxicab got him to headquarters for eighty cents.

This time he found the police commissioner in, and, being Simmie Leg, Dick Hammel's friend from college days, he was passed in ahead of a score of others who had been waiting anywhere from ten minutes to three hours.

Police Commissioner Richard Hammel was a tall, well-built man of middle age, with a fine-looking head, well carried, and piercing, cynical eyes. He was well connected socially, being a member of an old New York family that had been prominent in the life of the city for over a century.

"How are you, Simmie?" said he, rising from his chair with outstretched hand as Mr. Leg was ushered in. "Something new to see you around here."

"Hello, Dick!" The visitor took the proffered hand. "Yes, but you know what Devery said."

They chatted for ten minutes before the lawyer came to the purpose of his call. Then, pulling Dan's description of the missing janitor from his pocket, he explained the circumstances to the commissioner, saying that he wished a general alarm sent out for him all over the country.

Commissioner Hammel did not reply at once. He was apparently making a careful study of the length of a pencil he held in his hand, as he continued to gaze at it thoughtfully for some moments after Mr. Leg had stopped speaking. Finally he turned to his visitor.

"Simmie," he said slowly, "I'm sorry, but I can't do it."

"Why not," demanded the lawyer in surprise. "Of course, I know you might be working against yourself in case Cummings's testimony should free Mount, but justice—"

"It isn't that." The commissioner frowned. "Our esprit de corps doesn't go so far as to want to convict an innocent man of murder. But Mount isn't innocent." He eyed his visitor speculatively. "If it were anyone else, Simmie, I'd turn him off with evasion, but with you I can be frank.

"Of course Mount is guilty; the evidence is conclusive. I don't mean it's merely sufficient to convict; it's absolutely conclusive of his guilt. You know that as well as I do. But you think this man Cummings could throw new light on the affair. Well, you're right. He could."

The commissioner stopped to clear his throat.

"The fact is," he continued, "if Cummings were found and allowed to tell his story, he would bring notoriety on somebody. I don't know who. I really don't know, Simmie. But it's somebody that has a voice in high places, for word has come that

Cummings must not be found. You appreciate the circumstances. There's no use kicking up a scandal when it will do good to nobody."

There was a silence.

"Humph," grunted Mr. Leg finally, casting a thoughtful eye on the floor. "Of course, Dick, I don't like scandal any more than you do, especially when it hits one of my friends. But, in the first place, I don't know that this unknown person is my friend, and I don't admire this mystery stuff except in stories. And secondly, how do you know it wouldn't do any good?"

"Oh, come now, Simmie," replied the commissioner with a smile, "you know very well Mount's guilty. Don't be foolish."

"On the contrary," retorted the lawyer, "I believe he's innocent. And Dan—that is, a detective I've employed—believes it, too. I tell you, Dick, scandal or no scandal, Cummings must be found."

"If he is," said the commissioner decisively, "it will be without the help of the police."

"But, Dick—"

"No. A good friend of mine, and an invaluable member of this community, has asked me to stay off, and that's all there is to it. I don't know who he spoke for, and he wouldn't tell me; but since we unquestionably have the guilty man—"

"I tell you he's innocent!" repeated Mr. Leg warmly. He got up from his chair and put on his hat; he was dangerously near losing his temper for the first time in five years.

"Don't be an ass!" was the commissioner's reply.

"Is that so?" retorted Mr. Leg inelegantly. "I'll show you who's an ass, Dick Hammel! And let me tell you something: Patrick Cummings is going to be found if I have to hunt for him myself!"

And, leaving this awful threat to shake the walls behind him, he departed.

VI. The Name on the Screen

In the weeks that followed Mr. Simon Leg experienced for the first time in his life the sensation of mingled rage, helplessness, and doubt that attack a man when he grimly swears to do a thing and then fails in the execution. He said: "Patrick Cummings is going to be found if I have to hunt for him myself."

He hunted. Dan hunted. They hired detectives, and the detectives hunted. But three weeks after Mr. Leg had hurled his ultimatum at the commissioner of police the missing janitor was still missing.

The detectives were also set to work on other aspects of the case. They investigated the past lives of both Mount and his wife, but found out nothing of real value.

They discovered that for at least a year previous to her disappearance Mrs. Mount had been a more or less frequent visitor to cabarets, and once they thought they had found the man with whom she had run away, but he proved an alibi.

In all, Mr. Leg hired more than a dozen detectives, including the great Jim Dickinson himself, at a cost of several thousand dollars, but all he really got out of it was a huge stack of elaborate daily reports which, in fact, were absolutely useless.

They advised Mr. Leg to advertise a reward of five thousand dollars for Patrick Cummings, since he had expressed his willingness to spend ten times that sum if necessary, and Mr. Leg himself favored the idea. But Dan, who had surprised the lawyer on his return from the commissioner's office by not being surprised at what the commissioner had said, vetoed it, saying that it might be all right to offer a reward if the police were on their side, but utterly futile under the circumstances.

"Besides," argued the youth, "the first time Cummings saw the reward posted he would fly to cover, if he isn't there already. Public rewards are never any good, except to stimulate the police. And, besides that, I have a reason of my own."

Dan was the busiest of all. He spent a whole day going inch by inch through the basement where Cummings had lived, though he had previously searched it; he interviewed the Scotchman next door several times; he found and talked with everyone in the neighborhood who had ever seen the missing man; he pursued vainly a thousand avenues of information. It seemed that Patrick Cummings had come from nowhere and gone back to the same place.

His first appearance in the discoverable world had been the day when, nearly three years back, he had called at the office of Levis & Levis to ask for a job as janitor; his last, the evening of the murder. It got so that one thing, one name, one person, occupied Dan's mind like a mania; he thought, ate, slept, and breathed Patrick Cummings.

He forgot to open Miss Venner's desk for her of mornings; he forgot to comb his hair; he forgot to look when he crossed the street.

He came near to having cause to regret this latter neglect when one afternoon, hearing a warning honk, he jumped in the wrong direction and was knocked flat on his back by a touring car as it whizzed by. He scrambled to his feet in time to see the well-dressed figure of Judge Fraser Manton in the tonneau.

Finally, when there appeared to be nothing else to do, Dan would walk the streets for hours at time, cudgeling his brain for a scheme to find a man that evidently didn't want to be found, and meanwhile watching the passersby. He had followed many a gray-haired man with a scraggly mustache in the past three weeks; once he had found one named Cummings, but not Patrick.

The number of suspects rounded up by the detective mounted into the hundreds, so eager were they, for Mr. Leg had let it be known that the successful man would get a good-sized check.

Late one afternoon, a week before the date set for Mount's trial, Dan was walking down Eighth Avenue, tired, dejected, and ready to give up, but, nevertheless, with his eyes open. As he passed the tawdry front of a motion picture theater he stopped to glance over a group of men standing near, and then half unconsciously began to glance over the flaring posters displayed at the entrance to the theater. "The Scotchman said Cummings was a movie fan," he was thinking. Suddenly he gave a start, stopped still, as if transfixed by a sudden thought, and uttered the ejaculation of discovery.

"I never thought of that!" he exclaimed aloud, so that the girl in the ticket booth looked over him with an amused grin. He stood for several minutes, lost in consideration of the scheme that had entered his mind. Suddenly he pulled himself together, dashed into the avenue, and hopped on a downtown trolley car.

Fifteen minutes later he was in the office, explaining his plan to Mr. Leg with eager tongue. His enthusiasm was somewhat dampened by his employer's lack of it.

"All right," said the lawyer indifferently; "try it if you want to, though I don't think much of it. I'll foot the bill and stand for the reward if you find him. Write the letter yourself."

Dan went into the other room to ask Miss Venner for permission to use her machine. She granted it politely; she had had very little to say to Dan lately, since he had begun to neglect thousand little attentions he had always paid her. He sat down with a frown and began to click.

Half an hour later he submitted the following letter to his employer:

MANAGER OF THE EMPIRE MOTION PICTURE THEATER,
2168 EIGHTH AVENUE, NEW YORK

Dear Sir:

I am trying to find a man I need as a witness in an important case. I make you the following proposition:

You are to flash on your screen at every performance the words: "Patrick Cummings, formerly of 714 West 157th Street, is wanted on the telephone." If Cummings appears in response, tell him that the party rang off after asking that he wait till they call again. Then telephone at once to my office, 11902 Rector, and report that Cummings is there; and you are to hold Cummings, if possible, until someone from my office arrives. If it is impossible to hold him, have him followed by one of your employees when he leaves.

In case I find Cummings with this assistance from you, I will pay you five thousand dollars cash. As to my reliability and integrity, as well as ability to pay that amount, I refer you to the Murray National Bank of New York.

I am enclosing a detailed description of Cummings. This offer is good for only ten days from the date of this letter.

Yours truly,

"It's a pretty good idea," admitted Mr. Leg when he had finished reading it; "but what makes you think that Cummings will be fool enough to walk into the trap, provided he sees the bait?"

"That's just it," explained Dan. "I'm counting on his being somewhat of a fool. Put yourself in his place, sir. Here he is, sitting in the movies, when suddenly he sees his own name thrown on the screen, and, so that there may be no mistake about it, even the address where he lived. It won't occur to him that it is merely an attempt to find him; he will immediately conclude that whoever is asking for him must already know where he is, and the chances are that he'll be mighty anxious to find out who the call is from. At any rate, it's worth trying. It won't cost much unless we find him, and you won't care then."

"I certainly won't," agreed the lawyer grimly. "I didn't tell you, Dan, that I went to see Hammel again yesterday. Nothing doing."

"Of course not, sir." Dan took back the letter. "I'm going to take this right downstairs and have them run off ten thousand copies on the multigraph. Then I'll telephone to the Trow people for a list of motion picture theaters, and to an agency for ten or twelve girls to come and help us send them out. I think it would be best, sir, if you would sign the letters. If the signature were multigraphed perhaps they wouldn't feel so sure of the reward."

"By Jove, you've got it all down," observed Mr. Leg. "Yes, the letters ought to be signed, but you can do it as well as I. They won't know the difference." He looked at his watch. "I have to be uptown for dinner."

Thus was Dan's scheme set to work. Somewhat to his surprise, Miss Venner volunteered to stay and help; and, with the assistance of some dozen girls sent in by an agency, they had the ten thousand letters signed, addressed, sealed, and stamped by midnight. Dan carried them to the main post office, after which he escorted Miss Venner home.

Meanwhile, Mr. Leg was acquiring a fresh stock of indignation. His dinner engagement uptown was only half social; it was an informal meeting of a special committee of one of the most exclusive clubs of the city to arrange for a dinner to be given

in honor of one of their members on the occasion of his return from a high diplomatic position abroad. The membership of the committee included James Reynolds,
the banker; Alfred Cinnott and Corkran Updergraff, capitalists; Judge Fraser Manton,
and two or three others.

Although Mr. Leg had met Judge Manton several years before, and had of course
seen him many times since, they had never got beyond a bowing acquaintance. So
when, after dinner was over and they retired to the club library, Mr. Leg approached
the judge with a view to conversation, there was a slight tinge of formality in his manner. They talked a little on a topic that had been discussed earlier in the evening, on
which they had disagreed.

"By the way, Judge," observed Mr. Leg when a chance offered itself, "I want to
thank you for assigning me to that Mount case—the murder case, you know—though
I certainly can't guess why I was selected."

"Ah," Judge Manton's brow lifted. "Is it a matter for thanks?"

"It certainly is. Most interesting three weeks I've ever had. I've worked day and
night. Spent ten thousand dollars, and there's a chance I'll win it."

"M-m-m! Of course you know I can't discuss the case out of court."

"Oh, no! I understand that," agreed Mr. Leg hastily. "Only I just thought I'd let
you know that I'll probably be in court tomorrow with a request for postponement."

"Ah!" Again Judge Manton's brows were lifted. "I suppose you have a good
reason."

"No, I haven't. That is, no particular reason. But I haven't been able to get hold
of my most important witness, and I believe there is usually no difficulty in getting a
postponement when a man's life depends on it. I believe the district attorney will make
no objection."

For a moment there was no reply. Judge Manton took from his pocket a silk case
embroidered with gold, extracted a cigarette, and lit it. He blew a long column of
smoke slowly into the air, and another. Then he turned with startling suddenness and
spoke rapidly in a low voice, looking straight into Mr. Leg's eyes:

"I don't know if the district attorney will object, Mr. Leg. But I know that I will.
The calendar is too far behind already to permit of further postponements, except for
the most cogent reasons. You've had a month to prepare your case and find your witnesses. Of course you may come to court and enter your petition for a postponement
if you wish. But, my dear Leg, speaking merely as a private citizen, I wouldn't advise
you to bank much on it."

Judge Manton stopped abruptly, blew a third column of smoke into the air, turned
on his heel, and walked away.

"Well!" ejaculated Mr. Leg to himself in astonishment. "I'll be damned if they haven't got to Manton the same as they did to Dick Hammel Lord, how I'd love to show 'em all up!"

And he walked all the way home from downtown, a distance of over two miles, in order to inspect the faces of the passersby in search of Patrick Cummings. He was deadly in earnest, was Mr. Simon Leg. Think of walking over two miles when a mere uplifting of a finger would have brought a spirited taxi dashing to the curb!

The following morning at the office Mr. Leg lost no time in telling Dan of his conversation with Judge Manton. His indignation had increased during the night; he denounced the entire police force and judiciary of the city.

"Think of it!" he exclaimed. "They are willing to throw away an innocent man's life merely to save the good name of a friend! Or there may be politics in it. Whatever it is, it's rotten! I didn't think it of Dick Hammel, and now the judge himself—"

"I'm not surprised, sir," observed Dan. "I've half a mind to tell you—but it would do no good. Our only hope now is the movies. We've got ten thousand of them working for us. We've covered everything within five hundred miles of New York; the only trouble is, he's nearly as apt to be in San Francisco."

"Or dead."

"Yes, sir. For Mount's sake I hope not."

"Well, we've got just six days left. I'm going to call up Dickinson and tell him to send out more men. I don't know, Dan; I'm about ready to give up."

A little later telephone calls began to come in from the motion picture theaters. They asked every conceivable question under the sun, from the number of hairs on Patrick Cummings's head to the color his shoestrings. Dan finally gave up all thought of leaving the office, and all day long he sat at his desk with the telephone receiver at his ear. Toward the middle of the afternoon he made two calls on his own account: one to his mother to tell her that he would not be home that night, and the other to a furniture dealer on Fourteenth Street. An hour later Mr. Leg, hearing a most unusual noise in the outer office, stepped to his door to see a man setting up a cot with mattress, covers, and pillows.

"I sent for it," explained Dan to his astonished employer. "I'm going to sleep here, sir, to answer the telephone."

After that he refused to leave the office; he had his meals sent in from a nearby restaurant. The truth was, Dan's conscience was troubling him; he had begun to fear that he had done wrong not to tell his suspicions and his reasons for them to his employer, though he tried to console himself by reflecting that he would have only been laughed at.

But the poor boy felt that his desire for glory had jeopardized the life of an inno-cent man, and he was miserable. His whole hope now lay in the telephone. Would the word come? Every time the bell rang his nerves quivered.

The next day Mr. Leg went to court and requested a postponement of two weeks, having first gained the acquiescence of the district attorney's office. Judge Manton denied the petition, and the lawyer left in a rage.

Only five days were left before the trial.

Several false alarms came from the various motion picture theaters. Most of them were obviously mistakes, but one sent Dan flying for a train to Stamford. When he got there he found the manager of the theater seated in his office, chatting with a little, redhaired Irishman, whose name indeed proved to be Patrick Cummings, but who was certainly not the one wanted.

"Didn't you read the description of him?" Dan demanded.

"Sure," replied the manager, "but I wasn't taking any chances."

"You're a fool!" retorted the boy shortly as he started at a run to catch the next train back to New York."

That was Monday afternoon, and the trial was set for Wednesday.

Later that same afternoon Mr. Leg, wandering into the outer office, approached Dan's desk. The boy was seated there with the telephone at his elbow, apparently bur-ied deep in contemplation of some object spread out before him on the desk. Mr. Leg, going closer and looking over his shoulder, saw a white slip of paper with the words, "Bonneau et Mouet—Sec," written on it in ink, and besides it a large reproduction of a man's photograph.

"What in the name of goodness are you doing with that?" demanded Mr. Leg, pointing to the photograph.

Dan jumped with surprise.

"Oh, I—I didn't know you were there, sir!" He flushed. "Why, I—er—I was just looking at it." He managed a smile. "Studying human nature, sir."

The lawyer grunted. "If you ask me, Dan, I think you're getting kind of queer."

"Yes, sir." The boy folded the photograph with the slip of paper inside and placed it in his pocket. The lawyer regarded him sharply for a moment, then returned to the other room.

Tuesday morning came, the day before the trial. Dan did not move from his desk all day and evening. The telephone rang over and over, and each time he took up the receiver it was with a hand that trembled so that it could scarcely hold the receiver to his ear. The fact was, he had persuaded himself, or, rather, he felt that the little wire was certain to bring him the word he wanted. But it did not come.

The following morning at ten o'clock William Mount was called before the bar to stand trial for the murder of his wife.

The courtroom was not crowded, for the case was not a celebrated one; but there was a good-sized gathering of those people who may always be counted on to turn up at a murder trial, and there was much twisting of curious necks when the prisoner was led in. There was little change in Mount's appearance since the day a month previous, when he had been called before Judge Manton to plead.

His face was slightly paler and his cheeks more sunken; but he wore the same air of heavy, stolid indifference, and his eyes were sullen and devoid of hope.

Mr. Leg started proceedings by asking again for a postponement, declaring that he had been unable to locate his most important witness. Assistant District Attorney Thornton, for the prosecution, refrained from argument. Judge Manton denied the request, saying that counsel for the defense had had ample time to prepare his case.

There was little difficulty in selecting the jury, as neither side appeared to be particular, and the box was filled by noon. The addresses to the jury were short, and by the time court reconvened after lunch they were ready for the witnesses.

The prosecution opened with the young man who had been called to the scene of the murder by Mount's scream, and had found him standing over the body with the knife in his hand. His testimony, with that of three other tenants and as many policemen, consumed the afternoon.

When court adjourned a little before six Mr. Leg returned to his office to find Dan seated at his desk, staring moodily at the telephone.

"Nothing doing, Dan?" said Mr. Leg grimly.

"No, sir."

"Been here all day?"

"Yes, sir."

"It's funny you can't see," put in Miss Venner with a sudden sharpness, "that he's getting sick over it. He sits and stares at that telephone like a crazy man. He hasn't eaten a bite all day. Of course, not that I care, only I—I—"

She flushed and stopped.

"Can't help it," remarked Mr. Leg gloomily. "Come on in the other room, Dan, and I'll tell you how it went in court. Or wait, I'll sit here."

The following day at noon the prosecution finished. They had presented evidence that the murdered woman was the wife of the prisoner, and had left him, furnishing—as the assistant district attorney had said in his opening address—the strongest possible combination of motives—jealousy and revenge. When the prosecution's last witness left the stand it was easy to see from the expression of the jurors' faces as they stole glances at the prisoner that they regarded the case as already proven. Mr. Leg, following Dan's instructions, had attempted to gain time by prolonging the cross-examinations; but he was anything but an adept at the game, and several times he had been prodded by Judge Manton.

The first witness called by the defense was the prisoner himself. Aided—and sometimes retarded—by questions from Mr. Leg, he merely repeated the story he had previously told to the police, the coroner, and his lawyer. Again Mr. Leg attempted to drag out the proceedings by prolonging the examination; but at length his invention ran out and he was forced to let the witness go, reflecting, however, that the cross-examination would occupy another hour or two.

Therefore, was he struck with consternation when he heard the prosecuting attorney say calmly:

"I will not cross-examine, your honor."

"Call your next witness, Mr. Leg," said Judge Manton sharply.

Luckily Mr. Leg had one—a Mr. Rafter, of the firm by whom Mount had been employed as a bookkeeper. He was followed by two men who had known the prisoner in his earlier and happier days, who testified to his good character and mild temper. At that point court was adjourned till tomorrow.

Mr. Leg missed his dinner that evening. Long after darkness had fallen and windows had begun to make their tens of thousands of little squares of light against the huge black forms of the skyscrapers, the lawyer sat in his office talking with Dan between patches of silence, trying to invent something that could be applied as a desperate last resort.

Jim Dickinson, chief of the best detective bureau in the city, whose men had been employed on the case for the past month, was called in by telephone, but he had nothing to suggest, and soon left them. The lawyer had told Dan of the failure of the prosecution to cross-examine Mount, observing bitterly that their case was so strong they could afford to appear compassionate.

Trinity's chimes rang out for ten o'clock. Mr. Leg arose and put on his hat.

"Well, I guess we're done for," he observed. "We've only got two more witnesses, and they don't amount to anything. Three hours for the summing up; it will probably go to the jury by three o'clock tomorrow afternoon. It's no use, Dan. You're taking it too hard; it's not your fault, my boy. See you in the morning. Good night."

After his employer had gone, Dan sat motionless at his desk with his eyes on the telephone. He felt that it had betrayed him. Curious, how confident he had felt that the wire would bring him the word he awaited!

"Bum hunch," he muttered.

The little black instrument was distasteful to his sight. He hated it. An impulse entered his mind to seize the thing, jerk it from its cord, and hurl it out of the window; an impulse so strong that he actually got up from his chair and walked over and sat down on the cot for fear he would give way to it. He sat there for some time. Finally he bent over and began unlacing his shoes preparatory to lying down. The knot was tight and he jerked angrily at the string.

As he did so the telephone bell rang.

He hastened to the desk, took up the telephone, placed the receiver to his ear, and said "Hello!"

"Hello!" came a female voice. "Is this Rector 11902?"

"Yes."

"Wait a minute, please. This is long distance. Albany wants you."

There was a moment's wait, while Dan trembled with impatience. Then a man's voice came:

"Hello! Is this Simon Leg's office?"

"Yes," Dan replied.

"The lawyer, Broadway, New York?"

"Yes."

"This is the Royal Theater, No. 472 Jefferson Avenue, Albany. Four, seven, two Jefferson Avenue. I've got your man, Patrick Cummings."—"Yes, I tell you, I've got him. He's here—wait—wait a minute—I'm afraid he'll beat it—"

The last words came faintly. There was a buzzing on the line, a series of clicks, and the wire sounded dead. Dan moved the receiver hook frantically up and down; finally he got a reply from the local operator, who informed him that Albany had rung off. Yes, she could get them again, probably in a quarter of an hour; would he please hang up his receiver?

He did so, but took it off again immediately and asked for Grand Central Station. From the information bureau he learned that there would be no train to Albany for two hours, and then a slow one. Dan grabbed up his hat and, without stopping even to turn out the light, dashed from the office. He ran all the way to the subway station, where he boarded an uptown express train. At Fourteenth Street he got off and rushed up the steps to the sidewalk three at a time, and started east at breakneck speed, knocking over pedestrians and leaping across the path of streetcars and automobiles. Two minutes later he appeared, breathless and trembling, before two men who were seated in the entrance of a garage near Third Avenue.

"The fastest car in the place!" he hurled at them. "Quick!"

He thrust a bunch of twenty-dollar bills under the nose of one of the men.

"Don't look, get busy!" he commanded. "The fastest car you've got, and a chauffer that can drive!"

Finally they were moved to action. Lights were turned on in the rear of the garage, a limousine was wheeled to one side, disclosing to view a big touring car, and a sleepy-looking young man, wearing a cap and drab uniform, appeared from somewhere.

"Here's one hundred dollars!" cried Dan to one of the men, thrusting a roll of bills into his hand. "If that isn't enough, I'll pay the rest when I get back."

He scrambled into the tonneau and the chauffer mounted his seat in front. The powerful engine began to throb.

"Where to?" asked the chauffer.

"Albany," replied Dan as the car started forward. "And there's a fifty-dollar bill in it if we get there by four o'clock!"

VII. The End

Mr. Simon Leg arrived at his office early the following morning. After reaching home the night before he stayed up for four hours working on his address to the jury, though he felt it to be a hopeless task, and when he did go to bed he slept fitfully. That was the explanation of his red eyes and general appearance of discomfort as he opened his office door.

He found Miss Venner with her hat and coat still on, gazing at the cot in the corner.

"Where's Dan?" demanded Mr. Leg, stopping short after a glance around.

"I don't know." The stenographer turned a troubled countenance on him. "He wasn't here when I came in." She pointed to the cot. "The covers haven't been disturbed. I guess he didn't sleep here. And the electric lights were all turned on."

The lawyer grunted. "Strange. I left him here late last night, and he intended to stay then. There's no message anywhere?"

"No, sir; I looked." Miss Venner appeared to hesitate, then continued. "You don't think—he's done anything, do you, Mr. Leg? He acted queer yesterday. I know he felt responsible, somehow, about Mr. Mount. I—I'm afraid, sir."

Even Mr. Leg, who didn't pretend to be a student of human nature, realized suddenly that the quiver in the stenographer's voice and the expression in her eyes betokened more than ordinary concern. He crossed over and laid a fatherly hand on her shoulder.

"Don't you worry, Miss Venner," said he. "Nothing has happened to Dan and nothing is likely to happen. He's fully able to take care of himself, and someone else into the bargain."

And then, as Miss Venner caught the significance of his last words and began to flush indignantly, he speedily retreated into the other room.

He looked through the drawers on his desk, thinking Dan might have left a message there, but there was nothing. He glanced at his watch; it was 8:20, and court was to convene at nine.

"I suppose I ought to go over and have a talk with Mount first," he thought as he sat down at his desk and began to stuff papers into a portfolio. "Poor devil! Well, we've tried, anyway. I wonder where the deuce Dan can be? At that, I've got a pretty fair speech here, though I don't suppose it will do any good. It isn't possible Dan has gone somewhere after—but there's no use trying to guess."

A little later he departed for the courthouse, leaving Miss Venner alone in the office.

The door had no sooner closed behind him than the stenographer rushed to the telephone and asked for a number.

"Hello, Mrs. Culp?" she said presently. "This is Miss Venner, at the office."—"Yes. I—that is, Mr. Leg wants to speak to Dan."—"He isn't there?"—"I didn't know, only he went uptown some time ago, and I thought he might have gone home."—"You haven't seen him for four days?"—"Yes, I know he has been sleeping in the office."—"Yes, it's dreadful; I'm so glad it will be over today."—"Yes. Thank you, Mrs. Culp."

She slowly got up and returned to her own desk where she sat gazing at the cot in the corner. "I wish Mr. Leg *never* had got a case," she said aloud vehemently. She took out her embroidery and started to work on it. The minutes passed draggingly. She felt that an hour must have gone by when the sound of chimes entered at the open window. "Good Heavens, it's only nine o'clock!" she thought.

She went to the window and stood for some time looking down into the street far below, then returned to her sewing. Suddenly she stopped and gazed in astonishment at what she had done, then threw the thing down on her desk with a gasp of irritation. She had embroidered two whole figures on the wrong side of the cloth.

"I don't care!" she snapped. "I don't see how I can expect myself—"

She was interrupted by the ringing of the telephone bell.

She sprang to the instrument. "Hello."

"Hello," came the response. "Is this you, Miss Venner?"

"Oh!" The light of joy that leaped into her eyes! "Oh, Dan, it's you!"

"Yes." It was indeed Dan's voice, eager and rapid. "Has Mr. Leg gone to court yet?"

"Yes, half an hour ago. Where are you?"

"Yonkers. In an automobile. I've got Patrick Cummings."

"No!"

"Yes, I have. Found him at Albany. I got a call at the office last night, and I certainly didn't lose any time getting there. Made it in a little over four hours. A fellow named Saunders, manager of a moving picture theater, had him locked up in his office. Saunders was certainly out for that five thousand, and he deserves it. I would have been down there when the court opened only we were held up at Peekskill for speeding. Fool policeman wouldn't listen to reason."

"But, Dan, have you really got that Cummings? The right one?"

"I sure have. Listen, Miss Venner, here's what I want you to do. Go over to the courthouse as fast as you can—take a taxi—and tell Mr. Leg I'm coming. Tell him to hold things off—put some more witnesses on, do anything—till I get there. I'll come as fast as the police will let me."

"All right, I'll hurry. Oh, Dan, I'm so glad!"

"So am I. Good-by."

Miss Venner hung up the receiver and sprang to her feet. Her eyes dancing with excitement, and her flushed and joyous face were good to look at as she ran to the closet and took down her coat and hat. Of course, she had to examine herself in the mirror above the washbasin, but nevertheless she was out of the office and on the street in less than five minutes after Dan's last words had come over the wire.

She found a taxi in front of Raoul's and gave the driver the address of the courthouse. North, they crawled on Broadway; the crowds of hurrying people on the sidewalk, the noise of the traffic, and the May sunshine, all answered to Miss Venner's mood and made her feel that she was a part, and not the least important, of this busy world. She leaned forward and spoke over the driver's shoulder.

"I'm in a hurry, you know."

He nodded and made a quick turn to the left to get around a slow-moving truck. Skillfully and swiftly he made his way through Broadway's crowded traffic as far as Grand Street, where he turned east, and after that it was easier. Soon he drew up at the entrance of a large, gloomy building whose granite pillars had been blackened by time.

"Thank you, miss," said he, touching his cap as his fare alighted and handed him a dollar bill.

Inside the courthouse, Miss Venner was forced to ask the way of a uniformed attendant, who obligingly accompanied her up two flights of stairs and down a long, dark corridor, finally halting before a pair of double swinging doors bearing the inscription in plain black letters: "General Sessions, Part VI."

"There you are," said the attendant.

She pushed the open door and entered. At first she was bewildered by the unexpected spaciousness of the room as well as the throng of people—men and women—seated on the benches and chairs; but finally she saw Mr. Leg. He was standing at one end of the attorneys' table, listening to a reply to one of his questions from the witness in the chair, who was a young woman in a blue dress.

Miss Venner timidly made her way up the aisle, feeling two hundred eyes staring at her, and through the little swinging gate in front of the public benches. There she halted, hesitating, wondering what would happen to her if she dared interrupt Mr. Leg while he was examining a witness. Finally she sat down at the table, on which were lying some scattered sheets of paper, pulled a pencil from her hair, and scribbled a few lines.

She walked over and handed the paper to Mr. Leg. He took it with a glance of surprise at finding her there. He motioned her to a chair and she sat down, not ten feet from the prisoner. But she didn't notice that, for she was busy watching Mr. Leg's face as he read the slip of paper. It expressed doubt, stupefaction, incredulous joy; his face grew pale at the unexpectedness of it, and he stood looking at the paper, hardly believing his eyes.

"Go on with the witness, Mr. Leg," came the voice of Judge Manton from the bench.

"Yes, your honor—I—what—" the lawyer stammered. "That is, I'm through with the witness, your honor."

The prosecuting attorney bobbed up from his chair to say that he would not cross-examine, and sat down again. Mr. Leg hastened over to whisper to Miss Venner, pointing to the slip of paper:

"Is this true, is it possible?"

"Yes, sir," she whispered back. "He just telephoned from Yonkers. I came right over—"

She was interrupted by the voice of Judge Manton:

"Call your next witness, Mr. Leg."

He had just one left—a young woman who, like the preceding witness, had known Mrs. Mount during the time she had lived with her husband, and whose function it was to testify to the prisoner's excellent character during that period and the unfailing tenderness and affection he had shown his wife, even when she had begun to neglect her home. Mr. Leg asked many questions; he made them as long as possible, and he drawled his words.

In the past two days he had learned something about the art of killing time, and though the testimony of this particular witness would ordinarily have occupied barely fifteen minutes he succeeded in keeping her on the stand almost an hour. Finally he was forced to stop, and the witness was dismissed.

"Have you any more witnesses?" asked Judge Manton.

Mr. Leg didn't, but he did have an idea.

"I would like to recall Mount for a few questions, your honor."

The judge nodded impatiently, and the prisoner was summoned to the witness chair. Mr. Leg began questioning him concerning the disappearance of his wife four years before. Then he switched to the night of the murder, and once more Mount told of his entry into the apartment house, of the man he saw in the hall, and of the finding of his wife's body. This consumed some time, until finally an interruption came from Judge Manton:

"This has all been gone over before, Mr. Leg."

"Yes, your honor, I—"

The lawyer stopped and turned. His ear caught the sound of the almost noiseless opening of the swinging door of the courtroom. Every eye in the room followed the direction of his gaze, and what they saw was the entrance of a little, gray-haired man with a scraggly mustache, followed by a twenty-year-old youth, who had a firm grip on the other's arm.

Mr. Leg turned to address the court:

"I am through with the witness—"

Again he was interrupted, this time by a cry of amazement from the lips of the gray-haired man who had just entered. There was an instant commotion; the spectators rose to their feet and craned their necks to see the man who had uttered the cry, and who was now saying to the youth:

"You didn't tell me—you didn't tell me—"

The face of Judge Manton had turned pale with irritation at this disorder in his court. He rapped the desk with his gavel and called out sharply:

"Order! Silence! Sit down!"

But by this time Mr. Leg had met Dan's eyes and read their message of assurance and triumph. He turned to the judge:

"Your honor, that man is my next witness. I apologize for the disturbance." Again he turned to look at Dan.

"Patrick Cummings to the stand!"

The spectators sat down again, though whispers were still going back and forth over the room. The prosecuting attorney was leaning back in his chair with the amused and bored smile he had worn through the presentation of the defense. (It must be admitted that Mr. Leg had shown himself a fearful tyro.) William Mount was looking indifferently across the table at Miss Venner; as for her, she was gazing with bright eyes at Dan as he led Patrick Cummings up to the rail and turned him over to the court attendant, who conducted him to the witness chair.

Dan crossed over to Mr. Leg and murmured in his ear:

"Just get him started on his story. He'll do the rest. I'll prompt you if you need it."

Then he took a chair at the lawyer's elbow.

The witness gave his name to the clerk and was sworn in. His voice trembled, his hands were nervously gripping the arms of the chair, and his eyes were shifting constantly from side to side with an expression of fear. In answer to Mr. Leg's first question, he said his name was Patrick Cummings, his address No. 311 Murray Street, Albany, and his occupation janitor, though he was not working at present.

"Did you ever work in New York City?" asked Mr. Leg.

"Yes, sir."

"As janitor?"

"Yes, sir."

"At what address?"

"No. 714 West One Hundred and Fifty-seventh Street."

"When did you start work there?"

The witness thought a moment.

"I don't know exactly; but it was sometime in July 1912."

One of the jurors in the last row interrupted to say that the witness was not speaking loud enough for him to hear. Judge Manton, who had been gazing directly at Cummings ever since he took the chair, admonished him to speak louder.

"Where did you work before that?" continued Mr. Leg.

"In Philadelphia, sir. That was my first job in New York."

"How long were you janitor at No. 714 West One Hundred and Fifty-seventh Street?"

"Nearly three years."

"Were you there on April 3, 1915?"

"Yes, sir."

Dan got up from his chair to whisper something in Mr. Leg's ear. The lawyer nodded and returned to the witness.

"Cummings, did you ever see Mrs. Elaine Mount, known as Alice Reeves, a tenant in the house where you were janitor?"

"I knew Miss Reeves, yes, sir."

"She lived there quite a while, didn't she?"

"Yes, sir. I don't know how long; she was there when I came."

"Did you see Miss Reeves often?"

"Oh, yes, I saw her every day; sometimes two or three times." Again, Dan got up to whisper a suggestion in the lawyer's ear; from this time on, indeed, half the questions were suggested by him. As for the witness, he was losing, little by little, the nervous fright that had possessed him when he took the chair. His voice was becoming stronger and louder, and his eyes had gained an expression of determination and defiance.

"Now, Cummings, do you know if Miss Reeves ever had any callers?"

"Yes, sir."

"Well, did she?"

"She had one."

"Only one?"

"There were others, sir, but not very often; but this man came every two or three days, sometimes oftener than that."

"So it was a man?"

"Yes, sir."

"Can you describe him?"

The witness hesitated, then spoke in a louder voice than before:

"He was a man about thirty-eight or forty, with dark hair and dark eyes. He was a good-looking man."

"And you say he would call often on Miss Reeves. How do you know he was calling on her?"

"Why, he would go in her flat."

"Did you see him go in?"

"Of course I did. And besides, he would often send me out for something at the restaurant or delicatessen; and I'd take it up, and he'd be there in the flat, and he'd give me a dollar, or sometimes even five."

"So he was liberal, was he?"

"Sir?"

"He was good to you, was he?"

"Oh, yes; he always gave me something. He always had lots of money."

"Do you know who this man was?"

"No, sir. That is, I don't know his name."

"Do you know where he lived?"

"No, sir."

"I see. And did he continue to call on Miss Reeves all the time you were there?"

"Yes, sir. Two or three times a week, except toward the last, when he didn't come quite so often."

The lawyer stopped to confer with Dan a moment. Then, with a nod of satisfaction, he turned again to the witness.

"Now, Cummings, do you remember whether this man whom you have described called at No. 714 West One Hundred and Fifty-seventh Street on the evening of Saturday, April 3, 1915?"

The witness's answer was lost in a sudden stir which passed over the courtroom as the speculators leaned forward. Judge Manton took advantage of the interruption to beckon to an attendant for a glass of water. When he came he drank a little and placed the glass, still half full, before him on his desk. The last question was reread by the clerk, and the witness repeated his answer:

"Yes, sir; he was there."

"What time did he arrive?"

"I don't know; I didn't see him come in."

"Did you see him at all that evening?"

"Yes, sir."

"What time?"

"About half past eight, I think it was, the bell rang for the dumbwaiter. That was the way he always sent for me to come up when he wanted something. I went up and rang the bell at Miss Reeve's door, and he opened it."

"How was he dressed?"

"Why, he had on a black suit, except he had taken off his coat and put on a smoking jacket. He always did that."

"Did you see Miss Reeves?"

"Yes, sir; I went inside the hall to wait, while he went to the desk to write something, and I saw Miss Reeves in the front room. She was sitting by the table, crying. She had her handkerchief up to her eyes."

"Did she say anything to you?"

"No, sir; she didn't even look at me."

"I see. What did the man go to the desk for?"

"He went for some paper to write down something. I remember he didn't find any there, and he took a piece out of his pocket. He wanted to write down the name of some wine he wanted me to get. He wrote it down and gave it to me, and gave me a ten-dollar bill to get it with."

Mr. Leg turned to find Dan at his elbow with a slip of paper in his hand. The lawyer took it, and examined it while the boy whispered in his ear. By this time every spectator in the room was listening intently to the witness's every word. The prosecuting attorney had leaned forward in his chair with a new expression of interest for this unexpected Irishman. Judge Manton sat up straight, gazing at the prisoner Mount with an expressionless countenance.

"I have here," Mr. Leg resumed, "a slip of paper bearing in ink the words, Bonneau et Mouet—Sec. Now, Cummings, is this the paper which this man in Miss Reeves's apartment handed to you on the night of April third?"

The witness took the slip and examined it. "Yes, sir, that's it," he said finally. "That's the name of the wine he wanted me to get."

"And that's the paper he wrote on and handed to you?"

"Yes, sir; it's the same one," answered Cummings. "It's got that funny thing in the corner."

Mr. Leg turned to the judge:

"You honor, I wish to introduce this paper in evidence."

Judge Manton merely inclined his head. The clerk took the slip and marked it.

"Now, Cummings," went on the lawyer, "after this man gave you the slip of paper, what did you do?"

"I went out after the wine."

"Did you get it?"

"Yes, sir, but I had a hard time. I always went to a wine store at the corner of One Hundred Fifty-eighth Street and Broadway, but they didn't have this kind, so I went down to One Hundred Twenty-fifth Street, and I had to go to four or five stores before I could find it. I was gone about an hour, or maybe more, because when I got back it was nearly ten o'clock."

"All right, go on. You took the wine upstairs?"

"Yes, sir. I went up to Miss Reeves's apartment, and I was about to ring the bell when I heard her crying inside. She was crying and talking very loud."

"Could you hear what she was saying?"

"Some of it, yes, sir. I heard her say, 'Let me go! I love him! Let me go!' then I heard the man's voice, only he didn't talk as loud as she did; but I could hear him even plainer than her. He was saying, 'You'll stay right here; do you hear? I won't let you go back to him, do you hear? Let him wait all night if he wants to.' I didn't want to ring the bell while they were going on like that, so I stood and listened for a long while. Miss Reeves kept crying, and the man kept swearing at her. He kept saying, 'I won't let you go back to him!'"

"Finally I got tired waiting and rang the bell. I guess I stood there half an hour. The man opened the door, and he told me to come in, and go and put the wine in the refrigerator. I went back to the kitchen and unwrapped it, and put the bottle on the ice. Then I went out again. As soon as I closed the door behind me I heard them fighting again inside."

"Do you remember what became of the slip of paper on which this man had written the name of the wine?"

"Yes, sir; I remember they had wrapped it up with the wine. I threw it on the floor with the wrapping paper."

"I see. What did you do after you left the apartment?"

"I turned down the lights in the halls, and then went down to the basement and got ready to go to bed."

"Do you know what time that was?"

"Yes, sir; when I wound my clock it was twenty minutes past ten. I put some coal on the hot-water furnace and locked the basement doors and went to bed."

"Well?"

"Well, I'd been in bed, I guess, about half an hour and was nearly asleep when there was a knock on the door. I went—"

"You mean the door of your room?"

"Yes, sir; the room in the basement where I was sleeping. I got up and lit the gas and opened the door, and there stood the colonel."

"The colonel?"

"That's what I called the man who called on Miss Reeves. He stepped inside the room, and I saw that he had a big bundle of papers and things in his hand. He had on his hat and light overcoat, and the muffler he always wore around the lower part of his face. He told me to close the door because he had the bundle in his hands, then he said, 'Hurry up, Cummings; dress yourself. Don't ask me any questions.'

"I knew at once from his funny voice and the way he looked at me that something had happened. I didn't say a word, but dressed myself as quick as I could. When I was done he said, 'Where's the furnace? I want to burn this stuff.' I went back and opened the furnace door, and he threw the papers and things on the fire. He wouldn't let me help him."

"Did you see any of the articles? Do you know what they were?"

"No, sir; only there was a lot of letters and other papers. I supposed they came from Miss Reeves's—"

"Never mind what you supposed. Go on."

"Well, after the stuff was burned up we went back in front. He had me sit down in a chair, and then he said, 'Cummings, I've got a proposition to make to you. I'll give you a thousand dollars cash to leave New York immediately and put yourself where nobody can find you.'

"I didn't know what to answer, I was so surprised, and he went on to say that that was all he happened to have with him, and that it was lucky he had that much. He said he wouldn't tell me who he was, but he told me how to have something printed in the Herald if I ever needed money, and he would send me some. He said I'd have to take his word for that. I decided to do it when I saw him count out the thousand dollars on the table. I promised to leave right away, in ten minutes, without stopping to take anything but my clothes."

Mr. Leg interrupted:

"Didn't you suspect that a crime had been committed?"

"Yes, sir; of course I knew something had happened, but all that money was too much for me. After he had gone——"

"Didn't he wait to see you go?"

"No, sir; he went right away. I guess he knew that I'd certainly beat it with the money. I let him out at the basement door, and in less than no time I had my clothes packed and was all ready. I went out by the basement door, too, but I couldn't make myself go. I stood there on the sidewalk maybe two minutes calling myself a fool, but I couldn't help it. I wanted to see what had happened in that flat upstairs.

"I went up to the ground floor by the front steps, leaving the outer door open as I entered, dropped my suitcase in the front hall, and went up two more flights to the door of Miss Reeves's flat. It was locked. I ran down to the basement for my duplicate key, came back up and unlocked the door. The flat was dark. I switched on the lights, and there on the floor I saw Miss Reeves. The hilt of a knife was sticking from her breast, and there was blood on her dress, and her face looked awful. It scared me so I didn't know what I was doing. I ran out without turning off the lights, and I think I forgot to lock the door.

"I ran back to the ground floor as fast as I could and picked up my suitcase. I started for the outside door, and then I suddenly saw a man coming up the stoop. I was so scared I didn't know what to do. I stepped back into the corner of the hall as the man entered the door, and, scared as I was, I was surprised to see that it wasn't one of the tenants, or anyone I had ever seen before. He came in and started upstairs without saying anything, just glancing at me. I picked up——"

"Just a minute, Cummings," Mr. Leg interrupted. He turned and pointed at William Mount. "Is that the man you saw enter and go upstairs, after you had seen Miss Reeve's dead body on the floor?"

The witness examined the prisoner for a moment..

"Yes, sir, I think so. The light in the hall was dim, so I couldn't be sure, but it looks like him."

"All right. Go on."

"That's all, sir. I picked up the suitcase and ran. I took the subway to the end of the line, and there I got on a trolley for Yonkers. The next day I went on to Albany, and I've been hiding there ever since."

"And don't you know that you have made yourself an accessory to this murder and are liable to punishment?" asked the lawyer.

"Yes, sir, I know that. I didn't care at first, until I saw in the papers that some man that I knew was innocent had been arrested for it. Then I wanted to come and tell all I knew—I really did, sir—but I was afraid, and I couldn't ever make myself start. When that young man came after me this morning"—he pointed to Dan—"I was only too glad to come, sir. Ask him. I hope I won't be punished, sir."

At this point Judge Manton interrupted the examination. He leaned forward in his chair as he spoke, while the fingers of his right hand were toying with the edge of the glass which had remained on his desk, half full of water.

"I think we had better adjourn for luncheon, Mr. Leg," he observed. "It's one o'clock. You may continue with the witness after the recess."

Dan sprang up to murmur something in Mr. Leg's ear. The lawyer looked astonished and bewildered, but finally nodded in acquiescence.

"Very well, your honor," he said to the court. "But I would like to ask the witness just two more questions before adjournment, if your honor please."

"Let them be short," the judge said curtly.

Mr. Leg turned to the witness.

"Cummings, I want to ask you if this man whom you called the colonel, whom you saw and heard quarreling with Alice Reeves, and who gave you a thousand dollars to flee from the scene of the murder—I want to ask you if that man is now in this courtroom?"

Cummings hesitated a moment and glanced from side to side, then suddenly straightened up and said in a loud and distinct tone:

"Yes, sir, he is here."

A gasp of astonishment came from every side.

"Will you point him out to the judge and jury?"

For reply, Cummings turned and leveled his finger straight at the face of Judge Manton.

But the wave of astonishment and incredulity that swept over the courtroom was swiftly drowned in a great cry of alarm. Judge Manton, looking over the accusing finger straight into Cummings's face, had lifted the glass of water to his lips; and Dan, springing up and knocking Mr. Leg out of his way, had leaped like a panther over the rails to the daïs and with one sweep of his arm dashed the glass from the judge's hand to the floor.

Court attendants ran forward, shouting; the jury stood up in their box; several of them leaped over the partition and rushed onto the platform of justice; the spectators tumbled over the rail by scores, trampling one another; screams were heard from a hundred throats. Dan was hanging desperately on to Judge Manton's gown, calling at the top of his voice:

"The water was poisoned! Quick! Hold him! You fools! He'll kill himself! Help!"

But the officers and attendants shrank back before the look of mad rage and passion on Judge Manton's face. With a violent movement he threw Dan off; the boy fell on his knees on the platform, still calling out for help. Judge Manton seized the heavy wooden gavel from his desk and raised it high.

"Damn you!" he snarled in a voice of savage fury, and brought the gavel down on Dan's head. The boy toppled over with a moan.

The next moment a dozen men had sprung over and borne Judge Manton to the floor.

The following morning Mr. Leg and Dan sat talking in the lawyer's office. Nearby was Miss Venner, listening to them; her eyes never left Dan's face. The blow from Judge Manton's gavel had, luckily, not seriously injured him; he had been unconscious for more than an hour, but when he finally came to, was none the worse for it.

"Yes, I let Mount have two thousand dollars," Mr. Leg was saying. "He's going to buy a little cigar store or something somewhere and try to forget things. Poor devil! I hope he succeeds."

"Yes, sir," Dan agreed. "But he really hasn't anything left to live for." And quite unconsciously the boy's eyes turned to meet those of Miss Venner, who flushed and looked the other way.

"And so you saw Manton take something from his pocket and put it in that glass of water," Mr. Leg observed in a voice filled with undisguised admiration.

"Yes, sir. Of course, I was watching him all the time."

"And you think it was with him that Mount's wife left home. But why wouldn't some of his friends have known about her?"

"Perhaps they did," was the reply. "But it's evident that the judge was pretty cagey; he doesn't seem ever to have taken anybody up there. He probably met her in a cabaret, or somewhere, and simply fell in love with her. As for his willingness to sacrifice Mount, well, some men are made that way. He probably said to himself, 'What does this broken-down creature amount to compared to a man like me—wealthy, intellectual, cultured, of high position?' You must remember that he murdered her in a fit of passion, just as when he hit me with that gavel."

"There's one thing I don't understand yet," observed Mr. Leg. "I've got to believe you when you say you thought it was Judge Manton all the time, because I saw you carrying his photograph around. And you say you found that slip of paper was in his handwriting by comparing it with his signature and the postscript on the letter he sent me assigning me to the case. But what the dickens made you compare it with his handwriting? What made you suspect him in the first place?"

"You remember what I quoted from Montaigne," replied Dan, with a smile. " 'The passions smothered by modern civilization are doubly ferocious when awakened.' "

"Yes; but what made you suspect him?"

"What's the difference, sir, so long as we got him? It certainly made a fuss, didn't it?" Dan grinned with delight as he glanced at a pile of morning papers on his desk, the front page of each of which carried under scare headlines pictures of Manton, the murderer, and Dan, his boy Nemesis, side by side.

"There's no doubt about his being convicted," Dan went on, "unless he manages to find some way of committing suicide before his trial, which is likely. We have a dozen corroborative items from Cummings's story. By the way, I'm glad the district attorney offered him immunity."

"So am I," Mr. Leg agreed; "but don't try to change the subject, young man. Clever as you are, you can't evade me. What made you first suspect Judge Manton?"

"I see I'll have to tell you, sir," grinned Dan. "Well, it was on account of you."

"On account of me?"

"Yes, sir. I wondered about it from the very first, when you called me in that morning and told me the judge had assigned you to the case. I couldn't understand it, because I know the practice in such cases is to give it to a man fairly well up in the profession. And men, especially judges, don't play jokes in murder cases. So I knew there must be some good reason why he assigned you to Mount's defense, and the most probable one was that he wanted him convicted."

"But I don't see—"

Again Dan grinned. "You know I think you're a mighty fine man, Mr. Leg. You've been really good to me, sir. But you hadn't had a case in ten years, and you certainly are a bum lawyer."

Mr. Leg frowned. A peal of mischievous laughter came from behind him in Miss Venner's silvery voice. And Dan, because he was looking at her dancing eyes and parted lips and wavy hair, and found it such an agreeable and delightful sight, began to laugh with her. Mr. Leg looked from one to the other, trying hard to maintain his frown; but who can frown at a boy and a fun-loving girl when they are looking at and laughing with each other?

And so Mr. Leg joined in and began to laugh, too.

THE ROPE OF FEAR

Mary E. Hanshew AND Thomas W. Hanshew

I F YOU KNOW ANYTHING OF THE COUNTRY OF WESTMORELAND, YOU WILL KNOW the chief market-town of Merton Sheppard, and if you know Merton Sheppard, you will know there is only one important building in that town besides the massive Town Hall, and that building is the Westmoreland Union Bank—a private concern, well backed by every wealthy magnate in the surrounding district, and patronized by everyone from the highest to the lowest degree.

Anybody will point the building out to you, firstly because of its imposing exterior, and secondly because everyone in the whole county brings his money to Mr. Naylor-Brent, to do with it what he wills. For Mr. Naylor-Brent is the manager, and besides being known far and wide for his integrity, his uprightness of purpose, and his strict sense of justice, he acts to the poorer inhabitants of Merton Sheppard as a sort of father-confessor in all their troubles, both of a social and a financial character.

It was toward the last of September that the big robbery happened, and upon one sunny afternoon at the end of that month Mr. Naylor-Brent was pacing the narrow confines of his handsomely appointed room in the bank, visibly disturbed. That he was awaiting the arrival of someone was evident by his frequent glances at the marble clock which stood upon the mantel-shelf, and which bore across its base a silver plate upon which were inscribed the names of some fifteen or more "grateful customers" whose money had passed successfully through his managerial hands.

At length the door opened, after a discreet knock upon its oaken panels, and an old, bent, and almost decrepit clerk ushered in the portly figure of Mr. Maverick Narkom, Superintendent of Scotland Yard, followed by a heavily-built, dull-looking person in navy blue.

Mr. Naylor-Brent's good-looking, rugged face took on an expression of the keenest relief.

"Mr. Narkom himself! This is indeed more than I expected!" he said with extended hand. "We had the pleasure of meeting once in London, some years ago. Perhaps you have forgotten—?"

Mr. Narkom's bland face wrinkled into a smile of appreciation.

"Oh no, I haven't," he returned pleasantly, "I remember quite distinctly. I decided to answer your letter in person, and bring with me one of my best men—friend and colleague, you know—Mr. George Headland."

"Pleased to meet you, sir. And if you'll both sit down we can go into the matter at once. That's a comfortable chair over there, Mr. Headland."

They seated themselves, and Mr. Narkom, clearing his throat, proceeded in his usual official manner to "take the floor."

"I understand from headquarters," said he, "that you have had an exceptionally large deposit of banknotes sent up from London for payments in connection with your new canal. Isn't that so, Mr. Brent? I trust the trouble you mentioned in your letter has nothing to do with this money."

Mr. Naylor-Brent's face paled considerably, and his voice had an anxious note in it when he spoke.

"Gad, sir, but it has!" he ejaculated. "That's the trouble itself. Every single banknote is gone. £200,000 is gone and not a trace of it! Heaven only knows what I'm going to do about it, Mr. Narkom, but that's how the matter stands. Every penny is *gone*."

"Gone!"

Mr. Narkom drew out a red silk handkerchief and wiped his forehead vigorously—a sure sign of nervous excitement—while Mr. Headland exclaimed loudly, "Well, I'm hanged!"

"Someone certainly will be," rapped out Mr. Brent sharply. "For not only have the notes vanished, but I've lost the best night-watchman I ever had, a good, trustworthy man—"

"Lost him?" put in Mr. Headland curiously. "What exactly do you mean by that, Mr. Brent? Did he vanish with the notes?"

"What? Will Simmons? Never in this world! He's not that kind. The man that offered Will Simmons a bribe to betray his trust would answer for it with his life. A more faithful servant, or better fellow never drew breath. No it's dead he is, Mr. Headland, and—I can hardly speak of it yet! I feel so much to blame for putting him on the job at all, but you see we've had a regular series of petty thefts lately; small sums unable to be accounted for, safes opened in the most mysterious manner, and money abstracted—though never any large sums fortunately—even the clerks' coats had not been left untouched. I have had a constant watch kept, but all in vain. So, naturally, when this big deposit came to hand on Tuesday morning, I determined that special precautions should be taken at night, and put poor old Simmons down in the vault with the bank's watchdog for company. That was the last time I saw him alive! He was found writhing in convulsions and by the time that the doctor arrived upon the scene he was dead; the safe was found open, and every note was *gone!*"

"Bad business indeed!" declared Mr. Headland with a shake of the head. "No idea as to the cause of death, Mr. Brent? What was the doctor's verdict?"

Mr. Naylor-Brent's face clouded.

"That's the very dickens of it, he didn't quite know. Said it was evidently a case of poisoning, but was unable to decide further, or to find out what sort of poison—if any—had been used."

"Hmm. I see. And what did the local police say? Have they found any clues yet?"

The manager flushed, and he gave vent to a forced laugh.

"As a matter of fact," he responded, "the local police know nothing about it. I have kept the loss an entire secret until I could call in the help of Scotland Yard."

"A secret, Mr. Brent, with *such* a loss!" ejaculated Mr. Narkom. "That's surely an unusual course to pursue. When a bank loses such a large sum of money, and in banknotes—the most easily handled commodity in the world—and in addition a mysterious murder takes place, one would naturally expect that the first act would be to call in the officers of the law, that is—unless—I see—"

"Well, it's more than I do!" responded Mr. Brent sadly. "Do you see any light, however?"

"Hardly that. But it stands to reason that if you are prepared to make good the loss—a course to which there seems no alternative—there is an obvious possibility that you yourself have some faint idea as to who the criminal is, and are anxious that your suspicions should not be verified."

Mr. Headland (otherwise Cleek) looked at his friend with considerable admiration shining in his eyes. "Beginning to use his old head at last!" he thought as he watched the Superintendent's keen face. "Well, well, it's never too late to mend, anyhow." And then aloud, "Exactly my thought, Mr. Narkom. Perhaps Mr. Brent could enlighten us as to his own suspicions, for I'm positive that he has some tucked away somewhere in his mind."

"Jove, if you're not almost supernatural, Mr. Headland!" returned that gentleman with a heavy sigh. "You have certainly unearthed something which I thought was hidden only in my own soul. That is exactly the reason I have kept silent; my suspicions were I to voice them, might—er—drag the person accused still deeper into the mire of his own foolishness. There's Patterson, for instance, he would arrest him on sight without the slightest compunction."

"Patterson?" threw in Cleek quickly. "Patterson—the name's familiar. Don't suppose though, that it would be the same one—it is a common enough name.

Company promoter who made a pile on copper, the first year of the war, and retired with 'the swag'—to put it brutally. 'Tisn't that chap I suppose?"

"The identical man!" returned Mr. Brent, excitedly. "He came here some five years ago, bought up Mount Morris Court—a fine place having a view of the whole town—and he has lately started to run an opposition bank to ours, doing everything in his power to overthrow my position here. It's—it's spite I believe, against myself as well as George. The young fool had the impudence to ask his daughter's hand, and what was more, ran off with her and they were married, which increased Patterson's hatred of us both almost to insanity."

"Hmm. I see," said Cleek. "Who is George?"

"My stepson, Mr. Headland—unfortunately for me—my late wife's boy by her first marriage. I have to admit it regretfully enough, he was the cause of his mother's death. He literally broke her heart by his wild living, and I was only too glad to give him a small allowance—which however helped him with his unhappy marriage—and hoped to see the last of George Barrington."

Cleek twitched up an inquiring eyebrow.

"Unhappy, Mr. Brent?" he queried. "But I understood from you a moment ago it was a love match."

"In the beginning it was purely a question of love, Mr. Headland," responded the manager gravely. "But as you know, when poverty comes in at the door, love sometimes flies out of the window, and from all accounts, the late Miss Patterson never ceases to regret the day she became Mrs. George Barrington. George has been hanging about here this last week or two, and I noticed him trying to renew acquaintance with old Simmons only a day or two ago in the bar of the Rose and Anchor. He—he was also seen prowling round the bank on Tuesday night. So now you know why I was loath to set the ball rolling; old man Patterson would lift the sky to get the chance to have that young waster imprisoned, to say nothing of defaming my personal character at the same time.

"Sooner than that I must endeavour to raise sufficient money by private means to replace the notes—but the death of old Simmons is, of course, another matter. His murderer must and shall be brought to justice, while I have a penny piece in my pocket."

His voice broke suddenly into a harsh sob, and for a moment his hands covered his face. Then he shook himself free of his emotion.

"We will all do our best on that score, Mr. Brent," said Mr. Narkom, after a somewhat lengthy silence. "It is a most unfortunate tragedy indeed, almost a dual one, one might say, but I think you can safely trust yourself in our hands, eh, Headland?"

Cleek bowed his head, while Mr. Brent smiled appreciation of the Superintendent's kindly sympathy.

"I know I can," he said warmly. "Believe me, Mr. Narkom, and you, too, Mr. Headland, I am perfectly content to leave myself with you. But I have my suspicions, and strong ones they are too, and I would not mind laying a bet that Patterson has engineered the whole scheme and is quietly laughing up his sleeve at me."

"That's a bold assertion, Mr. Brent," put in Cleek quietly.

"But justified by facts, Mr. Headland. He has twice tried to bribe Simmons away from me, and last year offered Calcott, my head clerk, a sum of £5,000 to let him have the list of our clients."

"Oho!" said Cleek in two different tones. "One of that sort is he? Not content with a fortune won by profiteering, he must try and ruin others; and having failed to get hold of your list of clients, he tries the bogus theft game, and gambles on that. Hmm! Well, Young Barrington may be only a coincidence after all, Mr. Brent. I shouldn't worry too much about him if I were you. Suppose you tell Mr. Narkom and myself the details, right from the beginning, please? When was the murder discovered and who discovered it?"

Mr. Naylor-Brent leaned back in his chair and sighed heavily, as he polished his gold glasses.

"For an affair of such tragic importance, Mr. Headland," he said, "it is singularly lacking in details. There is really nothing more to tell you than that at 6 o'clock, when I myself retired from the bank to my private rooms overhead, I left poor Simmons on guard over the safe; at nine o'clock I was fetched down by the inspector on the beat, who had left young Wilson with the body. After that—"

Cleek lifted a silencing hand.

"One moment," he said. "Who is young Wilson, Mr. Brent, and why should he instead of the inspector have been left alone with the body?"

"Wilson is one of the cashiers, Mr. Headland—a nice lad, but of no particular education. It seems he found the bank's outer door unlatched, and called up the constable on the beat; as luck would have it the inspector happened along, and down they went into the vaults together. But as to why the inspector left young Wilson with the body instead of sending him up for me—well, frankly I had never given the thing a thought until now."

"I see. Funny thing this chap Wilson should have made straight for the vaults though. Did he expect a murder or robbery beforehand? Was he acquainted with the fact that the notes were there, Mr. Brent?"

"No. He knew nothing whatever about them. No one did—that is no one but the head clerk, Mr. Calcott, myself and old Simmons. In bank matters you know the less said about such things the better, and—"

Mr. Narkom nodded.

"Very wise, very wise indeed!" he said, approvingly. "One can't be too careful in money matters, and if I may say so, bank pay being none too high, the temptation must sometimes be rather great. I've a couple of nephews in the bank myself—"

Cleek's eyes suddenly silenced him as though there had been a spoken word.

"This Wilson, Mr. Brent," Cleek asked quietly, "is he a young man?"

"Oh—quite young. Not more than four or five and twenty, I should say. Came from London with an excellent reference, and so far has given every satisfaction. Universal favourite with the firm, and also with old Simmons himself. I believe the two used sometimes to lunch together, and were firm friends. It seems almost a coincidence that the old man should have died in the boy's arms."

"He made no statement, I suppose, before he died, to give an idea of the assassin? But of course you wouldn't know that, as you weren't there."

"As it happens I do, Mr. Headland. Young Wilson, who is frightfully upset—in fact the shock of the thing has completely shattered his nerves, never very strong at the best of times—says that the old man just writhed and writhed, and muttered something about a rope. Then he fell back dead."

"A rope?" said Cleek in surprise. "Was he tied or bound then?"

"That's just it. There was no sign of anything whatever to do with a rope about him. It was possibly a death delusion, or something of the sort. Perhaps the poor old chap was semi-conscious."

"Undoubtedly. And now just one more question, Mr. Brent, before I tire your patience out. We policemen, you know, are terrible nuisances. What time was it when young Wilson discovered the door of the bank unlatched?"

"About half-past nine. I had just noticed my clock striking the half hour, when I was disturbed by the inspector—"

"And wasn't it a bit unusual for a clerk to come back to the bank at that hour—unless he was working overtime?"

Mr. Naylor-Brent's fine head went back with a gesture which conveyed to Cleek the knowledge that he was not in a habit of working any of his employees beyond the given hours.

"He was doing nothing of the sort, Mr. Headland," he responded, a trifle brusquely. "Our firm is particularly keen about the question of working hours. Wilson tells me he came back for his watch which he left behind him, and—"

"And the door was conveniently unlatched and ready, so he simply fetched in the inspector, and took him straight down into the vaults. Didn't get his watch, I suppose?"

Mr. Naylor-Brent jumped suddenly to his feet, all his self-possession gone for the moment.

"Gad! I never thought of that. Hang it! man, you're making a bigger puzzle of it than ever. You're not insinuating that that boy murdered old Simmons, are you? I can't believe that."

"I'm not insinuating anything," responded Cleek blandly, "but I have to look at things from every angle there is. When you got downstairs with the inspector, Mr. Brent, did you happen to notice the safe or not?"

"Yes, I did. Indeed, I fear that was my first thought—it was natural, with £200,000 Bank of England notes to be responsible for—and at first I thought everything was all rights Then young Wilson told me that he himself had closed the safe door . . . What are you smiling at, Mr. Headland? It's no laughing matter, I assure you!"

The queer little one-sided smile, so indicative of the man, travelled for a moment up Cleek's cheek and was gone again in a twinkling.

"Nothing," he responded briefly. "Just a passing thought. Then you mean to say young Wilson closed the safe. Did he know the notes had vanished? But of course you said he knew nothing of them. But if they were there when he looked in—"

His voice trailed off into silence, and he let the rest of the sentence go by default. Mr. Brent's face flushed crimson with excitement.

"Why, at that rate," he ejaculated, "the money wasn't stolen until young Wilson sent the inspector up for me. And we let him walk quietly out! You were right, Mr. Headland, if I had only done my duty and told Inspector Corkran at once—"

"Steady man, steady. I don't say it *is* so," put in Cleek with a quiet little smile. "I'm only trying to find light—"

"And making it a dashed sight blacker still, begging your pardon," returned Mr. Brent briskly.

"That's as may be. But the devil isn't always as black as he is painted," responded Cleek. "I'd like to see this Wilson, Mr. Brent, unless he is so ill he hasn't been able to attend the office."

"Oh he's back at work to-day, and I'll have him here in a twinkling."

And almost in a twinkling he arrived—a young, slim, pallid youngster, rather given to over-brightness in his choice of ties, and somewhat better dressed than is the lot of most bank clerks. Cleek noted the pearl pin, the well-cut suit he wore, and for a moment his face wore a strange look.

Mr. Naylor-Brent's brisk voice broke the silence.

"These gentlemen are from Scotland Yard, Wilson," he said sharply, "and they want to know just what happened here on Tuesday night. Tell them all you know, please."

Young Wilson's pale face went a queer drab shade like newly baked bread. He began to tremble visibly.

"Happened, sir—happened?" he stammered. "How should I know what happened? I—I only got there just in time and—"

"Yes, yes. We know just when you got there, Mr. Wilson," said Cleek, "but what we want to know is what induced you to go down into the vaults when you fetched the inspector? It seemed a rather unnecessary journey to say the least of it."

"I heard a cry—at least—"

"Right through the closed door of a nine-inch concrete-walled vault, Wilson?" struck in Mr. Brent promptly. "Simmons had been shut in there by myself, Mr. Headland, and—"

"Shut in, Mr. Brent? Shut in, did you say? Then how did Mr. Wilson here, and the inspector enter?"

Young Wilson stretched out his hand imploringly.

"The door was open," he stammered. "I swear it on my honour. And the safe was open, and—and the notes were gone!"

"What notes?" It was Mr. Brent's voice which broke the momentary silence, as he realized the significance of the admission. For answer the young man dropped his face into his shaking hands.

"Oh, the notes—the £200,000! You may think what you like, sir, but I swear I am innocent! I never touched the money, nor did I touch my—Mr. Simmons. I swear it, I swear it!"

"Don't swear too strongly, or you may have to 'un-swear' again," struck in Cleek, severely. "Mr. Narkom and I would like to have a look at the vault itself, and see the body, if you have no objection."

"Certainly. Wilson, you had better come along with us, we might need you. This way, gentlemen."

Speaking, the manager rose to his feet, opened the door of his private office, and proceeded downstairs by way of an equally private staircase to the vaults below. Cleek, Mr. Narkom and young Wilson—very much agitated at the coming ordeal—brought up the rear. As they passed the door leading into the bank, for the use of the clerks, old Calcott came out, and paused respectfully in front of the manager.

"If you excuse me, sir," he said, "I thought perhaps you might like to see this."

He held out a Bank of England £5 note, and Mr. Brent took it and examined it critically. Then a little cry broke from his lips.

"A. 541063!" he exclaimed. "Good Heavens, Calcott, where did this come from? Who—?"

Calcott rubbed his old hands together as though he were enjoying a tit-bit with much satisfaction.

"Half-an-hour ago, sir, Mr. George Barrington brought it in, and wanted smaller change."

George Barrington! The members of the little party looked at one another in amazement, and Cleek noticed for a moment that young Wilson's tense face relaxed. Mr. George Barrington, eh? The curious little one-sided smile travelled up Cleek's cheek and was gone. The party continued their way downstairs, somewhat silenced by this new development.

A narrow, dark corridor led to the vault itself, which was by no means a large chamber, but remarkable for the extreme solidity of its building. It was concrete, as most vaults are, and lit only by a single electric light, which, when switched on, shone dully against the gray stone walls. The only ventilation it boasted was provided by means of a row of small holes, about an inch in diameter, across one wall—that nearest to the passage—and exactly facing the safe. So small were they that it seemed almost as if not even a mouse could get through one of them, should a mouse be so minded. These holes were placed so low down that it was physically impossible to see through them, and though Cleek's eyes noted their appearance there in the vault, he said nothing and seemed to pay them little attention.

A speedy glance round the room gave him all the details of it! The safe against the wall, the figure of the old bank servant beside it, sleeping his last sleep, and guarding the vault in death as he had not been able to do in life. Cleek crossed toward him, and then stopped suddenly, peering down at what seemed a little twist of paper.

"Hullo!" he said. "Surely you don't allow smoking in the vault, Mr. Brent? Not that it could do much harm but—"

"Certainly not, Mr. Headland," returned the manager warmly. "That is strictly against orders." He glared at young Wilson, who, nervous as he had been before, became obviously more flustered than ever.

"I don't smoke, sir," he stammered in answer to that managerial look of accusation.

"Glad to hear it." Cleek stroked his cigarette case lovingly inside his pocket as though in apology for the libel. "But it's my mistake; not a cigarette end at all, just a twist of paper. Of no account anyway." He stooped to pick it up, and then giving his hand a flirt, appeared to have tossed it away. Only Mr. Narkom, used to the ways of his famous associate, saw that he had "palmed" it into his pocket. Then Cleek crossed the room and stood a moment looking down at the body, lying there huddled and distorted in the death agony that had so cruelly and mysteriously seized it.

So this was Will Simmons. Well, if the face is any index to the character—which in nine cases out of ten it isn't—then Mr. Naylor-Brent's confidence had certainly not been misplaced. A fine, clean, rugged face this, with set lips, a face that would never fail a friend, and never forgive an enemy. Young Wilson, who had stepped up beside Cleek, shivered suddenly as he looked down at the body, and closed his eyes.

Mr. Brent's voice broke the silence that the sight of death so often brings.

"I think," he said quietly, "if you don't mind, gentlemen, I'll get back to my office. There are important matters at stake just now, so if you'll excuse me—It's near closing time you know, and there are many important matters to see to. Wilson, you stay here with these gentlemen, and render any assistance that you can. Show them round if they wish it. You need not resume work to-day. Anything which you wish to know, please call upon me."

"Thanks. We'll remember," Cleek bowed ceremoniously, as the manager retreated, "but no doubt Mr. Wilson here will give us all the assistance we require, Mr. Brent. We'll make an examination of the body first, and let you know the verdict."

The door closed on Mr. Brent's figure, and Cleek and Mr. Narkom and young Wilson were alone with the dead.

Cleek went down upon his knees before the still figure, and examined it from end to end. The clenched hands were put to the keenest scrutiny, but he passed no comment, only glancing now and again from those same hands to the figure of the young cashier who stood trembling beside him.

"Hmm, convulsions," he finally said softly to himself, and Mr. Narkom watched his face with intense eagerness. "Might be aconite—but how administered?" Again he stood silent, his brain moving swiftly down an avenue of thought, and if the thoughts could have been seen, they should have shown something like this: Convulsions—writhing—twisting—tied up in knots of pain—a *rope*.

Suddenly he wheeled swiftly upon Wilson, his face a mask for his emotions.

"Look here," he said sternly, "I want you to tell me the exact truth, Mr. Wilson. It's the wisest way when dealing with the police, you know. Are you positively certain Simmons said nothing as to the cause of his death? What exactly were his last words to you?"

"I begged him to tell me who it was who had injured him," replied Wilson, in a shaking voice, "but all he could say was, 'The rope—mind the Rope—the Rope of Fear—the Rope of Fear,' and then he was gone. But there was no sign of any rope, Mr. Headland, and I can't imagine what the dear old man was driving at. And now to think he is dead—dead—"

His voice broke and was silent for a moment. Once again Cleek spoke.

"And you saw nothing, heard nothing?"

"Well—I hardly know. There was a sound—a faint whisper, reedlike and thin, almost like a long drawn sigh. I really thought I must have imagined it, and when I listened again it had gone. After that I rushed to the safe and—"

"Why did you do that?"

"Because he had told me at dinner-time about the notes, and made me promise I wouldn't mention it, and I was afraid someone had stolen them."

"Is it likely that anyone overheard your conversation then? Where were you lunching?"

"In the Rose and Crown," Wilson's voice trembled again as though the actual recalling of the thing terrified him anew. "Simmons and I often had lunch together. There was no one else at our table, and the place was practically empty. The only person near was old Ramagee, the black chap who keeps the Indian bazaar in the town. He's an old inhabitant, but even now hardly understands English, and most of the time he's so drugged with opium, that if did hear he'd never understand. He was certainly blind to the world that lunch time, because my—my friend, Simmons, I mean, noticed it."

"Indeed!" Cleek stroked his chin thoughtfully for some moments. Then he sniffed the air, and uttered a casual remark: "Fond of sweets still, are you Mr. Wilson? Peppermint drops, or aniseed balls, eh?"

Mr. Narkom's eyes fairly bulged with amazement, and young Wilson flushed angrily.

"I am not such a fool as all that, Mr. Headland," he said quickly. "If I don't smoke, I certainly don't go about sucking candy like a Kid. I never cared for 'em as a youngster, and I haven't had any for a cat's age. What made you ask?"

"Nothing, simply my fancy." But, nevertheless, Cleek continued to sniff, and then suddenly with a little excited sound went down on his hands and knees and began examining the stone floor.

"It's not possible—and yet—and yet, I must be right," he said softly, getting to his feet at last. " 'A rope of fear' was what he said, wasn't it? 'A rope of fear.' " He crossed suddenly to the safe, and bending over it, examined the handle and doors critically. And at the moment Mr. Brent reappeared. Cleek switched round upon his heel, and smiled across at him.

"Able to spare us a little more of your valuable time, Mr. Brent?" he said politely. "Well, I was just coming up. There's nothing really to be gained here. I have been looking over the safe for finger-prints, and there's not much doubt about whose they are. Mr. Wilson here had better come upstairs and tell us just exactly what he did with the notes, and—"

Young Wilson's face went suddenly gray. He clenched his hands together and breathed hard like a spent runner.

"I tell you, they were gone," he cried desperately. "They were gone. I looked for them, and didn't find them. They were gone—gone—gone!"

But Cleek seemed not to take the slightest notice of him, and swinging upon his heel followed in the wake of the manager's broad back, while Wilson perforce had to return with Mr. Narkom. Half way up the stairs, however, Cleek suddenly stopped, and gave vent to a hurried ejaculation.

"Silly idiot that I am!" he said crossly. "I have left my magnifying glass on top of the safe—and it's the most necessary tool we policemen have. Don't bother to come, Mr. Brent, if you'll just lend me the keys of the vault. Thanks, I'll be right back."

It was certainly not much more than a moment when he did return, and the other members of the little party had barely reached the private office when he fairly rushed in after them. There was a look of supreme satisfaction in his eyes.

"Here it is," he said, lifting the glass up for all to see. "And look here, Mr. Brent, I've changed my mind about discussing the matter any further here. The best thing you can do is to go down in a cab with Mr. Narkom to the police station, and get a warrant for this young man's arrest—no, don't speak, Mr. Wilson, I've not finished yet—and take him along with you. I will stay here and just scribble down the facts. It'll save no end of bother, and we can take our man straight up to London with us, under proper arrest. I shan't be more than ten minutes at the most."

Mr. Brent nodded assent.

"As you please, Mr. Headland," he said gravely. "We'll go along at once. Wilson, you understand you are to come with us? It's no use trying to get away from it, man, you're up against it now. You'd better just keep a stiff upper lip and face the music. I'm ready, Mr. Narkom."

Quietly they took their departure, in a hastily found cab, leaving Cleek, the picture of stolid policemanism, with notebook and pencil in hand, busily inscribing what he was pleased to call "the facts."

Only "ten minutes" Cleek had asked for, but it was nearer twenty before he was ushered out of the side entrance of the bank by the old housekeeper, and though perhaps it was only sheer luck that caused him to nearly tumble into the arms of Mr. George Barrington—whom he recognized from the word picture of that gentleman given by Mr. Brent some time before—it was decidedly by arrangement that, after a few careless words on the part of Cleek, Barrington, his face blank with astonishment, accompanied this stranger down to the police station.

They found a grim little party awaiting them but at sight of Cleek's face Mr. Narkom started forward, and put a hand upon his friend's arm.

"What have you found, Headland?" he asked excitedly.

"Just what I expected to find," came the triumphant reply. "Now, Mr. Wilson, you are going to hear the end of the story. Do you want to see what I found, gentlemen?

Here it is." He fumbled in his big coat pocket for a moment and pulled out a parcel which crackled crisply. "The notes!"

"Good God!"

It was young Wilson who spoke.

"Yes, a *very* good God—even to sinners, Mr. Wilson. We don't always deserve all the goodness we get, you know," Cleek went on. "The notes are found you see; the notes, you murderer, you despicable thief, the notes which were entrusted to your care by the innocent people who pinned their faith to you."

Speaking, he leaped forward, past the waiting inspector and Mr. Narkom, past the shabby, down-at-heel figure of George Barrington, past the slim, shaking Wilson, and straight at the substantial figure of Mr. Naylor-Brent, as he stood leaning with one arm upon the inspector's high desk.

So surprising, so unexpected was the attack, that this victim was overpowered and the bracelets snapped upon his wrists before anyone present had begun to realize exactly what had happened.

Then Cleek rose to his feet.

"What's that, Inspector?" he said in answer to a hurriedly spoken query. "A mistake? Oh dear, no. No mistake whatever. Our friend here understands that quite well. Thought you'd have escaped with that £200,000 and left your confederate to bear the brunt of the whole thing, did you? Or else young Wilson here whom you'd so terrorized! A very pretty plot indeed, only Hamilton Cleek happened to come along instead of Mr. George Headland, and show you a thing or two about plots."

"Hamilton Cleek!" The name fell from every pair of lips, and even Brent himself stared at this wizard whom all the world knew, and who unfortunately had crossed his path when he least wanted him.

"Yes, Hamilton Cleek, gentlemen. Cleek of Scotland Yard. And a very good thing for you, Mr. Wilson, that I happened to come along. Things looked very black for you, you know, and those beastly nerves of yours made it worse. And if it hadn't been for this cad's confederate—"

"Confederate, Mr. Cleek?" put in Wilson shakily. "I—I don't understand. Who could have been his confederate?"

"None other than old Ramagee," responded Cleek. "You'll find him drugged as usual, in the Rose and Crown. I've seen him there only a while ago. But now he is minus a constant companion of his. . . . And here is the actual murderer."

He put his hand into another capacious pocket and drew forth a smallish, glass box.

"The Rope of Fear, gentlemen," he said quietly, "a vicious little rattler of the most deadly sort. And it won't be long before that gentleman there becomes acquainted with another sort of rope. Take him away, Inspector. The bare sight of him hurts an honest man's eyes."

And they took him away forthwith, a writhing, furious Thing, utterly transformed from the genial personality which had for so long swindled and outwitted a trusting public.

As the door closed upon them, Cleek turned to young Wilson and held out his hand.

"I'm sorry to have accused you as I did," he said softly, with a little smile, "but that is a policeman's way, you know. Strategy is part of the game—though it was a poor trick of mine to cause you additional pain. You must forgive me. I don't doubt the death of your father was a great shock, although you tried manfully to conceal the relationship. No doubt it was his wish—not yours."

A sudden transformation came over Wilson's pale, haggard face. It was like the sun shining after a heavy storm.

"You—knew?" he said, over and over again. "You *knew?* Oh, Mr. Cleek, now I can speak out at last. Father always made me promise to be silent, he—he wanted me to be a gentleman, and he'd spent every penny he possessed to get me well enough educated to enter the bank. He was mad for money, mad for anything which was going to better my position. And—and I was afraid when he told me about the notes, he might be tempted—Oh! It was dreadful of me, I know, to think of it, but I knew he doted upon me, I was afraid he might try and take one or two of them, hoping they wouldn't be missed out of so great an amount. You see we'd been in money difficulties and were still paying my college fees off after all this time. So I went back to keep watch with him—and found him dying—though how you *knew*—"

His voice trailed off into silence, and Cleek smiled kindly.

"By the identical shape of your hands, my boy. I never saw two pairs of hands so much alike in all my life. And then your agitation made me risk the guess. . . . What's that, Inspector? How was the murder committed, and what did this little rattler have to do with it? Well, quite simple. The snake was put in the safe with the notes, and a trail of aniseed—of which snakes are very fond, you know—laid from there to the foot of old Simmons. The safe door was left ajar—though in the half dusk the old man certainly never noticed it. I found all this out from those few words of Wilson's about 'the rope,' and from his having heard a reedlike sound. I had to do some hard thinking, I can tell you. When I went downstairs again, Mr. Narkom, after my magnifying glass, I turned down poor Summons's sock and found the mark I expected—the snake had crawled up his leg and struck home.

"Why did I suspect Mr. Brent? Well, it was obvious almost from the very first, for he was so anxious to throw suspicion upon Mr. Barrington here, and Wilson—with Patterson thrown in for good measure. Then again it was certain that no one else would have been allowed into the vault by Simmons, much less to go to the safe itself, and open it with the keys. That he did go to the safe was apparent by the finger-prints upon it, and as they too smelt of aniseed, the whole thing began to look decidedly funny. The trail of aniseed led straight up to where Simmons lay, so I can only suppose that after Brent released the snake—the trail of course having been laid beforehand, when he was alone—Brent must have stood and waited until he saw it actually strike, and—How do I know that, Mr. Wilson? Well, he smoked a cigarette there, anyhow. The stub I found bore the same name as those in his box, and it was smoked identically the same way as a couple which lay in his ashtray.

"I could only conclude that he was waiting for something to happen, and as the snake struck, he grabbed up the bundle of notes, quite forgetting to close the safe-door, and rushed out of the vault. Ramagee was in the corridor outside, and probably whistled the snake back through the ventilating holes near the floor, instead of venturing near the body himself. You remember, you heard the sound of that pipe, Mr. Wilson? Ramagee probably made his escape while the Inspector was upstairs. Unfortunately for him, he ran right into Mr. George Barrington here, and when, as he tells me, he later told Brent about seeing Ramagee, well, the whole thing became as plain as a pikestaff."

"Yes," put in George Barrington, excitedly, taking up the tale in his weak, rather silly voice, "my step-father refused to believe me, and gave me £20 in notes to go away. I suppose he didn't notice they were some of the stolen ones. I changed one of them at the bank this morning, but I had no idea how important they were until I knocked into Mr.—Mr. Cleek here. And he made me come along with him."

Mr. Narkom looked at Cleek, and Cleek looked at Mr. Narkom, and the blank wonder in the Superintendent's eyes caused him to smile.

"Another feather in the cap of foolish old Scotland Yard, isn't it?" he said. "Time we made tracks I think. Coming our way, Mr. Wilson? We'll see you back home if you like. You're too upset to go on alone. Good afternoon, Inspector and—good-bye. I'll leave the case with you. It's safe enough in your hands, but if you take my tip you'll put that human beast in as tight a lock-up as the station affords."

Then he linked one arm in Mr. Narkom's and the other arm in that of the admiring, and wholly speechless Wilson, and went out into the sunshine.

THE MYSTERIOUS AFFAIR
AT STYLES

Agatha Christie

I. I Go to Styles

The intense interest aroused in the public by what was known at the time as "The Styles Case" has now somewhat subsided. Nevertheless, in view of the worldwide notoriety which attended it, I have been asked, both by my friend Poirot and the family themselves, to write an account of the whole story. This, we trust, will effectually silence the sensational rumours which still persist.

I will therefore briefly set down the circumstances which led to my being connected with the affair.

I had been invalided home from the Front; and, after spending some months in a rather depressing Convalescent Home, was given a month's sick leave. Having no near relations or friends, I was trying to make up my mind what to do, when I ran across John Cavendish. I had seen very little of him for some years. Indeed, I had never known him particularly well. He was a good fifteen years my senior, for one thing, though he hardly looked his forty-five years. As a boy, though, I had often stayed at Styles, his mother's place in Essex.

We had a good yarn about old times, and it ended in his inviting me down to Styles to spend my leave there.

"The mater will be delighted to see you again—after all those years," he added.

"Your mother keeps well?" I asked.

"Oh, yes. I suppose you know that she has married again?"

I am afraid I showed my surprise rather plainly. Mrs. Cavendish, who had married John's father when he was a widower with two sons, had been a handsome woman of middle-age as I remembered her. She certainly could not be a day less than seventy now. I recalled her as an energetic, autocratic personality, somewhat inclined to charitable and social notoriety, with a fondness for opening bazaars and playing the Lady Bountiful. She was a most generous woman, and possessed a considerable fortune of her own.

Their country-place, Styles Court, had been purchased by Mr. Cavendish early in their married life. He had been completely under his wife's ascendancy, so much so that, on dying, he left the place to her for her lifetime, as well as the larger part of his income; an arrangement that was distinctly unfair to his two sons. Their step-mother, however, had always been most generous to them; indeed, they were so young at the time of their father's remarriage that they always thought of her as their own mother.

Lawrence, the younger, had been a delicate youth. He had qualified as a doctor but early relinquished the profession of medicine, and lived at home while pursuing literary ambitions; though his verses never had any marked success.

John practised for some time as a barrister, but had finally settled down to the more congenial life of a country squire. He had married two years ago, and had taken his wife to live at Styles, though I entertained a shrewd suspicion that he would have preferred his mother to increase his allowance, which would have enabled him to have a home of his own. Mrs. Cavendish, however, was a lady who liked to make her own plans, and expected other people to fall in with them, and in this case she certainly had the whip hand, namely: the purse strings.

John noticed my surprise at the news of his mother's remarriage and smiled rather ruefully.

"Rotten little bounder too!" he said savagely. "I can tell you, Hastings, it's making life jolly difficult for us. As for Evie—you remember Evie?"

"No."

"Oh, I suppose she was after your time. She's the mater's factotum, companion, Jack of all trades! A great sport—old Evie! Not precisely young and beautiful, but as game as they make them."

"You were going to say—?"

"Oh, this fellow! He turned up from nowhere, on the pretext of being a second cousin or something of Evie's, though she didn't seem particularly keen to acknowledge the relationship. The fellow is an absolute outsider, anyone can see that. He's got a great black beard, and wears patent leather boots in all weathers! But the mater cottoned to him at once, took him on as secretary—you know how she's always running a hundred societies?"

I nodded.

"Well, of course the war has turned the hundreds into thousands. No doubt the fellow was very useful to her. But you could have knocked us all down with a feather when, three months ago, she suddenly announced that she and Alfred were engaged! The fellow must be at least twenty years younger than she is! It's simply bare-faced fortune hunting; but there you are—she is her own mistress, and she's married him."

"It must be a difficult situation for you all."

"Difficult! It's damnable!"

Thus it came about that, three days later, I descended from the train at Styles St. Mary, an absurd little station, with no apparent reason for existence, perched up in the midst of green fields and country lanes. John Cavendish was waiting on the platform, and piloted me out to the car.

"Got a drop or two of petrol still, you see," he remarked. "Mainly owing to the mater's activities."

The village of Styles St. Mary was situated about two miles from the little station, and Styles Court lay a mile the other side of it. It was a still, warm day in early July. As one looked out over the flat Essex country, lying so green and peaceful under the afternoon sun, it seemed almost impossible to believe that, not so very far away, a great war was running its appointed course. I felt I had suddenly strayed into another world. As we turned in at the lodge gates, John said:

"I'm afraid you'll find it very quiet down here, Hastings."

"My dear fellow, that's just what I want."

"Oh, it's pleasant enough if you want to lead the idle life. I drill with the volunteers twice a week, and lend a hand at the farms. My wife works regularly 'on the land.' She is up at five every morning to milk, and keeps at it steadily until lunchtime. It's a jolly good life taking it all round—if it weren't for that fellow Alfred Inglethorp!" He checked the car suddenly, and glanced at his watch. "I wonder if we've time to pick up Cynthia. No, she'll have started from the hospital by now."

"Cynthia! That's not your wife?"

"No, Cynthia is a protégée of my mother's, the daughter of an old schoolfellow of hers, who married a rascally solicitor. He came a cropper, and the girl was left an orphan and penniless. My mother came to the rescue, and Cynthia has been with us nearly two years now. She works in the Red Cross Hospital at Tadminster, seven miles away."

As he spoke the last words, we drew up in front of the fine old house. A lady in a stout tweed skirt, who was bending over a flowerbed, straightened herself at our approach.

"Hullo, Evie, here's our wounded hero! Mr. Hastings—Miss Howard."

Miss Howard shook hands with a hearty, almost painful, grip. I had an impression of very blue eyes in a sunburnt face. She was a pleasant-looking woman of about forty, with a deep voice, almost manly in its stentorian tones, and had a large sensible square body, with feet to match—these last encased in good thick boots. Her conversation, I soon found, was couched in the telegraphic style.

"Weeds grow like house afire. Can't keep even with 'em. Shall press you in. Better be careful."

"I'm sure I shall be only too delighted to make myself useful," I responded.

"Don't say it. Never does. Wish you hadn't later."

"You're a cynic, Evie," said John, laughing. "Where's tea today—inside or out?"

"Out. Too fine a day to be cooped up in the house."

"Come on then, you've done enough gardening for today. 'The labourer is worthy of his hire,' you know. Come and be refreshed."

"Well," said Miss Howard, drawing off her gardening gloves, "I'm inclined to agree with you."

She led the way round the house to where tea was spread under the shade of a large sycamore.

A figure rose from one of the basket chairs, and came a few steps to meet us.

"My wife, Hastings," said John.

I shall never forget my first sight of Mary Cavendish. Her tall, slender form, outlined against the bright light; the vivid sense of slumbering fire that seemed to find expression only in those wonderful tawny eyes of hers, remarkable eyes, different from any other woman's that I have ever known; the intense power of stillness she possessed, which nevertheless conveyed the impression of a wild untamed spirit in an exquisitely civilised body—all these things are burnt into my memory. I shall never forget them.

She greeted me with a few words of pleasant welcome in a low clear voice, and I sank into a basket chair feeling distinctly glad that I had accepted John's invitation. Mrs. Cavendish gave me some tea, and her few quiet remarks heightened my first impression of her as a thoroughly fascinating woman. An appreciative listener is always stimulating, and I described, in a humorous manner, certain incidents of my Convalescent Home, in a way which, I flatter myself, greatly amused my hostess. John, of course, good fellow though he is, could hardly be called a brilliant conversationalist.

At that moment a well remembered voice floated through the open French window near at hand:

"Then you'll write to the Princess after tea, Alfred? I'll write to Lady Tadminster for the second day, myself. Or shall we wait until we hear from the Princess? In case of a refusal, Lady Tadminster might open it the first day, and Mrs. Crosbie the second. Then there's the Duchess—about the school fête."

There was the murmur of a man's voice, and then Mrs. Inglethorp's rose in reply:

"Yes, certainly. After tea will do quite well. You are so thoughtful, Alfred dear."

The French window swung open a little wider, and a handsome white-haired old lady, with a somewhat masterful cast of features, stepped out of it on to the lawn. A man followed her, a suggestion of deference in his manner.

Mrs. Inglethorp greeted me with effusion.

"Why, if it isn't too delightful to see you again, Mr. Hastings, after all these years. Alfred, darling, Mr. Hastings—my husband."

I looked with some curiosity at "Alfred darling." He certainly struck a rather alien note. I did not wonder at John objecting to his beard. It was one of the longest and blackest I have ever seen. He wore gold-rimmed pince-nez, and had a curious impassivity of feature. It struck me that he might look natural on a stage, but was strangely out of place in real life. His voice was rather deep and unctuous. He placed a wooden hand in mine and said:

"This is a pleasure, Mr. Hastings." Then, turning to his wife: "Emily dearest, I think that cushion is a little damp."

She beamed fondly on him, as he substituted another with every demonstration of the tenderest care. Strange infatuation of an otherwise sensible woman!

With the presence of Mr. Inglethorp, a sense of constraint and veiled hostility seemed to settle down upon the company. Miss Howard, in particular, took no pains to conceal her feelings. Mrs. Inglethorp, however, seemed to notice nothing unusual. Her volubility, which I remembered of old, had lost nothing in the intervening years, and she poured out a steady flood of conversation, mainly on the subject of the forthcoming bazaar which she was organizing and which was to take place shortly. Occasionally she referred to her husband over a question of days or dates. His watchful and attentive manner never varied. From the very first I took a firm and rooted dislike to him, and I flatter myself that my first judgments are usually fairly shrewd.

Presently Mrs. Inglethorp turned to give some instructions about letters to Evelyn Howard, and her husband addressed me in his painstaking voice:

"Is soldiering your regular profession, Mr. Hastings?"

"No, before the war I was in Lloyd's."

"And you will return there after it is over?"

"Perhaps. Either that or a fresh start altogether."

Mary Cavendish leant forward.

"What would you really choose as a profession, if you could just consult your inclination?"

"Well, that depends."

"No secret hobby?" she asked. "Tell me—you're drawn to something? Every one is—usually something absurd."

"You'll laugh at me."

She smiled.

"Perhaps."

"Well, I've always had a secret hankering to be a detective!"

"The real thing—Scotland Yard? Or Sherlock Holmes?"

"Oh, Sherlock Holmes by all means. But really, seriously, I am awfully drawn to it. I came across a man in Belgium once, a very famous detective, and he quite inflamed me. He was a marvellous little fellow. He used to say that all good detective work was a mere matter of method. My system is based on his—though of course I have progressed rather further. He was a funny little man, a great dandy, but wonderfully clever."

"Like a good detective story myself," remarked Miss Howard. "Lots of nonsense written, though. Criminal discovered in last chapter. Everyone dumbfounded. Real crime—you'd know at once."

"There have been a great number of undiscovered crimes," I argued.

"Don't mean the police, but the people that are right in it. The family. You couldn't really hoodwink them. They'd know."

"Then," I said, much amused, "you think that if you were mixed up in a crime, say a murder, you'd be able to spot the murderer right off?"

"Of course I should. Mightn't be able to prove it to a pack of lawyers. But I'm certain I'd know. I'd feel it in my fingertips if he came near me."

"It might be a 'she,'" I suggested.

"Might. But murder's a violent crime. Associate it more with a man."

"Not in a case of poisoning." Mrs. Cavendish's clear voice startled me. "Dr. Bauerstein was saying yesterday that, owing to the general ignorance of the more uncommon poisons among the medical profession, there were probably countless cases of poisoning quite unsuspected."

"Why, Mary, what a gruesome conversation!" cried Mrs. Inglethorp. "It makes me feel as if a goose were walking over my grave. Oh, there's Cynthia!"

A young girl in V. A. D. uniform ran lightly across the lawn.

"Why, Cynthia, you are late today. This is Mr. Hastings—Miss Murdoch."

Cynthia Murdoch was a fresh-looking young creature, full of life and vigour. She tossed off her little V. A. D. cap, and I admired the great loose waves of her auburn hair, and the smallness and whiteness of the hand she held out to claim her tea. With dark eyes and eyelashes she would have been a beauty.

She flung herself down on the ground beside John, and as I handed her a plate of sandwiches she smiled up at me.

"Sit down here on the grass, do. It's ever so much nicer."

I dropped down obediently.

"You work at Tadminster, don't you, Miss Murdoch?"

She nodded.

"For my sins."

"Do they bully you, then?" I asked, smiling.

"I should like to see them!" cried Cynthia with dignity.

"I have got a cousin who is nursing," I remarked. "And she is terrified of 'Sisters.'"

"I don't wonder. Sisters *are*, you know, Mr. Hastings. They simp-ly *are*! You've no idea! But I'm not a nurse, thank heaven, I work in the dispensary."

"How many people do you poison?" I asked, smiling.

Cynthia smiled too.

"Oh, hundreds!" she said.

"Cynthia," called Mrs. Inglethorp, "do you think you could write a few notes for me?"

"Certainly, Aunt Emily."

She jumped up promptly, and something in her manner reminded me that her position was a dependent one, and that Mrs. Inglethorp, kind as she might be in the main, did not allow her to forget it.

My hostess turned to me.

"John will show you your room. Supper is at half-past seven. We have given up late dinner for some time now. Lady Tadminster, our Member's wife—she was the late Lord Abbotsbury's daughter—does the same. She agrees with me that one must set an example of economy. We are quite a war household; nothing is wasted here—every scrap of waste paper, even, is saved and sent away in sacks."

I expressed my appreciation, and John took me into the house and up the broad staircase, which forked right and left halfway to different wings of the building. My room was in the left wing, and looked out over the park.

John left me, and a few minutes later I saw him from my window walking slowly across the grass arm in arm with Cynthia Murdoch. I heard Mrs. Inglethorp call "Cynthia" impatiently, and the girl started and ran back to the house. At the same moment, a man stepped out from the shadow of a tree and walked slowly in the same direction. He looked about forty, very dark with a melancholy clean-shaven face. Some violent emotion seemed to be mastering him. He looked up at my window as he passed, and I recognized him, though he had changed much in the fifteen years that had elapsed since we last met. It was John's younger brother, Lawrence Cavendish. I wondered what it was that had brought that singular expression to his face.

Then I dismissed him from my mind, and returned to the contemplation of my own affairs.

The evening passed pleasantly enough; and I dreamed that night of that enigmatical woman, Mary Cavendish.

The next morning dawned bright and sunny, and I was full of the anticipation of a delightful visit.

I did not see Mrs. Cavendish until lunchtime, when she volunteered to take me for a walk, and we spent a charming afternoon roaming in the woods, returning to the house about five.

As we entered the large hall, John beckoned us both into the smoking-room. I saw at once by his face that something disturbing had occurred. We followed him in, and he shut the door after us.

"Look here, Mary, there's the deuce of a mess. Evie's had a row with Alfred Inglethorp, and she's off."

"Evie? Off?"

John nodded gloomily.

"Yes; you see she went to the mater, and—Oh, here's Evie herself."

Miss Howard entered. Her lips were set grimly together, and she carried a small suitcase. She looked excited and determined, and slightly on the defensive.

"At any rate," she burst out, "I've spoken my mind!"

"My dear Evelyn," cried Mrs. Cavendish, "this can't be true!"

Miss Howard nodded grimly.

"True enough! Afraid I said some things to Emily she won't forget or forgive in a hurry. Don't mind if they've only sunk in a bit. Probably water off a duck's back, though. I said right out: 'You're an old woman, Emily, and there's no fool like an old fool. The man's twenty years younger than you, and don't you fool yourself as to what he married you for. Money! Well, don't let him have too much of it. Farmer Raikes has got a very pretty young wife. Just ask your Alfred how much time he spends over there.' She was very angry. Natural! I went on, 'I'm going to warn you, whether you like it or not. That man would as soon murder you in your bed as look at you. He's a bad lot. You can say what you like to me, but remember what I've told you. He's a bad lot!'"

"What did she say?"

Miss Howard made an extremely expressive grimace.

"'Darling Alfred'—'dearest Alfred'—'wicked calumnies'—'wicked lies'—'wicked woman'—to accuse her 'dear husband'! The sooner I left her house the better. So I'm off."

"But not now?"

"This minute!"

For a moment we sat and stared at her. Finally John Cavendish, finding his persuasions of no avail, went off to look up the trains. His wife followed him, murmuring something about persuading Mrs. Inglethorp to think better of it.

As she left the room, Miss Howard's face changed. She leant towards me eagerly.

"Mr. Hastings, you're honest. I can trust you?"

I was a little startled. She laid her hand on my arm, and sank her voice to a whisper.

"Look after her, Mr. Hastings. My poor Emily. They're a lot of sharks—all of them. Oh, I know what I'm talking about. There isn't one of them that's not hard up and trying to get money out of her. I've protected her as much as I could. Now I'm out of the way, they'll impose upon her."

"Of course, Miss Howard," I said, "I'll do everything I can, but I'm sure you're excited and overwrought."

She interrupted me by slowly shaking her forefinger.

"Young man, trust me. I've lived in the world rather longer than you have. All I ask you is to keep your eyes open. You'll see what I mean."

The throb of the motor came through the open window, and Miss Howard rose and moved to the door. John's voice sounded outside. With her hand on the handle, she turned her head over her shoulder, and beckoned to me.

"Above all, Mr. Hastings, watch that devil—her husband!"

There was no time for more. Miss Howard was swallowed up in an eager chorus of protests and good-byes. The Inglethorps did not appear.

As the motor drove away, Mrs. Cavendish suddenly detached herself from the group, and moved across the drive to the lawn to meet a tall bearded man who had been evidently making for the house. The colour rose in her cheeks as she held out her hand to him.

"Who is that?" I asked sharply, for instinctively I distrusted the man.

"That's Dr. Bauerstein," said John shortly.

"And who is Dr. Bauerstein?"

"He's staying in the village doing a rest cure, after a bad nervous breakdown. He's a London specialist; a very clever man—one of the greatest living experts on poisons, I believe."

"And he's a great friend of Mary's," put in Cynthia, the irrepressible.

John Cavendish frowned and changed the subject.

"Come for a stroll, Hastings. This has been a most rotten business. She always had a rough tongue, but there is no stauncher friend in England than Evelyn Howard."

He took the path through the plantation, and we walked down to the village through the woods which bordered one side of the estate.

As we passed through one of the gates on our way home again, a pretty young woman of gipsy type coming in the opposite direction bowed and smiled.

"That's a pretty girl," I remarked appreciatively.

John's face hardened.

"That is Mrs. Raikes."

"The one that Miss Howard——"

"Exactly," said John, with rather unnecessary abruptness.

I thought of the white-haired old lady in the big house, and that vivid wicked little face that had just smiled into ours, and a vague chill of foreboding crept over me. I brushed it aside.

"Styles is really a glorious old place," I said to John.

He nodded rather gloomily.

"Yes, it's a fine property. It'll be mine some day—should be mine now by rights, if my father had only made a decent will. And then I shouldn't be so damned hard up as I am now."

"Hard up, are you?"

"My dear Hastings, I don't mind telling you that I'm at my wit's end for money."

"Couldn't your brother help you?"

"Lawrence? He's gone through every penny he ever had, publishing rotten verses in fancy bindings. No, we're an impecunious lot. My mother's always been awfully good to us, I must say. That is, up to now. Since her marriage, of course—" he broke off, frowning.

For the first time I felt that, with Evelyn Howard, something indefinable had gone from the atmosphere. Her presence had spelt security. Now that security was removed—and the air seemed rife with suspicion. The sinister face of Dr. Bauerstein recurred to me unpleasantly. A vague suspicion of everyone and everything filled my mind. Just for a moment I had a premonition of approaching evil.

II. The 16th and 17th of July

I had arrived at Styles on the 5th of July. I come now to the events of the 16th and 17th of that month. For the convenience of the reader I will recapitulate the incidents of those days in as exact a manner as possible. They were elicited subsequently at the trial by a process of long and tedious cross-examinations.

I received a letter from Evelyn Howard a couple of days after her departure, telling me she was working as a nurse at the big hospital in Middlingham, a manufacturing town some fifteen miles away, and begging me to let her know if Mrs. Inglethorp should show any wish to be reconciled.

The only fly in the ointment of my peaceful days was Mrs. Cavendish's extraordinary, and, for my part, unaccountable preference for the society of Dr. Bauerstein. What she saw in the man I cannot imagine, but she was always asking him up to the house, and often went off for long expeditions with him. I must confess that I was quite unable to see his attraction.

The 16th of July fell on a Monday. It was a day of turmoil. The famous bazaar had taken place on Saturday, and an entertainment, in connection with the same charity, at which Mrs. Inglethorp was to recite a War poem, was to be held that night. We were all busy during the morning arranging and decorating the Hall in the village where it was to take place. We had a late luncheon and spent the afternoon resting in the garden. I noticed that John's manner was somewhat unusual. He seemed very excited and restless.

After tea, Mrs. Inglethorp went to lie down to rest before her efforts in the evening and I challenged Mary Cavendish to a single at tennis.

About a quarter to seven, Mrs. Inglethorp called us that we should be late as supper was early that night. We had rather a scramble to get ready in time; and before the meal was over the motor was waiting at the door.

The entertainment was a great success, Mrs. Inglethorp's recitation receiving tremendous applause. There were also some tableaux in which Cynthia took part. She did not return with us, having been asked to a supper party, and to remain the night with some friends who had been acting with her in the tableaux.

The following morning, Mrs. Inglethorp stayed in bed to breakfast, as she was rather over-tired; but she appeared in her briskest mood about 12:30, and swept Lawrence and myself off to a luncheon party.

"Such a charming invitation from Mrs. Rolleston. Lady Tadminster's sister, you know. The Rollestons came over with the Conqueror—one of our oldest families."

Mary had excused herself on the plea of an engagement with Dr. Bauerstein.

We had a pleasant luncheon, and as we drove away Lawrence suggested that we should return by Tadminster, which was barely a mile out of our way, and pay a visit to Cynthia in her dispensary. Mrs. Inglethorp replied that this was an excellent idea, but as she had several letters to write she would drop us there, and we could come back with Cynthia in the pony-trap.

We were detained under suspicion by the hospital porter, until Cynthia appeared to vouch for us, looking very cool and sweet in her long white overall. She took us up to her sanctum, and introduced us to her fellow dispenser, a rather awe-inspiring individual, whom Cynthia cheerily addressed as "Nibs."

"What a lot of bottles!" I exclaimed, as my eye travelled round the small room. "Do you really know what's in them all?"

"Say something original," groaned Cynthia. "Every single person who comes up here says that. We are really thinking of bestowing a prize on the first individual who does *not* say: 'What a lot of bottles!' And I know the next thing you're going to say is: 'How many people have you poisoned?'"

I pleaded guilty with a laugh.

"If you people only knew how fatally easy it is to poison some one by mistake, you wouldn't joke about it. Come on, let's have tea. We've got all sorts of secret stories in that cupboard. No, Lawrence—that's the poison cupboard. The big cupboard—that's right."

We had a very cheery tea, and assisted Cynthia to wash up afterwards. We had just put away the last teaspoon when a knock came at the door. The countenances of Cynthia and Nibs were suddenly petrified into a stern and forbidding expression.

"Come in," said Cynthia, in a sharp professional tone.

A young and rather scared looking nurse appeared with a bottle which she proffered to Nibs, who waved her towards Cynthia with the somewhat enigmatical remark:

"*I*'m not really here today."

Cynthia took the bottle and examined it with the severity of a judge.

"This should have been sent up this morning."

"Sister is very sorry. She forgot."

"Sister should read the rules outside the door."

I gathered from the little nurse's expression that there was not the least likelihood of her having the hardihood to retail this message to the dreaded "Sister."

"So now it can't be done until tomorrow," finished Cynthia.

"Don't you think you could possibly let us have it tonight?"

"Well," said Cynthia graciously, "we are very busy, but if we have time it shall be done."

The little nurse withdrew, and Cynthia promptly took a jar from the shelf, refilled the bottle, and placed it on the table outside the door.

I laughed.

"Discipline must be maintained?"

"Exactly. Come out on our little balcony. You can see all the outside wards there."

I followed Cynthia and her friend and they pointed out the different wards to me. Lawrence remained behind, but after a few moments Cynthia called to him over her shoulder to come and join us. Then she looked at her watch.

"Nothing more to do, Nibs?"

"No."

"All right. Then we can lock up and go."

I had seen Lawrence in quite a different light that afternoon. Compared to John, he was an astoundingly difficult person to get to know. He was the opposite of his brother in almost every respect, being unusually shy and reserved. Yet he had a certain charm of manner, and I fancied that, if one really knew him well, one could have a deep affection for him. I had always fancied that his manner to Cynthia was rather constrained, and that she on her side was inclined to be shy of him. But they were both gay enough this afternoon, and chatted together like a couple of children.

As we drove through the village, I remembered that I wanted some stamps, so accordingly we pulled up at the post office.

As I came out again, I cannoned into a little man who was just entering. I drew aside and apologised, when suddenly, with a loud exclamation, he clasped me in his arms and kissed me warmly.

"*Mon ami* Hastings!" he cried. "It is indeed *mon ami* Hastings!"

"Poirot!" I exclaimed.

I turned to the pony-trap.

"This is a very pleasant meeting for me, Miss Cynthia. This is my old friend, Monsieur Poirot, whom I have not seen for years."

"Oh, we know Monsieur Poirot," said Cynthia gaily. "But I had no idea he was a friend of yours."

"Yes, indeed," said Poirot seriously. "I know Mademoiselle Cynthia. It is by the charity of that good Mrs. Inglethorp that I am here." Then, as I looked at him inquiringly: "Yes, my friend, she had kindly extended hospitality to seven of my countrypeople who, alas, are refugees from their native land. We Belgians will always remember her with gratitude."

Poirot was an extraordinary looking little man. He was hardly more than five feet, four inches, but carried himself with great dignity. His head was exactly the shape of an egg, and he always perched it a little on one side. His moustache was very stiff and military. The neatness of his attire was almost incredible. I believe a speck of dust would have caused him more pain than a bullet wound. Yet this quaint dandyfied little man who, I was sorry to see, now limped badly, had been in his time one of the most celebrated members of the Belgian police. As a detective, his *flair* had been extraordinary, and he had achieved triumphs by unravelling some of the most baffling cases of the day.

He pointed out to me the little house inhabited by him and his fellow Belgians, and I promised to go and see him at an early date. Then he raised his hat with a flourish to Cynthia, and we drove away.

"He's a dear little man," said Cynthia. "I'd no idea you knew him."

"You've been entertaining a celebrity unawares," I replied.

And, for the rest of the way home, I recited to them the various exploits and triumphs of Hercule Poirot.

We arrived back in a very cheerful mood. As we entered the hall, Mrs. Inglethorp came out of her boudoir. She looked flushed and upset.

"Oh, it's you," she said.

"Is there anything the matter, Aunt Emily?" asked Cynthia.

"Certainly not," said Mrs. Inglethorp sharply. "What should there be?" Then catching sight of Dorcas, the parlourmaid, going into the dining room, she called to her to bring some stamps into the boudoir.

"Yes, m'm." The old servant hesitated, then added diffidently: "Don't you think, m'm, you'd better get to bed? You're looking very tired."

"Perhaps you're right, Dorcas—yes—no—not now. I've some letters I must finish by post-time. Have you lighted the fire in my room as I told you?"

"Yes, m'm."

"Then I'll go to bed directly after supper."

She went into the boudoir again, and Cynthia stared after her.

"Goodness gracious! I wonder what's up?" she said to Lawrence.

He did not seem to have heard her, for without a word he turned on his heel and went out of the house.

I suggested a quick game of tennis before supper and, Cynthia agreeing, I ran upstairs to fetch my racquet.

Mrs. Cavendish was coming down the stairs. It may have been my fancy, but she, too, was looking odd and disturbed.

"Had a good walk with Dr. Bauerstein?" I asked, trying to appear as indifferent as I could.

"I didn't go," she replied abruptly. "Where is Mrs. Inglethorp?"

"In the boudoir."

Her hand clenched itself on the banisters, then she seemed to nerve herself for some encounter, and went rapidly past me down the stairs across the hall to the boudoir, the door of which she shut behind her.

As I ran out to the tennis court a few moments later, I had to pass the open boudoir window, and was unable to help overhearing the following scrap of dialogue. Mary Cavendish was saying in the voice of a woman desperately controlling herself:

"Then you won't show it to me?"

To which Mrs. Inglethorp replied:

"My dear Mary, it has nothing to do with that matter."

"Then show it to me."

"I tell you it is not what you imagine. It does not concern you in the least."

To which Mary Cavendish replied, with a rising bitterness:

"Of course, I might have known you would shield him."

Cynthia was waiting for me, and greeted me eagerly with:

"I say! There's been the most awful row! I've got it all out of Dorcas."

"What kind of a row?"

"Between Aunt Emily and *him*. I do hope she's found him out at last!"

"Was Dorcas there, then?"

"Of course not. She 'happened to be near the door.' It was a real old bust-up. I do wish I knew what it was all about."

I thought of Mrs. Raikes's gipsy face, and Evelyn Howard's warnings, but wisely decided to hold my peace, whilst Cynthia exhausted every possible hypothesis, and cheerfully hoped, "Aunt Emily will send him away, and will never speak to him again."

I was anxious to get hold of John, but he was nowhere to be seen. Evidently something very momentous had occurred that afternoon. I tried to forget the few words I had overheard; but, do what I would, I could not dismiss them altogether from my mind. What was Mary Cavendish's concern in the matter?

Mr. Inglethorp was in the drawing room when I came down to supper. His face was impassive as ever, and the strange unreality of the man struck me afresh.

Mrs. Inglethorp came down last. She still looked agitated, and during the meal there was a somewhat constrained silence. Inglethorp was unusually quiet. As a rule, he surrounded his wife with little attentions, placing a cushion at her back, and altogether playing the part of the devoted husband. Immediately after supper, Mrs. Inglethorp retired to her boudoir again.

"Send my coffee in here, Mary," she called. "I've just five minutes to catch the post."

Cynthia and I went and sat by the open window in the drawing room. Mary Cavendish brought our coffee to us. She seemed excited.

"Do you young people want lights, or do you enjoy the twilight?" she asked. "Will you take Mrs. Inglethorp her coffee, Cynthia? I will pour it out."

"Do not trouble, Mary," said Inglethorp. "I will take it to Emily." He poured it out, and went out of the room carrying it carefully.

Lawrence followed him, and Mrs. Cavendish sat down by us.

We three sat for some time in silence. It was a glorious night, hot and still. Mrs. Cavendish fanned herself gently with a palm leaf.

"It's almost too hot," she murmured. "We shall have a thunderstorm."

Alas, that these harmonious moments can never endure! My paradise was rudely shattered by the sound of a well known, and heartily disliked, voice in the hall.

"Dr. Bauerstein!" exclaimed Cynthia. "What a funny time to come."

I glanced jealously at Mary Cavendish, but she seemed quite undisturbed, the delicate pallor of her cheeks did not vary.

In a few moments, Alfred Inglethorp had ushered the doctor in, the latter laughing, and protesting that he was in no fit state for a drawing room. In truth, he presented a sorry spectacle, being literally plastered with mud.

"What have you been doing, doctor?" cried Mrs. Cavendish.

"I must make my apologies," said the doctor. "I did not really mean to come in, but Mr. Inglethorp insisted."

"Well, Bauerstein, you are in a plight," said John, strolling in from the hall. "Have some coffee, and tell us what you have been up to."

"Thank you, I will." He laughed rather ruefully, as he described how he had discovered a very rare species of fern in an inaccessible place, and in his efforts to obtain it had lost his footing, and slipped ignominiously into a neighbouring pond.

"The sun soon dried me off," he added, "but I'm afraid my appearance is very disreputable."

At this juncture, Mrs. Inglethorp called to Cynthia from the hall, and the girl ran out.

"Just carry up my despatch-case, will you, dear? I'm going to bed."

The door into the hall was a wide one. I had risen when Cynthia did, John was close by me. There were therefore three witnesses who could swear that Mrs. Inglethorp was carrying her coffee, as yet untasted, in her hand.

My evening was utterly and entirely spoilt by the presence of Dr. Bauerstein. It seemed to me the man would never go. He rose at last, however, and I breathed a sigh of relief.

"I'll walk down to the village with you," said Mr. Inglethorp. "I must see our agent over those estate accounts." He turned to John. "No one need sit up. I will take the latchkey."

III. THE NIGHT OF THE TRAGEDY

To make this part of my story clear, I append the following plan of the first floor of Styles. The servants' rooms are reached through the door B. They have no communication with the right wing, where the Inglethorps' rooms were situated.

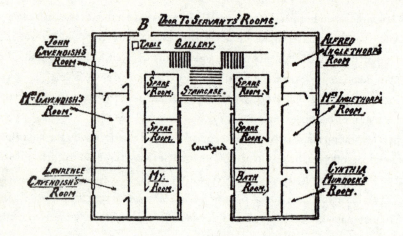

It seemed to be the middle of the night when I was awakened by Lawrence Cavendish. He had a candle in his hand, and the agitation of his face told me at once that something was seriously wrong.

"What's the matter?" I asked, sitting up in bed, and trying to collect my scattered thoughts.

"We are afraid my mother is very ill. She seems to be having some kind of fit. Unfortunately she has locked herself in."

"I'll come at once."

I sprang out of bed; and, pulling on a dressing gown, followed Lawrence along the passage and the gallery to the right wing of the house.

John Cavendish joined us, and one or two of the servants were standing round in a state of awe-stricken excitement. Lawrence turned to his brother.

"What do you think we had better do?"

Never, I thought, had his indecision of character been more apparent.

John rattled the handle of Mrs. Inglethorp's door violently, but with no effect. It was obviously locked or bolted on the inside. The whole household was aroused by now. The most alarming sounds were audible from the interior of the room. Clearly something must be done.

"Try going through Mr. Inglethorp's room, sir," cried Dorcas. "Oh, the poor mistress!"

Suddenly I realized that Alfred Inglethorp was not with us—that he alone had given no sign of his presence. John opened the door of his room. It was pitch dark, but Lawrence was following with the candle, and by its feeble light we saw that the bed had not been slept in, and that there was no sign of the room having been occupied.

We went straight to the connecting door. That, too, was locked or bolted on the inside. What was to be done?

"Oh, dear, sir," cried Dorcas, wringing her hands, "what ever shall we do?"

"We must try and break the door in, I suppose. It'll be a tough job, though. Here, let one of the maids go down and wake Baily and tell him to go for Dr. Wilkins at once. Now then, we'll have a try at the door. Half a moment, though, isn't there a door into Miss Cynthia's rooms?"

"Yes, sir, but that's always bolted. It's never been undone."

"Well, we might just see."

He ran rapidly down the corridor to Cynthia's room. Mary Cavendish was there, shaking the girl—who must have been an unusually sound sleeper—and trying to wake her.

In a moment or two he was back.

"No good. That's bolted too. We must break in the door. I think this one is a shade less solid than the one in the passage."

We strained and heaved together. The framework of the door was solid, and for a long time it resisted our efforts, but at last we felt it give beneath our weight, and finally, with a resounding crash, it was burst open.

We stumbled in together, Lawrence still holding his candle. Mrs. Inglethorp was lying on the bed, her whole form agitated by violent convulsions, in one of which she must have overturned the table beside her. As we entered, however, her limbs relaxed, and she fell back upon the pillows.

John strode across the room, and lit the gas. Turning to Annie, one of the house-maids, he sent her downstairs to the dining room for brandy. Then he went across to his mother whilst I unbolted the door that gave on the corridor.

I turned to Lawrence, to suggest that I had better leave them now that there was no further need of my services, but the words were frozen on my lips. Never have I seen such a ghastly look on any man's face. He was white as chalk, the candle he held in his shaking hand was sputtering onto the carpet, and his eyes, petrified with terror, or some such kindred emotion, stared fixedly over my head at a point on the further wall. It was as though he had seen something that turned him to stone. I instinctively followed the direction of his eyes, but I could see nothing unusual. The still feebly flickering ashes in the grate, and the row of prim ornaments on the mantelpiece, were surely harmless enough.

The violence of Mrs. Inglethorp's attack seemed to be passing. She was able to speak in short gasps.

"Better now—very sudden—stupid of me—to lock myself in."

A shadow fell on the bed and, looking up, I saw Mary Cavendish standing near the door with her arm around Cynthia. She seemed to be supporting the girl, who looked utterly dazed and unlike herself. Her face was heavily flushed, and she yawned repeatedly.

"Poor Cynthia is quite frightened," said Mrs. Cavendish in a low clear voice. She herself, I noticed, was dressed in her white land smock. Then it must be later than I thought. I saw that a faint streak of daylight was showing through the curtains of the windows, and that the clock on the mantelpiece pointed to close upon five o'clock.

A strangled cry from the bed startled me. A fresh access of pain seized the unfortunate old lady. The convulsions were of a violence terrible to behold. Everything was confusion. We thronged round her, powerless to help or alleviate. A final convulsion lifted her from the bed, until she appeared to rest upon her head and her heels, with her body arched in an extraordinary manner. In vain Mary and John tried to administer more brandy. The moments flew. Again the body arched itself in that peculiar fashion.

At that moment, Dr. Bauerstein pushed his way authoritatively into the room. For one instant he stopped dead, staring at the figure on the bed, and, at the same instant, Mrs. Inglethorp cried out in a strangled voice, her eyes fixed on the doctor:

"Alfred—Alfred—" Then she fell back motionless on the pillows.

With a stride, the doctor reached the bed, and seizing her arms worked them energetically, applying what I knew to be artificial respiration. He issued a few short sharp orders to the servants. An imperious wave of his hand drove us all to the door. We watched him, fascinated, though I think we all knew in our hearts that it was too late, and that nothing could be done now. I could see by the expression on his face that he himself had little hope.

Finally he abandoned his task, shaking his head gravely. At that moment, we heard footsteps outside, and Dr. Wilkins, Mrs. Inglethorp's own doctor, a portly, fussy little man, came bustling in.

In a few words Dr. Bauerstein explained how he had happened to be passing the lodge gates as the car came out, and had run up to the house as fast as he could, whilst the car went on to fetch Dr. Wilkins. With a faint gesture of the hand, he indicated the figure on the bed.

"Ve—ry sad. Ve—ry sad," murmured Dr. Wilkins. "Poor dear lady. Always did far too much—far too much—against my advice. I warned her. Her heart was far from strong. 'Take it easy,' I said to her, 'Take—it—easy'. But no—her zeal for good works was too great. Nature rebelled. Na—ture—re—belled."

Dr. Bauerstein, I noticed, was watching the local doctor narrowly. He still kept his eyes fixed on him as he spoke.

"The convulsions were of a peculiar violence, Dr. Wilkins. I am sorry you were not here in time to witness them. They were quite—tetanic in character."

"Ah!" said Dr. Wilkins wisely.

"I should like to speak to you in private," said Dr. Bauerstein. He turned to John. "You do not object?"

"Certainly not."

We all trooped out into the corridor, leaving the two doctors alone, and I heard the key turned in the lock behind us.

We went slowly down the stairs. I was violently excited. I have a certain talent for deduction, and Dr. Bauerstein's manner had started a flock of wild surmises in my mind. Mary Cavendish laid her hand upon my arm.

"What is it? Why did Dr. Bauerstein seem so—peculiar?"

I looked at her.

"Do you know what I think?"

"What?"

"Listen!" I looked round, the others were out of earshot. I lowered my voice to a whisper. "I believe she has been poisoned! I'm certain Dr. Bauerstein suspects it."

"*What?*" She shrank against the wall, the pupils of her eyes dilating wildly. Then, with a sudden cry that startled me, she cried out: "No, no—not that—not that!" And breaking from me, fled up the stairs. I followed her, afraid that she was going to faint. I found her leaning against the bannisters, deadly pale. She waved me away impatiently.

"No, no—leave me. I'd rather be alone. Let me just be quiet for a minute or two. Go down to the others."

I obeyed her reluctantly. John and Lawrence were in the dining room. I joined them. We were all silent, but I suppose I voiced the thoughts of us all when I at last broke it by saying:

"Where is Mr. Inglethorp?"

John shook his head.

"He's not in the house."

Our eyes met. Where *was* Alfred Inglethorp? His absence was strange and inexplicable. I remembered Mrs. Inglethorp's dying words. What lay beneath them? What more could she have told us, if she had had time?

At last we heard the doctors descending the stairs. Dr. Wilkins was looking important and excited, and trying to conceal an inward exultation under a manner of decorous calm. Dr. Bauerstein remained in the background, his grave bearded face unchanged. Dr. Wilkins was the spokesman for the two. He addressed himself to John:

"Mr. Cavendish, I should like your consent to a postmortem."

"Is that necessary?" asked John gravely. A spasm of pain crossed his face.

"Absolutely," said Dr. Bauerstein.

"You mean by that—?"

"That neither Dr. Wilkins nor myself could give a death certificate under the circumstances."

John bent his head.

"In that case, I have no alternative but to agree."

"Thank you," said Dr. Wilkins briskly. "We propose that it should take place tomorrow night—or rather tonight." And he glanced at the daylight. "Under the circumstances, I am afraid an inquest can hardly be avoided—these formalities are necessary, but I beg that you won't distress yourselves."

There was a pause, and then Dr. Bauerstein drew two keys from his pocket, and handed them to John.

"These are the keys of the two rooms. I have locked them and, in my opinion, they would be better kept locked for the present."

The doctors then departed.

I had been turning over an idea in my head, and I felt that the moment had now come to broach it. Yet I was a little chary of doing so. John, I knew, had a horror of any kind of publicity, and was an easygoing optimist, who preferred never to meet trouble halfway. It might be difficult to convince him of the soundness of my plan. Lawrence, on the other hand, being less conventional, and having more imagination, I felt I might count upon as an ally. There was no doubt that the moment had come for me to take the lead.

"John," I said, "I am going to ask you something."

"Well?"

"You remember my speaking of my friend Poirot? The Belgian who is here? He has been a most famous detective."

"Yes."

"I want you to let me call him in—to investigate this matter."

"What—now? Before the postmortem?"

"Yes, time is an advantage if—if—there has been foul play."

"Rubbish!" cried Lawrence angrily. "In my opinion the whole thing is a mare's nest of Bauerstein's! Wilkins hadn't an idea of such a thing, until Bauerstein put it into his head. But, like all specialists, Bauerstein's got a bee in his bonnet. Poisons are his hobby, so of course he sees them everywhere."

I confess that I was surprised by Lawrence's attitude. He was so seldom vehement about anything.

John hesitated.

"I can't feel as you do, Lawrence," he said at last. "I'm inclined to give Hastings a free hand, though I should prefer to wait a bit. We don't want any unnecessary scandal."

"No, no," I cried eagerly, "you need have no fear of that. Poirot is discretion itself."

"Very well, then, have it your own way. I leave it in your hands. Though, if it is as we suspect, it seems a clear enough case. God forgive me if I am wronging him!"

I looked at my watch. It was six o'clock. I determined to lose no time.

Five minutes' delay, however, I allowed myself. I spent it in ransacking the library until I discovered a medical book which gave a description of strychnine poisoning.

IV. POIROT INVESTIGATES

The house which the Belgians occupied in the village was quite close to the park gates. One could save time by taking a narrow path through the long grass, which cut off the detours of the winding drive. So I, accordingly, went that way. I had nearly reached the lodge, when my attention was arrested by the running figure of a man approaching me. It was Mr. Inglethorp. Where had he been? How did he intend to explain his absence?

He accosted me eagerly.

"My God! This is terrible! My poor wife! I have only just heard."

"Where have you been?" I asked.

"Denby kept me late last night. It was one o'clock before we'd finished. Then I found that I'd forgotten the latchkey after all. I didn't want to arouse the household, so Denby gave me a bed."

"How did you hear the news?" I asked.

"Wilkins knocked Denby up to tell him. My poor Emily! She was so self-sacrific-ing—such a noble character. She overtaxed her strength."

A wave of revulsion swept over me. What a consummate hypocrite the man was!

"I must hurry on," I said, thankful that he did not ask me whither I was bound.

In a few minutes I was knocking at the door of Leastways Cottage.

Getting no answer, I repeated my summons impatiently. A window above me was cautiously opened, and Poirot himself looked out.

He gave an exclamation of surprise at seeing me. In a few brief words, I explained the tragedy that had occurred, and that I wanted his help.

"Wait, my friend, I will let you in, and you shall recount to me the affair whilst I dress."

In a few moments he had unbarred the door, and I followed him up to his room. There he installed me in a chair, and I related the whole story, keeping back nothing, and omitting no circumstance, however insignificant, whilst he himself made a careful and deliberate toilet.

I told him of my awakening, of Mrs. Inglethorp's dying words, of her husband's absence, of the quarrel the day before, of the scrap of conversation between Mary and her mother-in-law that I had overheard, of the former quarrel between Mrs. Inglethorp and Evelyn Howard, and of the latter's innuendoes.

I was hardly as clear as I could wish. I repeated myself several times, and occasionally had to go back to some detail that I had forgotten. Poirot smiled kindly on me.

"The mind is confused? Is it not so? Take time, *mon ami*. You are agitated; you are excited—it is but natural. Presently, when we are calmer, we will arrange the facts, neatly, each in his proper place. We will examine—and reject. Those of importance we will put on one side; those of no importance, pouf!"—he screwed up his cherub-like face, and puffed comically enough—"blow them away!"

"That's all very well," I objected, "but how are you going to decide what is important, and what isn't? That always seems the difficulty to me."

Poirot shook his head energetically. He was now arranging his moustache with exquisite care.

"Not so. *Voyons!* One fact leads to another—so we continue. Does the next fit in with that? A *merveille!* Good! We can proceed. This next little fact—no! Ah, that is curious! There is something missing—a link in the chain that is not there. We examine. We search. And that little curious fact, that possibly paltry little detail that will not tally, we put it here!" He made an extravagant gesture with his hand. "It is significant! It is tremendous!"

"Y—es—"

"Ah!" Poirot shook his forefinger so fiercely at me that I quailed before it. "Beware! Peril to the detective who says: 'It is so small—it does not matter. It will not agree. I will forget it.' That way lies confusion! Everything matters."

"I know. You always told me that. That's why I have gone into all the details of this thing whether they seemed to me relevant or not."

"And I am pleased with you. You have a good memory, and you have given me the facts faithfully. Of the order in which you present them, I say nothing—truly, it is deplorable! But I make allowances—you are upset. To that I attribute the circumstance that you have omitted one fact of paramount importance."

"What is that?" I asked.

"You have not told me if Mrs. Inglethorp ate well last night."

I stared at him. Surely the war had affected the little man's brain. He was carefully engaged in brushing his coat before putting it on, and seemed wholly engrossed in the task.

"I don't remember," I said. "And, anyway, I don't see——"

"You do not see? But it is of the first importance."

"I can't see why," I said, rather nettled. "As far as I can remember, she didn't eat much. She was obviously upset, and it had taken her appetite away. That was only natural."

"Yes," said Poirot thoughtfully, "it was only natural."

He opened a drawer, and took out a small despatch-case, then turned to me.

"Now I am ready. We will proceed to the château, and study matters on the spot. Excuse me, *mon ami*, you dressed in haste, and your tie is on one side. Permit me." With a deft gesture, he rearranged it.

"*Ça y est!* Now, shall we start?"

We hurried up the village, and turned in at the lodge gates. Poirot stopped for a moment, and gazed sorrowfully over the beautiful expanse of park, still glittering with morning dew.

"So beautiful, so beautiful, and yet, the poor family, plunged in sorrow, prostrated with grief."

He looked at me keenly as he spoke, and I was aware that I reddened under his prolonged gaze.

Was the family prostrated by grief? Was the sorrow at Mrs. Inglethorp's death so great? I realized that there was an emotional lack in the atmosphere. The dead woman had not the gift of commanding love. Her death was a shock and a distress, but she would not be passionately regretted.

Poirot seemed to follow my thoughts. He nodded his head gravely.

"No, you are right," he said, "it is not as though there was a blood tie. She has been kind and generous to these Cavendishes, but she was not their own mother. Blood tells—always remember that—blood tells."

"Poirot," I said, "I wish you would tell me why you wanted to know if Mrs. Inglethorp ate well last night? I have been turning it over in my mind, but I can't see how it has anything to do with the matter."

He was silent for a minute or two as we walked along, but finally he said:

"I do not mind telling you—though, as you know, it is not my habit to explain until the end is reached. The present contention is that Mrs. Inglethorp died of strychnine poisoning, presumably administered in her coffee."

"Yes?"

"Well, what time was the coffee served?"

"About eight o'clock."

"Therefore she drank it between then and half-past eight—certainly not much later. Well, strychnine is a fairly rapid poison. Its effects would be felt very soon, probably in about an hour. Yet, in Mrs. Inglethorp's case, the symptoms do not manifest themselves until five o'clock the next morning: nine hours! But a heavy meal, taken at about the same time as the poison, might retard its effects, though hardly to that extent. Still, it is a possibility to be taken into account. But, according to you, she ate very little for supper, and yet the symptoms do not develop until early the next morning! Now that is a curious circumstance, my friend. Something may arise at the autopsy to explain it. In the meantime, remember it."

As we neared the house, John came out and met us. His face looked weary and haggard.

"This is a very dreadful business, Monsieur Poirot," he said. "Hastings has explained to you that we are anxious for no publicity?"

"I comprehend perfectly."

"You see, it is only suspicion so far. We have nothing to go upon."

"Precisely. It is a matter of precaution only."

John turned to me, taking out his cigarette case, and lighting a cigarette as he did so.

"You know that fellow Inglethorp is back?"

"Yes. I met him."

John flung the match into an adjacent flower bed, a proceeding which was too much for Poirot's feelings. He retrieved it, and buried it neatly.

"It's jolly difficult to know how to treat him."

"That difficulty will not exist long," pronounced Poirot quietly.

John looked puzzled, not quite understanding the portent of this cryptic saying. He handed the two keys which Dr. Bauerstein had given him to me.

"Show Monsieur Poirot everything he wants to see."

"The rooms are locked?" asked Poirot.

"Dr. Bauerstein considered it advisable."

Poirot nodded thoughtfully.

"Then he is very sure. Well, that simplifies matters for us."

We went up together to the room of the tragedy. For convenience I append a plan of the room and the principal articles of furniture in it.

Poirot locked the door on the inside, and proceeded to a minute inspection of the room. He darted from one object to the other with the agility of a grasshopper.

I remained by the door, fearing to obliterate any clues. Poirot, however, did not seem grateful to me for my forbearance.

"What have you, my friend?" he cried, "that you remain there like—how do you say it?—? ah yes, the stuck pig?"

I explained that I was afraid of obliterating any foot-marks.

"Foot-marks? But what an idea! There has already been practically an army in the room! What foot-marks are we likely to find? No, come here and aid me in my search. I will put down my little case until I need it."

He did so, on the round table by the window, but it was an ill-advised proceeding; for, the top of it being loose, it tilted up, and precipitated the despatch-case on the floor.

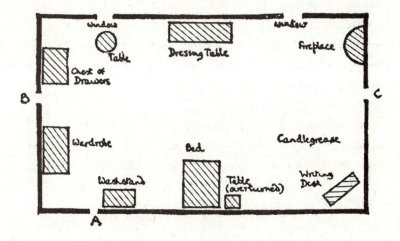

MRS. INGLETHORPE'S BEDROOM
A. Door into Passage
B. Door into Mr. Inglethorpe's Room
C. Door into Cynthia's Room

"*Eh voilà une table!*" cried Poirot. "Ah, my friend, one may live in a big house and yet have no comfort."

After which piece of moralizing, he resumed his search.

A small purple despatch-case, with a key in the lock, on the writing- table, engaged his attention for some time. He took out the key from the lock, and passed it to me to inspect. I saw nothing peculiar, however. It was an ordinary key of the Yale type, with a bit of twisted wire through the handle.

Next, he examined the framework of the door we had broken in, assuring himself that the bolt had really been shot. Then he went to the door opposite leading into Cynthia's room. That door was also bolted, as I had stated. However, he went to the length of unbolting it, and opening and shutting it several times; this he did with the utmost precaution against making any noise. Suddenly something in the bolt itself seemed to rivet his attention. He examined it carefully, and then, nimbly whipping out a pair of small forceps from his case, he drew out some minute particle which he carefully sealed up in a tiny envelope.

On the chest of drawers there was a tray with a spirit lamp and a small saucepan on it. A small quantity of a dark fluid remained in the saucepan, and an empty cup and saucer that had been drunk out of stood near it.

I wondered how I could have been so unobservant as to overlook this. Here was a clue worth having. Poirot delicately dipped his finger into the liquid, and tasted it gingerly. He made a grimace.

"Coco—with—I think—rum in it."

He passed on to the debris on the floor, where the table by the bed had been overturned. A reading lamp, some books, matches, a bunch of keys, and the crushed fragments of a coffee cup lay scattered about.

"Ah, this is curious," said Poirot.

"I must confess that I see nothing particularly curious about it."

"You do not? Observe the lamp—the chimney is broken in two places; they lie there as they fell. But see, the coffee cup is absolutely smashed to powder."

"Well," I said wearily, "I suppose someone must have stepped on it."

"Exactly," said Poirot, in an odd voice. "Someone stepped on it."

He rose from his knees, and walked slowly across to the mantelpiece, where he stood abstractedly fingering the ornaments, and straightening them—a trick of his when he was agitated.

"*Mon ami*," he said, turning to me, "somebody stepped on that cup, grinding it to powder, and the reason they did so was either because it contained strychnine or—which is far more serious—because it did not contain strychnine!"

I made no reply. I was bewildered, but I knew that it was no good asking him to explain. In a moment or two he roused himself, and went on with his investigations. He picked up the bunch of keys from the floor, and twirling them round in his fingers finally selected one, very bright and shining, which he tried in the lock of the purple despatch-case. It fitted, and he opened the box, but after a moment's hesitation, closed and relocked it, and slipped the bunch of keys, as well as the key that had originally stood in the lock, into his own pocket.

"I have no authority to go through these papers. But it should be done—at once!"

He then made a very careful examination of the drawers of the washstand. Crossing the room to the left-hand window, a round stain, hardly visible on the dark brown carpet, seemed to interest him particularly. He went down on his knees, examining it minutely—even going so far as to smell it.

Finally, he poured a few drops of the coco into a test tube, sealing it up carefully. His next proceeding was to take out a little notebook.

"We have found in this room," he said, writing busily, "six points of interest. Shall I enumerate them, or will you?"

"Oh, you," I replied hastily.

"Very well, then. One, a coffee cup that has been ground into powder; two, a despatch-case with a key in the lock; three, a stain on the floor."

"That may have been done some time ago," I interrupted.

"No, for it is still perceptibly damp and smells of coffee. Four, a fragment of some dark green fabric—only a thread or two, but recognizable."

"Ah!" I cried. "That was what you sealed up in the envelope."

"Yes. It may turn out to be a piece of one of Mrs. Inglethorp's own dresses, and quite unimportant. We shall see. Five, *this*!" With a dramatic gesture, he pointed to a large splash of candle grease on the floor by the writing-table. "It must have been done since yesterday, otherwise a good housemaid would have at once removed it with blotting-paper and a hot iron. One of my best hats once—but that is not to the point."

"It was very likely done last night. We were very agitated. Or perhaps Mrs. Inglethorp herself dropped her candle."

"You brought only one candle into the room?"

"Yes. Lawrence Cavendish was carrying it. But he was very upset. He seemed to see something over here"—I indicated the mantelpiece—"that absolutely paralysed him."

"That is interesting," said Poirot quickly. "Yes, it is suggestive"—his eye sweeping the whole length of the wall—"but it was not his candle that made this great patch, for you perceive that this is white grease; whereas Monsieur Lawrence's candle, which is still on the dressing table, is pink. On the other hand, Mrs. Inglethorp had no candlestick in the room, only a reading lamp."

"Then," I said, "what do you deduce?"

To which my friend only made a rather irritating reply, urging me to use my own natural faculties.

"And the sixth point?" I asked. "I suppose it is the sample of coco."

"No," said Poirot thoughtfully. "I might have included that in the six, but I did not. No, the sixth point I will keep to myself for the present."

He looked quickly round the room. "There is nothing more to be done here, I think, unless"—he stared earnestly and long at the dead ashes in the grate. "The fire burns—and it destroys. But by chance—there might be—let us see!"

Deftly, on hands and knees, he began to sort the ashes from the grate into the fender, handling them with the greatest caution. Suddenly, he gave a faint exclamation.

"The forceps, Hastings!"

I quickly handed them to him, and with skill he extracted a small piece of half charred paper.

"There, *mon ami*!" he cried. "What do you think of that?"

I scrutinized the fragment. This is an exact reproduction of it:

I was puzzled. It was unusually thick, quite unlike ordinary notepaper. Suddenly an idea struck me.

"Poirot!" I cried. "This is a fragment of a will!"

"Exactly."

I looked up at him sharply.

"You are not surprised?"

"No," he said gravely, "I expected it."

I relinquished the piece of paper, and watched him put it away in his case, with the same methodical care that he bestowed on everything. My brain was in a whirl. What was this complication of a will? Who had destroyed it? The person who had left the candle grease on the floor? Obviously. But how had anyone gained admission? All the doors had been bolted on the inside.

"Now, my friend," said Poirot briskly, "we will go. I should like to ask a few questions of the parlourmaid—Dorcas, her name is, is it not?"

We passed through Alfred Inglethorp's room, and Poirot delayed long enough to make a brief but fairly comprehensive examination of it. We went out through that door, locking both it and that of Mrs. Inglethorp's room as before.

I took him down to the boudoir which he had expressed a wish to see, and went myself in search of Dorcas.

When I returned with her, however, the boudoir was empty.

"Poirot," I cried, "where are you?"

"I am here, my friend."

He had stepped outside the French window, and was standing, apparently, lost in admiration, before the various shaped flower beds.

"Admirable!" he murmured. "Admirable! What symmetry! Observe that crescent; and those diamonds—their neatness rejoices the eye. The spacing of the plants, also, is perfect. It has been recently done; is it not so?"

"Yes, I believe they were at it yesterday afternoon. But come in—Dorcas is here."

"*Eh bien, eh bien!* Do not grudge me a moment's satisfaction of the eye."

"Yes, but this affair is more important."

"And how do you know that these fine begonias are not of equal importance?"

I shrugged my shoulders. There was really no arguing with him if he chose to take that line.

"You do not agree? But such things have been. Well, we will come in and interview the brave Dorcas."

Dorcas was standing in the boudoir, her hands folded in front of her, and her grey hair rose in stiff waves under her white cap. She was the very model and picture of a good old-fashioned servant.

In her attitude towards Poirot, she was inclined to be suspicious, but he soon broke down her defences. He drew forward a chair.

"Pray be seated, mademoiselle."

"Thank you, sir."

"You have been with your mistress many years, is it not so?"

"Ten years, sir."

"That is a long time, and very faithful service. You were much attached to her, were you not?"

"She was a very good mistress to me, sir."

"Then you will not object to answering a few questions. I put them to you with Mr. Cavendish's full approval."

"Oh, certainly, sir."

"Then I will begin by asking you about the events of yesterday afternoon. Your mistress had a quarrel?"

"Yes, sir. But I don't know that I ought—" Dorcas hesitated.

Poirot looked at her keenly.

"My good Dorcas, it is necessary that I should know every detail of that quarrel as fully as possible. Do not think that you are betraying your mistress's secrets. Your mistress lies dead, and it is necessary that we should know all—if we are to avenge her. Nothing can bring her back to life, but we do hope, if there has been foul play, to bring the murderer to justice."

"Amen to that," said Dorcas fiercely. "And, naming no names, there's *one* in this house that none of us could ever abide! And an ill day it was when first *he* darkened the threshold."

Poirot waited for her indignation to subside, and then, resuming his business-like tone, he asked:

"Now, as to this quarrel? What is the first you heard of it?"

"Well, sir, I happened to be going along the hall outside yesterday—"

"What time was that?"

"I couldn't say exactly, sir, but it wasn't teatime by a long way. Perhaps four o'clock—or it may have been a bit later. Well, sir, as I said, I happened to be passing along, when I heard voices very loud and angry in here. I didn't exactly mean to listen, but—well, there it is. I stopped. The door was shut, but the mistress was speaking very sharp and clear, and I heard what she said quite plainly. 'You have lied to me, and deceived me,' she said. I didn't hear what Mr. Inglethorp replied. He spoke a good bit lower than she did—but she answered: 'How dare you? I have kept you and clothed you and fed you! You owe everything to me! And this is how you repay me! By bringing disgrace upon our name!' Again I didn't hear what he said, but she went on: 'Nothing that you can say will make any difference. I see my duty clearly. My mind is made up. You need not think that any fear of publicity, or scandal between husband and wife will deter me.' Then I thought I heard them coming out, so I went off quickly."

"You are sure it was Mr. Inglethorp's voice you heard?"

"Oh, yes, sir, whose else's could it be?"

"Well, what happened next?"

"Later, I came back to the hall; but it was all quiet. At five o'clock, Mrs. Inglethorp rang the bell and told me to bring her a cup of tea—nothing to eat—to the boudoir. She was looking dreadful—so white and upset. 'Dorcas,' she says, 'I've had a great shock.' 'I'm sorry for that, m'm,' I says. 'You'll feel better after a nice hot cup of tea, m'm.' She had something in her hand. I don't know if it was a letter, or just a piece of paper, but it had writing on it, and she kept staring at it, almost as if she couldn't believe what was written there. She whispered to herself, as though she had forgotten I was there: 'These few words—and everything's changed.' And then she says to me: 'Never trust a man, Dorcas, they're not worth it!' I hurried off, and got her a good strong cup of tea, and she thanked me, and said she'd feel better when she'd drunk it. 'I don't know what to do,' she says. 'Scandal between husband and wife is a dreadful thing, Dorcas. I'd rather hush it up if I could.' Mrs. Cavendish came in just then, so she didn't say any more."

"She still had the letter, or whatever it was, in her hand?"

"Yes, sir."

"What would she be likely to do with it afterwards?"

"Well, I don't know, sir, I expect she would lock it up in that purple case of hers."

"Is that where she usually kept important papers?"

"Yes, sir. She brought it down with her every morning, and took it up every night."

"When did she lose the key of it?"

"She missed it yesterday at lunchtime, sir, and told me to look carefully for it. She was very much put out about it."

"But she had a duplicate key?"

"Oh, yes, sir."

Dorcas was looking very curiously at him and, to tell the truth, so was I. What was all this about a lost key? Poirot smiled.

"Never mind, Dorcas, it is my business to know things. Is this the key that was lost?" He drew from his pocket the key that he had found in the lock of the despatch-case upstairs.

Dorcas's eyes looked as though they would pop out of her head.

"That's it, sir, right enough. But where did you find it? I looked everywhere for it."

"Ah, but you see it was not in the same place yesterday as it was today. Now, to pass to another subject, had your mistress a dark green dress in her wardrobe?"

Dorcas was rather startled by the unexpected question.

"No, sir."

"Are you quite sure?"

"Oh, yes, sir."

"Has anyone else in the house got a green dress?"

Dorcas reflected.

"Miss Cynthia has a green evening dress."

"Light or dark green?"

"A light green, sir; a sort of chiffon, they call it."

"Ah, that is not what I want. And nobody else has anything green?"

"No, sir—not that I know of."

Poirot's face did not betray a trace of whether he was disappointed or otherwise. He merely remarked:

"Good, we will leave that and pass on. Have you any reason to believe that your mistress was likely to take a sleeping powder last night?"

"Not *last* night, sir, I know she didn't."

"Why do you know so positively?"

"Because the box was empty. She took the last one two days ago, and she didn't have any more made up."

"You are quite sure of that?"

"Positive, sir."

"Then that is cleared up! By the way, your mistress didn't ask you to sign any paper yesterday?"

"To sign a paper? No, sir."

"When Mr. Hastings and Mr. Lawrence came in yesterday evening, they found your mistress busy writing letters. I suppose you can give me no idea to whom these letters were addressed?"

"I'm afraid I couldn't, sir. I was out in the evening. Perhaps Annie could tell you, though she's a careless girl. Never cleared the coffee cups away last night. That's what happens when I'm not here to look after things."

Poirot lifted his hand.

"Since they have been left, Dorcas, leave them a little longer, I pray you. I should like to examine them."

"Very well, sir."

"What time did you go out last evening?"

"About six o'clock, sir."

"Thank you, Dorcas, that is all I have to ask you." He rose and strolled to the window. "I have been admiring these flower beds. How many gardeners are employed here, by the way?"

"Only three now, sir. Five, we had, before the war, when it was kept as a gentleman's place should be. I wish you could have seen it then, sir. A fair sight it was. But now there's only old Manning, and young William, and a new-fashioned woman gardener in breeches and such-like. Ah, these are dreadful times!"

"The good times will come again, Dorcas. At least, we hope so. Now, will you send Annie to me here?"

"Yes, sir. Thank you, sir."

"How did you know that Mrs. Inglethorp took sleeping powders?" I asked, in lively curiosity, as Dorcas left the room. "And about the lost key and the duplicate?"

"One thing at a time. As to the sleeping powders, I knew by this." He suddenly produced a small cardboard box, such as chemists use for powders.

"Where did you find it?"

"In the washstand drawer in Mrs. Inglethorp's bedroom. It was Number Six of my catalogue."

"But I suppose, as the last powder was taken two days ago, it is not of much importance?"

"Probably not, but do you notice anything that strikes you as peculiar about this box?"

I examined it closely.

"No, I can't say that I do."

"Look at the label."

I read the label carefully: " 'One powder to be taken at bedtime, if required. Mrs. Inglethorp.' No, I see nothing unusual."

"Not the fact that there is no chemist's name?"

"Ah!" I exclaimed. "To be sure, that is odd!"

"Have you ever known a chemist to send out a box like that, without his printed name?"

"No, I can't say that I have."

I was becoming quite excited, but Poirot damped my ardour by remarking:

"Yet the explanation is quite simple. So do not intrigue yourself, my friend."

An audible creaking proclaimed the approach of Annie, so I had no time to reply.

Annie was a fine, strapping girl, and was evidently labouring under intense excitement, mingled with a certain ghoulish enjoyment of the tragedy.

Poirot came to the point at once, with a business-like briskness.

"I sent for you, Annie, because I thought you might be able to tell me something about the letters Mrs. Inglethorp wrote last night. How many were there? And can you tell me any of the names and addresses?"

Annie considered.

"There were four letters, sir. One was to Miss Howard, and one was to Mr. Wells, the lawyer, and the other two I don't think I remember, sir—oh, yes, one was to Ross's, the caterers in Tadminster. The other one, I don't remember."

"Think," urged Poirot.

Annie racked her brains in vain.

"I'm sorry, sir, but it's clean gone. I don't think I can have noticed it."

"It does not matter," said Poirot, not betraying any sign of disappointment. "Now I want to ask you about something else. There is a saucepan in Mrs. Inglethorp's room with some coco in it. Did she have that every night?"

"Yes, sir, it was put in her room every evening, and she warmed it up in the night—whenever she fancied it."

"What was it? Plain coco?"

"Yes, sir, made with milk, with a teaspoonful of sugar, and two teaspoonfuls of rum in it."

"Who took it to her room?"

"I did, sir."

"Always?"

"Yes, sir."

"At what time?"

"When I went to draw the curtains, as a rule, sir."

"Did you bring it straight up from the kitchen then?"

"No, sir, you see there's not much room on the gas stove, so Cook used to make it early, before putting the vegetables on for supper. Then I used to bring it up, and put it on the table by the swing door, and take it into her room later."

"The swing door is in the left wing, is it not?"

"Yes, sir."

"And the table, is it on this side of the door, or on the farther—servants' side?"

"It's this side, sir."

"What time did you bring it up last night?"

"About quarter-past seven, I should say, sir."

"And when did you take it into Mrs. Inglethorp's room?"

"When I went to shut up, sir. About eight o'clock. Mrs. Inglethorp came up to bed before I'd finished."

"Then, between seven-fifteen and eight o'clock, the cocoa was standing on the table in the left wing?"

"Yes, sir." Annie had been growing redder and redder in the face, and now she blurted out unexpectedly:

"And if there *was* salt in it, sir, it wasn't me. I never took the salt near it."

"What makes you think there was salt in it?" asked Poirot.

"Seeing it on the tray, sir."

"You saw some salt on the tray?"

"Yes. Coarse kitchen salt, it looked. I never noticed it when I took the tray up, but when I came to take it into the mistress's room I saw it at once, and I suppose I ought to have taken it down again, and asked Cook to make some fresh. But I was in a hurry, because Dorcas was out, and I thought maybe the coco itself was all right, and the salt had only gone on the tray. So I dusted it off with my apron, and took it in."

I had the utmost difficulty in controlling my excitement. Unknown to herself, Annie had provided us with an important piece of evidence. How she would have gaped if she had realized that her "coarse kitchen salt" was strychnine, one of the most deadly poisons known to mankind. I marvelled at Poirot's calm. His self-control was astonishing. I awaited his next question with impatience, but it disappointed me.

"When you went into Mrs. Inglethorp's room, was the door leading into Miss Cynthia's room bolted?"

"Oh! Yes, sir; it always was. It had never been opened."

"And the door into Mr. Inglethorp's room? Did you notice if that was bolted too?" Annie hesitated.

"I couldn't rightly say, sir; it was shut but I couldn't say whether it was bolted or not."

"When you finally left the room, did Mrs. Inglethorp bolt the door after you?"

"No, sir, not then, but I expect she did later. She usually did lock it at night. The door into the passage, that is."

"Did you notice any candle grease on the floor when you did the room yesterday?"

"Candle grease? Oh, no, sir. Mrs. Inglethorp didn't have a candle, only a reading lamp."

"Then, if there had been a large patch of candle grease on the floor, you think you would have been sure to have seen it?"

"Yes, sir, and I would have taken it out with a piece of blotting-paper and a hot iron."

Then Poirot repeated the question he had put to Dorcas:

"Did your mistress ever have a green dress?"

"No, sir."

"Nor a mantle, nor a cape, nor a—how do you call it?—a sports coat?"

"Not green, sir."

"Nor anyone else in the house?"

Annie reflected.

"No, sir."

"You are sure of that?"

"Quite sure."

"*Bien!* That is all I want to know. Thank you very much."

With a nervous giggle, Annie took herself creakingly out of the room. My pent-up excitement burst forth.

"Poirot," I cried, "I congratulate you! This is a great discovery."

"What is a great discovery?"

"Why, that it was the coco and not the coffee that was poisoned. That explains everything! Of course it did not take effect until the early morning, since the coco was only drunk in the middle of the night."

"So you think that the coco—mark well what I say, Hastings, the *coco*—contained strychnine?"

"Of course! That salt on the tray, what else could it have been?"

"It might have been salt," replied Poirot placidly.

I shrugged my shoulders. If he was going to take the matter that way, it was no good arguing with him. The idea crossed my mind, not for the first time, that poor old Poirot was growing old. Privately I thought it lucky that he had associated with him someone of a more receptive type of mind.

Poirot was surveying me with quietly twinkling eyes.

"You are not pleased with me, *mon ami*?"

"My dear Poirot," I said coldly, "it is not for me to dictate to you. You have a right to your own opinion, just as I have to mine."

"A most admirable sentiment," remarked Poirot, rising briskly to his feet. "Now I have finished with this room. By the way, whose is the smaller desk in the corner?"

"Mr. Inglethorp's."

"Ah!" He tried the roll top tentatively. "Locked. But perhaps one of Mrs. Inglethorp's keys would open it." He tried several, twisting and turning them with a practised hand, and finally uttering an ejaculation of satisfaction. "*Voila!* It is not the key, but it will open it at a pinch." He slid back the roll top, and ran a rapid eye over the neatly filed papers. To my surprise, he did not examine them, merely remarking approvingly as he relocked the desk: "Decidedly, he is a man of method, this Mr. Inglethorp!"

A "man of method" was, in Poirot's estimation, the highest praise that could be bestowed on any individual.

I felt that my friend was not what he had been as he rambled on disconnectedly:

"There were no stamps in his desk, but there might have been, eh, *mon ami*? There might have been? Yes"—his eyes wandered round the room—"this boudoir has nothing more to tell us. It did not yield much. Only this."

He pulled a crumpled envelope out of his pocket, and tossed it over to me. It was rather a curious document. A plain, dirty looking old envelope with a few words scrawled across it, apparently at random. The following is a facsimile of it.

pressed

I am possessed

He is possessed

I am possessed

possessed

V. "It Isn't Strychnine, Is It?"

"Where did you find this?" I asked Poirot, in lively curiosity.

"In the wastepaper basket. You recognise the handwriting?"

"Yes, it is Mrs. Inglethorp's. But what does it mean?"

Poirot shrugged his shoulders.

"I cannot say—but it is suggestive."

A wild idea flashed across me. Was it possible that Mrs. Inglethorp's mind was deranged? Had she some fantastic idea of demoniacal possession? And, if that were so, was it not also possible that she might have taken her own life?

I was about to expound these theories to Poirot, when his own words distracted me.

"Come," he said, "now to examine the coffee cups!"

"My dear Poirot! What on earth is the good of that, now that we know about the coco?"

"Oh, *là là*! That miserable coco!" cried Poirot flippantly.

He laughed with apparent enjoyment, raising his arms to heaven in mock despair, in what I could not but consider the worst possible taste.

"And, anyway," I said, with increasing coldness, "as Mrs. Inglethorp took her coffee upstairs with her, I do not see what you expect to find, unless you consider it likely that we shall discover a packet of strychnine on the coffee tray!"

Poirot was sobered at once.

"Come, come, my friend," he said, slipping his arms through mine. "*Ne vous fâchez pas!* Allow me to interest myself in my coffee cups, and I will respect your coco. There! Is it a bargain?"

He was so quaintly humorous that I was forced to laugh; and we went together to the drawing room, where the coffee cups and tray remained undisturbed as we had left them.

Poirot made me recapitulate the scene of the night before, listening very carefully, and verifying the position of the various cups.

"So Mrs. Cavendish stood by the tray—and poured out. Yes. Then she came across to the window where you sat with Mademoiselle Cynthia. Yes. Here are the three cups. And the cup on the mantelpiece, half drunk, that would be Mr. Lawrence Cavendish's. And the one on the tray?"

"John Cavendish's. I saw him put it down there."

"Good. One, two, three, four, five—but where, then, is the cup of Mr. Inglethorp?"

"He does not take coffee."

"Then all are accounted for. One moment, my friend."

With infinite care, he took a drop or two from the grounds in each cup, sealing them up in separate test tubes, tasting each in turn as he did so. His physiognomy underwent a curious change. An expression gathered there that I can only describe as half puzzled, and half relieved.

"*Bien!*" he said at last. "It is evident! I had an idea—but clearly I was mistaken. Yes, altogether I was mistaken. Yet it is strange. But no matter!"

And, with a characteristic shrug, he dismissed whatever it was that was worrying him from his mind. I could have told him from the beginning that this obsession of his over the coffee was bound to end in a blind alley, but I restrained my tongue. After all, though he was old, Poirot had been a great man in his day.

"Breakfast is ready," said John Cavendish, coming in from the hall. "You will breakfast with us, Monsieur Poirot?"

Poirot acquiesced. I observed John. Already he was almost restored to his normal self. The shock of the events of the last night had upset him temporarily, but his equable poise soon swung back to the normal. He was a man of very little imagination, in sharp contrast with his brother, who had, perhaps, too much.

Ever since the early hours of the morning, John had been hard at work, sending telegrams—one of the first had gone to Evelyn Howard—writing notices for the papers, and generally occupying himself with the melancholy duties that a death entails.

"May I ask how things are proceeding?" he said. "Do your investigations point to my mother having died a natural death—or—or must we prepare ourselves for the worst?"

"I think, Mr. Cavendish," said Poirot gravely, "that you would do well not to buoy yourself up with any false hopes. Can you tell me the views of the other members of the family?"

"My brother Lawrence is convinced that we are making a fuss over nothing. He says that everything points to its being a simple case of heart failure."

"He does, does he? That is very interesting—very interesting," murmured Poirot softly. "And Mrs. Cavendish?"

A faint cloud passed over John's face.

"I have not the least idea what my wife's views on the subject are."

The answer brought a momentary stiffness in its train. John broke the rather awkward silence by saying with a slight effort:

"I told you, didn't I, that Mr. Inglethorp has returned?"

Poirot bent his head.

"It's an awkward position for all of us. Of course one has to treat him as usual—but, hang it all, one's gorge does rise at sitting down to eat with a possible murderer!"

Poirot nodded sympathetically.

"I quite understand. It is a very difficult situation for you, Mr. Cavendish. I would like to ask you one question. Mr. Inglethorp's reason for not returning last night was, I believe, that he had forgotten the latchkey. Is not that so?"

"Yes."

"I suppose you are quite sure that the latchkey *was* forgotten—that he did not take it after all?"

"I have no idea. I never thought of looking. We always keep it in the hall drawer. I'll go and see if it's there now."

Poirot held up his hand with a faint smile.

"No, no, Mr. Cavendish, it is too late now. I am certain that you would find it. If Mr. Inglethorp did take it, he has had ample time to replace it by now."

"But do you think—"

"I think nothing. If anyone had chanced to look this morning before his return, and seen it there, it would have been a valuable point in his favour. That is all."

John looked perplexed.

"Do not worry," said Poirot smoothly. "I assure you that you need not let it trouble you. Since you are so kind, let us go and have some breakfast."

Every one was assembled in the dining room. Under the circumstances, we were naturally not a cheerful party. The reaction after a shock is always trying, and I think we were all suffering from it. Decorum and good breeding naturally enjoined that our demeanour should be much as usual, yet I could not help wondering if this self-control were really a matter of great difficulty. There were no red eyes, no signs of secretly indulged grief. I felt that I was right in my opinion that Dorcas was the person most affected by the personal side of the tragedy.

I pass over Alfred Inglethorp, who acted the bereaved widower in a manner that I felt to be disgusting in its hypocrisy. Did he know that we suspected him, I wondered. Surely he could not be unaware of the fact, conceal it as we would. Did he feel some secret stirring of fear, or was he confident that his crime would go unpunished? Surely the suspicion in the atmosphere must warn him that he was already a marked man.

But did everyone suspect him? What about Mrs. Cavendish? I watched her as she sat at the head of the table, graceful, composed, enigmatic. In her soft grey frock, with white ruffles at the wrists falling over her slender hands, she looked very beautiful. When she chose, however, her face could be sphinx-like in its inscrutability. She was very silent, hardly opening her lips, and yet in some queer way I felt that the great strength of her personality was dominating us all.

And little Cynthia? Did she suspect? She looked very tired and ill, I thought. The heaviness and languor of her manner were very marked. I asked her if she were feeling ill, and she answered frankly:

"Yes, I've got the most beastly headache."

"Have another cup of coffee, mademoiselle?" said Poirot solicitously. "It will revive you. It is unparalleled for the *mal de tête*." He jumped up and took her cup.

"No sugar," said Cynthia, watching him, as he picked up the sugar-tongs.

"No sugar? You abandon it in the wartime, eh?"

"No, I never take it in coffee."

"*Sacré!*" murmured Poirot to himself, as he brought back the replenished cup.

Only I heard him, and glancing up curiously at the little man I saw that his face was working with suppressed excitement, and his eyes were as green as a cat's. He had heard or seen something that had affected him strongly—but what was it? I do not usually label myself as dense, but I must confess that nothing out of the ordinary had attracted *my* attention.

In another moment, the door opened and Dorcas appeared.

"Mr. Wells to see you, sir," she said to John.

I remembered the name as being that of the lawyer to whom Mrs. Inglethorp had written the night before.

John rose immediately.

"Show him into my study." Then he turned to us. "My mother's lawyer," he explained. And in a lower voice: "He is also Coroner—you understand. Perhaps you would like to come with me?"

We acquiesced and followed him out of the room. John strode on ahead and I took the opportunity of whispering to Poirot:

"There will be an inquest then?"

Poirot nodded absently. He seemed absorbed in thought; so much so that my curiosity was aroused.

"What is it? You are not attending to what I say."

"It is true, my friend. I am much worried."

"Why?"

"Because Mademoiselle Cynthia does not take sugar in her coffee."

"What? You cannot be serious?"

"But I am most serious. Ah, there is something there that I do not understand. My instinct was right."

"What instinct?"

"The instinct that led me to insist on examining those coffee cups. *Chut!* No more now!"

We followed John into his study, and he closed the door behind us.

Mr. Wells was a pleasant man of middle-age, with keen eyes, and the typical lawyer's mouth. John introduced us both, and explained the reason of our presence.

"You will understand, Wells," he added, "that this is all strictly private. We are still hoping that there will turn out to be no need for investigation of any kind."

"Quite so, quite so," said Mr. Wells soothingly. "I wish we could have spared you the pain and publicity of an inquest, but of course it's quite unavoidable in the absence of a doctor's certificate."

"Yes, I suppose so."

"Clever man, Bauerstein. Great authority on toxicology, I believe."

"Indeed," said John with a certain stiffness in his manner. Then he added rather hesitatingly: "Shall we have to appear as witnesses—all of us, I mean?"

"You, of course—and ah—er—Mr.—er—Inglethorp."

A slight pause ensued before the lawyer went on in his soothing manner:

"Any other evidence will be simply confirmatory, a mere matter of form."

"I see."

A faint expression of relief swept over John's face. It puzzled me, for I saw no occasion for it.

"If you know of nothing to the contrary," pursued Mr. Wells, "I had thought of Friday. That will give us plenty of time for the doctor's report. The postmortem is to take place tonight, I believe?"

"Yes."

"Then that arrangement will suit you?"

"Perfectly."

"I need not tell you, my dear Cavendish, how distressed I am at this most tragic affair."

"Can you give us no help in solving it, monsieur?" interposed Poirot, speaking for the first time since we had entered the room.

"I?"

"Yes, we heard that Mrs. Inglethorp wrote to you last night. You should have received the letter this morning."

"I did, but it contains no information. It is merely a note asking me to call upon her this morning, as she wanted my advice on a matter of great importance."

"She gave you no hint as to what that matter might be?"

"Unfortunately, no."

"That is a pity," said John.

"A great pity," agreed Poirot gravely.

There was silence. Poirot remained lost in thought for a few minutes. Finally he turned to the lawyer again.

"Mr. Wells, there is one thing I should like to ask you—that is, if it is not against professional etiquette. In the event of Mrs. Inglethorp's death, who would inherit her money?"

The lawyer hesitated a moment, and then replied:

"The knowledge will be public property very soon, so if Mr. Cavendish does not object—"

"Not at all," interpolated John.

"I do not see any reason why I should not answer your question. By her last will, dated August of last year, after various unimportant legacies to servants, etc., she gave her entire fortune to her stepson, Mr. John Cavendish."

"Was not that—pardon the question, Mr. Cavendish—rather unfair to her other stepson, Mr. Lawrence Cavendish?"

"No, I do not think so. You see, under the terms of their father's will, while John inherited the property, Lawrence, at his stepmother's death, would come into a considerable sum of money. Mrs. Inglethorp left her money to her elder stepson, knowing that he would have to keep up Styles. It was, to my mind, a very fair and equitable distribution."

Poirot nodded thoughtfully.

"I see. But I am right in saying, am I not, that by your English law that will was automatically revoked when Mrs. Inglethorp remarried?"

Mr. Wells bowed his head.

"As I was about to proceed, Monsieur Poirot, that document is now null and void."

"*Hein!*" said Poirot. He reflected for a moment, and then asked: "Was Mrs. Inglethorp herself aware of that fact?"

"I do not know. She may have been."

"She was," said John unexpectedly. "We were discussing the matter of wills being revoked by marriage only yesterday."

"Ah! One more question, Mr. Wells. You say 'her last will.' Had Mrs. Inglethorp, then, made several former wills?"

"On an average, she made a new will at least once a year," said Mr. Wells imperturbably. "She was given to changing her mind as to her testamentary dispositions, now benefiting one, now another member of her family."

"Suppose," suggested Poirot, "that, unknown to you, she had made a new will in favour of someone who was not, in any sense of the word, a member of the family—we will say Miss Howard, for instance—would you be surprised?"

"Not in the least."

"Ah!" Poirot seemed to have exhausted his questions.

I drew close to him, while John and the lawyer were debating the question of going through Mrs. Inglethorp's papers.

"Do you think Mrs. Inglethorp made a will leaving all her money to Miss Howard?" I asked in a low voice, with some curiosity.

Poirot smiled.

"No."

"Then why did you ask?"

"Hush!"

John Cavendish had turned to Poirot.

"Will you come with us, Monsieur Poirot? We are going through my mother's papers. Mr. Inglethorp is quite willing to leave it entirely to Mr. Wells and myself."

"Which simplifies matters very much," murmured the lawyer. "As technically, of course, he was entitled——" He did not finish the sentence.

"We will look through the desk in the boudoir first," explained John, "and go up to her bedroom afterwards. She kept her most important papers in a purple despatch-case, which we must look through carefully."

"Yes," said the lawyer, "it is quite possible that there may be a later will than the one in my possession."

"There *is* a later will." It was Poirot who spoke.

"What?" John and the lawyer looked at him startled.

"Or, rather," pursued my friend imperturbably, "there *was* one."

"What do you mean—there was one? Where is it now?"

"Burnt!"

"Burnt?"

"Yes. See here." He took out the charred fragment we had found in the grate in Mrs. Inglethorp's room, and handed it to the lawyer with a brief explanation of when and where he had found it.

"But possibly this is an old will?"

"I do not think so. In fact I am almost certain that it was made no earlier than yesterday afternoon."

"What?" "Impossible!" broke simultaneously from both men.

Poirot turned to John.

"If you will allow me to send for your gardener, I will prove it to you."

"Oh, of course—but I don't see—"

Poirot raised his hand.

"Do as I ask you. Afterwards you shall question as much as you please."

"Very well." He rang the bell.

Dorcas answered it in due course.

"Dorcas, will you tell Manning to come round and speak to me here."

"Yes, sir."

Dorcas withdrew.

We waited in a tense silence. Poirot alone seemed perfectly at his ease, and dusted a forgotten corner of the bookcase.

The clumping of hobnailed boots on the gravel outside proclaimed the approach of Manning. John looked questioningly at Poirot. The latter nodded.

"Come inside, Manning," said John, "I want to speak to you."

Manning came slowly and hesitatingly through the French window, and stood as near it as he could. He held his cap in his hands, twisting it very carefully round and round. His back was much bent, though he was probably not as old as he looked, but his eyes were sharp and intelligent, and belied his slow and rather cautious speech.

"Manning," said John, "this gentleman will put some questions to you which I want you to answer."

"Yessir," mumbled Manning.

Poirot stepped forward briskly. Manning's eye swept over him with a faint contempt.

"You were planting a bed of begonias round by the south side of the house yesterday afternoon, were you not, Manning?"

"Yes, sir, me and Willum."

"And Mrs. Inglethorp came to the window and called you, did she not?"

"Yes, sir, she did."

"Tell me in your own words exactly what happened after that."

"Well, sir, nothing much. She just told Willum to go on his bicycle down to the village, and bring back a form of will, or such-like—I don't know what exactly—she wrote it down for him."

"Well?"

"Well, he did, sir."

"And what happened next?"

"We went on with the begonias, sir."

"Did not Mrs. Inglethorp call you again?"

"Yes, sir, both me and Willum, she called."

"And then?"

"She made us come right in, and sign our names at the bottom of a long paper—under where she'd signed."

"Did you see anything of what was written above her signature?" asked Poirot sharply.

"No, sir, there was a bit of blotting paper over that part."

"And you signed where she told you?"

"Yes, sir, first me and then Willum."

"What did she do with it afterwards?"

"Well, sir, she slipped it into a long envelope, and put it inside a sort of purple box that was standing on the desk."

"What time was it when she first called you?"

"About four, I should say, sir."

"Not earlier? Couldn't it have been about half-past three?"

"No, I shouldn't say so, sir. It would be more likely to be a bit after four—not before it."

"Thank you, Manning, that will do," said Poirot pleasantly.

The gardener glanced at his master, who nodded, whereupon Manning lifted a finger to his forehead with a low mumble, and backed cautiously out of the window.

We all looked at each other.

"Good heavens!" murmured John. "What an extraordinary coincidence."

"How—a coincidence?"

"That my mother should have made a will on the very day of her death!"

Mr. Wells cleared his throat and remarked drily:

"Are you so sure it is a coincidence, Cavendish?"

"What do you mean?"

"Your mother, you tell me, had a violent quarrel with—someone yesterday afternoon—"

"What do you mean?" cried John again. There was a tremor in his voice, and he had gone very pale.

"In consequence of that quarrel, your mother very suddenly and hurriedly makes a new will. The contents of that will we shall never know. She told no one of its provisions. This morning, no doubt, she would have consulted me on the subject—but she had no chance. The will disappears, and she takes its secret with her to her grave. Cavendish, I much fear there is no coincidence there. Monsieur Poirot, I am sure you agree with me that the facts are very suggestive."

"Suggestive, or not," interrupted John, "we are most grateful to Monsieur Poirot for elucidating the matter. But for him, we should never have known of this will. I suppose, I may not ask you, monsieur, what first led you to suspect the fact?"

Poirot smiled and answered:

"A scribbled over old envelope, and a freshly planted bed of begonias."

John, I think, would have pressed his questions further, but at that moment the loud purr of a motor was audible, and we all turned to the window as it swept past.

"Evie!" cried John. "Excuse me, Wells." He went hurriedly out into the hall.

Poirot looked inquiringly at me.

"Miss Howard," I explained.

"Ah, I am glad she has come. There is a woman with a head and a heart too, Hastings. Though the good God gave her no beauty!"

I followed John's example, and went out into the hall, where Miss Howard was endeavouring to extricate herself from the voluminous mass of veils that enveloped her head. As her eyes fell on me, a sudden pang of guilt shot through me. This was the woman who had warned me so earnestly, and to whose warning I had, alas, paid no heed! How soon, and how contemptuously, I had dismissed it from my mind. Now that she had been proved justified in so tragic a manner, I felt ashamed. She had known Alfred Inglethorp only too well. I wondered whether, if she had remained at Styles, the tragedy would have taken place, or would the man have feared her watchful eyes?

I was relieved when she shook me by the hand, with her well remembered painful grip. The eyes that met mine were sad, but not reproachful; that she had been crying bitterly, I could tell by the redness of her eyelids, but her manner was unchanged from its old blunt gruffness.

"Started the moment I got the wire. Just come off night duty. Hired car. Quickest way to get here."

"Have you had anything to eat this morning, Evie?" asked John.

"No."

"I thought not. Come along, breakfast's not cleared away yet, and they'll make you some fresh tea." He turned to me. "Look after her, Hastings, will you? Wells is waiting for me. Oh, here's Monsieur Poirot. He's helping us, you know, Evie."

Miss Howard shook hands with Poirot, but glanced suspiciously over her shoulder at John.

"What do you mean—helping us?"

"Helping us to investigate."

"Nothing to investigate. Have they taken him to prison yet?"

"Taken who to prison?"

"Who? Alfred Inglethorp, of course!"

"My dear Evie, do be careful. Lawrence is of the opinion that my mother died from heart seizure."

"More fool, Lawrence!" retorted Miss Howard. "Of course Alfred Inglethorp murdered poor Emily—as I always told you he would."

"My dear Evie, don't shout so. Whatever we may think or suspect, it is better to say as little as possible for the present. The inquest isn't until Friday."

"Not until fiddlesticks!" The snort Miss Howard gave was truly magnificent. "You're all off your heads. The man will be out of the country by then. If he's any sense, he won't stay here tamely and wait to be hanged."

John Cavendish looked at her helplessly.

"I know what it is," she accused him, "you've been listening to the doctors. Never should. What do they know? Nothing at all—or just enough to make them dangerous. I ought to know—my own father was a doctor. That little Wilkins is about the greatest fool that even I have ever seen. Heart seizure! Sort of thing he would say. Anyone with any sense could see at once that her husband had poisoned her. I always said he'd murder her in her bed, poor soul. Now he's done it. And all you can do is to murmur silly things about 'heart seizure' and 'inquest on Friday.' You ought to be ashamed of yourself, John Cavendish."

"What do you want me to do?" asked John, unable to help a faint smile. "Dash it all, Evie, I can't haul him down to the local police station by the scruff of his neck."

"Well, you might do something. Find out how he did it. He's a crafty beggar. Dare say he soaked fly papers. Ask Cook if she's missed any."

It occurred to me very forcibly at that moment that to harbour Miss Howard and Alfred Inglethorp under the same roof, and keep the peace between them, was likely to prove a Herculean task, and I did not envy John. I could see by the expression of his face that he fully appreciated the difficulty of the position. For the moment, he sought refuge in retreat, and left the room precipitately.

Dorcas brought in fresh tea. As she left the room, Poirot came over from the window where he had been standing, and sat down facing Miss Howard.

"Mademoiselle," he said gravely, "I want to ask you something."

"Ask away," said the lady, eyeing him with some disfavour.

"I want to be able to count upon your help."

"I'll help you to hang Alfred with pleasure," she replied gruffly. "Hanging's too good for him. Ought to be drawn and quartered, like in good old times."

"We are at one then," said Poirot, "for I, too, want to hang the criminal."

"Alfred Inglethorp?"

"Him, or another."

"No question of another. Poor Emily was never murdered until *he* came along. I don't say she wasn't surrounded by sharks—she was. But it was only her purse they were after. Her life was safe enough. But along comes Mr. Alfred Inglethorp—and within two months—hey presto!"

"Believe me, Miss Howard," said Poirot very earnestly, "if Mr. Inglethorp is the man, he shall not escape me. On my honour, I will hang him as high as Haman!"

"That's better," said Miss Howard more enthusiastically.

"But I must ask you to trust me. Now your help may be very valuable to me. I will tell you why. Because, in all this house of mourning, yours are the only eyes that have wept."

Miss Howard blinked, and a new note crept into the gruffness of her voice.

"If you mean that I was fond of her—yes, I was. You know, Emily was a selfish old woman in her way. She was very generous, but she always wanted a return. She never let people forget what she had done for them—and, that way, she missed love. Don't think she ever realized it, though, or felt the lack of it. Hope not, anyway. I was on a different footing. I took my stand from the first. 'So many pounds a year I'm worth to you. Well and good. But not a penny piece besides—not a pair of gloves, nor a theatre ticket.' She didn't understand—was very offended sometimes. Said I was foolishly proud. It wasn't that—but I couldn't explain. Anyway, I kept my self-respect. And so, out of the whole bunch, I was the only one who could allow myself to be fond of her. I watched over her. I guarded her from the lot of them. And then a glib-tongued scoundrel comes along, and pooh! All my years of devotion go for nothing."

Poirot nodded sympathetically.

"I understand, mademoiselle, I understand all you feel. It is most natural. You think that we are lukewarm—that we lack fire and energy—but trust me, it is not so."

John stuck his head in at this juncture, and invited us both to come up to Mrs. Inglethorp's room, as he and Mr. Wells had finished looking through the desk in the boudoir.

As we went up the stairs, John looked back to the dining room door, and lowered his voice confidentially:

"Look here, what's going to happen when these two meet?"

I shook my head helplessly.

"I've told Mary to keep them apart if she can."

"Will she be able to do so?"

"The Lord only knows. There's one thing, Inglethorp himself won't be too keen on meeting her."

"You've got the keys still, haven't you, Poirot?" I asked, as we reached the door of the locked room.

Taking the keys from Poirot, John unlocked it, and we all passed in. The lawyer went straight to the desk, and John followed him.

"My mother kept most of her important papers in this despatch-case, I believe," he said.

Poirot drew out the small bunch of keys.

"Permit me. I locked it, out of precaution, this morning."

"But it's not locked now."

"Impossible!"

"See." And John lifted the lid as he spoke.

"*Milles tonnerres!*" cried Poirot, dumbfounded. "And I—who have both the keys in my pocket!" He flung himself upon the case. Suddenly he stiffened. "*En voilà une affaire!* This lock has been forced."

"What?"

Poirot laid down the case again.

"But who forced it? Why should they? When? But the door was locked?" These exclamations burst from us disjointedly.

Poirot answered them categorically—almost mechanically.

"Who? That is the question. Why? Ah, if I only knew. When? Since I was here an hour ago. As to the door being locked, it is a very ordinary lock. Probably any other of the doorkeys in this passage would fit it."

We stared at one another blankly. Poirot had walked over to the mantelpiece. He was outwardly calm, but I noticed his hands, which from long force of habit were mechanically straightening the spill vases on the mantelpiece, were shaking violently.

"See here, it was like this," he said at last. "There was something in that case— some piece of evidence, slight in itself perhaps, but still enough of a clue to connect the murderer with the crime. It was vital to him that it should be destroyed before it was discovered and its significance appreciated. Therefore, he took the risk, the great risk, of coming in here. Finding the case locked, he was obliged to force it, thus betraying his presence. For him to take that risk, it must have been something of great importance."

"But what was it?"

"Ah!" cried Poirot, with a gesture of anger. "That, I do not know! A document of some kind, without doubt, possibly the scrap of paper Dorcas saw in her hand yesterday afternoon. And I—" his anger burst forth freely—"miserable animal that I am! I guessed nothing! I have behaved like an imbecile! I should never have left that case here. I should have carried it away with me. Ah, triple pig! And now it is gone. It is destroyed—but is it destroyed? Is there not yet a chance—we must leave no stone unturned—"

He rushed like a madman from the room, and I followed him as soon as I had sufficiently recovered my wits. But, by the time I had reached the top of the stairs, he was out of sight.

Mary Cavendish was standing where the staircase branched, staring down into the hall in the direction in which he had disappeared.

"What has happened to your extraordinary little friend, Mr. Hastings? He has just rushed past me like a mad bull."

"He's rather upset about something," I remarked feebly. I really did not know how much Poirot would wish me to disclose. As I saw a faint smile gather on Mrs. Cavendish's expressive mouth, I endeavoured to try and turn the conversation by saying: "They haven't met yet, have they?"

"Who?"

"Mr. Inglethorp and Miss Howard."

She looked at me in rather a disconcerting manner.

"Do you think it would be such a disaster if they did meet?"

"Well, don't you?" I said, rather taken aback.

"No." She was smiling in her quiet way. "I should like to see a good flare up. It would clear the air. At present we are all thinking so much, and saying so little."

"John doesn't think so," I remarked. "He's anxious to keep them apart."

"Oh, John!"

Something in her tone fired me, and I blurted out:

"Old John's an awfully good sort."

She studied me curiously for a minute or two, and then said, to my great surprise:

"You are loyal to your friend. I like you for that."

"Aren't you my friend too?"

"I am a very bad friend."

"Why do you say that?"

"Because it is true. I am charming to my friends one day, and forget all about them the next."

I don't know what impelled me, but I was nettled, and I said foolishly and not in the best of taste:

"Yet you seem to be invariably charming to Dr. Bauerstein!"

Instantly I regretted my words. Her face stiffened. I had the impression of a steel curtain coming down and blotting out the real woman. Without a word, she turned and went swiftly up the stairs, whilst I stood like an idiot gaping after her.

I was recalled to other matters by a frightful row going on below. I could hear Poirot shouting and expounding. I was vexed to think that my diplomacy had been in vain. The little man appeared to be taking the whole house into his confidence, a proceeding of which I, for one, doubted the wisdom. Once again I could not help regretting that my friend was so prone to lose his head in moments of excitement. I stepped briskly down the stairs. The sight of me calmed Poirot almost immediately. I drew him aside.

"My dear fellow," I said, "is this wise? Surely you don't want the whole house to know of this occurrence? You are actually playing into the criminal's hands."

"You think so, Hastings?"

"I am sure of it."

"Well, well, my friend, I will be guided by you."

"Good. Although, unfortunately, it is a little too late now."

"True."

He looked so crestfallen and abashed that I felt quite sorry, though I still thought my rebuke a just and wise one.

"Well," he said at last, "let us go, *mon ami*."

"You have finished here?"

"For the moment, yes. You will walk back with me to the village?"

"Willingly."

He picked up his little suitcase, and we went out through the open window in the drawing room. Cynthia Murdoch was just coming in, and Poirot stood aside to let her pass.

"Excuse me, mademoiselle, one minute."

"Yes?" she turned inquiringly.

"Did you ever make up Mrs. Inglethorp's medicines?"

A slight flush rose in her face, as she answered rather constrainedly:

"No."

"Only her powders?"

The flush deepened as Cynthia replied:

"Oh, yes, I did make up some sleeping powders for her once."

"These?"

Poirot produced the empty box which had contained powders.

She nodded.

"Can you tell me what they were? Sulphonal? Veronal?"

"No, they were bromide powders."

"Ah! Thank you, mademoiselle; good morning."

As we walked briskly away from the house, I glanced at him more than once. I had often before noticed that, if anything excited him, his eyes turned green like a cat's. They were shining like emeralds now.

"My friend," he broke out at last, "I have a little idea, a very strange, and probably utterly impossible idea. And yet—it fits in."

I shrugged my shoulders. I privately thought that Poirot was rather too much given to these fantastic ideas. In this case, surely, the truth was only too plain and apparent.

"So that is the explanation of the blank label on the box," I remarked. "Very simple, as you said. I really wonder that I did not think of it myself."

Poirot did not appear to be listening to me.

"They have made one more discovery, *là-bas*," he observed, jerking his thumb over his shoulder in the direction of Styles. "Mr. Wells told me as we were going upstairs."

"What was it?"

"Locked up in the desk in the boudoir, they found a will of Mrs. Inglethorp's, dated before her marriage, leaving her fortune to Alfred Inglethorp. It must have been made just at the time they were engaged. It came quite as a surprise to Wells—and to John Cavendish also. It was written on one of those printed will forms, and witnessed by two of the servants—not Dorcas."

"Did Mr. Inglethorp know of it?"

"He says not."

"One might take that with a grain of salt," I remarked sceptically. "All these wills are very confusing. Tell me, how did those scribbled words on the envelope help you to discover that a will was made yesterday afternoon?"

Poirot smiled.

"*Mon ami*, have you ever, when writing a letter, been arrested by the fact that you did not know how to spell a certain word?"

"Yes, often. I suppose every one has."

"Exactly. And have you not, in such a case, tried the word once or twice on the edge of the blotting-paper, or a spare scrap of paper, to see if it looked right? Well, that is what Mrs. Inglethorp did. You will notice that the word 'possessed' is spelt first with one 's' and subsequently with two—correctly. To make sure, she had further tried it in a sentence, thus: 'I am possessed.' Now, what did that tell me? It told me that Mrs. Inglethorp had been writing the word 'possessed' that afternoon, and, having the fragment of paper found in the grate fresh in my mind, the possibility of a will—(a document almost certain to contain that word)—occurred to me at once. This possibility was confirmed by a further circumstance. In the general confusion, the boudoir had not been swept that morning, and near the desk were several traces of brown mould and earth. The weather had been perfectly fine for some days, and no ordinary boots would have left such a heavy deposit.

"I strolled to the window, and saw at once that the begonia beds had been newly planted. The mould in the beds was exactly similar to that on the floor of the boudoir, and also I learnt from you that they *had* been planted yesterday afternoon. I was now sure that one, or possibly both of the gardeners—for there were two sets of footprints in the bed—had entered the boudoir, for if Mrs. Inglethorp had merely wished to speak to them she would in all probability have stood at the window, and they would not have come into the room at all. I was now quite convinced that she had made a fresh will, and had called the two gardeners in to witness her signature. Events proved that I was right in my supposition."

"That was very ingenious," I could not help admitting. "I must confess that the conclusions I drew from those few scribbled words were quite erroneous."

He smiled.

"You gave too much rein to your imagination. Imagination is a good servant, and a bad master. The simplest explanation is always the most likely."

"Another point—how did you know that the key of the despatch-case had been lost?"

"I did not know it. It was a guess that turned out to be correct. You observed that it had a piece of twisted wire through the handle. That suggested to me at once that it had possibly been wrenched off a flimsy key-ring. Now, if it had been lost and recovered, Mrs. Inglethorp would at once have replaced it on her bunch; but on her bunch I found what was obviously the duplicate key, very new and bright, which led me to the hypothesis that somebody else had inserted the original key in the lock of the despatch-case."

"Yes," I said, "Alfred Inglethorp, without doubt."

Poirot looked at me curiously.

"You are very sure of his guilt?"

"Well, naturally. Every fresh circumstance seems to establish it more clearly."

"On the contrary," said Poirot quietly, "there are several points in his favour."

"Oh, come now!"

"Yes."

"I see only one."

"And that?"

"That he was not in the house last night."

"'Bad shot!' as you English say! You have chosen the one point that to my mind tells against him."

"How is that?"

"Because if Mr. Inglethorp knew that his wife would be poisoned last night, he would certainly have arranged to be away from the house. His excuse was an obviously trumped up one. That leaves us two possibilities: either he knew what was going to happen or he had a reason of his own for his absence."

"And that reason?" I asked sceptically.

Poirot shrugged his shoulders.

"How should I know? Discreditable, without doubt. This Mr. Inglethorp, I should say, is somewhat of a scoundrel—but that does not of necessity make him a murderer."

I shook my head, unconvinced.

"We do not agree, eh?" said Poirot. "Well, let us leave it. Time will show which of us is right. Now let us turn to other aspects of the case. What do you make of the fact that all the doors of the bedroom were bolted on the inside?"

"Well—" I considered. "One must look at it logically."

"True."

"I should put it this way. The doors *were* bolted—our own eyes have told us that—yet the presence of the candle grease on the floor, and the destruction of the will, prove that during the night someone entered the room. You agree so far?"

"Perfectly. Put with admirable clearness. Proceed."

"Well," I said, encouraged, "as the person who entered did not do so by the window, nor by miraculous means, it follows that the door must have been opened from inside by Mrs. Inglethorp herself. That strengthens the conviction that the person in question was her husband. She would naturally open the door to her own husband."

Poirot shook his head.

"Why should she? She had bolted the door leading into his room—a most unusual proceeding on her part—she had had a most violent quarrel with him that very afternoon. No, he was the last person she would admit."

"But you agree with me that the door must have been opened by Mrs. Inglethorp herself?"

"There is another possibility. She may have forgotten to bolt the door into the passage when she went to bed, and have got up later, towards morning, and bolted it then."

"Poirot, is that seriously your opinion?"

"No, I do not say it is so, but it might be. Now, to turn to another feature, what do you make of the scrap of conversation you overheard between Mrs. Cavendish and her mother-in-law?"

"I had forgotten that," I said thoughtfully. "That is as enigmatical as ever. It seems incredible that a woman like Mrs. Cavendish, proud and reticent to the last degree, should interfere so violently in what was certainly not her affair."

"Precisely. It was an astonishing thing for a woman of her breeding to do."

"It is certainly curious," I agreed. "Still, it is unimportant, and need not be taken into account."

A groan burst from Poirot.

"What have I always told you? Everything must be taken into account. If the fact will not fit the theory—let the theory go."

"Well, we shall see," I said, nettled.

"Yes, we shall see."

We had reached Leastways Cottage, and Poirot ushered me upstairs to his own room. He offered me one of the tiny Russian cigarettes he himself occasionally smoked. I was amused to notice that he stowed away the used matches most carefully in a little china pot. My momentary annoyance vanished.

Poirot had placed our two chairs in front of the open window which commanded a view of the village street. The fresh air blew in warm and pleasant. It was going to be a hot day.

Suddenly my attention was arrested by a weedy looking young man rushing down the street at a great pace. It was the expression on his face that was extraordinary—a curious mingling of terror and agitation.

"Look, Poirot!" I said.

He leant forward.

"*Tiens!*" he said. "It is Mr. Mace, from the chemist's shop. He is coming here."

The young man came to a halt before Leastways Cottage, and, after hesitating a moment, pounded vigorously at the door.

"A little minute," cried Poirot from the window. "I come."

Motioning to me to follow him, he ran swiftly down the stairs and opened the door. Mr. Mace began at once.

"Oh, Mr. Poirot, I'm sorry for the inconvenience, but I heard that you'd just come back from the Hall?"

"Yes, we have."

The young man moistened his dry lips. His face was working curiously.

"It's all over the village about old Mrs. Inglethorp dying so suddenly. They do say—" he lowered his voice cautiously—"that it's poison?"

Poirot's face remained quite impassive.

"Only the doctors can tell us that, Mr. Mace."

"Yes, exactly—of course—" The young man hesitated, and then his agitation was too much for him. He clutched Poirot by the arm, and sank his voice to a whisper: "Just tell me this, Mr. Poirot, it isn't—it isn't strychnine, is it?"

I hardly heard what Poirot replied. Something evidently of a non-committal nature. The young man departed, and as he closed the door Poirot's eyes met mine.

"Yes," he said, nodding gravely. "He will have evidence to give at the inquest."

We went slowly upstairs again. I was opening my lips, when Poirot stopped me with a gesture of his hand.

"Not now, not now, *mon ami*. I have need of reflection. My mind is in some disorder—which is not well."

For about ten minutes he sat in dead silence, perfectly still, except for several expressive motions of his eyebrows, and all the time his eyes grew steadily greener. At last he heaved a deep sigh.

"It is well. The bad moment has passed. Now all is arranged and classified. One must never permit confusion. The case is not clear yet—no. For it is of the most complicated! It puzzles *me*. *Me*, Hercule Poirot! There are two facts of significance."

"And what are they?"

"The first is the state of the weather yesterday. That is very important."

"But it was a glorious day!" I interrupted. "Poirot, you're pulling my leg!"

"Not at all. The thermometer registered 80° in the shade. Do not forget that, my friend. It is the key to the whole riddle!"

"And the second point?" I asked.

"The important fact that Monsieur Inglethorp wears very peculiar clothes, has a black beard, and uses glasses."

"Poirot, I cannot believe you are serious."

"I am absolutely serious, my friend."

"But this is childish!"

"No, it is very momentous."

"And supposing the Coroner's jury returns a verdict of Wilful Murder against Alfred Inglethorp. What becomes of your theories, then?"

"They would not be shaken because twelve stupid men had happened to make a mistake! But that will not occur. For one thing, a country jury is not anxious to take responsibility upon itself, and Mr. Inglethorp stands practically in the position of local squire. Also," he added placidly, "*I* should not allow it!"

"*You* would not allow it?"

"No."

I looked at the extraordinary little man, divided between annoyance and amusement. He was so tremendously sure of himself. As though he read my thoughts, he nodded gently.

"Oh, yes, *mon ami*, I would do what I say." He got up and laid his hand on my shoulder. His physiognomy underwent a complete change. Tears came into his eyes. "In all this, you see, I think of that poor Mrs. Inglethorp who is dead. She was not extravagantly loved—no. But she was very good to us Belgians—I owe her a debt."

I endeavoured to interrupt, but Poirot swept on.

"Let me tell you this, Hastings. She would never forgive me if I let Alfred Inglethorp, her husband, be arrested now—when a word from me could save him!"

VI. THE INQUEST

In the interval before the inquest, Poirot was unfailing in his activity. Twice he was closeted with Mr. Wells. He also took long walks into the country. I rather resented his not taking me into his confidence, the more so as I could not in the least guess what he was driving at.

It occurred to me that he might have been making inquiries at Raikes's farm; so, finding him out when I called at Leastways Cottage on Wednesday evening, I walked over there by the fields, hoping to meet him. But there was no sign of him, and I hesitated to go right up to the farm itself. As I walked away, I met an aged rustic, who leered at me cunningly.

"You'm from the Hall, bain't you?" he asked.

"Yes. I'm looking for a friend of mine whom I thought might have walked this way."

"A little chap? As waves his hands when he talks? One of them Belgies from the village?"

"Yes," I said eagerly. "He has been here, then?"

"Oh, ay, he's been here, right enough. More'n once too. Friend of yours, is he? Ah, you gentlemen from the Hall—you'n a pretty lot!" And he leered more jocosely than ever.

"Why, do the gentlemen from the Hall come here often?" I asked, as carelessly as I could.

He winked at me knowingly.

"*One* does, mister. Naming no names, mind. And a very liberal gentleman too! Oh, thank you, sir, I'm sure."

I walked on sharply. Evelyn Howard had been right then, and I experienced a sharp twinge of disgust, as I thought of Alfred Inglethorp's liberality with another woman's money. Had that piquant gipsy face been at the bottom of the crime, or was it the baser mainspring of money? Probably a judicious mixture of both.

On one point, Poirot seemed to have a curious obsession. He once or twice observed to me that he thought Dorcas must have made an error in fixing the time of the quarrel. He suggested to her repeatedly that it was 4:30, and not 4 o'clock when she had heard the voices.

But Dorcas was unshaken. Quite an hour, or even more, had elapsed between the time when she had heard the voices and 5 o'clock, when she had taken tea to her mistress.

The inquest was held on Friday at the Stylites Arms in the village. Poirot and I sat together, not being required to give evidence.

The preliminaries were gone through. The jury viewed the body, and John Cavendish gave evidence of identification.

Further questioned, he described his awakening in the early hours of the morning, and the circumstances of his mother's death.

The medical evidence was next taken. There was a breathless hush, and every eye was fixed on the famous London specialist, who was known to be one of the greatest authorities of the day on the subject of toxicology.

In a few brief words, he summed up the result of the postmortem. Shorn of its medical phraseology and technicalities, it amounted to the fact that Mrs. Inglethorp had met her death as the result of strychnine poisoning. Judging from the quantity recovered, she must have taken not less than three-quarters of a grain of strychnine, but probably one grain or slightly over.

"Is it possible that she could have swallowed the poison by accident?" asked the Coroner.

"I should consider it very unlikely. Strychnine is not used for domestic purposes, as some poisons are, and there are restrictions placed on its sale."

"Does anything in your examination lead you to determine how the poison was administered?"

"No."

"You arrived at Styles before Dr. Wilkins, I believe?"

"That is so. The motor met me just outside the lodge gates, and I hurried there as fast as I could."

"Will you relate to us exactly what happened next?"

"I entered Mrs. Inglethorp's room. She was at that moment in a typical tetanic convulsion. She turned towards me, and gasped out: 'Alfred—Alfred—' "

"Could the strychnine have been administered in Mrs. Inglethorp's after-dinner coffee which was taken to her by her husband?"

"Possibly, but strychnine is a fairly rapid drug in its action. The symptoms appear from one to two hours after it has been swallowed. It is retarded under certain conditions, none of which, however, appear to have been present in this case. I presume Mrs. Inglethorp took the coffee after dinner about eight o'clock, whereas the symptoms did not manifest themselves until the early hours of the morning, which, on the face of it, points to the drug having been taken much later in the evening."

"Mrs. Inglethorp was in the habit of drinking a cup of coco in the middle of the night. Could the strychnine have been administered in that?"

"No, I myself took a sample of the coco remaining in the saucepan and had it analysed. There was no strychnine present."

I heard Poirot chuckle softly beside me.

"How did you know?" I whispered.

"Listen."

"I should say"—the doctor was continuing—"that I would have been considerably surprised at any other result."

"Why?"

"Simply because strychnine has an unusually bitter taste. It can be detected in a solution of 1 in 70,000, and can only be disguised by some strongly flavoured substance. Coco would be quite powerless to mask it."

One of the jury wanted to know if the same objection applied to coffee.

"No. Coffee has a bitter taste of its own which would probably cover the taste of the strychnine."

"Then you consider it more likely that the drug was administered in the coffee, but that for some unknown reason its action was delayed."

"Yes, but, the cup being completely smashed, there is no possibility of analyzing its contents."

This concluded Dr. Bauerstein's evidence. Dr. Wilkins corroborated it on all points. Sounded as to the possibility of suicide, he repudiated it utterly. The deceased, he said, suffered from a weak heart, but otherwise enjoyed perfect health, and was of a cheerful and well-balanced disposition. She would be one of the last people to take her own life.

Lawrence Cavendish was next called. His evidence was quite unimportant, being a mere repetition of that of his brother. Just as he was about to step down, he paused, and said rather hesitatingly:

"I should like to make a suggestion if I may?"

He glanced deprecatingly at the Coroner, who replied briskly:

"Certainly, Mr. Cavendish, we are here to arrive at the truth of this matter, and welcome anything that may lead to further elucidation."

"It is just an idea of mine," explained Lawrence. "Of course I may be quite wrong, but it still seems to me that my mother's death might be accounted for by natural means."

"How do you make that out, Mr. Cavendish?"

"My mother, at the time of her death, and for some time before it, was taking a tonic containing strychnine."

"Ah!" said the Coroner.

The jury looked up, interested.

"I believe," continued Lawrence, "that there have been cases where the cumulative effect of a drug, administered for some time, has ended by causing death. Also, is it not possible that she may have taken an overdose of her medicine by accident?"

"This is the first we have heard of the deceased taking strychnine at the time of her death. We are much obliged to you, Mr. Cavendish."

Dr. Wilkins was recalled and ridiculed the idea.

"What Mr. Cavendish suggests is quite impossible. Any doctor would tell you the same. Strychnine is, in a certain sense, a cumulative poison, but it would be quite impossible for it to result in sudden death in this way. There would have to be a long period of chronic symptoms which would at once have attracted my attention. The whole thing is absurd."

"And the second suggestion? That Mrs. Inglethorp may have inadvertently taken an overdose?"

"Three, or even four doses, would not have resulted in death. Mrs. Inglethorp always had an extra large amount of medicine made up at a time, as she dealt with Coot's, the Cash Chemists in Tadminster. She would have had to take very nearly the whole bottle to account for the amount of strychnine found at the postmortem."

"Then you consider that we may dismiss the tonic as not being in any way instrumental in causing her death?"

"Certainly. The supposition is ridiculous."

The same juryman who had interrupted before here suggested that the chemist who made up the medicine might have committed an error.

"That, of course, is always possible," replied the doctor.

But Dorcas, who was the next witness called, dispelled even that possibility. The medicine had not been newly made up. On the contrary, Mrs. Inglethorp had taken the last dose on the day of her death.

So the question of the tonic was finally abandoned, and the Coroner proceeded with his task. Having elicited from Dorcas how she had been awakened by the violent ringing of her mistress's bell, and had subsequently roused the household, he passed to the subject of the quarrel on the preceding afternoon.

Dorcas's evidence on this point was substantially what Poirot and I had already heard, so I will not repeat it here.

The next witness was Mary Cavendish. She stood very upright, and spoke in a low, clear, and perfectly composed voice. In answer to the Coroner's question, she told how, her alarm clock having aroused her at 4:30 as usual, she was dressing, when she was startled by the sound of something heavy falling.

"That would have been the table by the bed?" commented the Coroner.

"I opened my door," continued Mary, "and listened. In a few minutes a bell rang violently. Dorcas came running down and woke my husband, and we all went to my mother-in-law's room, but it was locked—"

The Coroner interrupted her.

"I really do not think we need trouble you further on that point. We know all that can be known of the subsequent happenings. But I should be obliged if you would tell us all you overheard of the quarrel the day before."

"I?"

There was a faint insolence in her voice. She raised her hand and adjusted the ruffle of lace at her neck, turning her head a little as she did so. And quite spontaneously the thought flashed across my mind: "She is gaining time!"

"Yes. I understand," continued the Coroner deliberately, "that you were sitting reading on the bench just outside the long window of the boudoir. That is so, is it not?"

This was news to me and glancing sideways at Poirot, I fancied that it was news to him as well.

There was the faintest pause, the mere hesitation of a moment, before she answered:

"Yes, that is so."

"And the boudoir window was open, was it not?"

Surely her face grew a little paler as she answered:

"Yes."

"Then you cannot have failed to hear the voices inside, especially as they were raised in anger. In fact, they would be more audible where you were than in the hall."

"Possibly."

"Will you repeat to us what you overheard of the quarrel?"

"I really do not remember hearing anything."

"Do you mean to say you did not hear voices?"

"Oh, yes, I heard the voices, but I did not hear what they said." A faint spot of colour came into her cheek. "I am not in the habit of listening to private conversations."

The Coroner persisted.

"And you remember nothing at all? *Nothing*, Mrs. Cavendish? Not one stray word or phrase to make you realize that it *was* a private conversation?"

She paused, and seemed to reflect, still outwardly as calm as ever.

"Yes; I remember. Mrs. Inglethorp said something—I do not remember exactly what—about causing scandal between husband and wife."

"Ah!" the Coroner leant back satisfied. "That corresponds with what Dorcas heard. But excuse me, Mrs. Cavendish, although you realized it was a private conversation, you did not move away? You remained where you were?"

I caught the momentary gleam of her tawny eyes as she raised them. I felt certain that at that moment she would willingly have torn the little lawyer, with his insinuations, into pieces, but she replied quietly enough:

"No. I was very comfortable where I was. I fixed my mind on my book."

"And that is all you can tell us?"

"That is all."

The examination was over, though I doubted if the Coroner was entirely satisfied with it. I think he suspected that Mary Cavendish could tell more if she chose.

Amy Hill, shop assistant, was next called, and deposed to having sold a will form on the afternoon of the 17th to William Earl, under-gardener at Styles.

William Earl and Manning succeeded her, and testified to witnessing a document. Manning fixed the time at about 4:30, William was of the opinion that it was rather earlier.

Cynthia Murdoch came next. She had, however, little to tell. She had known nothing of the tragedy, until awakened by Mrs. Cavendish.

"You did not hear the table fall?"

"No. I was fast asleep."

The Coroner smiled.

"A good conscience makes a sound sleeper," he observed. "Thank you, Miss Murdoch, that is all."

"Miss Howard."

Miss Howard produced the letter written to her by Mrs. Inglethorp on the evening of the 17th. Poirot and I had, of course, already seen it. It added nothing to our knowledge of the tragedy. The following is a facsimile:

It was handed to the jury who scrutinized it attentively.

"I fear it does not help us much," said the Coroner, with a sigh. "There is no mention of any of the events of that afternoon."

"Plain as a pikestaff to me," said Miss Howard shortly. "It shows clearly enough that my poor old friend had just found out she'd been made a fool of!"

"It says nothing of the kind in the letter," the Coroner pointed out.

"No, because Emily never could bear to put herself in the wrong. But *I* know her. She wanted me back. But she wasn't going to own that I'd been right. She went round about. Most people do. Don't believe in it myself."

Mr. Wells smiled faintly. So, I noticed, did several of the jury. Miss Howard was obviously quite a public character.

"Anyway, all this tomfoolery is a great waste of time," continued the lady, glancing up and down the jury disparagingly. "Talk—talk—talk! When all the time we know perfectly well—"

The Coroner interrupted her in an agony of apprehension:

"Thank you, Miss Howard, that is all."

I fancy he breathed a sigh of relief when she complied.

Then came the sensation of the day. The Coroner called Albert Mace, chemist's assistant.

It was our agitated young man of the pale face. In answer to the Coroner's questions, he explained that he was a qualified pharmacist, but had only recently come to this particular shop, as the assistant formerly there had just been called up for the army.

These preliminaries completed, the Coroner proceeded to business.

"Mr. Mace, have you lately sold strychnine to any unauthorized person?"

"Yes, sir."

"When was this?"

"Last Monday night."

"Monday? Not Tuesday?"

"No, sir, Monday, the 16th."

"Will you tell us to whom you sold it?"

You could have heard a pin drop.

"Yes, sir. It was to Mr. Inglethorp."

Every eye turned simultaneously to where Alfred Inglethorp was sitting, impassive and wooden. He started slightly, as the damning words fell from the young man's lips. I half thought he was going to rise from his chair, but he remained seated, although a remarkably well acted expression of astonishment rose on his face.

"You are sure of what you say?" asked the Coroner sternly.

"Quite sure, sir."

"Are you in the habit of selling strychnine indiscriminately over the counter?"

The wretched young man wilted visibly under the Coroner's frown.

"Oh, no, sir—of course not. But, seeing it was Mr. Inglethorp of the Hall, I thought there was no harm in it. He said it was to poison a dog."

Inwardly I sympathized. It was only human nature to endeavour to please "The Hall"—especially when it might result in custom being transferred from Coot's to the local establishment.

"Is it not customary for anyone purchasing poison to sign a book?"

"Yes, sir, Mr. Inglethorp did so."

"Have you got the book here?"

"Yes, sir."

It was produced; and, with a few words of stern censure, the Coroner dismissed the wretched Mr. Mace.

Then, amidst a breathless silence, Alfred Inglethorp was called. Did he realize, I wondered, how closely the halter was being drawn around his neck?

The Coroner went straight to the point.

"On Monday evening last, did you purchase strychnine for the purpose of poisoning a dog?"

Inglethorp replied with perfect calmness:

"No, I did not. There is no dog at Styles, except an outdoor sheepdog, which is in perfect health."

"You deny absolutely having purchased strychnine from Albert Mace on Monday last?"

"I do."

"Do you also deny *this*?"

The Coroner handed him the register in which his signature was inscribed.

"Certainly I do. The handwriting is quite different from mine. I will show you."

He took an old envelope out of his pocket, and wrote his name on it, handing it to the jury. It was certainly utterly dissimilar.

"Then what is your explanation of Mr. Mace's statement?"

Alfred Inglethorp replied imperturbably:

"Mr. Mace must have been mistaken."

The Coroner hesitated for a moment, and then said:

"Mr. Inglethorp, as a mere matter of form, would you mind telling us where you were on the evening of Monday, July 16th?"

"Really—I cannot remember."

"That is absurd, Mr. Inglethorp," said the Coroner sharply. "Think again."

Inglethorp shook his head.

"I cannot tell you. I have an idea that I was out walking."

"In what direction?"

"I really can't remember."

The Coroner's face grew graver.

"Were you in company with anyone?"

"No."

"Did you meet anyone on your walk?"

"No."

"That is a pity," said the Coroner dryly. "I am to take it then that you decline to say where you were at the time that Mr. Mace positively recognized you as entering the shop to purchase strychnine?"

"If you like to take it that way, yes."

"Be careful, Mr. Inglethorp."

Poirot was fidgeting nervously.

"*Sacré!*" he murmured. "Does this imbecile of a man *want* to be arrested?"

Inglethorp was indeed creating a bad impression. His futile denials would not have convinced a child. The Coroner, however, passed briskly to the next point, and Poirot drew a deep breath of relief.

"You had a discussion with your wife on Tuesday afternoon?"

"Pardon me," interrupted Alfred Inglethorp, "you have been misinformed. I had no quarrel with my dear wife. The whole story is absolutely untrue. I was absent from the house the entire afternoon."

"Have you anyone who can testify to that?"

"You have my word," said Inglethorp haughtily.

The Coroner did not trouble to reply.

"There are two witnesses who will swear to having heard your disagreement with Mrs. Inglethorp."

"Those witnesses were mistaken."

I was puzzled. The man spoke with such quiet assurance that I was staggered. I looked at Poirot. There was an expression of exultation on his face which I could not understand. Was he at last convinced of Alfred Inglethorp's guilt?

"Mr. Inglethorp," said the Coroner, "you have heard your wife's dying words repeated here. Can you explain them in any way?"

"Certainly I can."

"You can?"

"It seems to me very simple. The room was dimly lighted. Dr. Bauerstein is much of my height and build, and, like me, wears a beard. In the dim light, and suffering as she was, my poor wife mistook him for me."

"Ah!" murmured Poirot to himself. "But it is an idea, that!"

"You think it is true?" I whispered.

"I do not say that. But it is truly an ingenious supposition."

"You read my wife's last words as an accusation"—Inglethorp was continuing—"they were, on the contrary, an appeal to me."

The Coroner reflected a moment, then he said:

"I believe, Mr. Inglethorp, that you yourself poured out the coffee, and took it to your wife that evening?"

"I poured it out, yes. But I did not take it to her. I meant to do so, but I was told that a friend was at the hall door, so I laid down the coffee on the hall table. When I came through the hall again a few minutes later, it was gone."

This statement might, or might not, be true, but it did not seem to me to improve matters much for Inglethorp. In any case, he had had ample time to introduce the poison.

At that point, Poirot nudged me gently, indicating two men who were sitting together near the door. One was a little, sharp, dark, ferret-faced man, the other was tall and fair.

I questioned Poirot mutely. He put his lips to my ear.

"Do you know who that little man is?"

I shook my head.

"That is Detective Inspector James Japp of Scotland Yard—Jimmy Japp. The other man is from Scotland Yard too. Things are moving quickly, my friend."

I stared at the two men intently. There was certainly nothing of the policeman about them. I should never have suspected them of being official personages.

I was still staring, when I was startled and recalled by the verdict being given:

"Wilful Murder against some person or persons unknown."

VII. Poirot Pays His Debts

As we came out of the Stylites Arms, Poirot drew me aside by a gentle pressure of the arm. I understood his object. He was waiting for the Scotland Yard men.

In a few moments, they emerged, and Poirot at once stepped forward, and accosted the shorter of the two.

"I fear you do not remember me, Inspector Japp."

"Why, if it isn't Mr. Poirot!" cried the Inspector. He turned to the other man. "You've heard me speak of Mr. Poirot? It was in 1904 he and I worked together—the Abercrombie forgery case—you remember, he was run down in Brussels. Ah, those were great days, moosier. Then, do you remember 'Baron' Altara? There was a pretty rogue for you! He eluded the clutches of half the police in Europe. But we nailed him in Antwerp—thanks to Mr. Poirot here."

As these friendly reminiscences were being indulged in, I drew nearer, and was introduced to Detective-Inspector Japp, who, in his turn, introduced us both to his companion, Superintendent Summerhaye.

"I need hardly ask what you are doing here, gentlemen," remarked Poirot.

Japp closed one eye knowingly.

"No, indeed. Pretty clear case I should say."

But Poirot answered gravely:

"There I differ from you."

"Oh, come!" said Summerhaye, opening his lips for the first time. "Surely the whole thing is clear as daylight. The man's caught red-handed. How he could be such a fool beats me!"

But Japp was looking attentively at Poirot.

"Hold your fire, Summerhaye," he remarked jocularly. "Me and Moosier here have met before—and there's no man's judgment I'd sooner take than his. If I'm not greatly mistaken, he's got something up his sleeve. Isn't that so, moosier?"

Poirot smiled.

"I have drawn certain conclusions—yes."

Summerhaye was still looking rather sceptical, but Japp continued his scrutiny of Poirot.

"It's this way," he said, "so far, we've only seen the case from the outside. That's where the Yard's at a disadvantage in a case of this kind, where the murder's only out, so to speak, after the inquest. A lot depends on being on the spot first thing, and that's where Mr. Poirot's had the start of us. We shouldn't have been here as soon as this even, if it hadn't been for the fact that there was a smart doctor on the spot, who gave us the tip through the Coroner. But you've been on the spot from the first, and you may have picked up some little hints. From the evidence at the inquest, Mr. Inglethorp murdered his wife as sure as I stand here, and if anyone but you hinted the contrary I'd laugh in his face. I must say I was surprised the jury didn't bring it in Wilful Murder against him right off. I think they would have, if it hadn't been for the Coroner—he seemed to be holding them back."

"Perhaps, though, you have a warrant for his arrest in your pocket now," suggested Poirot.

A kind of wooden shutter of officialdom came down from Japp's expressive countenance.

"Perhaps I have, and perhaps I haven't," he remarked dryly.

Poirot looked at him thoughtfully.

"I am very anxious, Messieurs, that he should not be arrested."

"I dare say," observed Summerhaye sarcastically.

Japp was regarding Poirot with comical perplexity.

"Can't you go a little further, Mr. Poirot? A wink's as good as a nod—from you. You've been on the spot—and the Yard doesn't want to make any mistakes, you know."

Poirot nodded gravely.

"That is exactly what I thought. Well, I will tell you this. Use your warrant: Arrest Mr. Inglethorp. But it will bring you no kudos—the case against him will be dismissed at once! *Comme ça!*" And he snapped his fingers expressively.

Japp's face grew grave, though Summerhaye gave an incredulous snort.

As for me, I was literally dumb with astonishment. I could only conclude that Poirot was mad.

Japp had taken out a handkerchief, and was gently dabbing his brow.

"I daren't do it, Mr. Poirot. *I*'d take your word, but there's others over me who'll be asking what the devil I mean by it. Can't you give me a little more to go on?"

Poirot reflected a moment.

"It can be done," he said at last. "I admit I do not wish it. It forces my hand. I would have preferred to work in the dark just for the present, but what you say is very just—the word of a Belgian policeman, whose day is past, is not enough! And Alfred Inglethorp must not be arrested. That I have sworn, as my friend Hastings here knows. See, then, my good Japp, you go at once to Styles?"

"Well, in about half an hour. We're seeing the Coroner and the doctor first."

"Good. Call for me in passing—the last house in the village. I will go with you. At Styles, Mr. Inglethorp will give you, or if he refuses—as is probable—I will give you such proofs that shall satisfy you that the case against him could not possibly be sustained. Is that a bargain?"

"That's a bargain," said Japp heartily. "And, on behalf of the Yard, I'm much obliged to you, though I'm bound to confess I can't at present see the faintest possible loophole in the evidence, but you always were a marvel! So long, then, moosier."

The two detectives strode away, Summerhaye with an incredulous grin on his face.

"Well, my friend," cried Poirot, before I could get in a word, "what do you think? *Mon Dieu!* I had some warm moments in that court; I did not figure to myself that the man would be so pig-headed as to refuse to say anything at all. Decidedly, it was the policy of an imbecile."

"H'm! There are other explanations besides that of imbecility," I remarked. "For, if the case against him is true, how could he defend himself except by silence?"

"Why, in a thousand ingenious ways," cried Poirot. "See; say that it is I who have committed this murder, I can think of seven most plausible stories! Far more convincing than Mr. Inglethorp's stony denials!"

I could not help laughing.

"My dear Poirot, I am sure you are capable of thinking of seventy! But, seriously, in spite of what I heard you say to the detectives, you surely cannot still believe in the possibility of Alfred Inglethorp's innocence?"

"Why not now as much as before? Nothing has changed."

"But the evidence is so conclusive."

"Yes, too conclusive."

We turned in at the gate of Leastways Cottage, and proceeded up the now familiar stairs.

"Yes, yes, too conclusive," continued Poirot, almost to himself. "Real evidence is usually vague and unsatisfactory. It has to be examined—sifted. But here the whole thing is cut and dried. No, my friend, this evidence has been very cleverly manufactured—so cleverly that it has defeated its own ends."

"How do you make that out?"

"Because, so long as the evidence against him was vague and intangible, it was very hard to disprove. But, in his anxiety, the criminal has drawn the net so closely that one cut will set Inglethorp free."

I was silent. And in a minute or two, Poirot continued:

"Let us look at the matter like this. Here is a man, let us say, who sets out to poison his wife. He has lived by his wits as the saying goes. Presumably, therefore, he has some wits. He is not altogether a fool. Well, how does he set about it? He goes boldly to the village chemist's and purchases strychnine under his own name, with a trumped up story about a dog which is bound to be proved absurd. He does not employ the poison that night. No, he waits until he has had a violent quarrel with her, of which the whole household is cognisant, and which naturally directs their suspicions upon him. He prepares no defence—no shadow of an alibi, yet he knows the chemist's assistant must necessarily come forward with the facts. Bah! Do not ask me to believe that any man could be so idiotic! Only a lunatic, who wished to commit suicide by causing himself to be hanged, would act so!"

"Still—I do not see—" I began.

"Neither do I see. I tell you, *mon ami*, it puzzles me. *Me*—Hercule Poirot!"

"But if you believe him innocent, how do you explain his buying the strychnine?"

"Very simply. He did *not* buy it."

"But Mace recognized him!"

"I beg your pardon, he saw a man with a black beard like Mr. Inglethorp's, and wearing glasses like Mr. Inglethorp, and dressed in Mr. Inglethorp's rather noticeable clothes. He could not recognize a man whom he had probably only seen in the distance, since, you remember, he himself had only been in the village a fortnight, and Mrs. Inglethorp dealt principally with Coot's in Tadminster."

"Then you think—"

"*Mon ami*, do you remember the two points I laid stress upon? Leave the first one for the moment, what was the second?"

"The important fact that Alfred Inglethorp wears peculiar clothes, has a black beard and uses glasses," I quoted.

"Exactly. Now suppose anyone wished to pass himself off as John or Lawrence Cavendish. Would it be easy?"

"No," I said thoughtfully. "Of course an actor—"

But Poirot cut me short ruthlessly.

"And why would it not be easy? I will tell you, my friend: Because they are both clean-shaven men. To make up successfully as one of these two in broad daylight, it would need an actor of genius, and a certain initial facial resemblance. But in the case of Alfred Inglethorp, all that is changed. His clothes, his beard, the glasses which hide his eyes—those are the salient points about his personal appearance. Now, what is the first instinct of the criminal? To divert suspicion from himself, is it not so? And how can he best do that? By throwing it on some one else. In this instance, there was a man ready to his hand. Everybody was predisposed to believe in Mr. Inglethorp's guilt. It was a foregone conclusion that he would be suspected; but, to make it a sure thing there must be tangible proof—such as the actual buying of the poison, and that, with a man of the peculiar appearance of Mr. Inglethorp, was not difficult. Remember, this young Mace had never actually spoken to Mr. Inglethorp. How should he doubt that the man in his clothes, with his beard and his glasses, was not Alfred Inglethorp?"

"It may be so," I said, fascinated by Poirot's eloquence. "But, if that was the case, why does he not say where he was at six o'clock on Monday evening?"

"Ah, why indeed?" said Poirot, calming down. "If he were arrested, he probably would speak, but I do not want it to come to that. I must make him see the gravity of his position. There is, of course, something discreditable behind his silence. If he did not murder his wife, he is, nevertheless, a scoundrel, and has something of his own to conceal, quite apart from the murder."

"What can it be?" I mused, won over to Poirot's views for the moment, although still retaining a faint conviction that the obvious deduction was the correct one.

"Can you not guess?" asked Poirot, smiling.

"No, can you?"

"Oh, yes, I had a little idea sometime ago—and it has turned out to be correct."

"You never told me," I said reproachfully.

Poirot spread out his hands apologetically.

"Pardon me, *mon ami*, you were not precisely *sympathique*." He turned to me earnestly. "Tell me—you see now that he must not be arrested?"

"Perhaps," I said doubtfully, for I was really quite indifferent to the fate of Alfred Inglethorp, and thought that a good fright would do him no harm.

Poirot, who was watching me intently, gave a sigh.

"Come, my friend," he said, changing the subject, "apart from Mr. Inglethorp, how did the evidence at the inquest strike you?"

"Oh, pretty much what I expected."

"Did nothing strike you as peculiar about it?"

My thoughts flew to Mary Cavendish, and I hedged:

"In what way?"

"Well Mr. Lawrence Cavendish's evidence for instance?"

I was relieved.

"Oh, Lawrence! No, I don't think so. He's always a nervous chap."

"His suggestion that his mother might have been poisoned accidentally by means of the tonic she was taking, that did not strike you as strange—*hein?*"

"No, I can't say it did. The doctors ridiculed it of course. But it was quite a natural suggestion for a layman to make."

"But Monsieur Lawrence is not a layman. You told me yourself that he had started by studying medicine, and that he had taken his degree."

"Yes, that's true. I never thought of that." I was rather startled. "It *is* odd."

Poirot nodded.

"From the first, his behaviour has been peculiar. Of all the household, he alone would be likely to recognize the symptoms of strychnine poisoning, and yet we find him the only member of the family to uphold strenuously the theory of death from natural causes. If it had been Monsieur John, I could have understood it. He has no technical knowledge, and is by nature unimaginative. But Monsieur Lawrence—no! And now, today, he puts forward a suggestion that he himself must have known was ridiculous. There is food for thought in this, *mon ami*!"

"It's very confusing," I agreed.

"Then there is Mrs. Cavendish," continued Poirot. "That's another who is not telling all she knows! What do you make of her attitude?"

"I don't know what to make of it. It seems inconceivable that she should be shielding Alfred Inglethorp. Yet that is what it looks like."

Poirot nodded reflectively.

"Yes, it is queer. One thing is certain, she overheard a good deal more of that 'private conversation' than she was willing to admit."

"And yet she is the last person one would accuse of stooping to eavesdrop!"

"Exactly. One thing her evidence *has* shown me. I made a mistake. Dorcas was quite right. The quarrel did take place earlier in the afternoon, about four o'clock, as she said."

I looked at him curiously. I had never understood his insistence on that point.

"Yes, a good deal that was peculiar came out today," continued Poirot. "Dr. Bauerstein, now, what was *he* doing up and dressed at that hour in the morning? It is astonishing to me that no one commented on the fact."

"He has insomnia, I believe," I said doubtfully.

"Which is a very good, or a very bad explanation," remarked Poirot. "It covers everything, and explains nothing. I shall keep my eye on our clever Dr. Bauerstein."

"Any more faults to find with the evidence?" I inquired satirically.

"*Mon ami*," replied Poirot gravely, "when you find that people are not telling you the truth—look out! Now, unless I am much mistaken, at the inquest today only one—at most, two persons were speaking the truth without reservation or subterfuge."

"Oh, come now, Poirot! I won't cite Lawrence, or Mrs. Cavendish. But there's John—and Miss Howard, surely they were speaking the truth?"

"Both of them, my friend? One, I grant you, but both—!"

His words gave me an unpleasant shock. Miss Howard's evidence, unimportant as it was, had been given in such a downright straightforward manner that it had never occurred to me to doubt her sincerity. Still, I had a great respect for Poirot's sagacity—except on the occasions when he was what I described to myself as "foolishly pig-headed."

"Do you really think so?" I asked. "Miss Howard had always seemed to me so essentially honest—almost uncomfortably so."

Poirot gave me a curious look, which I could not quite fathom. He seemed to speak, and then checked himself.

"Miss Murdoch too," I continued, "there's nothing untruthful about *her*."

"No. But it was strange that she never heard a sound, sleeping next door; whereas Mrs. Cavendish, in the other wing of the building, distinctly heard the table fall."

"Well, she's young. And she sleeps soundly."

"Ah, yes, indeed! She must be a famous sleeper, that one!"

I did not quite like the tone of his voice, but at that moment a smart knock reached our ears, and looking out of the window we perceived the two detectives waiting for us below.

Poirot seized his hat, gave a ferocious twist to his moustache, and, carefully brushing an imaginary speck of dust from his sleeve, motioned me to precede him down the stairs; there we joined the detectives and set out for Styles.

I think the appearance of the two Scotland Yard men was rather a shock—especially to John, though of course, after the verdict, he had realized that it was only a matter of time. Still, the presence of the detectives brought the truth home to him more than anything else could have done.

Poirot had conferred with Japp in a low tone on the way up, and it was the latter functionary who requested that the household, with the exception of the servants, should be assembled together in the drawing room. I realized the significance of this. It was up to Poirot to make his boast good.

Personally, I was not sanguine. Poirot might have excellent reasons for his belief in Inglethorp's innocence, but a man of the type of Summerhaye would require tangible proofs, and these I doubted if Poirot could supply.

Before very long we had all trooped into the drawing room, the door of which Japp closed. Poirot politely set chairs for everyone. The Scotland Yard men were the cynosure of all eyes. I think that for the first time we realized that the thing was not a bad dream, but a tangible reality. We had read of such things—now we ourselves were actors in the drama. Tomorrow the daily papers, all over England, would blazon out the news in staring headlines:

MYSTERIOUS TRAGEDY IN ESSEX
WEALTHY LADY POISONED

There would be pictures of Styles, snapshots of "The family leaving the Inquest"— the village photographer had not been idle! All the things that one had read a hundred times—things that happen to other people, not to oneself. And now, in this house, a murder had been committed. In front of us were "the detectives in charge of the case." The well known glib phraseology passed rapidly through my mind in the interval before Poirot opened the proceedings.

I think every one was a little surprised that it should be he and not one of the official detectives who took the initiative.

"*Mesdames* and *messieurs*," said Poirot, bowing as though he were a celebrity about to deliver a lecture, "I have asked you to come here all together, for a certain object. That object, it concerns Mr. Alfred Inglethorp."

Inglethorp was sitting a little by himself—I think, unconsciously, everyone had drawn his chair slightly away from him—and he gave a faint start as Poirot pronounced his name.

"Mr. Inglethorp," said Poirot, addressing him directly, "a very dark shadow is resting on this house—the shadow of murder."

Inglethorp shook his head sadly.

"My poor wife," he murmured. "Poor Emily! It is terrible."

"I do not think, monsieur," said Poirot pointedly, "that you quite realize how terrible it may be—for you." And as Inglethorp did not appear to understand, he added: "Mr. Inglethorp, you are standing in very grave danger."

The two detectives fidgeted. I saw the official caution "Anything you say will be used in evidence against you," actually hovering on Summerhaye's lips. Poirot went on.

"Do you understand now, monsieur?"

"No. What do you mean?"

"I mean," said Poirot deliberately, "that you are suspected of poisoning your wife."

A little gasp ran round the circle at this plain speaking.

"Good heavens!" cried Inglethorp, starting up. "What a monstrous idea! I—poison my dearest Emily!"

"I do not think"—Poirot watched him narrowly—"that you quite realize the unfavourable nature of your evidence at the inquest. Mr. Inglethorp, knowing what I have now told you, do you still refuse to say where you were at six o'clock on Monday afternoon?"

With a groan, Alfred Inglethorp sank down again and buried his face in his hands. Poirot approached and stood over him.

"Speak!" he cried menacingly.

With an effort, Inglethorp raised his face from his hands. Then, slowly and deliberately, he shook his head.

"You will not speak?"

"No. I do not believe that anyone could be so monstrous as to accuse me of what you say."

Poirot nodded thoughtfully, like a man whose mind is made up.

"Soit!" he said. "Then I must speak for you."

Alfred Inglethorp sprang up again.

"You? How can you speak? You do not know—" he broke off abruptly.

Poirot turned to face us. "Mesdames and messieurs! I speak! Listen! I, Hercule Poirot, affirm that the man who entered the chemist's shop, and purchased strychnine at six o'clock on Monday last was not Mr. Inglethorp, for at six o'clock on that day

Mr. Inglethorp was escorting Mrs. Raikes back to her home from a neighbouring farm. I can produce no less than five witnesses to swear to having seen them together, either at six or just after and, as you may know, the Abbey Farm, Mrs. Raikes's home, is at least two and a half miles distant from the village. There is absolutely no question as to the alibi!"

VIII. Fresh Suspicions

There was a moment's stupefied silence. Japp, who was the least surprised of any of us, was the first to speak.

"My word," he cried, "you're the goods! And no mistake, Mr. Poirot! These witnesses of yours are all right, I suppose?"

"*Voilà!* I have prepared a list of them—names and addresses. You must see them, of course. But you will find it all right."

"I'm sure of that." Japp lowered his voice. "I'm much obliged to you. A pretty mare's nest arresting him would have been." He turned to Inglethorp. "But, if you'll excuse me, sir, why couldn't you say all this at the inquest?"

"I will tell you why," interrupted Poirot. "There was a certain rumour—"

"A most malicious and utterly untrue one," interrupted Alfred Inglethorp in an agitated voice.

"And Mr. Inglethorp was anxious to have no scandal revived just at present. Am I right?"

"Quite right." Inglethorp nodded. "With my poor Emily not yet buried, can you wonder I was anxious that no more lying rumours should be started."

"Between you and me, sir," remarked Japp, "I'd sooner have any amount of rumours than be arrested for murder. And I venture to think your poor lady would have felt the same. And, if it hadn't been for Mr. Poirot here, arrested you would have been, as sure as eggs is eggs!"

"I was foolish, no doubt," murmured Inglethorp. "But you do not know, Inspector, how I have been persecuted and maligned." And he shot a baleful glance at Evelyn Howard.

"Now, sir," said Japp, turning briskly to John, "I should like to see the lady's bedroom, please, and after that I'll have a little chat with the servants. Don't you bother about anything. Mr. Poirot, here, will show me the way."

As they all went out of the room, Poirot turned and made me a sign to follow him upstairs. There he caught me by the arm, and drew me aside.

"Quick, go to the other wing. Stand there—just this side of the baize door. Do not move till I come." Then, turning rapidly, he rejoined the two detectives.

I followed his instructions, taking up my position by the baize door, and wondering what on earth lay behind the request. Why was I to stand in this particular spot on guard? I looked thoughtfully down the corridor in front of me. An idea struck me. With the exception of Cynthia Murdoch's, everyone's room was in this left wing. Had that anything to do with it? Was I to report who came or went? I stood faithfully at my post. The minutes passed. Nobody came. Nothing happened.

It must have been quite twenty minutes before Poirot rejoined me.

"You have not stirred?"

"No, I've stuck here like a rock. Nothing's happened."

"Ah!" Was he pleased, or disappointed? "You've seen nothing at all?"

"No."

"But you have probably heard something? A big bump—eh, *mon ami*?"

"No."

"Is it possible? Ah, but I am vexed with myself! I am not usually clumsy. I made but a slight gesture"—I know Poirot's gestures—"with the left hand, and over went the table by the bed!"

He looked so childishly vexed and crestfallen that I hastened to console him.

"Never mind, old chap. What does it matter? Your triumph downstairs excited you. I can tell you, that was a surprise to us all. There must be more in this affair of Inglethorp's with Mrs. Raikes than we thought, to make him hold his tongue so persistently. What are you going to do now? Where are the Scotland Yard fellows?"

"Gone down to interview the servants. I showed them all our exhibits. I am disappointed in Japp. He has no method!"

"Hullo!" I said, looking out of the window. "Here's Dr. Bauerstein. I believe you're right about that man, Poirot. I don't like him."

"He is clever," observed Poirot meditatively.

"Oh, clever as the devil! I must say I was overjoyed to see him in the plight he was in on Tuesday. You never saw such a spectacle!" And I described the doctor's adventure. "He looked a regular scarecrow! Plastered with mud from head to foot."

"You saw him, then?"

"Yes. Of course, he didn't want to come in—it was just after dinner—but Mr. Inglethorp insisted."

"What?" Poirot caught me violently by the shoulders. "Was Dr. Bauerstein here on Tuesday evening? Here? And you never told me? Why did you not tell me? Why? Why?"

He appeared to be in an absolute frenzy.

"My dear Poirot," I expostulated, "I never thought it would interest you. I didn't know it was of any importance."

"Importance? It is of the first importance! So Dr. Bauerstein was here on Tuesday night—the night of the murder. Hastings, do you not see? That alters everything—everything!"

I had never seen him so upset. Loosening his hold of me, he mechanically straightened a pair of candlesticks, still murmuring to himself: "Yes, that alters everything—everything."

Suddenly he seemed to come to a decision.

"*Allons!*" he said. "We must act at once. Where is Mr. Cavendish?"

John was in the smoking-room. Poirot went straight to him.

"Mr. Cavendish, I have some important business in Tadminster. A new clue. May I take your motor?"

"Why, of course. Do you mean at once?"

"If you please."

John rang the bell, and ordered round the car. In another ten minutes, we were racing down the park and along the high road to Tadminster.

"Now, Poirot," I remarked resignedly, "perhaps you will tell me what all this is about?"

"Well, *mon ami*, a good deal you can guess for yourself. Of course you realize that, now Mr. Inglethorp is out of it, the whole position is greatly changed. We are face to face with an entirely new problem. We know now that there is one person who did not buy the poison. We have cleared away the manufactured clues. Now for the real ones. I have ascertained that anyone in the household, with the exception of Mrs. Cavendish, who was playing tennis with you, could have personated Mr. Inglethorp on Monday evening. In the same way, we have his statement that he put the coffee down in the hall. No one took much notice of that at the inquest—but now it has a very different significance. We must find out who did take that coffee to Mrs. Inglethorp eventually, or who passed through the hall whilst it was standing there. From your account, there are only two people whom we can positively say did not go near the coffee—Mrs. Cavendish, and Mademoiselle Cynthia."

"Yes, that is so." I felt an inexpressible lightening of the heart. Mary Cavendish could certainly not rest under suspicion.

"In clearing Alfred Inglethorp," continued Poirot, "I have been obliged to show my hand sooner than I intended. As long as I might be thought to be pursuing him, the criminal would be off his guard. Now, he will be doubly careful. Yes—doubly careful." He turned to me abruptly. "Tell me, Hastings, you yourself—have you no suspicions of anybody?"

I hesitated. To tell the truth, an idea, wild and extravagant in itself, had once or twice that morning flashed through my brain. I had rejected it as absurd, nevertheless it persisted.

"You couldn't call it a suspicion," I murmured. "It's so utterly foolish."

"Come now," urged Poirot encouragingly. "Do not fear. Speak your mind. You should always pay attention to your instincts."

"Well then," I blurted out, "it's absurd—but I suspect Miss Howard of not telling all she knows!"

"Miss Howard?"

"Yes—you'll laugh at me—"

"Not at all. Why should I?"

"I can't help feeling," I continued blunderingly; "that we've rather left her out of the possible suspects, simply on the strength of her having been away from the place. But, after all, she was only fifteen miles away. A car would do it in half an hour. Can we say positively that she was away from Styles on the night of the murder?"

"Yes, my friend," said Poirot unexpectedly, "we can. One of my first actions was to ring up the hospital where she was working."

"Well?"

"Well, I learnt that Miss Howard had been on afternoon duty on Tuesday, and that—a convoy coming in unexpectedly—she had kindly offered to remain on night duty, which offer was gratefully accepted. That disposes of that."

"Oh!" I said, rather nonplussed. "Really," I continued, "it's her extraordinary vehemence against Inglethorp that started me off suspecting her. I can't help feeling she'd do anything against him. And I had an idea she might know something about the destroying of the will. She might have burnt the new one, mistaking it for the earlier one in his favour. She is so terribly bitter against him."

"You consider her vehemence unnatural?"

"Y—es. She is so very violent. I wondered really whether she is quite sane on that point."

Poirot shook his head energetically.

"No, no, you are on a wrong tack there. There is nothing weak-minded or degenerate about Miss Howard. She is an excellent specimen of well-balanced English beef and brawn. She is sanity itself."

"Yet her hatred of Inglethorp seems almost a mania. My idea was—a very ridiculous one, no doubt—that she had intended to poison him—and that, in some way,

Mrs. Inglethorp got hold of it by mistake. But I don't at all see how it could have been done. The whole thing is absurd and ridiculous to the last degree."

"Still you are right in one thing. It is always wise to suspect everybody until you can prove logically, and to your own satisfaction, that they are innocent. Now, what reasons are there against Miss Howard's having deliberately poisoned Mrs. Inglethorp?"

"Why, she was devoted to her!" I exclaimed.

"Tcha! Tcha!" cried Poirot irritably. "You argue like a child. If Miss Howard were capable of poisoning the old lady, she would be quite equally capable of simulating devotion. No, we must look elsewhere. You are perfectly correct in your assumption that her vehemence against Alfred Inglethorp is too violent to be natural; but you are quite wrong in the deduction you draw from it. I have drawn my own deductions, which I believe to be correct, but I will not speak of them at present." He paused a minute, then went on. "Now, to my way of thinking, there is one insuperable objection to Miss Howard's being the murderess."

"And that is?"

"That in no possible way could Mrs. Inglethorp's death benefit Miss Howard. Now there is no murder without a motive."

I reflected.

"Could not Mrs. Inglethorp have made a will in her favour?"

Poirot shook his head.

"But you yourself suggested that possibility to Mr. Wells?"

Poirot smiled.

"That was for a reason. I did not want to mention the name of the person who was actually in my mind. Miss Howard occupied very much the same position, so I used her name instead."

"Still, Mrs. Inglethorp might have done so. Why, that will, made on the afternoon of her death may—"

But Poirot's shake of the head was so energetic that I stopped.

"No, my friend. I have certain little ideas of my own about that will. But I can tell you this much—it was not in Miss Howard's favour."

I accepted his assurance, though I did not really see how he could be so positive about the matter.

"Well," I said, with a sigh, "we will acquit Miss Howard, then. It is partly your fault that I ever came to suspect her. It was what you said about her evidence at the inquest that set me off."

Poirot looked puzzled.

"What did I say about her evidence at the inquest?"

"Don't you remember? When I cited her and John Cavendish as being above suspicion?"

"Oh—ah—yes." He seemed a little confused, but recovered himself. "By the way, Hastings, there is something I want you to do for me."

"Certainly. What is it?"

"Next time you happen to be alone with Lawrence Cavendish, I want you to say this to him. 'I have a message for you, from Poirot. He says: "Find the extra coffee cup, and you can rest in peace!"' Nothing more. Nothing less."

"'Find the extra coffee cup, and you can rest in peace.' Is that right?" I asked, much mystified.

"Excellent."

"But what does it mean?"

"Ah, that I will leave you to find out. You have access to the facts. Just say that to him, and see what he says."

"Very well—but it's all extremely mysterious."

We were running into Tadminster now, and Poirot directed the car to the "Analytical Chemist."

Poirot hopped down briskly, and went inside. In a few minutes he was back again.

"There," he said. "That is all my business."

"What were you doing there?" I asked, in lively curiosity.

"I left something to be analysed."

"Yes, but what?"

"The sample of coco I took from the saucepan in the bedroom."

"But that has already been tested!" I cried, stupefied. "Dr. Bauerstein had it tested, and you yourself laughed at the possibility of there being strychnine in it."

"I know Dr. Bauerstein had it tested," replied Poirot quietly.

"Well, then?"

"Well, I have a fancy for having it analysed again, that is all."

And not another word on the subject could I drag out of him.

This proceeding of Poirot's, in respect of the coco, puzzled me intensely. I could see neither rhyme nor reason in it. However, my confidence in him, which at one time had rather waned, was fully restored since his belief in Alfred Inglethorp's innocence had been so triumphantly vindicated.

The funeral of Mrs. Inglethorp took place the following day, and on Monday, as I came down to a late breakfast, John drew me aside, and informed me that Mr. Inglethorp was leaving that morning, to take up his quarters at the Stylites Arms until he should have completed his plans.

"And really it's a great relief to think he's going, Hastings," continued my honest friend. "It was bad enough before, when we thought he'd done it, but I'm hanged if it isn't worse now, when we all feel guilty for having been so down on the fellow. The fact is, we've treated him abominably. Of course, things did look black against him. I don't see how anyone could blame us for jumping to the conclusions we did. Still, there it is, we were in the wrong, and now there's a beastly feeling that one ought to make amends; which is difficult, when one doesn't like the fellow a bit better than one did before. The whole thing's damned awkward! And I'm thankful he's had the tact to take himself off. It's a good thing Styles wasn't the mater's to leave to him. Couldn't bear to think of the fellow lording it here. He's welcome to her money."

"You'll be able to keep up the place all right?" I asked.

"Oh, yes. There are the death duties, of course, but half my father's money goes with the place, and Lawrence will stay with us for the present, so there is his share as well. We shall be pinched at first, of course, because, as I once told you, I am in a bit of a hole financially myself. Still, the Johnnies will wait now."

In the general relief at Inglethorp's approaching departure, we had the most genial breakfast we had experienced since the tragedy. Cynthia, whose young spirits were naturally buoyant, was looking quite her pretty self again, and we all, with the exception of Lawrence, who seemed unalterably gloomy and nervous, were quietly cheerful, at the opening of a new and hopeful future.

The papers, of course, had been full of the tragedy. Glaring headlines, sandwiched biographies of every member of the household, subtle innuendoes, the usual familiar tag about the police having a clue. Nothing was spared us. It was a slack time. The war was momentarily inactive, and the newspapers seized with avidity on this crime in fashionable life: "The Mysterious Affair at Styles" was the topic of the moment.

Naturally it was very annoying for the Cavendishes. The house was constantly besieged by reporters, who were consistently denied admission, but who continued to haunt the village and the grounds, where they lay in wait with cameras, for any unwary members of the household. We all lived in a blast of publicity. The Scotland Yard men came and went, examining, questioning, lynx-eyed and reserved of tongue. Towards what end they were working, we did not know. Had they any clue, or would the whole thing remain in the category of undiscovered crimes?

After breakfast, Dorcas came up to me rather mysteriously, and asked if she might have a few words with me.

"Certainly. What is it, Dorcas?"

"Well, it's just this, sir. You'll be seeing the Belgian gentleman today perhaps?"
I nodded. "Well, sir, you know how he asked me so particular if the mistress, or anyone else, had a green dress?"

"Yes, yes. You have found one?" My interest was aroused.

"No, not that, sir. But since then I've remembered what the young gentlemen"—
John and Lawrence were still the "young gentlemen" to Dorcas—"call the 'dressing-up
box.' It's up in the front attic, sir. A great chest, full of old clothes and fancy dresses, and
whatnot. And it came to me sudden like that there might be a green dress amongst them.
So, if you'd tell the Belgian gentleman—"

"I will tell him, Dorcas," I promised.

"Thank you very much, sir. A very nice gentleman he is, sir. And quite a different class from them two detectives from London, what goes prying about, and asking
questions. I don't hold with foreigners as a rule, but from what the newspapers say I
make out as how these brave Belges isn't the ordinary run of foreigners, and certainly
he's a most polite spoken gentleman."

Dear old Dorcas! As she stood there, with her honest face upturned to mine,
I thought what a fine specimen she was of the old-fashioned servant that is so fast
dying out.

I thought I might as well go down to the village at once, and look up Poirot;
but I met him halfway, coming up to the house, and at once gave him Dorcas's
message.

"Ah, the brave Dorcas! We will look at the chest, although—but no matter—we
will examine it all the same."

We entered the house by one of the windows. There was no one in the hall, and
we went straight up to the attic.

Sure enough, there was the chest, a fine old piece, all studded with brass nails, and
full to overflowing with every imaginable type of garment.

Poirot bundled everything out on the floor with scant ceremony. There were one
or two green fabrics of varying shades; but Poirot shook his head over them all. He
seemed somewhat apathetic in the search, as though he expected no great results from
it. Suddenly he gave an exclamation.

"What is it?"

"Look!"

The chest was nearly empty, and there, reposing right at the bottom, was a magnificent black beard.

"*Ohó!*" said Poirot. "*Ohó!*" He turned it over in his hands, examining it closely.
"New," he remarked. "Yes, quite new."

After a moment's hesitation, he replaced it in the chest, heaped all the other things on top of it as before, and made his way briskly downstairs. He went straight to the pantry, where we found Dorcas busily polishing her silver.

Poirot wished her good morning with Gallic politeness, and went on:

"We have been looking through that chest, Dorcas. I am much obliged to you for mentioning it. There is, indeed, a fine collection there. Are they often used, may I ask?"

"Well, sir, not very often nowadays, though from time to time we do have what the young gentlemen call 'a dress-up night.' And very funny it is sometimes, sir. Mr. Lawrence, he's wonderful. Most comic! I shall never forget the night he came down as the Char of Persia, I think he called it—a sort of Eastern King it was. He had the big paper knife in his hand, and 'Mind, Dorcas,' he says, 'you'll have to be very respectful. This is my specially sharpened scimitar, and it's off with your head if I'm at all displeased with you!' Miss Cynthia, she was what they call an Apache, or some such name—a Frenchified sort of cutthroat, I take it to be. A real sight she looked. You'd never have believed a pretty young lady like that could have made herself into such a ruffian. Nobody would have known her."

"These evenings must have been great fun," said Poirot genially. "I suppose Mr. Lawrence wore that fine black beard in the chest upstairs, when he was Shah of Persia?"

"He did have a beard, sir," replied Dorcas, smiling. "And well I know it, for he borrowed two skeins of my black wool to make it with! And I'm sure it looked wonderfully natural at a distance. I didn't know as there was a beard up there at all. It must have been got quite lately, I think. There was a red wig, I know, but nothing else in the way of hair. Burnt corks they use mostly—though 'tis messy getting it off again. Miss Cynthia was a nigger once, and, oh, the trouble she had."

"So Dorcas knows nothing about that black beard," said Poirot thoughtfully, as we walked out into the hall again.

"Do you think it is *the* one?" I whispered eagerly.

Poirot nodded.

"I do. You notice it had been trimmed?"

"No."

"Yes. It was cut exactly the shape of Mr. Inglethorp's, and I found one or two snipped hairs. Hastings, this affair is very deep."

"Who put it in the chest, I wonder?"

"Someone with a good deal of intelligence," remarked Poirot drily. "You realize that he chose the one place in the house to hide it where its presence would not be remarked? Yes, he is intelligent. But we must be more intelligent. We must be so intelligent that he does not suspect us of being intelligent at all."

I acquiesced.

"There, *mon ami*, you will be of great assistance to me."

I was pleased with the compliment. There had been times when I hardly thought that Poirot appreciated me at my true worth.

"Yes," he continued, staring at me thoughtfully, "you will be invaluable."

This was naturally gratifying, but Poirot's next words were not so welcome.

"I must have an ally in the house," he observed reflectively.

"You have me," I protested.

"True, but you are not sufficient."

I was hurt, and showed it. Poirot hurried to explain himself.

"You do not quite take my meaning. You are known to be working with me. I want somebody who is not associated with us in any way."

"Oh, I see. How about John?"

"No, I think not."

"The dear fellow isn't perhaps very bright," I said thoughtfully.

"Here comes Miss Howard," said Poirot suddenly. "She is the very person. But I am in her black books, since I cleared Mr. Inglethorp. Still, we can but try."

With a nod that was barely civil, Miss Howard assented to Poirot's request for a few minutes' conversation.

We went into the little morning-room, and Poirot closed the door.

"Well, Monsieur Poirot," said Miss Howard impatiently, "what is it? Out with it. I'm busy."

"Do you remember, mademoiselle, that I once asked you to help me?"

"Yes, I do." The lady nodded. "And I told you I'd help you with pleasure—to hang Alfred Inglethorp."

"Ah!" Poirot studied her seriously. "Miss Howard, I will ask you one question. I beg of you to reply to it truthfully."

"Never tell lies," replied Miss Howard.

"It is this. Do you still believe that Mrs. Inglethorp was poisoned by her husband?"

"What do you mean?" she asked sharply. "You needn't think your pretty explanations influence me in the slightest. I'll admit that it wasn't he who bought strychnine at the chemist's shop. What of that? I dare say he soaked fly paper, as I told you at the beginning."

"That is arsenic—not strychnine," said Poirot mildly.

"What does that matter? Arsenic would put poor Emily out of the way just as well as strychnine. If I'm convinced he did it, it doesn't matter a jot to me *how* he did it."

"Exactly. *If* you are convinced he did it," said Poirot quietly. "I will put my question in another form. Did you ever in your heart of hearts believe that Mrs. Inglethorp was poisoned by her husband?"

"Good heavens!" cried Miss Howard. "Haven't I always told you the man is a villain? Haven't I always told you he would murder her in her bed? Haven't I always hated him like poison?"

"Exactly," said Poirot. "That bears out my little idea entirely."

"What little idea?"

"Miss Howard, do you remember a conversation that took place on the day of my friend's arrival here? He repeated it to me, and there is a sentence of yours that has impressed me very much. Do you remember affirming that if a crime had been committed, and anyone you loved had been murdered, you felt certain that you would know by instinct who the criminal was, even if you were quite unable to prove it?"

"Yes, I remember saying that. I believe it too. I suppose you think it nonsense?"

"Not at all."

"And yet you will pay no attention to my instinct against Alfred Inglethorp?"

"No," said Poirot curtly. "Because your instinct is not against Mr. Inglethorp."

"What?"

"No. You wish to believe he committed the crime. You believe him capable of committing it. But your instinct tells you he did not commit it. It tells you more—shall I go on?"

She was staring at him, fascinated, and made a slight affirmative movement of the hand.

"Shall I tell you why you have been so vehement against Mr. Inglethorp? It is because you have been trying to believe what you wish to believe. It is because you are trying to drown and stifle your instinct, which tells you another name—"

"No, no, no!" cried Miss Howard wildly, flinging up her hands. "Don't say it! Oh, don't say it! It isn't true! It can't be true. I don't know what put such a wild—such a dreadful—idea into my head!"

"I am right, am I not?" asked Poirot.

"Yes, yes; you must be a wizard to have guessed. But it can't be so—it's too monstrous, too impossible. It *must* be Alfred Inglethorp."

Poirot shook his head gravely.

"Don't ask me about it," continued Miss Howard, "because I shan't tell you. I won't admit it even to myself. I must be mad to think of such a thing."

Poirot nodded, as if satisfied.

"I will ask you nothing. It is enough for me that it is as I thought. And I—I, too, have an instinct. We are working together towards a common end."

"Don't ask me to help you, because I won't. I wouldn't lift a finger to—to—" She faltered.

"You will help me in spite of yourself. I ask you nothing—but you will be my ally. You will not be able to help yourself. You will do the only thing that I want of you."

"And that is?"

"You will watch!"

Evelyn Howard bowed her head.

"Yes, I can't help doing that. I am always watching—always hoping I shall be proved wrong."

"If we are wrong, well and good," said Poirot. "No one will be more pleased than I shall. But, if we are right? If we are right, Miss Howard, on whose side are you then?"

"I don't know, I don't know—"

"Come now."

"It could be hushed up."

"There must be no hushing up."

"But Emily herself—" She broke off.

"Miss Howard," said Poirot gravely, "this is unworthy of you."

Suddenly she took her face from her hands.

"Yes," she said quietly, "that was not Evelyn Howard who spoke!" She flung her head up proudly. "*This* is Evelyn Howard! And she is on the side of Justice! Let the cost be what it may." And with these words, she walked firmly out of the room.

"There," said Poirot, looking after her, "goes a very valuable ally. That woman, Hastings, has got brains as well as a heart."

I did not reply.

"Instinct is a marvellous thing," mused Poirot. "It can neither be explained nor ignored."

"You and Miss Howard seem to know what you are talking about," I observed coldly. "Perhaps you don't realize that *I* am still in the dark."

"Really? Is that so, *mon ami*?"

"Yes. Enlighten me, will you?"

Poirot studied me attentively for a moment or two. Then, to my intense surprise, he shook his head decidedly.

"No, my friend."

"Oh, look here, why not?"

"Two is enough for a secret."

"Well, I think it is very unfair to keep back facts from me."

"I am not keeping back facts. Every fact that I know is in your possession. You can draw your own deductions from them. This time it is a question of ideas."

"Still, it would be interesting to know."

Poirot looked at me very earnestly, and again shook his head.

"You see," he said sadly, "*you* have no instincts."

"It was intelligence you were requiring just now," I pointed out.

"The two often go together," said Poirot enigmatically.

The remark seemed so utterly irrelevant that I did not even take the trouble to answer it. But I decided that if I made any interesting and important discoveries—as no doubt I should—I would keep them to myself, and surprise Poirot with the ultimate result.

There are times when it is one's duty to assert oneself.

IX. Dr. Bauerstein

I had had no opportunity as yet of passing on Poirot's message to Lawrence. But now, as I strolled out on the lawn, still nursing a grudge against my friend's high-handedness, I saw Lawrence on the croquet lawn, aimlessly knocking a couple of very ancient balls about, with a still more ancient mallet.

It struck me that it would be a good opportunity to deliver my message. Otherwise, Poirot himself might relieve me of it. It was true that I did not quite gather its purport, but I flattered myself that by Lawrence's reply, and perhaps a little skillful cross-examination on my part, I should soon perceive its significance. Accordingly I accosted him.

"I've been looking for you," I remarked untruthfully.

"Have you?"

"Yes. The truth is, I've got a message for you—from Poirot."

"Yes?"

"He told me to wait until I was alone with you," I said, dropping my voice significantly, and watching him intently out of the corner of my eye. I have always been rather good at what is called, I believe, creating an atmosphere.

"Well?"

There was no change of expression in the dark melancholic face. Had he any idea of what I was about to say?

"This is the message." I dropped my voice still lower. "'Find the extra coffee cup, and you can rest in peace.'"

"What on earth does he mean?" Lawrence stared at me in quite unaffected astonishment.

"Don't you know?"

"Not in the least. Do you?"

I was compelled to shake my head.

"What extra coffee cup?"

"I don't know."

"He'd better ask Dorcas, or one of the maids, if he wants to know about coffee cups. It's their business, not mine. I don't know anything about the coffee cups, except that we've got some that are never used, which are a perfect dream! Old Worcester. You're not a connoisseur, are you, Hastings?"

I shook my head.

"You miss a lot. A really perfect bit of old china—it's pure delight to handle it, or even to look at it."

"Well, what am I to tell Poirot?"

"Tell him I don't know what he's talking about. It's double Dutch to me."

"All right."

I was moving off towards the house again when he suddenly called me back.

"I say, what was the end of that message? Say it over again, will you?"

" 'Find the extra coffee cup, and you can rest in peace.' Are you sure you don't know what it means?" I asked him earnestly.

He shook his head.

"No," he said musingly, "I don't. I—I wish I did."

The boom of the gong sounded from the house, and we went in together. Poirot had been asked by John to remain to lunch, and was already seated at the table.

By tacit consent, all mention of the tragedy was barred. We conversed on the war, and other outside topics. But after the cheese and biscuits had been handed round, and Dorcas had left the room, Poirot suddenly leant forward to Mrs. Cavendish.

"Pardon me, madame, for recalling unpleasant memories, but I have a little idea"—Poirot's "little ideas" were becoming a perfect byword—"and would like to ask one or two questions."

"Of me? Certainly."

"You are too amiable, madame. What I want to ask is this: the door leading into Mrs. Inglethorp's room from that of Mademoiselle Cynthia, it was bolted, you say?"

"Certainly it was bolted," replied Mary Cavendish, rather surprised. "I said so at the inquest."

"Bolted?"

"Yes." She looked perplexed.

"I mean," explained Poirot, "you are sure it was bolted, and not merely locked?"

"Oh, I see what you mean. No, I don't know. I said bolted, meaning that it was fastened, and I could not open it, but I believe all the doors were found bolted on the inside."

"Still, as far as you are concerned, the door might equally well have been locked?"

"Oh, yes."

"You yourself did not happen to notice, madame, when you entered Mrs. Inglethorp's room, whether that door was bolted or not?"

"I—I believe it was."

"But you did not see it?"

"No. I—never looked."

"But *I* did," interrupted Lawrence suddenly. "I happened to notice that it *was* bolted."

"Ah, that settles it." And Poirot looked crestfallen.

I could not help rejoicing that, for once, one of his "little ideas" had come to naught.

After lunch Poirot begged me to accompany him home. I consented rather stiffly.

"You are annoyed, is it not so?" he asked anxiously, as we walked through the park.

"Not at all," I said coldly.

"That is well. That lifts a great load from my mind."

This was not quite what I had intended. I had hoped that he would have observed the stiffness of my manner. Still, the fervour of his words went towards the appeasing of my just displeasure. I thawed.

"I gave Lawrence your message," I said.

"And what did he say? He was entirely puzzled?"

"Yes. I am quite sure he had no idea of what you meant."

I had expected Poirot to be disappointed; but, to my surprise, he replied that that was as he had thought, and that he was very glad. My pride forbade me to ask any questions.

Poirot switched off on another tack.

"Mademoiselle Cynthia was not at lunch today? How was that?"

"She is at the hospital again. She resumed work today."

"Ah, she is an industrious little demoiselle. And pretty too. She is like pictures I have seen in Italy. I would rather like to see that dispensary of hers. Do you think she would show it to me?"

"I am sure she would be delighted. It's an interesting little place."

"Does she go there every day?"

"She has all Wednesdays off, and comes back to lunch on Saturdays. Those are her only times off."

"I will remember. Women are doing great work nowadays, and Mademoiselle Cynthia is clever—oh, yes, she has brains, that little one."

"Yes. I believe she has passed quite a stiff exam."

"Without doubt. After all, it is very responsible work. I suppose they have very strong poisons there?"

"Yes, she showed them to us. They are kept locked up in a little cupboard. I believe they have to be very careful. They always take out the key before leaving the room."

"Indeed. It is near the window, this cupboard?"

"No, right the other side of the room. Why?"

Poirot shrugged his shoulders.

"I wondered. That is all. Will you come in?"

We had reached the cottage.

"No. I think I'll be getting back. I shall go round the long way through the woods."

The woods round Styles were very beautiful. After the walk across the open park, it was pleasant to saunter lazily through the cool glades. There was hardly a breath of wind, the very chirp of the birds was faint and subdued. I strolled on a little way, and finally flung myself down at the foot of a grand old beech tree. My thoughts of mankind were kindly and charitable. I even forgave Poirot for his absurd secrecy. In fact, I was at peace with the world. Then I yawned.

I thought about the crime, and it struck me as being very unreal and far off.

I yawned again.

Probably, I thought, it really never happened. Of course, it was all a bad dream. The truth of the matter was that it was Lawrence who had murdered Alfred Inglethorp with a croquet mallet. But it was absurd of John to make such a fuss about it, and to go shouting out: "I tell you I won't have it!"

I woke up with a start.

At once I realized that I was in a very awkward predicament. For, about twelve feet away from me John and Mary Cavendish were standing facing each other, and they were evidently quarrelling. And, quite as evidently, they were unaware of my vicinity, for before I could move or speak John repeated the words which had aroused me from my dream.

"I tell you, Mary, I won't have it."

Mary's voice came, cool and liquid:

"Have *you* any right to criticize my actions?"

"It will be the talk of the village! My mother was only buried on Saturday, and here you are gadding about with the fellow."

"Oh," she shrugged her shoulders, "if it is only village gossip that you mind!"

"But it isn't. I've had enough of the fellow hanging about. He's a Polish Jew, anyway."

"A tinge of Jewish blood is not a bad thing. It leavens the"—she looked at him—"stolid stupidity of the ordinary Englishman."

Fire in her eyes, ice in her voice. I did not wonder that the blood rose to John's face in a crimson tide.

"Mary!"

"Well?" Her tone did not change.

The pleading died out of his voice.

"Am I to understand that you will continue to see Bauerstein against my express wishes?"

"If I choose."

"You defy me?"

"No, but I deny your right to criticize my actions. Have *you* no friends of whom I should disapprove?"

John fell back a pace. The colour ebbed slowly from his face.

"What do you mean?" he said, in an unsteady voice.

"You see!" said Mary quietly. "You *do* see, don't you, that *you* have no right to dictate to *me* as to the choice of my friends?"

John glanced at her pleadingly, a stricken look on his face.

"No right? Have I *no* right, Mary?" he said unsteadily. He stretched out his hands. "Mary—"

For a moment, I thought she wavered. A softer expression came over her face, then suddenly she turned almost fiercely away.

"None!"

She was walking away when John sprang after her, and caught her by the arm.

"Mary"—his voice was very quiet now—"are you in love with this fellow Bauerstein?"

She hesitated, and suddenly there swept across her face a strange expression, old as the hills, yet with something eternally young about it. So might some Egyptian sphinx have smiled.

She freed herself quietly from his arm, and spoke over her shoulder.

"Perhaps," she said; and then swiftly passed out of the little glade, leaving John standing there as though he had been turned to stone.

Rather ostentatiously, I stepped forward, crackling some dead branches with my feet as I did so. John turned. Luckily, he took it for granted that I had only just come upon the scene.

"Hullo, Hastings. Have you seen the little fellow safely back to his cottage? Quaint little chap! Is he any good, though, really?"

"He was considered one of the finest detectives of his day."

"Oh, well, I suppose there must be something in it, then. What a rotten world it is, though!"

"You find it so?" I asked.

"Good Lord, yes! There's this terrible business to start with. Scotland Yard men in and out of the house like a jack-in-the-box! Never know where they won't turn up next. Screaming headlines in every paper in the country—damn all journalists, I say! Do you know there was a whole crowd staring in at the lodge gates this morning. Sort of Madame Tussaud's chamber of horrors business that can be seen for nothing. Pretty thick, isn't it?"

"Cheer up, John!" I said soothingly. "It can't last for ever."

"Can't it, though? It can last long enough for us never to be able to hold up our heads again."

"No, no, you're getting morbid on the subject."

"Enough to make a man morbid, to be stalked by beastly journalists and stared at by gaping moon-faced idiots, wherever he goes! But there's worse than that."

"What?"

John lowered his voice:

"Have you ever thought, Hastings—it's a nightmare to me—who did it? I can't help feeling sometimes it must have been an accident. Because—because—who could have done it? Now Inglethorp's out of the way, there's no one else; no one, I mean, except—one of us."

Yes, indeed, that was nightmare enough for any man! One of us? Yes, surely it must be so, unless—

A new idea suggested itself to my mind. Rapidly, I considered it. The light increased. Poirot's mysterious doings, his hints—they all fitted in. Fool that I was not to have thought of this possibility before, and what a relief for us all.

"No, John," I said, "it isn't one of us. How could it be?"

"I know, but, still, who else is there?"

"Can't you guess?"

"No."

I looked cautiously round, and lowered my voice.

"Dr. Bauerstein!" I whispered.

"Impossible!"

"Not at all."

"But what earthly interest could he have in my mother's death?"

"That I don't see," I confessed, "but I'll tell you this: Poirot thinks so."

"Poirot? Does he? How do you know?"

I told him of Poirot's intense excitement on hearing that Dr. Bauerstein had been at Styles on the fatal night, and added:

"He said twice: 'That alters everything.' And I've been thinking. You know Inglethorp said he had put down the coffee in the hall? Well, it was just then that Bauerstein arrived. Isn't it possible that, as Inglethorp brought him through the hall, the doctor dropped something into the coffee in passing?"

"H'm," said John. "It would have been very risky."

"Yes, but it was possible."

"And then, how could he know it was her coffee? No, old fellow, I don't think that will wash."

But I had remembered something else.

"You're quite right. That wasn't how it was done. Listen." And I then told him of the coco sample which Poirot had taken to be analysed.

John interrupted just as I had done.

"But, look here, Bauerstein had had it analysed already?"

"Yes, yes, that's the point. I didn't see it either until now. Don't you understand? Bauerstein had it analysed—that's just it! If Bauerstein's the murderer, nothing could be simpler than for him to substitute some ordinary coco for his sample, and send that to be tested. And of course they would find no strychnine! But no one would dream of suspecting Bauerstein, or think of taking another sample—except Poirot," I added, with belated recognition.

"Yes, but what about the bitter taste that coco won't disguise?"

"Well, we've only his word for that. And there are other possibilities. He's admittedly one of the world's greatest toxicologists—"

"One of the world's greatest what? Say it again."

"He knows more about poisons than almost anybody," I explained. "Well, my idea is, that perhaps he's found some way of making strychnine tasteless. Or it may not have been strychnine at all, but some obscure drug no one has ever heard of, which produces much the same symptoms."

"H'm, yes, that might be," said John. "But look here, how could he have got at the coco? That wasn't downstairs?"

"No, it wasn't," I admitted reluctantly.

And then, suddenly, a dreadful possibility flashed through my mind. I hoped and prayed it would not occur to John also. I glanced sideways at him. He was frowning perplexedly, and I drew a deep breath of relief, for the terrible thought that had flashed across my mind was this: that Dr. Bauerstein might have had an accomplice.

Yet surely it could not be! Surely no woman as beautiful as Mary Cavendish could be a murderess. Yet beautiful women had been known to poison.

And suddenly I remembered that first conversation at tea on the day of my arrival, and the gleam in her eyes as she had said that poison was a woman's weapon. How agitated she had been on that fatal Tuesday evening! Had Mrs. Inglethorp discovered something between her and Bauerstein, and threatened to tell her husband? Was it to stop that denunciation that the crime had been committed?

Then I remembered that enigmatical conversation between Poirot and Evelyn Howard. Was this what they had meant? Was this the monstrous possibility that Evelyn had tried not to believe?

Yes, it all fitted in.

No wonder Miss Howard had suggested "hushing it up." Now I understood that unfinished sentence of hers: "Emily herself——" And in my heart I agreed with her. Would not Mrs. Inglethorp have preferred to go unavenged rather than have such terrible dishonour fall upon the name of Cavendish.

"There's another thing," said John suddenly, and the unexpected sound of his voice made me start guiltily. "Something which makes me doubt if what you say can be true."

"What's that?" I asked, thankful that he had gone away from the subject of how the poison could have been introduced into the coco.

"Why, the fact that Bauerstein demanded a postmortem. He needn't have done so. Little Wilkins would have been quite content to let it go at heart disease."

"Yes," I said doubtfully. "But we don't know. Perhaps he thought it safer in the long run. Some one might have talked afterwards. Then the Home Office might have ordered exhumation. The whole thing would have come out, then, and he would have been in an awkward position, for no one would have believed that a man of his reputation could have been deceived into calling it heart disease."

"Yes, that's possible," admitted John. "Still," he added, "I'm blest if I can see what his motive could have been."

I trembled.

"Look here," I said, "I may be altogether wrong. And, remember, all this is in confidence."

"Oh, of course—that goes without saying."

We had walked, as we talked, and now we passed through the little gate into the garden. Voices rose near at hand, for tea was spread out under the sycamore tree, as it had been on the day of my arrival.

Cynthia was back from the hospital, and I placed my chair beside her, and told her of Poirot's wish to visit the dispensary.

"Of course! I'd love him to see it. He'd better come to tea there one day. I must fix it up with him. He's such a dear little man! But he *is* funny. He made me take the brooch out of my tie the other day, and put it in again, because he said it wasn't straight."

I laughed.

"It's quite a mania with him."

"Yes, isn't it?"

We were silent for a minute or two, and then, glancing in the direction of Mary Cavendish, and dropping her voice, Cynthia said:

"Mr. Hastings."

"Yes?"

"After tea, I want to talk to you."

Her glance at Mary had set me thinking. I fancied that between these two there existed very little sympathy. For the first time, it occurred to me to wonder about the girl's future. Mrs. Inglethorp had made no provisions of any kind for her, but I imagined that John and Mary would probably insist on her making her home with them—at any rate until the end of the war. John, I knew, was very fond of her, and would be sorry to let her go.

John, who had gone into the house, now reappeared. His good-natured face wore an unaccustomed frown of anger.

"Confound those detectives! I can't think what they're after! They've been in every room in the house—turning things inside out, and upside down. It really is too bad! I suppose they took advantage of our all being out. I shall go for that fellow Japp, when I next see him!"

"Lot of Paul Prys," grunted Miss Howard.

Lawrence opined that they had to make a show of doing something.

Mary Cavendish said nothing.

After tea, I invited Cynthia to come for a walk, and we sauntered off into the woods together.

"Well?" I inquired, as soon as we were protected from prying eyes by the leafy screen.

With a sigh, Cynthia flung herself down, and tossed off her hat. The sunlight, piercing through the branches, turned the auburn of her hair to quivering gold.

"Mr. Hastings—you are always so kind, and you know such a lot."

It struck me at this moment that Cynthia was really a very charming girl! Much more charming than Mary, who never said things of that kind.

"Well?" I asked benignantly, as she hesitated.

"I want to ask your advice. What shall I do?"

"Do?"

"Yes. You see, Aunt Emily always told me I should be provided for. I suppose she forgot, or didn't think she was likely to die—anyway, I am *not* provided for! And I don't know what to do. Do you think I ought to go away from here at once?"

"Good heavens, no! They don't want to part with you, I'm sure."

Cynthia hesitated a moment, plucking up the grass with her tiny hands. Then she said: "Mrs. Cavendish does. She hates me."

"Hates you?" I cried, astonished.

Cynthia nodded.

"Yes. I don't know why, but she can't bear me; and *he* can't, either."

"There I know you're wrong," I said warmly. "On the contrary, John is very fond of you."

"Oh, yes—*John*. I meant Lawrence. Not, of course, that I care whether Lawrence hates me or not. Still, it's rather horrid when no one loves you, isn't it?"

"But they do, Cynthia dear," I said earnestly. "I'm sure you are mistaken. Look, there is John—and Miss Howard—"

Cynthia nodded rather gloomily. "Yes, John likes me, I think, and of course Evie, for all her gruff ways, wouldn't be unkind to a fly. But Lawrence never speaks to me if he can help it, and Mary can hardly bring herself to be civil to me. She wants Evie to stay on, is begging her to, but she doesn't want me, and—and—I don't know what to do." Suddenly the poor child burst out crying.

I don't know what possessed me. Her beauty, perhaps, as she sat there, with the sunlight glinting down on her head; perhaps the sense of relief at encountering some-one who so obviously could have no connection with the tragedy; perhaps honest pity for her youth and loneliness. Anyway, I leant forward, and taking her little hand, I said awkwardly:

"Marry me, Cynthia."

Unwittingly, I had hit upon a sovereign remedy for her tears. She sat up at once, drew her hand away, and said, with some asperity:

"Don't be silly!"

I was a little annoyed.

"I'm not being silly. I am asking you to do me the honour of becoming my wife."

To my intense surprise, Cynthia burst out laughing, and called me a "funny dear."

"It's perfectly sweet of you," she said, "but you know you don't want to!"

"Yes, I do. I've got—"

"Never mind what you've got. You don't really want to—and I don't either."

"Well, of course, that settles it," I said stiffly. "But I don't see anything to laugh at. There's nothing funny about a proposal."

"No, indeed," said Cynthia. "Somebody might accept you next time. Good-bye, you've cheered me up *very* much."

And, with a final uncontrollable burst of merriment, she vanished through the trees.

Thinking over the interview, it struck me as being profoundly unsatisfactory.

It occurred to me suddenly that I would go down to the village, and look up Bauerstein. Somebody ought to be keeping an eye on the fellow. At the same time, it would be wise to allay any suspicions he might have as to his being suspected. I remembered how Poirot had relied on my diplomacy. Accordingly, I went to the little house with the "Apartments" card inserted in the window, where I knew he lodged, and tapped on the door.

An old woman came and opened it.

"Good afternoon," I said pleasantly. "Is Dr. Bauerstein in?"

She stared at me.

"Haven't you heard?"

"Heard what?"

"About him."

"What about him?"

"He's took."

"Took? Dead?"

"No, took by the perlice."

"By the police!" I gasped. "Do you mean they've arrested him?"

"Yes, that's it, and—"

I waited to hear no more, but tore up the village to find Poirot.

X. The Arrest

To my extreme annoyance, Poirot was not in, and the old Belgian who answered my knock informed me that he believed he had gone to London.

I was dumbfounded. What on earth could Poirot be doing in London! Was it a sudden decision on his part, or had he already made up his mind when he parted from me a few hours earlier?

I retraced my steps to Styles in some annoyance. With Poirot away, I was uncertain how to act. Had he foreseen this arrest? Had he not, in all probability, been the cause of it? Those questions I could not resolve. But in the meantime what was I to do? Should I announce the arrest openly at Styles, or not? Though I did not acknowledge it to myself, the thought of Mary Cavendish was weighing on me. Would it not be a terrible shock to her? For the moment, I set aside utterly any suspicions of her. She could not be implicated—otherwise I should have heard some hint of it.

Of course, there was no possibility of being able permanently to conceal Dr. Bauerstein's arrest from her. It would be announced in every newspaper on the morrow. Still, I shrank from blurting it out. If only Poirot had been accessible, I could have asked his advice. What possessed him to go posting off to London in this unaccountable way?

In spite of myself, my opinion of his sagacity was immeasurably heightened. I would never have dreamt of suspecting the doctor, had not Poirot put it into my head. Yes, decidedly, the little man was clever.

After some reflecting, I decided to take John into my confidence, and leave him to make the matter public or not, as he thought fit.

He gave vent to a prodigious whistle, as I imparted the news.

"Great Scot! You *were* right, then. I couldn't believe it at the time."

"No, it is astonishing until you get used to the idea, and see how it makes everything fit in. Now, what are we to do? Of course, it will be generally known tomorrow."

John reflected.

"Never mind," he said at last, "we won't say anything at present. There is no need. As you say, it will be known soon enough."

But to my intense surprise, on getting down early the next morning, and eagerly opening the newspapers, there was not a word about the arrest! There was a column of mere padding about "The Styles Poisoning Case," but nothing further. It was rather inexplicable, but I supposed that, for some reason or other, Japp wished to keep it out of the papers. It worried me just a little, for it suggested the possibility that there might be further arrests to come.

After breakfast, I decided to go down to the village, and see if Poirot had returned yet; but, before I could start, a well-known face blocked one of the windows, and the well-known voice said:

"*Bon jour, mon ami!*"

"Poirot," I exclaimed, with relief, and seizing him by both hands, I dragged him into the room. "I was never so glad to see anyone. Listen, I have said nothing to anybody but John. Is that right?"

"My friend," replied Poirot, "I do not know what you are talking about."

"Dr. Bauerstein's arrest, of course," I answered impatiently.

"Is Bauerstein arrested, then?"

"Did you not know it?"

"Not the least in the world." But, pausing a moment, he added: "Still, it does not surprise me. After all, we are only four miles from the coast."

"The coast?" I asked, puzzled. "What has that got to do with it?"

Poirot shrugged his shoulders.

"Surely, it is obvious!"

"Not to me. No doubt I am very dense, but I cannot see what the proximity of the coast has got to do with the murder of Mrs. Inglethorp."

"Nothing at all, of course," replied Poirot, smiling. "But we were speaking of the arrest of Dr. Bauerstein."

"Well, he is arrested for the murder of Mrs. Inglethorp—"

"What?" cried Poirot, in apparently lively astonishment. "Dr. Bauerstein arrested for the murder of Mrs. Inglethorp?"

"Yes."

"Impossible! That would be too good a farce! Who told you that, my friend?"

"Well, no one exactly told me," I confessed. "But he is arrested."

"Oh, yes, very likely. But for espionage, *mon ami*."

"Espionage?" I gasped.

"Precisely."

"Not for poisoning Mrs. Inglethorp?"

"Not unless our friend Japp has taken leave of his senses," replied Poirot placidly.

"But—but I thought you thought so too?"

Poirot gave me one look, which conveyed a wondering pity, and his full sense of the utter absurdity of such an idea.

"Do you mean to say," I asked, slowly adapting myself to the new idea, "that Dr. Bauerstein is a spy?"

Poirot nodded.

"Have you never suspected it?"

"It never entered my head."

"It did not strike you as peculiar that a famous London doctor should bury himself in a little village like this, and should be in the habit of walking about at all hours of the night, fully dressed?"

"No," I confessed, "I never thought of such a thing."

"He is, of course, a German by birth," said Poirot thoughtfully, "though he has practised so long in this country that nobody thinks of him as anything but an Englishman. He was naturalized about fifteen years ago. A very clever man."

"The blackguard!" I cried indignantly.

"Not at all. He is, on the contrary, a patriot. Think what he stands to lose. I admire the man myself."

But I could not look at it in Poirot's philosophical way.

"And this is the man with whom Mrs. Cavendish has been wandering about all over the country!" I cried indignantly.

"Yes. I should fancy he had found her very useful," remarked Poirot. "So long as gossip busied itself in coupling their names together, any other vagaries of the doctor's passed unobserved."

"Then you think he never really cared for her?" I asked eagerly—rather too eagerly, perhaps, under the circumstances.

"That, of course, I cannot say, but—shall I tell you my own private opinion, Hastings?"

"Yes."

"Well, it is this: that Mrs. Cavendish does not care, and never has cared one little jot about Dr. Bauerstein!"

"Do you really think so?" I could not disguise my pleasure.

"I am quite sure of it. And I will tell you why."

"Yes?"

"Because she cares for some one else, *mon ami.*"

"Oh!" What did he mean? In spite of myself, an agreeable warmth spread over me. I am not a vain man where women are concerned, but I remembered certain evidences, too lightly thought of at the time, perhaps, but which certainly seemed to indicate—

My pleasing thoughts were interrupted by the sudden entrance of Miss Howard. She glanced round hastily to make sure there was no one else in the room, and quickly produced an old sheet of brown paper. This she handed to Poirot, murmuring as she did so the cryptic words:

"On top of the wardrobe." Then she hurriedly left the room.

Poirot unfolded the sheet of paper eagerly, and uttered an exclamation of satisfaction. He spread it out on the table.

"Come here, Hastings. Now tell me, what is that initial—J. or L.?"

It was a medium sized sheet of paper, rather dusty, as though it had lain by for some time. But it was the label that was attracting Poirot's attention. At the top, it bore the printed stamp of Messrs. Parkson's, the well-known theatrical costumiers, and it was addressed to "—(the debatable initial) Cavendish, Esq., Styles Court, Styles St. Mary, Essex."

"It might be T., or it might be L.," I said, after studying the thing for a minute or two. "It certainly isn't a J."

"Good," replied Poirot, folding up the paper again. "I, also, am of your way of thinking. It is an L., depend upon it!"

"Where did it come from?" I asked curiously. "Is it important?"

"Moderately so. It confirms a surmise of mine. Having deduced its existence, I set Miss Howard to search for it, and, as you see, she has been successful."

"What did she mean by 'On the top of the wardrobe'?"

"She meant," replied Poirot promptly, "that she found it on top of a wardrobe."

"A funny place for a piece of brown paper," I mused.

"Not at all. The top of a wardrobe is an excellent place for brown paper and cardboard boxes. I have kept them there myself. Neatly arranged, there is nothing to offend the eye."

"Poirot," I asked earnestly, "have you made up your mind about this crime?"

"Yes—that is to say, I believe I know how it was committed."

"Ah!"

"Unfortunately, I have no proof beyond my surmise, unless—" With sudden energy, he caught me by the arm, and whirled me down the hall, calling out in French in his excitement: "Mademoiselle Dorcas, Mademoiselle Dorcas, *un moment, s'il vous plaît*!"

Dorcas, quite flurried by the noise, came hurrying out of the pantry.

"My good Dorcas, I have an idea—a little idea—if it should prove justified, what magnificent chance! Tell me, on Monday, not Tuesday, Dorcas, but Monday, the day before the tragedy, did anything go wrong with Mrs. Inglethorp's bell?"

Dorcas looked very surprised.

"Yes, sir, now you mention it, it did; though I don't know how you came to hear of it. A mouse, or some such, must have nibbled the wire through. The man came and put it right on Tuesday morning."

With a long drawn exclamation of ecstasy, Poirot led the way back to the morning-room.

"See you, one should not ask for outside proof—no, reason should be enough. But the flesh is weak, it is consolation to find that one is on the right track. Ah, my friend, I am like a giant refreshed. I run! I leap!"

And, in very truth, run and leap he did, gambolling wildly down the stretch of lawn outside the long window.

"What is your remarkable little friend doing?" asked a voice behind me, and I turned to find Mary Cavendish at my elbow. She smiled, and so did I. "What is it all about?"

"Really, I can't tell you. He asked Dorcas some question about a bell, and appeared so delighted with her answer that he is capering about as you see!"

Mary laughed.

"How ridiculous! He's going out of the gate. Isn't he coming back today?"

"I don't know. I've given up trying to guess what he'll do next."

"Is he quite mad, Mr. Hastings?"

"I honestly don't know. Sometimes, I feel sure he is as mad as a hatter; and then, just as he is at his maddest, I find there is method in his madness."

"I see."

In spite of her laugh, Mary was looking thoughtful this morning. She seemed grave, almost sad.

It occurred to me that it would be a good opportunity to tackle her on the subject of Cynthia. I began rather tactfully, *I* thought, but I had not gone far before she stopped me authoritatively.

"You are an excellent advocate, I have no doubt, Mr. Hastings, but in this case your talents are quite thrown away. Cynthia will run no risk of encountering any unkindness from me."

I began to stammer feebly that I hoped she hadn't thought— But again she stopped me, and her words were so unexpected that they quite drove Cynthia, and her troubles out of my mind.

"Mr. Hastings," she said, "do you think I and my husband are happy together?"

I was considerably taken aback, and murmured something about it's not being my business to think anything of the sort.

"Well," she said quietly, "whether it is your business or not, I will tell you that we are *not* happy."

I said nothing, for I saw that she had not finished.

She began slowly, walking up and down the room, her head a little bent, and that slim, supple figure of hers swaying gently as she walked. She stopped suddenly, and looked up at me.

"You don't know anything about me, do you?" she asked. "Where I come from, who I was before I married John—anything, in fact? Well, I will tell you. I will make a father confessor of you. You are kind, I think—yes, I am sure you are kind."

Somehow, I was not quite as elated as I might have been. I remembered that Cynthia had begun her confidences in much the same way. Besides, a father confessor should be elderly, it is not at all the rôle for a young man.

"My father was English," said Mrs. Cavendish, "but my mother was a Russian."

"Ah," I said, "now I understand—"

"Understand what?"

"A hint of something foreign—different—that there has always been about you."

"My mother was very beautiful, I believe. I don't know, because I never saw her. She died when I was quite a little child. I believe there was some tragedy connected with her death—she took an overdose of some sleeping draught by mistake. However that may be, my father was broken-hearted. Shortly afterwards, he went into the Consular Service. Everywhere he went, I went with him. When I was twenty-three, I had been nearly all over the world. It was a splendid life—I loved it."

There was a smile on her face, and her head was thrown back. She seemed living in the memory of those old glad days.

"Then my father died. He left me very badly off. I had to go and live with some old aunts in Yorkshire." She shuddered. "You will understand me when I say that it was a deadly life for a girl brought up as I had been. The narrowness, the deadly monotony of it, almost drove me mad." She paused a minute, and added in a different tone: "And then I met John Cavendish."

"Yes?"

"You can imagine that, from my aunts' point of view, it was a very good match for me. But I can honestly say it was not this fact which weighed with me. No, he was simply a way of escape from the insufferable monotony of my life."

I said nothing, and after a moment, she went on:

"Don't misunderstand me. I was quite honest with him. I told him, what was true, that I liked him very much, that I hoped to come to like him more, but that I was not in any way what the world calls 'in love' with him. He declared that that satisfied him, and so—we were married."

She waited a long time, a little frown had gathered on her forehead. She seemed to be looking back earnestly into those past days.

"I think—I am sure—he cared for me at first. But I suppose we were not well matched. Almost at once, we drifted apart. He—it is not a pleasing thing for my pride, but it is the truth—tired of me very soon." I must have made some murmur of dissent, for she went on quickly: "Oh, yes, he did! Not that it matters now—now that we've come to the parting of the ways."

"What do you mean?"

She answered quietly:

"I mean that I am not going to remain at Styles."

"You and John are not going to live here?"

"John may live here, but I shall not."

"You are going to leave him?"

"Yes."

"But why?"

She paused a long time, and said at last:

"Perhaps—because I want to be—free!"

And, as she spoke, I had a sudden vision of broad spaces, virgin tracts of forests, untrodden lands—and a realization of what freedom would mean to such a nature as Mary Cavendish. I seemed to see her for a moment as she was, a proud wild creature, as untamed by civilization as some shy bird of the hills. A little cry broke from her lips:

"You don't know, you don't know, how this hateful place has been prison to me!"

"I understand," I said, "but—but don't do anything rash."

"Oh, rash!" Her voice mocked at my prudence.

Then suddenly I said a thing I could have bitten out my tongue for:

"You know that Dr. Bauerstein has been arrested?"

An instant coldness passed like a mask over her face, blotting out all expression.

"John was so kind as to break that to me this morning."

"Well, what do you think?" I asked feebly.

"Of what?"

"Of the arrest?"

"What should I think? Apparently he is a German spy; so the gardener had told John."

Her face and voice were absolutely cold and expressionless. Did she care, or did she not?

She moved away a step or two, and fingered one of the flower vases.

"These are quite dead. I must do them again. Would you mind moving—thank you, Mr. Hastings." And she walked quietly past me out of the window, with a cool little nod of dismissal.

No, surely she could not care for Bauerstein. No woman could act her part with that icy unconcern.

Poirot did not make his appearance the following morning, and there was no sign of the Scotland Yard men.

But, at lunchtime, there arrived a new piece of evidence or rather lack of evidence. We had vainly tried to trace the fourth letter, which Mrs. Inglethorp had written on the evening preceding her death. Our efforts having been in vain, we had abandoned the matter, hoping that it might turn up of itself one day. And this is just what did happen, in the shape of a communication, which arrived by the second post from a firm of French music publishers, acknowledging Mrs. Inglethorp's cheque, and regretting they had been unable to trace a certain series of Russian folk songs. So the last hope of solving the mystery, by means of Mrs. Inglethorp's correspondence on the fatal evening, had to be abandoned.

Just before tea, I strolled down to tell Poirot of the new disappointment, but found, to my annoyance, that he was once more out.

"Gone to London again?"

"Oh, no, monsieur, he has but taken the train to Tadminster. 'To see a young lady's dispensary,' he said."

"Silly ass!" I ejaculated. "I told him Wednesday was the one day she wasn't there! Well, tell him to look us up tomorrow morning, will you?"

"Certainly, monsieur."

But, on the following day, no sign of Poirot. I was getting angry. He was really treating us in the most cavalier fashion.

After lunch, Lawrence drew me aside, and asked if I was going down to see him.

"No, I don't think I shall. He can come up here if he wants to see us."

"Oh!" Lawrence looked indeterminate. Something unusually nervous and excited in his manner roused my curiosity.

"What is it?" I asked. "I could go if there's anything special."

"It's nothing much, but—well, if you are going, will you tell him—" he dropped his voice to a whisper—"I think I've found the extra coffee cup!"

I had almost forgotten that enigmatical message of Poirot's, but now my curiosity was aroused afresh.

Lawrence would say no more, so I decided that I would descend from my high horse, and once more seek out Poirot at Leastways Cottage.

This time I was received with a smile. Monsieur Poirot was within. Would I mount? I mounted accordingly.

Poirot was sitting by the table, his head buried in his hands. He sprang up at my entrance.

"What is it?" I asked solicitously. "You are not ill, I trust?"

"No, no, not ill. But I decide an affair of great moment."

"Whether to catch the criminal or not?" I asked facetiously.

But, to my great surprise, Poirot nodded gravely.

"'To speak or not to speak,' as your so great Shakespeare says, 'that is the question.'"

I did not trouble to correct the quotation.

"You are not serious, Poirot?"

"I am of the most serious. For the most serious of all things hangs in the balance."

"And that is?"

"A woman's happiness, *mon ami*," he said gravely.

I did not quite know what to say.

"The moment has come," said Poirot thoughtfully, "and I do not know what to do. For, see you, it is a big stake for which I play. No one but I, Hercule Poirot, would attempt it!" And he tapped himself proudly on the breast.

After pausing a few minutes respectfully, so as not to spoil his effect, I gave him Lawrence's message.

"Aha!" he cried. "So he has found the extra coffee cup. That is good. He has more intelligence than would appear, this long-faced Monsieur Lawrence of yours!"

I did not myself think very highly of Lawrence's intelligence; but I forebore to contradict Poirot, and gently took him to task for forgetting my instructions as to which were Cynthia's days off.

"It is true. I have the head of a sieve. However, the other young lady was most kind. She was sorry for my disappointment, and showed me everything in the kindest way."

"Oh, well, that's all right, then, and you must go to tea with Cynthia another day."

I told him about the letter.

"I am sorry for that," he said. "I always had hopes of that letter. But no, it was not to be. This affair must all be unravelled from within." He tapped his forehead. "These little grey cells. It is 'up to them'—as you say over here." Then, suddenly, he asked: "Are you a judge of finger-marks, my friend?"

"No," I said, rather surprised, "I know that there are no two finger-marks alike, but that's as far as my science goes."

"Exactly."

He unlocked a little drawer, and took out some photographs which he laid on the table.

"I have numbered them, 1, 2, 3. Will you describe them to me?"

I studied the proofs attentively.

"All greatly magnified, I see. No. 1, I should say, are a man's finger-prints; thumb and first finger. No. 2 are a lady's; they are much smaller, and quite different in every way. No. 3"—I paused for some time—"there seem to be a lot of confused finger-marks, but here, very distinctly, are No. 1's."

"Overlapping the others?"

"Yes."

"You recognize them beyond fail?"

"Oh, yes; they are identical."

Poirot nodded, and gently taking the photographs from me locked them up again.

"I suppose," I said, "that as usual, you are not going to explain?"

"On the contrary. No. 1 were the finger-prints of Monsieur Lawrence. No. 2 were those of Mademoiselle Cynthia. They are not important. I merely obtained them for comparison. No. 3 is a little more complicated."

"Yes?"

"It is, as you see, highly magnified. You may have noticed a sort of blur extending all across the picture. I will not describe to you the special apparatus, dusting powder, etc., which I used. It is a well known process to the police, and by means of it you can obtain a photograph of the fingerprints of any object in a very short space of time. Well, my friend, you have seen the finger-marks—it remains to tell you the particular object on which they had been left."

"Go on—I am really excited."

"*Eh bien!* Photo No. 3 represents the highly magnified surface of a tiny bottle in the top poison cupboard of the dispensary in the Red Cross Hospital at Tadminster—which sounds like the house that Jack built!"

"Good heavens!" I exclaimed. "But what were Lawrence Cavendish's finger-marks doing on it? He never went near the poison cupboard the day we were there?"

"Oh, yes, he did!"

"Impossible! We were all together the whole time."

Poirot shook his head.

"No, my friend, there was a moment when you were not all together. There was a moment when you could not have been all together, or it would not have been necessary to call to Monsieur Lawrence to come and join you on the balcony."

"I'd forgotten that," I admitted. "But it was only for a moment."

"Long enough."

"Long enough for what?"

Poirot's smile became rather enigmatical.

"Long enough for a gentleman who had once studied medicine to gratify a very natural interest and curiosity."

Our eyes met. Poirot's were pleasantly vague. He got up and hummed a little tune. I watched him suspiciously.

"Poirot," I said, "what was in this particular little bottle?"

Poirot looked out of the window.

"Hydrochloride of strychnine," he said, over his shoulder, continuing to hum.

"Good heavens!" I said it quite quietly. I was not surprised. I had expected that answer.

"They use the pure hydrochloride of strychnine very little—only occasionally for pills. It is the official solution, Liq. Strychnine Hydroclor. that is used in most medicines. That is why the finger-marks have remained undisturbed since then."

"How did you manage to take this photograph?"

"I dropped my hat from the balcony," explained Poirot simply. "Visitors were not permitted below at that hour, so, in spite of my many apologies, Mademoiselle Cynthia's colleague had to go down and fetch it for me."

"Then you knew what you were going to find?"

"No, not at all. I merely realized that it was possible, from your story, for Monsieur Lawrence to go to the poison cupboard. The possibility had to be confirmed, or eliminated."

"Poirot," I said, "your gaiety does not deceive me. This is a very important discovery."

"I do not know," said Poirot. "But one thing does strike me. No doubt it has struck you too."

"What is that?"

"Why, that there is altogether too much strychnine about this case. This is the third time we run up against it. There was strychnine in Mrs. Inglethorp's tonic. There is the strychnine sold across the counter at Styles St. Mary by Mace. Now we have more strychnine, handled by one of the household. It is confusing; and, as you know, I do not like confusion."

Before I could reply, one of the other Belgians opened the door and stuck his head in.

"There is a lady below, asking for Mr. Hastings."

"A lady?"

I jumped up. Poirot followed me down the narrow stairs. Mary Cavendish was standing in the doorway.

"I have been visiting an old woman in the village," she explained, "and as Lawrence told me you were with Monsieur Poirot I thought I would call for you."

"Alas, madame," said Poirot, "I thought you had come to honour me with a visit!"

"I will some day, if you ask me," she promised him, smiling.

"That is well. If you should need a father confessor, madame"—she started ever so slightly—"remember, Papa Poirot is always at your service."

She stared at him for a few minutes, as though seeking to read some deeper meaning into his words. Then she turned abruptly away.

"Come, will you not walk back with us too, Monsieur Poirot?"

"Enchanted, madame."

All the way to Styles, Mary talked fast and feverishly. It struck me that in some way she was nervous of Poirot's eyes.

The weather had broken, and the sharp wind was almost autumnal in its shrewishness. Mary shivered a little, and buttoned her black sports coat closer. The wind through the trees made a mournful noise, like some great giant sighing.

We walked up to the great door of Styles, and at once the knowledge came to us that something was wrong.

Dorcas came running out to meet us. She was crying and wringing her hands. I was aware of other servants huddled together in the background, all eyes and ears.

"Oh, m'am; oh, m'am! I don't know how to tell you—"

"What is it, Dorcas?" I asked impatiently. "Tell us at once."

"It's those wicked detectives. They've arrested him—they've arrested Mr. Cavendish!"

"Arrested Lawrence?" I gasped.

I saw a strange look come into Dorcas's eyes.

"No, sir. Not Mr. Lawrence—Mr. John."

Behind me, with a wild cry, Mary Cavendish fell heavily against me, and as I turned to catch her I met the quiet triumph in Poirot's eyes.

XI. THE CASE FOR THE PROSECUTION

The trial of John Cavendish for the murder of his stepmother took place two months later.

Of the intervening weeks I will say little, but my admiration and sympathy went out unfeignedly to Mary Cavendish. She ranged herself passionately on her husband's side, scorning the mere idea of his guilt, and fought for him tooth and nail.

I expressed my admiration to Poirot, and he nodded thoughtfully.

"Yes, she is of those women who show at their best in adversity. It brings out all that is sweetest and truest in them. Her pride and her jealousy have—"

"Jealousy?" I queried.

"Yes. Have you not realized that she is an unusually jealous woman? As I was saying, her pride and jealousy have been laid aside. She thinks of nothing but her husband, and the terrible fate that is hanging over him."

He spoke very feelingly, and I looked at him earnestly, remembering that last afternoon, when he had been deliberating whether or no to speak. With his tenderness for "a woman's happiness," I felt glad that the decision had been taken out of his hands.

"Even now," I said, "I can hardly believe it. You see, up to the very last minute, I thought it was Lawrence!"

Poirot grinned.

"I know you did."

"But John! My old friend John!"

"Every murderer is probably somebody's old friend," observed Poirot philosophically. "You cannot mix up sentiment and reason."

"I must say I think you might have given me a hint."

"Perhaps, *mon ami*, I did not do so, just because he *was* your old friend."

I was rather disconcerted by this, remembering how I had busily passed on to John what I believed to be Poirot's views concerning Bauerstein. He, by the way, had been acquitted of the charge brought against him. Nevertheless, although he had been too clever for them this time, and the charge of espionage could not be brought home to him, his wings were pretty well clipped for the future.

I asked Poirot whether he thought John would be condemned. To my intense surprise, he replied that, on the contrary, he was extremely likely to be acquitted.

"But, Poirot——" I protested.

"Oh, my friend, have I not said to you all along that I have no proofs. It is one thing to know that a man is guilty, it is quite another matter to prove him so. And, in this case, there is terribly little evidence. That is the whole trouble. I, Hercule Poirot, know, but I lack the last link in my chain. And unless I can find that missing link——" He shook his head gravely.

"When did you first suspect John Cavendish?" I asked, after a minute or two.

"Did you not suspect him at all?"

"No, indeed."

"Not after that fragment of conversation you overheard between Mrs. Cavendish and her mother-in-law, and her subsequent lack of frankness at the inquest?"

"No."

"Did you not put two and two together, and reflect that if it was not Alfred Inglethorp who was quarrelling with his wife—and you remember, he strenuously denied it at the inquest—it must be either Lawrence or John. Now, if it was Lawrence, Mary Cavendish's conduct was just as inexplicable. But if, on the other hand, it was John, the whole thing was explained quite naturally."

"So," I cried, a light breaking in upon me, "it was John who quarrelled with his mother that afternoon?"

"Exactly."

"And you have known this all along?"

"Certainly. Mrs. Cavendish's behaviour could only be explained that way."

"And yet you say he may be acquitted?"

Poirot shrugged his shoulders.

"Certainly I do. At the police court proceedings, we shall hear the case for the prosecution, but in all probability his solicitors will advise him to reserve his defence. That will be sprung upon us at the trial. And—ah, by the way, I have a word of caution to give you, my friend. I must not appear in the case."

"What?"

"No. Officially, I have nothing to do with it. Until I have found that last link in my chain, I must remain behind the scenes. Mrs. Cavendish must think I am working for her husband, not against him."

"I say, that's playing it a bit low down," I protested.

"Not at all. We have to deal with a most clever and unscrupulous man, and we must use any means in our power—otherwise he will slip through our fingers. That is why I have been careful to remain in the background. All the discoveries have been made by Japp, and Japp will take all the credit. If I am called upon to give evidence at all"—he smiled broadly—"it will probably be as a witness for the defence."

I could hardly believe my ears.

"It is quite *en règle*," continued Poirot. "Strangely enough, I can give evidence that will demolish one contention of the prosecution."

"Which one?"

"The one that relates to the destruction of the will. John Cavendish did not destroy that will."

Poirot was a true prophet. I will not go into the details of the police court proceedings, as it involves many tiresome repetitions. I will merely state baldly that John Cavendish reserved his defence, and was duly committed for trial.

September found us all in London. Mary took a house in Kensington, Poirot being included in the family party.

I myself had been given a job at the War Office, so was able to see them continually.

As the weeks went by, the state of Poirot's nerves grew worse and worse. That "last link" he talked about was still lacking. Privately, I hoped it might remain so, for what happiness could there be for Mary, if John were not acquitted?

On September 15th John Cavendish appeared in the dock at the Old Bailey, charged with "The Wilful Murder of Emily Agnes Inglethorp," and pleaded "Not Guilty."

Sir Ernest Heavywether, the famous K. C., had been engaged to defend him.

Mr. Philips, K. C., opened the case for the Crown.

The murder, he said, was a most premeditated and cold-blooded one. It was neither more nor less than the deliberate poisoning of a fond and trusting woman by the stepson to whom she had been more than a mother. Ever since his boyhood, she had supported him. He and his wife had lived at Styles Court in every luxury, surrounded by her care and attention. She had been their kind and generous benefactress.

He proposed to call witnesses to show how the prisoner, a profligate and spendthrift, had been at the end of his financial tether, and had also been carrying on an intrigue with a certain Mrs. Raikes, a neighbouring farmer's wife. This having come to his stepmother's ears, she taxed him with it on the afternoon before her death, and a quarrel ensued, part of which was overheard. On the previous day, the prisoner had purchased strychnine at the village chemist's shop, wearing a disguise by means of which he hoped to throw the onus of the crime upon another man—to wit, Mrs. Inglethorp's husband, of whom he had been bitterly jealous. Luckily for Mr. Inglethorp, he had been able to produce an unimpeachable alibi.

On the afternoon of July 17th, continued Counsel, immediately after the quarrel with her son, Mrs. Inglethorp made a new will. This will was found destroyed in the grate of her bedroom the following morning, but evidence had come to light which showed that it had been drawn up in favour of her husband. Deceased had already made a will in his favour before her marriage, but—and Mr. Philips wagged an expressive forefinger—the prisoner was not aware of that. What had induced the deceased to make a fresh will, with the old one still extant, he could not say. She was old lady, and might possibly have forgotten the former one; or—this seemed to him more likely—she may have had an idea that it was revoked by her marriage, as there had been some conversation on the subject. Ladies were not always very well versed in legal knowledge. She had, about a year before, executed a will in favour of the prisoner. He would call evidence to show that it was the prisoner who ultimately handed his stepmother her coffee on the fatal night. Later in the evening, he had sought admission to her room, on which occasion, no doubt, he found an opportunity of destroying the will which, as far as he knew, would render the one in his favour valid.

The prisoner had been arrested in consequence of the discovery, in his room, by Detective Inspector Japp—a most brilliant officer—of the identical phial of strychnine which had been sold at the village chemist's to the supposed Mr. Inglethorp on the day before the murder. It would be for the jury to decide whether or not these damning facts constituted an overwhelming proof of the prisoner's guilt.

And, subtly implying that a jury which did not so decide, was quite unthinkable, Mr. Philips sat down and wiped his forehead.

The first witnesses for the prosecution were mostly those who had been called at the inquest, the medical evidence being again taken first.

Sir Ernest Heavywether, who was famous all over England for the unscrupulous manner in which he bullied witnesses, only asked two questions.

"I take it, Dr. Bauerstein, that strychnine, as a drug, acts quickly?"

"Yes."

"And that you are unable to account for the delay in this case?"

"Yes."

"Thank you."

Mr. Mace identified the phial handed him by Counsel as that sold by him to "Mr. Inglethorp." Pressed, he admitted that he only knew Mr. Inglethorp by sight. He had never spoken to him. The witness was not cross-examined.

Alfred Inglethorp was called, and denied having purchased the poison. He also denied having quarrelled with his wife. Various witnesses testified to the accuracy of these statements.

The gardeners' evidence, as to the witnessing of the will was taken, and then Dorcas was called.

Dorcas, faithful to her "young gentlemen," denied strenuously that it could have been John's voice she heard, and resolutely declared, in the teeth of everything, that it was Mr. Inglethorp who had been in the boudoir with her mistress. A rather wistful smile passed across the face of the prisoner in the dock. He knew only too well how useless her gallant defiance was, since it was not the object of the defence to deny this point. Mrs. Cavendish, of course, could not be called upon to give evidence against her husband.

After various questions on other matters, Mr. Philips asked:

"In the month of June last, do you remember a parcel arriving for Mr. Lawrence Cavendish from Parkson's?"

Dorcas shook her head.

"I don't remember, sir. It may have done, but Mr. Lawrence was away from home part of June."

"In the event of a parcel arriving for him whilst he was away, what would be done with it?"

"It would either be put in his room or sent on after him."

"By you?"

"No, sir, I should leave it on the hall table. It would be Miss Howard who would attend to anything like that."

Evelyn Howard was called and, after being examined on other points, was questioned as to the parcel.

"Don't remember. Lots of parcels come. Can't remember one special one."

"You do not know if it was sent after Mr. Lawrence Cavendish to Wales, or whether it was put in his room?"

"Don't think it was sent after him. Should have remembered it if it was."

"Supposing a parcel arrived addressed to Mr. Lawrence Cavendish, and afterwards it disappeared, should you remark its absence?"

"No, don't think so. I should think someone had taken charge of it."

"I believe, Miss Howard, that it was you who found this sheet of brown paper?" He held up the same dusty piece which Poirot and I had examined in the morning-room at Styles.

"Yes, I did."

"How did you come to look for it?"

"The Belgian detective who was employed on the case asked me to search for it."

"Where did you eventually discover it?"

"On the top of—of—a wardrobe."

"On top of the prisoner's wardrobe?"

"I—I believe so."

"Did you not find it yourself?"

"Yes."

"Then you must know where you found it?"

"Yes, it was on the prisoner's wardrobe."

"That is better."

An assistant from Parkson's, Theatrical Costumiers, testified that on June 29th, they had supplied a black beard to Mr. L. Cavendish, as requested. It was ordered by letter, and a postal order was enclosed. No, they had not kept the letter. All transactions were entered in their books. They had sent the beard, as directed, to "L. Cavendish, Esq., Styles Court."

Sir Ernest Heavywether rose ponderously.

"Where was the letter written from?"

"From Styles Court."

"The same address to which you sent the parcel?"

"Yes."

"And the letter came from there?"

"Yes."

Like a beast of prey, Heavywether fell upon him:

"How do you know?"

"I—I don't understand."

"How do you know that letter came from Styles? Did you notice the postmark?"

"No—but—"

"Ah, you did *not* notice the postmark! And yet you affirm so confidently that it came from Styles. It might, in fact, have been any postmark?"

"Y—es."

"In fact, the letter, though written on stamped notepaper, might have been posted from anywhere? From Wales, for instance?"

The witness admitted that such might be the case, and Sir Ernest signified that he was satisfied.

Elizabeth Wells, second housemaid at Styles, stated that after she had gone to bed she remembered that she had bolted the front door, instead of leaving it on the latch as Mr. Inglethorp had requested. She had accordingly gone downstairs again to rectify her error. Hearing a slight noise in the West wing, she had peeped along the passage, and had seen Mr. John Cavendish knocking at Mrs. Inglethorp's door.

Sir Ernest Heavywether made short work of her, and under his unmerciful bullying she contradicted herself hopelessly, and Sir Ernest sat down again with a satisfied smile on his face.

With the evidence of Annie, as to the candle grease on the floor, and as to seeing the prisoner take the coffee into the boudoir, the proceedings were adjourned until the following day.

As we went home, Mary Cavendish spoke bitterly against the prosecuting counsel.

"That hateful man! What a net he has drawn around my poor John! How he twisted every little fact until he made it seem what it wasn't!"

"Well," I said consolingly, "it will be the other way about tomorrow."

"Yes," she said meditatively; then suddenly dropped her voice. "Mr. Hastings, you do not think—surely it could not have been Lawrence—Oh, no, that could not be!"

But I myself was puzzled, and as soon as I was alone with Poirot I asked him what he thought Sir Ernest was driving at.

"Ah!" said Poirot appreciatively. "He is a clever man, that Sir Ernest."

"Do you think he believes Lawrence guilty?"

"I do not think he believes or cares anything! No, what he is trying for is to create such confusion in the minds of the jury that they are divided in their opinion as to which brother did it. He is endeavouring to make out that there is quite as much evidence against Lawrence as against John—and I am not at all sure that he will not succeed."

Detective-Inspector Japp was the first witness called when the trial was reopened, and gave his evidence succinctly and briefly. After relating the earlier events, he proceeded:

"Acting on information received, Superintendent Summerhaye and myself searched the prisoner's room, during his temporary absence from the house. In his chest of drawers, hidden beneath some underclothing, we found: first, a pair of gold-rimmed pince-nez similar to those worn by Mr. Inglethorp"—these were exhibited—"secondly, this phial."

The phial was that already recognized by the chemist's assistant, a tiny bottle of blue glass, containing a few grains of a white crystalline powder, and labelled: "Strychnine Hydrochloride. POISON."

A fresh piece of evidence discovered by the detectives since the police court proceedings was a long, almost new piece of blotting-paper. It had been found in Mrs. Inglethorp's cheque book, and on being reversed at a mirror, showed clearly the words: ". . . erything of which I die possessed I leave to my beloved husband Alfred Ing . . ." This placed beyond question the fact that the destroyed will had been in favour of the deceased lady's husband. Japp then produced the charred fragment of paper recovered from the grate, and this, with the discovery of the beard in the attic, completed his evidence.

But Sir Ernest's cross-examination was yet to come.

"What day was it when you searched the prisoner's room?"

"Tuesday, the 24th of July."

"Exactly a week after the tragedy?"

"Yes."

"You found these two objects, you say, in the chest of drawers. Was the drawer unlocked?"

"Yes."

"Does it not strike you as unlikely that a man who had committed a crime should keep the evidence of it in an unlocked drawer for anyone to find?"

"He might have stowed them there in a hurry."

"But you have just said it was a whole week since the crime. He would have had ample time to remove them and destroy them."

"Perhaps."

"There is no perhaps about it. Would he, or would he not have had plenty of time to remove and destroy them?"

"Yes."

"Was the pile of underclothes under which the things were hidden heavy or light?"

"Heavyish."

"In other words, it was winter underclothing. Obviously, the prisoner would not be likely to go to that drawer?"

"Perhaps not."

"Kindly answer my question. Would the prisoner, in the hottest week of a hot summer, be likely to go to a drawer containing winter underclothing. Yes, or no?"

"No."

"In that case, is it not possible that the articles in question might have been put there by a third person, and that the prisoner was quite unaware of their presence?"

"I should not think it likely."

"But it is possible?"

"Yes."

"That is all."

More evidence followed. Evidence as to the financial difficulties in which the prisoner had found himself at the end of July. Evidence as to his intrigue with Mrs. Raikes—poor Mary, that must have been bitter hearing for a woman of her pride. Evelyn Howard had been right in her facts, though her animosity against Alfred Inglethorp had caused her to jump to the conclusion that he was the person concerned.

Lawrence Cavendish was then put into the box. In a low voice, in answer to Mr. Philips's questions, he denied having ordered anything from Parkson's in June. In fact, on June 29th, he had been staying away, in Wales.

Instantly, Sir Ernest's chin was shooting pugnaciously forward.

"You deny having ordered a black beard from Parkson's on June 29th?"

"I do."

"Ah! In the event of anything happening to your brother, who will inherit Styles Court?"

The brutality of the question called a flush to Lawrence's pale face. The judge gave vent to a faint murmur of disapprobation, and the prisoner in the dock leant forward angrily.

Heavywether cared nothing for his client's anger.

"Answer my question, if you please."

"I suppose," said Lawrence quietly, "that I should."

"What do you mean by you 'suppose'? Your brother has no children. You *would* inherit it, wouldn't you?"

"Yes."

"Ah, that's better," said Heavywether, with ferocious geniality. "And you'd inherit a good slice of money too, wouldn't you?"

"Really, Sir Ernest," protested the judge, "these questions are not relevant."

Sir Ernest bowed, and having shot his arrow proceeded.

"On Tuesday, the 17th July, you went, I believe, with another guest, to visit the dispensary at the Red Cross Hospital in Tadminster?"

"Yes."

"Did you—while you happened to be alone for a few seconds—unlock the poison cupboard, and examine some of the bottles?"

"I—I—may have done so."

"I put it to you that you did do so?"

"Yes."

Sir Ernest fairly shot the next question at him.

"Did you examine one bottle in particular?"

"No, I do not think so."

"Be careful, Mr. Cavendish. I am referring to a little bottle of Hydrochloride of Strychnine."

Lawrence was turning a sickly greenish colour.

"N—o—I am sure I didn't."

"Then how do you account for the fact that you left the unmistakable impress of your fingerprints on it?"

The bullying manner was highly efficacious with a nervous disposition.

"I—I suppose I must have taken up the bottle."

"I suppose so too! Did you abstract any of the contents of the bottle?"

"Certainly not."

"Then why did you take it up?"

"I once studied to be a doctor. Such things naturally interest me."

"Ah! So poisons 'naturally interest' you, do they? Still, you waited to be alone before gratifying that 'interest' of yours?"

"That was pure chance. If the others had been there, I should have done just the same."

"Still, as it happens, the others were not there?"

"No, but—"

"In fact, during the whole afternoon, you were only alone for a couple of minutes, and it happened—I say, it happened—to be during those two minutes that you displayed your 'natural interest' in Hydrochloride of Strychnine?"

Lawrence stammered pitiably.

"I—I—"

With a satisfied and expressive countenance, Sir Ernest observed:

"I have nothing more to ask you, Mr. Cavendish."

This bit of cross-examination had caused great excitement in court. The heads of the many fashionably attired women present were busily laid together, and their whispers became so loud that the judge angrily threatened to have the court cleared if there was not immediate silence.

There was little more evidence. The handwriting experts were called upon for their opinion of the signature of "Alfred Inglethorp" in the chemist's poison register. They all declared unanimously that it was certainly not his handwriting, and gave it as their view that it might be that of the prisoner disguised. Cross-examined, they admitted that it might be the prisoner's handwriting cleverly counterfeited.

Sir Ernest Heavywether's speech in opening the case for the defence was not a long one, but it was backed by the full force of his emphatic manner. Never, he said, in the course of his long experience, had he known a charge of murder rest on slighter evidence. Not only was it entirely circumstantial, but the greater part of it was practically unproved. Let them take the testimony they had heard and sift it impartially. The strychnine had been found in a drawer in the prisoner's room. That drawer was an unlocked one, as he had pointed out, and he submitted that there was no evidence to prove that it was the prisoner who had concealed the poison there. It was, in fact, a wicked and malicious attempt on the part of some third person to fix the crime on the prisoner. The prosecution had been unable to produce a shred of evidence in support of their contention that it was the prisoner who ordered the black beard from Parkson's. The quarrel which had taken place between prisoner and his stepmother was freely admitted, but both it and his financial embarrassments had been grossly exaggerated.

His learned friend—Sir Ernest nodded carelessly at Mr. Philips—had stated that if prisoner were an innocent man, he would have come forward at the inquest to explain that it was he, and not Mr. Inglethorp, who had been the participator in the quarrel. He thought the facts had been misrepresented. What had actually occurred was this. The prisoner, returning to the house on Tuesday evening, had been authoritatively told that there had been a violent quarrel between Mr. and Mrs. Inglethorp. No suspicion had entered the prisoner's head that anyone could possibly have mistaken his voice for that of Mr. Inglethorp. He naturally concluded that his stepmother had had two quarrels.

The prosecution averred that on Monday, July 16th, the prisoner had entered the chemist's shop in the village, disguised as Mr. Inglethorp. The prisoner, on the contrary, was at that time at a lonely spot called Marston's Spinney, where he had been summoned by an anonymous note, couched in blackmailing terms, and threatening to reveal certain matters to his wife unless he complied with its demands. The prisoner had, accordingly, gone to the appointed spot, and after waiting there vainly for half an hour had returned home. Unfortunately, he had met with no one on the way there or back who could vouch for the truth of his story, but luckily he had kept the note, and it would be produced as evidence.

As for the statement relating to the destruction of the will, the prisoner had formerly practised at the Bar, and was perfectly well aware that the will made in his favour a year before was automatically revoked by his stepmother's remarriage. He would call evidence to show who did destroy the will, and it was possible that that might open up quite a new view of the case.

Finally, he would point out to the jury that there was evidence against other people besides John Cavendish. He would direct their attention to the fact that the evidence against Mr. Lawrence Cavendish was quite as strong, if not stronger than that against his brother.

He would now call the prisoner.

John acquitted himself well in the witness-box. Under Sir Ernest's skilful handling, he told his tale credibly and well. The anonymous note received by him was produced, and handed to the jury to examine. The readiness with which he admitted his financial difficulties, and the disagreement with his stepmother, lent value to his denials.

At the close of his examination, he paused, and said:

"I should like to make one thing clear. I utterly reject and disapprove of Sir Ernest Heavywether's insinuations against my brother. My brother, I am convinced, had no more to do with the crime than I have."

Sir Ernest merely smiled, and noted with a sharp eye that John's protest had produced a very favourable impression on the jury.

Then the cross-examination began.

"I understand you to say that it never entered your head that the witnesses at the inquest could possibly have mistaken your voice for that of Mr. Inglethorp. Is not that very surprising?"

"No, I don't think so. I was told there had been a quarrel between my mother and Mr. Inglethorp, and it never occurred to me that such was not really the case."

"Not when the servant Dorcas repeated certain fragments of the conversation— fragments which you must have recognized?"

"I did not recognize them."

"Your memory must be unusually short!"

"No, but we were both angry, and, I think, said more than we meant. I paid very little attention to my mother's actual words."

Mr. Philips's incredulous sniff was a triumph of forensic skill. He passed on to the subject of the note.

"You have produced this note very opportunely. Tell me, is there nothing familiar about the handwriting of it?"

"Not that I know of."

"Do you not think that it bears a marked resemblance to your own handwriting—carelessly disguised?"

"No, I do not think so."

"I put it to you that it is your own handwriting!"

"No."

"I put it to you that, anxious to prove an alibi, you conceived the idea of a fictitious and rather incredible appointment, and wrote this note yourself in order to bear out your statement!"

"No."

"Is it not a fact that, at the time you claim to have been waiting about at a solitary and unfrequented spot, you were really in the chemist's shop in Styles St. Mary, where you purchased strychnine in the name of Alfred Inglethorp?"

"No, that is a lie."

"I put it to you that, wearing a suit of Mr. Inglethorp's clothes, with a black beard trimmed to resemble his, you were there—and signed the register in his name!"

"That is absolutely untrue."

"Then I will leave the remarkable similarity of handwriting between the note, the register, and your own, to the consideration of the jury," said Mr. Philips, and sat down with the air of a man who has done his duty, but who was nevertheless horrified by such deliberate perjury.

After this, as it was growing late, the case was adjourned till Monday.

Poirot, I noticed, was looking profoundly discouraged. He had that little frown between the eyes that I knew so well.

"What is it, Poirot?" I inquired.

"Ah, *mon ami*, things are going badly, badly."

In spite of myself, my heart gave a leap of relief. Evidently there was a likelihood of John Cavendish being acquitted.

When we reached the house, my little friend waved aside Mary's offer of tea.

"No, I thank you, madame. I will mount to my room."

I followed him. Still frowning, he went across to the desk and took out a small pack of patience cards. Then he drew up a chair to the table, and, to my utter amazement, began solemnly to build card houses!

My jaw dropped involuntarily, and he said at once:

"No, *mon ami*, I am not in my second childhood! I steady my nerves, that is all. This employment requires precision of the fingers. With precision of the fingers goes precision of the brain. And never have I needed that more than now!"

"What is the trouble?" I asked.

With a great thump on the table, Poirot demolished his carefully built up edifice.

"It is this, *mon ami*! That I can build card houses seven stories high, but I cannot"—thump—"find"—thump—"that last link of which I spoke to you."

I could not quite tell what to say, so I held my peace, and he began slowly building up the cards again, speaking in jerks as he did so.

"It is done—so! By placing—one card—on another—with mathematical—precision!"

I watched the card house rising under his hands, story by story. He never hesitated or faltered. It was really almost like a conjuring trick.

"What a steady hand you've got," I remarked. "I believe I've only seen your hand shake once."

"On an occasion when I was enraged, without doubt," observed Poirot, with great placidity.

"Yes indeed! You were in a towering rage. Do you remember? It was when you discovered that the lock of the despatch-case in Mrs. Inglethorp's bedroom had been forced. You stood by the mantelpiece, twiddling the things on it in your usual fashion, and your hand shook like a leaf! I must say—"

But I stopped suddenly. For Poirot, uttering a hoarse and inarticulate cry, again annihilated his masterpiece of cards, and putting his hands over his eyes swayed backwards and forwards, apparently suffering the keenest agony.

"Good heavens, Poirot!" I cried. "What is the matter? Are you taken ill?"

"No, no," he gasped. "It is—it is—that I have an idea!"

"Oh!" I exclaimed, much relieved. "One of your 'little ideas'?"

"Ah, *ma foi*, no!" replied Poirot frankly. "This time it is an idea gigantic! Stupendous! And you—*you*, my friend, have given it to me!"

Suddenly clasping me in his arms, he kissed me warmly on both cheeks, and before I had recovered from my surprise ran headlong from the room.

Mary Cavendish entered at that moment.

"What is the matter with Monsieur Poirot? He rushed past me crying out: 'A garage! For the love of Heaven, direct me to a garage, madame!' And, before I could answer, he had dashed out into the street."

I hurried to the window. True enough, there he was, tearing down the street, hatless, and gesticulating as he went. I turned to Mary with a gesture of despair.

"He'll be stopped by a policeman in another minute. There he goes, round the corner!"

Our eyes met, and we stared helplessly at one another.

"What can be the matter?"

I shook my head.

"I don't know. He was building card houses, when suddenly he said he had an idea, and rushed off as you saw."

"Well," said Mary, "I expect he will be back before dinner."

But night fell, and Poirot had not returned.

XII. THE LAST LINK

Poirot's abrupt departure had intrigued us all greatly. Sunday morning wore away, and still he did not reappear. But about three o'clock a ferocious and prolonged hooting outside drove us to the window, to see Poirot alighting from a car, accompanied by Japp and Summerhaye. The little man was transformed. He radiated an absurd complacency. He bowed with exaggerated respect to Mary Cavendish.

"Madame, I have your permission to hold a little *rèunion* in the *salon?* It is necessary for every one to attend."

Mary smiled sadly.

"You know, Monsieur Poirot, that you have *carte blanche* in every way."

"You are too amiable, madame."

Still beaming, Poirot marshalled us all into the drawing room, bringing forward chairs as he did so.

"Miss Howard—here. Mademoiselle Cynthia. Monsieur Lawrence. The good Dorcas. And Annie. *Bien!* We must delay our proceedings a few minutes until Mr. Inglethorp arrives. I have sent him a note."

Miss Howard rose immediately from her seat.

"If that man comes into the house, I leave it!"

"No, no!" Poirot went up to her and pleaded in a low voice.

Finally Miss Howard consented to return to her chair. A few minutes later Alfred Inglethorp entered the room.

The company once assembled, Poirot rose from his seat with the air of a popular lecturer, and bowed politely to his audience.

"*Messieurs, mesdames,* as you all know, I was called in by Monsieur John Cavendish to investigate this case. I at once examined the bedroom of the deceased which, by the advice of the doctors, had been kept locked, and was consequently exactly as it had been when the tragedy occurred. I found: first, a fragment of green material; second, a stain on the carpet near the window, still damp; thirdly, an empty box of bromide powders.

"To take the fragment of green material first, I found it caught in the bolt of the communicating door between that room and the adjoining one occupied by Mademoiselle Cynthia. I handed the fragment over to the police who did not consider it of much importance. Nor did they recognize it for what it was—a piece torn from a green land armlet."

There was a little stir of excitement.

"Now there was only one person at Styles who worked on the land—Mrs. Cavendish. Therefore it must have been Mrs. Cavendish who entered deceased's room through the door communicating with Mademoiselle Cynthia's room."

"But that door was bolted on the inside!" I cried.

"When I examined the room, yes. But in the first place we have only her word for it, since it was she who tried that particular door and reported it fastened. In the ensuing confusion she would have had ample opportunity to shoot the bolt across. I took an early opportunity of verifying my conjectures. To begin with, the fragment corresponds exactly with a tear in Mrs. Cavendish's armlet. Also, at the inquest, Mrs. Cavendish declared that she had heard, from her own room, the fall of the table by the bed. I took an early opportunity of testing that statement by stationing my friend Monsieur Hastings in the left wing of the building, just outside Mrs. Cavendish's door. I myself, in company with the police, went to the deceased's room, and whilst there I, apparently accidentally, knocked over the table in question, but found that, as I had expected, Monsieur Hastings had heard no sound at all. This confirmed my belief that Mrs. Cavendish was not speaking the truth when she declared that she had been dressing in her room at the time of the tragedy. In fact, I was convinced that, far from having been in her own room, Mrs. Cavendish was actually in the deceased's room when the alarm was given."

I shot a quick glance at Mary. She was very pale, but smiling.

"I proceeded to reason on that assumption. Mrs. Cavendish is in her mother-in-law's room. We will say that she is seeking for something and has not yet found it. Suddenly Mrs. Inglethorp awakens and is seized with an alarming paroxysm. She flings out her arm, overturning the bed table, and then pulls desperately at the bell. Mrs. Cavendish, startled, drops her candle, scattering the grease on the carpet. She picks it up, and retreats quickly to Mademoiselle Cynthia's room, closing the door behind her. She hurries out into the passage, for the servants must not find her where she is. But it is too late! Already footsteps are echoing along the gallery which connects the two wings. What can she do? Quick as thought, she hurries back to the young girl's room, and starts shaking her awake. The hastily aroused household come trooping down the passage. They are all busily battering at Mrs. Inglethorp's door. It occurs to nobody that Mrs. Cavendish has not arrived with the rest, but—and this is significant—I can find no one who saw her come from the other wing." He looked at Mary Cavendish. "Am I right, madame?"

She bowed her head.

"Quite right, monsieur. You understand that, if I had thought I would do my husband any good by revealing these facts, I would have done so. But it did not seem to me to bear upon the question of his guilt or innocence."

"In a sense, that is correct, madame. But it cleared my mind of many misconceptions, and left me free to see other facts in their true significance."

"The will!" cried Lawrence. "Then it was you, Mary, who destroyed the will?"

She shook her head, and Poirot shook his also.

"No," he said quietly. "There is only one person who could possibly have destroyed that will—Mrs. Inglethorp herself!"

"Impossible!" I exclaimed. "She had only made it out that very afternoon!"

"Nevertheless, *mon ami*, it was Mrs. Inglethorp. Because, in no other way can you account for the fact that, on one of the hottest days of the year, Mrs. Inglethorp ordered a fire to be lighted in her room."

I gave a gasp. What idiots we had been never to think of that fire as being incongruous! Poirot was continuing:

"The temperature on that day, messieurs, was 80° in the shade. Yet Mrs. Inglethorp ordered a fire! Why? Because she wished to destroy something, and could think of no other way. You will remember that, in consequence of the War economics practised at Styles, no waste paper was thrown away. There was therefore no means of destroying a thick document such as a will. The moment I heard of a fire being lighted in Mrs. Inglethorp's room, I leaped to the conclusion that it was to destroy some important document—possibly a will. So the discovery of the charred fragment in the grate was no surprise to me. I did not, of course, know at the time that the will in question had only been made that afternoon, and I will admit that, when I learnt that fact, I fell into a grievous error. I came to the conclusion that Mrs. Inglethorp's determination to destroy her will arose as a direct consequence of the quarrel she had that afternoon, and that therefore the quarrel took place after, and not before the making of the will.

"Here, as we know, I was wrong, and I was forced to abandon that idea. I faced the problem from a new standpoint. Now, at 4 o'clock, Dorcas overheard her mistress saying angrily: 'You need not think that any fear of publicity, or scandal between husband and wife will deter me." I conjectured, and conjectured rightly, that these words were addressed, not to her husband, but to Mr. John Cavendish. At 5 o'clock, an hour later, she uses almost the same words, but the standpoint is different. She admits to Dorcas, 'I don't know what to do; scandal between husband and wife is a dreadful thing.' At 4 o'clock she has been angry, but completely mistress of herself. At 5 o'clock she is in violent distress, and speaks of having had 'a great shock.'

"Looking at the matter psychologically, I drew one deduction which I was convinced was correct. The second 'scandal' she spoke of was not the same as the first—and it concerned herself!

"Let us reconstruct. At 4 o'clock, Mrs. Inglethorp quarrels with her son, and threatens to denounce him to his wife—who, by the way, overheard the greater part of the conversation. At 4:30, Mrs. Inglethorp, in consequence of a conversation on the validity of wills, makes a will in favour of her husband, which the two gardeners witness. At 5 o'clock, Dorcas finds her mistress in a state of considerable agitation, with a slip of paper—'a letter,' Dorcas thinks—in her hand, and it is then that she orders the fire in her room to be lighted. Presumably, then, between 4:30 and 5 o'clock, something has occurred to occasion a complete revolution of feeling, since she is now as anxious to destroy the will, as she was before to make it. What was that something?

"As far as we know, she was quite alone during that half-hour. Nobody entered or left that boudoir. What then occasioned this sudden change of sentiment?

"One can only guess, but I believe my guess to be correct. Mrs. Inglethorp had no stamps in her desk. We know this, because later she asked Dorcas to bring her some. Now in the opposite corner of the room stood her husband's desk—locked. She was anxious to find some stamps, and, according to my theory, she tried her own keys in the desk. That one of them fitted I know. She therefore opened the desk, and in searching for the stamps she came across something else—that slip of paper which Dorcas saw in her hand, and which assuredly was never meant for Mrs. Inglethorp's eyes. On the other hand, Mrs. Cavendish believed that the slip of paper to which her mother-in-law clung so tenaciously was a written proof of her own husband's infidelity. She demanded it from Mrs. Inglethorp who assured her, quite truly, that it had nothing to do with that matter. Mrs. Cavendish did not believe her. She thought that Mrs. Inglethorp was shielding her stepson. Now Mrs. Cavendish is a very resolute woman, and, behind her mask of reserve, she was madly jealous of her husband. She determined to get hold of that paper at all costs, and in this resolution chance came to her aid. She happened to pick up the key of Mrs. Inglethorp's despatch-case, which had been lost that morning. She knew that her mother-in-law invariably kept all important papers in this particular case.

"Mrs. Cavendish, therefore, made her plans as only a woman driven desperate through jealousy could have done. Some time in the evening she unbolted the door leading into Mademoiselle Cynthia's room. Possibly she applied oil to the hinges, for I found that it opened quite noiselessly when I tried it. She put off her project until the early hours of the morning as being safer, since the servants were accustomed to hearing her move about her room at that time. She dressed completely in her land kit, and made her way quietly through Mademoiselle Cynthia's room into that of Mrs. Inglethorp."

He paused a moment, and Cynthia interrupted:

"But I should have woken up if anyone had come through my room?"

"Not if you were drugged, mademoiselle."

"Drugged?"

"*Mais, oui!*"

"You remember"—he addressed us collectively again—"that through all the tumult and noise next door Mademoiselle Cynthia slept. That admitted of two possibilities. Either her sleep was feigned—which I did not believe—or her unconsciousness was indeed by artificial means.

"With this latter idea in my mind, I examined all the coffee cups most carefully, remembering that it was Mrs. Cavendish who had brought Mademoiselle Cynthia her coffee the night before. I took a sample from each cup, and had them analysed—with no result. I had counted the cups carefully, in the event of one having been removed. Six persons had taken coffee, and six cups were duly found. I had to confess myself mistaken.

"Then I discovered that I had been guilty of a very grave oversight. Coffee had been brought in for seven persons, not six, for Dr. Bauerstein had been there that evening. This changed the face of the whole affair, for there was now one cup missing. The servants noticed nothing, since Annie, the housemaid, who took in the coffee, brought in seven cups, not knowing that Mr. Inglethorp never drank it, whereas Dorcas, who cleared them away the following morning, found six as usual—or strictly speaking she found five, the sixth being the one found broken in Mrs. Inglethorp's room.

"I was confident that the missing cup was that of Mademoiselle Cynthia. I had an additional reason for that belief in the fact that all the cups found contained sugar, which Mademoiselle Cynthia never took in her coffee. My attention was attracted by the story of Annie about some 'salt' on the tray of coco which she took every night to Mrs. Inglethorp's room. I accordingly secured a sample of that coco, and sent it to be analysed."

"But that had already been done by Dr. Bauerstein," said Lawrence quickly.

"Not exactly. The analyst was asked by him to report whether strychnine was, or was not, present. He did not have it tested, as I did, for a narcotic."

"For a narcotic?"

"Yes. Here is the analyst's report. Mrs. Cavendish administered a safe, but effectual, narcotic to both Mrs. Inglethorp and Mademoiselle Cynthia. And it is possible that she had a *mauvais quart d'heure* in consequence! Imagine her feelings when her mother-in-law is suddenly taken ill and dies, and immediately after she hears the word 'Poison'! She has believed that the sleeping draught she administered was perfectly harmless, but there is no doubt that for one terrible moment she must have feared that Mrs. Inglethorp's death lay at her door. She is seized with panic, and under its influence she hurries downstairs, and quickly drops the coffee cup and saucer used by Mademoiselle Cynthia into a large brass vase, where it is discovered later by Monsieur Lawrence. The remains of the coco she dare not touch. Too many eyes are upon her. Guess at her relief when strychnine is mentioned, and she discovers that after all the tragedy is not her doing.

"We are now able to account for the symptoms of strychnine poisoning being so long in making their appearance. A narcotic taken with strychnine will delay the action of the poison for some hours."

Poirot paused. Mary looked up at him, the colour slowly rising in her face.

"All you have said is quite true, Monsieur Poirot. It was the most awful hour of my life. I shall never forget it. But you are wonderful. I understand now——"

"What I meant when I told you that you could safely confess to Papa Poirot, eh? But you would not trust me."

"I see everything now," said Lawrence. "The drugged coco, taken on top of the poisoned coffee, amply accounts for the delay."

"Exactly. But was the coffee poisoned, or was it not? We come to a little difficulty here, since Mrs. Inglethorp never drank it."

"What?" The cry of surprise was universal.

"No. You will remember my speaking of a stain on the carpet in Mrs. Inglethorp's room? There were some peculiar points about that stain. It was still damp, it exhaled a strong odour of coffee, and imbedded in the nap of the carpet I found some little splinters of china. What had happened was plain to me, for not two minutes before I had placed my little case on the table near the window, and the table, tilting up, had deposited it upon the floor on precisely the identical spot. In exactly the same way, Mrs. Inglethorp had laid down her cup of coffee on reaching her room the night before, and the treacherous table had played her the same trick.

"What happened next is mere guess work on my part, but I should say that Mrs. Inglethorp picked up the broken cup and placed it on the table by the bed. Feeling in need of a stimulant of some kind, she heated up her coco, and drank it off then and there. Now we are faced with a new problem. We know the coco contained no strychnine. The coffee was never drunk. Yet the strychnine must have been administered between seven and nine o'clock that evening. What third medium was there—a medium so suitable for disguising the taste of strychnine that it is extraordinary no one has thought of it?" Poirot looked round the room, and then answered himself impressively. "Her medicine!"

"Do you mean that the murderer introduced the strychnine into her tonic?" I cried.

"There was no need to introduce it. It was already there—in the mixture. The strychnine that killed Mrs. Inglethorp was the identical strychnine prescribed by Dr. Wilkins. To make that clear to you, I will read you an extract from a book on dispensing which I found in the Dispensary of the Red Cross Hospital at Tadminster:

"'The following prescription has become famous in text books:

Strychninae Sulph.	ggr. I
Potass Bromide.	3zv i
Aqua ad.	3zv iii

Fiat Mistura

This solution deposits in a few hours the greater part of the strychnine salt as an insoluble bromide in transparent crystals. A lady in England lost her life by taking a similar mixture: the precipitated strychnine collected at the bottom, and in taking the last dose she swallowed nearly all of it!

"Now there was, of course, no bromide in Dr. Wilkins's prescription, but you will remember that I mentioned an empty box of bromide powders. One or two of those powders introduced into the full bottle of medicine would effectually precipitate the strychnine, as the book describes, and cause it to be taken in the last dose. You will learn later that the person who usually poured out Mrs. Inglethorp's medicine was always extremely careful not to shake the bottle, but to leave the sediment at the bottom of it undisturbed.

"Throughout the case, there have been evidences that the tragedy was intended to take place on Monday evening. On that day, Mrs. Inglethorp's bell wire was neatly cut, and on Monday evening Mademoiselle Cynthia was spending the night with friends, so that Mrs. Inglethorp would have been quite alone in the right wing, completely shut off from help of any kind, and would have died, in all probability, before medical aid could have been summoned. But in her hurry to be in time for the village entertainment Mrs. Inglethorp forgot to take her medicine, and the next day she lunched away from home, so that the last—and fatal—dose was actually taken twenty-four hours later than had been anticipated by the murderer; and it is owing to that delay that the final proof—the last link of the chain—is now in my hands."

Amid breathless excitement, he held out three thin strips of paper.

"A letter in the murderer's own hand-writing, *mes amis*! Had it been a little clearer in its terms, it is possible that Mrs. Inglethorp, warned in time, would have escaped. As it was, she realized her danger, but not the manner of it."

In the deathly silence, Poirot pieced together the slips of paper and, clearing his throat, read:

> Dearest Evelyn:
> You will be anxious at hearing nothing. It is all right—only it will be tonight instead of last night. You understand. There's a good time coming once the old woman is dead and out of the way. No one can possibly bring home the crime to me. That idea of yours about the bromides was a stroke of genius! But we must be very circumspect. A false step—

"Here, my friends, the letter breaks off. Doubtless the writer was interrupted; but there can be no question as to his identity. We all know this handwriting and—"

A howl that was almost a scream broke the silence.

"You devil! How did you get it?"

A chair was overturned. Poirot skipped nimbly aside. A quick movement on his part, and his assailant fell with a crash.

"*Messieurs, mesdames*," said Poirot, with a flourish, "let me introduce you to the murderer, Mr. Alfred Inglethorp!"

XIII. POIROT EXPLAINS

Poirot, you old villain," I said, "I've half a mind to strangle you! What do you mean by deceiving me as you have done?"

We were sitting in the library. Several hectic days lay behind us. In the room below, John and Mary were together once more, while Alfred Inglethorp and Miss Howard were in custody. Now at last, I had Poirot to myself, and could relieve my still burning curiosity.

Poirot did not answer me for a moment, but at last he said:

"I did not deceive you, *mon ami*. At most, I permitted you to deceive yourself."

"Yes, but why?"

"Well, it is difficult to explain. You see, my friend, you have a nature so honest, and a countenance so transparent, that—*enfin*, to conceal your feelings is impossible! If I had told you my ideas, the very first time you saw Mr. Alfred Inglethorp that astute gentleman would have—in your so expressive idiom—'smelt a rat'! And then, *bon jour* to our chances of catching him!"

"I think that I have more diplomacy than you give me credit for."

"My friend," besought Poirot, "I implore you, do not enrage yourself! Your help has been of the most invaluable. It is but the extremely beautiful nature that you have, which made me pause."

"Well," I grumbled, a little mollified. "I still think you might have given me a hint."

"But I did, my friend. Several hints. You would not take them. Think now, did I ever say to you that I believed John Cavendish guilty? Did I not, on the contrary, tell you that he would almost certainly be acquitted?"

"Yes, but—"

"And did I not immediately afterwards speak of the difficulty of bringing the murderer to justice? Was it not plain to you that I was speaking of two entirely different persons?"

"No," I said, "it was not plain to me!"

"Then again," continued Poirot, "at the beginning, did I not repeat to you several times that I didn't want Mr. Inglethorp arrested *now*? That should have conveyed something to you."

"Do you mean to say you suspected him as long ago as that?"

"Yes. To begin with, whoever else might benefit by Mrs. Inglethorp's death, her husband would benefit the most. There was no getting away from that. When I went up to Styles with you that first day, I had no idea as to how the crime had been committed, but from what I knew of Mr. Inglethorp I fancied that it would be very hard to find anything to connect him with it. When I arrived at the château, I realized at once that it was Mrs. Inglethorp who had burnt the will; and there, by the way, you cannot complain, my friend, for I tried my best to force on you the significance of that bedroom fire in midsummer."

"Yes, yes," I said impatiently. "Go on."

"Well, my friend, as I say, my views as to Mr. Inglethorp's guilt were very much shaken. There was, in fact, so much evidence against him that I was inclined to believe that he had not done it."

"When did you change your mind?"

"When I found that the more efforts I made to clear him, the more efforts he made to get himself arrested. Then, when I discovered that Inglethorp had nothing to do with Mrs. Raikes, and that in fact it was John Cavendish who was interested in that quarter, I was quite sure."

"But why?"

"Simply this. If it had been Inglethorp who was carrying on an intrigue with Mrs. Raikes, his silence was perfectly comprehensible. But, when I discovered that it was known all over the village that it was John who was attracted by the farmer's pretty wife, his silence bore quite a different interpretation. It was nonsense to pretend that he was afraid of the scandal, as no possible scandal could attach to him. This attitude of his gave me furiously to think, and I was slowly forced to the conclusion that Alfred Inglethorp wanted to be arrested. *Eh bien!* From that moment, I was equally determined that he should not be arrested."

"Wait a minute. I don't see why he wished to be arrested?"

"Because, *mon ami*, it is the law of your country that a man once acquitted can never be tried again for the same offence. Aha! But it was clever—his idea! Assuredly, he is a man of method. See here, he knew that in his position he was bound to be suspected, so he conceived the exceedingly clever idea of preparing a lot of manufactured evidence against himself. He wished to be suspected. He wished to be arrested. He would then produce his irreproachable alibi—and, hey presto, he was safe for life!"

"But I still don't see how he managed to prove his alibi, and yet go to the chemist's shop?"

Poirot stared at me in surprise.

"Is it possible? My poor friend! You have not yet realized that it was Miss Howard who went to the chemist's shop?"

"Miss Howard?"

"But, certainly. Who else? It was most easy for her. She is of a good height, her voice is deep and manly; moreover, remember, she and Inglethorp are cousins, and there is a distinct resemblance between them, especially in their gait and bearing. It was simplicity itself. They are a clever pair!"

"I am still a little fogged as to how exactly the bromide business was done," I remarked.

"*Bon!* I will reconstruct for you as far as possible. I am inclined to think that Miss Howard was the master mind in that affair. You remember her once mentioning that her father was a doctor? Possibly she dispensed his medicines for him, or she may have taken the idea from one of the many books lying about when Mademoiselle Cynthia was studying for her exam. Anyway, she was familiar with the fact that the addition of a bromide to a mixture containing strychnine would cause the precipitation of the latter. Probably the idea came to her quite suddenly. Mrs. Inglethorp had a box of bromide powders, which she occasionally took at night. What could be easier than quietly to dissolve one or more of those powders in Mrs. Inglethorp's large sized bottle of medicine when it came from Coot's? The risk is practically nil. The tragedy will not take place until nearly a fortnight later. If anyone has seen either of them touching the medicine, they will have forgotten it by that time. Miss Howard will have engineered her quarrel, and departed from the house. The lapse of time, and her absence, will defeat all suspicion. Yes, it was a clever idea! If they had left it alone, it is possible the crime might never have been brought home to them. But they were not satisfied. They tried to be too clever—and that was their undoing."

Poirot puffed at his tiny cigarette, his eyes fixed on the ceiling.

"They arranged a plan to throw suspicion on John Cavendish, by buying strychnine at the village chemist's, and signing the register in his handwriting.

"On Monday Mrs. Inglethorp will take the last dose of her medicine. On Monday, therefore, at six o'clock, Alfred Inglethorp arranges to be seen by a number of people at a spot far removed from the village. Miss Howard has previously made up a cock and bull story about him and Mrs. Raikes to account for his holding his tongue afterwards. At six o'clock, Miss Howard, disguised as Alfred Inglethorp, enters the chemist's shop, with her story about a dog, obtains the strychnine, and writes the name of Alfred Inglethorp in John's handwriting, which she had previously studied carefully.

"But, as it will never do if John, too, can prove an alibi, she writes him an anonymous note—still copying his handwriting—which takes him to a remote spot where it is exceedingly unlikely that anyone will see him.

"So far, all goes well. Miss Howard goes back to Middlingham. Alfred Inglethorp returns to Styles. There is nothing that can compromise him in any way, since it is Miss Howard who has the strychnine, which, after all, is only wanted as a blind to throw suspicion on John Cavendish.

"But now a hitch occurs. Mrs. Inglethorp does not take her medicine that night. The broken bell, Cynthia's absence—arranged by Inglethorp through his wife—all these are wasted. And then—he makes his slip.

"Mrs. Inglethorp is out, and he sits down to write to his accomplice, who, he fears, may be in a panic at the non-success of their plan. It is probable that Mrs. Inglethorp returned earlier than he expected. Caught in the act, and somewhat flurried he hastily shuts and locks his desk. He fears that if he remains in the room he may have to open it again, and that Mrs. Inglethorp might catch sight of the letter before he could snatch it up. So he goes out and walks in the woods, little dreaming that Mrs. Inglethorp will open his desk, and discover the incriminating document.

"But this, as we know, is what happened. Mrs. Inglethorp reads it, and becomes aware of the perfidy of her husband and Evelyn Howard, though, unfortunately, the sentence about the bromides conveys no warning to her mind. She knows that she is in danger—but is ignorant of where the danger lies. She decides to say nothing to her husband, but sits down and writes to her solicitor, asking him to come on the morrow, and she also determines to destroy immediately the will which she has just made. She keeps the fatal letter."

"It was to discover that letter, then, that her husband forced the lock of the despatch-case?"

"Yes, and from the enormous risk he ran we can see how fully he realized its importance. That letter excepted, there was absolutely nothing to connect him with the crime."

"There's only one thing I can't make out, why didn't he destroy it at once when he got hold of it?"

"Because he did not dare take the biggest risk of all—that of keeping it on his own person."

"I don't understand."

"Look at it from his point of view. I have discovered that there were only five short minutes in which he could have taken it—the five minutes immediately before our own arrival on the scene, for before that time Annie was brushing the stairs, and would have seen anyone who passed going to the right wing. Figure to yourself the scene! He enters the room, unlocking the door by means of one of the other doorkeys—they were all much alike. He hurries to the despatch-case—it is locked, and the keys are nowhere to be seen. That is a terrible blow to him, for it means that his presence in the room cannot be concealed as he had hoped. But he sees clearly that everything must be risked for the sake of that damning piece of evidence. Quickly, he forces the lock with a penknife, and turns over the papers until he finds what he is looking for.

"But now a fresh dilemma arises: he dare not keep that piece of paper on him. He may be seen leaving the room—he may be searched. If the paper is found on him, it is certain doom. Probably, at this minute, too, he hears the sounds below of Mr. Wells and John leaving the boudoir. He must act quickly. Where can he hide this terrible slip of paper? The contents of the wastepaper-basket are kept and in any case, are sure to be examined. There are no means of destroying it; and he dare not keep it. He looks round, and he sees—what do you think, *mon ami*?"

I shook my head.

"In a moment, he has torn the letter into long thin strips, and rolling them up into spills he thrusts them hurriedly in amongst the other spills in the vase on the mantelpiece."

I uttered an exclamation.

"No one would think of looking there," Poirot continued. "And he will be able, at his leisure, to come back and destroy this solitary piece of evidence against him."

"Then, all the time, it was in the spill vase in Mrs. Inglethorp's bedroom, under our very noses?" I cried.

Poirot nodded.

"Yes, my friend. That is where I discovered my 'last link,' and I owe that very fortunate discovery to you."

"To me?"

"Yes. Do you remember telling me that my hand shook as I was straightening the ornaments on the mantelpiece?"

"Yes, but I don't see—"

"No, but I saw. Do you know, my friend, I remembered that earlier in the morning, when we had been there together, I had straightened all the objects on the mantelpiece. And, if they were already straightened, there would be no need to straighten them again, unless, in the meantime, someone else had touched them."

"Dear me," I murmured, "so that is the explanation of your extraordinary behaviour. You rushed down to Styles, and found it still there?"

"Yes, and it was a race for time."

"But I still can't understand why Inglethorp was such a fool as to leave it there when he had plenty of opportunity to destroy it."

"Ah, but he had no opportunity. *I* saw to that."

"You?"

"Yes. Do you remember reproving me for taking the household into my confidence on the subject?"

"Yes."

"Well, my friend, I saw there was just one chance. I was not sure then if Inglethorp was the criminal or not, but if he was I reasoned that he would not have the paper on him, but would have hidden it somewhere, and by enlisting the sympathy of the household I could effectually prevent his destroying it. He was already under suspicion, and by making the matter public I secured the services of about ten amateur detectives, who would be watching him unceasingly, and being himself aware of their watchfulness he would not dare seek further to destroy the document. He was therefore forced to depart from the house, leaving it in the spill vase."

"But surely Miss Howard had ample opportunities of aiding him."

"Yes, but Miss Howard did not know of the paper's existence. In accordance with their prearranged plan, she never spoke to Alfred Inglethorp. They were supposed to be deadly enemies, and until John Cavendish was safely convicted they neither of them dared risk a meeting. Of course I had a watch kept on Mr. Inglethorp, hoping that sooner or later he would lead me to the hiding place. But he was too clever to take any chances. The paper was safe where it was; since no one had thought of looking there in the first week, it was not likely they would do so afterwards. But for your lucky remark, we might never have been able to bring him to justice."

"I understand that now; but when did you first begin to suspect Miss Howard?"

"When I discovered that she had told a lie at the inquest about the letter she had received from Mrs. Inglethorp."

"Why, what was there to lie about?"

"You saw that letter? Do you recall its general appearance?"

"Yes—more or less."

"You will recollect, then, that Mrs. Inglethorp wrote a very distinctive hand, and left large clear spaces between her words. But if you look at the date at the top of the letter you will notice that 'July 17th' is quite different in this respect. Do you see what I mean?"

"No," I confessed, "I don't."

"You do not see that that letter was not written on the 17th, but on the 7th—the day after Miss Howard's departure? The '1' was written in before the '7' to turn it into the '17th'."

"But why?"

"That is exactly what I asked myself. Why does Miss Howard suppress the letter written on the 17th, and produce this faked one instead? Because she did not wish to show the letter of the 17th. Why, again? And at once a suspicion dawned in my mind. You will remember my saying that it was wise to beware of people who were not telling you the truth."

"And yet," I cried indignantly, "after that, you gave me two reasons why Miss Howard could not have committed the crime!"

"And very good reasons too," replied Poirot. "For a long time they were a stumbling-block to me until I remembered a very significant fact: that she and Alfred

Inglethorp were cousins. She could not have committed the crime single-handed, but the reasons against that did not debar her from being an accomplice. And, then, there was that rather over-vehement hatred of hers! It concealed a very opposite emotion. There was, undoubtedly, a tie of passion between them long before he came to Styles. They had already arranged their infamous plot—that he should marry this rich, but rather foolish old lady, induce her to make a will leaving her money to him, and then gain their ends by a very cleverly conceived crime. If all had gone as they planned, they would probably have left England, and lived together on their poor victim's money.

"They are a very astute and unscrupulous pair. While suspicion was to be directed against him, she would be making quiet preparations for a very different *dénouement*. She arrives from Middlingham with all the compromising items in her possession. No suspicion attaches to her. No notice is paid to her coming and going in the house. She hides the strychnine and glasses in John's room. She puts the beard in the attic. She will see to it that sooner or later they are duly discovered."

"I don't quite see why they tried to fix the blame on John," I remarked. "It would have been much easier for them to bring the crime home to Lawrence."

"Yes, but that was mere chance. All the evidence against him arose out of pure accident. It must, in fact, have been distinctly annoying to the pair of schemers."

"His manner was unfortunate," I observed thoughtfully.

"Yes. You realize, of course, what was at the back of that?"

"No."

"You did not understand that he believed Mademoiselle Cynthia guilty of the crime?"

"No," I exclaimed, astonished. "Impossible!"

"Not at all. I myself nearly had the same idea. It was in my mind when I asked Mr. Wells that first question about the will. Then there were the bromide powders which she had made up, and her clever male impersonations, as Dorcas recounted them to us. There was really more evidence against her than anyone else."

"You are joking, Poirot!"

"No. Shall I tell you what made Monsieur Lawrence turn so pale when he first entered his mother's room on the fatal night? It was because, whilst his mother lay there, obviously poisoned, he saw, over your shoulder, that the door into Mademoiselle Cynthia's room was unbolted."

"But he declared that he saw it bolted!" ?" I cried.

"Exactly," said Poirot dryly. "And that was just what confirmed my suspicion that it was not. He was shielding Mademoiselle Cynthia."

"But why should he shield her?"

"Because he is in love with her."

I laughed.

"There, Poirot, you are quite wrong! I happen to know for a fact that, far from being in love with her, he positively dislikes her."

"Who told you that, *mon ami?*"

"Cynthia herself."

"*La pauvre petite!* And she was concerned?"

"She said that she did not mind at all."

"Then she certainly did mind very much," remarked Poirot. "They are like that—*les femmes!*"

"What you say about Lawrence is a great surprise to me," I said.

"But why? It was most obvious. Did not Monsieur Lawrence make the sour face every time Mademoiselle Cynthia spoke and laughed with his brother? He had taken it into his long head that Mademoiselle Cynthia was in love with Monsieur John. When he entered his mother's room, and saw her obviously poisoned, he jumped to the conclusion that Mademoiselle Cynthia knew something about the matter. He was nearly driven desperate. First he crushed the coffee cup to powder under his feet, remembering that *she* had gone up with his mother the night before, and he determined that there should be no chance of testing its contents. Thenceforward, he strenuously, and quite uselessly, upheld the theory of 'Death from natural causes.'"

"And what about the 'extra coffee cup'?"

"I was fairly certain that it was Mrs. Cavendish who had hidden it, but I had to make sure. Monsieur Lawrence did not know at all what I meant; but, on reflection, he came to the conclusion that if he could find an extra coffee cup anywhere his lady love would be cleared of suspicion. And he was perfectly right."

"One thing more. What did Mrs. Inglethorp mean by her dying words?"

"They were, of course, an accusation against her husband."

"Dear me, Poirot," I said with a sigh, "I think you have explained everything. I am glad it has all ended so happily. Even John and his wife are reconciled."

"Thanks to me."

"How do you mean—thanks to you?"

"My dear friend, do you not realize that it was simply and solely the trial which has brought them together again? That John Cavendish still loved his wife, I was convinced. Also, that she was equally in love with him. But they had drifted very far apart. It all arose from a misunderstanding. She married him without love. He knew it. He is a sensitive man in his way, he would not force himself upon her if she did not want him.

And, as he withdrew, her love awoke. But they are both unusually proud, and their pride held them inexorably apart. He drifted into an entanglement with Mrs. Raikes, and she deliberately cultivated the friendship of Dr. Bauerstein. Do you remember the day of John Cavendish's arrest, when you found me deliberating over a big decision?"

"Yes, I quite understood your distress."

"Pardon me, *mon ami*, but you did not understand it in the least. I was trying to decide whether or not I would clear John Cavendish at once. I could have cleared him—though it might have meant a failure to convict the real criminals. They were entirely in the dark as to my real attitude up to the very last moment—which partly accounts for my success."

"Do you mean that you could have saved John Cavendish from being brought to trial?"

"Yes, my friend. But I eventually decided in favour of 'a woman's happiness.' Nothing but the great danger through which they have passed could have brought these two proud souls together again."

I looked at Poirot in silent amazement. The colossal cheek of the little man! Who on earth but Poirot would have thought of a trial for murder as a restorer of conjugal happiness!

"I perceive your thoughts, *mon ami*," said Poirot, smiling at me. "No one but Hercule Poirot would have attempted such a thing! And you are wrong in condemning it. The happiness of one man and one woman is the greatest thing in all the world."

His words took me back to earlier events. I remembered Mary as she lay white and exhausted on the sofa, listening, listening. There had come the sound of the bell below. She had started up. Poirot had opened the door, and meeting her agonized eyes had nodded gently. "Yes, madame," he said. "I have brought him back to you." He had stood aside, and as I went out I had seen the look in Mary's eyes, as John Cavendish had caught his wife in his arms.

"Perhaps you are right, Poirot," I said gently. "Yes, it is the greatest thing in the world."

Suddenly, there was a tap at the door, and Cynthia peeped in.

"I—I only—"

"Come in," I said, springing up.

She came in, but did not sit down.

"I—only wanted to tell you something—"

"Yes?"

Cynthia fidgeted with a little tassel for some moments, then, suddenly exclaiming: "You dears!," kissed first me and then Poirot, and rushed out of the room again.

"What on earth does this mean?" I asked, surprised.

It was very nice to be kissed by Cynthia, but the publicity of the salute rather impaired the pleasure.

"It means that she has discovered Monsieur Lawrence does not dislike her as much as she thought," replied Poirot philosophically.

"But—"

"Here he is."

Lawrence at that moment passed the door.

"Eh! Monsieur Lawrence," called Poirot. "We must congratulate you, is it not so?"

Lawrence blushed, and then smiled awkwardly. A man in love is a sorry spectacle. Now Cynthia had looked charming.

I sighed.

"What is it, *mon ami?*"

"Nothing," I said sadly. "They are two delightful women!"

"And neither of them is for you?" finished Poirot. "Never mind. Console yourself, my friend. We may hunt together again, who knows? And then—"

ORIGINAL SOURCES

Bailey, H. C. "The Business Minister," *Call Mr. Fortune* (New York: E. P. Dutton & Company, 1921).

Bramah, Ernest. "The Tragedy at Brookbend Cottage," *Max Carrados* (London: Methuen, 1914).

Chesterton, G.K. "The Invisible Man," *The Innocence of Father Brown* (London: Cassell and Company, Ltd., 1911).

Christie, Agatha. *The Mysterious Affair at Styles* (London: John Lane, 1920).

Collins, Wilkie. "The Traveller's Story of a Very Strange Bed," *After Dark* (London: Smith, Elder and Co., 1856).

Doyle, Arthur Conan. *The Hound of the Baskervilles* (London: George Newnes, 1902).

Freeman, R. Austin. "A Case of Premeditation," *McClure's Magazine*, August 1910.

Futrelle, Jacques. "The Scarlet Thread," *The Thinking Machine* (New York: Dodd, Mead and Company, 1907).

Gaboriau, Émile. "Missing," *The Little Old Man of Batignolles and Other Stories* (London: Vizetelly & Co., 1886).

Green, Anna Katherine. "Room No. 3," *Room Number 3 and Other Detective Stories* (New York: Dodd, Mead and Company 1913).

Hansew, Thomas and Mary. "The Rope of Fear," *Short Stories*, December 1919.

Leblanc, Maurice. "The Red Silk Scarf," *The Confessions of Arsène Lupin* (London: Mills and Boon, Ltd., 1912).

Moffatt, Cleveland. "The Mysterious Card," *The Mysterious Card* (Boston: Small, Maynard and Company, 1912)

Morrison, Arthur. "The Ivy Cottage Mystery," *The Chronicles of Martin Hewitt* (New York: D. Appleton and Company, 1896).

Orczy, Baronness. "The Fenchurch Street Mystery," *The Man in the Corner* (London: Greening & Co., Ltd., 1909).

Poe, Edgar Allan. "Murders in the Rue Morgue," *Tales* (New York: Wiley & Putnam, 1845).

Post, Melville Davisson. "The Doomsdorf Mystery," *Uncle Abner, Master of Mysteries* (New York: D. Appleton and Company, 1919).

Reeve, Arthur B. "The Poisoned Pen," *The Poisoned Pen* (New York: Harper & Brothers, 1911).

Rohmer, Sax. "The Ten-Thirty Folkestone Express," *Lippincott's Magazine*, December 1914.

Shiel, M. P. "The S. S." *Prince Zaleski* (London: John Lane, 1895).

Stout, Rex. "Justice Ends at Home," *All-Story Weekly*, December 4, 1915.

Wallace, Edgar. "The Murder of Bennett Sandman," *The Novel Magazine*, September 1919.

Zangwill, Israel. "The Big Bow Mystery," *The Grey Wig* (London: The Macmillan Company, 1903).